THE THREE MUSKETEERS

(The Three Guardsmen)

By ALEXANDRE DUMAS

Author of
"The Count of Monte Cristo," "The Man in the Iron Mask,"
"Twenty Years After," etc.

THE CRESCENT LIBRARY

A. L. BURT COMPANY
Publishers
New York   Chicago

4/72

THE THREE MUSKETEERS

CHAPTER I.

THE THREE PRESENTS OF M. D'ARTAGNAN THE ELDER.

ON THE first Monday of the month of April, 1625, the bourg, of Meung, in which the author of the "Romance of the Rose" was born, appeared to be in as perfect a state of revolution as if the Huguenots had just made a second Rochelle of it. Many citizens, seeing the women flying toward the High Street, leaving their children crying at the open doors, hastened to don the cuirass, and, supporting their somewhat uncertain courage with a musket or a partizan, directed their steps toward the hostelry of the Franc-Meunier, before which was gathered, increasing every minute, a compact group, vociferous and full of curiosity.

In those times panics were common, and few days passed without some city or other enregistering in its archives an event of this kind. There were nobles who made war against each other; there was the king, who made war against the cardinal; there was Spain, which made war against the king. Then, in addition to these, concealed or public, secret or patent wars, there were, moreover, robbers, mendicants, Huguenots, wolves, and scoundrels who made war upon everybody. The citizens always took up arms readily against thieves, wolves, or scoundrels—often against nobles or Huguenots—sometimes against the king—but never against the cardinal or Spain. It resulted, then, from this habit, that on the said first Monday of the month of April, 1625, the citizens, on hearing the clamor, and seeing neither the red and yellow standard, nor the livery of the Duke de Richelieu, rushed toward the hostel of the Franc-Meunier.

When arrived there, the cause of this hubbub was apparent to all.

A young man—we can sketch his portrait at a dash—imagine to yourself a Don Quixote of eighteen; a Don Quixote

1

without his corselet, without his coat of mail, without his
cuistres; a Don Quixote clothed in a woolen doublet, the blue
color of which had faded into a nameless shade between lees
of wine and a heavenly azure; face long and brown; high
cheek-bones, a sign of astucity; the maxillary muscles enormously developed, an infallible sign by which a Gascon may
always be detected, even without his barret-cap—and our
young man wore a barret-cap, set off with a sort of feather; the
eye open and intelligent; the nose hooked, but finely chiseled.
Too big for a youth, too small for a grown man, an experienced eye might have taken him for a farmer's son upon a
journey, had it not been for the long sword, which, dangling
from a leathern baldrick, hit against the calves of its owner
as he walked, and against the rough side of his steed when he
was on horseback.

For our young man had a steed, which was the observed of
all observers. It was a Béarn pony, from twelve to fourteen
years old, yellow in his hide, without a hair in his tail, but
not without wind-galls on his legs, which, though going with
his head lower than his knees, rendering a martingale quite
unnecessary, contrived, nevertheless, to perform his eight
leagues a day. Unfortunately, the qualities of this horse
were so well concealed under his strange-colored hide and his
unaccountable gait, that at a time when everybody was a connoisseur in horseflesh, the appearance of the said pony at
Meung, which place he had entered about a quarter of an
hour before, by the gate of Beaugency, produced an unfavor-
able feeling, which extended to his master.

And this feeling had been the more painfully perceived by
young D'Artagnan—for so was the Don Quixote of this second Rosinate named—from his not being able to conceal
from himself the ridiculous appearance that such a steed
gave him, good horseman as he was. He had sighed deeply,
therefore, when accepting the gift of the pony from M. d'Artagnan the elder. He was not ignorant that such a beast was
worth at least twenty livres; and the words which accompanied the present were above all price.

"My son," said the old Gascon gentleman, in that pure
Béarn *patois* of which Henry IV. could never get rid—"my
son, this horse was born in the house of your father, about
thirteen years ago, and has remained in it ever since, which
ought to make you love it. Never sell it—allow it to die
tranquilly and honorably of old age; and if you make a campaign with it, take as much care of it as you would of an old
servant. At court, provided you have ever the honor to go

there," continued M. d'Artagnan the elder, "an honor to which, remember, your ancient nobility gives you right, sustain worthily your name of *gentleman,* which has been worthily borne by your ancestors during five hundred years, both for your own sake and that of those that belong to you. By these I mean your relations and friends. Endure nothing from any one but M. le Cardinal and the king. It is by his courage, please to observe, by his courage alone, that a gentleman can make his way nowadays. Whoever trembles for a second perhaps allows the bait to escape, which, during that exact second, fortune held out to him. You are young; you ought to be brave for two reasons—the first is that you are a Gascon, and the second is that you are my son. Never fear quarrels, but seek hazardous adventures. I have taught you how to handle a sword; you have thews of iron, a wrist of steel: fight on all occasions; fight the more for duels being forbidden, since, consequently there is twice as much courage in fighting. I have nothing to give you, my son, but fifteen crowns, my horse, and the counsels you have just heard. Your mother will add to them a recipe for a certain balsam, which she had from a Bohemian, and which has the miraculous virtue of curing all wounds that do not reach the heart. Take advantage of all, and live happily and long. I have but one word to add, and thàt is to propose an example to you—not mine, for I myself have never appeared at court, and have only taken part in religious wars as a volunteer; I speak of M. de Tréville, who was formerly my neighbor, and who had the honor to be as a child the playfellow of our king, Louis XIII., whom God preserve! Sometimes their play degenerated into battles, and in these battles the king was not always the stronger. The blows which he received from him gave him a great esteem and friendship for M. de Tréville. Afterward, M. de Tréville fought with others: in his first journey to Paris, five times; from the death of the late king to the majority of the young one, without reckoning wars and sieges, seven times; and from that majority up to the present day, a hundred times perhaps! So that in spite of edicts, ordinances, and decrees, there he is captain of the musketeers—that is to say, leader of a legion of Cæsars, whom the king holds in great esteem, and whom the cardinal dreads —he who dreads nothing, as it is said. Still further, M. de Tréville gains ten thousand crowns a year; he is, therefore, a great noble. He began as you begin; go to him with this letter, and make him your model, in order that you may do as he has done."

Upon which M. d'Artagnan the elder girded his own sword round his son, kissed him tenderly on both cheeks, and gave him his benediction.

On leaving the paternal chamber, the young man found his mother, who was waiting for him with the famous recipe, of which the counsels we have just repeated would necessitate the so frequent employment. The adieux were on this side longer and more tender than they had been on the other; not that M. d'Artagnan did not love his son, who was his only offspring, but M. d'Artagnan was a man, and he would have considered it unworthy of a man to give way to his feelings; whereas Madame d'Artagnan was a woman, and, still more, a mother. She wept abundantly, and, let us speak it to the praise of M. d'Artagnan the younger, notwithstanding the efforts he made to be as firm as a future musketeer ought to be, nature prevailed, and he shed many tears, of which he succeeded with great difficulty in concealing the half.

The same day the young man set forward on his journey, furnished with the three paternal presents, which consisted, as we have said, of fifteen crowns, the horse, and the letter for M. de Tréville, the counsels being thrown into the bargain.

With such a *vade mecum* D'Artagnan was, morally and physically, an exact copy of the hero of Cervantes, to whom we so happily compared him, when our duty of an historian placed us under the necessity of sketching his portrait. Don Quixote took windmills for giants, and sheep for armies; D'Artagnan took every smile for an insult, and every look as a provocation; whence it resulted that from Tarbes to Meung his fist was constantly doubled, or his hand on the hilt of his sword; and yet the fist did not descend upon any jaw, nor did the sword issue from its scabbard. It was not that the sight of the wretched pony did not excite numerous smiles on the countenances of passers by; but as against the side of this pony rattled a sword of respectable length, and as over this sword gleamed an eye rather ferocious than haughty, these said passers-by repressed their hilarity, or, if hilarity prevailed over prudence, they endeavored to laugh only on one side, like the masks of the ancients. D'Artagnan, then, remained majestic and intact in his susceptibility till he came to this unlucky city of Meung.

But there, as he was alighting from his horse at the gate of the Franc-Meunier, without any one, host, waiter, or hostler, coming to hold his stirrup or take his horse, D'Artagnan spied, through an open window on the ground floor, a gentleman well made and of good carriage, although of rather a stern countenance, talking with two persons who appeared to listen to him with respect. D'Artagnan fancied quite naturally, according to his custom, that he must be the object of their conversation and listened. This time D'Artagnan was only in part mistaken: he himself was not in question, but his horse was. The gentleman appeared to be enumerating all his qualities to his auditors, and, as I have said, the auditors seeming to have great deference for the narrator, they every moment burst into fits of laughter. Now, as a half smile was sufficient to awaken the irascibility of the young man, the effect produced upon him by this vociferous mirth may be easily imagined.

Nevertheless, D'Artagnan was desirous of examining the appearance of this impertient personage who was laughing at him. He fixed his haughty eye upon the stranger, and perceived a man of from forty to forty-five years of age, with black and piercing eyes, a pale complexion, a strongly-marked nose, and a black and well-shaped mustache. He was dressed in a doublet and hose of a violet color, with aiguillettes of the same without any other ornaments than the customary slashes through which the skirt appeared. This doublet and hose, though new, looked creased like traveling clothes for a long time packed up in a portmanteau. D'Artagnan made all these remarks with the rapidity of a most minute observer, and, doubtless, from an instinctive feeling that this unknown was destined to have a great influence over his future life.

Now, as at the moment in which D'Artagnan fixed his eyes upon the gentleman in the violet doublet, the gentleman made one of his most knowing and profound remarks respecting the Béarnese pony, his two auditors laughed even louder than before, and he himself, though contrary to his custom, allowed a pale smile (if I may be allowed to use such an expression) to stray over his countenance. This time, there could be no doubt, D'Artagnan was really insulted. Full, then, of this conviction, he pulled his cap down over his eyes, and, endeavoring to copy some of the court airs he had picked up in Gascony among young traveling nobles, he advanced, with one hand on the hilt of his sword and the other leaning on his hip. Unfortunately, as he advanced, his anger increased at every step, and, instead of the proper and lofty speech he had prepared, as a prelude to his challenge, he found nothing at the tip of his tongue but a gross personality, which he accompanied with a furious gesture.

"I say, sir, you, sir, who are hiding yourself behind that

shutter!—yes, you, sir, tell me what you are laughing at, and we will laugh together."

The gentleman withdrew his eyes slowly from the nag to his master, as if he required some time to ascertain whether it could be to him that such strange reproaches were addressed; then, when he could not possibly entertain any doubt of the matter, his eyebrows slightly bent, and, with an accent of irony and insolence impossible to be described, replied to D'Artagnan:

"I was not speaking to you, sir!"

"But I am speaking to you!" replied the young man, additionally exasperated with this mixture of insolence and good manners, of politeness and scorn.

The unknown looked at him again with a slight smile, and retiring from the window, came out of the hostelry with a slow step, and placed himself before the horse within two paces of D'Artagnan. His quiet manner and the ironical expression of his countenance redoubled the mirth of the persons with whom he had been talking, and who still remained at the window.

D'Artagnan, seeing him approach, drew his sword a foot out of the scabbard.

"This horse is decidedly, or rather has been in his youth, a *bouton d'or*" (buttercup), resumed the unknown, continuing the remarks he had begun, and addressing himself to his auditors at the window, without paying the least attention to the exasperation of D'Artagnan, who, however, placed himself between him and them. "It is a color very well known in botany, but till the present time very rare among horses."

"There are people who laugh at a horse that would not dare to laugh at the master of it," cried the young emulator of the furious Tréville.

"I do not often laugh, sir," replied the unknown, "as you may perceive by the air of my countenance; but, nevertheless, I retain the privilege of laughing when I please."

"And I," cried D'Artagnan "will allow no man to laugh when it displeases me!"

"Indeed, sir," continued the unknown, more calm than ever. "Well! that is perfectly right!" and, turning on his heel. was about to re-enter the hostelry by the front gate, under which D'Artagnan, on arriving, had observed a saddled horse.

But D'Artagnan was not of a character to allow a man to escape him thus, who had had the insolence to laugh at him.

He drew his sword entirely from the scabbard, and followed him, crying:

"Turn, turn, Master Joker, lest I strike you behind!"

"Strike me!" said the other, turning sharply round and surveying the young man with as much astonishment as contempt. "Why, my good fellow, you must be mad!" Then, in a suppressed tone, as if speaking to himself: "This is annoying," continued he. "What a God-send this would be for his majesty, who is seeking everywhere for brave fellows to recruit his musketeers!"

He had scarcely finished, when D'Artagnan made such a furious lunge at him that if he had not sprung nimbly backward, he would have jested for the last time. The unknown then, perceiving that the matter was beyond a joke, drew his sword, saluted his adversary, and placed himself on his guard. But at the same moment his two auditors, accompanied by the host, fell upon D'Artagnan with sticks, shovels, and tongs. This caused so rapid and complete a diversion to the attack, that D'Artagnan's adversary, while the latter turned round to face this shower of blows, sheathed his sword with the same precision, and from an actor, which he had nearly been, became a spectator of the fight, a part in which he acquitted himself with his usual impassibility, muttering, nevertheless:

"A plague upon these Gascons! Put him on his orange horse again, and let him begone!"

"Not before I have killed you, poltroon!" cried D'Artagnan, making the best face possible, and never giving back one step before his three assailants, who continued to shower their blows upon him.

"Another Gasconade!" murmured the gentleman. "By my honor, these Gascons are incorrigible! Keep up the dance, then, since he will have it so. When he is tired, he will, perhaps, tell us that he has enough of it."

But the unknown was not acquainted with the headstrong personage he had to do with; D'Artagnan was not the man ever to cry for quarter. The fight was, therefore, prolonged for some seconds; but at length D'Artagnan's sword was struck from his hand by the blow of a stick, and broken in two pieces. Another blow full upon his forehead, at the same moment, brought him to the ground, covered with blood and almost fainting.

It was at this period that people came flocking to the scene of action from all parts. The host, fearful of consequences, with the help of his servants, carried the wounded man into the kitchen, where some trifling attention was bestowed upon him.

As to the gentleman, he resumed his place at the window, and surveyed the crowd with a certain air of impatience, evidently annoyed by their remaining undispersed.

"Well, how is it with this madman?" exclaimed he, turning round as the opening door announced the entrance of the host, who came to inquire if he was unhurt.

"Your excellency is safe and sound?" asked the host.

"Oh, yes! perfectly safe and sound, my good host, and wish to know what is become of our young man."

"He is better," said the host; "he fainted quite away."

"Indeed!" said the gentleman.

"But before he fainted, he collected all his strength to challenge you, and to defy you while challenging you."

"Why, this fellow must be the devil in person!" cried the unknown.

"Oh, no, your excellency!" replied the host, with a grin of contempt; "he is not the devil, for during his fainting we rummaged his valise, and found nothing but a clean shirt and twelve crowns, which, however, did not prevent his saying, as he was fainting, that if such a thing had happened in Paris you should have instantly repented of it, while here you would only have cause to repent of it at a later period."

"Then," said the unknown coldly, "he must be some prince in disguise."

"I have told you this, good sir," resumed the host, "in order that you may be on your guard."

"Did he name no one in his passion?"

"Yes! he struck his pocket and said: 'We shall see what M. de Tréville will think of this insult offered to his *protégé.*'

"M. de Tréville?" said the unknown, becoming attentive: "he put his hand upon his pocket while pronouncing the name of M. de Tréville? Now, my dear host! while your young man was insensible, you did not fail, I am quite sure, to ascertain what that pocket contained. What was there in it?"

"A letter addressed to M. de Tréville, captain of the musketeers."

"Indeed!"

"Exactly as I have the honor to tell your excellency."

The host, who was not endowed with great perspicacity, did not observe the expression which his words had given to the physiognomy of the unknown. The latter rose from the front of the window, upon the sill of which he had leaned with his elbow, and knitted his brows like a man suddenly rendered uneasy.

"The devil!" murmured he, between his teeth. "Can Tréville have set this Gascon upon me? He is very young, but a sword-thrust is a sword-thrust, whatever be the age of him who gives it, and a youth is less to be suspected than an older man; a weak obstacle is sometimes sufficient to overthrow a great design."

And the unknown fell into a reverie which lasted some minutes.

"Host," said he, "could you not contrive to get rid of this frantic boy for me? In conscience, I cannot kill him; and yet," added he, with a coldly menacing expression, "and yet he annoys me. Where is he?"

"In my wife's chamber, where they are dressing his hurts, on the first floor."

"His things and his bag are with him? Has he taken off his doublet?"

"On the contrary, everything is in the kitchen. But if he annoys you, this young crazy fool——"

"To be sure he does. He causes a disturbance in your hostelry. Go make out my bill, and call my servant."

"What, sir! do you mean to leave us already?"

"You know I was going, as I ordered you to get my horse saddled. Has not my desire been complied with?"

"Yes, sir; and as your excellency may have observed, your horse is in the great gateway, ready saddled for your departure."

"That is well; do as I have directed you, then."

"What the devil!" said the host to himself, "can he be afraid of this boy?" He bowed humbly, and retired.

"Milady* must see nothing of this fellow," continued the stranger. "She will soon pass—she is already late. I had better get on horseback, and go and meet her. I should like, however, to know what this letter addressed to Tréville contains!"

And the unknown, muttering to himself, directed his steps toward the kitchen.

In the meantime, the host, who entertained no doubt that

---

* We are well aware that this term "milady" is only properly used when followed by a family name. But we find it thus in the manuscript, and we do not choose to take upon ourselves to alter it.

it was the presence of the young man that drove the unknown from his hostelry, reascended to his wife's chamber, and found D'Artagnan just recovering his senses. Giving him to understand that the police would deal with him pretty severely for having sought a quarrel with a great lord, for, in the opinion of the host, the unknown could be nothing less than a great lord, he insisted that, notwithstanding his weakness, he should get up and depart as quickly as possible. D'Artagnan, half stupefied, without his doublet, and with his head bound up in linen cloth, arose then, and, urged forward by the host, began to descend the stairs; but on arriving at the kitchen, the first thing he saw was his antagonist, talking calmly, at the step of a heavy carriage, drawn by two large Norman horses.

His interlocutor, whose head appeared through the carriage window, was a woman of from twenty to two-and-twenty years of age. We have already observed with what rapidity D'Artagnan seized the expression of a countenance: he perceived then, at a glance, that this woman was young and beautiful; and her style of beauty struck him the more forcibly from its being totally different from that of the southern countries in which D'Artagnan had hitherto resided. She was pale and fair, with long curls falling in profusion over her shoulders; had large blue, languishing eyes, rosy lips, and hands of alabaster. She was talking with great animation with the unknown.

"His eminence, then, orders me—" said the lady.

"To return instantly to England, and to inform him immediately the duke leaves London."

"And my other instructions?" asked the fair traveler.

"They are contained in this box, which you will not open until you are on the other side of the Channel."

"Very well; and you, what are you going to do?"

"I, oh! I shall return to Paris."

"What, without chastising this insolent boy?" asked the lady.

The unknown was about to reply, but at the moment he opened his mouth, D'Artagnan, who had heard all, rushed forward through the open door.

"This insolent boy chastises others," cried he, "and I have good hope that he whom he means to chastise will not escape him as he did before."

"Will not escape him?" replied the unknown, knitting his brow.

"No, before a woman, you would not dare to fly, I presume?"

"Remember," said milady, seeing the unknown lay his hand on his sword, "remember that the least delay may ruin everything."

"True," cried the gentleman; "begone then, on your part, and I will depart as quickly on mine." And bowing to the lady, he sprang into his saddle, her coachman at the same time applying his whip vigorously to his horses. The two interlocutors thus separated, taking opposite directions, at full gallop.

"Your reckoning! your reckoning!" vociferated the host, whose respect for the traveler was changed into profound contempt on seeing him depart without settling his bill.

"Pay him, booby!" cried the unknown to his servant, without checking the speed of his horse; and the man, after throwing two or three pieces of silver at the foot of mine host, galloped after his master.

"Base coward! false gentleman!" cried D'Artagnan, springing forward, in his turn, after the servant. But his wound had rendered him too weak to support such an exertion. Scarcely had he gone ten steps when his ears began to tingle, a faintness seized him, a cloud of blood passed over his eyes, and he fell in the middle of the street, crying still:

"Coward! coward! coward!"

"He is a coward indeed," grumbled the host, drawing near to D'Artagnan, and endeavoring by this little flattery to make up matters with the young man, as the heron of the fable did with the snail he had despised the evening before.

"Yes, a base coward," murmured D'Artagnan, "but she, she was very beautiful."

"What she?" demanded the host.

"Milady," faltered D'Artagnan, and fainted a second time.

"Ah! it's all one," said the host; "I have lost two customers, but this one remains, of whom I am pretty certain for some days to come; and that will be eleven crowns gained, at all events."

We must remember that eleven crowns was just the amount that was left in D'Artagnan's purse.

The host had reckoned upon eleven days of confinement at a crown a day, but he had reckoned without his guest. On the following morning, at five o'clock, D'Artagnan arose, and descending to the kitchen, without help, asked, among other ingredients the list of which has not come down to us, for some oil, some wine, and some rosemary, and with his mother's recipe in his hand, composed a balsam, with which he anointed his numerous wounds, replacing his bandages himself, and positively refusing the assistance of any doctor. Thanks, no doubt, to the efficacy of the Bohemian balsam; and perhaps also, thanks to the absence of any doctor. D'Artagnan walked about that same evening, and was almost cured by the morrow.

But when the time came to pay for this rosemary, this oil, and the wine, the only expense the master had incurred, as he had preserved a strict abstinence; while, on the contrary, the yellow horse, by the account of the hostler, at least, had eaten three times as much as a horse of his size could reasonably be supposed to have done, D'Artagnan found nothing in his pocket but his little old velvet purse with the eleven crowns it contained: as to the letter addressed to M. de Tréville, it had disappeared.

The young man commenced his search for the letter with the greatest patience, turning out his pockets of all kinds over and over again, rummaging and re-rummaging in his valise, and opening and re-opening his purse; but when he had come to the conviction that the letter was not to be found, he flew, for the third time, into such a rage as was near costing him a fresh consumption of wine, oil, and rosemary; for upon seeing this hot-headed youth become exasperated and threaten to destroy everything in the establishment if his letter were not found, the host seized a spit, his wife a broom-handle, and the servants the same sticks they had used the day before.

"My letter of recommendation!" cried D'Artagnan, "my letter of recommendation! or, by God's blood, I will spit you all like so many ortolans!"

Unfortunately there was one circumstance which created a powerful obstacle to the accomplishment of this threat; which was, as we have related, that his sword had been in his first conflict broken in two, and which he had perfectly forgotten. Hence it resulted, that when D'Artagnan proceeded to draw his sword in earnest, he found himself purely and simply armed with a stump of a sword of about eight or ten inches in length, which the host had carefully placed in the scabbard. As to the rest of the blade, the master had slyly put that on one side to make himself a larding pin.

But this deception would probably not have stopped our fiery young man if the host had not reflected that the reclamation which his guest made was perfectly just.

"But after all," said he, lowering the point of his spit, "where is this letter?"

"Yes, where is this letter?" cried D'Artagnan. "In the

first place I warn you that that letter is for M. de Tréville, and it must be found; if it be not quickly found, he will know how to cause it to be found, I'll answer for it!"

This threat completed the intimidation of the host. After the king and the cardinal, M. de Tréville was the man whose name was perhaps most frequently repeated by the military, and even by citizens. There was, to be sure, Father Joseph, but his name was never pronounced but with subdued voice, such was the terror inspired by his Gray Eminence, as the cardinal's familiar was called.

Throwing down his spit then, and ordering his wife to do the same with her broom-handle, and the servants with their sticks, he set the first example of commencing an earnest search for the lost letter.

"Does the letter contain anything valuable?" demanded the host, after a few minutes of useless investigation.

"Zounds! I think it does, indeed," cried the Gascon, who reckoned upon this letter for making his way at court; "it contained my fortune!"

"Bills upon Spain?" asked the disturbed host.

"Bills upon his majesty's private treasury," answered D'Artagnan, who, reckoning upon entering into the king's service in consequence of this recommendation, thought he could make this somewhat hazardous reply without telling a falsehood.

"The devil!" cried the host, at his wit's end.

"But it's of no importance," continued D'Artagnan, with national assurance; "it's of no importance, the money is nothing—that letter was everything; I would rather have lost a thousand pistoles than have lost it." He would not have risked more if he had said twenty thousand; but a certain juvenile modesty restrained him.

A ray of light all at once broke upon the mind of the host, as he was giving himself to the devil upon finding nothing.

"That letter is not lost!" cried he.

"What!" said D'Artagnan.

"No; it has been stolen from you."

"Stolen! by whom?"

"By the gentleman who was here yesterday. He came down into the kitchen, where your doublet was. He remained there some time alone. I would lay a wager he has stolen it."

"Do you think so?" answered D'Artagnan, but little convinced, as he knew better than any one else how entirely personal the value of this letter was, and saw nothing in it likely to tempt the cupidity of any one. The fact was that none of the servants, none of the travelers present, could have gained anything by being possessed of this paper.

"Do you say!" resumed D'Artagnan, "that you suspect that impertinent gentleman?"

"I tell you I am sure of it," continued the host; "when I informed him that your lordship was the *protégé* of M. de Tréville, and that you even had a letter for that illustrious gentleman, he appeared to be very much disturbed, and asked me where the letter was, and immediately came down into the kitchen, where he knew your doublet was."

"Then that's the man that has robbed me," replied D'Artagnan: "I will complain to M. de Tréville, and M. de Tréville will complain to the king." He then drew two crowns majestically from his purse, gave them to the host, who accompanied him cap in hand to the gate, remounted his yellow horse, which bore him without any further accident to the gate of St. Antoine at Paris, where his owner sold him for three crowns, which was a very good price, considering that D'Artagnan had ridden him hard from Meung. Thus the dealer to whom D'Artagnan sold him for the said nine livres did not conceal from the young man that he only gave that enormous sum for him on account of the originality of his color.

Thus D'Artagnan entered Paris on foot, carrying his little packet under his arm, and walked about till he found an apartment to let on terms suited to the scantiness of his means. This chamber was a sort of garret, situated in the Rue des Fossoyeurs, near the Luxembourg.

As soon as the earnest-penny was paid, D'Artagnan took possession of his lodging, and passed the remainder of the day in sewing on his doublet and hose some ornamental braiding which his mother had taken off from an almost new doublet of M. d'Artagnan's the elder, and which she had given to him secretly; next he went to the Quai de Ferraille, to have a new blade put to his sword, and then returned toward the Louvre, inquiring of the first musketeer he met with for the situation of the hotel of M. de Tréville, which proved to be in the Rue du Vieux-Colombier, in the immediate vicinity of the chamber hired by D'Artagnan; a circumstance which appeared to furnish a happy augury for the success of his journey.

After which, satisfied with the way in which he had conducted himself at Meung, without remorse for the past, confident in the present, and full of hope for the future, he retired to bed, and slept the sleep of the brave.

This sleep, provincial as it was, brought him to nine o'clock in the morning, at which hour he rose in order to repair to the residence of M. de Tréville, the third personage in the kingdom in paternal estimation.

CHAPTER II.

THE ANTECHAMBER OF M. DE TRÉVILLE.

M. DE TROISVILLE, as his family was still called in Gascony, or M. de Tréville, as he has ended by styling himself in Paris, had really commenced life as D'Artagnan now did, that is to say, without a sou in his pocket, but with a fund of courage, shrewdness, and intelligence, that makes the poorest Gascon gentleman often derive more in his hope from the paternal inheritance than the richest Pengordian or Berrichan gentleman derives in reality from his. His insolent bravery, his still more insolent success at a time when blows poured down like hail, had borne him to the top of that ladder called court favor, which he had climbed four steps at a time.

He was the friend of the king, who honored highly, as every one knows, the memory of his father, Henry IV. The father of M. de Tréville had served him so faithfully in his wars against the League, that for want of money—a thing to which the Béarnais was accustomed all his life, and who constantly paid his debts with that of which he never stood in need of borrowing, that is to say, with ready wit—for want of money, we repeat, he authorized him after the reduction of Paris to assume for his arms a golden lion passant upon gules with the device of: *Fidelis et fortis.* .This was a great matter in the way of honor, but very little in the way of wealth; so that when the illustrious companion of the great Henry died, the only inheritance he was able to leave his son was his sword and his device. Thanks to this double gift and the spotless name that accompanied them, M. de Tréville was admitted into the household of the young prince, where he made such good use of his sword, and was so faithful to his device, that Louis XIII., one of the good blades of his kingdom, was accustomed to say that, if he had a friend who was about to fight, he would advise him to choose as a second, himself first, and Tréville next, or even perhaps before him.

Thus Louis XIII. had a real liking for Tréville, a royal

liking, a selfish liking it is true, but which was still a liking.
At that unhappy period it was an important consideration to
be surrounded by such men as De Tréville. Many might
take for their device the epithet of *strong,* which formed the
second part of his motto, but very few gentlemen could lay
claim to the *faithful,* which constituted the first. Tréville
was one of these latter; his was one of those rare organiza-
tions, endowed with an obedient intelligence like that of the
dog, with a blind valor, a quick eye, and a prompt hand, to
whom sight appeared only to be given to see if the king were
dissatisfied with any one, and with the hand to strike this
displeasing any one, whether a Besme, a Maurevers, a Poltiot
de Méré, or a Vitry. In short, up to this period, nothing
had been wanting to De Tréville but opportunity; but he
was ever on the watch for it, and he promised himself that
he would never fail to seize it by its three hairs whenever it
came within reach of his hand. Louis XIII. then made De
Tréville the captain of his musketeers, who were to Louis
XIII., in devotedness, or rather in fanaticism, what his
Ordinaries had been to Henry III. and his Scotch Guard to
Louis XI.

On his part, and in this respect, the cardinal was not behindhand with the king. When he saw the formidable and
chosen body by which Louis XII. surrounded himself, this
second, or rather this first king of France, became desirous
that he too should have his guard. He had his musketeers
then, as Louis XIII. had his, and these two powerful rivals
vied with each other in procuring the most celebrated swordsmen, not only from all the provinces of France, but even from
all foreign states. It was not uncommon for Richelieu and
Louis XIII. to dispute over their evening game of chess upon
the merits of their servants. Each boasted the bearing and
the courage of his own people, and while exclaiming loudly
against duels and broils, they excited them secretly to quarrel, deriving an immoderate satisfaction or a true regret at
the success or defeat of their own combatants. We learn this
from the memoirs of a man who was concerned in some few
of these defeats and in many victories.

Tréville had seized on the weak side of his master, and it
was to this address that he owed the long and constant favor
of a king who has not left the reputation behind him of having been very faithful in his friendships. He paraded his
musketeers before the cardinal Aramand Duplessis with an insolent air, which made the gray mustache of his eminence
curl with ire. Tréville was a master of the war of that period,

in which he who did not live at the expense of the enemy, lived at the expense of his compatriots: his soldiers formed a legion of devil-may-care fellows, perfectly undisciplined as regarded every one but himself.

Loose, half-drunk, imposing, the king's musketeers, or rather M. de Tréville's, spread about in the cabarets, in the public walks, and the public sports, shouting, twisting their mustaches, clanking their swords, and "taking great pleasure in annoying the guards of M. le Cardinal when ever they could fall in with them; then drawing in the open streets, as if it were the best of all possible sports; sometimes killed, but sure in that case to be both wept and avenged; often killing others, but then certain of not rotting in prison, M. de Tréville being there to claim them. Thus M. de Tréville was praised to the highest note by these men, who absolutely adored him, and who, ruffians as they were, trembled before him like scholars before their master, obedient to his least word, and ready to sacrifice themselves to wash out the smallest insult.

M. de Tréville employed this powerful machine for the king in the first place, and the friends of the king—and then for himself and his own friends. For the rest, in none of the memoirs of this period, which has left so many memoirs, is this worthy gentleman accused even by his enemies, and he had many such among men of the pen, as well as among men of the sword; in no instance, we are told, was this worthy gentleman accused of deriving personal advantage from the co-operation of his minions. Endowed with a rare genius for intrigue, which rendered him the equal of the ablest intriguers, he remained an honest man. Still further, in spite of sword-thrusts which weaken, and painful exercises which fatigue, he had become one of the most gallant frequenters of revels, one of the most insinuating squires of dames, one of the softest whisperers of interesting nothings of his day: the *bonnes fortunes* of De Tréville were talked of as those of M. de Bassompierre had been talked of twenty years before, and that was not saying a little. The captain of the musketeers then, was admired, feared, and loved, which constitutes the apogee of human fortunes.

Louis XIV. absorbed all the smaller stars of his court in his own vast radiance; but his father, a sun *pluribus impar,* left his personal splendor to each of his favorites, his individual value to each of his courtiers. In addition to the *lever* of the king and that of the cardinal, there might be reckoned in Paris at that time more than two hundred smaller *levers,* each, in its degree, attended. Among these two hundred *levers,* that of De Tréville was one of the most thronged. The court of his hotel, situated in the Rue du Vieux-Colombier, resembled a camp, and that by six o'clock in the morning in summer and eight o'clock in winter. From fifty to sixty musketeers, who appeared to relieve each other in order always to present an imposing number, paraded constantly about, armed to the teeth and ready for anything. On one of those immense staircases upon whose space modern civilization would build a whole house, ascended and descended the solicitors of Paris, who were in search of favors of any kind: gentlemen from the provinces anxious to be enrolled, and servants in all sorts of liveries, bringing and carrying messages between their masters and M. de Tréville. In the antechamber upon long circular benches reposed the elect, that is to say, those who were called. In this apartment a continued buzzing prevailed from morning till night, while M. de Tréville, in his closet contiguous to this antechamber, received visits, listened to complaints, gave his orders, and like the king in his balcony at the Louvre, had only to place himself at the window to review both men and arms.

The day on which D'Artagnan presented himself, the assemblage was imposing, particularly for a provincial just arriving from his province: it is true that this provincial was a Gascon, and that particularly at this period, the compatriots of D'Artagnan had the reputation of not being easily intimidated. When he had once passed the massive door, covered with long square-headed nails, he fell into the midst of a troop of men of the sword, who crossed each other in their passage, calling out, quarreling, and playing tricks one among another. To make way through these turbulent and conflicting waves, it required to be an officer, a great noble, or a pretty woman.

It was, then, into the midst of this tumult and disorder that our young man advanced with a beating heart, ranging his long rapier up his lanky leg, and keeping one hand on the edge of his cap, with that provincial half-smile which affects confidence. When he had passed one group he began to breathe more freely; but he could not help observing that they turned round to look at him, and, for the first time in his life, D'Artagnan, who had till that day entertained a very good opinion of himself, felt that he was the object of ridicule.

When arrived at the staircase it was still worse; there were four musketeers on the bottom steps amusing themselves with the following exercise, while ten or twelve of their comrades waited upon the landing-place their turns to take their places in the sport.

One of them, placed upon the top stair, naked sword in hand, prevented, or at least endeavored to prevent, the three others from going up.

These three others fenced against him with their agile swords, which D'Artagnan at first took for foils, and believed to be buttoned; but he soon perceived, by certain scratches, that every weapon was pointed and sharpened, and that at each of these scratches, not only the spectators, but even the actors themselves laughed, like so many madmen.

He who at the moment occupied the upper step, kept his adversaries in check admirably. A circle was formed around them; the conditions required that at every hit the person hit should quite the game, losing his turn of audience to the advantage of the person who had hit him. In five minutes three were slightly wounded, one on the hand, another on the chin, and the third on the ear, by the defender of the stair, who himself remained intact: a piece of skill which was worth to him, according to agreement, three turns of favor.

However difficult it might be, or rather as he pretended it was, to astonish our young traveler, this pastime really astonished him; he had seen in his province—that land in which heads become so easily heated—a few of the preliminaries of duels, but the Gasconades of the four fences appeared to him the strongest he had ever heard, even in Gascony. He believed himself transported into that famous country of giants into which Gulliver since went and was so frightened; and yet he had not gained the goal, for there were still the landing-place and the antechamber.

On the landing they were no longer fighting, but amused themselves with stories about women, and in the antechamber with stories about the court. On the landing, D'Artagnan blushed; in the antechamber, he trembled. His warm and fickle imagination, which in Gascony had rendered him formidable to young chambermaids, and even sometimes to their mistresses, had never dreamed, even in moment of delirium, of half the amorous wonders, or a quarter of the feats of gallantry, which were here set forth, accompanied by names the best known, and with details the least delicate. But if his morals were shocked on the landing, his respect for the cardinal was scandalized in the antechamber. There, to his great astonishment, D'Artagnan heard the policy which made all Europe tremble, criticised aloud and openly, as well as the private life of the cardinal, which had brought about the punishment of so many great nobles for having dared to pry into: that great man, who was so revered by D'Artagnan the elder, served as an object of ridicule to the musketeers, who cracked their jokes upon his bandy legs and his humpback; some sang ballads upon Madame d'Aiguillon, his mistress, and Madame Cambalet, his niece; whilst others formed parties and plans to annoy the pages and guards of the cardinal duke—all things which appeared to D'Artagnan monstrous impossibilities.

Nevertheless, when the name of the king was now and then uttered unthinkingly amid all these cardinal jokes, a sort of gag seemed to close for a moment all the jeering mouths; they looked hesitatingly around them, and appeared to doubt the thickness of the partition between them and the closet of M. de Tréville; but a fresh allusion soon brought back the conversation to his eminence, and then the laughter recovered its loudness, and no coloring was spared to any of his actions.

"Certes, these fellows will all be either embastilled or hung," thought the terrified D'Artagnan, "and I, no doubt, with them; for from the moment I have either listened to or heard them, I shall be held to be an accomplice. What would my good father say, who so strongly pointed out to me the respect due to the cardinal, if he knew I was in the society of such pagans?"

We have no need, therefore, to say that D'Artagnan did not venture to join in the conversation; only he looked with all his eyes and listened with all his ears, stretching his five senses so as to lose nothing; and, in spite of his confidence in the paternal monitions, he felt himself carried by his tastes and led by his instincts to praise rather than to blame the unheard-of things which were passing before him.

D'Artagnan being, however, a perfect stranger in the crowd of M. de Tréville's courtiers, and this his first appearance in that place, he was at length noticed, and a person came to him and asked him his business there. At this demand, D'Artagnan gave his name very modestly, laid a stress upon the title of compatriot, and begged the servant who had put the question to him to request a moment's audience of M. de Tréville—a request which the other, with an air of protection, promised to convey in time and season.

D'Artagnan, a little recovered from his first surprise, had now leisure to study costumes and countenances.

The center of the most animated group was a musketeer of great height, of a haughty countenance, and dressed in a costume so peculiar as to attract general attention. He did not wear the uniform cloak—which, indeed, at that time, of less liberty and of still greater independence, was not obligatory —but a cerulean blue doublet, a little faded and worn, and over this a magnificent baldrick worked in gold, which shone like water-ripples in the sun. A long cloak of crimson velvet fell in graceful folds from his shoulders, disclosing in front the splendid baldrick, from which was suspended a gigantic rapier.

This musketeer had just come off guard, complained of having a cold, and coughed from time to time affectedly. It was for this reason, he said to those around him, he had put on his cloak, and while he spoke with a lofty air and twisted his mustache, all admired his embroidered baldrick, and D'Artagnan more than any one.

"What do you make a wonder about?" said the musketeer; "the fashion is coming in; it is a folly, I admit, but still it is the fashion. Besides one must lay out one's inheritance somehow."

"Ah, Porthos!" cried one of his companions, "don't think to palm upon us that you obtained that baldrick by paternal generosity; it was given to you by that veiled lady I met you with the other Sunday, near the gate Saint-Honore."

"No, 'pon honor; by the faith of a gentleman, I bought it with the contents of my own purse," answered he whom they designated under the name of Porthos.

"Yes, about in the same manner," said another musketeer, "as I bought this new purse with the money my mistress put into the old one."

"It's true, though," said Porthos; "and the proof is, that I paid twelve pistoles for it."

The wonder was increased, though the doubt continued to exist.

"Is it not true, Aramis?" said Porthos, turning toward another musketeer.

This other musketeer formed a perfect contrast with his interrogator, who had just designated him by the name of Aramis: he was a stout man, of about two or three-and-twenty, with an open, ingenuous countenance, a black, mild eye, and cheeks rosy and downy as an autumn peach; his delicate mustache marked a perfectly straight line upon his upper lip: he appeared to dread to lower his hands lest their veins should swell, and he pinched the tips of his ears from time to time to preserve their delicate pink transparency. Habitually he spoke little and slowly, bowed frequently, laughed without noise, showing his teeth, which were fine, and of which, as of the rest of his person, he appeared to take great care. He answered the appeal of his friend by an affirmative nod of the head.

This affirmation appeared to dispel all doubts with regard to the baldrick; they continued to admire it, but said no more about it; and, with one of the rapid changes of thought, the conversation passed suddenly to another subject.

"What do you think of the story Chalais' esquire relates?" asked another musketeer, without addressing any one in particular.

"And what does he say?" asked Porthos, in a self-sufficient tone.

"He relates that he met at Brussels Rochefort, the *âme damnée* of the cardinal, disguised as a capuchin; and that this cursed Rochefort, thanks to his disguise, had tricked M. de Laigues, like a simpleton as he is."

"A simpleton, indeed!" said Porthos; "but is the matter certain?"

"I had it from Aramis," replied the musketeer.

"Indeed!"

"Why, you know it is, Porthos," said Aramis; "I told you of it yesterday—say nothing more about it."

"Say nothing more about it—that's your opinion!" replied Porthos. "Say nothing more about it! *Peste!* you come to your conclusions quickly. What! the cardinal sets a spy upon a gentleman, has his letters stolen from him by means of a traitor, a brigand, a rascal—has, with the help of this spy, and thanks to this correspondence, Chalais' throat cut under the stupid pretext that he wanted to kill the king and marry monsieur to the queen! Nobody knew a word of this enigma. You unraveled it yesterday, to the great satisfaction of all; and while we are still gaping with wonder at the news, you come and tell us to day—'Let us say no more about it.'"

"'Well, then let us speak about it, since you desire it,'" replied Aramis patiently.

"This Rochforte," cried Porthos, "if I were poor Chalais' esquire, should pass a minute or two very uncomfortably with me."

"And you—you would pass rather a sad half-hour with the Red Duke," replied Aramis.

"Oh! oh! the Red Duke! bravo! bravo! the Red Duke!" cried Porthos, clapping his hands and nodding his head. "The Red Duke is capital. I'll circulate that saying, be assured, my dear fellow. Who says this Aramis is not a wit?

What a misfortune it is you did not follow your first vocation
—what a delightful abbé you would have made!"

"Oh, it's only a temporary postponement," replied Aramis;
"I shall be one, some day. You very well know, Porthos,
that I continue to study theology for that purpose."

"He will be one, as he says," cried Porthos; "he will be
one, sooner or later."

"Soon," said Aramis.

"He only waits for one thing to determine him to resume
his cassock, which hangs behind his uniform," said another
musketeer.

"What is he waiting for?" asked another.

"Only till the queen has given an heir to the crown of
France."

"No jokes upon that subject, gentlemen," said Porthos;
"thank God, the queen is still of an age to give one."

"They say that M. de Buckingham is in France," replied
Aramis, with a significant smile, which gave to this sentence,
apparently so simple, a tolerably scandalous meaning.

"Aramis, my good friend, this time you are wrong," interrupted Porthos, "your wit is always leading you astray; if
M. de Tréville heard you, you would repent of speaking thus."

"Are you going to teach me better, Porthos," cried Aramis,
from whose usually mild eye a flash passed like lightning.

"My dear fellow, be a musketeer or an abbé. Be one or
the other, but not both," replied Porthos. "You know what
Athos told you the other day: you eat at everybody's mess.
Ah! don't be angry, I beg of you, that would be useless; you
know what is agreed upon between you, Athos, and me. You
go to Madame d'Aiguillon's, and you pay your court to her;
you go to Madame de Bois-Tracy's, the cousin of Madame de
Chevreuse, and you pass for being far advanced in the good
graces of that lady. Oh, good Lord! don't trouble yourself
to reveal your good fortunes; no one asks for your secret—
all the world knows your discretion. But since you possess
that virtue, why the devil don't you make use of it with respect to her majesty? Let whoever likes talk of the king and
the cardinal, and how he likes; but the queen is sacred,
and if any one speaks of her, let it be well."

"Porthos, you are as vain as Narcissus, I plainly tell you
so," replied Aramis; "you know I hate moralizing, except
when it is done by Athos. As to you, good sir, you wear too
magnificent a baldrick to be strong on that head. I will be
an abbé if it suits me; in the meanwhile I am a musketeer:

in that quality I say what I please, and at this moment it
pleases me to say that you annoy me."

"Aramis!"

"Porthos!"

"Gentlemen! gentlemen!" cried the surrounding group.

"Monsieur de Tréville awaits M. d'Artagnan," cried a
servant, throwing open the door of the cabinet.

At this announcement, during which the door remained
open, every one became mute, and amid the general silence
the young man crossed the antechamber in a part of its length,
and entered the apartment of the captain of the musketeers,
congratulating himself with all his heart at having so narrowly
escaped the end of this strange quarrel.

CHAPTER III.

THE AUDIENCE.

M. DE TRÉVILLE was at the moment in rather an ill-
humor; nevertheless, he saluted the young man politely, who
bowed to the very ground, and he smiled on receiving his
compliment, the Béarnese accent of which recalled to him at
the same time his youth and his country, a double remembrance, which makes a man smile at all ages. But stepping
toward the antechamber, and making a sign to D'Artagnan
with his hand, as if to ask his permission to finish with others
before he began with him, he called three times, with a louder
voice at each time, so that he went through all the tones between the imperative accent and the angry accent.

"Athos! Porthos! Aramis!"

The two musketeers, with whom we have already made
acquaintance, and who answered to the last two of these three
names, immediately quitted the group of which they formed
a part, and advanced toward the cabinet, the door of which
closed after them as soon as they had entered. Their appearance, although it was not quite at ease, excited by its carelessness, at once full of dignity and submission, the admiration of D'Artagnan, who beheld in these two men demi-gods,
and in their leader an Olympian Jupiter, armed with all his
thunders.

When the two musketeers had entered, when the door was
closed behind them, when the buzzing murmur of the antechamber, to which the summons which had been made had

doubtless furnished fresh aliment, had recommenced; when
M. de Tréville had three or four times paced in silence, and
with a frowning brow, the whole length of his cabinet, passing each time before Porthos and Aramis, who were as upright
and silent as if on parade, he stopped all at once full in front
of them, and, covering them from head to foot with an angry
look:

"Do you know what the king said to me," cried he, "and
that no longer ago than yesterday evening—do you know,
gentlemen?"

"No," replied the two musketeers after a moment's silence
—"no, sir, we do not."

"But I hope that you will do us the honor to tell us," added
Aramis, in his politest tone, and with the most graceful bow.

"He told me that he should henceforth recruit his musketeers from among the guards of Monsieur the Cardinal."

"The guards of M. the Cardinal! and why so?" asked
Porthos warmly.

"Because he plainly perceives that his piquette* stands in
need of being enlivened by a mixture of good wine."

The two musketeers colored up to the eyes. D'Artagnan
did not know where he was, and would have wished to be a
hundred feet under ground.

"Yes, yes," continued M. de Tréville, growing warmer as
he spoke, "and his majesty was right, for, upon my honor, it
is true that the musketeers make but a miserable figure at
court. M. le Cardinal related yesterday, while playing with
the king, with an air of condolence not very pleasing to me,
that the day before yesterday those damned musketeers, those
dare-devils—he dwelt upon those words with an ironical tone
still more unpleasing to me—those braggarts, added he,
glancing at me with his tiger-cat's eye, had made a riot in
the Rue Ferou, in a cabaret, and that a party of his guards
(I thought he was going to laugh in my face) had been forced
to arrest the rioters. *Morbleu!* you must know something
about it! Arrest musketeers! You were among them—you
were! Don't deny it; you were recognized, and the cardinal
named you. But it's all my fault! yes, it's all my fault, because it is myself who select my men. You, now, Aramis,
why the devil did you ask me for a uniform, when you would
have been so much better in a cassock? And you, Porthos,
do you only wear such a fine golden baldrick to suspend a

* A liquor squeezed out of grapes, when they have been pressed,
and water poured upon them.

sword of straw from it? And Athos—I don't see Athos! Where is he?"

"Sir," replied Aramis, in a sorrowful tone, "he is ill, very ill!"

"Ill—very ill, say you? And what is his malady?"

"It is feared that it is the small-pox, sir," replied Porthos, desirous of getting a word in the conversation; "and, what is worse, that it will certainly spoil his face."

"The small-pox! That's a pretty glorious story to tell me, Porthos! Sick of the small-pox at his age! No, no; but wounded, without doubt—perhaps killed. Ah, if I knew! *Sang Dieu!* Messieurs musketeers, I will not have this haunting of bad places, this quarreling in the streets, this sword-play in cross-ways; and, above all, I will not have occasion given for the cardinal's guards, who are brave, quiet, skillful men, who never put themselves in a position to be arrested, and who, besides, never allow themselves to be arrested, to laugh at you! I am sure of it—they would prefer dying on the spot to being arrested, or to giving back a step. To save yourselves, to scamper away, to fly! a pretty thing to be said of the kings's musketeers!"

Porthos and Aramis trembled with rage; they could willingly have strangled M. de Tréville, if, at the bottom of all this, they had not felt it was the great love he bore them which made him speak thus. They stamped upon the carpet with their feet, they bit their lips till the blood sprang, and grasped the hilts of their swords with all their strength. Without, all had heard, as we have said, Athos, Porthos, and Aramis called, and had guessed from M. de Tréville's tone of voice that he was very angry about something. Ten curious heads were glued to the tapestry, and became pale with fury; for their ears, closely applied to the door, did not lose a syllable of what he said while their mouths repeated, as he went on, the insulting expressions of the captain to the whole population of the antechamber. In an instant, from the door of the cabinet to the street-gate, the whole hotel was in a state of commotion.

"Ah! the king's musketeers are arrested by the guards of M. the Cardinal, are they!" continued M. de Tréville, as furious within as his soldiers, but emphasizing his words, and plunging them, one by one, so to say, like so many blows of a stiletto, into the bossoms of his audtiors. "What! six of his eminence's guards arrest six of his majesty's muketeers! *Morbleu!* my part is taken! I will go straight to the Louvre; I will give in my resignation as captain of the king's musketeers, to take a lieutenancy in the cardinal's guards; and if he refuses me, *morbleu!* I will turn abbé."

At these words, the murmur without became an explosion; nothing was to be heard but oaths and blasphemies. The *morbleus!* the *sang Dieus!* the *morts de touts les diables!* crossed each other in the air. D'Artagnan looked round for some tapestry behind which he might hide himself, and felt an immense inclination to crawl under the table.

"Well, *mon capitaine,*" said Porthos, quite beside himself, "the truth is, that we were six against six; but we were not captured by fair means; and before we had time to draw our swords two of our party were dead; and Athos, grievously wounded, was very little better. For you know Athos. Well, captain, he endeavored twice to get up, and fell again twice. And we did not surrender—no! they dragged us away by force. On the way we escaped. As for Athos, they believed him to be dead, and left him very quietly on the field of battle, but not thinking it worth the trouble to carry him away. Now, that's the whole history. What the devil, captain, one cannot win all one's battles! The great Pompey lost that of Pharsalia; and Francis the First, who was, as I have heard say, as good as other folks, nevertheless lost the battle of Pavia."

"And I have the honor of assuring you that I killed one of them with his own sword," said Aramis, "for mine was broken at the first parry. Killed him, or poniarded him, sir, as is most agreeable to you."

"I did not know that," replied M. de Tréville, in a somewhat softened tone. "M. le Cardinal exaggerated, as I perceive."

"But pray, sir," continued Aramis, who, seeing his captain become appeased, ventured to risk a prayer—"pray, sir, do not say that Athos is wounded; he would be in despair if that should come to the ears of the king; and as the wound is very serious, seeing that after crossing the shoulder it penetrates into the chest, it is to be feared——"

At this instant the tapestry was raised, and a noble and handsome head, but frightfully pale, appeared under the fringe.

"Athos!" cried the two musketeers.

"Athos!" repeated M. de Tréville to himself.

"You have sent for me, sir," said Athos to M. de Tréville, in a feeble yet perfectly calm voice—"you have sent for me, as my comrades inform me, and I have hastened to receive your orders. I am here, monsieur; what do you want with me?"

And at these words the musketeer, in irreproachable costume, belted as usual, with a tolerably firm step, entered the cabinet. M. de Tréville, moved to the bottom of his heart by this proof of courage, sprang toward him.

"I was about to say to these gentlemen," added he, "that I forbid my musketeers to expose their lives needlessly; for brave men are very dear to the king, and the king knows that his musketeers are the bravest fellows on earth. Your hand, Athos!"

And without waiting for the answer of the newly-arrived to this proof of affection, M. de Tréville seized his right hand, and pressed it with all his might, without perceiving that Athos, whatever might be his self-command, allowed a slight murmur of pain to escape him, and, if possible, grew paler than he was before.

The door had remained open, so strong was the excitement produced by the arrival of Athos, whose wound, though kept as secret as possible, was known to all. A burst of satisfaction hailed the last words of the captain; and two or three heads, carried away by the enthusiasm of the moment, appeared through the openings of the tapestry. M. de Tréville was about to reprehend this infraction of the rules of etiquette when he felt the hand of Athos stiffen within his and upon turning his eyes toward him, perceived he was about to faint. At the same instant Athos, who had rallied all his energies to contend against pain, at length overcome by it, fell upon the floor as if he was dead.

"A surgeon!" cried M. de Tréville, "mine! the king's! the best that can be found—a surgeon! or, *sang Dieu!* my brave Athos will die!"

At the cries of M. de Tréville, the whole assemblage rushed into the cabinet without his thinking of shutting the door against any one, and all crowded round the wounded man. But all this eager attention might have been useless if the doctor so loudly called for had not chanced to be in the hotel. He pushed through the crowd, approached Athos, still insensible, and, as all this noise and commotion inconvenienced him greatly, he required, as the first and most urgent thing that the musketeer should be carried into another chamber. Immediately M. de Tréville opened the door, and pointed the way to Porthos and Aramis, who bore their comrade in their arms. Behind this group walked the surgeon, and as the surgeon passed through, the door closed.

The cabinet of M. de Tréville, generally held so sacred, became in an instant the recipient of the antechamber. Every one spoke, harangued, and vociferated, swearing, cursing, and consigning the cardinal and his guards to all the devils. An instant after, Porthos and Aramis re-entered, the surgeon and M. de Tréville alone remaining with the wounded man.

At length M. de Tréville himself returned. Athos had recovered his senses; the surgeon declared that the situation of the musketeer had nothing in it to render his friends uneasy, his weakness having been purely and simply caused by loss of blood.

Then M. de Tréville made a sign with his hand, and all retired except D'Artagnan, who did not forget that he had an audience, and, with the tenacity of a Gascon, remained in his place.

When all had gone out, and the door was closed, M. de Tréville, on turning round, found himself alone with the young man. The stirring event which had just passed had in some degree broken the thread of his ideas. He inquired what was the will of his persevering visitor. D'Artagnan then repeated his name, and in an instant, recovering all his remembrances of the present and the past, M. de Tréville was in possession of the current circumstances.

"Pardon me," said he, smiling, "pardon me, my dear compatriot, but I had perfectly forgotten you. But what help is there for it! a captain is nothing but a father of a family, charged with even a greater responsibility than the father of an ordinary family. Soldiers are great children; but as I maintain that the orders of the king, and more particularly the orders of M. the Cardinal should be executed——"

D'Artagnan could not restrain a smile. By this smile, M. de Tréville judged that he had not to deal with a fool, and changing the subject, came straight to the point.

"I respected your father very much," said he. "What can I do for the son? Tell me quickly, my time is not my own."

"Monsieur," said D'Artagnan, "on quitting Tarbes, and coming hither, it was my intention to request of you, in remembrance of the friendship which you have not forgotten, the uniform of a musketeer; but after all that I have seen, during the last two hours, I have become aware of the value of such a favor, and tremble lest I should not merit it."

"Well, young man," replied M. de Tréville, "it is, in fact, a favor, but it may not be so far beyond your hopes as you believe, or rather as you appear to believe; but his majesty's

decision is always necessary: and I inform you with regret,
that no one becomes a musketeer without the preliminary
ordeal of several campaigns, certain brilliant actions, or a
service of two years in some regiment of less reputation than
ours."

D'Artagnan bowed without replying, feeling his desire to
don the musketeer's uniform vastly increased by the difficulties which he learned preceded the attainment of it.

"But," continued M. de Tréville, fixing upon his compatriot a look so piercing, that it might be said he wished to
read the thoughts of his heart; "but, on account of my old
companion, your father, as I have said, I will do something
for you, young man. Our cadets from Béarn are not generally very rich, and I have no reason to think matters have
much changed in this respect since I left the province. I
dare say you have not brought too large a stock of money
with you?"

D'Artagnan drew himself up with an air that plainly said,
"I ask charity of no man."

"Oh! that's all very well, young man," continued M. de
Tréville, "that's all very well. I am well acquainted with
all those lofty airs; I myself came to Paris with four crowns
in my purse, and would have fought with any one who would
have dared to tell me I was not in a condition to purchase
the Louvre."

D'Artagnan's carriage became still more imposing; thanks
to the sale of his horse, he commenced his career with four
crowns more than M. de Tréville had possessed at the commencement of his.

"You ought, I say, then to husband the means you have,
however large the sum may be; but you ought also to endeavor to perfect yourself in the exercises becoming a gentleman. I will write a letter to-day to the director of the Royal
Academy, and to-morrow he will admit you without any expense to yourself. Do not refuse this little service. Our
best born and richest gentlemen sometimes solicit it, without
being able to obtain it. You will be learning riding, swords-
manship in all its branches, and dancing; you will make some
desirable acquaintances, and from time to time you can call
upon me, just to tell me how you are going on, and to say
whether I can be of further service to you."

D'Artagnan, stranger as he was to all the manners of a
court, could not but perceive a little coldness in this reception.

"Alas! sir," said he, "I cannot but perceive how sadly I

miss the letter of introduction which my father gave me to present to you."

"I certainly am surprised," replied M. de Tréville, "that you should undertake so long a journey without that necessary viaticum, the only resource of us poor Béarnese."

"I had one, sir, and, thank God, such as I could wish, but it was perfidiously stolen from me."

He then related the adventure of Meung, described the unknown gentleman with the greatest minuteness, and all with a warmth and truthfulness that delighted M. de Tréville.

"This is all very strange," said M. de Tréville, after meditating a minute; "you mentioned my name, then, aloud?"

"Yes, sir, I certainly committed that imprudence; but why should I have done otherwise? A name like yours must be as a buckler to me on my way. Why should I not avail myself of it?"

Flattery was at that period very current, and M. de Tréville loved incense as well as a king, or even a cardinal. He could not refrain from a smile of visible satisfaction, but this smile soon disappeared; and returning to the adventure of Meung:

"Tell me," continued he, "had not this gentleman a slight scar on his cheek?"

"Yes, such a one as would be made by the grazing of a ball."

"Was he not a fine-looking man?"

"Yes."

"Of lofty stature?"

"Yes."

"Of pale complexion and brown hair?"

"Yes, yes, that is he; how is it, sir, that you are acquainted with this man? If ever I should meet him again, and I will find him, I swear—were it in hell."

"He was waiting for a woman," continued Tréville.

"He, at least, departed immediately after having conversed for a minute with the one for whom he appeared to have been waiting."

"You did not gather the subject of their discourse?"

"He gave her a box; told her that that box contained her instructions, and desired her not to open it before she arrived in London."

"Was this woman English?"

"He called her Milady."

"It is he! it must be he!" murmured Tréville; "I thought he was still at Brussels!"

"Oh! sir; you know who and what this man is," cried

D'Artagnan, "tell me who he is, and whence he is. I will then release you from all your promises—even that of procuring my admission into the musketeers; for, before everything, I am desirous to avenge myself."

"Beware, young man!" cried De Tréville; "if you see him coming on one side of the street, pass by on the other! Do not cast yourself against such a rock; he would break you like glass."

"That thought will not prevent me," replied D'Artagnan, "if ever I should happen to meet with him."

"In the meantime, if you will take my advice, you will not seek him," said Tréville.

All at once, the captain stopped, as if struck by a sudden suspicion. This great hatred which the young traveler manifested so loudly for this man, who—a rather improbable thing—had stolen his father's letter from him! Was there not some perfidy concealed under this hatred? might not this young man be sent by his eminence? might he not have come for the purpose of laying a snare for him? this pretended D'Artagnan! was he not an emisarry of the cardinal's whom he sought to introduce into his house, to place near him, and win his confidence, and afterward to bring about his ruin, as had been practiced in a thousand other instances? He fixed his eyes upon D'Artagnan, even more earnestly than before. He was moderately reassured, however, by the aspect of that countenance, full of shrewd intelligence and affected humility.

I know he is a Gascon, reflected he; but he may be one for the cardinal as well as for me. Let us try him. "My friend," said he slowly, "I wish, as the son of an ancient friend—for I consider this story of the lost letter perfectly true—I wish, I say, in order to repair the coldness you may have remarked in my reception of you, to make you acquainted with the secrets of our policy. The king and the cardinal are the best of friends; their apparent bickerings are only feints to deceive fools. I am not willing that a compatriot, a handsome cavalier, a brave youth, quite fit to make his way, should become the dupe all of these artifices, and fall into the snare, after the example of so many others, who have been ruined by it. Be assured that I am devoted to both these all-powerful masters, and that my earnest endeavors have no other aim than the service of the king, and that of the cardinal, one of the most illustrious geniuses that France has ever produced.

"Now, young man, regulate your conduct accordingly; and if you entertain, whether from your family, your relations, or even from your instincts, any of these enmities which we see constantly breaking out against the cardinal, bid me adieu, and let us separate. I will aid you in many ways, but without attaching you to my person. I hope that my frankness, at least, will make you my friend; for you are the only young man to whom I have hitherto spoken as I have done to you."

Tréville said to himself:

"If the cardinal has set this young fox upon me, he will certainly not have failed, he, who knows how bitterly I execrate him, to tell his spy that the best means of making his court to me is to rail at him; therefore in spite of all my protestations, if it be as I suspect, my cunning gossip here will launch out in abuse of his eminence."

It, however, proved otherwise. D'Artagnan answered, with the greatest simplicity:

"I am come to Paris with exactly such intentions, sir. My father advised me to stoop to nobody but the king, Monsieur the Cardinal, and you—whom he considered the three first personages in France."

D'Artagnan added M. de Tréville to the others, as may be perceived; but he thought this adjunction would do no harm. "I hold, therefore, M. the Cardinal in the greatest veneration," continued he; "and have the greatest respect for his actions. So much the better for me, sir, if you speak to me, as you say, with frankness—for then you will do me the honor to esteem the resemblance of our opinions; but if you have entertained any doubt, as naturally you may, I feel that I am ruining myself by speaking the truth. But I still trust you will not esteem me the less for it, and that is my object beyond all others."

M. de Tréville was surprised to the greatest degree. So much penetration—so much frankness—created admiration, but did not entirely remove his suspicions; the more this young man was superior to others, the more he was to be dreaded, if he meant to deceive him. Nevertheless, he pressed D'Artagnan's hand, and said to him:

"You are an honest youth; but, at the present moment, I can only do for you that which I just now offered. My hotel will be always open to you. Hereafter, being able to ask for me at all hours, and consequently to take advantage of all opportunities, you will probably obtain that which you desire."

"That is to say, sir," replied D'Artagnan, "that you will wait till I have proved myself worthy of it. Well! be assured," added he, with the familiarity of a Gascon, "you shall not wait long." And he bowed on retiring, as if he considered the future was left in his own hands.

"But, wait a minute," said M. de Tréville, stopping him. "I promised you a letter for the director of the academy; are you too proud to accept it, young gentleman?"

"No, sir," said D'Artagnan; "and I will answer for it that this one shall not fare like the other. I will guard it so carefully that I will be sworn it shall arrive at its address, and woe be to him who shall attempt to take it from me!"

M. de Tréville smiled at this little flourish; and, leaving his young companion in the embrasure of the window, where they had talked together, he seated himself at a table, in order to write the promised letter of recommendation. While he was doing this, D'Artagnan, having no better employment, amused himself with beating a march upon the window, and with looking at the musketeers, who went away, one after another, following them with his eyes till they disappeared at the turning of the street.

M. de Tréville, after having written the letter, sealed it; and, rising, approached the young man, in order to give it to him. But, at the very moment that D'Artagnan stretched out his hand to receive it, M. de Tréville was highly astonished to see his *protégé* make a sudden spring, become crimson with passion, and rush from the cabinet, crying: "Ah! *Sang Dieu!* he shall not escape me this time!"

"Who? who?" asked M. de Tréville.

"He, my thief!" replied D'Artagnan. "Ah! the traitor!" and he disappeared.

"The devil take the madman!" murmured M. de Tréville, "unless," added he, "this is a cunning mode of escaping, seeing that he has failed in his purpose!"

CHAPTER IV.

THE SHOULDER OF ATHOS, THE BALDRICK OF PORTHOS, AND THE HANDKERCHIEF OF ARAMIS.

D'ARTAGNAN, in a state of fury, crossed the antechamber at three bounds, and was darting toward the stairs, which he reckoned upon descending four at a time, when, in his heedless course, he ran headforemost against a musketeer, who was coming out of one of M. de Tréville's back rooms, and striking his shoulder violently, made him utter a cry, or rather a howl.

"Excuse me," said D'Artagnan, endeavoring to resume his course, "excuse me, but I am in a hurry."

Scarcely had he descended the first stair, when a hand of iron seized him by the belt and stopped him.

"You are in a hurry," said the musketeer, as pale as a sheet; "under that pretense, you run against me; you say, 'Excuse me!' and you believe that that is sufficient? Not at all, my young man. Do you fancy that because you have heard M. de Tréville speak to us a little cavalierly to-day that other people are to treat us as he speaks to us? Undeceive yourself, my merry companion, you are not M. de Tréville."

"Ma foi!" replied D'Artagnan, recognizing Athos, who, after the dressing performed by the doctor, was going to his own apartment, "ma foi! I did not do it intentionally, and, not doing it intentionally, I said, 'Excuse me!' It appears to me that that is quite enough. I repeat to you, however, and this time, *parole d'honneur*—I think, perhaps, too often—that I am in great haste—great haste. Leave your hold then, I beg of you, and let me go where my business calls me."

"Monsieur," said Athos, letting him go, "you are not polite; it is easy to perceive that you come from a distance."

D'Artagnan had already strode down three or four stairs, when Athos' last remark stopped him short.

"*Morbleu*, monsieur!" said he, "however far I may come, it is not you who can give me a lesson in good manners, I warn you."

"Perhaps!" said Athos.

"Ah! if I were not in such haste, and if I were not running after some one," said D'Artagnan.

"Mister gentleman in a hurry, you can find me without running after me; me! do you understand me?"

"And where, I pray you?"

"Near the Carmes Deschaux."

"At what hour?"

"About noon."

"About noon; that will do, I will be there."

"Endeavor not to make me wait, for at a quarter past twelve I will cut off your ears as you run."

"Good!" cried D'Artagnan, "I will be there ten minutes before twelve."

And he set off running as if the devil possesssed him, hoping that he might yet find the unknown, whose slow pace could not have carried him far.

But at the street-gate Porthos was talking with the soldier on guard. Between the two talkers there was just room for a man to pass. D'Artagnan thought it would suffice for him, and he sprang forward like a dart between them. But D'Artagnan had reckoned without the wind. As he was about to pass, the wind blew out Porthos' long cloak, and D'Artagnan rushed straight into the middle of it. Without doubt, Porthos had reasons for not abandoning this part of his vestments, for, instead of quitting his hold of the flap in his hand, he pulled it toward him, so that D'Artagnan rolled himself up in the velvet, by a movement of rotation explained by the persistency of Porthos.

D'Artagnan, hearing the musketeer swear, wished to escape from under the cloak which blinded him, and endeavored to make his way up the folds of it. He was particularly anxious to avoid marring the freshness of the magnificent baldrick we are acquainted with; but on timidly opening his eyes, he found himself with his nose fixed between the two shoulders of Porthos, that is to say, exactly upon the baldrick.

Alas! how most of the things in this world have nothing in their favor but appearances! the baldrick was glittering with gold in the front, but was nothing but simple buff behind. Vainglorious as he was, Porthos could not afford to have an entirely gold-worked baldrick, but had, at least, half one; the care on account of the cold, and the necessity for the cloak became intelligible.

"*Vertubleu!*" cried Porthos, making strong efforts to get rid of D'Artagnan, who was wriggling about his back, "the fellow must be mad to run against people in this manner!"

"Excuse me!" said D'Artagnan, reappearing under the shoulder of the giant, "but I am in such haste—I was running after some one and——"

"And do you always forget your eyes when you happen to be in a hurry?" asked Porthos.

"No," replied D'Artagnan, piqued, "no, and thanks to my eyes, I can see what other people cannot see."

Whether Porthos understood him or did not understand him, giving way to his anger:

"Monsieur," said he, "you stand a chance of getting chastised if you run against musketeers in this fashion."

"Chastised, monsieur!" said D'Artagnan, "the expression is strong."

"It is one that becomes a man accustomed to look his enemies in the face."

"Ah! *pardieu!* I know full well that you don't turn your back to yours!"

And the young man, delighted with his joke, went away laughing loudly.

Porthos foamed with rage, and made a movement to rush after D'Artagnan.

"Presently, presently," cried the latter, "when you haven't your cloak on."

"At one o'clock then, behind the Luxembourg."

"Very well, at one o'clock, then," replied D'Artagnan, turning the angle of the street.

But neither in the street he had passed through, nor in the one which his eager glance pervaded, could he see any one; however slowly the unknown had walked, he was gone on his way, or perhaps had entered some house. D'Artagnan inquired of every one he met with, went down to the ferry, came up again by the Rue de Seine, and the Croix Rouge; but nothing, absolutely nothing! This chase was, however, advantageous to him in one sense, for in proportion as the perspiration broke from his forehead, his heart began to cool.

He began to reflect upon the events that had passed; they were numerous and inauspicious; it was scarcely eleven o'clock in the morning, and yet this morning had already brought him into disgrace with M. de Tréville, who could not fail to think the manner in which D'Artagnan had left him a little cavalier.

Besides this, he had drawn upon himself two good duels with two men, each capable of killing three D'Artagnans, with two musketeers, in short, with two of those beings whom he esteemed so greatly that he placed them in his mind and heart above all other men.

Appearances were sad. Sure of being killed by Athos, it may easily be understood that the young man was not very uneasy about Porthos. As hope, however, is the last thing extinguished in the heart of man, he finished by hoping that he might survive, although terribly wounded in both these duels, and in case of surviving, he made the following reprehensions upon his own conduct.

"What a hare-brained, stupid fellow I am! That brave and unfortunate Athos was wounded exactly on that shoulder against which I must run head-formost, like a ram. The only thing that astonishes me is that he did not strike me dead at once: he had good cause to do so, the pain I gave

him must have been atrocious. As to Porthos, oh! as to
Porthos, *ma foi!* that's a droll affair!"

And, in spite of himself, the young man began to laugh
aloud, looking round carefully, however, to see if his solitary
laugh, without an apparent cause, in the eyes of passers-by,
offended no one.

"As to Porthos, that is certainly droll, but I am not the less
a giddy fool. Are people to be run against without warning?
No! and have I any right to go and peep under their cloaks
to see what is not there? He would have pardoned me, he
would certainly have pardoned me, if I had not said anything
to him about that cursed baldrick, in ambiguous words, it is
true, but rather drolly ambiguous! Ah! cursed Gascon that
I am, I get from one hobble into another. Friend D'Artagnan," continued he, speaking to himself with all the
amenity that he thought due to himself, "if you escape, of
which there is not much chance, I would advise you to practice perfect politeness for the future. You must henceforth
be admired and quoted as a model of it. To be obliging and
polite does not necessarily make a man a coward. Look at
Aramis now: Aramis is mildness and grace personified. Well!
did ever anybody dream of saying that Aramis is a coward?
No, certainly not, and from this moment I will endeavor to
model myself after him. Ah! that's strange! here he is!"

D'Artagnan, walking and solioquizing had arrived within
a few steps of the Hotel d'Arguillon, and in front of that
hotel perceived Aramis chatting gayly with three gentlemen
of the king's guards. On this part Aramis perceived D'Artagnan; but as he had not forgotten that it was before this
young man that M. de Tréville had been so angry in the
morning, and that a witness of the rebuke the musketeers
had received was not likely to be at all agreeable, he pretended
not to see him. D'Artagnan, on the contrary, quite full of
his plans of conciliation and courtesy, approached the young
men, with a profound bow, accompanied by a most gracious
smile. Aramis bowed his head slightly, but did not smile.
All four, besides, immediately broke off their conversation.

D'Artagnan was not so dull as not to perceive that he was
not wanted; but he was not sufficiently broken into the
fashions of the world to know how to extricate himself gallantly from a false position, as that of a man generally is who
comes up and mingles with people he is scarcely acquainted
with, and in a conversation that does not concern him. He
was seeking in his mind, then, for the least awkward means
of retreat, when he remarked that Aramis had let his hand-

kerchief fall, and, by mistake, no doubt, had placed his foot upon it, and it appeared a favorable opportunity to repair his intrusion: he stooped, and with the most gracious air he could assume, drew the handerchief from under the foot of the musketeer, in spite of the efforts the latter made to detain it, and holding it out to him, said:

"I believe, monsieur, that this is a handkerchief you would be sorry to lose?"

The handkerchief was, in fact, richly embroidered, and had a coronet and arms at one of its corners. Aramis blushed excessively, and snatched rather than took the handkerchief from D'Artagnan's hand.

"Ah! ah!" cried one of the guards, "will you persist in saying, most discreet Aramis, that you are not on good terms with Madame de Bois-Tracy, when that gracious lady has the kindness to lend you her handkerchief?"

Aramis darted at D'Artagnan one of those looks which inform a man that he has acquired a mortal enemy; then, resuming his mild air:

"You are deceived, gentlemen," said he, "this handkerchief is not mine, and I cannot fancy why monsieur has taken it into his head to offer it to me rather than to one of you, and as a proof of what I say, here is mine in my pocket."

So saying, he pulled out his own handkerchief, which was likewise a very elegant handkerchief, and of fine cambric, though cambric was then dear, but a handkerchief with embroidery and without arms, only ornamented with a single cipher, that of the musketeer.

This time D'Artagnan was not hasty, he perceived his mistake; but the friends of Aramis were not at all convinced by his assertion, and one of them, addressing the young musketeer with affected seriousness:

"If it were as you pretend it is," said he, "I should be forced, my dear Aramis, to reclaim it myself; for, as you very well know, Bois-Tracy is an intimate friend of mine, and I cannot allow the property of his wife to be sported as a trophy."

"You make the demand badly," replied Aramis; "and while acknowledging the justice of your reclamation, I refuse it on account of the form."

"The fact is," hazarded D'Artagnan timidly, "I did not see the handkerchief fall from the pocket of M. Aramis. He had his foot upon it, that is all, and I thought from his having his foot upon it, the handkerchief was his."

"And, you were deceived, my dear sir," replied Aramis

coldly, very little sensible to the reparation; then turning toward that one of the guards who had declared himself the friend of Bois-Tracy; "besides," continued he, "I have reflected, my dear intimate friend of Bois-Tracy, that I am not less tenderly his friend than you can possibly be, so that decidedly this handkerchief is as likely to have fallen from your pocket as mine."

"No, upon my honor!" cried his majesty's guard.

"You are about to swear upon your honor and I upon my word, and then it will be pretty evident that one of us will have lied. Now, here, Montaran, we will do better than that, let each take a half."

"Of the handkerchief?"

"Yes."

"Perfectly just," cried the two other guards—"the judgment of King Solomon! Aramis, you certainly are cram-full of wisdom!"

The young men burst into a loud laugh, and, as may be supposed, the affair had no other consequence. In a moment or two the conversation ceased, and the three guards and the musketeer, after having cordially shaken hands, separated, the guards going one way, and Aramis another.

"Now is my time to make my peace with this gentleman," said D'Artagnan to himself, having stood on one side during the whole of the latter part of the conversation; and with this good feeling drawing near to Aramis, who was going without paying any attention to him.

"Monsieur," said he, "you will excuse me, I hope."

"Ah! monsieur," interrupted Aramis, "permit me to observe to you, that you have not acted in this affair as a man of good breeding ought to have done."

"What, monsieur!" cried D'Artagnan, "you suppose——"

"I suppose, monsieur, that you are not a fool, and that you knew very well, although coming from Gascony, that people do not tread upon pocket-handkerchiefs without a reason. What the devil! Paris is not paved with cambric!"

"Monsieur, you act wrongly in endeavoring to mortify me," said D'Artagnan, with whom the natural quarrelsome spirit began to speak more loudly than his pacific resolutions. "I am from Gascony, it is true; and since you know it, there is no occasion to tell you that Gascons are not very enduring, so that when they have begged to be excused at once, were it even for a folly, they are convinced that they have done already at least as much again as they ought to have done."

"Monsieur, what I say to you about the matter," said Aramis, "is not for the sake of seeking a quarrel. Thank God! I am not a spadasin, and, being a musketeer but for a time, I only fight when I am forced to do so, and always with great repugnance; but this time the affair is serious, for here is a lady compromised by you."

"By us, you mean," cried D'Artagnan.

"Why did you so injudiciously restore me the handkerchief?"

"Why did you so awkwardly let it fall?"

"I have said, monsieur, that the handkerchief did not fall from my pocket."

"Well, and by saying so, you have lied twice, monsieur, for I saw it fall."

"Oh, oh! you take it up in that way, do you, Master Gascon? Well, I will teach you how to behave yourself."

"And I will send you back to your mass-book, Master Abbé. Draw, if you please, and instantly——"

"Not so, if you please, my good friend, not here, at least. Do you not perceive that we are opposite the Hotel d'Arguillon, which is full of the cardinal's creatures? How do I know that it is not his eminence who has honored you with the commission to bring him in my head? Now I entertain a ridiculous partiality for my head, it seems to suit my shoulders so admirably. I have no objection to killing you, depend upon that, but quietly, in a snug remote place, where you will not be able to boast of your death to anybody."

"I agree, monsieur, but do not be too confident. Take away your handkerchief; whether it belongs to you or another, you may, perhaps, stand in need of it."

"Monsieur is a Gascon?" asked Aramis.

"Yes. Monsieur does not postpone an interview through prudence?"

"Prudence, monsieur, is a virtue sufficiently useless to musketeers, I know, but indispensable to churchmen; and as I am only a musketeer provisionally, I hold it good to be prudent. At two o'clock I shall have the honor of expecting you at the hotel of M. de Tréville. There I will point out to you the best place and time."

The two young men bowed and separated, Aramis ascending the street which led to the Luxembourg, while D'Artagnan, perceiving the appointed hour was approaching, took the road to the Carmes-Deschaux, saying to himself, "Decidedly I can't draw back; but at least, if I am killed, I shall be killed by a musketeer!"

CHAPTER V.

THE KING'S MUSKETEERS AND THE CARDINAL'S GUARDS.

D'ARTAGNAN was acquainted with nobody in Paris. He went, therefore, to his appointment with Athos, without a second, determined to be satisfied with those his adversary should choose. Besides, his intention was formed to make the brave musketeer all suitable apologies, but without meanness or weakness, fearing that that might result from this duel which generally results from an affair of the kind, when a young and vigorous man fights with an adversary who is wounded and weakened: if conquered, he doubles the triumph of his antagonist; if a conqueror, he is accused of foul play and want of courage.

Now, we must have badly painted the character of our adventurer, or our readers must have already perceived that D'Artagnan was not a common man; therefore, while repeating to himself that his death was inevitable, he did not make up his mind to die so quietly as another, less courageous and less moderate than he might have done in his place. He reflected upon the different characters of the men he had to fight with, and began to view his situation more clearly. He hoped, by means of loyal excuses to make a friend of Athos, whose nobleman air, and austere courage pleased him much. He flattered himself he should be able to frighten Porthos with the adventure of the baldrick, which he might, if not killed upon the spot, relate to everybody—a recital which, well managed, would cover Porthos with ridicule; as to the astute Aramis, he did not entertain much dread of him, and if he should be able to get so far as him, he determined to despatch him in good style, or, at least, by hitting him in the face, as Cæsar recommended his soldiers to do to those of Pompey, damage the beauty of which he was so proud forever.

In addition to this, D'Artagnan possessed that invincible stock of resolution which the counsels of his father had implanted in his heart—Endure nothing from any one but the king, the cardinal, and M. de Tréville. He flew, then, rather than walked, toward the convent of the Carmes Déchaussés, or rather Dechaux, as it was called at that period, a sort of building without a window, surrounded by barren fields, an accessory to the Pré-aux-Clercs, and which was generally employed as the place for the rencounters of men who had no time to lose.

THE THREE MUSKETEERS

When D'Artagnan arrived in sight of the bare spot of ground which extended along the foot of the monastery, Athos had been waiting about five minutes, and twelve o'clock was striking; he was, then, as punctual as the Samaritan woman, and the most rigorous casuist with regard to duels could have nothing to say.

Athos, who still suffered grievously from his wound, though it had been dressed by M. de Tréville's surgeon at nine, was seated on a post and waiting for his adversary with that placid countenance and that noble air which never forsook him. At sight of D'Artagnan, he arose and came politely a few steps to meet him. The latter, on his side, saluted his adversary with hat in hand, and his feather even touching the ground.

"Monsieur," said Athos, "I have engaged two of my friends as seconds; but these two friends are not yet come, at which I am astonished, as it is not at all their custom to be behindhand."

"I have no seconds on my part, monsieur," said D'Artagnan; "for, having only arrived yesterday in Paris, I as yet know no one but M. de Tréville, to whom I was recommended by my father, who has the honor to be, in some degree, one of his friends."

Athos reflected for an instant.

"You know no one but M. de Tréville?" he asked.

"No, monsieur; I only know him."

"Well, but then," continued Athos, speaking partly to himself, "well, but then, if I kill you, I shall have the air of a boy-slayer."

"Not too much so," replied D'Artagnan, with a bow that was not deficient in dignity, "not too much so, since you do me the honor to draw a sword with me while suffering from a wound which is very painful."

"Very painful, upon my word, and you hurt me devilishly, I can tell you; but I will take the left hand—I usually do so in such circumstances. Do not fancy that I favor you—I use both hands equally; and it will be even a disadvantage to you —a left-handed man is very troublesome to people who are not used to it. I regret I did not inform you sooner of this circumstance."

"You are truly, monsieur," said D'Artagnan, bowing again, "of a courtesy, for which, I assure you, I am very grateful."

"You confuse me," replied Athos, with his gentlemanly

air; "let us talk of something else, if you please. Ah, *sang Dieu!* how you have hurt me! my shoulder quite burns."

"If you would permit me—" said D'Artagnan, with timidity.

"What, monsieur?"

"I have a miraculous balsam for wounds—a balsam given to me by my mother, and of which I have made a trial upon myself."

"Well?"

"Well, I am sure that in less than three days this balsam would cure you; and at the end of three days, when you would be cured—well, sir, it would still do me a great honor to be your man."

D'Artagnan spoke these words with a simplicity that did honor to his courtesy, without throwing the least doubt upon his courage.

"*Pardieu,* monsieur!" said Athos, "that's a proposition that pleases me; not that I accept it, but it savors of the gentleman a league off. It was thus that spoke the gallant knights of the time of Charlemagne, in whom every knight ought to seek his model. Unfortunately, we do not live in the time of the great emperor; we live in the times of Monsieur the Cardinal, and three days hence, however well the secret might be guarded, it would be known, I say, that we were to fight, and our combat would be prevented. I think these fellows will never come."

"If you are in haste, monsieur," said D'Artagnan, with the same simplicity with which a moment before he had proposed to him to put off the duel for three days, "if you are in haste, and if it be your will to despatch me at once, do not inconvenience yourself—I am ready."

"Well, that is again well said," cried Athos, with a gracious nod to D'Artagnan, that did not come from a man without brains, and certainly not from a man without a heart. "Monsieur, I love men of your kidney, and I foresee plainly that, if we don't kill each other, I shall hereafter have much pleasure in your conversation. We will wait for these gentlemen, if you please; I have plenty of time, and it will be more correct. Ah! here is one of them, I think."

In fact, at the end of the Rue Vanguard, the gigantic form of Porthos began to appear.

"What!" cried D'Artagnan, "is your first second M Porthos?"

"Yes. Is that unpleasant to you?"

"Oh, not at all."

"And here comes the other."

D'Artagnan turned in the direction pointed to by Athos and perceived Aramis.

"What!" cried he, in an accent of greater astonishment than before, "is your second witness M. Aramis?"

"Doubtless he is. Are you not aware that we are never seen one without the others, and that we are called in the musketeers and the guards, at court and in the city, Athos, Porthos, and Aramis, or the three inseparables? And yet, as you come from Dax or Pau——."

"From Tarbes," said D'Artagnan.

"It is probable you are ignorant of this circumstance," said Athos.

"*Ma foi!*" replied D'Artagnan, "you are well named, gentlemen, and my adventure, if it should make any noise, will prove at least that your union is not founded upon contrasts."

In the meantime Porthos had come up, waved his hand to Athos, and then turning toward D'Artagnan, stood quite astonished.

Permit us to say, in passing, that he had changed his baldrick, and was without his cloak.

"Ah, ah!" said he, "what does this mean?"

"This is the gentleman I am going to fight with," said Athos, pointing to D'Artagnan with his hand, and saluting him with the same gesture.

"Why, it is with him I am also going to fight," said Porthos.

"But not before one o'clock," replied D'Artagnan.

"Well, and I also am going to fight with that gentleman," said Aramis, coming on to the ground as he spoke.

"But not till two o'clock," said D'Artagnan, with the same calmness.

"But what are you going to fight about, Athos?" asked Aramis.

Ma foi! I don't very well know; he hurt my shoulder. And you, Porthos?"

"*Ma foi!* I am going to fight, because I am going to fight," answered Porthos, coloring deeply.

Athos, whose keen eye lost nothing, perceived a faintly sly smile pass over the lips of the young Gascon, as he replied:

"We had a short discussion upon dress."

"And you, Aramis?" asked Athos.

"Ah, ours is a theological quarrel," replied Aramis, making a sign to D'Artagnan to keep secret the cause of their dispute.

Athos saw a second smile on the lips of D'Artagnan.
"Indeed?" said Athos.
"Yes; a passage of St. Augustin, upon which we could
not agree," said the Gascon.
"By Jove! this a clever fellow," murmured Athos.
"And now you are all assembled, gentlemen," said D'Artagnan, "permit me to offer you my excuses."
At this word *excuses,* a cloud passed over the brow of
Athos, a haughty smile curled the lips of Porthos, and a nega-
tive sign was the reply of Aramis.
"You do not understand me, gentlemen," said D'Artagnan,
throwing up his head, the sharp and bold lines of which were
at the moment gilded by a bright sun ray. "I ask to be
excused in case I should not be able to discharge my debt to
all three; for M. Athos has the right to kill me first, which
must abate your valor in your own estimation, M. Porthos,
and render yours almost null, M. Aramis. And now, gentlemen, I repeat, excuse me, but on that account only, and—
guard!"
At these words, with the most gallant air possible, D'Artagnan drew his sword.
The blood had mounted to the head of D'Artagnan, and at
that moment he would have drawn his sword against all the
musketeers in the kingdom, as willingly as he now did against
Athos, Porthos, and Aramis.
It was a quarter past midday. The sun was in its zenith,
and the spot chosen for the theater of the duel was exposed
to its full power.
"It is very hot," said Athos, drawing his sword in his turn,
"and yet I cannot take off my doublet for I just now felt my
wound begin to bleed again, and I should not like to annoy
monsieur with the sight of blood which he has not drawn
from me himself."
"That is true, monsieur," replied D'Artagnan, "and,
whether drawn by myself or another, I assure you I shall
always view with regret the blood of so brave a gentleman;
I will therefore fight in my doublet, as you do."
"Come, come, enough of compliments," cried Porthos;
"please to remember we are waiting for our turns."
"Speak for yourself, when you are inclined to utter such
incongruities," interrupted Aramis. "For my part, I think
what they say is very well said, and quite worthy of two gentlemen."
"When you please, monsieur," said Athos, putting himself on guard.

"I waited your orders," said D'Artagnan, crossing swords. But scarcely had the two rapiers sounded on meeting, when a company of the guards of his eminence, commanded by M. de Jussac, turned the angle of the convent.

"The cardinal's guards! the cardinal's guards!" cried Aramis and Porthos at the same time. "Sheathe swords! gentlemen! sheathe swords!"

But it was too late. The two combatants had been seen in a position which left no doubt of their intentions.

"Hola!" cried Jussac, advancing toward them, and making a sign to his men to do so likewise, "hola! musketeers, fighting here, then, are you? And the edicts, what is become of them?"

"You are very generous, gentlemen of the guards," said Athos, with acrimony, for Jussac was one of the aggressors of the preceding day. "If we were to see you fighting, I can assure you that we would make no effort to prevent you. Leave us alone then, and you will enjoy a little amusement without cost to yourselves."

"Gentlemen," said Jussac, "it is with great regret that I pronounce the thing impossible. Duty before everything. Sheathe, then, if you please, and follow us."

"Monsieur," said Aramis, parodying Jussac, "it would afford us great pleasure to obey your polite invitation, if it depended upon ourselves; but, unfortunately, the thing is impossible; M. de Tréville has forbidden it. Pass on your way, then; it is the best thing you can do."

This raillery exasperated Jussac.

"We will charge upon you, then," said he, "if you disobey."

"There are five of them," said Athos, half aloud, "and we are but three; we shall be beaten again, and must die on the spot, for, on my part, I declare I will never appear before the captain again as a conquered man."

Athos, Porthos, and Aramis, instantly closed in, and Jussac drew up his soldiers.

This short interval was sufficient to determine D'Artagnan on the part he was to take; it was one of those events which decide the life of a man; it was a choice between the king and the cardinal; the choice made, it must be persisted in. To fight was to disobey the law, to risk his head, to make at once an enemy of a minister more powerful than the king himself; all this the young man perceived, and yet, to his praise we speak it, he did not hesitate a second. Turning toward Athos and his friends:

"Gentlemen," said he, "allow me to correct your words, if you please. You said you were but three, but it appears to me we are four."

"But you are not one of us," said Porthos.

"That's true," replied D'Artagnan; "I do not wear the uniform, but I am in spirit. My heart is that of a musketeer; I feel it, monsieur, and that impels me on."

"Withdraw, young man," cried Jussac, who, doubtless, by his gesture and the expression of his countenance, had guessed D'Artagnan's design. "You may retire, we allow you to do so. Save your skin; begone quickly."

D'Artagnan did not move.

"Decidedly you are a pretty fellow," said Athos, pressing the young man's hand.

"Come, come, decide one way or the other," replied Jussac.

"Well," said Porthos to Aramis, "we must do something."

"Monsieur is very generous," said Athos.

But all three reflected upon the youth of D'Artagnan, and dreaded his inexperience.

"We should only be three, one of whom is wounded, with the addition of a boy," resumed Athos, "and yet it will be not the less said we were four men."

"Yes, but to yield!" said Porthos.

"That's rather difficult," replied Athos.

D'Artagnan comprehended whence a part of this irresolution arose.

"Try me, gentlemen," said he, "and I swear to you by my honor that I will not go hence if we are conquered."

"What is your name, my brave fellow?" said Athos.

"D'Artagnan, monsieur."

"Well, then! Athos, Porthos, Aramis, and D'Artagnan, forward!" cried Athos.

"Come, gentlemen, have you made your minds up?" cried Jussac, for the third time.

"It is done, gentlemen," said Athos.

"And what do you mean to do?" asked Jussac.

"We are about to have the honor of charging you," replied Aramis, lifting his hat with one hand, and drawing his sword with the other.

"Oh! you resist, do you!" cried Jussac.

"*Sang Dieu!* does that astonish you?"

And the nine combatants rushed upon each other with a fury which, however, did not exclude a certain degree of method.

Athos fixed upon a certain Cahusac, a favorite of the cardi-

nal's; Porthos had Bicarat, and Aramis found himself opposed to two adversaries. As to D'Artagnan, he sprang
toward Jussac himself. The heart of the young Gascon
beat as if it would burst through his side, not from fear, God
be thanked—he had not the shade of it—but with emulation;
he fought like a furious tiger, turning ten times round his
adversary, and changing his ground and his guard twenty
times. Jussac was, as was then said, a fine blade, and had
had much practice; nevertheless, it required all his skill to
defend himself against an adversary, who, active and ener-
getic, departed every instant from received rules, attacking
him on all sides at once, and yet parrying like a man who
had the greatest respect for his own epidermis.

This contest at length exhausted Jussac's patience. Furious at being held in check by him whom he had considered a
boy, he became warm, and began to commit faults. D'Artagnan, who, though wanting in practice, had a profound
theory, redoubled his agility. Jussac, anxious to put an end
to this, springing forward, aimed a terrible thrust at his adversary, but the latter parried it; and while Jussac was recovering himself, glided like a serpent beneath his blade, and
passed his sword through his body. Jussac fell like a dead
mass.

D'Artagnan then cast an anxious and rapid glance over the
field of battle.

Aramis had killed one of his adversaries, but the other
pressed him warmly. Nevertheless, Aramis was in a good
situation, and able to defend himself.

Bicarat and Porthos had just made counter-hits; Porthos
had received a thrust through his arm, and Bicarat one
through his thigh. But neither of the wounds was serious,
and they only fought the more earnestly for them.

Athos, wounded again by Cahusac, became evidently paler,
but did not give way a foot: he had only changed his sword-
hand, and fought with his left hand.

According to the laws of duelling at that period, D'Artagnan was at liberty to assist the one he pleased. While he
was endeavoring to find out which of his companions stood
in greatest need, he caught a glance from Athos. This glance
was of sublime eloquence. Athos would have died rather
than appeal for help; but he could look, and with that look
ask assistance. D'Artagnan interpreted it; with a terrible
bound, he sprang to the side of Cahusac, crying:

"To me, monsieur! guard, or I will slay you!"

Cahusac turned; it was time, for Athos, whose great courage alone supported him, sank upon his knee.

"*Sang Dieu!*" cried he to D'Artagnan, "do not kill him, young man, I beg of you; I have an old affair to settle with him, when I am cured and sound again. Disarm him only— make sure of his sword; that's it, that's it! well done! very well done!"

This exclamation was drawn from Athos by seeing the sword of Cahusac fly twenty paces from him. D'Artagnan and Cahusac sprang forward at the same instant, the one to recover, the other to obtain the sword; but D'Artagnan, being the more active, reached it first, and placed his foot upon it.

Cahusac immediately ran to that of one of the guards that Aramis had killed, and returned toward D'Artagnan; but on his way he met Athos, who, during this relief which D'Artagnan had procured him, had recovered his breath, and who, for fear that D'Artagnan should kill his enemy, wished to resume the fight.

D'Artagnan perceived that it would be disobliging Athos not to leave him alone; and in a few minutes Cahusac fell, with a sword-thrust through his throat.

At the same instant Aramis placed his sword-point on the breast of his fallen enemy, and compelled him to ask for mercy.

There only then remained Porthos and Bicarat. Porthos made a thousand fanfaronnades, asking Bicarat what o'clock it could be, and offering him his compliments upon his brother's having just obtained a company in the regiment of Navarre; but, joke as he might, he gained no advantage— Bicarat was one of those iron men who never fall dead.

Nevertheless, it was necessary to put an end to the affair. The watch might come up, and take all the combatants, wounded or not, royalists or cardinalists. Athos, Aramis, and D'Artagnan surrounded Bicarat, and required him to surrender. Though alone against all, and with a wound in his thigh, Bicarat wished to hold out; but Jussac, who had risen upon his elbow, cried out to him to yield. Bicarat was a Gascon, as D'Artagnan was; he turned a deaf ear, and contented himself with laughing; and, between two parries, finding time to point to a spot of earth with his sword:

"Here," cried he, parodying a verse of the Bible, "here will Bicarat die, the only one of those who are with him!"

"But there are four against you; leave off, I command you."

"Ah! if you command me, that's another thing," said Bicarat; "you being my brigadier, it is my duty to obey."

And, springing backward, he broke his sword across his knee, to avoid the necessity of surrendering it, threw the pieces over the convent wall, and crossed his arms, whistling a cardinalist air.

Bravery is always respected, even in an enemy. The musketeers saluted Bicarat with their swords, and returned them to their sheaths. D'Artagnan did the same; then, assisted by Bicarat, the only one left standing, he bore Jussac, Cahusac, and that one of Aramis' adversaries who was only wounded, under the porch of the convent. The fourth as we have said was dead. They then rang the bell, and, carrying away four swords out of five, they took their road, intoxicated with joy, toward the hotel of M. de Tréville.

They walked arm in arm, occupying the whole width of the street, and accosting every musketeer they met, so that it in the end became a triumphal march. The heart of D'Artagnan swam in delight; he marched between Athos and Porthos, pressing them tenderly.

"If I am not yet a musketeer," said he to his new friends, as he passed through the gateway of M. de Tréville's hotel, "at least I have entered upon my apprenticeship, haven't I?"

CHAPTER VI.

HIS MAJESTY KING LOUIS XIII.

THIS affair made a great noise. M. de Tréville scolded his musketeers in public, and congratulated them in private; but as no time was to be lost in gaining the king, M. de Tréville made all haste to the Louvre. But he was too late: the king was closeted with the cardinal, and M. de Tréville was informed that the king was busy, and could not receive him. In the evening, M. de Tréville attended the king's play-table. The king was winning, and, as the king was very avaricious, he was in an excellent humor; thus, perceiving M. de Tréville at a distance:

"Come here, monsieur le capitaine," said he, "come here, that I may scold you. Do you know that his eminence has just been to make fresh complaints against your musketeers, and that with so much emotion that his eminence is indisposed this evening? Why, these musketeers of yours are very devils!"

"No, sire," replied Tréville, who saw at the first glance which way things would take—"no, sire; on the contrary, they are good creatures, as meek as lambs, and have but one desire, I'll be their warranty; and that is, that their swords may never leave their scabbards but in your majesty's service. But what are they to do? the guards of monsieur the cardinal are forever seeking quarrels with them, and for the honor of the corps even, the poor young men are obliged to defend themselves."

"Listen to M. de Tréville," said the king, "listen to him! would not one say he was speaking of a religious community! In truth, my dear captain, I have a great mind to take away your commission, and give it to Mademoiselle de Chemerault, to whom I promised an abbey. But don't fancy that I am going to take you on your bare word; I am called Louis the Just, Monsieur de Tréville, and by and by, by and by, we will see."

"Ah! it is because I have a perfect reliance upon that justice that I shall wait patiently and quietly the good pleasure of your majesty."

"Wait, then, monsieur, wait," said the king "I will not detain you long."

In fact, fortune changed, and as the king began to lose what he had won, he was not sorry to find an excuse for leaving off. The king then arose a minute after, and putting the money which lay before him into his pocket, the major part of which arose from his winnings:

"La Vieuville," said he, "take my place; I must speak to M. de Tréville on an affair of importance. Ah, I had eighty louis before me; put down the same sum, so that they who have lost may have nothing to complain of—justice before everything." Then turning toward M. de Tréville, and walking with him toward the embrasure of a window:

"Well, monsieur," continued he, "you say it is his eminence's guards who have sought a quarrel with your musketeers?"

"Yes, sire, as they always do."

"And how did the thing happen? let us see, for you know, my dear captain, a judge must hear both sides."

"Good lord! in the most simple and natural manner possible. Three of my best soldiers, whom your majesty knows by name, and whose devotedness you have more than once appreciated, and who have, I dare affirm to the king, his service much at heart; three of my best soldiers, I say—MM. Athos, Porthos, and Aramis—had made a party of pleasure with a young cadet from Gascony, whom I had introduced to them the same morning. The party was to take place at St. Germain, I believe, and they had appointed to meet at the Carmes-Deschaux, when they were disturbed by M. de Jussac, MM. Cahusac, Bicarat, and two other guards, who certainly did not go there in such a numerous company without some ill intention against the edicts."

"Ah, ah! you incline me to think so," said the king: "there is no doubt they went thither to fight themselves."

"I do not accuse them, sire; but I leave your majesty to judge what five armed men could possibly be going to do in such a retired spot as the environs of the Convent des Carmes."

"You are right, Tréville—you are right!"

"Then, upon seeing my musketeers, they changed their minds, and forgot their private hatred for the hatred *de corps,* for your majesty cannot be ignorant that the musketeers, who belong to the king, and to nobody but the king, are the natural enemies of the guards, who belong to the cardinal."

"Yes, Tréville, yes," said the king, in a melancholy tone; "and it is very sad, believe me, to see thus two parties in France, two heads to royalty. But all this will come to an end, Tréville, will come to an end. You say, then, that the guards sought a quarrel with the musketeers?"

"I say that it is probable that things have fallen out so, but I will not swear to it, sire. You know how difficult it is to discover the truth; and unless a man be endowed with that admirable instinct which causes Louis XIII. to be termed the Just——"

"You are right, Tréville; but they were not alone, your musketeers—they had a youth with them?"

"Yes, sire, and one wounded man; so that three of the king's musketeers—one of whom was wounded, and a youth —not only maintained their ground against five of the most terrible of his eminence's guards, but absolutely brought four of them to the earth."

"Why, this is a victory!" cried the king, glowing with delight, "a complete victory!"

"Yes, sire; as complete as that of the bridge of Ce."

"Four men, one of them wounded, and a youth, say you?"

"One scarcely attained the age of a young man; but who, however, behaved himself so admirably on this occasion that I will take the liberty of recommending him to your majesty."

"What is his name?"

"D'Artagnan, sire; he is the son of one of my oldest
friends—the son of a man who served under your father of
glorious memory, in the partisan war."

"And you say that this young man behaved himself well?
Tell me how, De Tréville—you know how I delight in accounts of war and fights."

And Louis XIII. twisted his moustache proudly, placing
his hand upon his hip.

"Sire," resumed Tréville, "as I told you, M. d'Artagnan
is little more than a boy, and as he has not the honor of being
a musketeer, he was dressed as a private citizen; the guards
of M. the Cardinal, perceiving his youth, and still more
that he did not belong to the corps, pressed him to retire before they attacked."

"So you may plainly see, Tréville," interrupted the king,
"it was they who attacked?"

"That is true, sire; there can be no more doubt on that
head. They called upon him then to retire, but he answered
that he was a musketeer at heart, entirely devoted to your
majesty, and that he would therefore remain with messieurs
the musketeers."

"Brave young man!" murmured the king.

"Well, he did remain with them; and your majesty has in
him so firm a champion that it was he who gave Jussac the
terrible sword-thrust which has made M. the Cardinal so
angry."

"He who wounded Jussac!" cried the king—"he, a boy!
Tréville, that's impossible!"

"It is as I have the honor to relate it to your majesty."

"Jussac, one of the first swordsmen in the kingdom?"

"Well, sire, for once he found his master."

"I should like to see this young man, Tréville—I should
like to see him; and if anything can be done—well, we will
make it our business."

"When will your majesty deign to receive him?"

"To-morrow, at midday, Tréville."

"Shall I bring him alone?"

"No; bring me all four together; I wish to thank them all
at once. Devoted men are so rare, Tréville, we must recompense devotedness."

"At twelve o'clock, sire, we will be at the Louvre."

"Ah! by the back staircase, Tréville, by the back staircase;
it is useless to let the cardinal know."

"Yes, sire."

"You understand, Tréville; an edict is still an edict—it is
forbidden to fight, after all."

"But this encounter, sire, is quite out of the ordinary conditions of a duel; it is a brawl, and the proof is that there
were five of the cardinal's guards against my three musketeers
and M. d'Artagnan."

"That is true," said the king; "but never mind, Tréville,
come still by the back staircase."

Tréville smiled. But as it was already something to have
prevailed upon this child to rebel against his master, he
saluted the king respectfully, and, with this agreement, took
leave of him.

That evening the three musketeers were informed of the
honor which was granted them. As they had long been acquainted with the king, they were not much excited by the
circumstances; but D'Artagnan, with his Gascon imagination,
saw in it his future fortune, and passed the night in golden
dreams. As early, then, as eight o'clock he was at the apartment of Athos.

D'Artagnan found the musketeer dressed and ready to go
out. As the hour to wait upon the king was not till twelve,
he had made a party with Porthos and Aramis to play a game
at tennis, in a tennis-court situated near the stables of the
Luxembourg. Athos invited D'Artagnan to follow them;
and, although ignorant of the game, which he had never
played, he accepted the invitation, not knowing what to do
with his time from nine o'clock in the morning, as it then
scarcely was, till twelve.

The two musketeers were already there, and were playing
together. Athos, who was very expert in all bodily exercises,
passed with D'Artagnan to the opposite side, and challenged
them; but at the first effort he made, although he played
with his left hand, he found that his wound was yet too re-
cent to allow of such exertion. D'Artagnan remained, therefore, alone; and as he declared he was too ignorant of the
game to play it regularly, they only continued giving balls
to each other, without counting; but one of these balls,
launched by Porthos' Herculean hand, passed so close to
D'Artagnan's face that he thought if, instead of passing
near, it had hit him, his audience would have been probably
lost, as it would have been impossible for him to have presented himself before the king. Now, as upon this audience,
in his Gascon imagination, depended his future life, he saluted
Aramis and Porthos politely, declaring that he would not
resume the game until he should be prepared to play with

them on more equal terms; and he went and took his place near the cord and in the gallery.

Unfortunately for D'Artagnan, among the spectators was one of his eminence's guards, who, still irritated by the defeat of his companions, which had happened only the day before, had promised himself to seize the first opportunity of avenging it. He believed this opportunity was now come, and addressing his neighbor:

"It is not astonishing," said he, "that that young man should be afraid of a ball; he is doubtless a musketeer apprentice."

D'Artagnan turned round as if a serpent had stung him, and fixed his eyes intensely upon the guard who had just made this insolent speech.

"*Pardieu!*" resumed the latter, twisting his moustache, "look at me as long as you like, my little gentleman, I have said what I have said."

"And as since that which you have said is too clear to require any explanation," replied D'Artagnan, in a low voice, "I beg you will follow me."

"And when?" asked the guard, with the same jeering air.

"Immediately, if you please."

"And you know who I am, without doubt?"

"I! no, I assure you I am completely ignorant; nor does it much concern me."

"You're in the wrong there; for if you knew my name, perhaps you would not be in such a hurry."

"What is your name, then?"

"Bernajoux, at your service."

"Well, then, Monsieur Bernajoux," said D'Artagnan quietly, "I will wait for you at the door."

"Go on, monsieur, I will follow you."

"Do not appear to be in a hurry, monsieur, so as to cause it to be observed that we go out together; you must be aware that for that which we have in hand company would be inconvenient."

"That's true," said the guard, astonished that his name had not produced more effect upon the young man.

In fact, the name of Bernajoux was known to everybody, D'Artagnan alone excepted, perhaps; for it was one of those which figured most frequently in the daily brawls, which all the edicts of the cardinal had not been able to repress.

Porthos and Aramis were so engaged with their game, and Athos was watching them with so much attention, that they did not even perceive their young companion go out, who, as he had told his eminence's guard he would, stopped outside the door; an instant after, the guard descended. As D'Artagnan had no time to lose, on account of the audience of the king, which was fixed for midday, he cast his eyes around, and seeing that the street was empty:

"*Ma foi!*" said he to his adversary, "it is fortunate for you, although your name is Bernajoux, to have only to deal with an apprentice musketeer; never mind, be content, I will do my best. Guard!"

"But," said he whom D'Artagnan thus provoked, "it appears to me that this place is very ill-chosen, and that we should be better behind the Abbey St. Germain or in the Pré-aux-Clercs."

"What you say is very sensible," replied D'Artagnan; "but unfortunately, I have very little time to spare, having an appointment at twelve precisely. Guard! then, monsieur, guard!"

Bernajoux was not a man to have such a compliment paid to him twice. In an instant his sword glittered in his hand, and he sprang upon his adversary, whom, from his youth, he hoped to intimidate.

But D'Artagnan had on the preceding day gone through his apprenticeship. Fresh sharpened by his victory, full of the hopes of future favor, he was resolved not to give back a step; so the two swords were crossed close to the hilts, and as D'Artagnan stood firm, it was his adversary who made the retreating step; but D'Artagnan seized the moment at which, in this movement, the sword of Bernajoux deviated from the line; he freed his weapon, made a lunge, and touched his adversary on the shoulder. D'Artagnan immediately made a step backward and raised his sword; but Bernajoux cried out that it was nothing, and rushing blindly upon him, absolutely spitted himself upon D'Artagnan's sword. As, however, he did not fall, as he did not declare himself conquered, but only broke away toward the hotel of M. de Trémouille, in whose service he had a relation, D'Artagnan was ignorant of the seriousness of the last wound his adversary had received, pressed him warmly, and without doubt would soon have completed his work with a third blow, when the noise which arose from the street being heard in the tennis-court, two of the friends of the guard, who had seen him go out after exchanging some words with D'Artagnan, rushed, sword in hand, from the court, and fell upon the conqueror. But Athos, Porthos, and Aramis quickly appeared in their turn, and the moment the two guards attacked their young companion, drove them back. Bernajoux now fell, and as the guards were only two against four, they began to cry, "To the rescue! the hotel de Trémouille!" At these cries, all who were in the hotel rushed out, falling upon the four companions, who on their side cried aloud, "To the rescue! musketeers!"

This cry was generally attended to; for the musketeers were known to be enemies to the cardinal and were beloved on account of the hatred they bore to his enemies. Thus the guards of other companies than those which belonged to the Red Duke, as Aramis had called him, in general, in these quarrels took part with the king's musketeers. Of three guards of the company of M. Dessessart, who were passing, two came to the assistance of the four companions, while the other ran toward the hotel of M. de Tréville, crying: "To the rescue! musketeers! to the rescue!" As usual, this hotel was full of soldiers of this corps who hastened to the succor of their comrades; the *mêlée* became general, but strength was on the side of the musketeers; the cardinal's guards and M. de la Trémouille's people retreated into the hotel, the doors of which they closed just in time to prevent their enemies from entering with them. As to the wounded man, he had been taken in at once, and as we have said, in a very bad state.

Excitement was at its height among the musketeers and their allies, and they even began to deliberate whether they should not set fire to the hotel to punish the insolence of M. de la Trémouille's domestics, in daring to make a *sortie* upon the king's musketeers. The proposition had been made, and received with enthusiasm, when fortunately eleven o'clock struck; D'Artagnan and his companions remembered their audience, and as they would very much have regretted that such a feat should be performed without them, they succeeded in quieting their coadjutors. The latter contented themselves with hurling some paving stones against the gates, but the gates were too strong; they then grew tired of the sport; besides, those who must be considered as the leaders of the enterprise had quitted the group and were making their way toward the hotel of M. de Tréville, who was waiting for them, already informed of this fresh disturbance.

"Quick, to the Louvre," said he, "to the Louvre without losing an instant, and let us endeavor to see the king before he is prejudiced by the cardinal: we will describe the thing to him as a consequence of the affair of yesterday, and the two will pass off together."

M. de Tréville, accompanied by his four young men, directed his course toward the Louvre; but to the great astonishment of the captain of the musketeers, he was informed that the king was gone stag-hunting in the forest of St. Germain. M. de Tréville required this intelligence to be repeated to him twice, and each time his companions saw his brow become darker.

"Had his majesty," asked he, "any intention of holding this hunting party yesterday?"

"No, your excellency," replied the valet de chambre, "the grand veneur came this morning to inform him that he had marked down a stag. He, at first, answered that he would not go, but could not resist his love of sport, and set out after dinner."

"Has the king seen the cardinal?" asked M. de Tréville.

"Most probably he has," replied the valet de chambre, "for I saw the horses harnessed to his eminence's carriage this morning, and when I asked where he was going, I was told to St. Germain."

"He is beforehand with us," said M. de Tréville. "Gentlemen, I will see the king this evening; but as to you, I do not advise you to risk doing so."

This advice was too reasonable, and, moreover, came from a man who knew the king too well, to allow the four young men to dispute it. M. de Tréville recommended them each to retire to his apartment, and wait for news from him.

On entering his hotel, M. de Tréville thought it best to be first in making the complaint. He sent one of his servants to M. de la Trémouille with a letter, in which he begged of him to eject the cardinal's guard from his house, and to reprimand his people for their audacity in making *sortie* against the king's musketeers. But M. de la Trémouille, already prejudiced by his esquire, whose relation, as we already know, Bernajoux was, replied that it was neither for M. de Tréville nor the musketeers to complain, but on the contrary, he, whose people the musketeers had assaulted and whose hotel they had endeavored to burn. Now, as the debate between these two nobles might last a long time, each becoming, naturally, more firm in his own opinion, M. de Tréville thought of an expedient which might terminate it quietly; which was to go himself to M. de la Trémouille.

He repaired, then, immediately to his hotel, and caused himself to be announced.

The two nobles saluted each other politely, for if no friendship existed between them, there was at least esteem. Both were men of courage and honor; and as M. de la Trémouille, a Protestant, and seeing the king seldom, was of no party, he did not, in general, carry any bias into his social relations This time, however, his address, although polite, was colder than usual.

"Monsieur!" said M. de Tréville, "we fancy that we have each cause to complain of the other, and I am come to endeavor to clear up this affair."

"I have no objection," replied M. de la Trémouille, "but I warn you that I have inquired well into it, and all the fault lies with your musketeers."

"You are too just and reasonable a man, monsieur!" said De Tréville, "not to accept the proposal I am about to make to you."

"Make it, monsieur. I am attentive."

"How is M. Bernajoux, your esquire's relation?"

"Why, monsieur, very ill, indeed! In addition to the sword thrust in his arm, which is not dangerous, he has received another right through his lungs, of which the doctor speaks very unfavorably."

"But is the wounded man sensible?"

"Perfectly."

"Can he speak?"

"With difficulty, but he can speak."

"Well, monsieur, let us go to him; let us adjure him, in the name of the God before whom he is called upon, perhaps quickly, to appear, to speak the truth. I will take him for judge in his own cause, monsieur, and will believe what he will say."

M. de la Trémouille reflected for an instant, then, as it was difficult to make a more reasonable proposal, agreed to it.

Both descended to the chamber in which the wounded man lay. The latter, on seeing these two noble lords who came to visit him, endeavored to raise himself up in his bed, but he was too weak, and exhausted by the effort he fell back again almost insensible.

M. de la Trémouille approached him, and made him respire some salts, which recalled him to life. Then M. de Tréville, unwilling that it should be thought that he had influenced he wounded man, requested M. de la Trémouille to interrogate him himself.

That which M. de Tréville had forseen, happened. Placed between life and death, as Bernajoux was, he had no idea for a moment of concealing the truth; and he described to the two nobles the affair exactly as it had passed.

This was all that M. de Tréville wanted; he wished Bernjoux a speedy recovery, took leave of M. de la. Trémouille, returned to his hotel, and immediately sent word to the four friends that he awaited their company to dinner.

M. de Tréville received very good company, quite anticardinalist though. It may easily be understood, therefore, that the conversation, during the whole dinner, turned upon the two checks that his eminence's guards had received. Now, as D'Artagnan had been the hero of these two fights, it was upon him that all the felicitations fell, which Athos Porthos, and Aramis abandoned to him; not only as good comrades, but as men who had so often had their turn that they could very well afford him his.

Toward six o'clock M. de Tréville announced that it was time to go to the Louvre; but as the hour of audience granted by his majesty was past, instead of claiming the *entrée* by the back stairs, he placed himself with the four young men in the antechamber. The king was not yet returned from hunting. Our young men had been waiting about half an hour, mingled with the crowd of courtiers, when all the doors were thrown open, and his majesty was announced.

At this announcement D'Artagnan felt himself tremble to the very marrow of his bones. The instant which was about to follow would, in all probability, decide his future life. His eyes, therefore, were fixed in a sort of agony upon the door through which the king would pass.

Louis XIII. appeared, walking fast; he was in hunting costume, covered with dust, wearing large boots, and had a whip in his hand. At the first glance, D'Artagnan judged that the mind of the king was stormy.

This disposition, visible as it was in his majesty, did not prevent the courtiers from ranging themselves upon his passage. In royal antechambers it is better to be looked upon with an angry eye than not to be looked upon at all. The three musketeers, therefore, did not hesitate to make a step forward; D'Artagnan, on the contrary, remained concealed behind them; but although the king knew Athos, Porthos, and Aramis personally, he passed before them without speaking or looking—indeed, as if he had never seen them before. As for M. de Tréville, when the eyes of the king fell upon him, he sustained the look with so much firmness that it was the king who turned aside; after which his majesty, grumbling, entered his apartment.

"Matters go but badly," said Athos smiling; "and we shall not be made knights of the order this time."

"Wait here ten minutes," said M. de Tréville; "and if, at the expiration of ten minutes, you do not see me come out. return to my hotel, for it will be useless for you to wait for me longer."

The four young men waited ten minutes, a quarter of an hour, twenty minutes; and, seeing that M. de Tréville did not return, went away very uneasy as to what was going to happen.

M. de Tréville entered the king's closet boldly, and found his majesty in a very ill humor, seated on a *fauteuil,* beating his boot with the handle of his whip; which, however, did not prevent his asking, with the greatest coolness, after his majesty's health.

"Bad! monsieur—bad! *je m'ennuie!*" (I grow weary.)

This was, in fact, the worst complaint of Louis XIII., who would sometimes take one of his courtiers to a window, and say, "Monsieur So-and-so, *ennuyons-nous ensemble."* (Let us weary one another.)

"How! your majesty is becoming dull! Have you not enjoyed the pleasures of the chase to-day?"

"A fine pleasure, indeed, monsieur! Upon my soul, everything degenerates; and I don't know whether it is the game leaves no scent, or the dogs that have no noses. We started a stag of ten-tine; we chased him for six hours, and when he was near being taken—when St. Simon was already putting his horn to his mouth to sound the *halali*—crack, all the pack takes the wrong scent, and sets off after a two-tine. I shall be obliged to give up hunting, as I have given up hawking. Ah! I am an unfortunate king, Monsieur de Tréville! I had but one gerfalcon, and he died the day before yesterday."

"Indeed, sire, I enter into your annoyance perfectly; the misfortune is great; but I think you have still a good number of falcons, sparrow-hawks, and tiercets."

"And not a man to instruct them. Falconers are declining; I know no one but myself who is acquainted with the noble art of venery. After me it will be all over, and people will hunt with gins, snares, and traps. If I had but the time to form pupils! but there is M. le Cardinal always at hand, who does not leave me a moment's repose; who talks to me perpetually about Spain, about Austria, about England. Ah! *à propos* of M. le Cardinal, Monsieur de Tréville, I am vexed with you."

This was the place at which M. de Tréville waited for the king. He knew the king of old, and he knew that all these complaints were but a preface—a sort of excitation to encourage himself—and that he had now come to his point at last.

"And in what have I been so unfortunate as to displease your majesty?" asked M. de Tréville, feigning the most profound astonishment.

"Is it thus you perform your charge, monsieur?" continued the king, without directly replying to De Tréville's question; "is it for this I name you captain of my musketeers, that they should assassinate a man, disturb a whole quarter, and endeavor to set fire to Paris, without your saying a word? But yet," continued the king, "without doubt, my haste accuses you wrongly, without doubt the rioters are in prison, and you come to tell me justice is done."

"Sire," replied M. de Tréville calmly, "I come to demand it of you."

"And against whom, pray?" cried the king.

"Against calumniators," said M. de Tréville.

"Ah! this is something new," replied the king. "Will you tell me that your three damned musketeers, Athos Porthos, and Aramis, and your cadet from Béarn, have not fallen, like so many furies, upon poor Bernajoux, and have not maltreated him in such a fashion that probably by this time he is dead? Will you tell me that they did not lay siege to the hotel of the Duc de la Trémouille, and that they did not endeavor to burn it?—which would not, perhaps, have been a great misfortune in time of war, seeing that it is nothing but a nest of Huguenots; but which is, in time of peace, a frightful example. Tell me, now—can you deny all this?"

"And who has told you this fine story, sire?" asked De Tréville quietly.

"Who has told me this fine story, monsieur? Who should it be but him who watches while I sleep, who labors while I amuse myself, who conducts everything at home and abroad —in Europe as well as in France?"

"Your majesty must speak of God, without doubt," said M. de Tréville; "for I know no one but God that can be so far above your majesty."

"No, monsieur; I speak of the prop of the state—of my only servant—of my only friend—of M. de Cardinal."

"His eminence is not his holiness, sire."

"What do you mean by that, monsieur?"

"That it is only the pope that is infallible, and that this infallibility does not extend to the cardinals."

"You mean to say that he deceived me—you mean to say

that he betrays me? You accuse him, then? Come, speak —confess freely that you accuse him!"

"No, sire; but I say that he deceives himself; I say that he is ill informed; I say that he has hastily accused your majesty's musketeers, toward whom he is unjust, and that he has not obtained his information from good sources."

"The accusation comes from M. de la Trémouille—from the duke himself. What do you answer to that?"

"I might answer, sire, that he is too deeply interested in the question to be a very impartial evidence; but so far from that, sire, I know the duke to be a loyal gentleman, and I refer the matter to him—but upon one condition, sire."

"What is that?"

"It is, that your majesty will make him come here, will interrogate him yourself, *tête-à-tête*, without witnesses, and that I shall see your majesty as soon as you have seen the duke."

"What then! and you will be bound," cried the king, "by what M. de la Trémouille shall say?"

"Yes, sire."

"You will abide by his judgment?"

"Doubtless, I will."

"And you will submit to the reparation he may require?"

"Certainly."

"La Chesnaye!" cried the king; "La Chesnaye!"

Louis XIII.'s confidential valet de chambre, who never left the door, entered in reply to the call.

"La Chesnaye," said the king, "let some one go instantly and find M. de la Trémouille; I wish to speak with him this evening."

"Your majesty gives me your word that you will not see any one between M. de la Trémouille and me?"

"Nobody—by the word of a gentleman."

"To-morrow then, sire?"

"To-morrow, monsieur."

"At what o'clock, please your majesty?"

"At whatsoever time you like."

"But I should be afraid of awakening your majesty, if I came too early."

"Awaken me! Do you think I ever sleep, then? I sleep no longer, monsieur. I sometimes dream, that's all. Come, then, as early as you like—at seven o'clock, but beware, if you and your musketeers are guilty."

"If my musketeers are guilty, sire, the guilty shall be placed in your majesty's hands, who will dispose of them at your good pleasure. Does your majesty require anything further? Speak, I am ready to obey."

"No, monsieur, no; I am not called Louis the Just without reason. To-morrow, then, monsieur—to-morrow."

"Till, then, God preserve your majesty."

However ill the king might sleep, M. de Tréville slept still worse; he had ordered his three musketeers and their companion to be with him at half-past six in the morning. He took them with him, without encouraging them or promising them anything, and without concealing from them that their favor, and even his own, depended upon this cast of the dice.

When arrived at the bottom of the back stairs, he desired them to wait. If the king was still irritated against them, they would depart without being seen; if the king consented to see them, they would only have to be called.

On arriving at the king's private antechamber, M. de Tréville found La Chesnaye, who informed him that they had not been able to find M. de Trémouille on the preceding evening at his hotel, that he came in too late to present himself at the Louvre, that he had only that moment arrived, and that he was then with the king.

This circumstance pleased M. de Tréville much, as he thus became certain that no foreign suggestion could insinuate itself between M. de la Trémouille's disposition and himself.

In fact, ten minutes had scarcely passed away, when the door of the king's closet opened, and M. de Tréville saw M. de la Trémouille come out; the duke came straight up to him, and said:

"M. de Tréville, his majesty has just sent for me in order to inquire respecting the circumstances which took place yesterday at my hotel. I have told him the truth, that is to say, that the fault lay with my people, and that I was ready to offer you my excuses. Since I have the good fortune to meet you, I beg you to receive them, and to consider me always as one of your friends."

"Monsieur le Duc," said M. de Tréville, "I was so confident of your loyalty, that I required no other defender before his majesty than yourself. I find that I have not been mistaken, and I am gratified to think that there is still one man in France of whom may be said, without disappointment, what I have said of you."

"That's well said," said the king, who had heard all these compliments through the open door; "only tell him, Tréville, since he wishes to be considered as your friend, that I also wish to be one of his, but he neglects me; that it is nearly three years since I have seen him, and that I never do see him unless I send for him. Tell him all this for me, for these are things which a king cannot say himself."

"Thanks, sire, thanks," said M. de la Trémouille; "but your majesty may be assured that it is not those—I do not speak of M. de Tréville—that is not those whom your majesty sees at all hours of the day that are the most devoted to you."

"Ah! you heard what I said? so much the better, duke, so much the better," said the king, advancing toward the door. "Ah! that's you, Tréville. Where are your musketeers? I told you the day before yesterday to bring them with you, why have you not done so?"

"They are below, sire, and with your permission La Chesnaye will tell them to come up."

"Yes, yes, let them come up immediately; it is nearly eight o'clock, and at nine I expect a visit. Go, monsieur le duc, and return often. Come in, Tréville."

The duke bowed and retired. At the moment he opened the door, the three musketeers and D'Artagnan, conducted by La Chesnaye, appeared at the top of the staircase.

"Come in, my braves," said the king, "come in; I am going to scold you."

The musketeers advanced, bowing, D'Artagnan following closely behind them.

"How the devil!" continued the king, "seven of his eminence's guards placed *hors de combat* by you four in two days! That's too many, gentlemen, too many! If you go on so, his eminence will be forced to renew his company in three weeks, and I to put the edicts in force in all their rigor. One, now and then, I don't say much about; but seven in two days, I repeat, it is too many, it is far too many!"

"Therefore, sire, your majesty sees that they are come quite contrite and repentant to offer you their excuses."

"Quite contrite and repentant! Hem!" said the king, "I place no confidence in their hypocritical faces; in particular, there is one yonder of a Gascon look. Come hither, monsieur."

D'Artagnan, who understood that it was to him this compliment was addressed, approached, assuming a most deprecating air.

"Why, you told me he was a young man? This is a boy, Tréville, a mere boy! Do you mean to say that it was he who bestowed that severe thrust upon Jussac? And those two equally fine thrusts upon Bernajoux?"

"Truly!"

"Without reckoning," said Athos, "that if he had not rescued me from the hands of Cahusac, I should not now have the honor of making my very humble reverence to your majesty."

"Why, this Béarnais is a very devil! *Ventre-saint-gris!* Monsieur de Tréville, as the king my father would have said. But at this sort of work many doublets must be slashed and many swords broken. Now Gascons are always poor, are they not?"

"Sire, I can assert that they have hitherto discovered no gold mines in their mountains; though the Lord owes them this miracle in recompense of the manner in which they supported the pretensions of the king, your father."

"Which is to say, that the Gascons made a king of me, myself, seeing that I am my father's son, is it not, Tréville? Well, in good faith, I don't say nay to it. La Chesnaye, go and see if, by rummaging all my pockets, you can find forty pistoles; and if you can find them, bring them to me. And now, let us see, young man, with your hand upon your conscience, how did all this come to pass?"

D'Artagnan related the adventure of the preceding day in all its details: how, not having been able to sleep for the joy he felt in the expectation of seeing his majesty, he had gone to his three friends three hours before the hour of audience; how they had gone together to the fives-court, and how, upon the fear he had manifested of receiving a ball in the face, he had been jeered at by Bernajoux, who had nearly paid for his jeer with his life, and M. de la Trémouille, who had nothing to do with the matter, with the loss of his hotel.

"This is all very well," murmured the king; "yes, this is just the account the duke gave me of the affair. Poor cardinal! seven men in two days, and those of his very best! but that's quite enough, gentlemen; please to understand, that's enough: you have taken your revenge for the Rue Ferou, and even exceeded it; you ought to be satisfied."

"If your majesty is so," said Tréville, "we are."

"Oh, yes, I am," added the king, taking a handful of gold from La Chesnaye, and putting it into the hand of D'Artagnan. "Here," said he, "is a proof of my satisfaction."

At this period the ideas of pride which are in fashion in our days did not yet prevail. A gentleman received from hand to hand, money from the king, and was not in the least in the world humiliated. D'Artagnan put his forty pistoles into his pocket without any scruple; on the contrary, thanking his majesty greatly.

"There," said the king, looking at a clock, "there, now, as it is half-past eight, you may retire; for, as I told you, I expect some one at nine. Thanks for your devotedness, gentlemen. I may continue to rely upon it, may I not?"

"Oh, sir!" cried the four companions, with one voice, "we would allow ourselves to be cut to pieces in your majesty's service!"

"Well, well, but keep whole: that will be better, and you will be more useful to me. Tréville," added the king, in a low voice, as the others were retiring, "as you have no room in the musketeers, and as we have besides decided that a novitiate is necessary before entering that corps, place this young man in the company of the guards of M. Dessessart, your brother-in-law. Ah! *Pardieu!* I enjoy beforehand the face the cardinal will make; he will be furious; but I don't care; I am doing what is right."

And the king waved his hand to Tréville, who left him and rejoined the musketeers, whom he found sharing the forty pistoles with D'Artagnan.

And the cardinal, as his majesty had said, was really furious, so furious that during eight days he absented himself from the king's play-table, which did not prevent the king from being as complacent to him as possible, or whenever he met him from asking in the kindest tone:

"Well, monsieur the cardinal, how fares it with that poor Jussac, and that poor Bernajoux of yours?"

CHAPTER VII.

THE INTERIOR OF "THE MUSKETEERS."

WHEN D'Artagnan was out of the Louvre, and consulted his friends upon the use he had best make of his share of the forty pistoles, Athos advised him to order a good repast at the Pomme-de-Pin, Porthos to engage a lackey, and Aramis to provide himself with a suitable mistress.

The repast was carried into effect that very day, and the lackey waited at table. The repast had been ordered by Athos, and the lackey furnished by Porthos. He was a Picard, whom the glorious musketeer had picked up on the bridge De la Tournelle, making his rounds and spitting in the water.

Porthos pretended that this occupation was a proof of a reflective and contemplative organization, and he had brought him away without any other recommendation. The noble carriage of this gentleman, on whose account he believed himself to be engaged, had seduced Planchet—that was the name of the Picard: he felt a slight disappointment, however, when he saw that the place was already taken by a compeer named Mousqueton, and when Porthos signified to him that the state of his household, though great, would not support two servants, and that he must enter into the service of D'Artagnan. Nevertheless, when he waited at the dinner given by his master, and saw him take out a handful of gold to pay for it, he believed his fortune made, and returned thanks to heaven for having thrown him into the service of such a Crœsus; he preserved this opinion even after the feast, with the remnants of which he repaired his long abstinences. But when in the evening he made his master's bed, the chimeras of Planchet faded away. The bed was the only one in the apartments, which consisted of an antechamber and a bedroom. Planchet slept in the antechamber upon a coverlet taken from the bed of D'Artagnan, and which D'Artagnan from that time made shift without.

Athos, on his part, had a valet whom he had trained in his service in a perfectly peculiar fashion, and who was named Grimaud. He was very taciturn, this worthy signor. Be it understood we are speaking of Athos. During the five or six years that he had lived in the strictest intimacy with his companions, Porthos and Aramis, they could remember having often seen him smile, but had never heard him laugh. His words were brief and expressive—conveying all that was meant—and no more: no embellishments, no embroidery, no arabesques. His conversation was a fact without any episodes.

Although Athos was scarcely thirty years old, and was of great personal beauty, and intelligence of mind, no one knew that he had ever had a mistress. He never spoke of women. He certainly did not prevent others from speaking of them before him, although it was easy to perceive that this kind of conversation, in which he only mingled by bitter words and misanthropic remarks, was perfectly disagreeable to him. His reserve, his roughness, and his silence made almost an old man of him; he had then, in order not to disturb his habits, accustomed Grimaud to obey him upon a single gesture, or upon the mere movement of his lips. He never spoke to him but upon most extraordinary occasions.

Sometimes Grimaud, who feared his master as he did fire, while entertaining a strong attachment to his person, and a

great veneration for his talents, believed he perfectly understood what he wanted, flew to execute the order received, and
did precisely the contrary. Athos then shrugged his shoulders, and without putting himself in a passion, gave Grimaud
a good thrashing. On these days he spoke a little.

Porthos, as we have seen, was of a character exactly opposite to that of Athos: he not only talked much, but he talked
loudly; little caring, we muster render him that justice, whether
anybody listened to him or not; he talked for the pleasure of
talking, and for the pleasure of hearing himself talk; he
spoke upon all subjects except the sciences, alleging in this
respect the inveterate hatred he had borne to the learned
from his childhood. He had not so noble an air as Athos, and
the consciousness of his inferiority in this respect had, at the
commencement of their intimacy, often rendered him 'unjust
toward that gentleman, whom he endeavored to eclipse by his
splendid dress. But with his simple musketeer's uniform
and nothing but the manner in which he threw back his head
and advanced his foot, Athos instantly took the place which
was his due, and consigned the ostentatious Porthos to the
second rank. Porthos consoled himself by filling the antechamber of M. de Tréville and the guard-room of the Louvre
with the accounts of his *bonnes fortunes,* of which Athos never
spoke, and at the present moment, after having passed from
the noblesse of the robe to the noblesse of the sword, from
the lawyer's dame to the baroness, there was question of
nothing less with Porthos than a foreign princess, who was
enormously fond of him.

An old proverb says, "Like master like man." Let us pass
then from the valet of Athos to the valet of Porthos, from
Grimaud to Mousqueton.

Mousqueton was a Norman, whose pacific name of Boniface
his master had changed into the infinitely more sonorous one
of Mousqueton. He had entered Porthos' service upon condition that he should only be clothed and lodged, but in a
handsome manner; he claimed but two hours a day to himself, to consecrate to an employment which would provide for
his other wants. Porthos agreed to the bargain; the thing
suited him wonderfully well. He had doublets for Mousqueton cut out of his old clothes and cast-off cloaks, and thanks
to a very intelligent tailor, who made his clothes look as good
as new by turning them, and whose wife was suspected of
wishing to make Porthos descend from his aristocratic habits,
Mousqueton made a very good figure when attending on his
master.

As for Aramis, of whom we believe we have sufficiently explained the character, a character besides which, like that of his companions, we shall be able to follow in its development, his lackey was called Bazin. Thanks to the hopes which his master entertained of some day entering into orders, he was always clothed in black, as became the servant of a churchman. This was a Berrichon of from thirty-five to forty years of age, mild, peaceable, sleek, employing the leisure his master left him in the perusal of pious works, providing rigorously for two, a dinner of few dishes but excellent. For the rest, he was dumb, blind, and deaf, and of unimpeachable fidelity.

And now that we are acquainted, superficially at least, with the masters and the valets, let us pass on to the dwellings occupied by each of them.

Athos dwelt in the Rue Férou, within two steps of the Luxembourg: his apartments consisted of two small chambers, very nicely fitted up, in a furnished house, the hostess of which, still young, and still really handsome, cast tender glances uselessly at him. Some fragments of great past splendor appeared here and there upon the walls of this modest lodging; a sword, for example, richly damascened, which belonged by its make to the times of Francis I., the hilt of which alone, incrusted with precious stones, might be worth two hundred pistoles, and which, nevertheless, in his moments of greatest distress, Athos had never pledged nor offered for sale. This sword had long been an object of ambition for Porthos. Porthos would have given ten years of his life to possess this sword.

One day when he had an appointment with a duchess, he endeavored even to borrow it of Athos. Athos, without saying anything, emptied his pockets, got together all his jewels, purses, aiguillettes, and gold chains, and offered them all to Porthos; but as to the sword, he said, it was sealed to its place, and should never quit it until its master should himself quit his lodgings. In addition to the sword there was a portrait representing a nobleman of the time of Henry III., dressed with the greatest elegance, and who wore the order of the Holy Ghost; and his portrait had with Athos certain resemblances of lines, certain family likenesses, which indicated that this great noble, a knight of the orders of the king, was his ancestor.

Besides these, a casket of magnificent goldsmith's work, with the same arms as the sword and the portrait, formed a middle ornament to the mantelpiece, which assorted badly with the rest of the furniture. Athos always carried the key of this coffer about him, but he one day opened it before Porthos, and Porthos was convinced that this coffer contained nothing but letters and papers—love letters and family papers, no doubt.

Porthos lived in apartments, large in size, and of a very sumptuous appearance, in the Rue du Vieux-Colombier. Every time he passed with a friend before his windows, at one of which Mousqueton was sure to be placed in full livery, Porthos raised his head and his hand, and said, *"That is my abode!"* But he was never to be found at home, he never invited anybody to go up with him, and no one could form an idea of what these sumptuous apartments contained in the shape of real riches.

As to Aramis, he dwelt in a little lodging composed of a boudoir, an eating-room, and a bedroom, which room, situated, as the others were, on the ground-floor, looked out upon a little fresh, green garden, shady and impenetrable to the eyes of his neighbors.

With regard to D'Artagnan, we know how he was lodged, and we have already made acquaintance with his lackey, Master Planchet.

D'Artagnan, who was by nature very curious, as people generally are who possess the genius of intrigue, did all he could to make out who Athos, Porthos, and Aramis really were; for under these *noms de guerre* each of these young men concealed his family name. Athos in particular, who savored of the noble a league off. He addressed himself then to Porthos, to gain information respecting Athos and Aramis, and to Aramis, in order to learn something of Porthos.

Unfortunately Porthos knew nothing of the life of his silent companion but that which had transpired. It was said he had met with great crosses in an affair of the heart, and that a frightful treachery had forever poisoned the life of this gallant young man. What could this treachery be? All the world was ignorant of it.

As to Porthos, except his real name, which no one but M. de Tréville was acquainted with, as well as with those of his two comrades, his life was very easily known. Vain and indiscreet, it was as easy to see through him as through a crystal. The only thing to mislead the investigator would have been for him to believe all the good he said of himself.

With respect to Aramis, while having the air of having nothing secret about him, he was a young fellow made up of mysteries, answering little to questions put to him about others, and eluding those that concerned himself. One day, D'Artagnan, having for a long time interrogated him about Porthos, and having learned from him the report which prevailed concerning the *bonne fortune* of the musketeer with a princess, wished to gain a little insight into the amorous adventures of his interlocutor.

"And you, my dear companion," said he, "you who speak of the baronesses, countesses, and princesses of others?"

"*Pardieu!* I spoke of them because Porthos talked of them himself, because he has cried all these fine things before me. But, be assured, my dear Monsieur d'Artagnan, that if I had obtained them from any other source, or if they had been confided to me, there exists no confessor more discreet than I am."

"Oh! I don't doubt that," replied D'Artagnan; "but it seems to me that you are tolerably familiar with coats of arms, a certain embroidered handkerchief, for instance, to which I owe the honor of your acquaintance?"

This time Aramis was not angry, but assumed the most modest air, and replied in a friendly tone:

"My dear friend, do not forget that I wish to belong to the church, and that I avoid all mundane opportunities. The handkerchief you saw had not been given to me, but it had been forgotten, and left at my house by one of my friends. I was obliged to pick it up, in order not to compromise him and the lady he loves. As for myself, I neither have nor desire to have a mistress, following, in that respect, the very judicious example of Athos, who has none, any more than I have."

"But, what the devil! you are not an abbé, you are a musketeer!"

"A musketeer for a time, my friend, as the cardinal says, a musketeer against my will, but a churchman at heart, believe me. Athos and Porthos dragged me into this to occupy me. I had, at the moment of being ordained, a little difficulty with— But that would not interest you, and I am taking up your valuable time."

"Oh! not at all; it interests me very much," cried D'Artagnan, "and at this moment I have absolutely nothing to do."

"Yes, but I have my breviary to repeat," answered Aramis; "then some verses to compose, which Madame d'Aiguillon begged of me. Then I must go to Rue St. Honoré, in order to purchase some rouge for Madame de Chevreuse: so you see, my dear friend, that if you are not in a hurry, I am."

And Aramis held out his hand in a cordial manner to his young companion, and took leave of him.

Notwithstanding all the pains he took, D'Artagnan was unable to learn any more concerning his young friends. He formed, therefore, the resolution of believing in the present all that was said of their past, hoping for more certain and extended revelations from the future. In the meanwhile, he looked upon Athos as an Achilles, Porthos as an Ajax, and Aramis as a Joseph.

As to the rest, the life of our four young friends was joyous enough. Athos played, and that generally unfortunately. Nevertheless, he never borrowed a sou of his companions, although his purse was ever at their service; and when he had played upon honor, he always awakened his creditor by six o'clock the next morning to pay the debt of the preceding evening.

Porthos played by fits: on the days he won he was insolent and ostentatious; if he lost, he disappeared completely for several days, after which he reappeared with a pale face and thinner person, but with money in his purse.

As to Aramis, he never played. He was the worst musketeer and the most unconvivial companion imaginable. He had always something or other to do. Sometimes, in the midst of dinner, when every one, under the attraction of wine and in the warmth of conversation, believed they had two or three hours longer to enjoy themselves at table, Aramis looked at his watch, arose with a bland smile, and took leave of the company, to go, as he said, to consult a casuist with whom he had an appointment. At other times he would return home to write a treatise, and requested his friends not to disturb him.

At this Athos would smile, with his charming, melancholy smile, which so became his noble countenance, and Porthos would drink, swearing that Aramis would never be anything but a village *curé*.

Planchet, D'Artagnan's valet, supported his good fortune nobly; he received thirty sous per day, and during a month he returned home gay as a chaffinch, and affable toward his master. When the wind of adversity began to blow upon the housekeeping of Rue des Fossoyeurs, that is to say, when the forty pistoles of King Louis XIII. were consumed, or nearly so, he commenced complaints which Athos thought nauseous, Porthos unseemly, and Aramis ridiculous. Athos advised D'Artagnan to dismiss the fellow, Porthos was of opinion that he should give him a good thrashing first, and Aramis contended that a master should never attend to anything but the civilities paid him.

"This is all very easy for you to say," replied D'Artagnan; "for you, Athos, who live like a dumb man with Grimaud, who forbid him to speak, and consequently never exchange ill words with him; for you, Porthos, who carry matters in such magnificent style, and are a god for your valet Mousqueton; and for you, Aramis, who, always abstracted by your theological studies, inspire your servant Bazin, a mild, religious man, with a profound respect; but for me—who am without any settled means, and without resources—for me, who am neither a musketeer, nor even a guard, what am I to do to inspire either affection, terror, or respect in Planchet?"

"The thing is serious," answered the three friends; "it is a family affair; it is with valets as with wives, they must be placed at once upon the footing in which you wish them to remain. Reflect upon it."

D'Artagnan did reflect, and resolved to thrash Planchet in the interim, which was executed with the conscience that D'Artagnan placed in everything; then, after having well beaten him, he forbade him to leave his service without his permission; for, added he, "the future cannot fail to mend; I inevitably look for better times. Your fortune is therefore made if you remain with me, and I am too good a master to allow you to miss such a chance by granting you the dismissal you require."

This manner of acting created much respect for D'Artagnan's policy among the musketeers. Planchet was equally seized with admiration, and said no more about going away.

The life of the four young men had become common; D'Artagnan, who had no settled habits of his own, as he came from his province into the midst of a world quite new to him, fell easily into the habits of his friends.

They rose about eight o'clock in the winter, about six in summer, and went to take the orderly words and see how things went on at M. de Tréville's. D'Artagnan, although he was not a musketeer, performed the duty of one with remarkable punctuality: he went on guard, because he always kept company with that one of his friends who mounted his. He was well known at the hotel of the musketeers, where every one considered him a good comrade; M. de Tréville, who had appreciated him at the first glance, and who bore him a real affection, never ceased recommending him to the king.

On their side, the three musketeers were much attached to

their young comrade. The friendship which united these four men, and the want they felt of seeing each other three or four times a day, whether for duel, business, or pleasure, caused them to be continually running after one another like shadows, and the inseparables were constantly to be met with seeking each other, from the Luxembourg to the Place Saint-Sulpice, or from the Rue du Vieux-Colombier to the Luxembourg.

In the meanwhile the promises of M. de Tréville went on prosperously. One fine morning the king commanded M. le Chevalier Dessessarts to admit D'Artagnan as a cadet in his company of guards. D'Artagnan, with a sigh, donned his uniform, which he would have exchanged for that of a musketeer, at the expense of ten years of his existence. But M. de Tréville promised this favor after a noviate of two years, a novitiate which might, besides, be abridged if an opportunity should present itself for D'Artagnan to render the king any signal service, or to distinguish himself by some brilliant action. Upon this promise D'Artagnan retired, and the next day entered upon his duties.

Then it became the turn of Athos, Porthos and Aramis to mount guard with D'Artagnan, when he was on duty. By admitting D'Artagnan, the company of M. le Chevalier Dessessarts thus received four instead of one.

CHAPTER VIII.

A COURT INTRIGUE.

IN THE meantime, the forty pistoles of King Louis XIII., like all other things of this world, after having had a beginning had an end, and after this end our four companions began to be somewhat embarrassed. At first Athos supported the association for a time with his own means. Porthos succeeded him, and thanks to one of these disappearances to which he was accustomed, he was able to provide for the wants of all for a fortnight; at last it became Aramis' turn, who performed it with a good grace, and who succeeded, as he said, by selling some theological books, in procuring a few pistoles.

They then, as they had been accustomed to do, had recourse to M. de Tréville, who made some advances on their pay; but these advances could not go far with three musketeers who were already much in arrears, and a guard who as yet had no pay at all.

At length, when they found they were likely to be quite in want, they got together, as a last effort, eight or ten pistoles, with which Porthos went to the gaming-table. Unfortunately he was in a bad vein; he lost all, together with twenty-five pistoles upon his parole.

Then the inconvenience became distress; the hungry friends, followed by their lackeys, were seen haunting the quays and guard-rooms, picking up among their friends abroad all the dinners they could meet with; for, according to the advice of Aramis, it was prudent to sow repasts right and left in prosperity in order to reap a few in time of need.

Athos was invited four times, and each time took his friends and their lackeys with him; Porthos had six occasions, and contrived in the same manner that his friends should partake of them; Aramis had eight of them. He was a man, as must have been already perceived, who made but little noise, and yet was much sought after.

As to D'Artagnan, who as yet knew nobody in the capital, he only found one breakfast of chocolate at the house of a priest who was his countryman, and one dinner at the house of a cornet of the guards. He took his army to the priest's, where they devoured as much provision as would have lasted him for two months; and to the cornet's, who performed wonders; but, as Planchet said, "People only eat once at a time, even though they eat much."

D'Artagnan then felt himself humiliated in having only procured one meal and a half for his companions, as the breakfast at the priest's could only be counted as half a repast, in return for the feasts which Athos, Porthos, and Aramis had procured him. He fancied himself a burden to the society, forgetting in his perfectly juvenile good faith that he had fed this society for a month, and he set his mind actively to work. He reflected that this coalition of four young, brave, enterprising, and active men ought to have some other object than swaggering walks, fencing lessons, and practical jokes, more or less sensible.

In fact, four men, such as they were, four men devoted to each other, from their purses to their lives, four men always supporting each other, never yielding, executing singly or together the resolutions formed in common; four arms threatening the four cardinal points, or turning toward a single point, must inevitably, either subterraneously, in open day, by mining, in the trench, by cunning, or by force, open themselves a way toward the object they wished to attain, however well it might be defended, or however distant it might seem. The only thing that astonished D'Artagnan was, that his friends had never yet thought of this.

He was thinking alone, and seriously racking his brain to find a direction for this single force four times multiplied, with which he did not doubt, as with the lever for which Archimedes sought, they should succeed in moving the world, when some one tapped gently at his door. D'Artagnan awakened Planchet and desired him to go and see who was there.

Let not the reader, from this phrase—"D'Artagnan awakened Planchet," suppose that it was night, or that the day was not yet come. No, it had just struck four. Planchet, two hours before, had asked his master for some dinner, and he had answered him with the proverb, "He who sleeps dines." And Planchet dined sleeping.

A man was introduced of a common mien, with the appearance of a bourgeois.

Planchet, by way of dessert, would have liked to hear the conversation, but the bourgeois declared to D'Artagnan that that which he had to say being important and confidential, he desired to be left alone with him.

D'Artagnan dismissed Planchet, and requested his visitor to be seated.

There was a moment of silence, during which the two men looked at each other, as if to make a preliminary acquaintance, after which D'Artagnan bowed as a sign that he was attentive.

"I have heard speak of M. D'Artagnan as of a very brave young man," said the bourgeois, "and this reputation, which he justly enjoys, has determined me to confide a secret to him."

"Speak, monsieur, speak," said D'Artagnan, who instinctively scented something advantageous.

The bourgeois made a fresh pause and continued:

"I have a wife, who is seamstress to the queen, monsieur, and who is not deficient in either good conduct or beauty. I was induced to marry her, about three years ago, although she had but very little dowry, because M. Laporte, the queen's cloak-bearer, is her godfather, and patronizes her."

"Well, monsieur?" asked D'Artagnan.

"Well!" resumed the bourgeois, "well! monsieur, my wife was carried off, yesterday morning, as she was coming out of her work-room."

"And by whom was your wife carried off?"

"I know nothing certain about the matter, monsieur, but I suspect some one."

"And who is the person you suspect?"

"A man who pursued her a long time ago."

"The devil!"

"But allow me to tell you, monsieur," continued the citizen, "that I am convinced that there is less love than policy in all this."

"Less love than policy," replied D'Artagnan, with a very serious air, "and what do you suspect?"

"I do not know whether I ought to tell you what I suspect."

"Monsieur, I beg you to observe that I ask you absolutely nothing. It is you who have come to me. It is you who have told me that you had a secret to confide to me. Act then as you think proper; there is still time to withhold it."

"No, monsieur, no; you appear to be an honest young man, and I will place confidence in you. I believe, then, that love has nothing to do with the carrying off of my wife, as regards herself, but that it has been done on account of the amours of a much greater lady than she is."

"Ah! ah! can it be on account of the amours of Madame de Bois-Tracy?" said D'Artagnan, wishing to have the air, in the eyes of the bourgeois, of being acquainted with the affairs of the court.

"Higher, monsieur, higher."

"Of Madame d'Aiguillon?"

"Still higher."

"Of Madame de Chevreuse?"

"Higher; much higher!"

"Of the ——" D'Artagnan stopped.

"Yes, monsieur," replied the terrified bourgeois, in a tone so low that he was scarcely audible.

"And with whom?"

"With whom can it be, if not with the duke of——"

"The duke of——"

"Yes, monsieur," replied the bourgeois, giving a still lower intonation to his voice.

"But how do you know all this?"

"How do I know it?"

"Yes, how do you know it? No half-confidence, or—You understand!"

"I know it from my wife, monsieur—from my wife herself."

"Who knows it—she herself—from whom?"

"From M. Laporte. Did I not tell you that she was the

goddaughter of M. Laporte, the confidential man of the queen? Well, M. Laporte placed her near her majesty, in order that our poor queen might at least have some one in whom she could place confidence, abandoned as she is by the king, watched as she is by the cardinal, betrayed as she is by everybody.

"Ah! ah! it begins to develop itself," said D'Artagnan.

"Now my wife came home four days ago, monsieur; one of her conditions was that she should come and see me twice a week; for, as I had the honor to tell you, my wife loves me dearly; my wife, then, came and confided to me that the queen, at this very moment, entertained great fears."

"Indeed!"

"Yes. M. le Cardinal, as it appears, pursues her and persecutes her more than ever. He cannot pardon her the history of the Saraband. You know the history of the Saraband?"

"*Pardieu!* know it!" replied D'Artagnan, who knew nothing about it, but who wished to appear to know everything that was going on.

"So that now it is no longer hatred, but vengeance."

"Indeed!"

"And the queen believes——"

"Well, what does the queen believe?"

"She believes that some one has written to the Duke of Buckingham in her name."

"In the queen's name?"

"Yes, to make him come to Paris; and when once come to Paris, to draw him into some snare."

"The devil! But your wife, monsieur, what has she to do with all this?"

"Her devotion to the queen is known, and they wish either to remove her from her mistress, or to intimidate her, in order to obtain her majesty's secrets, or to seduce her and make use of her as a spy."

"That is all very probable," said D'Artagnan; "but the man who has carried her off—do you know him?"

"I have told you that I believe I know him."

"His name?"

"I do not know that; what I do know is that he is a creature of the cardinal's, his *âme damnée*."

"But you have seen him?"

"Yes, my wife pointed him out to me one day."

"Has he anything remarkable about him, by which he may be recognized?"

"Oh! certainly; he is a noble of very lofty carriage, black

hair, swarthy complexion, piercing eye, white teeth, and a scar on his temple."

"A scar on his temple," cried D'Artagnan; "and with that, white teeth, a piercing eye, dark complexion, black hair, and haughty carriage; why, that's my man of Meung."

"He is your man, do you say?"

"Yes, yes; but that has nothing to do with it. No, I am mistaken; that simplifies the matter greatly; on the contrary, if your man is mine, with one blow I shall obtain two revenges, that's all; but where is this man to be met with?"

"I cannot inform you."

"Have you no information respecting his dwelling?"

"None; one day, as I was conveying my wife back to the Louvre, he was coming out as she was going in, and she showed him to me."

"The devil! the devil!" murmured D'Artagnan; "all this is vague enough; from whom did you learn the abduction of your wife?"

"From M. Laporte."

"Did he give you any of the particulars?"

"He knew none himself."

"And you have learned none from any other quarter?"

"Yes, I have received——"

"What?"

"I fear I am committing a great imprudence."

"You still keep harping upon that; but I beg leave to observe to you this time that it is too late now to retreat."

"I do not retreat, *mordieu!*" cried the bourgeois, swearing to keep his courage up. "Besides, by the word of Bonacieux——"

"Your name is Bonacieux?" interrupted D'Artagnan.

"Yes, that is my name."

"You said then, by the word of Bonacieux! Pardon me for interrupting you, but it appears to me that that name is familiar to me."

"Very possibly, monsieur. I am your *propriétaire.*"

"Ah! ah!" said D'Artagnan, half rising and bowing; "you are my *propriétaire?*"

"Yes, monsieur, yes. And as it is three months since you came, and engaged as you must be in your important occupations, you have forgotten to pay me my rent; as, I say, I have not tormented you a single instant, I thought you would appreciate my delicacy."

"How can it be otherwise, my dear Bonacieux?" replied D'Artagnan; "trust me, I am fully grateful for such con-

duct, and if, as I have told you, I can be of any service to
you——"

"I believe you, monsieur, I believe you; and as I was about
to say, by the word of Bonacieux! I have confidence in you."

"Finish, then, that which you were about to say."

The bourgeois took a paper from his pocket, and presented
it to D'Artagnan.

"A letter?" said the young man.

"Which I received this morning."

D'Artagnan opened it, and as the day was beginning to
decline, he drew near to the window to read it, and the bourgeois followed him.

"Do not seek for your wife," read D'Artagnan; "she will
be restored to you when there is no longer occasion for her.
If you make a single step to find her you are lost."

"That's pretty positive," continued D'Artagnan; "but
after all, it is but a threat."

"Yes; but that threat terrifies me. I am not a man of the
sword at all, monsieur; and I am afraid of the Bastille."

"Hum!" said D'Artagnan. "I have no greater regard
for the Bastille than you. If it were nothing but a sword-
thrust——"

"I have depended upon you on this occasion, monsieur."

"You have?"

"Seeing you constantly surrounded by musketeers of a very
superb appearance, and knowing that these musketeers belonged to M. de Tréville, and were consequently enemies of
the cardinal, I thought that you and your friends, while rendering justice to our poor queen, would not be displeased at
having an opportunity of giving his eminence an ill-turn."

"Without doubt."

"And then I thought that owing me three months' rent,
which I have said nothing about——"

"Yes, yes; you have already given me that reason, and I
find it excellent."

"Reckoning still further, that as long as you do me the
honor to remain in my house, that I shall never name to you
your future rent."

"Very kind!"

"And adding to this, if there be need of it, meaning to
offer you fifty pistoles, if against all probability you should
be short at the present moment."

"Admirable! but you are rich then, my dear Monsieur
Bonacieux?"

"I am comfortably off, monsieur, that's all: I have scraped

together some such thing as an income of two or three thousand crowns in the mercery business, but more particularly in venturing some funds in the last voyage of the celebrated navigator, Jean Moquet: so that you understand, monsieur—But!" cried the bourgeois.

"What!" demanded D'Artagnan.

"Whom do I see yonder?"

"Where?"

"In the street, fronting your window, in the embrasure of that door: a man enveloped in a cloak."

"It is he!" cried D'Artagnan and the bourgeois at the same time, having each recognized his man.

"Ah! this time," cried D'Artagnan, springing to his sword, "this time he does not escape me!"

Drawing his sword from the sheath, he rushed out of the apartment.

On the staircase he met Athos and Porthos, who were coming to see him. They separated, and D'Artagnan rushed between them like lightning.

"Where the devil are you going?" cried the two musketeers in a breath.

"The man of Meung!" replied D'Artagnan, and disappeared.

D'Artagnan had more than once related to his friends his adventure with the unknown, as well as the apparition of the beautiful foreigner to whom this man had confided some important missive.

The opinion of Athos was that D'Artagnan had lost his letter in the skirmish. A gentleman, in his opinion, and according to D'Artagnan's portrait of him the unknown must be a gentleman, a gentleman would be incapable of the baseness of stealing a letter.

Porthos saw nothing in all this but a love-meeting, given by a lady to a cavalier, or by a cavalier to a lady, which had been disturbed by the presence of D'Artagnan and his yellow horse.

Aramis said that as these sorts of affairs were mysterious, it was better not to attempt to unravel them.

They understood then, from the few words which escaped from D'Artagnan, what affair was in hand, and as they thought that after having overtaken his man or lost sight of him, D'Artagnan would return to his rooms again, they went in.

When they entered D'Artagnan's chamber, it was empty; the *propriétaire*, dreading the consequences of the rencounter which was, doubtless, about to take place between the young man and the unknown, had, consistently with the character he had given himself, judged it most prudent to decamp.

CHAPTER IX.

D'ARTAGNAN BEGINS TO DEVELOP HIMSELF.

As Athos and Porthos had foreseen, at the expiration of half an hour D'Artagnan returned. He had this time again missed his man, who had disappeared as if by enchantment. D'Artagnan had run, sword in hand, through all the neighboring streets, but had found nobody resembling the man he sought for; then he did that by which, perhaps, he ought to have begun, which was to knock at the door against which the unknown was leaning; but it had proved useless to knock ten or twelve times running, for no one answered, and some of the neighbors, who put their noses out of their windows, or were brought to their doors by the noise, had assured him that that house, all the openings of which were tightly closed, had been for six months completely uninhabited.

While D'Artagnan was running through the streets and knocking at doors, Aramis had joined his companions, so that on returning home D'Artagnan found the meeting complete.

"Well!" cried the three musketeers all together, on seeing D'Artagnan enter with his brow covered with perspiration, and his face clouded with anger.

"Well!" 'cried he, throwing his sword upon the bed; "this man must be the devil in person; he has disappeared like a phantom, like a shade, like a spectre."

"Do you believe in apparitions?" asked Athos of Porthos.

"I never believe in anything I have not seen, and as I never have seen an apparition, I don't believe in them."

"The Bible," said Aramis, "makes our belief in them a law; the shade of Samuel appeared to Saul, and it is an article of faith that I should be very sorry to see any doubt thrown upon, Porthos."

"At all events, man or devil, body or shadow, illusion or reality, this man is born for my damnation, for his flight has caused us to miss a glorious affair, gentlemen, an affair by which there were a hundred pistoles, and perhaps more to be gained."

"How is that?" cried Porthos and Aramis in a breath.

As to Athos, faithful to his system of mutism, he satisfied himself with interrogating D'Artagnan by a look.

"Planchet," said D'Artagnan, to his domestic, who just then insinuated his head through the half-open door, in order to catch some fragments of the conversation, "go down to my *propriétare*, M. Bonacieux, and tell him to send me half a dozen bottles of Beaugency wine; I prefer that."

"Ah! ah! what, are you in credit with your *propriétaire*, then?" asked Porthos.

"Yes," replied D'Artagnan, "from this very day, and mind! if the wine be not good, we will send to him to find better."

"We must use, and not abuse, said Aramis sententiously.

"I always said that D'Artagnan had the longest head of the four," said Athos, who, after having uttered his opinion, to which D'Artagnan replied with a bow, immediately resumed his habitual silence.

"But, come, tell us, what is this about?" asked Porthos.

"Yes," said Aramis, "impart it to us, my dear friend, unless the honor of any lady be hazarded by this confidence; in that case you would do better to keep it to yourself."

"Be satisfied," replied D'Artagnan, "the honor of no one shall have to complain of that which I have to tell you."

He then related to his friends, word for word, all that had passed between him and his landlord, and how the man who had carried off the wife of his worthy *propriétaire* was the same with whom he had had a difference at the hostelry of the Franc-Meunier.

"Your affair is not a bad one," said Athos, after having tasted the wine like a connoisseur, and indicated by a nod of his head that he thought it good, "and fifty or sixty pistoles may be got out of this good man. Then, there only remains to ascertain whether these fifty or sixty pistoles are worth the risk of four heads."

"But please to observe," cried D'Artagnan, "that there is a woman in the affair, a woman carried off, a woman who is doubtless threatened, tortured perhaps, and all because she is faithful to her mistress."

"Beware, D'Artagnan, beware," said Aramis, "you grow a little too warm in my opinion, about the fate of Madame Bonacieux. Woman was created for our destruction, and it is from her we inherit all our miseries."

At this speech of Aramis the brow of Athos became clouded, and he bit his lips.

"It is not Madame Bonacieux about whom I am anxious,"

cried D'Artagnan, "but the queen, whom the king abandons, whom the cardinal persecutes, and who sees the heads of all her friends fall one after the other."

"Why does she love what we hate most in the world, the Spaniards and the English?"

"Spain is her country," replied D'Artagnan; "and it is very natural that she should love the Spanish, who are the children of the same soil as herself. As to the second reproach, I have heard say that she does not love the English, but an Englishman."

"Well, and by my faith!" said Athos, "it must be confessed that this Englishman was worthy of being loved. I never saw a man with a nobler air than his."

"Without reckoning that he dresses as nobody else can," said Porthos. "I was at the Louvre on the day that he scattered his pearls; and, *pardieu!* I picked up two that I sold for ten pistoles each. Do you know him, Aramis?"

"As well as you do, gentlemen; for I was among those who seized him in the garden at Amiens, into which M. Putange, the queen's equerry, introduced me. I was at school at the time, and the adventure appeared to me to be cruel for the king."

"Which would not prevent me," said D'Artagnan, "if I knew where the Duke of Buckingham was, to take him by the hand and conduct him to the queen, were it only to enrage the cardinal; for our true, our only, our eternal enemy, gentlemen, is the cardinal, and if we could find means to play him a sharp turn, I confess that I would voluntarily risk my head in doing it."

"And did the mercer," rejoined Athos, "tell you, D'Artagnan, that the queen thought that Buckingham had been brought over by a forged letter?"

"She is afraid so."

"Wait a minute, then," said Aramis.

"What for?" demanded Porthos.

"Go on. I am endeavoring to remember some circumstances."

"And now I am convinced," said D'Artagnan, "that this abduction of the queen's woman is connected with the events of which we are speaking; and perhaps with the presence of Monsieur de Buckingham at Paris."

"The Gascon is full of ideas," said Porthos, with admiration.

"I like to hear him talk," said Athos, "his *patois* amuses me."

"Gentlemen," cried Aramis, "listen to this."

"Listen to Aramis," said his three friends.

"Yesterday I was at the house of a doctor of theology whom I sometimes consult about my studies."

Athos smiled.

"He resides in a quiet quarter," continued Aramis: "his tastes and his profession require it. Now, at the moment that I left his house——"

Here Aramis stopped.

"Well," cried his auditors; "at the moment you left his house?"

Aramis appeared to make a strong inward effort, like a man who, in the full relation of a falsehood, finds himself stopped by some unforseen obstacle; but the eyes of his three companions were fixed upon him, their ears were wide open, and there were no means of retreating.

"This doctor has a niece," continued Aramis.

"A niece! has he?" said Porthos.

"A very respectable lady," said Aramis.

The three friends burst into a loud laugh.

"Ah! if you laugh, or doubt what I say," replied Aramis, "you shall know nothing."

"We are as stanch believers as Mahometans, and as mute as catafalques," said Athos.

"I will go on then," resumed Aramis. "This niece comes sometimes to see her uncle; and, by chance, was there yesterday at the same time that I was, and I could do no less than offer to conduct her to her carriage."

"Oh! oh! Then this niece of the doctor's keeps a carriage, does she?" interrupted Porthos, one of whose faults was a great incontinence of tongue; "a very nice acquaintance, my friend!"

"Porthos," replied Aramis, "I have had occasion to observe to you, more than once, that you are very indiscreet; and that is injurious to you among the women."

"Gentlemen, gentlemen," cried D'Artagnan, who began to get a glimpse of the result of the adventure, "the thing is serious; endeavor, then, not to joke, if possible. Go on Aramis, go on."

"All at once, a tall, dark gentleman—just like yours, D'Artagnan."

"The same, perhaps," said he.

"Possibly," continued Aramis—"came toward me, accompanied by five or six men, who followed at about ten paces behind him; and, in the politest tone, 'Monsieur the Duke,' said he to me, 'and you, madame,' continued he, addressing the lady, who had hold of my arm——"

"The doctor's niece?"

"Hold your tongue, Porthos," said Athos; "you are insupportable."

"'Be so kind as to get into this carriage; and that without offering the slightest resistance, or making the least noise.'"

"He took you for Buckingham!" cried D'Artagnan.

"I believe so," replied Aramis.

"But the lady?" asked Porthos.

"He took her for the queen!" said D'Artagnan.

"Just so," replied Aramis.

"The Gascon is the devil!" cried Athos; "nothing escapes him."

"The fact is," said Porthos, "Aramis is of the same height, and something of the shape of the duke; but it nevertheless appears to me that the uniform of a musketeer——"

"I wore a very large cloak," said Aramis.

"In the month of July; the devil!" said Porthos. "Is the doctor afraid you should be recognized?"

"I can comprehend that the spy may have been deceived by the person; but the face——"

"I had a very large hat on," said Aramis.

"Oh! good lord!" cried Porthos, "what precautions to study theology!"

"Gentlemen, gentlemen," said D'Artagnan, "do not let us lose our time in jesting; let us separate, and let us seek the mercer's wife; that is the key of the intrigue."

"A woman of such inferior condition! can you believe so?" said Porthos, protruding his lip with contempt.

"She is goddaughter to Laporte, the confidential valet of the queen. Have I not told you so, gentlemen? Besides, it has perhaps been a scheme of her majesty's to have sought, on this occasion, for support so lowly. High heads expose themselves sometimes; and the cardinal is farsighted."

"Well," said Porthos, "in the first place make a bargain with the mercer; and a good bargain, too."

"That's useless," said D'Artagnan; "for I believe if he does not pay us, we shall be well enough paid by another party."

At this moment a sudden noise of footsteps was heard upon the stairs, the door was thrown violently open, and the unfortunate mercer rushed into the chamber in which the council was held.

"Save me! gentlemen! save me!" cried he. "There are

four men come to arrest me; save me! for the love of heaven save me!"

Porthos and Aramis arose.

"A moment," cried D'Artagnan, making them a sign to replace their half-drawn swords: "on this occasion we don't require courage; we must exercise prudence."

"And yet," cried Porthos, "we will not leave——"

"You will leave D'Artagnan to act as he thinks proper; he has, I repeat, the longest head of the four, and for my part, I declare I obey him. Do as you think best, D'Artagnan."

At this moment the four guards appeared at the door of the antechamber, but seeing four musketeers standing, and their swords by their sides, they hesitated to advance further.

"Come in, gentlemen, come in; you are here in my apartment, and we are all faithful servants of the king and Monsieur le Cardinal."

"Then, gentlemen, you will not oppose our executing the orders we have received?" asked the one who appeared to be the leader of the party.

"On the contrary, gentlemen, we would assist you if it were necessary."

"*What* does he say?" grumbled Porthos.

"That you are a simpleton," said Athos; "hold your tongue."

"But you promised me," said the poor mercer, in a very low voice.

"We can only save you by being free ourselves," replied D'Artagnan, in a rapid, low tone, "and if we appear inclined to defend you, they will arrest us with you."

"It seems—nevertheless——"

"Come in, gentlemen! come in!" said D'Artagnan; "I have no motive for defending monsieur. I saw him to-day for the first time, and he can tell you on what occasion; he came to demand the rent of my lodging. Is not that true, M. Bonacieux? Answer?"

"That's the very truth," cried the mercer, "but monsieur does not tell you——"

"Silence, with respect to me! silence, with respect to my friends! silence about the queen above all, or you will ruin everybody without saving yourself. Now, gentlemen, you are at liberty to take away this man!"

And D'Artagnan pushed the half-stupefied mercer among the guards, saying to him:

"You are a shabby old fellow, my dear! you come to demand money of me! of a musketeer! to prison with him! gentlemen, once more, take him to prison, and keep him under key as long as possible—that will give me time to pay him."

The *sbirri* were full of thanks, and took away their prey.

At the moment they were going down, D'Artagnan laid his hand on the shoulder of their leader.

"Shall I not have the pleasure of drinking to your health, and you to mine?" said D'Artagnan, filling two glasses with the Beaugency wine which he had obtained from the liberality of M. Bonacieux.

"That will do me great honor," said the leader of the *sbirri,* "and I consent thankfully."

"Then to yours, monsieur—what is your name?"

"Boisrenard."

"Monsieur Boisrenard!"

"To yours, my good sir—in your turn, what is your name, if you please?"

"D'Artagnan."

"To yours, Monsieur d'Artagnan."

"And above all others," cried D'Artagnan, as if carried away by his enthusiasm, "to that of the king and the cardinal."

The leader of the *sbirri* would perhaps have doubted the sincerity of D'Artagnan if the wine had been bad, but the wine was good, and he was convinced.

"Why, what a devil of a villiany have you performed there," said Porthos, when the alguazil-in-chief had rejoined his companions, and the four friends were left alone. "Shame! shame! for four musketeers to allow an unfortunate devil who cried out for help to be arrested from among them, And a gentleman to hob-nob with a bailiff!"

"Porthos," said Aramis, "Athos has already told you, you are a simpleton, and I am quite of his opinion. D'Artagnan, you are a great man, and when you occupy M. de Tréville's place, I will come and ask your influence to secure me an abbey."

"Well! I am quite lost!" said Porthos, "do *you* approve of what D'Artagnan has done?"

"*Parbleu!* indeed I do!" said Athos, "I not only approve of what he has done, but I congratulate him upon it."

"And now, gentlemen," said D'Artagnan, without stopping to explain his conduct to Porthos—"all for one, one for all, that is our device, is it not?"

"And yet!" said Porthos.

"Hold out your hand and swear!" cried Athos and Aramis at once.

Overcome by example, grumbling to himself, nevertheless, Porthos stretched out his hand, and the four friends repeated with one voice the formula dictated by D'Artagnan.

"All for one, one for all."

"That's well! Now let every one retire to his own home," said D'Artagnan, as if he had done nothing but command all his life—"and attention! for from this moment we are at feud with the cardinal."

CHAPTER X.

A MOUSE-TRAP IN THE SEVENTEENTH CENTURY.

THE invention of the mouse-trap does not date from our days; as soon as societies, in forming, had invented any kind of police, that police in its turn, invented mouse-traps.

As perhaps our readers are not familiar with the slang of the Rue de Jerusalem, and that it is fifteen years since we applied this word, for the first time, to this thing, allow us to explain to them what a mouse-trap is.

When in a house, of whatever kind it may be, an individual suspected of any crime be arrested, the arrest is held secret; four or five men are placed in ambuscade, in the first apartment, the door is opened to all that knock, it is closed after them, and they are arrested: so that at the end of two or three days they have in their power almost all the familiars of the establishment. And that is a mouse-trap.

The apartment of Master Bonacieux then became a mouse-trap, and whoever appeared there was taken and interrogated by the cardinal's people. It must be observed that as a private passage led to the first floor, in which D'Artagnan lodged, those who called to see him were exempted from this.

Besides, nobody came thither but the three musketeers; they had all been engaged in earnest search and inquiries, but had discovered nothing. Athos had even gone so far as to question M. de Tréville, a thing which, considering the habitual mutism of the worthy musketeer, had very much astonished his captain. But M. de Tréville knew nothing, except that the last time he had seen the cardinal, the king and the queen, the cardinal looked very thoughtful, the king uneasy, and the redness of the queen's eyes denoted that she had been

deprived of sleep, or had been weeping. But this last circumstance was not at all striking, as the queen, since her
marriage, had slept badly and wept much.

M. de Tréville requested Athos, whatever might happen,
to be observant of his duty to the king, but more particularly
to the queen, begging him to convey his desires to his comrades.

As to D'Artagnan, he did not stir from his apartment. He
converted his chamber into an observatory. From his windows he saw all come who were caught; then, having removed
some of the boarding of his floor, and nothing remaining but
a simple ceiling between him and the room beneath, in which
the interrogatories were made, he heard all that passed between the inquisitors and the accused.

The interrogatories, preceded by a minute search operated
upon the persons arrested, were almost all thus conceived.

"Has Madame Bonacieux sent anything to you for her husband, or any other person?

"Has Monsieur Bonacieux sent anything to you for his
wife, or for any other person?

"Has either the one or the other confided anything to you
by word of mouth?"

"If they were acquainted with anything, they would not
question people in this manner," said D'Artagnan to himself.
"Now, what is it they want to know? Why, if the Duke of
Buckingham is in Paris, and if he has not had, or is not to
have, some interview with the queen."

D'Artagnan was satisfied with this idea, which, after all he
had heard, was not wanting in probability.

In the meantime, the mouse-trap continued in operation,
as likewise did D'Artagnan's vigilance.

On the evening of the day after the arrest of poor Bonacieux, as Athos had just left D'Artagnan to go to M. de
Tréville's as nine o'clock had just struck, and as Planchet,
who had not yet made the bed, was beginning his task, a
knocking was heard at the street-door; the door was instantly
opened and shut: some one was taken in the mouse-trap.

D'Artagnan flew to his hole, and laid himself down on the
floor at full length to listen.

Cries were soon heard, and then moans, which some one
appeared to be endeavoring to stifle. There were no interrogatories.

"The devil!" said D'Artagnan to himself, "it's a woman
—they are searching her—she resists—they use force—the
scoundrels!"

In spite of all his prudence, D'Artagnan restrained himself with great difficulty from taking a part in the scene that was going on below.

"But I tell you that I am the mistress of the house, gentlemen! I tell you I am Madame Bonacieux—I tell you I belong to the queen!" said the unfortunate woman.

"Madame Bonacieux!" murmured D'Artagnan; "can I have been so lucky as to have found what everybody is seeking for?"

The voice became more and more indistinct; a tumultuous movement shook the wainscoting. The victim resisted as much as a woman could resist four men.

"Pardon, gentlemen—par——" murmured the voice, which could now be only heard in inarticulate sounds.

"They are binding her, they are going to drag her away," cried D'Artagnan to himself, springing up from the floor. "My sword! good, it is by my side. Planchet!"

"Monsieur."

"Run and seek Athos, Porthos, and Aramis. One of the three will certainly be at home, perhaps all three are. Tell them to arm, to come here, and be quick! Ah! I remember, Athos is at M. de Tréville's."

"But where are you going, monsieur, where are you going?"

"I am going down by the window, in order to be there the sooner," cried D'Artagnan: "on your part, put back the boards, sweep the floor, go out at the door, and run where I bid you."

"Oh! monsieur! monsieur! you will kill yourself," cried Planchet.

"Hold your tongue, you stupid fellow," said D'Artagnan, and laying hold of the window-frame, he let himself gently down, and the height not being great, he did not sustain the least injury.

He then went straight to the door and knocked, murmuring:

"I will go myself and be caught in the mouse-trap, but woe be to the cats that shall pounce upon such a mouse!"

The knocker had scarcely sounded under the hand of the young man, than the tumult ceased, steps approached, the door was opened, and D'Artagnan, sword in hand, rushed into the apartment of Master Bonacieux, the door of which, doubtless, acted upon by a spring, closed after him.

Then those who dwelt in Bonacieux's unfortunate house, together with the nearest neighbors, heard loud cries, stamping of feet, clashing of swords, and breaking of furniture.

Then, a moment after, such as, surprised by this tumult, had gone to their windows to learn the cause of it, could see the door open, and four men, clothed in black, not come out of it, but fly, like so many frightened crows, leaving on the ground, and on the corners of the furniture, feathers from their wings; that is to say, portions of their clothes and fragments of their cloaks.

D'Artagnan was conqueror, without much trouble, it must be confessed, for only one of the alguazils was armed, and defended himself for form's sake. It is true that the three others had endeavored to knock the young man down with chairs, stools, and crockery ware; but two or three scratches made by the Gascon's blade terrified them. Ten minutes had sufficed for their defeat, and D'Artagnan remained master of the field of battle.

The neighbors who had opened their windows, with *sang froid* peculiar to the inhabitants of Paris in these times of perpetual riots and disturbances, closed them again as soon as they saw the four men in black fly away: their instinct telling them that, for the moment, all was over.

Besides, it began to grow late, and then, as at the present day, people went to bed early in the quarter of the Luxembourg.

On being left alone with Madame Bonacieux, D'Artagnan turned toward her; the poor woman reclined, where she had been left, upon a *fauteuil,* in a half-fainting state. D'Artagnan examined her with a rapid but an earnest glance.

She was a charming woman, of about twenty-five years of age, dark hair, blue eyes, and a nose slightly turned up, admirable teeth and a complexion marbled with rose and opal. There, however, stopped the signs which might have confounded her with a lady of rank. The hands were white, but without delicacy: the feet did not bespeak the woman of quality. Fortunately D'Artagnan was, as yet, not acquainted with such niceties.

While D'Artagnan was examining Madame Bonacieux, and was, as we have said, close to her, he saw on the ground a fine cambric handkerchief, which he mechanically picked up, and at the corner of which he recognized the same cipher that he had seen on the handkerchief which had nearly caused him and Aramis to cut each other's throats.

From that time D'Artagnan had been cautious with respect to handkerchiefs with arms on them, and he therefore placed the one he had just picked up in Madame Bonacieux's pocket.

At that moment Madame Bonacieux recovered her senses.

She opened her eyes, looked around her with terror, saw that the apartment was empty, and that she was alone with her liberator. She immediately held out her hands to him with a smile—Madame Bonacieux had the sweetest smile in the world!

"Ah! monsieur!" said she, "you have saved me: permit me to thank you."

"Madame," said D'Artagnan, "I have only done what every gentleman would have done in my place—you owe me no thanks."

"Oh! yes, monsieur, oh! yes; and I hope to prove to you that you have not served an ingrate. But what could these men, whom I at first took for robbers, want with me, and why is M. Bonacieux not here?"

"Madame, those men were much more dangerous than any robbers could have been, for they are the agents of M. the Cardinal: and as to your husband, M. Bonacieux, he is not here, because he was yesterday evening taken away to the Bastille."

"My husband in the Bastlile!" cried Madame Bonacieux. "Oh! good God! what can he have done? Poor dear man! he is innocence itself!"

And something like a faint smile glided over the still terrified features of the young woman.

"What has he done, madame?" said D'Artagnan. "I believe that his only crime is to have at the same time the good fortune and the misfortune be to your husband."

"But, monsieur, you know then——"

"I know that you have been carried off, madame."

"And by whom? Do you know? Oh! if you know, tell me!"

"By a man of from forty to forty-five years of age, with black hair, a dark complexion, and a scar on his left temple."

"That is he, that is he; but his name?"

"Ah! his name? I do not know that."

"And did my husband know I had been carried off?"

"He was informed of it by a letter written to him by the ravisher himself."

"And does he suspect," said Madame Bonacieux, with some embarrassment, "the cause of this event?"

"He attributed it, I believe, to a political cause."

"I suspected so myself at first, and now I think entirely as he does. My dear M. Bonacieux has not then for an instant suspected me?"

"So far from it, madame, he was too proud of your prudence, and particularly of your love."

A second smile stole almost imperceptibly over the rosy lips of the pretty young woman."

"But," continued D'Artagnan, "how did you escape?"

"I took advantage of a moment at which they left me alone; and as I knew from this morning what to think of my abduction, with the help of the sheets I let myself down from the window; then, as I concluded my husband would be at home, I hastened hither."

"To place yourself under his protection?"

"Oh! no, poor dear man! I knew very well that he was incapable of defending me; but, as he could be otherwise useful to us, I wished to inform him."

"Of what?"

"Oh! that is not my secret; I must not, therefore, tell you."

"Besides," said D'Artagnan—"pardon me, madam, if, guard as I am, I remind you of prudence—besides, I believe we are not here in a very proper place for imparting confidences. The men I have put to flight will return reinforced; if they find us here, we are lost. I have sent for three of my friends, but who knows whether they may at home?"

"Yes! yes! you are right," cried the terrified Madame Bonacieux; "let us fly! let us save ourselves."

At these words she passed her arm under that of D'Artagnan, and pulled him forward eagerly.

"But whither shall we fly? whither escape to?"

"Let us in the first place get away from this house; when clear of it we shall see."

And the young woman and the young man, without taking the trouble to shut the door after them, descended the Rue des Fossoyeurs rapidly, turned into the Rue des Fossés-Monsieur-le-Prince, and did not stop till they came to the Place-Saint-Surpree.

"And now, what are we to do, and whither do you wish me to conduct you?" asked D'Artagnan.

"I am quite at a loss how to answer you, I confess," said Madame Bonacieux; "my intention was to inform M. Laporte, by means of my husband, in order that M. Laporte might tell us exactly what has taken place at the Louvre in the course of the last three days, and whether there were any danger in presenting myself there."

"But I," said D'Artagnan, "can go and inform M. Laporte."

"No doubt you could; only there is one misfortune in it, and that is that M. Bonacieux is known at the Louvre, and would be allowed to pass; whereas you are not known there, and the gate would be closed against you."

"Ah! bah!" said D'Artagnan; "there is no doubt you have at some wicket of the Louvre a concierge who is devoted to you, and who, thanks to a password, would——"

Madame Bonacieux looked earnestly at the young man.

"And if I give you this password," said she, "would you forget it as soon as you had made use of it?"

"*Parole d'honneur!* by the faith of a gentleman!" said D'Artagnan, with an accent so truthful no one could mistake it.

"Then, I believe you; you appear to be a brave young man; besides, your fortune, perhaps, is at the end of your devotedness."

"I will do, without a promise, and voluntarily all that I can do to serve the king and be agreeable to the queen: dispose of me, then, as a friend."

"But I? where shall I go in the meanwhile?"

"Do you know no one from whose house M. Laporte can come and fetch you?"

"No, I know no one to whom I dare trust."

"Stop," said D'Artagnan; "we are near Athos' door. Yes, here it is."

"Who is this Athos?"

"One of my friends."

"But, if he should be at home, and see me?"

"He is not at home, and I will carry away the key, after having placed you in his apartment."

"But if he should return?"

"Oh! he won't return; and if he should, he will be told that I have brought a lady with me, and that lady is in his apartment."

"But that will compromise me sadly, you know."

"Of what consequence can it be to you? nobody knows you! besides, we are in a situation in which we must not be too particular."

"Come, then, let us go to your friend's house; where does he live?"

"Rue Férou, within two steps."

"Come, then!"

And both resumed their way. As D'Artagnan had foreseen, Athos was not at home; he took the key, which was customarily given him as one of the family, ascended the stairs, and introduced Madame Bonacieux in to the little apartment of which we gave a description.

"Here, make yourself at home," said he, "wait here, fasten the door within, and open it to nobody unless you hear three taps like these;" and he tapped thrice; "two taps close together and pretty hard, the other at a considerable distance and more light."

"That is all well," said Madame Bonacieux; "now, in my turn, let me give you my orders."

"I am all attention."

"Present yourself at the wicket of the Louvre, on the side of the Rue de l'Echelle, and ask for Germain."

"Well; and then?"

"He will ask you what you want, and you will answer by these two words—Tours and Bruxelles. He will immediately be at your command."

"And what shall I order him to do?"

"To go and fetch M. Laporte, the queen's *valet de chambre.*"

"And when he shall have informed him, and M. Laporte is come?"

"You will send him to me."

"That is all very well; but where and how shall I see you again?"

"Do you, then, wish much—to see me again?"

"Certainly, I do."

"Well, let that care be mine, and be at ease."

"I depend upon your word."

"You may."

D'Artagnan bowed to Madame Bonacieux, darting at her the most loving glance that he could possibly concentrate upon her charming little person; and while he descended the stairs, he heard the door closed and double-locked. In two bounds he was at the Louvre: as he entered the wicket of l'Echelle, ten o'clock struck. All the events we have described had taken place within an hour.

Everything fell out as Madame Bonacieux said it would On hearing the password Germain bowed; in a few minutes Laporte was at the lodge; in two words D'Artagnan informed him where Madame Bonacieux was. Laporte assured himself, by having it twice repeated, of the exactitude of the address, and set off at a run. He had, however, scarcely got ten steps before he returned.

"Young man," said he to D'Artagnan, "I have a piece of advice to give you."

"What is it?"

"You may get into trouble by what has taken place."

"Do you think so?"

"Yes. Have you any friend whose clock is too slow?"

"What then?"

"Go and call upon him, in order that he may give evidence of your having been with him at half-past nine. In a court of justice that is called an *alibi*."

D'Artagnan found his advice prudent he took to his heels, and was soon at M. de Tréville's; but instead of passing to the saloon with the rest of the world, he required to be introduced to M. de Tréville's closet. As D'Artagnan so constantly frequented the hotel, no difficulty was made in complying with his request, and a servant went to inform M. de Tréville that his young compatriot, having something important to communicate, solicited a private audience. Five minutes after M. de Tréville was asking D'Artagnan what he could do to serve him, and what caused his visit at so late an hour.

"Pardon me, monsieur," said D'Artagnan, who had profited by the moment he had been left alone to put back M. de Tréville's clock three-quarters of an hour, "but I thought, as it was yet only twenty minutes past nine, it was not too late to wait upon you."

"Twenty minutes past nine!" cried M. de Tréville, looking at the clock; "why, that's impossible!"

"Look, rather, monsieur," said D'Artagnan, "the clock shows it."

"That's true," said M. de Tréville; "I should have thought it had been later. But what can I do for you?"

Then D'Artagnan told M. de Tréville a long history about the queen. He expressed to him the fears he entertained with respect to her majesty; he related to him what he had heard of the projects of the cardinal with regard to Buckingham; and all with a tranquillity and sereneness of which M. de Tréville was the more the dupe, from having himself, as we have said observed something fresh between the cardinal, the king, and the queen.

As ten o'clock was striking, D'Artagnan left M. de Tréville, who thanked him for his information, recommended him to have the service of the king and queen always at heart, and returned to the saloon. But at the foot of the stairs, D'Artagnan remembered he had forgotten his cane: he consequently sprang up again, re-entered the closet, with a turn of his finger set the clock right again, that it might not be perceived the next day that it had been put wrong, and certain from that time that he had a witness to prove his *alibi,* he ran downstairs and soon gained the street.

CHAPTER XI.

THE PLOT THICKENS.

His visit to M. de Tréville being paid, D'Artagnan took his pensive but longest way homeward.

On what was D'Artagnan thinking, that he strayed thus from his path, gazing at the stars in the heaven, and sometimes sighing, sometimes smiling?

He was thinking of Madame Bonacieux. For an apprentice musketeer, the young woman was almost a loving ideality. Pretty, mysterious, initiated in almost all the secrets of the court, which spread such a charming gravity over her pleasing features, she was suspected of not being insensible, which is an irresistible charm for novices in love of the other sex; still further, D'Artagnan had delivered her from the hands of the demons who wished to search and ill-treat her; and this important service had established between them one of those sentiments of gratitude which so easily take another character.

D'Artagnan already fancied himself, so rapid is the progress of our dreams upon the wings of imagination, accosted by a messenger from the young woman, who brought him some billet appointing a meeting, a gold chain, or a diamond. We have observed that young cavaliers received presents from their king without shame; let us add that, in these times of lax morality, they had no more delicacy with respect to their mistresses, and that the latter almost always left them valuable and durable remembrances, as if they endeavored to conquer the fragility of their sentiments by the solidity of their gifts.

Men then made their way in the world by the means of women without blushing. Such as were only beautiful gave their beauty; whence, without doubt, comes the proverb, "That the most beautiful girl in the world can give no more than she has." Such as were rich, gave in addition a part of their money; and a vast number of heroes of that gallant period may be cited who would neither have won their spurs in the first place, nor their battles afterward, without the purse, more or less furnished, which their mistress fastened to the saddle-bow.

D'Artagnan possessed nothing; provincial diffidence, that slight varnish, that ephemeral flower, that down of the peach, had been borne to the winds by the but little orthodox counsels which the three musketeers gave their friend. D'Artagnan, following the strange custom of the times, considered himself at Paris as on a campaign, and that neither more nor less than if he had been in Flanders—Spain yonder, woman here. In each there was an enemy to contend with, and contributions to be levied.

But, we must say, at the present moment D'Artagnan was governed by a much more noble and disinterested feeling. The mercer had told him he was rich; the young man might easily guess that, with so weak a man as M. Bonacieux, it was most likely the young wife kept the purse. But all this had no influence upon the feeling produced by the sight of Madame Bonacieux, and interest remained nearly foreign to this commencement of love, which had been the consequence of it. We say nearly, for the idea that a young, handsome, kind and witty woman is at the same time rich, takes nothing from the charm of this beginning of love, but, on the contrary strengthens it.

There are in affluence a crowd of aristocratic cares and caprices which are highly becoming to beauty. A fine and white stocking, a silken robe, a lace kerchief, a pretty slipper on the foot, a tasty ribbon on the head, do not make an ugly woman pretty, but they make a pretty woman beautiful, without reckoning the hands which gain by all this; the hands, among women particularly, to be beautiful must be idle.

Then D'Artagnan, as the reader, from whom we have not concealed the state of his fortune, very well knows—D'Artagnan was not a millionaire; he hoped to become one some day, but the time which in his own mind he fixed upon for this happy change was still far distant. In the meanwhile, how disheartening to see the woman one loves long for those thousands of nothings which constitute a woman's happiness, and be unable to give her those thousands of nothings! At least, when the woman is rich and the lover is not, that which he cannot offer she offers to herself; and although it is generally with her husband's money that she procures herself this indulgence, the gratitude for it seldom reverts to him.

Then D'Artagnan, disposed to become the most tender of lovers, was at the same time a very devoted friend. In the midst of his amorous projects upon the mercer's wife, he did not forget his friends. The pretty Madame Bonacieux was just the woman to walk with in the' Plaine St. Denis, or in the fair of Saint-Germain, in company with Athos, Porthos and Aramis, to whom D'Artagnan would be so proud to display such a conquest. Then, when people walk for any length of time they become hungry, at least D'Artagnan had fancied so several times lately; and they could enjoy some of those little charming dinners, in which we, on one side, touch the hand of a friend, and on the other, the foot of a mistress. Besides, on pressing occasions, in extreme difficulties, D'Artagnan would become the preserver of his friends.

And Monsieur Bonacieux, whom D'Artagnan had pushed into the hands of the *sbirri* denying him aloud, although he had promised in a whisper to save him! We are compelled to admit to our readers that D'Artagnan thought nothing about him in any way; or that, if he did think of him, it was only to say to himself that he was very well where he was, wherever it might be. Love is the most selfish of all the passions.

Let our readers, however, be satisfied; if D'Artagnan forgets his host, or appears to forget him, under the pretense of not knowing where he has been taken to; we will not forget him, and we know where he is. But for the moment, let us do as the amorous Gascon did; we will see after the worthy mercer presently.

D'Artagnan, reflecting on his future loves, addressing himself to the beautiful night, and smiling at the stars, reascended the Rue Cherche-Midi, or Chasse-Midi, as it was then called. As he found himself in the quarter in which Aramis lived, he took it into his head to pay his friend a visit, in order to explain to him why he had sent Planchet to him, with a request that he would come instantly to the mouse-trap. Now, if Aramis was at home when Planchet came to his abode, he had doubtless hastened to the Rue des Fossoyeurs, and finding nobody there but his two other companions, perhaps they would not be able to conceive what all this meant. This mystery required an explanation; at least, so D'Artagnan thought.

And he likewise whispered to himself that he thought this was an opportunity for talking about pretty little Madame Bonacieux, of whom his head, if not his heart, was already full. We must never look for discretion in first love. First love is accompanied by such excessive joy, that unless this joy be allowed to overflow, it will stifle you.

Paris for two hours past had been dark, and began to be deserted. Eleven o'clock struck by all the clocks of the Faubourg Saint-Germain; it was delightful weather; D'Artagnan was passing along a lane upon the spot where the Rue d'Assas is now situated, respiring the balmy emanations which were borne upon the wind from the Rue Vaugirard, and which arose from the gardens refreshed by the dews of evening and the breeze of night. From a distance sounded, deadened, however, by good shutters, the songs of the tipples enjoying themselves in cabarets in the plain. When arrived at the end of the lane, D'Artagnan turned to the left. The house in which Aramis dwelt was situated between the Rue Cassette and the Rue Servandoni.

D'Artagnan had just passed the Rue Cassette, and already perceived the door of his friend's house, shaded by a mass of sycamores and clematis, which formed a vast arch opposite the front of it, when he perceived something like a shadow issuing from the Rue Servadoni. This something was enveloped in a cloak, and D'Artagnan at first believed it was a man; but by the smallness of the form, the hesitation of the progress, and the indecision of the step, he soon discovered that it was a woman. Further, this woman, as if not certain of the house she was seeking, lifted up her eyes to look around her, stopped, went a little back, and then returned again. D'Artagnan was perplexed.

"If I were to go and offer her my services!" thought he. "By her step she must be young, perhaps pretty. Oh! yes. But a woman who wanders about the streets at this hour seldoms does so but to meet the lover. Peste! to go and disturb an assignation would not be the best means of commencing an acquaintance."

The young woman, however, continued advancing slowly, counting the houses and windows. This was neither a long nor a difficult affair; there were but three hotels, in this part of the street, two windows looking out upon that street, and one of them was that of a pavilion parallel to that which Aramis occupied, the other was that of Aramis himself.

"*Pardieu!*" said D'Artagnan to himself, to whose mind the niece of the theologian reverted; "*Pardieu!* it would be droll if this late flying dove should be in search of our friend's house. But, by my soul, that seems more than probable. Ah! my dear friend Aramis, this time, I will find you out."

And D'Artagnan, making himself as small as he could, concealed himself in the darkest side of the street, near a stone bench placed at the back of a niche.

The young woman continued to advance, for, in addition to the lightness of her step, which had betrayed her, she had just emitted a little cough which announced a clear sweet voice. D'Artagnan believed this cough to be a signal.

Nevertheless, whether this cough had been answered to by an equivalent signal, which had removed the resolution of the nocturnal seeker, or whether she had recognized that she had arrived at the end of her journey, she boldly drew near to Aramis' shutter, and tapped at three equal intervals with her bent finger.

"This is all very fine, friend Aramis," murmured D'Artagnan. "Ah! master hypocrite! this is the way you study theology is it?"

The three blows were scarcely struck, when the inward casement was opened, and a light appeared through the apertures of the shutter.

"Ah! ah!" said the listener, "not through doors, but through windows! Ah! ah! this was an expected visit. We shall see the windows open, and the lady enter by escalade! Very pretty!"

But to the great astonishment of D'Artagnan, the shutter remained closed. Still more, the light which had shone out for an instant disappeared, and all was dark again.

D'Artagnan thought this could not last long, and continued to look with all his eyes, and listen with all his ears.

He was right: at the end of some seconds two sharp taps were heard in the interior; the young woman of the street replied by a single tap, and the shutter was opened a little way.

It may be judged whether D'Artagnan looked or listened with avidity. Unfortunately the light had been removed into another chamber. But the eyes of the young man were accustomed to the night. Besides, the eyes of Gascons have, as it is asserted, like those of cats, the faculty of seeing in the dark.

D'Artagnan then saw that the young woman took from her pocket a white object, which she unfolded quickly, and which took the form of a handkerchief. She made her interlocutor observe the corner of this unfolded object.

This immediately recalled to D'Artagnan's mind the handkerchief which he had found at the feet of Madame Bonacieux, which had reminded him of that which he had dragged from under Aramis' foot.

"What the devil could that handkerchief mean?"

Placed where he was, D'Artagnan could not perceive the

face of Aramis; we say Aramis, because the young man entertained no doubt that it was his friend who held this dialogue from the interior with the lady of the exterior; curiosity prevailed over prudence; and taking advantage of the preoccupation in which the sight of the handkerchief appeared to have plunged the two personages now on the scene, he stole from his hiding-place, and quick as lightning, but stepping with utmost caution, he went and placed himself close to the angle of the wall, from which his eye could plunge into the interior of the apartment.

Upon gaining this advantage, D'Artagnan was near uttering a cry of surprise; it was not Aramis who was conversing with the nocturnal visitor, it was a woman! D'Artagnan, however, could only see enough to recognize the form of her vestments, not enough to distinguish her features.

At the same instant the woman of the apartment drew a second handkerchief from her pocket, and exchanged it for that which had just been shown to her. Then some words were pronounced by the two women. At length the shutter was closed: the woman who was outside the window turned round, and passed within four steps of D'Artagnan, pulling down the hood of her cloak; but the precaution was too late, D'Artagnan had already recognized Madame Bonacieux!

Madame Bonacieux! The suspicion that it was she had crossed the mind of D'Artagnan when she drew the handkerchief from her pocket; but what probability was there that Madame Bonacieux, who had sent for M. Laporte, in order to be reconducted to the Louvre, should be running about the streets of Paris, at half-past eleven at night, at the risk of being carried off a second time?

It must be, then, for some affair of importance; and what is the affair of the greatest importance to a pretty woman of twenty-five? Love.

But was it on her own account or on account of another person that she exposed herself to such hazards? This was a question the young man asked himself, whom the demon of jealousy already gnawed to the heart, neither more nor less than a settled lover.

There was, besides, a very simple means of satisfying himself whither Madame Bonacieux was going: that was to follow her. This means was so simple that D'Artagnan employed it quite naturally and instinctively.

But at the sight of the young man, who detached himself from his wall like a statue walking from its niche, and at the noise of the steps which she heard resound behind her, Madame Bonacieux uttered a little cry and fled.

D'Artagnan ran after her. It was not a very difficult thing for him to overtake a woman embarrassed with her cloak. He came up to her before she had traversed a third of the street. The unfortunate woman was exhausted, not by fatigue, but by terror, and when D'Artagnan placed his hand upon her shoulder, she sank upon one knee, crying in a choking voice:

"Kill me, if you please, you shall know nothing!"

D'Artagnan raised her by passing his arm round her waist; but as he felt by her weight she was on the point of fainting, he made haste to reassure her by protestations of devotedness. These protestations were nothing for Madame Bonacieux, for such protestations may be made with the worst intentions in the world; but the voice was all. Madame Bonacieux thought she recognized the sound of that voice; she opened her eyes, cast a quick glance upon the man who had terrified her so, and at once perceiving it was D'Artagnan, she uttered a cry of joy.

"Oh! it is you! it is you! thank God! thank God!"

"Yes, it is I!" said D'Artagnan, "it is I, whom God has sent to watch over you."

"Was it with that intention you followed me?" asked the young woman, with a coquettish smile, whose somewhat bantering character resumed its influence, and with whom all fear had disappeared from the moment in which she recognized a friend in one she had taken for an enemy.

"No," said D'Artagnan; "no, I confess it: it was chance that threw me in your way; I saw a female knocking at the window of one of my friends."

"Of one of your friends?" interrupted Madame Bonacieux.

"Without doubt; Aramis is one of my most intimate friends."

"Aramis! who is he?"

"Come, come, you won't tell me you don't know Aramis?"

"This is the first time I ever heard his name pronounced."

"It is the first time, then, that you ever went to that house?"

"Certainly it is."

"And you did not know that it was inhabited by a young man?"

"No."

"By a musketeer?"

"Not at all."

"It was not him, then, you came to seek?"

"Not the least in the world. Besides, you must have seen that the person I spoke to was a woman."

"That is true; but this woman may be one of the friends of Aramis."

"I know nothing of that."

"Since she lodges with him."

"That does not concern me."

"But who is she?"

"Oh! that is not my secret."

"My dear Madame Bonacieux, you are charming; but at the same time you are one of the most mysterious women."

"Do I lose much by that?"

"No; you are, on the contrary, adorable!"

"Give me your arm, then."

"Most willingly. And now?"

"Now conduct me."

"Where?"

"Where I am going."

"But where are you going?"

"You will see, because you will leave me at the door."

"Shall I wait for you?"

"That will be useless."

"You will return alone, then?"

"Perhaps I may, perhaps I may not."

"But will the person who shall accompany you afterward be a man or a woman?"

"I don't know yet."

"But I will know it!"

"How?"

"I will wait for your coming out."

"In that case, adieu!"

"Why so?"

"I do not want you."

"But you have claimed——"

"The aid of a gentleman, not the watchfulness of a spy."

"The word is rather hard."

"How are they called who follow others in spite of them?"

"They are indiscreet."

"The word is too mild."

"Well, madame, I perceive I must act as you please."

"Why did you deprive yourself of the merit of doing so at once?"

"Is there no merit in repentance?"

"And you do really repent?"

"I know nothing about it myself. But what I know is, that I promise to do all you wish if you will allow me to accompany you where you are going."

"And you will leave me afterward?"

"Yes."

"Without waiting for my coming out again?"

"No."

"*Parole d'honneur?*"

"By the faith of a gentleman."

"Take my arm, then, and let us go on."

D'Artagnan offered his arm to Madame Bonacieux, who willingly took it, half laughing, half trembling, and both gained the top of Rue la Harpe. When arrived there the young woman seemed to hesitate, as she had before done in the Rue Vaugirard. She, however, appeared by certain signs to recognize a door; and approaching that door:

"And now, monsieur," said she, "it is here I have business; a thousand thanks for your honorable company, which has saved me from all the dangers to which, alone, I might have been exposed. But the moment is come to keep your word: I am arrived at the place of my destination."

"And you will have nothing to fear on your return?"

"I shall have nothing to fear but robbers."

"And is that nothing?"

"What could they take from me? I have not a denier about me."

"You forget that beautiful handkerchief, with the coat of arms."

"Which?"

"That which I found at your feet, and replaced in your pocket!"

"Silence! silence! imprudent man! Do you wish to destroy me?"

"You see very plainly that there is still danger for you, since a single word makes you tremble; and you confess that if that word were heard you would be ruined. Come, come, madame!" cried D'Artagnan, seizing her hands, and surveying her with an ardent glance; "come! be more generous—trust to me; have you not read in my eyes that there is nothing but devotion and sympathy in my heart?"

"Yes," replied Madame Bonacieux; "therefore, ask my own secrets, and I will tell them to you; but those of others—that is quite another thing."

"It is all very well," said D'Artagnan. "I shall discover

them; as these secrets may have an influence over your life, these secrets must become mine."

"Beware of what you do!" cried the young woman, in a manner so serious as made D'Artagnan start, in spite of himself. "Oh! meddle in nothing which concerns me; do not seek to assist me in that which I am accomplishing. And this I ask you in the name of the interest with which I inspire you; in the name of the service you have rendered me, and which I never shall forget while I have life. Rather place faith in what I tell you. Take no more concern about me; I exist no longer for you, any more than if you had never seen me."

"Must Aramis do as much as I, madame?" said D'Artagnan, deeply piqued.

"This is the second or third time, monsieur, that you have repeated that name, and yet I have told you that I do not know him."

"You do not know the man at whose shutter you went and knocked? Indeed, madame, you think me too credulous!"

"Confess, now, that it is for the sake of making me talk that you invent this history, and create this personage."

"I invent nothing, madame: I create nothing: I only speak the exact truth."

"And you say that one of your friends lives in that house?"

"I say so, and I repeat it for the third time; that house is that in which one of my friends lives; and that friend is Aramis."

"All this will be cleared up at a later period," murmured the young woman; "no, monsieur, be silent."

"If you could see my heart," said D'Artagnan, "you would there read so much curiosity that you would pity me; and so much love, that you would instantly satisfy my curiosity. We have nothing to fear from those who love us."

"You speak very quickly of love, monsieur!" said the young woman, shaking her head.

"That is because love has come suddenly upon me, and for the first time; and because I am only twenty years old."

The young woman looked at him furtively.

"Listen; I am already upon the scent," resumed D'Artagnan. "About three months ago I was near having a duel with Aramis, concerning a handkerchief resembling that you showed to the female in the house; for a handkerchief marked in the same manner, I am sure."

"Monsieur," said the young woman, "you fatigue me very much, I assure you, by your questions."

"But you, madame! prudent as you are, think, if you were to be arrested with that handkerchief, and that handkerchief were to be seized, would you not be compromised?"

"In what way: are not the initials mine—C. B.—Constance Bonacieux?"

"Or Camille de Bois-Tracy."

"Silence, monsieur! once again, silence! Ah! since the dangers I incur on my own account cannot stop you, think of those you may yourself run!"

"Danger for me?"

"Yes; there is risk of imprisonment, risk of life, in knowing me."

"Then I will not leave you."

"Monsieur!" said the young woman, supplicating him, and clasping her hands together; "monsieur, in the name of heaven, by the name of a soldier, by the courtesy of a gentleman, depart—there—there is midnight striking—that is the hour at which I am expected."

"Madame," said the young man, bowing; "I can refuse nothing asked of me thus; be satisfied, I will depart."

"But, you will not follow me; you will not watch me?"

"I will return home instantly."

"Ah! I was quite sure you were a good and brave young man," said Madame Bonacieux, holding out her hand to him, and placing the other upon the knocker of a little door almost hidden in the wall.

D'Artagnan seized the hand that was held out to him, and kissed it ardently.

"Ah! I wish I had never seen you!" cried D'Artagnan, with that ingenuous roughness, which women often prefer to the affectations of politeness, because it betrays the depth of the thought, and proves that feeling prevails over reason.

"Well!" resumed Madame Bonacieux, in a voice that was almost caressing, and pressing the hand of D'Artagnan, who had not left hold of hers, "well! I will not say as much as you do: what is lost for to-day may not be lost for ever. Who knows, when I shall be some day at liberty, that I may not satisfy your curiosity?"

"And, will you make the same promise to my love?" cried D'Artagnan, beside himself with joy.

"Oh! as to that, I do not engage myself; that depends upon the sentiments you may inspire me with."

"Then, to-day, madame——"

"Oh! to-day, I have got no further than gratitude."

"Ah! you are too charming," said D'Artagnan sorrowfully; "and you abuse my love."

"No, I use your generosity; that's all. But be of good cheer; with certain people, everything comes round."

"Oh! you render me the happiest of men! Do not forget this evening—do not forget that promise."

"Be satisfied, in time and place I will remember everything. Well! now then, go; go, in the name of heaven! I was expected exactly at midnight, and I am late."

"By five minutes."

"Yes; but in certain circumstances five minutes are five ages."

"When one loves."

"Well! and who told you I had not to do with some one in love!"

"It is a man, then, that expects you?" cried D'Artagnan —"a man!"

"Oh, Lord! oh, Lord! there is the discussion going to begin again!" said Madame Bonacieux, with a half-smile, which was not quite free from a tinge of impatience.

"No, no; I am going, I am going; I believe in you, and I would have all the merit of my devotedness, if that devotedness were even a stupidity. Adieu, madame, adieu!"

And as if he only felt the strength to detach himself from the hand he held, by a violent effort he sprang away, running, while Madame Bonacieux knocked, as she had done at the shutter, three light and regular taps; then, when he had gained the angle of the street, he returned: the door had been opened, and shut again—the mercer's pretty wife had disappeared.

D'Artagnan pursued his way; he had given his word not to watch Madame Bonacieux, and if his life had depended upon the spot to which she was going, or the person who should accompany her, D'Artagnan would have returned home, since he had promised that he would do so. In five minutes he was in the Rue des Fossoyeurs.

"Poor Athos!" said he; "he will never guess what all this means. He will have fallen asleep waiting for me, or else he will have returned home, where he will have learned that a woman had been there. A woman at Athos' house! After all," continued D'Artagnan, "there was certainly one in Aramis' house. All this is very strange; I should like to know how it will all end."

"Badly! monsieur—badly!" replied a voice, which the young man recognized as that of Planchet; for, soliloquizing aloud, as very preoccupied people do, he had entered the alley, at the bottom of which were the stairs which led to his chamber.

"How, badly? What do you mean by that, you stupid fellow?" asked D'Artagnan; "what has happened, then?"

"All sorts of misfortunes."

"What?"

"In the first place, M. Athos is arrested."

"Arrested! Athos arrested! What for?"

"He was found in your lodging—they took him for you."

"And by whom was he arrested?"

"By the guards whom the black men you put to flight fetched."

"Why did he not tell them his name? Why did he not tell them he knew nothing about his affair?"

"He took care not to do so, monsieur; on the contrary, he came up to me, and said, 'It is your master that wants his liberty at this moment, and not I, since he knows everything, and I know nothing. They will believe he is arrested, and that will give him time; in three days I will tell them who I am, and they cannot fail to set me at liberty again.'"

"Bravo, Athos! noble heart!" murmured D'Artagnan. "I know him well there! And what did the *sbirri* do?"

"Four conveyed him away, I don't know where—to the Bastille or Fort l'Evêque; two remained with the black men, who rummaged every place out, and took all the papers; the two last mounted guard at the door during this examination; then, when all was over, they went away, leaving the house empty and the doors open."

"And Porthos and Aramis?"

"I could not find them; they did not come."

"But they may come from one moment to the other, for you left word that I wanted them?"

"Yes, monsieur."

"Well, don't stir, then; if they come, tell them what has happened. Let them wait for me at the Pomme-de-Pin; here it would be dangerous—the house may be watched. I will run to M. de Tréville to tell him all this, and will join them there."

"Very well, monsieur," said Planchet.

"But you will remain, will you not? You are not afraid?" said D'Artagnan, coming back to recommend courage to his lackey.

"Be satisfied, monsieur," said Planchet; "you do not know

me yet. I am brave when I set about it—I have only to begin; besides, I am a Picard."

"Then that's understood," said D'Artagnan; "you would rather be killed than desert your post?"

"Yes, monsieur; and there is nothing I would not do to prove to monsieur that I am attached to him."

"Good!" said D'Artagnan to himself. "It appears that the method I have adopted with this boy is decidedly a good one; I shall employ it upon occasion."

And with all the swiftness of his legs, already a little fatigued, however, with the exercise of the day and night, D'Artagnan directed his course toward M. de Tréville's.

M. de Tréville was not at his hotel; his company was on guard at the Louvre; he was at the Louvre with his company.

He must get at M. de Tréville; it was of importance that he should be informed of what was going on. D'Artagnan resolved to endeavor to get into the Louvre. His costume of a guard in the company of M. Dessessarts would, he thought, be a passport for him.

He therefore went down the Rue des Petits Augustins, and came up to the quay, in order to take the Pont Neuf. He had an idea of passing over by the ferryboat; but, on gaining the riverside, he had mechanically put his hand into his pocket, and perceived that he had not wherewithal to pay the ferryman.

As he gained the top of the Rue Guénegaud, he saw two persons coming out of the Rue Dauphine whose appearance very much struck him. One was a man, and the other a woman: the latter very much like Madame Bonacieux in size and step, the former could be nobody but Aramis.

Besides, the woman had on that black cloak whose outline D'Artagnan could still see reflected upon the shutter of the Rue de Vaugirard, and upon the door of the Rue de la Harpe.

And still further, the man wore the uniform of a musketeer.

The woman's hood was pulled down, and the man held a handkerchief to his face; both, this double precaution indicated—both had an interest in not being known then.

They took the bridge; that was D'Artagnan's road, as D'Artagnan was going to the Louvre; D'Artagnan followed them.

He had not gone twenty steps before he became convinced that the woman was really Madame Bonacieux, and the man Aramis.

He felt himself doubly betrayed—by his friend, and by her whom he already loved as a mistress. Madame Bonacieux had declared to him, by all that was holy, that she did not know Aramis; and, a quarter of an hour after having made this assertion, he found her hanging on the arm of Aramis.

D'Artagnan did not reflect that he had only known the mercer's pretty wife for three hours; that she owed him nothing but a little gratitude for having delivered her from the black men who wished to carry her off, and that she had promised him nothing. He considered himself to be an outraged, betrayed, and ridiculed lover; blood and anger mounted to his face—he was resolved to unravel the mystery.

The young man and woman perceived they were watched, and redoubled their speed. D'Artagnan determined upon his course: he passed them, then returned, so as to meet them exactly before the *Samaritaine,* which was illuminated by a lamp, which threw its light over all that part of the bridge.

D'Artagnan stopped before them, and they stopped before him.

"What do you want, monsieur?" demanded the musketeer, drawing back a step, with a foreign accent, which proved to D'Artagnan that he was deceived in one part of his conjectures at least.

"It is not Aramis!" cried he.

"No, monsieur, it is not Aramis; and by your exclamation I perceive you have mistaken me for another, and pardon you."

"You pardon me!" cried D'Artagnan.

"Yes," replied the unknown. "Allow me, then, to pass on, since it is not with me you have anything to do."

"You are right, monsieur, it is not with you I have anything to do; it is with madame, here."

"With madame! You do not know her!" replied the stranger.

"You are deceived, monsieur; I know her very well."

"Ah," said Madame Bonacieux, in a tone of reproach, "ah, monsieur. I had the promise of a soldier and the word of a gentleman; I thought I might have depended upon them!"

"And I, madame!" said D'Artagnan, embarrassed—"you promised me——"

"Take my arm, madame," said the stranger, "and let us proceed on our way."

D'Artagnan, however, stupefied, cast down, annihilated by all that happened so strangely to him, still stood, with his arms crossed, before the musketeer and Madame Bonacieux.

The musketeer advanced two steps, and pushed D'Artagnan aside with his hand.

D'Artagnan made a spring backward, and drew his sword. At the same time, and with the rapidity of lightning, the unknown drew his.

"In the name of heaven, milord!" cried Madame Bonacieux, throwing herself between the combatants, and seizing the swords with her hands.

"Milord!" cried D'Artagnan, enlightened by a sudden idea, "milord! Pardon me, monsieur, but are you not——"

"Milord, the Duke of Buckingham!" said Madame Bonacieux, in an undertone; "and now you may ruin us all."

"Milord—madame, I ask a hundred pardons! but I love her, milord, and was jealous; you know what it is to love, milord. Pardon me, and then tell me how I can risk my life to serve your grace?"

"You are a brave young man!" said Buckingham, holding out his hand to D'Artagnan, who pressed it respectfully. "You offer me your services; with the same frankness I accept them. Follow us at a distance of twenty paces, to the Louvre, and if any one watches us, slay him!"

D'Artagnan placed his naked sword under his arm, allowed the duke and Madame Bonacieux to proceed twenty steps, and then followed them, ready to execute the instructions of the noble and elegant minister of Charles I.

But fortunately he had no opportunity to give the duke this proof of his devotion, and the young woman and the handsome musketeer entered the Louvre by the wicket of the Echelle, without meeting with any interruption.

As for D'Artagnan, he immediately repaired to the cabaret of the Pomme-de-Pin, where he found Porthos and Aramis. who were waiting for him. But, without giving them any explanation of the alarm and inconvenience he had caused them, he told them that he had terminated the affair alone, in which he had, for a moment, thought he should stand in need of their assistance.

And now, carried away as we are by our history, we must leave our three friends to return each to his own home, and follow the Duke of Buckingham and his guide through the labyrinth of the Louvre.

CHAPTER XII.

GEORGE VILLIERS, DUKE OF BUCKINGHAM.

MADAME BONACIEUX and the duke entered the Louvre without difficulty: Madame Bonacieux was known to belong to the queen, the duke wore the uniform of the musketeers of M. de Tréville, who were, as we have said, that evening on guard. Besides, Germain was in the interests of the queen, and, if anything should happen, Madame Bonacieux would only be accused of having introduced her lover into the Louvre. She took the risk upon herself; to be sure her reputation was jeopardized, but of what value in the world was the reputation of the little wife of a mercer?

Once entered into the interior of the court, the duke and the young woman kept along the wall for about twenty-five steps; this space passed, Madame Bonacieux pushed a little side-door, open by day, but generally closed at night. The door yielded: both entered, and found themselves in darkness; but Madame Bonacieux was acquainted with all the turnings and windings of this part of the Louvre, destined for the people of the household. She closed the door after her, took the duke by the hand, advanced a little, feeling her way, came to a balustrade, put her foot upon the bottom step, and began to ascend a flight of stairs; the duke counted two stories. She then turned to the right, followed the course of a long corridor, redescended a story, went a few steps further, introduced a key into a lock, opened a door, and pushed the duke into an apartment lighted only by a night lamp, saying, "Remain here, milord-duke; some one will come." She then went out by the same door, which she locked, so that the duke found himself literally a prisoner.

Nevertheless, isolated as he was, we must say that the Duke of Buckingham did not experience an instant of fear: one of the salient sides of his character was the seeking of adventures and a love of the romantic. Brave, even rash, and enterprising, this was not the first time he had risked his life in such attempts; he had learned that the pretended message from Anne of Austria, upon the faith of which he had come to Paris, was a snare, and instead of regaining England, he had, abusing the position in which he had been placed, declared to the queen that he would not go back again without having seen her. The queen had at first positively refused, but at length became afraid that the duke, if exasperated, would commit some rashness. She had already decided upon seeing him and urging his immediate departure, when, on the very evening of coming to this decision, Madame Bonacieux, who was charged with going to fetch the duke and conducting him to the Louvre, was carried off. During two days it was not known what had become of her, and everything remained in suspense. But when once free, and placed in communication with Laporte, matters having resumed their course, she accomplished the perilous enterprise, which, but for her abduction, would have been executed three days earlier.

Buckingham, on being left alone, walked toward a mirror. His musketeer's uniform became him wonderfully well.

At thirty-five, which was then his age, he passed with just title, for the handsomest gentleman and the most elegant cavalier of France or England.

The favorite of two kings, immensely rich, all powerful in a kingdom which he threw into disorder at his fancy, and calmed again at his caprice, George Villiers, Duke of Buckingham, passed through one of those fabulous existences which remain in the course of centuries as an astonishment for posterity.

Thus, sure of himself, convinced of his own power, certain that the laws which rule other men could not reach him, he went straight to the object he aimed at, even were this object so elevated and so dazzling that it would have been madness for any other even to have contemplated it. It was thus he had succeeded in gaining access several times to the beautiful and haughty Anne of Austria, and making himself loved by her, by astonishing her.

George Villiers then placed himself before the mirror, as we have said, restored the undulations to his beautiful hair, which the weight of his hat had disordered, turned his moustache, and, with a heart swelling with joy, happy and proud of being near the moment he had so long sighed for, he smiled upon himself with pride and hope.

At this moment a door concealed in the tapestry opened, and a woman appeared. Buckingham saw this apparition in the glass; he uttered a cry—it was the queen!

Anne of Austria was then from twenty-six to twenty-seven years of age—that is to say, she was in the full splendor of her beauty.

Her carriage was that of a queen or a goddess; her eyes, which cast the brilliancy of emeralds, were perfectly beautiful, and yet were, at the same time, full of sweetness and majesty.

Her mouth was small and rosy, and although her underlip, like that of the princes of the house of Austria, protruded slightly beyond the other, it was eminently lovely in its smile, but as profoundly disdainful in the expression of contempt.

Her skin was admired for its velvety softness, her hands and arms were of surpassing beauty, all the poets of the time singing them as incomparable.

Lastly, her hair, which, from being light in her youth, had
become chestnut, and which she wore curled very plain, and
with much powder, admirably set off her face, in which the
most rigid critic could only have descried a little less rouge,
and the most fastidious statuary a little more fineness in the
nose.

Buckingham remained for a moment dazzled; never had
Anne of Austria appeared to him so beautiful, amid balls,
fêtes, or carousals, as she appeared to him at this moment,
dressed in a simple robe of white satin, and accompanied by
Donna Estafania, the only one of her Spanish women that
had not been driven from her by the jealousy of the king, or
by the persecutions of the cardinal.

Anne of Austria made two steps forward; Buckingham
threw himself at her feet, and before the queen could prevent
him, kissed the hem of her robe.

"Duke, you already know that it is not I who have caused
you to be written to."

"Yes, yes, madame! yes, your majesty!" cried the duke;
"I know that I must have been mad, senseless, to believe that
snow would become animated or marble warm; but what
then! they who love easily believe in love—besides, this voyage is not a loss, since I see you."

"Yes," replied Anne, "but you know why and how I see
you, milord! I see you out of pity for yourself; I see you
because, insensible to all my sufferings, you persist in remaining in a city where, by remaining, you run the risk of your
own life, and make me run the risk of my honor; I see you
to tell you that everything separates us, the depths of the sea,
the enmity of kingdoms, the sanctity of vows. It is sacrilege to struggle against so many things, milord. In short, I
see you to tell you that we must never see each other again.

"Speak on, madame, speak on, queen," said Buckingham;
"the sweetness of your voice covers the harshness of your
words. You talk of sacrilege! why, the sacrilege is the separation of two hearts formed by God for each other."

"Milord," cried the queen, "you forget that I have never
told you I loved you."

"But you have never told me that you did not love me,
and truly, to speak such words to me would be, on the part
of your majesty, too great an ingratitude. For tell me, where
can you find a love like mine, a love which neither time, nor
absence, nor despair can extinguish; a love which contents
itself with a lost ribbon, a stray look, or a chance word? It
is now three years, madame, since I saw you for the first

time, and during those three years I have loved you thus.

"Shall I tell you how you were dressed the first time I saw you? shall I describe to you every one of the ornaments you wore? Mark! I see you now; you were seated upon cushions in the Spanish fashion; you wore a robe of green satin embroidered with gold and silver, hanging sleeves, fastened up upon your beautiful arms, upon those lovely arms, with large diamonds; you wore a close ruff, a small cap upon your head of the same color as your robe, and in that cap a heron's feather.

"Oh, madame! madame! I shut my eyes and I can see you such as you then were; I open them again and I see you such as you are now—a hundred times still more beautiful!"

"What folly!" murmured Anne of Austria, who had not the courage to find fault with the duke for having so well preserved her portrait in his heart; "what folly to feed a useless passion with such remembrances!"

"And upon what then must I live? I have nothing but remembrances. They are my happiness, my treasures, my hopes. Every time that I see you is a fresh diamond which I enclose in the casket of my heart. This is the fourth which you have let fall and I have picked up; for, in three years, madame, I have only seen you four times; the first which I have just described to you, the second at the mansion of Madame de Chevreuse, the third in the gardens of Amiens."

"Duke," said the queen, blushing, "never name that evening."

"Oh, yes! let me speak of it, on the contrary, let me speak of it; that is the most happy and brilliant evening of my life! Do you not remember what a beautiful night it was? How soft and perfumed the air was? and how lovely the blue star-enameled sky was?

"Ah! that time, madame, I was able for one instant to be alone with you; that time you were about to tell me all, the isolation of your life, the griefs of your heart. You leaned upon my arm; upon this, madame! I felt, as leaning my head toward you, your beautiful hair touched my cheek, and every time that it did touch me, I trembled from head to foot. Oh, queen, queen! you do not know what felicity from heaven, what joys from paradise, are comprised in a moment like that! I would give all my wealth, all my fortunes, all my glory, all the days I have to live, for such an instant, for a night like that! for that night, madame, that night you loved me, I will swear it."

"Milord, yes, it is possible that the influence of the place the charm of the beautiful evening, the fascination of your look, the thousand circumstances, in short, which sometimes unite to destroy a woman, were grouped around me on that fatal evening; but, milord, you saw the queen come to the aid of the woman who faltered: at the first word you dared to utter, at the first freedom to which I had to reply, I summoned my attendants."

"Yes, yes! that is true, and any other love but mine would have sunk beneath this ordeal, but my love came out from it more ardent and more eternal.   You believed you should fly from me by returning to Paris, you believed that I should not dare to quit the treasure over which my master had charged me to watch.   What to me were all the treasures in the world, or all the kings of the earth!   Eight days after I was back again, madame.   That time you had nothing to say to me; I had risked my life and my favor to see you but for a second; I did not even touch your hand, and you pardoned me on seeing me so submissive and so repentant."

"Yes, but calumny seized upon all those follies in which I took no part, as you well know, milord.   The king, excited by M. the Cardinal, made a terrible clamor; Madame de Vernet was driven from me, Putange was exiled, Madame de Chevreuse fell into disgrace, and when you wished to come back as ambassador to France, the king himself, remember, milord, the king himself opposed it."

"Yes, and France is about to pay for her king's refusal with a war.   I am not allowed to see you, madame, but you shall every day hear speak of me!   What object, think you, has this expedition to Ré and this league with the Protestants of Rochelle which I am projecting?   The pleasure of seeing you.

"I have no hope of penetrating sword in hand to Paris, I know that well; but this war may bring round a peace, this peace will require a negotiator, that negotiator will be me. They will not dare to refuse me then, and I will see you, and will be happy for an instant.   Thousands of men, it is true, will have to pay for my happiness with their lives, but what will that signify to me, provided I see you again!   All this is perhaps madness, folly, but tell me what woman has a lover more truly in love? what queen has a servant more faithful or more ardent?"

"Milord! milord! you invoke in your defense things which accuse you more strongly: milord, all these proofs of love that you boast are little better than crimes."

"Because you do not love me, madame: if you loved me,

you would view all this much otherwise: if you loved me, oh! if you loved me, that would be happiness too great, and I should run mad. Ah! Madame de Chevreuse, of whom you spoke but now, Madame de Chevreuse was less cruel than you. Holland loved her, and she responded to his love."

"Madame de Chevreuse was not a queen," murmured Anne of Austria, overcome in spite of herself by the expression of so profound a passion.

"You would love me, then, if you were no one; you, madame, say that you would love me then? I am then to believe that it is the dignity of your rank alone that makes you cruel to me: I may then believe that if you had been Madame de Chevreuse, the poor Buckingham might have hoped? Thanks for those sweet words! oh, my lovely queen! a hundred times, thanks!"

"Oh! milord! you have ill understood, wrongly interpreted; I did not mean to say——"

"Silence! silence!" cried the duke; "if I am happy in an error do not have the cruelty to deprive me of it. You have told me yourself, madame, that I have been drawn into a snare, and I, perhaps, shall leave my life in it; for, although it be strange, I have for some time had a presentiment that I shall shortly die." And the duke smiled, with a smile at once sad and charming.

"Oh! my God!" cried Anne of Austria, with an accent of terror which proved how much greater an interest she took in the duke than she ventured to tell.

"I do not tell you this, madame, to terrify you; no, it is even ridiculous for me to name it to you, and, believe me, I take no heed of such dreams. But the words you have just spoken, the hope you have almost given me, will have richly paid all—were it my life."

"Oh! but I," said Anne, "I, duke, have had presentiments likewise, I have had dreams. I dreamed that I saw you lying bleeding, wounded."

"In the left side, was it not, and with a knife" interrupted Buckingham.

"Yes, it was so, milord, it was so, in the left side, and with a knife. Who can possibly have told you I had had that dream; I have imparted it to no one but my God, and that in my prayers."

"I ask for no more; you love me, madame? it is enough."

"I love you! I!"

"Yes, yes. Would God send the same dreams to you as to me, if you did not love me? Should we have the same pre-

sentiments if our existences were not associated by our hearts?
You love me, my beautiful queen, and you will weep for me?"

"Oh! my God! my God!" cried Anne of Austria, "this is
more than I can bear! In the name of heaven, duke, leave
me, go! I do not know whether I love you or do not love
you, but what I know is that I will not be a perjured woman.
Take pity on me, then, and go. Oh! if you are struck in
France, if you die in France, if I could imagine that your
love for me was the cause of your death, nothing could console me, I should run mad. Depart, go then, I implore you!"

"Oh! how beautiful you are thus! Oh! how I love you!"
said Buckingham.

"Oh! but go! go! I implore you, and come back hereafter;
come back as ambassador, come back as minister, come back
surrounded with guards who will defend you, with servants
who will watch over you, and then—then I shall be no longer
in fear for your days, and I shall be happy in seeing you."

"Oh! is this true, is it true what you say?"

"Yes."

"Oh! then, some pledge of your indulgence, some object
which, coming from you, may assure me that I have not
dreamed; something you have worn, and that I may wear in
my turn—a ring, a necklace, a chain."

"Will you go then, will you go, if I give you that you ask
for?"

"Yes."

"This very instant?"

"Yes."

"You will leave France, you will return to England?"

"I will, I swear to you I will."

"Wait, then, wait."

And Anne of Austria re-entered her apartment, and came
out again almost immediately, holding a casket in her hand
made of rosewood, with her cipher upon it in gold letters.

"Here, milord, here," said she, "keep this in memory of
me."

Buckingham took the casket, and fell a second time on his
knees.

"You promised me you would go," said the queen.

"And I keep my word. Your hand, madame, your hand,
and I depart."

Anne of Austria stretched forth her hand, closing her eyes,
and leaning with the other upon Estafania, for she felt her
strength ready to fail her.

Buckingham applied his lips passionately to that beautiful hand, and then rising said:

"Within six months, if I am not dead, I shall have seen you again, madame; even if I have confounded the whole world for that object, I shall have seen you again."

Faithful to the promise he had made, with a desperate effort, he rushed out of the apartment.

In the corridor he met Madame Bonacieux, who waited for him, and who, with the same precautions and the same good fortune, conducted him out of the Louvre.

CHAPTER XIII.

MONSIEUR BONACIEUX.

THERE was in all this, as may have been observed, one personage concerned, of whom, notwithstanding his precarious position, we have appeared to take but very little notice; this personage is M. Bonacieux, the respectable martyr of the political and amorous intrigues which entangled themselves so nicely together at this gallant and chivalric period.

Fortunately, the reader may remember, or may not remember, fortunately, that we promised not to lose sight of him.

The officers who had arrested him conducted him straight to the Bastille, where he passed tremblingly before a party of soldiers who were loading their muskets.

Thence, introduced into a half-subterranean gallery, he became, on the part of those who had brought him, the object of the grossest insults and the harshest treatment. The *sbirri* perceived that they had not to deal with a gentleman, and they treated him like a very beggar.

At the end of half an hour, or thereabouts, an officer came to put an end to his tortures, but not to his inquietudes, by giving the order for M. Bonacieux's being led to the chamber of interrogatories.

Ordinarily, prisoners were interrogated in their own cells, but they did not pay so much respect to M. Bonacieux.

Two guards attended the mercer who made him traverse a court, and enter a corridor in which were three sentinels, opened a door and pushed him unceremoniously into an apartment, the whole furniture of which consisted of one table, one chair, and a commissary. The commissary was seated in the chair, and was busily writing upon the table.

The two guards led the prisoner toward the table, and upon a sign from the commissary, drew back so far as to be unable to hear the examination.

The commissary, who had till this time held his head down over his papers, looked up to see what sort of person he had to do with. This commissary was a man of very repulsive mien, with a pointed nose, yellow and salient cheek-bones, small, but keen penetrating eyes, and an expression of countenance partaking of the polecat and the fox. His head, supported by a long and flexible neck, issued from his large black robe, balancing itself with a motion very much like that of the tortoise when drawing his head out of his shell.

He began by asking M. Bonacieux his name, prenames, age, condition, and abode.

The accused replied that his name was Jacques Michel Bonacieux, that he was fifty-one years old, was a retired mercer, and lived Rue des Fossoyeurs, No. 14.

The commissary then, instead of continuing to interrogate him, made him a long speech upon the danger there is for an obscure bourgeois to meddle with public matters.

He complicated this exordium by an exposition in which he painted the power and the acts of M. the Cardinal, that incomparable minister, that conqueror of past ministers, that example for ministers to come—acts and power which no one would thwart with impunity.

After this second part of his discourse, fixing his hawk's-eyes upon poor Bonacieux, he bade him reflect upon the seriousness of his situation.

The reflections of the mercer were already made; he had consigned to the devil the instant at which M. Laporte had formed the idea of marrying him to his goddaughter, but more particularly that instant in which that goddaughter had been received lady of the *lingerie* to her majesty.

The character of M. Bonacieux was one of profound selfishness, mixed with sordid avarice, the whole seasoned with extreme cowardice. The love with which his young wife had inspired him was a secondary sentiment, and was not strong enough to contend with the primitive feelings we have just enumerated.

Bonacieux reflected, in fact, upon what had just been said to him.

"But, M. le Commissaire," said he timidly, "I beg you to believe that I know and appreciate more than anybody the merit of the incomparable eminence by whom we have the honor to be governed."

"Indeed?" asked the commissary, with an air of doubt, "indeed? if that is really the case, how came you in the Bastille?"

"How I came there or rather why I came there," replied Bonacieux, "is what it is impossible for me to tell you, because I don't know myself; but to a certainty it is not for having, knowingly at least, disobliged M. the Cardinal."

"You must, nevertheless, have committed a crime, since you are here, and are accused of high treason."

"Of high treason!" cried the terrified Bonacieux, "of high treason! How is it possible for a poor mercer, who detests all Huguenots, and who abhors all Spaniards, to be accused of high treason? Consider, monsieur, the thing is materially impossible."

"Monsieur Bonacieux," said the commissary, looking at the accused, as if his little eyes had the faculty of reading to the very depths of hearts, "Monsieur Bonacieux, you have a wife?"

"Yes, monsieur," replied the mercer, in a tremble, feeling that that was the point at which affairs were likely to become perplexing, "that is to say, I had one."

"What? you had one! what have you done with her then, if you have her no longer?"

"She has been carried off from me, monsieur."

"Been carried off from you?" said the commissary. "Ah!" Bonacieux felt, when he heard this "Ah," that matters were becoming more and more perplexing.

"She has been carried off?" resumed the commissary, "and do you know who the man is that has committed this outrage?"

"I think I know him."

"Who is he?"

"Remember that I affirm nothing, Monsieur le Commissaire, and that I only suspect."

"Whom do you suspect? Come, answer freely."

M. Bonacieux was in the greatest perplexity possible: had he better deny everything or tell everything? By denying all, it might be suspected that he must know too much to be so ignorant; by confessing all, he should prove his good will. He decided then upon telling all.

"I suspect," said he, "a tall, dark man, of lofty carriage, who has the air of a great lord; he has followed us several times, as I think, when I have waited for my wife at the wicket of the Louvre to fetch her home."

The commissary appeared to experience a little uneasiness.

"And his name?" said he.

"Oh! as to his name, I know nothing about it, but if I were ever to meet him, I should know him in an instant, I will answer for it, even if he were among a thousand persons."

The face of the commissary grew still darker.

"You should recognize him among a thousand, say you?" continued he.

"That is to say," cried Bonacieux, who saw he had gone wrong, "that is to say——"

"You have answered that you should recognize him," said the commissary; "that is all very well, and enough for to-day; before we proceed further, some one must be informed that you know the ravisher of your wife."

"But I have not told you that I know him!" cried Bonacieux in despair, "I told you, on the contrary——"

"Take away the prisoner," said the commissary to the two guards.

"Where must we place him?" demanded the officer.

"In a dungeon."

"Which?"

"Good Lord! in the first you come to, provided it be a safe one," said the commissary, with an indifference which penetrated poor Bonacieux with horror.

"Alas! alas!" said he to himself, "misfortune hangs over me; my wife must have committed some frightful crime; they believe that I am her accomplice, and will punish me with her! she must have spoken, she must have confessed everything, a woman is so weak! A dungeon, the first he comes to! that's it! one night is soon passed over; and to-morrow to the wheel, to the gallows! Oh! my God! my God! have pity on me!"

Without listening the least in the world to the lamentattions of Master Bonacieux, lamentations to which, besides, they must have been pretty well accustomed, the two guards took the prisoner, each by an arm, and led him away, while the commissary wrote a letter in haste, and dispatched it by an officer in waiting.

Bonacieux could not close his eyes; not because his dungeon was so very disagreeable, but because his uneasiness was too great to allow him to sleep. He sat up all night upon his stool, starting at the least noise; and when the first rays of the sun penetrated into his chamber, the dawn itself appeared to him to have taken a funereal tint.

All at once he heard his bolts drawn, and sprang up with a terrified bound, believing that they were come to fetch him to the scaffold; so that when he saw purely and simply that it

᠁as only his commissary of the preceding evening, attended by his officer, he was ready to embrace them both.

"Your affair has become more complicated since yesterday evening, my good man, and I advise you to tell the whole truth; for your repentance alone can remove the anger of the cardinal."

"Why, I am ready to tell everything," cried Bonacieux, "at least, all that I know. Interrogate me, I entreat you!"

"Where is your wife, in the first place?"

"Why, did not I tell you she had been stolen away from me?"

"Yes, but yesterday, at five o'clock in the afternoon, thanks to you, she escaped."

"My wife escaped!" cried Bonacieux. "Oh! unfortunate creature! Monsieur, if she has escaped, it is no fault of mine, I will swear."

"What business had you then to go into the chamber of M. d'Artagnan, your neighbor, with whom you had a long conference, in the course of the day?"

"Ah! yes, Monsieur le Commissaire; yes, that is true, and I confess that I was in the wrong. I did go to M. d'Artagnan's apartment."

"What was the object of that visit?"

"To beg him to assist me in finding my wife. I believed I had a right to endeavor to recover her; I was deceived, as it appears, and I ask your pardon for doing so."

"And what did M. d'Artagnan reply?"

"M. d'Artagnan promised me his assistance; but I soon found out that he was betraying me."

"You are imposing upon justice! M. d'Artagnan made an agreement with you, and in virtue of that agreement put to flight the men of the police who had arrested your wife, and has placed her out of reach of all inquiries."

"M. d'Artagnan has carried off my wife! What can that mean?"

"Fortunately M. d'Artagnan is in our hands, and you shall be confronted with him."

"Ah! *ma foi!* I ask no better," cried Bonacieux; "I shall not be sorry to see the face of an acquaintance."

"Bring in M. d'Artagnan," said the commissary to the guards. The two guards led in Athos.

"Monsieur d'Artagnan," said the commissary, addressing Athos, "declare all that passed yesterday between you and monsieur here."

"But!" cried Bonacieux, "this is not M. d'Artagnan that you have brought before me!"

"What! not M. d'Artagnan!" exclaimed the commissary.

"Not the least in the world like him," replied Bonacieux.

"What is this gentleman's name?" asked the commissary.

"I cannot tell you; I don't know him."

"How! you don't know him?"

"No."

"Did you never see him?"

"Yes, I have seen him, but I don't know what his name is."

"Your name?" asked the commissary.

"Athos," replied the musketeer.

"But that is not a man's name, that is the name of a mountain," cried the poor commissary, who began to feel a little bewildered.

"That is my name," said Athos quietly.

"But you said that your name was D'Artagnan."

"Who, I?"

"Yes, you."

"My guards said to me: 'You are Monsieur d'Artagnan?' I answered, 'You think so, do you?' My guards again exclaimed that they were sure I was. I did not think it worth while to contradict them. Besides, I might myself be deceived."

"Monsieur, you insult the majesty of justice."

"Not at all," said Athos calmly.

"You are Monsieur d'Artagnan."

"You see, monsieur, that you persist in saying that I am."

"But, I tell you, Monsieur le Commissaire," cried Bonacieux, in his turn, "there is not the least doubt about the matter. M. d'Artagnan is my tenant, although he does not pay me my rent, and even better on that account ought I to know him. M. d'Artagnan is a young man, scarcely nineteen, and this gentleman must be thirty at least. M. d'Artagnan is in M. Dessessart's guards, and monsieur is in the company of M. de Trêville's musketeers, look at his uniform, Monsieur le Commissaire, look at his uniform!"

"That's true," murmured the commissary; "*pardieu!* that's true."

At this moment th door was opened quickly, and a messenger, introduced by one of the gate-keepers of the Bastille, gave a letter to the commissary.

"Oh! unhappy woman!" cried the commissary.

"How! what do you say? of whom do you speak? It is not of my wife, I hope!"

"On the contrary, it is of her. Your affair is becoming a pretty one."

"But," said the agitated mercer, "do me the pleasure, monsieur, to tell me how my own proper affair can become the worse by anything my wife does while I am in prison?"

"Because that which she does is part of a plan concerted between you, of an infernal plan!"

"I swear to you, Monsieur le Commissaire, that you are in the profoundest error, that I know nothing in the world about what my wife had to do; that I am entirely a stranger to what she has done, and that if she has committed any follies I renounce her, I abjure her, I curse her!"

"Bah!" said Athos to the commissary, "if you have no more need of me, send me somewhere; your Monsieur Bonacieux is very unpleasant."

"Reconduct the prisoners to their dungeons," said the commissary, designating, by the same gesture, Athos and Bonacieux, "and let them be guarded more closely than ever."

"And yet," said Athos, with his habitual calmness, "if it be M. d'Artagnan who is concerned in this matter, I do not perceive too clearly how I can take his place."

"Do as I bade you," cried the commissary, "and preserve the profoundest secrecy! You undersand me!"

Athos shrugged his shoulders, and followed his guards silently, while Monsieur Bonacieux uttered lamentations enough to break the heart of a tiger.

They led back the mercer to the same dungeon in which he had passed the night, and left him to himself during the day. Bonacieux wept away the hours like a true mercer, not being at all a man of the sword, as he himself informed us. In the evening, at the moment he had made his mind up to lie down upon the bed, he heard steps in his corridor. These steps drew nearer to his dungeon, the door was thrown open, and the guards appeared.

"Follow me," said an exempt, who came behind the guards.

"Follow you!" cried Bonacieux, "follow you, at this hour! Where, in the name of God?"

"Where we have orders to lead you."

"But that is not an answer, that."

"It is, nevertheless, the only one we can give you."

"Ah! my God! my God!" murmured the poor mercer, "now, indeed, I am lost!" And he followed the guards who came for him mechanically and without resistance.

He passed along the same corridor as before, crossed a first court, then a second side of the building; at length at the gate of the entrance-court he found a carriage surrounded by four guards on horseback. They made him get into this carriage, the exempt placed himself by his side, the door was locked, and they were left in a rolling prison. The carriage was put in motion as slowly as a funeral car. Through the closely fastened windows the prisoner could perceive the houses and the pavement, that was all; but, true Parisian as he was, Bonacieux could recognize every street by the rails, the signs, and the lamps. At the moment of arriving at Saint Paul, the spot where such as were condemned at the Bastille were executed, he was near fainting and crossed himself twice. He thought the carriage was about to stop there. The carriage, however, passed on.

Further on, a still greater terror seized him on passing by the cemetery of Saint Jean, where state criminals were buried. One thing, however, reassured him: he remembered that before they were buried their heads were generally cut off, and he felt that his head was still on his shoulders. But when he saw the carriage take the way to La Grêve, when he perceived the pointed roof of the Hotel de Ville, and the carriage passed under the arcade, he then thought all was over with him, wished to confess to the exempt, and upon his refusal, uttered such pitiable cries that the exempt told him that if he continued to deafen him in that manner, he should put a gag in his mouth.

This measure somewhat reassured Bonacieux; if they meant to execute him at La Grêve, it could scarcely be worth while to gag him, as they had nearly reached the place of execution. In fact, the carriage crossed the fatal spot without stopping. There remained then no other place to fear but the Croix-du-Trahoir; the carriage was taking exactly the road to it.

This time there was no longer any doubt: it was at the Croix-du-Trahoir that obscure criminals were executed. Bonacieux had flattered himself in believing himself worthy of Saint Paul or of the Place de Grêve: it was the Croix-du-Trahoir that his journey and his destiny were about to be ended! He could not yet see that dreadful cross, but he felt as if it were in some sort coming to meet him. When he was within twenty paces of it, he heard a noise of people, and the carriage stopped. This was more than poor Bonacieux could endure depressed as he was by the successive emotions which he had experienced: he uttered a feeble groan which might have been taken for the last sigh of a dying man, and fainted.

CHAPTER XIV.

THE MAN OF MEUNG.

THE crowd was not produced by the expectation of a man who was to be hung, but by the contemplation of a man who was hung.

The carriage, which had been stopped for a minute, resumed its way, passed through the crowd, threaded the Rue Saint Honoré, turned the Rue des Bons Enfans, and stopped before a low door.

The door opened, two guards received Bonacieux in their arms from the exempt, who supported him; they carried him along an alley, up a flight of stairs, and deposited him in an antechamber.

All these movements had been effected, as far as he was concerned in them, mechanically. He had moved along as if in a dream; he had a glimpse of objects as if through a fog; his ears had perceived sounds without comprehending them; he might have been executed at that moment without his making a single gesture in his own defense, or his uttering a cry to implore mercy.

He remained upon the bench, with his back leaning against the wall and his hands hanging down, exactly in the spot where the guards had placed him.

On looking round him, however, as he could perceive no threatening object, as nothing indicated that he ran any real danger, as the bench was comfortably covered with a well-stuffed cushion, as the wall was ornamented with beautiful Cordova leather, and as large red damask curtains, fastened back by gold clasps, floated before the window, he perceived by degrees that his fear was exaggerated, and he began to turn his head to the right and the left, upward and downward.

At this movement, which nobody opposed, he resumed a little courage, and ventured to draw up one leg and then the other; at length, with the help of his two hands, he raised himself up upon the bench, and found himself upon his feet.

At this moment an officer of a sufficiently good appearance opened a door, continued to exchange some words with a person in the next chamber, and then came up to the prisoner:

"Is your name Bonacieux?" said he.

"Yes, Monsieur l'Officer," stammered the mercer, more dead than alive, "at your service."

"Come in," said the officer.

And he moved out of the way to let the mercer pass. The latter obeyed without reply, and entered the chamber, where he appeared to be expected.

It was a large cabinet, with the walls furnished with arms offensive and defensive, close and stifling; and in which there was already a fire, although it was scarcely the end of September. A square table, covered with books and papers, upon which was unrolled an immense plan of the city of La Rochelle, occupied the center of the apartment.

Standing before the chimney, was a man of middle height, of a haughty, proud mien; with piercing eyes, a large brow, and a thin face, which was made still longer by a royal (or imperial, as it is now called), surmounted by a pair of moustaches. Although this man was scarcely thirty-six or thirty-seven years of age, hair, moustaches, and royal, all began to be gray. This man, except a sword, had all the appearance of a soldier, and his buff boots, still slightly covered with dust, indicated that he had been on horseback in the course of the day.

This man was Armand Jean Duplessis, Cardinal de Richelieu, not such as he is now represented—broken down like an old man, suffering like a martyr, his body bent, his voice extinct—buried in a large *fauteuil*, as in an anticipated tomb; no longer living but by the strength of his genius, and no longer maintaining the struggle with Europe but by the eternal application of his thoughts—but such as he really was at this period; that is to say, an active and gallant cavalier, already weak of body, but sustained by that moral power which made of him one of the most extraordinary men that ever existed; preparing, after having supported the Duke de Nevers in his duchy of Mantua, after having taken Nimes, Castres, and Uzes—to drive the English from the isle of Ré, and lay seige to La Rochelle.

At first sight, nothing denoted the cardinal; and it was impossible for those who did not know his face to guess in whose presence they were.

The poor mercer remained standing at the door, while the eyes of the personage we have just described were fixed upon him, and appeared to wish to penetrate even into the depths of the past.

"Is this that Bonacieux?" asked he, after a moment of silence.

"Yes, monseigneur," replied the officer.

"That's well. Give me those papers, and leave us."

The officer took the papers pointed out from the table, gave them to him who asked for them, bowed to the ground, and retired.

Bonacieux recognized, in these papers, his interrogatories of the Bastille. From time to time, the man of the chimney raised his eyes from the writings, and plunged them like poniards into the heart of the poor mercer.

At the end of ten minutes' reading, and ten seconds of examination, the cardinal was satisfied.

"That head has never conspired," murmured he; "but it matters not; we will see, nevertheless."

"You are accused of high treason," said the cardinal slowly.

"So I have been told already, monseigneur," cried Bonacieux, giving his interrogator the title he had heard the officer give him, "but I swear to you that I know nothing about it."

The cardinal repressed a smile.

"You have conspired with your wife, with Madame de Chevreuse, and with milord Duke of Buckingham."

"In fact, monseigneur, I have heard her pronounce all those names."

"And on what occasion?"

"She said that the Cardinal de Richelieu had drawn the Duke of Buckingham to Paris to ruin him and to ruin the queen."

"She said that?" cried the cardinal, with violence.

"Yes, monseigneur, but I told her she was wrong to talk about such things; and that his eminence was incapable——"

"Hold your tongue! you are stupid," replied the cardinal.

"That's exactly what my wife said, monseigneur."

"Do you know who carried off your wife?"

"No, monseigneur."

"You have suspicions, nevertheless?"

"Yes, monseigneur; but these suspicions appeared to be disagreeable to monseigneur the commissary, and I no longer have them."

"Your wife has escaped! Did you know that?"

"No, monseigneur; I learned it since I have been in prison and that from the conversation of monsieur the commissary— a very good kind of man."

The cardinal repressed another smile.

"Then you are ignorant of what is become of your wife since her flight."

"Absolutely, monseigneur; but she has most likely returned to the Louvre."

"At one o'clock this morning she had not returned."

"Good God! what can have become of her then?"

"We shall know, be assured; nothing is concealed from the cardinal, the cardinal knows everything."

"In that case, monseigneur, do you believe the cardinal will be so kind as to tell me what has become of my wife?"

"Perhaps he may; but you must, in the first place, reveal to the cardinal all you know of your wife's relations with Madame de Chevreuse."

"But monseigneur, I know nothing about them; I have never seen her!"

"When you went to fetch your wife from the Louvre, did you always return directly home?"

"Scarcely ever; she had business to transact with linen drapers, to whose houses I conducted her."

"And how many were there of these linen drapers?"

"Two, monseigneur."

"And where did they live?"

"One Rue de Vaugirard, the other Rue de la Harpe."

"Did you go into these houses with her?"

"Never, monseigneur; I waited at the door."

"And what excuse did she make for going in in this manner alone?"

"She gave me none; she told me to wait, and I waited."

"You are a very complacent husband, my dear Monsieur Bonacieux," said the cardinal.

"He calls me his dear monsieur," said the mercer to himself. "Peste! matters are going all right!"

"Should you know those doors again?"

"Yes."

"Do you know the numbers?"

"Yes."

"What are they?"

"No. 25 in the Rue Vaugirard; 75 in the Rue de la Harpe."

"That's well," said the cardinal.

At these words, he took up a silver bell, and rang it: the officer entered.

"Go," said he, in a subdued voice, "and find Rochefort; tell him to come to me immediately, if he is returned."

"The count is here," said the officer, "and requests to speak with your eminence instantly."

"Let him come in, then; let him come in, then!" said the cardinal eagerly.

The officer sprang out of the apartment with that alacrity which all the servants of the cardinal displayed in obeying him.

"To your eminence!" murmured Bonacieux, rolling his eyes round in astonishment.

Five seconds had scarcely elapsed after the disappearance of the officer, when the door opened, and a new personage entered.

"It is he!" cried Bonacieux.

"He! what he?" asked the cardinal.

"The man that took away my wife!"

The cardinal rang a second time. The officer reappeared. "Place this man in the care of his guards again, and let him wait till I send for him."

"No, monseigneur! no! it is not he!" cried Bonacieux; "no, I was deceived: this is quite a different man, and does not resemble him at all. Monsieur is, I am sure, a very good sort of man!"

"Take away that fool!" said the cardinal.

The officer took Bonacieux by the arm, and led him into the antechamber, where he found his two guards.

The newly introduced personage followed Bonacieux impatiently with his eyes till he was gone out, and the moment the door closed, he advanced eagerly toward the cardinal, and said:

"They have seen each other!"

"Who?" asked his eminence.

"He and she!"

"The queen and the duke?" cried Richelieu.

"Yes."

"Where?"

"At the Louvre."

"Are you sure of it?"

"Perfectly sure."

"Who told you of it?"

"Madame Lannoy, who is devoted to your eminence, as you know."

"Why did she not let me know sooner?"

"Whether by chance or from mistrust, I don't know; but the queen made Madame de Surgis sleep in her chamber, and detained her all day."

"Well, we are beaten! Now let us try to take our revenge."

"I will assist you with all my heart, monseigneur; be assured of that."

"How did it take place?"

"At half-past twelve, the queen was with her women——"

"Where?"

"In her bedchamber——"

"Go on."

"When some one came and brought her a handkerchief from her *dame de lingerie*."

"And then!"

"The queen immediately exhibited strong emotion; and notwithstanding that her face was covered with rouge, evidently turned pale——"

"Well, go on!"

"She however, rose, and with a trembling voice: 'Ladies, said she, wait for me ten minutes, I shall soon return.' She then opened the door of her alcove, and went out."

"Why did not Madame Lannoy come and inform you instantly?"

"Nothing was certain; besides, her majesty had said: 'Ladies, wait for me;' and she did not dare to disobey the queen."

"How long did the queen remain out of the chamber?"

"Three-quarters of an hour."

"Did none of her women accompany her?"

"Only Donna Estafania."

"Did she afterward return?"

"Yes; but to take a little rosewood casket, with her cipher upon it; and went out again immediately."

"And when she finally returned, did she bring that casket with her?"

"No."

"Does Madame Lannoy know what was in that casket?"

"Yes; the diamond studs which his majesty gave the queen."

"And she came back without this casket?"

"Yes."

"Madame Lannoy, then, is of opinion that she gave them to Buckingham."

"She is sure of it."

"How can she be so?"

"In the course of the day, Madame de Lannoy, in her quality of tire-woman of the queen, looked for this casket, appeared uneasy at not finding it, and at length asked the queen if she knew anything about it."

"And the queen?"

"The queen became excedingly red, and replied, that having on the preceding evening broken one of those studs, she had sent it to her goldsmith to be repaired."

"He must be called upon, and so ascertain if the thing be true or not."

"I have just been with him."

"And the goldsmith says——"

"The goldsmith has heard of nothing of the kind."

"Right! right! Rochefort, all is not lost; and perhaps—perhaps—everything is for the best!"

"The fact is, that I do not doubt your eminence's genius——"

"Will repair the blunders of his agent—is that it?"

"That is exactly what I was going to say, if your eminence had permitted me to finish my sentence."

"Do you know where the Duchess de Chevreuse and the Duke of Buckingham are now concealed?"

"No, monseigneur; my people could tell me nothing on that head."

"But I know."

"You, monseigneur?"

"Yes; or at least I guess. They were, one in the Rue Vaugirard, No. 25; the other in the Rue de la Harpe, No. 75."

"Does your eminence command that they should be both instantly arrested?"

"It will be too late; they will be gone."

"But still, we can make sure that they are so."

"Take ten men of my guards, and search the house thoroughly."

"Instantly, monseigneur."

And Rochefort went hastily out of the apartment.

The cardinal, upon being left alone, reflected for an instant, and then rang the bell a third time. The same officer appeared.

"Bring the prisoner in again," said the cardinal.

Master Bonacieux was introduced afresh, and upon a sign from the cardinal the officer retired.

"You have deceived me!" said the cardinal sternly.

"I!" cried Bonacieux; "I! deceive your eminence!"

"Your wife, when going to Rue de Vaugirard and Rue de la Harpe, did not go to meet linen drapers."

"Then whom did she go to meet, in the name of God?"

"She went to meet the Duchess de Chevreuse and the Duke of Buckingham."

"Yes," cried Bonacieux, recalling all his remembrances of the circumstances, "yes, that's it. Your eminence is right. I told my wife, several times, that it was surprising that linen drapers should live in such houses as those—in houses that had no signs—but she only always laughed at me.

"Ah! monseigneur!" continued Bonacieux, throwing himself at his eminence's feet, "ah! how truly you are the cardinal, the great cardinal, the man of genius whom all the world reveres."

The cardinal, however contemptible might be the triumph gained over so vulgar a being as Bonacieux, did not the less enjoy it for an instant; then, almost immediately, as if a fresh thought had occurred, to the mercer:

"Rise, my good friend," said he; "you are a worthy man."

"The cardinal has touched me with his hand! I have touched the hand of the great man!" cried Bonacieux: "the great man has called me his friend!"

"Yes, my friend; yes!" said the cardinal, with that paternal tone which he sometimes knew how to assume, but which deceived none who knew him; "and as you have been unjustly suspected, well! you must be idemnified: here! take this purse of a hundred pistoles, and pardon me."

"I pardon you, monseigneur!" said Bonacieux, hesitating to take the purse, fearing, doubtless, that this pretended gift was but a joke. "But you are free to have me arrested, you are free to have me tortured, you are free to have me hung: you are the master, and I could not have the least word to say against it. Pardon you, monseigneur! you cannot mean that!"

"Ah! my dear Monsieur Bonacieux, you are generous in this matter, and I thank you for it. Thus, then, you will take this bag, and you will go away without being too much dissatisfied with your treatment."

"I shall go away enchanted."

"Farewell, then; that is to say, for the present, for I hope we shall meet again."

"Whenever monseigneur wishes: I am always at his emience's orders."

"And that will be frequently, I assure you, for I have found something extremely agreeable in your conversation."

"Oh! monseigneur!"

"Au revoir, Monsieur Bonacieux, au revoir!"

And the cardinal made him a sign with his hand, to which Bonacieux replied by bowing to the ground; he then went out backward, and when he was in the antechamber, the cardinal heard him, in his enthusiasm, crying aloud, "Vive monseigneur! Vive son eminence! Vive le grand cardinal!" The cardinal listened with a smile to this vociferous manifestation of the feelings of Bonacieux; and then, when Bonacieux's cries were no longer audible:

"Good!" said he, "that man would, henceforward, lay down his life for me."

And the cardinal began to examine with the greatest attention the map of La Rochelle, which, as we have said, lay open upon the table, tracing with a pencil the line in which the famous dyke was to pass, which, eighteen months later, shut up the port of the besieged city. As he was in the deepest of his strategic meditations, the door opened, and Rochefort returned.

"Well!" said the cardinal eagerly, rising with a promptitude which proved the degree of importance he attached to the commission with which he had charged the count.

"Well!" said the latter, "a young woman of about twenty-six or twenty-eight years of age, and a man of from thirty-five to forty, have lodged at the two houses pointed out by your eminence, but the woman left last night, and the man this morning."

"They were the persons!" cried the cardinal, looking at the clock; "and now it is too late to have them pursued: the duchess is at Tours, and the duke at Boulogne. It is at London they must be met with."

"What are your eminence's orders?"

"Not a word of what has passed; let the queen remain in perfect security; let her be ignorant that we know her secret; let her believe that we are in search of some conspiracy or other. Send me the keeper of the seals, Monseiur Séguier."

"And that man, what has your eminence done with him?"

"What man?" asked the cardinal.

"That Bonacieux."

"I have done with him all that could be done: I have made him a spy upon his wife."

The Count de Rochefort bowed like a man who acknowledges as great the superiority of the master, and retired.

"Tell Vitray to come to me," said he, "and tell him to get ready for a journey."

The instant after, the man he required was before him, booted and spurred.

"Vitray," said he, "you will go, with all speed, to London. You must not stop an instant on the way. You will deliver this letter to milady. Here is an order for two hundred pistoles; call upon my treasurer and get the money. You shall have as much again if you are back within six days, and have executed your commission well."

The messenger, without replying a single word, bowed, took

the letter, with the order for the two hundred pistoles, and retired.

These were the contents of the letter:

"MILADY: Be at the first ball at which the Duke of Buckingham shall be present. He will wear on his doublet twelve diamond studs; get as near to him as you can, and cut off two of them.

"As soon as these studs shall be in your possession, inform me."

CHAPTER XV.

MEN OF THE ROBE AND MEN OF THE SWORD.

ON the day after these events had taken place, Athos not having reappeared, M. de Tréville was informed by D'Artagnan and Porthos of the circumstance. As to Aramis, he had asked for leave of absence for five days, and was gone, it was said, to Rouen, on family business.

M. de Tréville was the father of his soldiers. The lowest or the most unknown of them, as soon as he assumed the uniform of the company, was as sure of his aid and support as his brother himself could have been.

He repaired then, instantly to the residence of the *lieutenant-criminel*. The officer who commanded the post of the Croix-Rouge was sent for, and by successive inquiries they found that Athos was at the time lodged in the Fort l'Evêque.

Athos had passed through all the examinations we have seen Bonacieux undergo.

We were present at the scene in which the two captives were confronted with each other. Athos, had till that time said nothing for fear that D'Artagnan, interrupted in his turn, should not have the time necessary; but from this moment Athos declared that his name was Athos, and not D'Artagnan. He added that he did not know either Monsieur or Madame Bonacieux; that he had never spoken to the one or the other; that he had come, at about ten o'clock in the evening, to pay a visit to his friend, M. d'Artagnan, but that till that hour he had been at M. de Tréville's, where he had dined; "twenty witnesses," added he, "could attest the fact," and he named several distinguished gentlemen, and among them was M. the duke de la Trémouille.

The second commissary was as much bewildered as the first

had been at the simple but firm declaration of the musketeer, upon whom he was anxious to take the revenge which men of the robe like at all times to gain over men of the sword; but the name of M. de Tréville, and that of M. de la Trémouille, commanded a little reflection.

Athos was then sent to the cardinal, but unfortunately the cardinal was at the Louvre with the king.

It was precisely at this moment, at which M. de Tréville, on leaving the residence of the *lieutenant-criminel,* and that of the governor of the Fort l'Evêque, without being able to find Athos, arrived at the palace.

As the captain of the musketeers, M. de Tréville had the right of *entrée* at all times.

It is well known how violent the king's prejudices were against the queen, and how carefully these prejudices were kept up by the cardinal, who, in affairs of intrigue, mistrusted women much more than men. One of the principal causes of this prejudice was the friendship of Anne of Austria for Madame de Chevreuse. These two women gave him more uneasiness than the war with Spain, the quarrel with England, or the embarrassment of the finances. In his eyes, and to his perfect conviction, Madame de Chevreuse not only served the queen in her political intrigues, but, which troubled him still more, in her love affairs.

At the first word the cardinal spoke of Madame de Chevreuse, who, though exiled to Tours, and who was believed to be in that city, had been at Paris, had remained there five days, and had outwitted the police, the king flew into a furious passion. Although capricious and unfaithful, the king wished to be called Louis the Just and Louis the Chaste. Posterity will find a difficulty in understanding this character, which history explains only by facts and never by reasonings.

But when the cardinal added, that not only had Madame de Chevreuse been in Paris, but, still further, that the queen had renewed with her, by the means of one of those mysterious correspondences which at that time was named a cabal; when he affirmed that he, the cardinal, was about to unravel the most closely twisted thread of this intrigue; when at the moment of arresting in the fact, with all the proofs about her, the queen's emissary to the exiled duchess, a musketeer, had dared to interrupt the course of justice violently, by falling, sword in hand, upon the honest men of the law charged with investigating impartially the whole affair, in order to place it before the eyes of the king, Louis XIII. could not contain himself, and he made a step toward the queen's apartment, with that pale and mute indignation, which when it broke out, led this prince to the commission of the coldest cruelty.

And yet, in all this, the cardinal had not yet said a word about the Duke of Buckingham.

At this instant M. de Tréville entered, cold, polite, and in irreproachable costume.

Rendered aware of what had passed by the presence of the cardinal, and the alteration in the king's countenance, M. de Tréville felt himself something like Samson before the Philistines.

Louis XIII. had already placed his hand on the button of the door; at the noise of M. de Tréville's entrance he turned round.

"You arrive in good time, monsieur," said the king, who, when his passions were raised to a certain point, could not dissemble; "I have learned some pretty things concerning your musketeers!"

"And I," said M. de Tréville, coldly, "I have some pretty things to inform your majesty of, concerning these men of the robe."

"What do you say?" said the king, with hauteur.

"I have the honor to inform your majesty," continued M. de Tréville in the same tone, "that a party of procureurs, commissaries, and the men of the police, very estimable people but very inveterate, as it appears, against the uniform, have taken upon themselves to arrest in a house, to lead away through the open street, and throw into the Fort l'Evêque, all upon an order which they have refused to show me, one of my, or rather your musketeers, sire, of irreproachable conduct, of an almost illustrious reputation, and whom your majesty knows favorably, M. Athos."

"Athos!" said the king mechanically; "yes, indeed, I know that name."

"Let your majesty remember," said M. de Tréville, "that M. Athos is the musketeer who, in the annoying duel which you are acquainted with, had the misfortune to wound M. de Cahusac so seriously. Apropos, monseigneur," continued De Tréville, addressing the cardinal, "M. de Cahusac is quite recovered, is he not?"

"Thank you!" said the cardinal, biting his lips with anger.

"M. Athos, then, went to pay a visit to one of his friends, at the time absent," continued M. de Tréville, "to a young Béarnais, a cadet in his majesty's guards, the company of M. Dessessarts, but scarcely had he arrived at his friend's, and taken up a book, while waiting his return, when a crowd of bailiffs and soldiers mixed, came and laid siege to the house, and broke open several doors——"

The cardinal made the king a sign, which signified, "That was on account of the affair about which I spoke to you."

"Oh! we all know that," interrupted the king; "for all that was done for our service."

"Then," said Tréville, "it was also for your majesty's service, that one of my musketeers, who was innocent, has been seized; that he has been placed between two guards, like a malefactor; and that this gallant man, who has ten times shed his blood in your majesty's service, and is ready to shed it again, has been paraded through the midst of an insolent populace!"

"Bah!" said the king, who began to be shaken, "was it managed so?"

"M. de Tréville," said the cardinal, with the greatest phlegm, "does not tell your majesty that this innocent musketeer, this gallant man, had only an hour before attacked, sword in hand four commissaires of inquiry, who were delegated by me to examine into an affair of the highest importance."

"I defy your eminence to prove it," cried M. de Tréville, with his Gascon freedom and military roughness; "for one hour before, M. Athos, who, I will confide it to your majesty, is really a man of the highest quality, did me the honor, after having dined with me, to be conversing in the salon of my hotel, with M. the Duke de la Trémouille and M. le Comte de Châlus, who happened to be there."

The king looked at the cardinal.

"A *procès-verbal* attests it," said the cardinal, replying aloud to the mute interrogation of his majesty; "and the ill-treated people have drawn up the following, which I have the honor to present to your majesty."

"And is the *procès-verbel* of men of the robe to be placed in comparison with the word of honor of a man of the sword?" replied Tréville haughtily.

"Come, come, Tréville, hold your tongue," said the king.

"If his eminence entertains any suspicion against one of my musketeers," said Tréville, "the justice of M. the Cardinal is sufficiently well known to induce me, myself, to demand an inquiry."

"In the house in which this judicial inquiry was made," continued the impassable cardinal, "there lodges, I believe, a young Béarnais, a friend of the musketeer's."

"Your eminence means M. d'Artagnan."

"I mean a young man whom you patronize, Monsieur de Tréville."

"Yes, your eminence, it is the same."

"Do you not suspect this young man of having given bad advice——"

"To M. Athos! to a man double his age?" interrupted M. de Tréville. "No, monseigneur. Besides, M. d'Artagnan passed the evening at my hotel."

"Well," said the cardinal, "everybody seems to have passed the evening at your hotel!"

"Does your eminence doubt my word?" said De Tréville, with a brow flushed with anger.

"No, God forbid!" said the cardinal; "but only let me inquire at what hour he was with you?"

"Oh, that I can speak to positively, your eminence; for as he came in I remarked that it was half-past nine by the clock, although I had believed it to be later."

"And at what hour did he leave your hotel?"

"At half-past ten; an hour after the event."

"Well, but," replied the cardinal, who could not for an instant suspect the loyalty of De Tréville, and who felt that the victory was escaping from his hands—"well, but Athos, *was* taken in the house of the Rue des Fossoyeurs."

"Is one friend forbidden to visit another? or a musketeer of my company to fraternize with a guard of M. Dessessart's company?"

"Yes, when the house in which he fraternizes is suspected."

"That house is suspected, Tréville," said the king; "perhaps you were not aware of that?"

"Indeed, sire, I knew nothing of the circumstances. The house may be suspected, but I deny that it is in the part of it inhabited by M. d'Artagnan; for I can affirm, sire, if I can believe what he says, that there does not exist a more devoted servant of your majesty, or a more profound admirer of Monsieur the Cardinal."

"Was it not this D'Artagnan who wounded, one day, Jussac, in that unfortunate encounter, which took place near the convent of the Carmes Déchaussés?" asked the king, looking at the cardinal, who colored with vexation.

"And the next day Bernajoux. Yes, sire, yes, it is the same. Your majesty has an excellent memory."

"Come, how shall we determine?" said the king.

"That concerns your majesty more than me," said the cardinal. "I should affirm the culpability."

"And I deny it," said De Tréville. "But his majesty has judges, and these judges will decide."

"That is best," said the king. "Send the case before the judges; it is their business to judge, and they will judge."

"Only," replied Tréville, "it is a sad thing that, in the unfortunate times in which we live, the purest life, the most incontestable virtue, cannot exempt a man from infamy and persecution. The army, I will answer for it, will be but little pleased at being exposed to rigorous treatment on account of affairs of police."

The expression was imprudent; but M. de Tréville launched it with a full knowledge of his cause. He was desirous of an explosion, because in that case the mine throws forth fire, and fire enlightens.

"Affairs of police!" cried the king, taking up De Tréville's words; "affairs of police! And what do you know about them, monsieur? Meddle with your musketeers, and do not annoy me in this way. It appears, according to your account, that if, unfortunately, a musketeer is arrested, France is in danger! Here's a piece of work about a musketeer! Why, I would arrest ten of them, *ventrebleu!* a hundred, even—all the company! and I would not allow a murmur!"

"From the moment they are suspected by your majesty," said Tréville, "the musketeers are guilty; therefore, you see me prepared to surrender my sword; for, after having accused my soldiers, there can be no doubt that M. the Cardinal will end by accusing me. It is best to constitute myself at once a prisoner with M. Athos, who is already arrested, and with M. d'Artagnan, who most probably will be arrested."

"Gascon-headed man! will you have done?" said the king.

"Sire," replied Tréville, without lowering his voice in the least, "either order my musketeer to be restored to me, or let him be tried."

"He shall be tried," said the cardinal.

"Well, so much the better; for in that case I shall demand of his majesty permission to plead for him."

The king became afraid of an outbreak.

"If his eminence," said he, "had not personal motives——"

The cardinal saw what the king was about to say, and interrupted him:

"Pardon me," said he; "but the instant your majesty considers me a prejudiced judge, I withdraw."

"Come," said the king, "will you swear by my father that M. Athos was at your residence during the event, and that he took no part in it?"

"By your glorious father, and by yourself—who are that which I love and venerate the most in the world—I swear it!"

"Be so kind as to reflect, sire," said the cardinal. "If we release the prisoner thus, we shall never be able to know the truth."

"M. Athos will always be to be found," replied Tréville—"always ready to answer, when it shall please the men of the long robe to interrogate him. He will not desert, Monsieur le Cardinal, be assured of that; I will answer for him."

"No, he will not desert," said the king; "he can always be found, as M. de Tréville says. Besides," added he, lowering his voice, and looking with a suppliant air at the cardinal, "let us give them apparent security: there is policy in that."

This policy of Louis XIII.'s made Richelieu smile.

"Order it as you please, sire; you possess the right of pardoning."

"The right of pardoning only applies to the guilty," said Tréville, who was determined to have the last word, "and my musketeer is innocent. It is not mercy, then, that you are about to accord, sire; it is justice."

"And he is in the Fort l'Evêque?" said the king.

"Yes, sire, in solitary confinement, in a dungeon, like the lowest criminal."

"The devil! the devil!" murmured the king—"what must be done?"

"Sign the order for his release, and all will be said," replied the cardinal. "I believe, with your majesty, that M. de Tréville's guarantee is more than sufficient."

Tréville bowed very respectfully, with a joy that was not unmixed with fear; he would have preferred an obstinate resistance on the part of the cardinal, to this sudden yielding.

The king signed the order for enlargement, and Tréville carried it away without delay.

At the moment he was about to leave the presence, the cardinal gave him a friendly smile, and said:

"A perfect harmony seems to prevail in your musketeers, sire, between the leader and the soldiers, which must be good for the service, and advantageous to all."

"Now he will play me some dog's trick or other, and that immediately," said Tréville; "there is no possibility of getting the last word with such a man. But let us be quick—the king may change his mind presently; and, at all events, it is more difficult to replace a man in the Fort l'Evêque, or the Bastille, who has got out, than to keep a prisoner there who is in."

M. de Tréville made his entrance triumphantly into the
Fort l'Evêque, whence he delivered the musketeer, whose
peaceful indifference had not for a moment abandoned him.

The first time he saw D'Artagnan, "You have come off
well," said he to him; "there is your Jussac thrust paid for.
There still remains that of Bernajoux, but you must not be
too confident."

As to the rest, M. de Tréville had good reason to mistrust
the cardinal, and to think that all was not over, for scarcely
had the captain of the musketeers closed the door after him,
than his eminence said to the king:

"Now that we are at length by ourselves, we will, if your
majesty pleases, converse seriously. Sire, Monsieur de Buckingham has been in Paris five days, and only left it this
morning."

CHAPTER XVI.

IN WHICH MONSIEUR SEGUIER, THE KEEPER OF THE SEALS,
LOOKS MORE THAN ONCE FOR THE BELL, IN ORDER TO
RING IT, AS HE DID BEFORE.

IT IS impossible to form an idea of the impression these
few words made upon Louis XIII. He grew pale and red
alternately; and the cardinal saw at once that he had recovered, by a single blow, all the ground he had lost.

"M. de Buckingham in Paris!" cried he, "and what does
he come to do there?"

"To conspire, no doubt, with your enemies the Huguenots
and the Spaniards."

"No, *pardieu!* no! To conspire against my honor, with
Madame de Chevreuse, Madame de Longueville, and the
Condés."

"Oh! sire, what an idea! The queen is too prudent, and,
besides, loves your majesty too well."

"Woman is weak, Monsieur le Cardinal," said the king;
"and as to loving me much, I have my own opinion respecting
that love."

"I not the less maintain," said the cardinal, "that the
Duke of Buckingham came to Paris for a project purely
political."

"And I am sure that he came for quite another purpose,
Monsieur le Cardinal, but if the queen be guilty, let her
tremble!"

"Indeed," said the cardinal, "whatever repugnance 1 may have to directing my mind to such a treason, your majesty compels me to think of it. Madame de Lannoy, whom, according to your majesty's command, I have frequently interrogated, told me this morning, that the night before last her majesty sat up very late, that this morning she wept much, and that she was writing all day."

"That's it!" cried the king; "to him, no doubt. Cardinal, I must have the queen's papers."

"But how to take them, sire? It seems to me that neither your majesty nor I can charge ourselves with such a mission."

"How did they act with regard to La Maréchale d'Ancre?" cried the king, in the highest state of irritation; "her *armoires* were thoroughly searched, and then she herself was searched."

"The Maréchale d'Ancre was no more than the Maréchale d'Ancre, a Florentine adventuress sire, and that was all; while the august spouse of your majesty is Anne of Austria, queen of France, that is to say, one of the greatest princesses in the world."

"She is not the less guilty, Monsieur le Duc! The more she has forgotten the high position in which she was placed, the more degrading is her fall. It is long since, besides, that I have determined to put an end to all these petty intrigues of policy and love. She has also about her a certain Laporte."

"Who, I believe, is the mainspring of all this, I confess," said the cardinal.

"You think, then, as I do, that she deceives me?" said the king.

"I believe, and I repeat it to your majesty, that the queen conspires against the power of the king, but I have not said against his honor."

"And I—I tell you against both; I tell you the queen does not love me; I tell you she loves another; I tell you she loves that infamous Buckingham! Why did you not cause him to be arrested while he was in Paris?"

"Arrest the duke! arrest the prime minister of King Charles I. Think of it, sire! What a scandal! And if then the suspicions of your majesty, which I still continue to doubt, should prove to have any foundation, what a terrible disclosure! what a fearful scandal!"

"But as he acted like a vagabond or a thief, he should have been——"

Louis XIII. stopped, terrified at what he was about to say, while Richelieu, stretching out his neck, waited uselessly for the word which had died on the lips of the king.

"He should have been?"

"Nothing," said the king, "nothing. But all the time he was in Paris, you, of course, did not lose sight of him?"

"No, sire."

"Where did he lodge?"

"Rue de la Harpe, No. 75."

"Where is that?"

"By the side of the Luxembourg."

"And you are certain that the queen and he did not see each other?"

"I believe the queen to have too high a sense of her duties, sire."

"But they have corresponded; it is to him that the queen has been writing all the day; Monsieur le Duc, I must have those letters!"

"Sire, notwithstanding——"

"Monsieur le Duc, at whatever price it may be, I will have them."

"I would, however, beg your majesty to observe——"

"Do you then also join in betraying me, Monsieur le Cardinal, by thus always opposing my will? Are you also in concert with Spain and England, with Madame de Chevreuse and the queen?"

"Sire," replied the cardinal, sighing, "I thought I was secure from such suspicion."

"Monsieur le Cardinal, you have heard me, I will have those letters."

"There is but one means."

"What is that?"

"That would be to charge M. de Séguier, the keeper of the seals, with this mission. The matter enters completely into the duties of his post."

"Let him be sent for instantly."

"He is most likely at my hotel; I requested him to call, and when I came to the Louvre, I left orders, if he came, to desire him to wait."

"Let him be sent for instantly."

"Your majesty's orders shall be executed; but——"

"But what?"

"But the queen will perhaps refuse to obey."

"What, my orders?"

"Yes, if she is ignorant that these orders come from the king."

"Well, that she may have no doubt on that head, I will go and inform her myself."

"Your majesty will not forget that I have done everything in my power to prevent a rupture."

"Yes, duke, yes, I know you are very indulgent toward the queen too indulgent perhaps; we shall have occasion I warn you, at some future period to speak of that."

"Whenever it shall please your majesty; but I shall be always happy and proud, sire, to sacrifice myself to the good harmony which I desire to see reign between you and the queen of France."

"It is all very well, cardinal, all very well; but, in the meantime, send for monsieur the keeper of the seals. I will go to the queen."

And Louis XIII., opening the door of communication, passed into the corridor which led to the apartments of Anne of Austria.

The queen was in the midst of her women, Madame de Guitant, Madame de Sable, Madame de Montbazon, and Madame de Guéméne. In a corner was the Spanish cameriste, Donna Estafania, who had followed her from Madrid. Madame Guéméne was reading aloud, and everybody was listening to her with attention, with the exception of the queen, who had, on the contrary, desired this reading in order that she might be able, while feigning to listen, to pursue the thread of her own thoughts.

These thoughts, gilded as they were by a last reflection of love, were not the less sad. Anne of Austria, deprived of the confidence of her husband, pursued by the hatred of the cardinal, who could not pardon her for having repulsed a more tender feeling, having before her eyes the example of the queen mother, whom that hatred had tormented all her life, though Mary de Medici, if the memoirs of the time are to be believed, had begun by according to the cardinal that sentiment which Anne of Austria always refused him; Anne of Austria had seen fall around her her most devoted servants, her most intimate confidants, her dearest favorites. Like those unfortunate persons endowed with a fatal gift, she brought misfortune upon everything she touched; her friendship was a fatal sign which called down persecution. Madame Chevreuse and Madame Vernet were exiled, and Laporte did not conceal from his mistress that he expected to be arrested every instant.

It was at the moment she was plunged in the deepest and darkest of these reflections, that the door of the chamber opened, and the king entered.

The reader was instantly silent, all the ladies rose, and

there was a profound silence. As to the king, he made no demonstration of politeness, only stopping before the queen.

"Madame," said he, "you are about to receive a visit from the chancellor, who will communicate certain matters to you, with which I have charged him."

The unfortunate queen, who was constantly threatened with divorce, exile, and trial even, turned pale under her rouge, and could not refrain from saying:

"But why this visit, sire? What can Monsieur the Chancellor have to say to me that your majesty could not say yourself?"

The king turned upon his heel without reply, and almost at the same instant the captain of the guards, M. de Guitant, announced the visit of Monsieur the Chancellor.

When the chancellor appeared, the king had already gone out by another door.

The chancellor entered, half smiling, half blushing. As we shall probably meet with him again in the course of our history, it would be quite as well for our readers to be made at once acquainted with him.

This chancellor was a pleasant man. It was Des Roches le Masle, canon of Notre Dame, and who had formerly been valet de chambre to the cardinal, who introduced him to his eminence as a perfectly devout man. The cardinal trusted him, and found his advantage in it.

There were many stories related of him, and among them this:

After a wild youth, he had retired into a convent, there to expiate, at least for some time, the follies of adolescence.

But, on entering this holy place, the poor penitent was unable to shut the door so close as to prevent the passions he fled from, from entering with him. He was incessantly attacked by them, and the superior, to whom he had confided this misfortune, wishing, as much as in him lay, to free him from them, had advised him, in order to conjure away the tempting demon, to have recourse to the bell-rope, and to ring with all his might. At the denunciating sound, the monks would be rendered aware that temptation was besieging a brother, and all the community would go to prayers.

This advice appeared good to the future chancellor. He conjured the evil spirit with abundance of prayers offered up by the monks. But the devil does not suffer himself to be easily disposed from a place in which he has fixed his garrison: in proportion as they redoubled the exorcisms he redoubled the temptations, so that day and night the bell was ringing full swing, announcing the extreme desire for mortification which the penitent experienced.

The monks had no longer an instant of repose. By day they did nothing but ascend and descend the steps which led to the chapel; at night, in addition to complins and matins, they were further obliged to leap twenty times out of their beds and prostrate themselves on the floor of their cells.

It is not known whether it was the devil who gave way, or the monks who grew tired; but within three months the penitent reappeared in the world with the reputation of being the most terrible *possessed* that ever existed.

On leaving the convent, he entered into the magistracy, became president à *mortier* in the place of his uncle, embraced the cardinal's party, which did not prove want of sagacity; became chancellor, served his eminence with zeal in his hatred against the queen-mother, and his vengeance against Anne of Austria; stimulated the judges in the affair of Chalais; encouraged the essays of M. de Laffemas, *grand gibecier* of France; then, at length, invested with the entire confidence of the cardinal, a confidence which he had so well earned, he received the singular commission for the execution of which he presented himself in the queen's apartments.

The queen was still standing when he entered, but scarcely had she perceived him than she reseated herslf in her *fauteuil,* and made a sign to her women to resume their cushions and stools, and, with an air of supreme hauteur, said:

"What do you desire, monsieur, and with what object do you present yourself here?"

"To make, madame, in the name of the king, and without prejudice to the respect which I have the honor to owe to your majesty, a close investigation into all your papers."

"How, monsieur! an investigation into my papers—mine! Truly, this is an unworthy proceeding!"

"Be kind enough to pardon me, madame; but in this circumstance I am but the instrument which the king employs. Has not his majesty just left you? and has he not himself desired you to prepare for this visit?"

"Examine, then, monsieur; I am a criminal, as it appears. Estafania, give the keys of my tables and my secretaries."

For form's sake the chancellor paid a visit to the pieces of furniture named, but he well knew that it was not in a piece of furniture that the queen would place the important letter she had written in the course of the day.

When the chancellor had opened and shut twenty times

the drawers of the secretaries, it became necessary, whatever hesitation he might experience, it bcame necessary, I say, to come to the conclusion of the affair—that is to say, to search the queen herself. The chancellor advanced, therefore, toward Anne of Austria, and, with a very perplexed and embarrassed air:

"And now," said he, "it remains for me to make the principal investigation."

"What is that?" asked the queen, who did not understand, or, rather, was not willing to understand.

"His majesty is certain that a letter has been written by you in the course of the day; he knows that it has not been sent to its address. This letter is not in your table-drawers, nor in your secretary; and yet this letter must be somewhere."

"Would you dare to lift your hand to your queen?" said Anne of Austria, drawing herself up to her full height, and fixing her eyes upon the chancellor with an expression almost threatening.

"I am an humble subject of the king, madame, and all that his majesty commands, I shall do."

"Well, that's true!" said Anne of Austria; "and the spies of the cardinal have served him faithfully. I have written a letter to-day; that letter is not yet gone. The letter is here."

And the queen laid her beautiful hand on her bosom.

"Then give me that letter, madame," said the chancellor.

"I will give it to none but the king, monsieur," said Anne.

"If the king had desired that the letter should be given to him, madame, he would have demanded it of you himself, and if you do not give it up——"

"Well?"

"He has, then, charged me to take it from you."

"How! what do you say?"

"That my orders go far, madame; and that I am authorized to seek for the suspected paper, even on the person of your majesty."

"What horror!" cried the queen.

"Be kind enough then, madame, to act more compliantly."

"This conduct is infamously violent! Do you know that, monsieur?"

"The king commands it, madame; excuse me."

"I will not suffer it! no, no, I would rather die!" cried the queen, with whom the imperious blood of Spain and Austria began to rise.

The chancellor made a profound reverence; then, with the intention quite patent of not drawing back a foot from the accomplishment of the commission with which he was charged, and as the attendant of an executioner might have done in the chamber of torture, he approached Anne of Austria, from whose eyes at the same instant sprang tears of rage.

The queen was, as we have said, of great beauty. The commission might then, pass for delicate; and the king had arrived, in his jealousy for Buckingham, at the point of being no longer jealous of any one.

Without doubt the Chancellor Séguier looked about at that moment for the rope of the famous bell; but, not finding it, he summoned his resolution, and stretched forth his hands toward the place where the queen had acknowledged the paper was to be found.

Anne of Austria made one step backward, became so pale that it might be said she was dying, and, leaning with her left hand, to keep herself from falling, upon a table behind her, she with her right hand drew the paper from her bosom, and held it out to the keeper of the seals.

"There, monsieur, there is that letter!" cried the queen, with a broken and trembling voice; "take it and deliver me from your odious presence."

The chancellor, who, on his part, trembled with an emotion easily to be conceived, took the letter, bowed to the ground, and retired.

The door was scarcely closed upon him, when the queen sank, half-fainting, into the arms of her women.

The chancellor carried the letter to the king without having read a single word of it. The king took it with a trembling hand, looked for the address, which was wanting, became very pale, opened it slowly, then, seeing by the first words that it was addressed to the king of Spain, he read it rapidly.

It was nothing but a plan of an attack against the cardinal. The queen pressed her brother and the emperor of Austria to appear to be wounded, as they really were, by the policy of Richelieu, the eternal object of which was the abasement of the house of Austria; to declare war against France, and, as a condition of peace, to insist upon the dismissal of the cardinal; but as to love, there was not a single word about it in all the letter.

The king, quite delighted, inquired if the cardinal was still at the Louvre: he was told that his eminence awaited the orders of his majesty in the business cabinet.

The king went straight to him.

"There, duke," said he, "you were right, and I was wrong:

the whole intrigue is political, and there is not the least question of love in this said letter. But, on the other hand, there is abundant question of you.

The cardinal took the letter, and read it with the greatest attention; then, when he had arrived at the end of it, he read it a second time.

"Well, your majesty," said he, "you see how far my enemies go; they threaten you with two wars if you do not dismiss me. In your place, in truth, sire, I should yield to such powerful instances; and, on my part, it would be a real happiness to withdraw from public affairs."

"What's that you say, duke?"

"I say, sire, that my health is sinking under these annoying struggles, and these never-ending labors. I say that, according to all probability, I shall not be able to undergo the fatigues of the siege of La Rochelle, and that it would be far better that you should appoint there, either M. de Condé, M. de Bassompierre, or some valiant gentleman whose business is war, and not me, who am a churchman, and who am constantly turned aside from my real vocation to look after matters for which I have no aptitude. You would be the happier for it at home, sire, and I do not doubt you would be the greater for it abroad."

"Monsieur le Duc," said the king, "I understand you. Be satisfied, all who are named in that letter shall be punished as they deserve; and the queen herself shall not be forgotten."

"What do you say, sire? God forbid that the queen should suffer the least inconvenience or uneasiness on my account! She has always believed me, sire, to be her enemy, although your majesty can bear witness that I have always taken her part warmly, even against you. Oh! if she betrayed your majesty on the side of your honor, it would be quite another thing, and I should be the first to say, 'No grace, sire—no grace for the guilty!' Fortunately, there is nothing of the kind, and your majesty has just acquired a fresh proof of it."

"That is true, Monsieur le Cardinal," said the king, "and you were right, as you always are; but the queen, not the less, deserves all my anger."

"It is you, sire, who have now incurred hers; and even if she were to be seriously offended, I could well understand it; your majesty has treated her with a severity——"

"It is thus I will always treat my enemies and yours, duke, however high they may be placed, and whatever peril I may incur in acting severely toward them."

"The queen is my enemy, but is not yours, sire; on the

contrary, she is a devoted, submissive, and irreproachable wife; allow me, then, sire, to intercede for her with your majesty."

"Let her humble herself, then, and come to me first."

"On the contrary, sire, set the example; you have committed the first wrong, since it was you who suspected the queen."

"What! I make advances first!" said the king, "never!"

"Sire, I entreat you to do so."

"Besides, in what manner can I make advances first?"

"By doing a thing which you know will be agreeable to her."

"What is that?"

"Give a ball; you know how much the queen loves dancing. I will answer for it, her resentment will not hold out against such an attention."

"Monsieur le Cardinal, you know that I do not like mundane pleasures."

"The queen will only be the more grateful to you, as she knows your antipathy for that amusement; besides, it will be an opportunity for her to wear those beautiful diamonds which you gave her recently, on her birthday, and with which she has since had no occasion to adorn herself."

"We shall see, Monsieur le Cardinal, we shall see," said the king, who, in his joy at finding the queen guilty of a crime which he cared little about, and innocent of a fault of which he had great dread, was ready to make up all differences with her; "we shall see, but, upon my honor, you are too indulgent toward her."

"Sire," said the cardinal, "leave severity to your ministers; clemency is a royal virtue; employ it, and you will find you derive advantage from it."

Upon which the cardinal, hearing the clock strike eleven, bowed lowly, demanding permission of the king to retire, and supplicating him to come to a good understanding with the queen.

Anne of Austria, who, in consequence of the seizure of her letter, expected reproaches, was much astonished the next day to see the king make some attempts at reconcilation with her. Her first movement was repulsive, her womanly pride and her queenly dignity had both been so cruelly outraged, that she could not come round at the first advance; but, overpersuaded by the advice of her women, she at last had the appearance of beginning to forget. The king took advantage of this favorable moment to tell her that he had the intention of shortly giving a fête.

A fête was so rare a thing for poor Anne of Austria, that at this announcement, as the cardinal had predicted, the last trace of her resentment disappeared, if not from her heart, at least from her countenance. She asked upon what day this fête would take place, but the king replied that he must consult the cardinal upon that head.

In fact, every day the king asked the cardinal when this fête should take place, and every day the cardinal, under some pretense or other, deferred fixing it. Ten days passed away thus.

On the eighth day after the scene we have described, the cardinal received a letter with the London stamp, which only contained these lines:

"I have them, but I am unable to leave London for want of money; send me five hundred pistoles, and four or five days after I have received them I shall be in Paris."

On the same day that the cardinal received this letter, the king put his customary question to him.

Richelieu counted on his fingers, and said to himself:

"She will arrive, she says, four or five days after having received the money; it will require four or five days for the transmission of the money, four or five days for her to return, that makes ten days; now, allowing for contrary winds, accidents, and a woman's weakness, we cannot make it, altogether, less than twelve days."

"Well, Monsieur le Duc," said the king, "have you made your calculations?"

"Yes, sire, to-day is the 20th of September; the *échevins* of the city give a fête on the 3d of October. That will fall in wonderfully well; you will not appear to have gone out of your way to please the queen."

Then the cardinal added:

"Apropos, sire, do not forget to tell her majesty, the evening before the fête, that you should like to see how her diamond studs become her."

CHAPTER XVII.

BONACIEUX AT HOME.

IT WAS the second time the cardinal had mentioned these diamond studs to the king. Louis XIII. was struck with these repetitions, and began to fancy that this recommendation concealed some mystery.

More than once the king had been humiliated by the cardinal, whose police, without having yet attained the perfection of the modern police, was excellent, being better informed than himself even upon what was going on in his own household. He hoped, then, in conversation with Anne of Austria, to obtain some information from that conversation, and afterward, to come upon his eminence with some secret, which the cardinal either knew or did not know, but which, in either case, would raise him infinitely in the eyes of his minister.

He went then to the queen, and, according to custom, accosted her with fresh menaces against those who surrounded her. Anne of Austria hung down her head, allowed the torrent to flow on without replying, and hoped that it would end by stopping of itself; but this was not what Louis XIII. meant; Louis XIII. wanted a discussion, from which some light or other might break, convinced as he was that the cardinal had some after-thought, and was preparing for him one of those terrible surprises which his eminence was so skillful in getting up. He arrived at this end by his persistence in accusing.

"But," cried Anne of Austria, tired of these vague attacks; "but, sire, you do not tell me all that you have in your heart. What have I done, then? Let me know what crime I have committed? It is impossible that your majesty can make all this to-do about a letter written to my brother!"

The king, attacked in a manner so direct, did not know what to answer; and he thought that this was the moment for expressing the desire which he was not to have made until the evening before the fête.

"Madame," said he, with dignity, "there will shortly be a ball at the Hotel de Ville; I wish that, to do honor to our worthy échevins, you should appear at it in ceremonial costume, and particularly ornamented with the diamond studs which I gave you on your birthday That is my answer."

The answer was terrible. Anne of Austria believed that Louis XIII. knew all, and that the cardinal had persuaded him to employ this long dissimulation of seven or eight days, which, likewise, was characteristic. She became excessively pale, leaned her beautiful hand upon a console, which hand appeared then like one of wax, and looking at the king with terror in her eyes, she was unable to reply by a single syllable.

"You hear, madame," said the king, who enjoyed this em-

barrassment to its full extent, but without guessing the cause
—"You hear, madame?"

"Yes, sire, I hear," stammered the queen.

"You will appear at this ball?"

"Yes."

"And with those studs?"

"Yes."

The queen's paleness, if possible, increased; the king perceived it and enjoyed it with that cold cruelty which was one of the worst sides of his character.

"Then that is agreed," said the king, "and that is all I had to say to you."

"But on what day will this ball take place?" asked Anne of Austria.

Louis XIII. felt instinctively that he ought not to reply to this question, the queen having put it in an almost inaudible voice.

"Oh! very shortly, madame," said he, "but I do not precisely recollect the date of the day; I will ask the cardinal."

"It was the cardinal, then, who informed you of this fête?"

"Yes, madame," replied the astonished king; "but why do you ask that?"

"It was he who told you to desire me to appear there with these studs?"

"That is to say, madame——"

"It was he, sire, it was he!"

"Well; and what does it signify whether it was he or I? is there any crime in this request?"

"No, sire."

"Then you will appear?"

"Yes, sire."

"That's well," said the king, retiring, "that's well, I depend upon you."

The queen made a courtesy, less from etiquette than because her knees were sinking under her.

"I am lost," murmured the queen, "lost! for the cardinal knows all, and it is he who urges on the king, who as yet knows nothing, but will soon know everything. I am lost! my God! my God! my God!"

She knelt upon a cushion and prayed, with her head buried between her palpitating arms.

In fact, her position was terrible. Buckingham had returned to London, Madame de Crevreuse was at Tours. More closely watched then ever, the queen felt certain that one of her women betrayed her, without knowing how to tell which. Laporte could not leave the Louvre; she had not a soul in the world in whom she could confide.

Thus, while contemplating the misfortune which threatened her, and the abandonment in which she was left, she broke out into sobs and tears.

"Can I be of no service to your majesty?" said all at once a voice full of sweetness and pity.

The queen turned sharply round, for there could be no deception in the expression of that voice: it was a friend who spoke thus.

In fact, at one of the doors which opened into the queen's apartment, appeared the pretty Madame Bonacieux; she had been engaged in arranging the dresses and linen in a closet, when the king entered; she could not get out, and had heard all.

The queen uttered a piercing cry at finding herself surprised, for in her trouble she did not at first recognize the young woman who had been given to her by Laporte.

"Oh! fear nothing, madame!" said the young woman, clasping her hands, and weeping herself at the queen's sorrows; "I am your majesty's, body and soul, and however far I may be from you, however inferior may be my position, I believe I have discovered a means of extricating your majesty from your trouble."

"You! oh heavens! you!" cried the queen; "but look me in the face; I am betrayed on all sides; can I trust in you?"

"Oh! madame!" cried the young woman, falling on her knees, "upon my soul, I am ready to die for your majesty!"

This expression sprang from the very bottom of the heart, and, like the first, there was no mistaking it.

"Yes," continued Madame Bonacieux, "yes, there are traitors here; but by the holy name of the Virgin, I swear that none is more devoted to your majesty than I am. Those studs, which the king speaks of, you gave them to the Duke of Buckingham, did you not? Those studs were in a little rosewood box, which he held under his arm? Am I deceived? Is it not so, madame?"

"Oh, my God! my God!" murmured the queen, whose teeth chattered with fright.

"Well, those studs," continued Madame Bonacieux, "we must have them back again."

"Yes, without doubt, it must be so," cried the queen, "but how am I to act? How can it be effected?"

"Some one must be sent to the duke."

"But who? who? in whom can I trust?"

"Place confidence in me, madame; do me that honor, my queen, and I will find a messenger."

"But I must write."

"Oh, yes; that is indispensable. Two words from the hands of your majesty and your own private seal."

"But these two words would bring about my condemnation, divorce, exile!"

"Yes, if they fell into infamous hands. But I will answer for these two words being delivered to their address."

"Oh, my God! I must then place my life, my honor, my reputation, all in your hands?"

"Yes, yes, madame, you must, and I will save them all."

"But how—tell me at least, how?"

"My husband has been set at liberty these two or three days; I have not yet had time to see him again. He is a worthy, honest man, who entertains neither love nor hatred for anybody. He will do anything I wish; he will set out upon receiving an order from me, without knowing what he carries, and he will remit your majesty's letter, without even knowing it is from your majesty, to the address which shall be upon it."

The queen took the two hands of the young woman with a burst of emotion, gazed at her as if to read her very heart, and seeing nothing but sincerity in her beautiful eyes, embraced her tenderly.

"Do that," cried she, "and you will have saved my life, you will have saved my honor!"

"Oh! do not exaggerate the service I have the happiness to render your majesty; I have nothing of your majesty's to save, who are only the victim of perfidious plots."

"That is true, that is true, my child," said the queen, "you are right."

"Give me then that letter, madame; time presses."

The queen ran to a little table, upon which were pens, ink, and paper; she wrote two lines, sealed the letter with her private seal, and gave it to Madame Bonacieux.

"And now," said the queen, "we are forgetting one very necessary thing."

"What is that, madame?"

"Money."

Madame Bonacieux blushed.

"Yes, that is true," said she, "and I will confess to your majesty that my husband——"

"Your husband has none; is that what you would say?"

"Oh! yes, he has some, but he is very avaricious, that is

his fault. Nevertheless, let not your majesty be uneasy, we will find means."

"And I have none, either," said the queen. Such as have read the Memoirs of Madame de Motteville will not be astonished at this reply. "But wait a minute."

Anne of Austria ran to her jewel case.

"Here," said she, "here is a ring of great value, as I have been assured; it came from my brother, the king of Spain; it is mine, and I am at liberty to dispose of it. Take this ring, make money of it, and let your husband set out."

"In an hour, you shall be obeyed, madame."

"You see the address," said the queen, speaking so low that Madame Bonacieux could hardly hear what she said— "To Milord Duke of Buckingham, London."

"The letter shall be given to him himself."

"Generous girl!" cried Anne of Austria.

Madame Bonacieux kissed the hands of the queen, concealed the paper in the bosom of her dress, and disappeared with the lightness of a bird.

Ten minutes afterward she was at home; as she told the queen, she had not seen her husband since his liberation, she was ignorant of the change that had taken place in him with respect to the cardinal, a change which had since been strengthened by two or three visits from the Count de Rochefort, who had become the best friend of Bonacieux, and had persuaded him that nothing culpable had been intended by the carrying off of his wife, but that it was only a piece of political precaution.

She found Bonacieux alone: the poor man was restoring with much trouble, order in his house, the furniture of which he had found mostly broken, and his chests and drawers mostly empty, justice not being one of the three things which King Solomon named as leaving no traces of their passage. As to the servant, she had run away at the moment of her master's arrest. Terror had had such an effect upon the poor girl, that she had never ceased walking from Paris till she got to Burgundy, her native place.

The worthy mercer had, immediately upon entering his house, communicated to his wife the news of his happy return, and his wife had replied by congratulating him, and telling him that the first moment she could steal from her duties should be devoted to paying him a visit.

The first moment had been delayed five days, which, under any other circumstances, might have appeared rather long to Master Bonacieux; but he had, in the visit he had made to

the cardinal, and in the visits Rochefort had made him, ample
subjects for reflection, and, as everybody knows, nothing
makes time pass more quickly than reflection.

This was all so much the more so from Bonacieux's reflections all being *couleur de rose.* Rochefort called him his friend,
his dear Bonacieux, and never ceased telling him that the
cardinal had a great respect for him. The mercer fancied
himself already in the high road to honors and fortune.

On her side, Madame Bonacieux had also reflected, but it
must be admitted, upon something widely different from ambition: in spite of herself, her thoughts constantly reverted
to that handsome young man, who was so brave, and appeared
to be so much in love. Married at eighteen to Monsieur
Bonacieux, having always lived among her husband's friends,
people very little susceptible of inspiring any sentiment whatever in a young woman whose heart was above her position,
Madame Bonacieux had remained insensible to vulgar seductions: but at this period the title of gentleman had a particularly great influence with the bourgeoise, or citizen class, and
D'Artagnan was a gentleman; besides, he wore the uniform
of the guards, which, next to that of the musketeers, was
most admired by the ladies. He was, we repeat, handsome,
young, and bold; he spoke of love like a man who did love,
and was anxious to be loved in return: there was certainly
enough in all this to turn a head only twenty-three years old,
and Madame Bonacieux had just attained that happy period
of life.

The married couple then, although they had not seen each
other for eight days, and during that time serious events
had taken place in which both were concerned, accosted each
other with a degree of preoccupation: nevertheless, M. Bonacieux manifested real joy, and advanced toward his wife with
open arms.

"Madame Bonacieux presented her cheek to him.

"Let us talk a little," said she.

"How!" said Bonacieux, astonished.

"Yes; I have something of great importance to tell you."

"True," said he, "and I have some questions sufficiently
serious to put to you. Describe to me how you were carried
off."

"Oh! that's of no consequence just now," said Madame
Bonacieux.

"And what does it allude to then? To my captivity!"

"I heard of it the day it happened; but as you were not
guilty of any crime, as you were not guilty of any intrigue,

as you, in short, knew nothing that could compromise your-self or anybody else, I attached little more importance to that event than it merited."

"You speak pretty much at your ease, madame," said Bon-acieux, hurt at the little interest his wife seemed to take in him; "do you know that I was plunged during a whole day and a whole night in a dungeon of the Bastille?"

"Oh! a day and night soon pass away; let us return to the object that brings me here."

"What! to that which brings you home to me! It it not the desire of seeing a husband again from whom you have been separated for a week?" asked the mercer, piqued to the quick.

"Yes, that first, and other things afterward."

"Speak then."

"It is a thing of the highest interest, and upon which our future fortune perhaps depends."

"The complexion of our fortune has changed very much since I saw you, Madame Bonacieux, and I should not be astonished if, in the course of a few months, it were to excite envy of many folks."

"Particularly if you obey the instructions I am about to give you."

"To me?"

"Yes, to you. There is a good and holy action to be per-formed, monsieur, and much money to be gained at the same time."

Madame Bonacieux knew that when naming money to her husband, she attacked him on his weak side. But a man, were he even a mercer, when he has talked for ten minutes with the Cardinal de Richelieu, is no longer the same man.

"Much money to be gained?" said Bonacieux, protruding his lip.

"Yes, much."

"About how much, pray?"

"A thousand pistoles, perhaps."

"Humph! What you have to ask me then is serious!"

"It is indeed."

"What is to be done?"

"You must set out immediately; I will give you a paper which you must not part with on any account, and which you will deliver into the proper hands."

"And where am I to go?"

"London."

'I go to London! You are joking, I have nothing to do
in London."

"But others require that you should go there."

"But who are those others? I warn you that I will never
again work in the dark, and that I will know not only to
what I expose myself, but for whom I expose myself."

"An illustrious person sends you, an illustrious person
awaits you; the recompense will exceed your expectations,
that is all I promise you."

"More intrigues! nothing but intrigues! Thank you, madame, I am aware of them now; Monsieur le Cardinal has
enlightened me on that head."

"The cardinal?" cried Madame Bonacieux; "have you seen
the cardinal!"

"He sent for me," answered the mercer proudly.

"And you went! you imprudent man!"

"Well, I can't say I had much choice in going or not going,
for I was taken to him between two guards. I must also
confess that as I did not then know his eminence, if I had
been able to have declined the visit, I should have been delighted to have done so."

"He ill-treated you, then? he threatened you?"

"He gave me his hand, and he called me his friend—his
friend! do you hear that, madame? I am the friend of the
great cardinal!"

"Of the great cardinal!"

"Perhaps you would dispute his right to that title, madame?"

"Oh! I would dispute his right to nothing; but I tell you
that the favor of a minister is ephemeral, and that a man
must be mad to attach himself to a minister; there are powers
above his which do not depend upon a man or the issue of an
event; it is around these powers we should endeavor to range
ourselves."

"I am sorry for it, madame, but I acknowledge no other
power but that of the great man whom I have the honor to
serve."

"You serve the cardinal?"

"Yes, madame, and as his servant, I will not allow you to
be concerned in plots against the safety of the state, or to
assist in the intrigues of a woman who is not a Frenchwoman,
and who has a Spanish heart. Fortunately, we have the
great cardinal, his vigilant eye watches over and penetrates
to the bottom of hearts."

Bonacieux was repeating, word for word, a sentence which

he had heard the Count de Rochefort make use of; but the poor wife, who had reckoned on her husband, and who, in that hope, had answered for him to the queen, did not tremble the less, both at the danger into which she had nearly cast herself, and at the helpless state to which she was reduced. Nevertheless, knowing the weakness of her husband, and more particularly his cupidity, she did not despair of bringing him round to her purpose.

"Ah! you are a cardinalist! then, monsieur, are you?" cried she, "and you serve the party who ill-treat your wife and insult your queen?"

"Private interests are as nothing before the interests of all. I am for those who save the state," said Bonacieux emphatically.

This was another of the Count de Rochefort's sentences which he had retained, and which he sought an occasion to make use of.

"And what do you know about the state you talk of?" said Madame Bonacieux, shrugging her shoulders. "Be satisfied with being a plain, straightforward bourgeois, and turn your attention to that side which holds out the greatest advantages."

"Eh! eh!" said Bonacieux, slapping a plump, round bag, which returned a sound of money; "what do you think of this, madame preacher?"

"Where does that money come from?"

"Can't you guess?"

"From the cardinal?"

"From him, and from my friend the Count de Rochefort."

"The Count de Rochefort! why, it was he who carried me off!"

"Perhaps it was, madame."

"And you receive money from that man!"

"Did you not yourself tell me that that carrying off was entirely political?"

"Yes, but that event had for its object to make me betray my mistress, to draw from me by tortures confessions that might have compromised the honor, and perhaps the life of my august mistress."

"Madame," replied Bonacieux, "your august mistress is a perfidious Spaniard, and what the cardinal does is well done."

"Monsieur," said the young woman, "I know you to be cowardly, avaricious, and weak, but I never till now believed you to be infamous!"

"Madame!" said Bonacieux, who had never seen his wife

in a passion, and who retreated before this conjugal anger;
"madame, what is that you say?"

"I say you are a miserable mean creature!" continued Madame Bonacieux, who saw she was regaining some little influence over her husband. "You meddle with politics, do you!
And still more, with cardinalist politics! Why, you are selling yourself, body and soul, to the devil, for money!"

"No, but to the cardinal."

"It's the same thing!" cried the young woman. "Who
says Richelieu says Satan!"

"Hold your tongue! hold your tongue, madame; we may
be overheard."

"Yes, you are right, I should be ashamed for any one to
know your baseness."

"But what do you require of me, then; come, let us see!"

"I have told you: you must set out instantly, monsieur;
you must accomplish loyally the commission with which I
deign to charge you, and on that condition I pardon everything, I forget everything; and still further"—and she held
out her hand to him—"I give you my love again."

Bonacieux was a coward, and he was avaricious, but he
loved his wife—he was softened. A man of fifty cannot long
bear malice with a pretty wife of twenty-three. Madame
Bonacieux saw that he hesitated.

"Come! have you made your mind up?" said she.

"But, my dear love! reflect a little upon what you require
of me. London is far from Paris, very far, and perhaps the
commission with which you charge me is not without
dangers?"

"Of what consequence is that, if you avoid them?"

"Well, then, Madame Bonacieux," said the mercer, "well,
then, I positively refuse: intrigues terrify me. I have seen
the Bastille; I—whew!—that's a frightful place, that Bastille!
only to think of it makes my flesh crawl. They threatened me
with torture! Do you know what the torture is? Wooden
points that they stick in between your legs till your bones
burst out! No, positively I will not go. And, *morbleu!* why
do you not go yourself? for, in truth, I think I have hitherto
been deceived in you; I really believe you are a man, and a
violent one too."

"And you, you are a woman, a miserable woman, stupid
and brutified. You are afraid, are you? Well, if you do
not go this very instant, I will have you arrested by the
queen's orders, and I will have you placed in that Bastille
which you dread so much."

Bonacieux fell into a profound reflection; he turned the two angers in his brain, that of the cardinal and that of the queen; that of the cardinal predominated enormously.

"Have me arrested on the part of the queen," said he, "and I, I will appeal to his eminence."

At once, Madame Bonacieux saw that she had gone too far, and she was terrified at having communicated so much. She for a moment contemplated, with terror, that stupid countenance, impressed with the invincible resolution of a fool that is overcome by fear.

"Well, be it so!" said she. "Perhaps, when all is considered, you are right: in the long run, a man knows more about politics than a woman does, particularly such as, like you, Monsieur Bonacieux, have conversed with the cardinal. And yet it is very hard," added she, "that a man upon whose affection I thought I might depend, treats me thus unkindly, and will not comply with any of my fancies."

"That is because your fancies might lead you too far," replied the triumphant Bonacieux, "and I mistrust them."

"Well, I will give it up, then," said the young woman, sighing; "it is as well as it is, say no more about it."

"Yes, at least you should tell me what I should have to do in London," replied Bonacieux, who remembered a little too late that Rochefort had desired him to endeavor to obtain his wife's secrets.

"It is of no use for you to know anything about it," said the young woman whom an instinctive mistrust now impelled to draw back: "it was about one of those purchases that interest women, a purchase by which much might have been gained."

But the more the young woman excused herself, the more important Bonacieux conceived the secret to be which she declined to communicate to him. He resolved, then, that instant to hasten to the residence of the Count de Rochefort and tell him that the queen was seeking for a messenger to send to London.

"Pardon me for leaving you, my dear Madame Bonacieux," said he; "but not knowing you would come to see me, I had made an engagement with a friend; I shall soon return, and if you will wait only a few minutes for me, as soon as I have concluded my business with that friend, as it is growing late, I will come and conduct you back to the Louvre."

"Thank you, monsieur, you are not obliging enough to be of any use to me whatever," replied Madame Bonacieux; "I shall return very safely to the Louvre by myself."

"As you please, Madame Bonacieux," said the ex-mercer, "shall I have the pleasure of seeing you soon again?"

"Yes, next week, "I hope my duties will afford me a little liberty, and I will take advantage of it to come and put things in order here, as they must, necessarily, be much deranged."

"Very well; I shall expect you. You are not angry with me?"

"Who, I? Oh! not the least in the world."

"Till then, then?"

"Till then, adieu!"

Bonacieux kissed his wife's hand and set off at a quick pace.

"Well!" said Madame Bonacieux when her husband had shut the street door, and she found herself alone, "there wanted nothing to complete that poor creature but being a cardinalist! And I, who have answered for him to the queen! I, who have promised my poor mistress! Ah! my God! my God! she will take me for one of those wretches with whom the palace swarms, and which are placed about her as spies! Ah! Monsieur Bonacieux! I never did love you much, but now, it is worse than ever: I hate you! and by my word, you shall pay for this!"

At the moment she spoke these words a rap on the ceiling made her raise her head, and a voice which reached her through the plaster, cried:

"Dear Madame Bonacieux, open the little passage-door for me, and I will come down to you."

CHAPTER XVIII.

THE LOVER AND THE HUSBAND.

"AH! madame," said D'Artagnan, as he entered by the door which the young woman had opened for him, "allow me to tell you that you have a bad sort of a husband there!"

"You have then overheard our conversation?" asked Madame Bonacieux eagerly, and looking at D'Artagnan with much uneasiness.

"The whole of it."

"But how, my God! could you do that?"

"By a mode of proceeding known to myself, and by which I likewise overheard the more animated conversation which you had with the cardinal's *sbirri*."

"And what did you understand by what you heard us say?"

"A thousand things; in the first place that, fortunately, your husband is a simpleton and a fool; in the next place you are in trouble, of which I am very glad, as it gives me an opportunity of placing myself at your service, and God knows I am ready to throw myself into the fire for you; and that the queen wants a brave, intelligent, devoted man to make a journey to London for her. I have, at least, two of the qualities you stand in need of—and here I am."

Madame Bonacieux made no reply, but her heart beat with joy, and secret hope shone in her eyes.

"And what pledge can you give me," asked she, "if I consent to confide this message to you?"

"My love for you. Speak! command! What must I do?"

"My God! my God!" murmured the young woman, "ought I to confide such a secret to you, monsieur? You are almost a boy!"

"I suppose, then, you require some one to answer for me?"

"I admit that that would reassure me greatly."

"Do you know Athos?"

"No."

"Porthos?"

"No."

"Aramis?"

"No; who are these gentlemen?"

"Three of the king's musketeers. Do you know M. de Tréville, their captain?"

"Oh! yes, him, I know him; not personally, but from having heard the queen speak of him more than once as a brave and loyal gentleman."

"You are not afraid that he would betray you for the sake of the cardinal?"

"Oh! no, certainly."

"Well, reveal your secret to him, and ask him, whether, however important, however valuable, however terrible it may be, you may not safely confide it to me."

"But this secret is not mine, and I cannot reveal it in this manner."

"Why, you were going to confide it to M. Bonacieux," said D'Artagnan, with an offended tone.

"As we confide a letter to the hollow of a tree, to the wing of a pigeon, or the collar of a dog."

"And yet me—you see plainly that I love you."

"You say so."

"I am an honorable man."

"I believe so."

"I am brave."

"Oh! I am sure of that."

"Then, put me to the proof."

Madame Bonacieux looked at the young man, restrained for a minute by a last hesitation; but there was such an ardor in his eyes, such persuasion in his voice, that she felt herself drawn on to place confidence in him. Besides, she was in one of those circumstances in which everything must be risked for the sake of everything. The queen also might be as much injured by too much discretion as by too much confidence—and let us admit it, the involuntary sentiment which she felt for her young protector, compelled her to speak.

"Listen," said she, "I yield to your protestations, I yield to your assurances. But I swear to you, before God who hears us, that if you betray me, and my enemies pardon me, I will kill myself, while accusing you of my death."

"And I, I swear to you before God, madame," said D'Artagnan, "that if I am taken while accomplishing the orders you give me, I will die sooner than do anything, or say anything, that may compromise any one."

Then the young woman confided to him the terrible secret of which chance had already communicated to him a part, in front of the *Samaritaine*.

This was their mutual declaration of love.

D'Artagnan was radiant with joy and pride. This secret which he possessed, this woman whom he loved! Confidence and love made him a giant.

"I will go," said he, "I will go at once."

"How! you will go!" said Madame Bonacieux; "and your regiment, your captain?"

"By my soul, you have made me forget all that, dear Constance! Yes, you are right, I must obtain leave of absence."

"There is still another obstacle," murmured Madame Bonacieux sorrowfully.

"Whatever it may be," cried D'Artagnan, after a moment of reflection, "I shall surmount it, be assured."

"How?"

"I will go this very evening to M. de Tréville, whom I will request to ask this favor for me of his brother-in-law, M. Dessessarts."

"But still, there is another thing."

"What is that?" asked D'Artagnan, seeing that Madame Bonacieux hesitated to continue.

"You have, perhaps, no money?"

"Perhaps is too much," said D'Artagnan, smiling.

"Then," replied Madame Bonacieux, opening a cupboard and taking from it the very bag which half an hour before her husband had caressed so affectionately, "take this bag."

"The cardinal's!" cried D'Artagnan, breaking into a loud laugh, he having heard, as may be remembered, thanks to his broken floor, every syllable of the conversation between the mercer and his wife.

"The cardinal's," replied Madame Bonacieux; "you see it makes a very respectable appearance."

"*Pardieu!*" cried D'Artagnan, "it will be a doubly amusing affair to save the queen with the cardinal's money!"

"You are an amiable and a charming young man!" said Madame Bonacieux. "Be assured you will not find her majesty ungrateful."

"Oh! I am already more than recompensed!" cried D'Artagnan. "I love you; you permit me to tell you that I do; that is already more happiness than I dared to hope for."

"Silence!" said Madame Bonacieux, starting.

"What!"

"Some one is talking in the street."

"It is the voice of——"

"Of my husband! Oh! yes; I recognized it!"

D'Artagnan ran to the door and drew the bolt.

"He shall not come in before I am gone," said he; "and when I am gone, you can open the door for him."

"But I ought to be gone, too. And the disappearance of his money, how am I to justify it, if I am here?"

"You are right; you must go out."

"Go out? How? He will see us if we go out."

"Then you must come up into my room."

"Ah!" said Madame Bonacieux, "you speak that in a tone that terrifies me!"

Madame Bonacieux pronounced these words with tears in her eyes. D'Artagnan saw those tears, and much disturbed, softened, he threw himself at her feet.

"In my apartment you will be as safe as in a temple; I give you my word of a gentleman."

"Let us go, then, I place full confidence in you, my friend!"

D'Artagnan drew back the bolt with precaution, and both, light as shadows, glided through the interior door into the passage, ascended the stairs as quietly as possible, and entered D'Artagnan's apartment.

Once in his apartment, for greater security, the young man

barricaded the door. They both went up to the window, and through a slit in the shutter, they saw M. Bonacieux talking with a man in a cloak.

At the sight of this man, D'Artagnan started, half drew his sword, and sprang toward the door.

It was the man of Meung.

"What are you going to do?" cried Madame Bonacieux; "you will ruin us all!"

"But I have sworn to kill that man!" said D'Artagnan.

"At this time your life is devoted, and does not belong to you! In the name of the queen I forbid you to throw yourself into any danger which is foreign to that of your voyage!"

"And do you command nothing in your own name?"

"In my name?" said Madame Bonacieux, with great emotion; "In my name I beg you! But listen; they appear to be speaking of me."

D'Artagnan drew near the window, and listened.

M. Bonacieux had opened his door, and seeing the apartment empty, had returned to the man in the cloak, whom he had left alone for an instant.

"She is gone," said he; "she must be gone back to the Louvre."

"You are sure," replied the stranger, "that she did not suspect the intention you went out with?"

"No," replied Bonacieux, with a self-sufficient air, "she is too superficial a woman."

"Is the young guardsman at home?"

"I do not think he is; as you see, his shutter is closed, and there is no light through the chinks of the shutters."

"That's true; but it's as well to be certain."

"How can we be so?"

"By knocking at his door."

"Go."

"I will ask his servant."

Bonacieux went into the house again, passed through the same door that had afforded a passage for the two fugitives, went up to D'Artagnan's door, and knocked.

No one answered. Porthos, to make a greater display, had that evening borrowed Planchet. As to D'Artagnan, he took care not to give the least sign of existence.

At the moment the finger of Bonacieux sounded on the door, the two young people felt their hearts bound within them.

"There is nobody within," said Bonacieux.

"Never mind; let us walk into your apartment; we shall be better there than in the doorway."

"Oh! Good God!" whispered Madame Bonacieux, we shall hear no more."

"On the contrary," said D'Artagnan, "we shall hear the better."

D'Artagnan raised the three or four boards which made another Dionysius' ear of his chamber, spread a carpet, went down upon his knees, and made a sign to Madame Bonacieux to do as he did, stooping down toward the opening.

"You are sure there is nobody there?" said the unknown.

"I will answer for it," said Bonacieux.

"And you think that your wife——"

"Is returned to the Louvre."

"Without speaking to any one but yourself?"

"I am sure of it."

"Please to understand, that is an important point."

"Then the news I brought you is valuable?"

"Very, my dear Bonacieux; I don't attempt to deny it."

"Then the cardinal will be pleased with me?"

"No doubt he will."

"The great cardinal!"

"Are you sure, that in her conversation with you, your wife mentioned no proper names?"

"I don't think she did."

"She did not name Madame de Chevreuse, the Duke of Buckingham, or Madame de Vernet?"

"No; she only told me she wished to send me to London, to further the interests of an illustrious personage."

"Oh! the traitor!" murmured Madame Bonacieux.

"Silence!" whispered D'Artagnan, taking a hand, which, without thinking of it, she suffered him to retain.

"Never mind," continued the man in the cloak; "it was very silly of you not to have feigned to accept the mission; you would now be in possession of the letter; the state, which is now threatened, would be safe; and you——"

"And I?"

"Well, you! The cardinal would have given you letters of nobility."

"Did he tell you so?"

"Yes, I know that he meant to afford you that agreeable surprise."

"Be satisfied," replied Bonacieux; "my wife adores me, and there is still plenty of time."

"The silly fool!" murmured Madame Bonacieux.

"Silence!" said D'Artagnan, pressing her hand more closely.

"What do you mean by its being still time?" asked the man in the cloak.

"I will go to the Louvre, I will ask for Madame Bonacieux, I will tell her I have reflected upon the matter, I will renew the affair, I will obtain the letter, and I will run directly to the cardinal's."

"Well! begone then! make all possible haste: I will shortly come back to learn the result of your plan."

The unknown went out.

"Base old fool!" said Madame Bonacieux, addressing this affectionate epithet to her husband.

"Silence, once more!" said D'Artagnan, pressing her hand still more warmly.

A terrible howling interrupted these reflections of D'Artagnan and Madame Bonacieux. It was her husband, who had discovered the disappearance of his money bag, and was screaming out, "Thieves! thieves!"

"Oh! good God," cried Madame Bonacieux, "he will rouse the whole quarter."

Bonacieux cried for a long time; but, as such cries, on account of their frequency, did not attract much notice in the Rue des Fossoyeurs, and as lately the mercer's house had not been in very good repute, finding that nobody came, he went out, crying aloud, his voice being heard fainter and fainter, in the direction of the Rue du Bac.

"Now he is gone, it is your turn to get out," said Madame Bonacieux: "courage, my friend, but, above all, prudence, and think what you owe to the queen!"

"To her and to you!" cried D'Artagnan. "Be satisfied, lovely Constance. I shall prove worthy of her gratitude; but shall I likewise return worthy of your love?"

The young woman only replied by the beautiful glow which mounted to her cheeks. A few seconds after, D'Artagnan went out in his turn, enveloped likewise in a large cloak, which ill-concealed the sheath of a long sword.

Madame Bonacieux followed him with her eyes, with that long, fond look with which a woman accompanies the man she loves; but when he had turned the angle of the street, she fell on her knees, and clasping her hands:

"Oh! my God!" cried she, "protect the queen, protect me!"

CHAPTER XIX.

PLAN OF THE CAMPAIGN.

D'ARTAGNAN went straight to the hotel of M. de Tréville. He had reflected that in a few minutes the cardinal would be warned by this cursed unknown, who appeared to be his agent, and he judged, with reason, he had not a moment to lose.

The heart of the young man overflowed with joy. An opportunity presented itself to him in which there would be both glory and money to be gained, and as a far higher encouragement still, which had brought him into close intimacy with a woman he adored. This chance did then for him, at once, more than he would have dared to ask of Providence.

M. de Tréville was in his saloon with his habitual court of gentlemen. D'Artagnan, who was known as a familiar of the house, went straight to his cabinet, and sent word to him that he wished to see him upon an affair of importance.

D'Artagnan had been there scarcely five minutes when M. de Tréville entered. At the first glance, and by the joy which was painted on his countenance, the worthy captain plainly perceived that something fresh and extraordinary was on foot.

All the way he came, D'Artagnan was consulting with himself whether he should place confidence in M. de Tréville, or whether he should only ask him to give him *carte blanche* for a second affair. But M. de Tréville had always been so perfectly his friend, had always been so devoted to the king and queen, and hated the cardinal so cordially, that the young man resolved to tell him everything.

"Did you ask for me, my young friend?" said M. de Tréville.

"Yes, monsieur," said D'Artagnan, "you will pardon me, I hope, for having disturbed you, when you know the importance of my business."

"Speak, then, I am attentive."

"It concerns nothing less," said D'Artagnan, lowering his voice, "than the honor, perhaps the life, of the queen."

"What do you say?" asked M. de Tréville, glancing round to see if they were alone, and then fixing his interrogative look upon D'Artagnan.

"I say, monsieur, that chance has rendered me master of a secret——"

"Which you will keep, I hope, young man, sacred as your life."

"But which I must impart to you, monsieur, for you alone can assist me in the mission I have just received from her majesty."

"Is this secret your own?"

"No, monsieur, it is her majesty's."

"Are you authorized by her majesty to communicate it to me?"

"No, monsieur, for on the contrary, I am desired to preserve the profoundest mystery."

"Why, then, are you about to betray it with respect to me?"

"Because, as I said, without you I can do nothing, and I was afraid that you would refuse me the favor I am come to ask, if you were not acquainted with the object for which I requested it of you."

"Keep your secret, young man, and tell me what you wish."

"I wish you to obtain for me, from M. Dessessarts, leave of absence for a fortnight."

"When?"

"This very night."

"You are leaving Paris?"

"I am going on a mission."

"May you tell me whither?"

"To London."

"Has any one an interest in preventing your arriving there?"

"The cardinal, I believe, would give anything in the world to prevent my success."

"And you are going alone?"

"I am going alone."

"In that case you will not get beyond Bondy; I tell you so, by the word of De Tréville."

"How so, monsieur?"

"You will be assassinated."

"And shall die in the performance of my duty."

"Yes, but please to recollect your mission will not be accomplished."

"That is true," replied D'Artagnan.

"You may take my word," continued Tréville, "in enterprises of this kind, in order that one may arrive, four must set out."

"Ah! you are right, monsieur," said D'Artagnan; "but you know Athos, Porthos, and Aramis, and you know if I can dispose of them."

"Without confiding to them the secret which I was not willing to know?"

"We are sworn, once forever, to implicit confidence and devotedness against all proof; besides, you can tell them that you have full confidence in me, and they will not be more incredulous than you."

"I can send to each of them leave of absence for a fortnight, that is all: Athos, whose wound still gives him inconvenience, to go to the waters of Forges; to Porthos and Aramis to accompany their friend, whom they are not willing to abandon in such a painful position. The sending of their leave of absence will be proof enough that I authorize their voyage."

"Thanks, monsieur! you are a hundred times kind!"

"Begone then, find them instantly, and let all be done tonight. Ha! but first write your request to M. Dessessarts. You, perhaps, had a spy at your heels, and your visit, if it should ever be known to the cardinal, will be thus legitimated."

D'Artagnan drew up his request, and M. de Tréville, on receiving it, assured him that by two o'clock in the morning, the four leaves of absence should be at the respective domiciles of the travelers.

"Have the goodness to send mine to Athos' residence. I should dread some disagreeable encounter if I were to go home."

"I will. Adieu! and a prosperous voyage! Apropos!" said M. de Tréville, calling him back.

D'Artagnan returned.

"Have you any money?"

D'Artagnan tapped the bag he had in his pocket.

"Enough?" asked M. de Tréville.

"Three hundred pistoles."

"Oh! plenty; that would carry you to the end of the world: begone then."

D'Artagnan bowed to M. de Tréville, who held out his hand to him; D'Artagnan pressed it with a respect mixed with gratitude. Since his first arrival at Paris, he had had constant occasion to honor this excellent man, whom he had always found worthy, loyal, and great.

His first visit was for Aramis, at whose residence he had not been since the famous evening on which he had followed Madame Bonacieux. Still further, he had seen the young musketeer but seldom, but every time he had seen him, he had remarked a deep sadness imprinted on his countenance.

He found Aramis this evening, sitting up, but melancholy and thoughtful; D'Artagnan risked a question or two about this prolonged melancholy; Aramis pleaded as his excuse a commentary upon the eighteenth chapter of St. Augustin, that he was forced to write in Latin, for the following week, and which preoccupied him a good deal.

After the two friends had been chatting a few instants, a servant from M. de Tréville entered, bringing a sealed packet.

"What is that," asked Aramis.

"The leave of absence monsieur has asked for," replied the lackey.

"For me! I have asked for no leave of absence!"

"Hold your tongue, and take it," said D'Artagnan. "And you, my friend, there is a demi-pistole for your trouble; you will tell M. de Tréville that M. Aramis is very much obliged to him. Go."

The lackey bowed to the ground and departed.

"What does all this mean?" asked Aramis.

"Pack up all you want for a journey of a fortnight, and follow me."

"But I cannot leave Paris, just now, without knowing——" Aramis stopped.

"What is become of her? I suppose you mean—" continued D'Artagnan.

"Become of whom?" replied Aramis.

"The lady who was here, the lady of the embroidered handkerchief."

"Who told you there was a lady here?" replied Aramis, becoming as pale as death.

"I saw her."

"And you know who she is?"

"Well, I think I can give a pretty good guess, at least."

"Then," said Aramis, "since you appear to know so many things, can you tell me what is become of that lady?"

"I presume that she is gone back to Tours."

"To Tours? yes, that may be; you evidently know her. But why did she return to Tours without telling me anything about it?"

"Because she was in fear of being arrested."

"Why did she not write to me then?"

"Because she was afraid of compromising you."

"D'Artagnan, you restore me to life!" cried Aramis. "I fancied myself despised, betrayed. I was so delighted to see her again! I could not have believed she would risk her liberty for me, and yet for what other cause could she have returned to Paris?"

"For the cause which, to-day, carries us to England."

"And what is this cause?" demanded Aramis.

"Oh! you'll know it some day, Aramis; but, at present, I must beg leave to imitate the discretion of *the doctor's niece.*"

Aramis smiled, as he remembered the tale he had related to his friends on a certain evening.

"Well, then, since she has left Paris, and you are sure of it, D'Artagnan, nothing prevents me, and I am ready to follow you. You say we are going——"

"To Athos' residence, now, and if you will come thither, I beg you to make haste, for we have lost much time already. Apropos, inform Bazin."

"Will Bazin go with us?" asked Aramis.

"Perhaps so. At all events, it is best that he should follow us to Athos'."

Aramis called Bazin, and after having ordered him to join them at Athos' residence: "Let us go, then," said he, taking his cloak, sword, and three pistoles, opening uselessly two or three drawers to see if he could not find some stray coin or other. When well assured this search was superfluous, he followed D'Artagnan, wondering to himself how this young guardsman should know so well who the lady was to whom he had given hospitality, and that he should know better than he did what was to become of her.

Only, as they went out, Aramis placed his hand upon the arm of D'Artagnan, and looking at him earnestly:

"You have not spoken of this lady?" said he.

"To nobody in the world."

"Not even to Athos or Porthos?"

"I have not breathed a syllable to them."

"That's well!"

And, at ease on this important point, Aramis continued his road with D'Artagnan, and both soon arrived at Athos' dwelling.

They found him holding his leave of absence in one hand, and M. de Tréville's note in the other.

"Can you explain to me what this leave of absence and this letter, which I have just received, mean?" said the astonished Athos: "'My dear Athos, I wish, as your health absolutely requires it, that you should rest for a fortnight. Go, then, and take the waters of Forges, or any that may be more agreeable to you, and re-establish yourself as quickly as possible. Your affectionate,   DE TRÉVILLE.'"

"Well; this leave of absence and that letter mean that you must follow me, Athos."

"To the waters of the Forges?"

"There or elsewhere."

"In the king's service?"

"Either the king's or the queen's; are we not their majesties' servants?"

At that moment Porthos entered.

"Pardieu!" said he; "here is a strange thing has happened! Since when, I wonder, in the musketeers, did they grant men leave of absence without its being asked for?"

"Since," said D'Artagnan, "they have friends who ask it for them."

"Ah, ah!" said Porthos, "it appears there's something fresh afoot?"

"Yes, we are going—" said Aramis.

"Going! to what country?" demanded Porthos.

"Ma foi! I don't know much about it," said Athos; "ask D'Artagnan here."

"To London, gentlemen," said D'Artagnan.

"To London!" cried Porthos; "and what the devil are we going to do in London?"

"That is what I am not at liberty to tell you, gentlemen; you must trust to me."

"But, in order to go to London, a man should have some money; and I have none."

"Nor I," said Aramis.

"Nor I," said Porthos.

"Well, I have," added D'Artagnan, pulling out his treasure from his pocket, and placing it on the table. There are in this bag three hundred pistoles. "Let each take seventy-five, which will be quite enough to take us to London and back. Besides, we may be sure that all of us will not arrive at London."

"Why so?"

"Because, according to all probability, some of us will be left on the road."

"What is this, then, a campaign upon which we are entering?"

"And a most dangerous one. I give you fair notice."

"Ah! ah! but if we do risk being killed," said Porthos, "at least I should like to know what for."

"You would be all the wiser!" said Athos.

"And yet," said Aramis, "I am somewhat of Porthos' opinion."

"Is the king accustomed to give you such reasons? No. He says to you, very simply: 'Gentlemen, there is fighting going on in Gascony or in Flanders; go and fight;' and you go there. Why? You need give yourselve no uneasiness about that."

"D'Artagnan is right," said Athos; "here are our three leaves of absence, which came from M. de Tréville; and here are three hundred pistoles, which came from I don't know where. So let us go and get killed where we are told to go. Is life worth the trouble of so many questions? D'Artagnan, I am ready to follow you."

"And I," said Porthos.

"And I, also," said Aramis. "And, indeed, I am not sorry to quit Paris; I stood in need of a little distraction."

"Well, you will have distractions enough, gentlemen, be assured," said D'Artagnan.

"And, now, when are we to go?" asked Athos.

"Immediately," replied D'Artagnan; "we have not a minute to lose."

"Hola! Grimaud, Planchet, Mousqueton, Bazin!" cried the four young men, calling their lackeys, "clean my boots, and fetch the horses from the hotel."

Each musketeer was accustomed to leave at the general hotel, as at a barrack, his own horse and that of his lackey.

Planchet, Grimaud, Mousqueton, and Bazin set off at full speed.

"Now let us lay down the plan of the campaign," said Porthos. "Where do we go first?"

"To Calais," said D'Artagnan; "that is the most direct line to London."

"Well," said Porthos, "this is my advice——"

"Speak—what is it?"

"Four men traveling together would be suspicious; D'Artagnan will give each of us his instructions; I will go by the way of Boulogne, to clear the way; Athos will set out two hours after, by that of Amiens; Aramis will follow us by that of Noyon; as to D'Artagnan, he will go by what route he thinks best, in Planchet's clothes, while Planchet will follow us like D'Artagnan, in the uniform of the guards."

"Gentlemen," said Athos, "my opinion is that it is not proper to allow lackeys to have anything to do in such an affair: a secret may, by chance, be betrayed by gentlemen; but it is almost always sold by lackeys."

"Porthos' plan appears to me to be impracticable," said D'Artagnan, "inasmuch as I am myself ignorant of what in-

structions I can give you. I am the bearer of a letter, that is
all. I have not, and I cannot make three copies of that letter, because it is sealed: we must then, as it appears to me,
travel in company. This letter is here, in this pocket;" and
he pointed to the pocket which contained the letter. "If I
should be killed, one of you must take it, and pursue the
route; if he be killed, it will be another's turn, and so on;
provided a single one arrives, that is all that is required."

"Bravo, D'Artagnan! your opinion is mine," cried Athos.
"Besides, we must be consistent; I am going to take the
waters, you will accompany me; instead of taking the waters
of Forges, I go and take sea waters; I am free to do so. If
any one wishes to stop us, I will show M. de Tréville's letter
and you will show your leaves of absence; if we are attacked,
we will defend ourselves; if we are tried, we will stoutly
maintain that we were only anxious to dip ourselves a certain
number of times in the sea. They would have an easy bargain of four isolated men; whereas four men together make
a troop. We will arm our four lackeys with pistols and musketoons; if they send an army out against us, we will give
battle, and the survivor, as D'Artagnan says, will carry the
letter."

"Well said," cried Aramis; "you don't often speak, Athos;
but when you do speak, it is like Saint John of the Golden
Mouth. I agree to Athos' plan. And you, Porthos?"

"I agree to it, too," said Porthos, "if D'Artagnan approves
of it. D'Artagnan, being bearer of the letter, is naturally
the head of the enterprise; let him decide, and we will
execute."

"Well!" said D'Artagnan; "I decide that we should adopt
Athos' plan, and that we set off in half an hour."

"Agreed!" shouted the three musketeers in chorus.

And every one, stretching out his hand to the bag, took his
seventy-five pistoles, and made his preparations to set out at
the time appointed.

CHAPTER XX.

THE JOURNEY.

AT two o'clock in the morning, our four adventurers left
Paris by the barrier St. Denis; as long as it was dark they
remained silent; in spite of themselves they felt the influence

of the obscurity, and apprehended ambushes everywhere.

With the first rays of the sun their tongues became loosened; with day their gayety revived; it was like the eve of a battle, the heart beat, the eyes laughed, and they felt that the life they were perhaps going to lose, was after all, worth something.

Besides, the appearance of the caravan was formidable; the black horses of the musketeers, their martial carriage, with the squadron-like step of these noble companions of the soldier, would have betrayed the most strict incognito. The lackeys followed, armed to the teeth.

All went well till they arrived at Chantilly, which place they reached about eight o'clock in the morning. They stood in need of breakfast; and alighted at the door of an auberge, recommended by a sign representing St. Martin giving half his cloak to a poor man. They ordered the lackeys not to unsaddle the horses, and to hold themselves in readiness to set off again immediately.

They entered the common room and placed themselves at table. A gentleman, who had just arrived by the route of Dammartin, was seated at the same table, and was taking his breakfast. He opened the conversation by talking of rain and fine weather; the travelers replied, he drank to their good health, and the travelers returned his politeness.

But at the moment Mousqueton came to announce that the horses were ready, and they were rising from table, the stranger proposed to Porthos to drink the health of the cardinal. Porthos replied that he asked no better, if the stranger in his turn, would drink the health of the king. The stranger cried that he acknowledged no other king but his eminence. Porthos told him he was drunk, and the stranger drew his sword.

"You have committed a piece of folly," said Athos, "but it can't be helped; there is no drawing back; kill the fellow, and rejoin us as soon as you can."

And all three mounted their horses, and set out at a good pace, while Porthos was promising his adversary to perforate him with all the thrusts known in the fencing schools.

"There goes one!" cried Athos, at the end of five hundred paces.

"But why did that man attack Porthos, rather than any other of us?" asked Aramis.

"Because Porthos talking louder than the rest, he took him for the leader of the party," said D'Artagnan.

"I always said that this cadet from Gascony was a well of wisdom," murmured Athos.

And the travelers continued their route.

At Beauvais they stopped two hours, as well to breathe their horses a little, as to wait for Porthos. At the end of the two hours, as Porthos did not come, and as they heard no news of him, they resumed their journey.

At a league from Beauvais, where the road was confined between two high banks, they fell in with eight or ten men who, taking advantage of the road being unpaved in this spot, appeared to be employed in digging holes and filling up the ruts with mud.

Aramis, not liking to soil his boots with this artificial mortar, apostrophized them rather sharply. Athos wished to restrain him, but it was too late. The laborers began to jeer the travelers, and by their insolence disturbed the equanimity even of the cool Athos, who urged on his horse against one of them.

The men all immediately drew back to the ditch, from which each took a concealed musket; the result was that our seven travelers were outnumbered in weapons. Aramis received a ball, which passed through his shoulder, and Mousqueton another ball which lodged in the fleshy part which prolongs the lower portion of the loins. Mousqueton alone fell from his horse, not because he was severely wounded, but from not being able to see the wound, he judged it to be more serious than it really was.

"It is an ambuscade!" shouted D'Artagnan, "don't waste a charge! forward!"

Aramis, wounded as he was, seized the mane of his horse which carried him on with the others. Mousqueton's horse rejoined them, and galloped by the side of his companions.

"That will serve us for a relay," said Athos.

"I would rather have had a hat," said D'Artagnan, "mine was carried away by a ball. By my faith, it is very fortunate that the letter was not in it."

"Well, but they'll kill poor Porthos, when he comes up." said Aramis.

"If Porthos were on his legs, he would have rejoined us by this time," said Athos, "my opinion is that when they came to the point, the drunken man proved to be sober enough."

They continued at their best speed for two hours, although the horses were so fatigued, that it was to be feared they would soon decline the service.

The travelers had chosen crossroads, in the hope that they might meet with less interruption; but at Crèvecœur, Aramis declared he could proceed no farther. In fact, it required all the courage which he concealed beneath his elegant form and polished manners to bear him so far. He every minute grew more pale, and they were obliged to support him on his horse. They lifted him off at the door of a cabaret, left Bazin with him, who besides, in a skirmish, was more embarrassing than useful, and set forward again in the hope of sleeping at Amiens.

"*Morbleu!*" said Athos, as soon as they were again in motion, "reduced to two masters, and Grimaud and Planchet! *Morbleu!* I won't be their dupe, I will answer for it; I will neither open my mouth nor draw my sword between this and Calais. I swear by——"

"Don't waste time in swearing," said D'Artagnan, "let us gallop, if our horses will consent to it."

And the travelers buried their rowels in their horses' flanks, who, thus vigorously stimulated, recovered their energies. They arrived at Amiens at midnight, and alighted at the auberge of the Lis d'Or.

The host had the appearance of as honest a man as any on earth; he received the travelers with his candlestick in one hand and his cotton nightcap in the other; he wished to lodge the two travelers each in a charming chamber, but, unfortunately, these charming chambers were at the opposite extremities of the hotel, and D'Artagnan and Athos declined them. The host replied that he had no other worthy of their execellencies; but his guests declared they would sleep in the common chamber, each upon a mattress, which might be thrown upon the ground. The host insisted, but the travelers were firm, and he was obliged to comply with their wishes.

They had just prepared their beds and barricaded their door within, when some one knocked at the yard-shutter; they demanded who was there, and, upon recognizing the voices of their lackeys, opened the shutter.

In fact, it was Planchet and Grimaud.

"Grimaud can take care of the horses," said Planchet; "if you are willing, gentlemen, I will sleep across your doorway, and you will then be certain that nobody can come to you."

"And what will you sleep upon?" said D'Artagnan.

"Here is my bed," replied Planchet, producing a bundle of straw.

"Come, then," said D'Artagnan, "you are right, mine host's face does not please me at all, it is too civil by half."

"Nor me neither," said Athos.

Planchet got up through the window, and installed himself across the doorway, while Grimaud went and shut himself up in the stable, undertaking that, by five o'clock in the morning, he and the four horses should be ready.

The night passed off quietly enough, it is true, till about two o'clock in the morning, when somebody endeavored to open the door, but as Planchet awoke in an instant, and cried, "Who is there?" this same somebody replied he was mistaken, and went away.

At four o'clock in the morning, there was a terrible riot in the stables. Grimaud had tried to waken the stable-boys, and the stable-boys had set upon him and beaten him. When they opened the window they saw the poor lad lying senseless, with his head split by a blow with a fork-handle.

Planchet went down into the yard, and proceeded to saddle the horses. But the horses were all knocked up. Mousqueton's horse, which had traveled for five or six hours without a rider the day before, alone might have been able to pursue the journey; but, by an inconceivable error, a veterinary surgeon, who had been sent for, as it appeared, to bleed one of the host's horses, had bled Mousqueton's.

This began to be annoying. All these successive accidents were, perhaps, the result of chance; but they might, quite as probably, be the fruits of a plot. Athos and D'Artagnan went out, while Planchet was sent to inquire if there were not three horses to be sold in the neighborhood. At the door stood two horses, fresh, strong, and fully equipped. These would just have suited them. He asked where the masters of them were, and was informed that they had passed the night in the auberge, and were then settling wtih the master.

Athos went down to pay the reckoning, while D'Artagnan and Planchet stood at the street-door. The host was in a lower and back chamber, to which Athos was requested to go.

Athos entered without the least mistrust, and took out two pistoles to pay the bill. The host was alone, seated before his desk, one of the drawers of which was partly open. He took the money which Athos offered to him, and, after turning it over and over in his hands, suddenly cried out that it was bad, and that he would have him and his companions arrested as coiners.

"You scoundrel!" cried Athos, stepping toward him, "I'll cut your ears off!"

But the host stooped, took two pistoles from the half-open drawer, pointed them at Athos, and called out for help.

At the same instant, four men, armed to the teeth, entered by lateral doors, and rushed upon Athos.

"I am taken!" shouted Athos, with all the power of his

lungs: "Go on, D'Artagnan! spur, spur!" and he fired two pistols.

D'Artagnan and Planchet did not require twice bidding: they unfastened the two horses that were waiting at the door, l aped upon them, buried their spurs in their sides, and set off at full gallop.

"Do you know what has become of Athos?" asked D'Artagnan of Planchet, as they galloped on.

"Ah, monsieur," said Planchet, "I saw one fall at each of his shots, and he appeared to me, through the glass door, to be fighting with his sword with the others."

"Brave Athos!" murmured D'Artagnan; "and to think that we are compelled to leave him, while the same fate awaits us, perhaps, two paces hence! Forward, Planchet, forward! you are a brave fellow!"

"Did not I tell you, monsieur," replied Planchet, "that we Picards are found out by being used? Besides, I am in my own country here, and that puts me on my mettle!"

And both, with free use of the spur, arrived at St. Omer, without drawing bit. At St. Omer they breathed their horses with their bridles passed under their arms, for fear of accident, and ate a morsel in their hands, standing in the road, after which they departed again.

At a hundred paces from the gates of Calais, D'Artagnan's horse sank under him, and could not by any means be got up again, the blood flowing from both his eyes and his nose. There still remained Planchet's horse, but, after he stopped, he remained quite still, and could not be urged to move a step.

Fortunately, as we have said, they were within a hundred paces of the city; they left their two nags upon the highroad, and ran toward the port. Planchet called his master's attention to a gentleman who had just arrived with his lackey, and preceded them by about fifty paces.

They made all speed to come up to this gentleman, who appeared to be in great haste. His boots were covered with dust, and he inquired if he could not instantly cross over to England.

"Nothing would be more easy," said the captain of a vessel ready to set sail; "but this morning an order arrived that no one should be allowed to cross without express permission from the cardinal."

"I have that permission," said the gentleman, drawing a paper from his pocket; "here it is."

"Have it examined by the governor of the port," said the captain, "and give me the preference."

"Where shall I find the governor?"

"At his country-house."

"Where is that situated?"

"At a quarter of a league from the city. Look, you may see it from here—at the foot of that little hill, that slated roof."

"Very well," said the gentleman.

And, with his lackey, he took the road to the governor's country-house.

D'Artagnan and Planchet followed the gentleman at a distance, not to be noticed; but when he was out of the city, D'Artagnan quickly came up with him, just as he was entering a little wood.

"Monsieur," said D'Artagnan, "you appear to be in great haste?"

"No one can be more so, monsieur."

"I am sorry for that," said D'Artagnan; "for, as I am in great haste likewise, I wished to beg you to render me a service."

"What service?"

"To let me go first."

"That's impossible," said the gentleman; "I have traveled sixty leagues in forty hours, and by to-morrow, at midday, I must be in London."

"I have performed the same distance in forty hours, and by to-morrow, at ten o'clock in the morning, I must be in London."

"Very sorry, monsieur; but I was here first, and will not go second."

"I am sorry too, monsieur; but I arrived second, and will go first."

"The king's service!" said the gentleman.

"My own service!" said D'Artagnan.

"But this is a needless quarrel you are fastening upon me, as I think."

"*Parbleu!* what do you desire it to be?"

"What do you want?"

"Would you like to know?"

"Certainly."

"Well, then, I want that order of which you are the bearer, seeing that I have not one of my own, and must have one."

"You are joking, I presume."

"I seldom joke."

"Let me pass!"

"You shall not pass."

"My brave young man, I will blow out your brains. Hola, Lubin! my pistols!"

"Planchet," called out D'Artagnan, "take care of the lackey; I will manage the master."

Planchet, emboldened by the first exploit, sprang upon Lubin, and, being strong and vigorous, he soon got him on the broad of his back, and placed his knee upon his breast.

"Go on with your affair, monsieur," cried Planchet; "I have finished mine."

Seeing this, the gentleman drew his sword, and sprang upon D'Artagnan; but he had more than he expected to deal with.

In three seconds, D'Artagnan had wounded him three times, exclaiming at each thrust:

"One for Athos! one for Porthos! and one for Aramis!"

At the third hit the gentleman fell heavily to the ground.

D'Artagnan believed him to be dead, or at least insensible, and went toward him for the purpose of taking the order; but at the moment he stretched out his hand to search for it, the wounded man, who had not dropped his sword, plunged the point into his breast, crying:

"And one for you!"

"And one for me! the best for the last!" cried D'Artagnan, in a rage, nailing him to the earth with a forth thrust through his body.

This time the gentleman closed his eyes and fainted. D'Artagnan searched his pockets, and took from one of them the order for the passage. It was in the name of the Count de Wardes.

Then, casting a glance on the handsome young man, who was scarcely twenty-five years of age, and whom he was leaving in his gore, deprived of sense, and perhaps dead, he gave a sigh to that unaccountable destiny which leads men to destroy each other for the interests of people who are strangers to them, and who often do not even know they exist.

But he was soon roused from these reflections by Lubin, who uttered loud cries, and screamed for help, with all his might.

Planchet grasped him by the throat, and pressed as hard as he could.

"Monsieur," said he, "as long as I hold him in this manner, he can't cry, I'll be bound; but as soon as I leave go, he will howl again as loud as ever. I have found out that he's a Norman, and Normans are all obstinate."

In fact, tightly held as he was, Lubin endeavored still to get out a cry.

"Stay!" said D'Artagnan, and, taking out his handkerchief, he gagged him.

"Now," said Planchet, "let us bind him to a tree."

This being properly done they drew the Count de Wardes close to his servant; and as night was approaching and as the wounded man and the bound man were at some little distance within the wood, it was evident they were likely to remain there till the next day.

"And now," said D'Artagnan, "to the governor's house."

"But you appear to me to be wounded," said Planchet.

"Oh, that's nothing! Let us despatch that which is most pressing first, and we will attend to my wound afterward; besides, I don't think it seems a very dangerous one."

And they both set forward as fast as they could toward the country-house of the worthy functionary.

The Count de Wardes was announced, and D'Artagnan was introduced.

"You have an order, signed by the cardinal?"

"Yes, monsieur," replied D'Artagnan; "here it is."

"Ah, ah! it is quite regular and explicit," said the governor.

"Most likely," said D'Artagnan; "I am one of his most faithful servants."

"It appears that his eminence is anxious to prevent some one from crossing to England?"

"Yes; a certain D'Artagnan, a Béarnese gentleman, who left Paris in company of three of his friends, with the intention of going to London."

"Do you him personally?" asked the governor.

"Whom?"

"This D'Artagnan."

"Oh, yes, perfectly well."

"Describe him to me, then."

"Nothing more easy."

And D'Artagnan gave, feature for feature, and in every way, the most minute description of the Count de Wardes.

"Is he accompanied by any one?"

"Yes, by a lackey, named Lubin."

"We will keep a sharp lookout for them; and if we lay hands upon them, his eminence may be assured they shall be reconducted to Paris under a good escort."

"And by doing so, Monsieur the Governor," said D'Artagnan, "you will have merited well of the cardinal."

"Shall you see him on your return?"

"Doubtless I shall."

"Tell him, I beg you, that I am his humble servant."

"I will not fail."

And delighted with this assurance, the governor signed the passport, and delivered it to D'Artagnan, who lost no time in useless compliments, but thanked the governor, bowed, and departed.

When once out, he and Planchet set off as fast as they could, and, by making a detour, avoided the wood, and re-entered the city by another gate.

The vessel was quite ready to sail, and the captain waiting in the port.

"Well?" said he, on perceiving D'Artagnan.

"Here is my pass, examined," said the latter.

"And that other gentleman?"

"He will not go to-day," said D'Artagnan; "but, here I'll pay you for us two."

"In that case we will be gone," said the captain.

"Yes, as soon as you please," replied D'Artagnan.

He leaped, with Planchet, into the boat, and five minutes after they were on board. And it was time; for they had scarcely sailed half a league, when D'Artagnan saw a flash and heard a detonation—it was the cannon which announced the closing of the port.

He had now leisure to look to his wound. Fortunately, as D'Artagnan had thought, it was not dangerous: the point of the sword had met with a rib, and glanced along the bone; still further, his shirt had stuck to the wound, and he had lost but very little blood.

D'Artagnan was worn out with fatigue. A mattress was laid upon the deck for him; he threw himself upon it, and fell fast asleep.

At break of day they were still three or four leagues from the coast of England; the breeze had been so light during the night they had made but little way.

At ten o'clock the vessel cast anchor in the port of Dover, and at half-past ten D'Artagnan placed his foot on English land, crying:

"Here I am at last!"

But that was not all, they had to get to London. In England the post was well served; D'Artagnan and Planchet took post-horses with a postilion, and who rode before them; and in a few hours were in the capital.

D'Artagnan did not know London, he was not acquainted with one word of English: but he wrote the name of Buck-

ingham on a piece of paper, and every one to whom he showed
it pointed out to him the way to the duke's hotel.

The duke was at Windsor hunting with the king.

D'Artagnan inquired for the confidential valet of the duke,
who having accompanied him in all his voyages, spoke French
perfectly well; he told him that he came from Paris, on an
affair of life and death, and that he must speak with his
master instantly.

The confidence with which D'Artagnan spoke convinced
Patrick, which was the name of this minister; he ordered
two horses to be saddled, and himself went as guide to the
young guardsman. As for Planchet, he had been lifted from
his horse as stiff as a rush; the poor lad's strength was almost
exhausted. D'Artagnan seemed to be made of iron.

On their arrival at the castle they inquired for the duke,
and learned that he was hawking with the king in the
marshes, at some distance.

They were quickly on the spot named, and Patrick almost
at the moment caught the sound of his master's voice, recalling his falcon.

"Whom must I announce to my lord duke?" asked Patrick.

"The young man who one evening sought a quarrel with
him on the Pont Neuf, opposite the *Samaritaine.*"

"Rather a singular introduction?"

"You will find that it is as good as another."

Patrick galloped off, reached the duke, and announced to
him, in the terms directed, that a messenger awaited him.

Buckingham at once remembered the circumstances, and
suspecting that something was going on in France, of which
it was necessary he should be informed, he only took the time
to inquire where the messenger was, and recognizing the uniform of the guards, he put his horse into a gallop, and rode
straight up to D'Artagnan; Patrick, discreetly, keeping in
the background.

"No misfortune has happened to the queen?" cried Buckingham, the instant he came up, throwing all his fear and
love into the question.

"I believe not; nevertheless, I believe she is in some great
peril from which your grace alone can extricate her."

"I!" cried Buckingham. "What is it? I should be but
too happy to render her any service! Speak! speak!"

"Take this letter," said D'Artagnan.

"This letter! from whom does this letter come?"

"From her majesty, as I think."

"From her majesty!" said Buckingham, becoming so pale

that D'Artagnan feared he would faint—and he broke the seal.

"What is this rent!" said he, showing D'Artagnan a place where it had been pierced through.

"Ah! ah!" said D'Artagnan, "I did not see that; it was the sword of the Count de Wardes that made that hole when he ran it into my breast."

"Are you wounded?" asked Buckingham, as he opened the letter.

"Oh! nothing! milord, only a scratch," said D'Artagnan.

"Just heavens! what have I read!" cried the duke. "Patrick, remain here, or rather join the king wherever he may be, and tell his majesty that I hereby beg him to excuse me, but an affair of the greatest importance calls me to London. Come, monsieur, come!" and both set off toward the capital at full gallop.

CHAPTER XXI.

THE COUNTESS DE WINTER.

As THEY rode along, the duke endeavored to draw from D'Artagnan, not what has passed, but what D'Artagnan himself knew. By adding all that he heard from the mouth of the young man to his own remembrances, he was enabled to form a pretty exact idea of a position of the seriousness of which, in addition, the queen's letter, however short and explicit, rendered him quite aware. But that which astonished him most was, that the cardinal, so deeply interested in preventing this young man from setting his foot on the soil of England, had not succeeded in arresting him on the road. It was then, and upon the manifestation of this astonishmennt, that D'Artagnan related to him the precaution taken, and how, thanks to his three friends, whom he had left scattered on the road, he had succeeded in coming off with a single sword-thrust, which had pierced the queen's letter, and for which he had repaid M. de Wardes in such terrible coin. While he was listening to this account, which was delivered with the greatest simplicity, the duke looked from time to time at the young man with astonishment, as if he could not comprehend how so much prudence, courage, and devotedness were allied with a countenance evidently not more than twenty years of age.

The horses went like the wind, and in an incredibly short time they were in London. D'Artagnan imagined that on arriving in the city the duke would slacken his pace. but it was not so: he kept on his way, heedless of whom he rode against. In fact, in crossing the city, two or three accidents of this kind happened; but Buckingham did not even turn his head to see what became of those he had knocked down. D'Artagnan followed him amid cries which very much resembled curses.

On entering the court of his hotel, Buckingham sprang from his horse and, without taking heed of the noble animal, threw the bridle on his neck, and sprang toward the vestibule. D'Artagnan did the same, with a little more concern, however, for the fine creatures, whose merits he fully appreciated; but he had the satisfaction to see three or four grooms run from the stables, and take charge of them.

The duke walked so fast that D'Artagnan had some trouble in keeping up with him. He passed through several apartments of an elegance of which even the greatest nobles of France had not even an idea, and arrived at length in a bedchamber which was at once a miracle of taste and of splendor. In the alcove of this chamber was a door practiced in the tapestry, which the duke opened with a small gold key, which he wore suspended from his neck by a chain of the same metal. From discretion, D'Artagnan remained behind; but at the moment of Buckingham's passing through the door, he turned round, and seeing the hesitation of the young man:

"Come in! come in!" cried he, "and if you have the good fortune to be admitted to her majesty's presence, tell her what you have seen."

Encouraged by this invitation, D'Artagnan followed the duke, who closed the door after them.

He found himself with the duke in a small chapel covered with a tapestry of Persian silk worked with gold, and brilliantly lit with a vast number of wax-lights. Over a species of altar, and beneath a canpoy of blue velvet, surmounted by white and red plumes, was a full-length portrait of Anne of Austria, so perfect in its resemblance that D'Artagnan uttered a cry of surprise on beholding it: it might be belived that the queen was about to speak.

Upon the altar and beneath the portrait, was the casket containing the diamond studs.

The duke approached the altar, fell on his knees as a priest might have done before a crucifix, and opened the casket.

"There," said he, drawing from the casket a large bow of

blue ribbon all sparkling with diamonds; "here," said he, "are the precious studs which I have taken an oath should be buried with me. The queen gave them to me, the queen requires them back again; her will be done, like that of God, in all things."

Then he began to kiss, one after the other, those dear studs with which he was about to part. All at once, he uttered a terrible cry.

"What is the matter?" exclaimed D'Artagnan anxiously, "what has happened to you, milord?"

"All is lost! all is lost!" cried Buckingham, turning as pale as death; "two of the studs are wanting! there are but ten of them!"

"Can you have lost them, milord, or do you think they have been stolen?"

"They have been stolen!" replied the duke, "and it is the cardinal who has dealt me this blow. See, the ribbons which held them have been cut with scissors."

"If milord suspects they have been stolen—perhaps the person who stole them still has them."

"Let me reflect," said the duke. "The only time I wore these studs was at a ball given by the king a week ago at Windsor. The Countess de Winter, with whom I had had a quarrel, became reconciled to me at that ball. That reconciliation was nothing but the vengeance of a jealous woman. I have never seen her from that day. The woman is an agent of the cardinal's."

"Why then, he has agents throughout the whole world!" cried D'Artagnan.

"Yes, yes," said Buckingham, gnashing his teeth with rage, "he is a terrible antagonist! But when is this ball to take place?"

"On Monday next."

"On Monday next! Still five days before us; that's more time than we want. Patrick!" cried the duke, opening the door of the chapel, "Patrick!"

His confidential valet, who had that moment returned appeared at his call.

"My jeweler and my secretary."

The valet de chambre went out with a mute promptitude that showed he was accustomed to obey implicity and without reply.

But although the jeweler had been mentioned first, it was the secretary that first made his appearance, simply because he lived in the hotel. He found Buckingham seated at a table in his bedchamber, writing orders with his own hand.

"Master Jackson," said he, "go instantly to the lord chancellor and tell him that I desire him to execute these orders. I wish them to be promulgated immediately."

"But, my lord, if the lord chancellor interrogates me upon the motives which may have led your grace to adopt such an extraordinary measure, what reply shall I make?"

"That such is my pleasure, and that I answer for my will to no man."

"Will that be the answer," replied the secretary, smiling, "which he must transmit to his majesty, if, by chance, his majesty should have the curiosity to know why no vessel is to leave any of the ports of Great Britain?"

"You are right, Master Jackson," replied Buckingham. "He will say, in that case, to the king, that I am determined on war, and that this measure is my first act of hostility against France."

The secretary bowed and retired.

"We are safe on that side," said Buckingham, turning toward D'Artagnan. "If the studs are not yet gone to Paris, they will not arrive till after you."

"How so, milord?"

"I have just placed an embargo on all vessels at present in his majesty's ports, and, without particular permission, not one can lift an anchor."

D'Artagnan looked with stupefaction at a man who thus employed the unlimited power with which he was clothed by the confidence of a king, in the prosecution of his amours. Buckingham saw by the expression of the young man's face what was passing in his mind, and he smiled.

"Yes," said he, "yes, Anne of Austria is my true queen; upon a word from her, I would betray my country, I would betray my king. I would betray my God. She asked me not to send the Protestants of La Rochelle the assistance, I promised them: I have not done so. I broke my word, it is true; but what signifies that? I obeyed my love; and have I not been richly paid for that obedience? It was to that obedience I owe her portrait!"

D'Artagnan admired by what fragile and unknown threads the destinies of nations and the lives of men are sometimes suspended.

He was lost in these reflections when the goldsmith entered. He was an Irishman, one of the most skillful of his craft, and who himself confessed that he gained a hundred thousand livres a year by the Duke of Buckingham.

"Master O'Reilly," said the duke to him, leading him into the chapel, "look at these diamond studs, and tell me what they are worth apiece."

The goldsmith cast a glance at the elegant manner in which they were set, calculated, one with another, what the diamonds were worth, and without hesitation:

"Fifteen hundred pistoles each, my lord," replied he.

"How many days would it require to make two studs exactly like them? You see there are two wanting."

"A week, my lord."

"I will give you three thousand pistoles each for two, if I can have them by the day after to-morrow."

"My lord, you shall have them."

"You are a jewel of a man, Master O'Reilly; but that is not all; these studs cannot be trusted to anybody: it must be effected in the palace."

"Impossible, my lord; there is no one but myself can execute them so that the new may not be distinguished from the old."

"Therefore, my dear Master O'Reilly, you are my prisoner; and if you wish ever to leave my palace, you cannot; so make the best of it. Name to me such of your workmen as you stand in need of, and point out the tools they must bring."

The goldsmith knew the duke; he knew all objection would be useless, and instantly determined how to act.

"May I be permitted to inform my wife?" said he.

"Oh! you may even see her if you like, my dear Master O'Reilly; your captivity shall be mild, be assured; and as every inconvenience deserves its indemnification, here is, in addition to the price of the studs, an order for a thousand pistoles, to make you forget the annoyance I cause you."

D'Artagnan could not get over the surprise created in him by this minister, who thus, open-handed, sported with men and millions.

As to the goldsmith, he wrote to his wife, sending her the order for the thousand pistoles, and charging her to send him, in exchange, his most skillful apprentice, an assortment of diamonds, of which he gave the names and the weight, and the necessary tools.

Buckingham led the goldsmith to the chamber destined for him, and which, at the end of half an hour, was transformed into a workshop. Then he placed a sentinel at each door, with an order to admit nobody, upon any pretense, but his *valet de chambre*, Patrick. We need not add that the goldsmith, O'Reilly, and his assistant, were prohibited from going out on any account.

All this being regulated, the duke turned to D'Artagnan.

"Now, my young friend," said he, "England is all our own. What do you wish for? What do you desire?"

"A bed, milord," replied D'Artagnan. "At present, I confess, that is the thing I stand most in need of."

Buckingham assigned D'Artagnan a chamber adjoining his own. He wished to have the young man at hand, not that he at all mistrusted him, but for the sake of having some one to whom he could constantly talk about the queen.

In one hour after, the ordinance was published in London that no vessel bound for France should leave the ports—not even the packet-boat with letters, in the eyes of everybody this was a declaration of war between the two kingdoms.

On the day after the morrow, by eleven o'clock, the two diamond studs were finished, and they were so completely imitated, so perfectly alike, that Buckingham could not tell the new ones from the old ones, and the most practiced in such matters would have been deceived as he was.

He immediately called D'Artagnan.

"Here," said he to him, "are the diamond studs that you came to fetch, and be my witness that I have done all that human power could do."

"Be satisfied, milord; I will tell all that I have seen. But does your grace mean to give me the studs without the casket?"

"The casket would only encumber you. Besides, the casket is the more precious from being all that is left to me. You will say that I keep it."

"I will perform your commission, word for word, milord."

"And now," resumed Buckingham, looking earnestly at the young man, "how shall I ever acquit myself of the debt I owe you?"

D'Artagnan colored up to the eyes. He saw that the duke was searching for a means of making him accept something, and the idea that the blood of himself and his friends was about to be paid for with English gold was strangely repugnant to him.

"Let us understand each other, milord," replied D'Artagnan, "and let us make things clear, in order that there may be no mistake. I am in the services of the king and queen of France, and form part of the company of M. Dessessarts, who, as well as his brother-in-law, M. de Tréville, is particularly attached to their majesties. What have I done, then, has

been for the queen, and not at all for your grace. And, still
further, it is very probable I should not have done anything
of this, if it had not been to make myself agreeable to some
one who is my lady, as the queen is yours."

"I understand," said the duke smiling, "and I even believe
that I know that other person; it is——"

"Milord! I have not named her!" interrupted the young
man warmly.

"That is true," said the duke, "and it is to this person I
am bound to discharge my debt of gratitude."

"You have said, milord; for truly, at this moment, when
there is question of war, I confess to you that I can see nothing
in your grace but an Englishman, and, consequently, an
enemy, whom I should have much greater pleasure in meeting on the field of battle than in the park at Windsor or the
chambers of the Louvre; all which, however, will not prevent
me from executing, to the very point, my commission, or
from laying down my life, if there be need of it, to accomplish it; but I repeat it to your grace, without your having
personally on that account more to thank me for in this second interview than that which I did for you in the first."

"We say, 'proud as a Scotchman,'" murmured the Duke
of Buckingham.

"And we say, 'proud as a Gascon,'" replied D'Artagnan;
"the Gascons are the Scots of France."

D'Artagnan bowed to the duke, and was retiring.

"Well! you are going away in that manner? But where?
and how?"

"That's true!"

"'Fore Gad, these Frenchmen have no consideration!"

"I had forgotten that England was an island, and that you
were the king of it."

"Go to the port, ask for the brig Sund, and give this letter
to the captain; he will convey you to a little port, where certainly you are not expected, and which is ordinarily only frequented by fishermen."

"What is the name of that port?"

"Saint-Valery; but listen. When you have arrived there,
you will go to a mean auberge, without a name and without
a sign, a mere fisherman's hut. You cannot be mistaken; there
is but one."

"And then?"

"You will ask for the host, and will repeat to him the word—
Forward!"

"Which means?"

"In Franch, *en avant;* that is the password. He will give
you a ready-saddled horse, and will point out to you the road
you are to take. You will find, in this manner, four relays
on your route. If you will give, at each of these relays, your
address in Paris, the four horses will follow you thither. You
already know two of them, and you appeared to appreciate
them like a judge. They were those we rode on, and you
may rely upon me for the others not being inferior to them.
These horses are equipped for the field. However proud you
may be, you will not refuse to accept one of them, and request your three companions to accept the others: that is in
order to make war against us, besides. The end excuses the
means, as you Frenchmen say, does it not?"

"Yes, milord, I accept them," said D'Artagnan, "and, if
it please God, we will make a good use of your presents."

"Well, now, your hand, young man; perhaps we shall soon
meet on the field of battle; but, in the meantime, we shall part
good friends, I hope?" ..

"Yes, milord; but with the hope of soon becoming enemies?"

"Be satisfied on that head; I promise you."

"I depend upon your parole, milord."

D'Artagnan bowed to the duke, and made his way as
quickly as possible to the port. Opposite the Tower he found
the vessel that had been named to him, delivered his letter to
the captain, who, after having it examined by the governor of
the port, made immediate preparation to sail.

Fifty vessels were waiting to set out, in momentary expectation of the removal of the prohibition. When passing
alongside of one of them, D'Artagnan fancied her perceived
on board of it the lady of Meung, the same whom the unknown gentleman had styled milady, and whom D'Artagnan
had thought so handsome; but thanks to the tide of the river
and a fair wind, his vessel passed so quickly that he had little
more than a glimpse of her.

The next day, about nine o'clock in the morning, he landed
as St. Valery. D'Artagnan went instantly in search of the
auberge, and easily discovered it by the riotous noise which
resounded from it; war between England and France was
then confidently talked of, and the sailors were carousing in
the hopes of it.

D'Artagnan made his way through the crowd, advanced
toward the host, and pronounced the word, *"Forward!"* The
host instantly made him a sign to follow him, went out with
him by a door which opened into a yard, led him to the stable.

where a ready saddled horse awaited him, and asked him if he stood in need of anything else.

"I want to know the route I am to follow," said D'Artagnan.

"Go from hence to Blangy, and from Blangy to Neufchâtel. At Neuchâtel, go to the auberge of the 'Herse d'Or', give the password to the host, and you will find, as you have done here, a horse ready saddled."

"Have I anything to pay?" demanded D'Artagnan.

"Everything is paid," replied the host, "and liberally. Begone then, and may God conduct you safely."

"Amen!" cried the young man, and set off at full gallop.

In four hours from starting he was in Neufchâtel. He strictly followed the instructions he had received; at Neufchâtel, as St. Valery, he found a horse quite ready awaiting him; he was about to remove the pistols from the saddle he had vacated to the one he was about to occupy, but he found the holsters furnished with similar pistols.

"Your address at Paris?"

"Hotel of the Guards, company of Dessessarts."

"Enough," replied the interrogator.

"Which route must I take?" demanded D'Artagnan, in his turn.

"That of Rouen; but you will leave the city on your right. You must stop at the little village of Eccuis, in which there is but one auberge, 'l'Ecu de France.' Don't condemn it from appearances, you will find a horse in the stables quite as good as this."

"The same password?"

"Exactly."

"Adieu, master!"

"A good journey, gentleman! Do you want anything?"

D'Artagnan shook his head in reply, and set off at full speed. At Eccuis, the same scene was repeated; he found as provident a host and a fresh horse. He left his address as he had done before, and set off again, at the same pace, for Pontoise. At Pontoise he changed his horse for the last time, and at nine o'clock galloped into the yard of M. de Tréville's hotel. He had performed nearly sixty leagues in little more than twelve hours.

M. de Tréville received him as if he had seen him that same morning; only, when pressing his hand a little more warmly than usual, he informed him that the company of M. Dessessarts was on duty at the Louvre, and that he might repair at once to his post.

CHAPTER XXII.

THE BALLET OF LA MERLAISON.

On the morrow, nothing was talked of in Paris but the ball which Messieurs the Echevins of the city were to give to the king and queen, and in which the king and queen were to dance the famous La Merlaison, the king's favorite ballet.

The whole of the last week had been occupied in preparations at the Hotel de Ville for this important evening. The city carpenters had erected scaffolds upon which the ladies invited were to be placed; the city grocer had ornamented the chambers with two hundred flambeaux of white wax, which was a piece of luxury unheard of at that period; and twenty violins were ordered, and the price paid for them fixed at double the usual rate, upon condition, said the report, that they should be played all night.

At ten o'clock in the morning, the Sieur de la Coste, ensign in the king's guards, followed by two exempts and several archers of that body, came to the city greffier (register or secretary), named Clement, and demanded of him all the keys of the chambers and offices at the hotel. These keys were given up to him instantly; and each of them had a ticket attached to it, by which it might be known, and from that moment the Sieur de la Coste was charged with the guarding of all the doors and all the avenues.

At eleven o'clock came in his turn Duhallier, captain of the guard, bringing with him fifty archers, who were distributed immediately, through the hotel, at the doors which had been assigned to them.

At three o'clock arrived two companies of the guards, one French, the other Swiss. The company of French guards was composed half of M. Duhallier's men, and half of M. Dessessart's men.

At nine o'clock, Madame la Première Présidente arrived. As, next to the queen, this was the most considerable personage of the fête, she was received by the city gentlemen, and placed in a box opposite to that which the queen was to occupy.

At ten o'clock, the king's collation, consisting of confitures and other delicacies, was prepared in the little chamber on the side of the church of St. Jean, in front of the silver buffet of the city, which was guarded by four archers.

At midnight, great cries and loud acclamations were heard;

it was the king, who was passing through the streets which led from the Louvre to the Hotel de Ville, and which were all illuminated with colored lamps.

Immediately Messieurs the Échevins, clothed in their cloth robes, and preceded by six sergeants, holding each a flambeau in his hand, went to attend upon the king, whom they met on the steps, where the provost of the merchants offered him the compliment of welcome; a compliment to which his majesty replied by an apology for coming so late, but laying the blame upon M. the Cardinal, who had detained him till eleven o'clock, talking of affairs of state.

His majesty, in full dress, was accompanied by his royal highness Monsieur the Count de Soissons, the Grand Prior, the Duke de Longueville, the Duke d'Elbœuf, the Count d'Harcourt, the Count de la Roche-Guyon, M. de Liancourt, M. de Baradas, the Count de Cramail, and the Chevalier de Souveray.

Everybody observed that the king looked dull and preoccupied.

A closet had been prepared for the king and another for monsieur. In each of these closets were placed masquerade habits. The same had been done with respect to the queen and Madame la Présidente. The nobles and ladies of their majesties' suites were to dress, two by two, in chambers prepared for the purpose.

Before entering his closet the king desired to be informed the moment the cardinal arrived.

Half an hour after the entrance of the king, fresh acclamations were heard: these announced the arrival of the queen. The *échevins* did as they had done before, and, preceded by their sergeants, went to receive their illustrious guest.

The queen entered the great hall; and it was remarked, that, like the king, she looked dull, and moreover, fatigued.

At the moment she entered, the curtain of a small gallery which to that time had been closed, was drawn, and the pale face of the cardinal appeared, he being dressed as a Spanish cavalier. His eyes were fixed upon those of the queen, and a smile of terrible joy passed over his lips: the queen did not wear her diamond studs.

The queen remained for a short time to receive the compliments of the city gentlemen and to reply to the salutations of the ladies.

All at once the king appeared at one of the doors of the hall. The cardinal was speaking to him in a low voice, and the king was very pale.

The king made his way through the crowd without a mask, and the ribbons of his doublet scarcely tied; he went straight to the queen, and in an altered voice, said:

"Why, madame, have you not thought proper to wear your diamond studs, when you know it would have given me so much gratification?"

The queen cast a glance around her, and saw the cardinal behind, with a diabolical smile on his countenance.

"Sire," replied the queen, with a faltering voice, "because, in the midst of such a crowd as this, I feared some accident might happen to them."

"And you were wrong, madame! if I made you that present it was that you might adorn yourself with them. I tell you, again, you were wrong."

And the voice of the king was tremulous with anger: the company looked and listened with astonishment, comprehending nothing of what passed.

"Sire," said the queen, "I can send for them to the Louvre, where they are, and thus your majesty's wishes will be complied with."

"Do so, madame! do so, and that at the quickest; for within an hour the ballet will commence."

The queen bent in token of submission, and followed the ladies who were to conduct her to her closet. On his part, the king returned to his.

A moment of trouble and confusion ensued in the assembly. Everybody had remarked that something had passed between the king and queen, but both of them had spoken so low that all out of respect had kept at a distance of several steps, so that nobody had heard anything. The violins began to sound with all their might, but nobody listened to them.

The king came out first from his closet; he was in a hunting costume of the most elegant description, and monsieur and the other nobles were dressed as he was. This was the costume that became the king the best, and when thus dressed, he really appeared the first gentleman of his kingdom.

The cardinal drew near to the king, and placed in his hand a small casket. The king opened it, and found in it two diamonds.

"What does this mean?" demanded he of the cardinal.

"Nothing," replied the latter; "only, if the queen has the studs, of which I very much doubt, count them, sire, and if you only find ten, ask her majesty who can have stolen from her the two studs that are here."

The king looked at the cardinal as if to interrogate him;

but he had not time to address any question to him; a cry of admiration burst from every mouth. If the king appeared to be the first gentleman of his kingdom, the queen was, without doubt, the most beautiful woman in France. It is true that the habit of a huntress became her admirably; she wore a beaver hat with blue feathers, a surtout of gray-pearl velvet, fastened with diamond clasps, and a petticoat of blue satin, embroidered with silver. On her left shoulder sparkled the diamond studs upon a bow of the same color as the plumes and the petticoat.

The king trembled with joy and the cardinal with vexation; nevertheless, distant as they were from the queen, they could not count the studs; the queen had them; the only question was, had she ten or twelve?

At that moment the violins sounded the signal for the ballet. The king advanced toward Madame la Présidente, with whom he was to dance, and his highness monsieur with the queen. They took their places, and the ballet began.

The king figured opposite the queen, and every time that he passed by her, he devoured with his eyes those studs, of which he could not ascertain the number. A cold sweat covered the brow of the cardinal.

The ballet lasted an hour, and had sixteen *entrées*.

The ballet ended amid the applauses of the whole assemblage, and every one reconducted his lady to her place; but the king took advantage of the privelege he had of leaving his lady, to advance eagerly toward the queen.

"I thank you, madame," said he, "for the deference you have shown to my wishes, but I think you want two of the studs, and I bring them back to you."

At these words he held out to the queen the two studs the cardinal had given him.

"How, sire!" cried the young queen, affecting surprise, "you are giving me then two more; but then I shall have fourteen!"

In fact, the king counted them, and the twelve studs were all on her majesty's shoulder.

The king called the cardinal to him.

"What does this mean, Monsieur the Cardinal?" asked the king in a severe tone.

"This means, sire," replied the cardinal, "that I was desirous of presenting her majesty with these two studs, and that not daring to offer them myself, I adopted these means of inducing her to accept them."

"And I am the more grateful to your eminence," replied

Anne of Austria, with a smile that proved she was not the dupe of this ingenious piece of gallantry, "from being certain these two studs have cost you as dearly as all the others cost his majesty."

Then, after bowing to the king and the cardinal, the queen resumed her way to the chamber in which she had dressed, and where she was to take off her ball costume.

The attention which we have been obliged to give, during the commencement of this chapter, to the illustrious personages we have introduced in it, has diverted us for an instant from him to whom Anne of Austria owed the extraordinary triumph she had obtained over the cardinal; and who, confounded, unknown, lost in the crowd gathered at one of the doors, looked on at this scene, comprehensible only to four persons, the king, the queen, his eminence, and himself.

The queen had just regained her chamber, and D'Artagnan was about to retire, when he felt his shoulder lightly touched; he turned round, and saw a young woman who made him a sign to follow her. The face of this young woman was covered with a black velvet mask, but, notwithstanding this precaution, which was, in fact, taken rather against others than against him, he at once recognized his usual guide, the light and intelligent Madame Bonacieux.

On the evening before, they had scarcely seen each other for a moment at the apartment of the Swiss Germain, whither D'Artagnan had sent for her. The haste which the young woman was in, to convey to her mistress the excellent news of the happy return of her messenger, prevented the two lovers from exchanging more than a few words. D'Artagnan then followed Madame Bonacieux, moved by a double sentiment, love and curiosity. During the whole of the way, and in proportion as the corridors became more deserted, D'Artagnan wished to stop the young woman, seize her, and gaze upon her, were it only for a minute; but quick as a bird, she glided between his hands, and when he wished to speak to her, her finger placed upon her mouth, with a little imperative gesture full of grace, reminded him that he was under the command of a power which he must blindly obey, and which forbade him even to make the slightest complaint; at length, after winding about for a minute or two, Madame Bonacieux opened the door of a closet, which was entirely dark, and led D'Artagnan into it. There she made a fresh sign of silence, and opening a second door concealed by a tapestry, and which opening spread at once a brilliant light, she disappeared.

D'Artagnan remained for a moment motionless, asking himself where he could be; but soon a ray of light which penetrated through the chamber, together with the warm and perfumed air which reached him from the same aperture, the conversation of two or three ladies in a language at once respectful and elegant, and the word "majesty" two or three times repeated, indicated clearly that he was in a closet attached to the queen's chamber.

The young man waited the event quietly in comparative darkness.

The queen appeared to be cheerful and happy, which seemed to astonish the persons who surrounded her, and who were accustomed to see her almost always sad and full of care. The queen attributed this joyous feeling to the beauty of the fête, to the pleasure she had experienced in the ballet, and as it is not permissible to contradict a queen, whether she smile or whether she weep, all rivaled each other in expatiating upon the gallantry of messieurs the *échevins* of the good city of Paris.

Although D'Artagnan did not at all know the queen, he soon distinguished her voice from the others, at first by a slightly foreign accent, and next by that tone of domination naturally impressed upon all sovereign expressions. He heard her approach, and withdraw from the partially open door, and twice or three times he even saw the shadow of a person intercept the light.

At length a hand and an arm, surpassingly beautiful in their form and whiteness, glided through the tapestry. D'Artagnan, at once, comprehended that this was his recompense: he cast himself on his knees, seized the hand, and touched it respectfully with his lips; then the hand was withdrawn, leaving in his an object which he perceived to be a ring; the door immediately closed, and D'Artagnan found himself again in complete darkness.

D'Artagnan placed the ring on his finger, and again waited: it was evident that all was not yet over. After the reward of his devotion that of his love was to come. Besides, although the ballet was danced, the evening's pleasures had scarcely begun; supper was to be served at three, and the clock of St. Jean had struck three-quarters past two.

The sound of voices diminished by degrees in the adjoining chamber; the company was then heard departing; then the door of the closet in which D'Artagnan was, was opened, and Madame Bonacieux entered quickly.

"You at last?" cried D'Artagnan.

"Silence!" said the young woman, placing her hand upon his lips; "silence! and begone the same way you came!"

"But where and when shall I see you again?" cried D'Artagnan.

"A note which you will find at home will tell you. Begone! begone!"

And at these words she opened the door of the corridor, and pushed D'Artagnan out of the closet. D'Artagnan obeyed like a child, without the least resistance or objection, which proved that he was downright really in love.

CHAPTER XXIII.

THE RENDEZVOUS.

D'ARTAGNAN ran home immediately, and although it was three o'clock in the morning, and he had some of the worst reputed quarters of Paris to pass through, he met with no misadventure. Every one knows that drunkards and lovers have a protecting deity.

He found the door of his passage open, sprang up the stairs, and knocked softly, in a manner agreed upon between him and his lackey. Planchet,* whom he had sent home two hours before from the Hotel de Ville, desiring him to be careful and sit up for him, opened the door to him.

"Has any one brought a letter for me?" asked D'Artagnan eagerly.

"No one has *brought* a letter, monsieur," replied Planchet; "but there is one come of itself."

"What do you mean by that, you stupid fellow?"

"I mean to say that when I came in, although I had the key of your apartment in my pocket, and that key had never been out of my possession, I found a letter upon the green table-cover in your bedchamber."

"And where is that letter?"

"I left it where I found it, monsieur. It is not natural for letters to enter in this manner into people's houses. If the window had been open, even in the smallest way, I should think nothing of it; but, no; all was as close as possible. Beware, monsieur, there is certainly some magic in it."

*There is no doubt the reader will ask, as the Translator does, "How came Planchet here?" We left him "stiff as a rush" from fatigue, being carried to bed in London.

While Planchet was saying this, the young man had darted
into his chamber, and seized and opened the letter; it was
from Madame Bonacieux, and was conceived in these terms:

"There are many thanks to be offered to you, and to be
transmitted to you. Be this evening about ten o'clock, at
St. Cloud, in front of the pavilion built at the corner of the
hotel of M. d'Estrées.—C. B."

While reading this letter, D'Artagnan felt his heart dilated
and compressed by that delicious spasm which tortures and
caresses the hearts of lovers.

It was the first billet he had received, it was the first rendezvous that had ever been granted him. His heart, swelled
by the intoxication of joy, felt ready to dissolve away at the
very gate of that terrestrial paradise called Love!

"Well, monsieur," said Planchet, who had observed his
master grow red and pale successively; "did I not guess
truly? is it not some bad business or other?"

"You are mistaken, Planchet," replied D'Artagnan; "and,
as a proof, there is a crown to drink my health."

"I am much obliged to monsieur, for the crown he has
given me, and I promise him I will obey his instructions exactly; but it is not the less true that letters which come in
this manner into shut-up houses——"

"Fall from heaven, my friend, fall from heaven."

"Then monsieur is satisfied?" asked Planchet.

"My dear Planchet, I am the happiest of men!"

"And I may profit by monsieur's happiness, and may go to
bed?"

"Yes, go."

"May the blessings of heaven fall upon monsieur; but it is
not the less true that that letter——"

And Planchet retired, shaking his head with an air of doubt,
which the liberality of D'Artagnan had not entirely removed

Left alone, D'Artagnan read and re-read his billet, then he
kissed and re-kissed twenty times the lines traced by the hand
of his beautiful mistress. At length he went to bed, fell
asleep, and had golden dreams.

At seven o'clock in the morning he arose and called Planchet, who, at the second summons, opened the door, his
countenance not yet quite free from the anxiety of the preceding night.

"Planchet," said D'Artagnan, "I am going out for all day,
perhaps; you are, therefore, your own master till seven o'clock

in the evening; but at seven o'clock you must hold yourself
in readiness with two horses."

"There!" said Planchot, "we are going again, it appears,
to have our skins pierced through, and rubbed off in all directions!"

"You will take your musketoon and your pistols."

"There now! did I not say so?" cried Planchet. "I was
sure of it; that cursed letter."

"Come, don't be afraid! you silly fellow; there is nothing
in hand but a party of pleasure."

"Ah! like the charming journey the other day, when it
rained billets, and produced a crop of steel-traps!"

"Well, if you are really afraid, Monsieur Planhcet," resumed
D'Artagnan. "I will go without you; I prefer traveling
alone to having a companion who entertains the least fear."

"Monsieur does me wrong," said Planchet; "I thought he
had seen me at work."

"Yes, but I do not know whether you had not worn out all
your courage the first time."

"Monsieur shall see, upon occasion, that I have some left;
only I beg monsieur not to be too prodigal of it, if he wishes
it to last long."

"Do you believe you have still a certain amount of it to expend
this evening?"

"I hope I have monsieur."

"Well, then, I depend upon you."

"At the appointed hour I shall be ready; only I believe
that monsieur had but one horse in the guard stables."

"Perhaps there is but one at this moment; but by this evening
there will be four."

"It appears that our journey was a remounting journey
then?"

"Exactly so," said D'Artagnan; and nodding to Planchet,
he went out.

M. Bonacieux was standing at his door. D'Artagnan's
intention was to go out without speaking to the worthy mercer; but the latter made so polite and friendly a salutation, that
his tenant felt obliged, not only to stop, but to enter into
conversation with him.

Besides, how was it possible to avoid a little condescension
toward a husband, whose pretty wife had appointed a meeting
with you that same evening at St. Cloud, opposite the pavilion
of M. d'Estrées? D'Artagnan approached him with the most
amiable air he could assume.

The conversation naturally fell upon the incarceration of

the poor man. M. Bonacieux, who was ignorant that D'Artagnan had overheard his conversation with the unknown of Meung, related to his young tenant the persecutions of that monster, M. de Laffemas, whom he never ceased to qualify, during his account, with the title of the cardinal's executioner, and expatiated at great length upon the Bastille, the bolts, the wickets, the dungeons, the loopholes, the gratings, and the instruments of torture.

D'Artagnan listened to him with exemplary complaisance, and when he had finished said:

"And Madame Bonacieux, do you know who carried her off? for I do not forget that I owe to that unpleasant circumstance the good fortune of having made your acquaintance."

"Ah!" said Bonacieux, "they took good care not to tell me that, and my wife, on her part, has sworn to me by all that's sacred, that she does not know. But you," continued M. Bonacieux, in a tone of perfect bonhomie, "what has become of you for several days past? I have not seen either you or any of your friends, and I don't think you could pick up all that dust on the pavement of Paris that I saw Planchet brush off your boots yesterday."

"You are right, my dear M. Bonacieux, my friends and I have been on a little journey."

"Far from Paris?"

"Oh lord, no! about forty leagues only. We went to take M. Athos to the waters of Forges, where my friends have remained."

"And you have returned, have you not?" replied M. Bonacieux, giving to his countenance the most jocular air. "A handsome young fellow like you does not obtain long leaves of absence from his mistress; and we were impatiently waited for at Paris, were we not?"

"*Ma foi!*" said the young man, laughing, "I am fain to confess it, and so much the more readily, my dear Bonacieux, as I see there is no concealing anything from you. Yes, I was expected, and impatiently, I assure you."

A slight shade passed over the brow of Bonacieux, but so slight that D'Artagnan did not perceive it.

"And we are going to be recompensed for our diligence?" said Bonacieux, with a trifling alteration in his voice—so trifling, indeed, that D'Artagnan did not perceive it any more than he had the shade which, an instant before, had darkened the countenance of the worthy man.

"Ah, I hope you are a true prophet!" said D'Artagnan, laughing.

"No; that which I say is only that I may know whether you will be late."

"Why do you ask me that question, my dear host? Do you intend to sit up for me?"

"No; only since my arrest and the robbery that was committed in my house, I am alarmed every time I hear a door opened, particularly in the night. What the deuce can you expect? I told you I was no man of the sword."

"Well, don't be alarmed if I come home at one, two or three o'clock in the morning; indeed, do not be alarmed if I do not come at all.'"

This time Bonacieux became so pale that D'Artagnan could not do otherwise than perceive it, and asked him what was the matter?

"Nothing," replied Bonacieux, "nothing; only since my misfortunes I have been subject to faintness, which seizes me all at once, and I have just felt a cold shiver. Pay no attention to it; you have nothing to occupy yourself with but being happy."

"Then I have a full occupation, for I am so."

"Not yet—wait a little; this evening, you said."

'Well, this evening will come, thank God! And perhaps you look for it with as much impatience as I do; perhaps this evening Madame Bonacieux will visit the conjugal domicile."

"Madame Bonacieux is not at liberty this evening," replied the husband seriously; "she is detained at the Louvre this evening by her duties."

"So much the worse for you, my dear host, so much the worse for you! When I am happy, I wish all the world to be so; but it appears that it is not possible."

And the young man departed, laughing at the joke, which he thought he alone could comprehend.

"Ah, have your laugh out!" replied Bonacieux, in a sepulchral tone.

But D'Artagnan was too far off to hear him, and if he had heard him, in the disposition of mind he then enjoyed he, certes would not have remarked it.

He took his way toward the hotel of M. de Tréville: his visit of the day before had been very short and very little explicative.

He found M. de Tréville in the joy of his heart. He had thought the king and queen charming at the ball. It is true the cardinal had been particularly ill-tempered; he had retired at one o'clock under the pretense of being indisposed. As to their majesties, they did not return to the Louvre till six o'clock.

"Now," said M. de Tréville, lowering his voice, and looking round to every corner of the apartment to see if they were alone, "now let us talk about you, my young friend; for it is evident that your fortunate return has something to do with the joy of the king, the triumph of the queen, and the humiliation of the cardinal. You must take care of yourself."

"What have I to fear," replied D'Artagnan, "as long as I shall have the good fortune to enjoy the favor of their majesties?"

"Everything, believe me. The cardinal is not the man to forget a mystification until he has settled his accounts with the mystifier; and the mystifier appears to me to have the air of being a certain young Gascon of my acquaintance."

"Do you think that the cardinal knows as much as you do, and knows that I have been to London?"

"The devil! you said London! Was it from London you brought that beautiful diamond that glitters on your finger? Beware, my dear D'Artagnan! a present from an enemy is not a good thing. Are there not some Latin verses upon that subject? Stop!"

"Yes, doubtless," replied D'Artagnan, who had never been able to cram the first rudiments even of that language into his head, and who had by his ignorance driven his master to despair —"yes, doubtless there is one."

"There certainly is one," said M. de Tréville, who had a tincture of letters, "and M. Benserade was quoting it to me the other day. Stop a minute—ah, this is it: 'Timeo Danaos et dona ferentes,' which means, 'Beware of the enemy who makes you presents.'"

"This diamond does not come from an enemy, monsieur," replied D'Artagnan; "it comes from the queen."

"From the queen! oh, oh!" said M. de Tréville. "Why it is, indeed, a true royal jewel, which is worth a thousand pistoles if it is worth a denier. By whom did the queen send you this jewel?"

"She gave it to me herself."

"Where?"

"In the closet adjoining the chamber in which she changed her toilet."

"How?"

"Giving me her hand to kiss."

"What! you have kissed the queen's hand?" said M. de Tréville, looking earnestly at D'Artagnan.

"Her majesty did me the honor to grant me that favor."

"And that in the presence of witnesses! Imprudent woman! thrice imprudent!"

"No, monsieur; be satisfied, nobody saw her," replied D'Artagnan, and he related to M. de Tréville how the affair had passed.

"Oh, the women, the women!" cried the old soldier. "I know them by their romantic imaginations; everything that savors of mystery charms them. So you have seen the arm, that was all; you would meet the queen and you would not know her; she might meet you and she would not know who you were?"

"No; but thanks to this diamond," replied the young man.

"Listen to me," said M. de Tréville; "shall I give you a good piece of advice— a piece of friendly advice?"

"You will do me honor, monsieur," said D'Artagnan.

"Well, then, go to the nearest goldsmith's, and sell that diamond for the highest price you can get from him; however much of a Jew he may be, he will give you at least eight hundred pistoles. Pistoles have no name, young man, and that ring has a terrible one, which may betray him who wears it."

"Sell this ring—a ring which comes from my sovereign! never!" said D'Artagnan.

"Then at least turn the collet inside, you silly fellow; for everybody must be aware that a cadet from Gascony does not find such gems in his mother's jewel-case."

"You think, then, that I have something to dread?" asked D'Artagnan.

"I mean to say, young man, that he who sleeps over a mine, the match of which is already lighted, may consider himself in safety in comparison with you."

"The devil!" said D'Artagnan, whom the positive tone of M. de Tréville began to make a little uneasy—"the devil what must I do?"

"Be particularly, and at all times, on your guard. The cardinal has a tenacious memory and a long arm; you may depend upon it, he will repay you by some ill turn."

"But what sort of one?"

"Eh! how can I tell? Has he not all the devil's tricks at command? The least that can be expected is that you will be arrested."

"What! will they dare to arrest a man in his majesty's service?"

"*Pardieu!* they did not scruple much in the case of Athos. At all events, young man, depend upon one who has been thirty years at court. Do not lull yourself in security, or you will be lost; but, on the contrary—and it is I who tell you so—see enemies in all directions. If anyone seeks a quarrel with you, shun it, were it with a child of ten years old; if you are attacked by day or by night, fight, but retreat, without shame; if you cross a bridge, feel every plank of it with your foot, lest one should give way beneath you; if you pass before a house which is being built, look up, for fear a stone should fall upon your head; if you stay out late, be always followed by your lackey, and let your lackey be armed, if, by the by, you can be sure of your lackey. Mistrust everybody, your friend, your brother, your mistress—your mistress in particular."

D'Artagnan blushed.

"Of my mistress," repeated he mechanically; "and why rather her than any other?"

"Because a mistress is one of the cardinal's favorite means —he has not one that is more expeditious; a woman will sell you for ten pistoles, witness Dalila. You are acquainted with the Scriptures, eh?"

D'Artagnan thought of the appointment Madame Bonacieux had made with him for that very evening; but we are bound to say, to the credit of our hero, that the bad opinion entertained by M. de Tréville of women in general, did not inspire him with the least suspicion of his pretty hostess.

"But, à propos," resumed M. de Tréville, "what has become of your three companions?"

"I was about to ask you if you had heard any news of them."

"None whatever, monsieur."

"Well, I left them on my road: Porthos at Chantilly, with a duel on his hands; Aramis at Crèvecœur, with a ball in his shoulder; and Athos at Amiens, detained by an accusation of coining!"

"See there, now!" said M. de Tréville; "and how the devil did you escape?"

"By a miracle, monsieur, I must acknowledge, with a sword-thrust in my breast, and by nailing M. le Comte de Wardes, on the by-road to Calais, like a butterfly on a tapestry."

"There again! De Wardes, one of the cardinal's men, a cousin of Rochefort's. But stop, my friend, I have an idea."

"Speak, monsieur."

"In your place, 1 would do one thing."

"What, monsieur?"

"While his eminence was seeking for me in Paris, I would take, without sound of drum or trumpet, the road to Picardy, and would go and make some inquiries concerning my three companions. What the devil! they merit richly that piece of attention on your part."

"The advice is good, monsieur, and to-morrow I will set out."

"To-morrow! and why not this evening?"

"This evening, monsieur, I am detained in Paris by an indispensable business."

"Ah, young man, young man! some love-passage or other! Take care, I repeat to you, take care! it is woman who was the ruin of us all, is the ruin of us all, and will be the ruin of us all as long as the world stands. Take my advice, and set out this evening."

"It is impossible, monsieur."

"You have given your word, then?"

"Yes, monsieur."

"Ah, that's quite another thing; but promise me, if you should not happen to be killed to-night, that you will go to-morrow."

"I promise you, monsieur."

"Do you want money?"

"I still have fifty pistoles. That, I think, is as much as I shall want."

"But your companions?"

"I don't think they can be in need of any. We left Paris with each seventy-five pistoles in his pocket."

"Shall I see you again before your departure?"

"I think not, monsieur, unless anything fresh should happen."

"Well, a pleasant journey to you then."

"Thank you, monsieur."

And D'Artagnan left M. de Tréville, penetrated more than ever by his paternal solicitude for his musketeers.

He called successively at the abodes of Athos, Porthos, and Aramis. Neither of them had returned. Their lackeys likewise were absent, and nothing had been heard of either masters or servants.

He would have inquired after them at their mistress', but he was neither acquainted with Porthos' nor Aramis' and as to Athos, he had not one.

As he passed the Hotel des Gardes, he took a glance into the stables. Three out of the four horses were already arrived. Planchet, all astonishment, was busy grooming them, and had already finished two.

"Ah, monsieur," said Planchet, on perceiving D'Artagnan, "how glad I am to see you."

"Why so, Planchet?" asked the young man.

"Do you place confidence in our landlord, Mr. Bonacieux?"

"I? Not the least in the world."

"Oh, you do quite right, monsieur."

"But, why do you ask?"

"Because, while you were talking with him, I watched you without listening to you; and, monsieur, his countenance changed so, two to three times!"

"Bah!"

"Preoccupied as monsieur was with the letter he had received, he did not observe that; but I, whom the strange fashion in which that letter came into the house had placed on my guard, I did not lose a movement of his feature."

"And you found it?"

"Traitorous, monsieur."

"Indeed!"

'Still more; as soon as monsieur had left, and disappeared round the corner of the street, M. Bonacieux took his hat, shut his door, and set off at a quick pace in an opposite direction."

"It seems you are right, Planchet; all this appears to be a little mysterious; and be assured that we will not pay him our rent until the matter shall be categorically explained to us."

"Monsieur jokes, but monsieur will see."

"What would you have, Planchet? It is written, that what must be must!"

"Monsieur has not then renounced his excursion for this evening?"

"Quite the contrary, Planchet; the more ill-wind I have reason to entertain toward M. Bonacieux, the more punctual I shall be in keeping the appointment made with me in that letter which makes you so uneasy."

"Then that is monsieur's determination?"

"Most decidedly, my friend; at nine o'clock, then, be ready here, at the hotel, I will come and take you."

Planchet seeing there was no longer any hope of making his master renounce his project, heaved a profound sigh, and set to work to groom the third horse.

As to D'Artagnan, being at bottom a prudent youth instead of returning home, he went and dined with the Gascon priest, who, at the time of the distress of the four friends, had given them a breakfast of chocolate.

CHAPTER XXIV.

THE PAVILION.

At NINE o'clock D'Artagnan was at the Hotel des Gardes; he found Planchet under arms. The fourth horse had arrived. Planchet was armed with his musketoon and a pistol. D'Artagnan had his sword, and placed two pistols in his belt; then both mounted, and departed quietly. It was quite dark, and no one saw them go out. Planchet took his place behind his master, and kept at a distance of about ten paces from him.

D'Artagnan crossed the quays, went out by the gate of La Conference, and proceeded along the road, much more beautiful then than it is now, which leads to St. Cloud.

As long as he was in the city, Planchet kept at the respectful distance he had imposed upon himself; but as soon as the road began to be more lonely and dark, he drew softly nearer; so that when they entered the Bois de Boulogne, he found himself riding quite naturally side by side with his master. In fact, we must not dissemble, that the oscillation of the tall trees, and the reflection of the moon in the dark underwood, gave him serious uneasiness. D'Artagnan could not help perceiving that more than usual was passing in the mind of his lackey, and said:

"Well, Master Planchet! what is the matter with us now?"

"Don't you think, monsieur, that woods are like churches?"

"How so, Planchet!"

"Because we dare not speak aloud in one or the other."

"But why do you not dare speak aloud, Planchet?—because you are afraid?"

"Afraid of being heard?—yes, monsieur."

"Afraid of being heard! Why there is nothing improper in our conversation, my dear Planchet, and no one could find fault with it."

"Ah, monsieur!" replied Planchet, recurring to his besetting idea, "that M. Bonacieux has something vicious in his eyebrows, and something very unpleasant in the play of his lips."

"What the devil makes you think of Bonacieux now?"

"Monsieur, we think of what we can, and not of what we will."

"Because you are a coward, Planchet."

"Monsieur, we must not confound prudence with cow-ardice; prudence is a virtue."

"And you are very virtuous, are you not, Planchet?"

"Monsieur, is not that the barrel of a musket which glitters yonder? Had we not better lower our heads?"

"In truth," murmured D'Artagnan, to whom M. de Tré-ville's recommendation recurred, "in truth, this animal will end by making me afraid." And he put his horse into a trot.

Planchet followed the movements of his master, as if he had been his shadow, and was soon trotting by his side.

"Are we going to continue this pace all night?" asked Planchet.

"No, for you, on your part, are at your journey's end."

"I, monsieur, am arrived! and monsieur?"

"Why, I am going a few steps farther."

"And does monsieur intend to leave me here alone?"

"You certainly are afraid, Planchet?"

"No but I only beg leave to observe to monsieur, that the night will be very cold, that chills bring on rheumatism, and that a lackey who has the rheumatism makes but a poor servant particularly to a master as active as monsieur."

"Well, if you are cold, Planchet, you can go into one of those cabarets that you see yonder, and be waiting for me at the door by six o'clock in the morning."

"Monsieur, I have eaten and drunk respectfully the crown you gave me this morning; so that I have not a sou left, in case I should be cold."

"Here's a half a pistole. To-morrow morning, then."

D'Artagnan sprang from his horse, threw the bridle to Planchet, and departed at a quick pace, folding his cloak round him.

"Good Lord, how cold I am!" cried Planchet, as soon as he had lost sight of his master; and in such haste was he to warm himself, that he went straight to a house set out with all the attributes of a suburban auberge, and knocked at the door.

In the meantime D'Artagnan, who had plunged into a by-path, continued his route, and gained St. Cloud; but instead of following the high street, he turned behind the chateau, reached a sort of retired lane, and found himself soon in front of the pavilion named. It was situated in a very private spot. A high wall, at the angle of which was the pavilion, ran along one side of this lane, and on the other was a little garden, connected with a poor cottage, which was protected from passengers by a hedge.

He gained the place appointed, and as no signal had been given him by which to announce his presence, he waited.

Not the least noise was to be heard; it might be imagined that he was a hundred miles from the capital.   D'Artagnan leaned against the hedge, after having cast a glance behind him.   Beyond that hedge, that garden, and that cottage, a dark mist enveloped with its folds that immensity in which sleeps Paris, a vast void from which glittered a few luminous points, the funeral stars of that hell!

But for D'Artagnan all aspects were clothed happily, all ideas wore a smile, all darknesses were diaphanous. The appointed hour was about to strike.

In fact, at the end of a few minutes, the belfry of St. Cloud let fall slowly ten strokes from its sonorous jaws.

There was something melancholy in this brazen voice pouring out its lamentations amid the night.

But every one of those hours which composed the expected hour, vibrated harmoniously to the heart of the young man.

His eyes were fixed upon the little pavilion situated at the angle of the wall, of which all the windows were closed with shutters, except one on the first story.   Through this window shone a mild light which silvered the foliage of two or three linden trees, which formed a group outside the park.   There could be no doubt that behind this little window, which threw forth such friendly beams, the pretty Madame Bonacieux expected him.

Wrapt in this sweet idea, D'Artagnan waited half an hour without the least impatience, his eyes fixed upon that charming little abode of which he could perceive a part of the ceiling with its gilded moldings, attesting the elegance of the rest of the apartment.

The belfry of St. Cloud struck half-past ten.

This time, without at all knowing why, D'Artagnan felt a cold shiver run through his veins. Perhaps the cold began to affect him, and he took a perfectly physical sensation for a moral impression.

Then the idea seized him that he had read incorrectly, and that the appointment was for eleven o'clock.   He drew near to the window, and placing himself so that a ray of light should fall upon the letter as he held it, he drew it from his pocket, and read it again; but he had not been mistaken, the appointment was for ten o'clock.

He went and resumed his post, beginning to be pretty uneasy at this silence and this solitude.

Eleven o'clock struck!

D'Artagnan began now really to fear that something had happened to Madame Bonacieux. He clapped his hands three times, the ordinary signal of lovers; but nobody replied to him—not even an echo.

He then thought, with a touch of vexation, that perhaps the young woman had fallen asleep while waiting for him.

He approached the wall, and endeavored to climb up it; but the wall had been recently pointed, and he could obtain no hold.

At that moment he thought of the trees, upon whose leaves the light still shone, and as one of them drooped over the road, he thought that from its branches he might succeed in getting a glimpse of the interior of the room.

The tree was easy to climb. Besides, D'Artagnan was but twenty years old, and consequently had not yet forgotten his schoolboy habits. In an instant he was among the branches, and his keen eyes plunged through the transparent window into the interior of the pavilion.

It was a strange thing, and one which made D'Artagnan tremble from the sole of his foot to the roots of his hair, to find that this soft light, this calm lamp, enlightened a scene of fearful disorder: one of the windows was broken, the door of the chamber had been beaten in, and hung, split in two, on its hinges; a table, which had been covered with an elegant supper, was overturned; the decanters, broken in pieces, and the fruits crushed, strewed the floor; everything in the apartment gave evidence of a violent and desperate struggle; D'Artagnan even fancied he could recognize amid this strange disorder, fragments of garments, and some bloody spots staining the cloth and the curtains.

He hastened down into the street, with a frightful beating at his heart; he wished to see if he could find any other traces of violence.

The little soft light continued to shine in the calm of the night. D'Artagnan then perceived, a thing that he had not before remarked, for nothing had led him to the examination, that the ground, trampled here, and hoof-marked there, presented confused traces of men and horses. Besides, the wheels of a carriage, which appeared to have come from Paris, had made a deep impression in the soft earth, which did not extend beyond the pavilion, but turned again toward Paris.

At length D'Artagnan, in following up his researches, found near the wall a woman's torn glove; which glove, wherever it had not touched the muddy ground, was of irreproachable freshness. It was one of those perfumed gloves that lovers like to snatch from a pretty hand.

As D'Artagnan pursued his investigations, at every fresh discovery a more abundant and more icy sweat broke in large drops from his forehead; his heart was oppressed by a horrible anguish, his respiration was broken and short; and yet he said, to reassure himself, that this pavilion, perhaps, had nothing in common with Madame Bonacieux; that the young woman had made an appointment with him before the pavilion, and not in the pavilion; that she might have been detained in Paris by her duties, or perhaps by the jealousy of her husband.

But all these reasons were combated, destroyed, overthrown, by that feeling of intimate pain which, on certain occasions, takes possession of our being, and cries to us, so as to be understood unmistakably, that some great misfortune is hanging over us.

Then D'Artagnan became almost wild; he ran along the high road, took the path he had before taken, and, coming to the ferry, closely interrogated the boatman.

About seven o'clock in the evening, the boatman said he had taken over a young woman, enveloped in a black mantle, who appeared to be very anxious not to be seen; but, entirely on account of her precautions, the boatman had paid more attention to her, and discovered that she was young and pretty.

There was then, as there is now, a crowd of young and pretty women who came to St. Cloud, and who had great reasons for not being seen, and yet D'Artagnan did not for an instant doubt that it was Madame Bonacieux whom the boatman had remarked.

D'Artagnan took advantage of the lamp which burned in the cabin of the boatman to read the billet of Madame Bonacieux once again, and satisfy himself that he had not been mistaken, that the appointment was at St. Cloud and not elsewhere, before the pavilion of M. d'Estrées and not in another street.

Everything conspired to prove to D'Artagnan that his presentiments had not deceived him, and that a great misfortune had happened.

He again ran back to the château; it appeared to him that something might have happened at the pavilion in his absence, and that fresh information awaited him.

The lane was still empty, and the same soft light shone from the window.

D'Artagnan then thought of that silent, obscure cottage;

some one from it might have seen, no doubt, and might tell of something.

The gate of the enclosure was shut, but he leaped over the hedge, and in spite of the barking of a chained-up dog, went up to the cabin.

No one answered to his first knocking. A silence of death reigned in the cabin as in the pavilion; the cabin, however, was his last resource; he knocked again.

It soon appeared to him that he heard a slight noise within, a timid noise, which seemed itself to tremble lest it should be heard.

Then D'Artagnan ceased to knock, and prayed with an accent so full of anxiety and promises, terror and cajolery, that his voice was of a nature to reassure the most fearful. At length an old, worm-eaten shutter was opened, or rather pushed ajar, but closed again as soon as the light from a miserable lamp which burned in the corner had shone upon the baldrick, sword-belt, and pistol pummels of D'Artagnan. Nevertheless, rapid as the movement had been, D'Artagnan had time to get a glimpse of the head of an old man.

"In the name of heaven!" cried he, "listen to me: I have been waiting for some one who is not come; I am dying with anxiety. Has anything particular happened in the neighborhood? Speak!"

The window was again opened slowly, and the same face appeared again; only it was still more pale than before.

D'Artagnan related his history simply, with the omission of names: he told how he had an appointment with a young woman before that pavilion, and how, not seeing her come, he had climbed the linden tree, and by the light of the lamp had seen the disorder of the chamber.

The old man listened attentively, making a sign only that it all was so; and then, when D'Artagnan had ended, he shook his head with an air that announced nothing good.

"What do you mean?" cried D'Artagnan, "in the name of heaven, tell me, explain yourself."

"Oh! monsieur," said the old man, "ask me nothing; for if I told you what I have seen, certainly no good would befall me."

"You have then seen something?" replied D'Artagnan. "In that case, in the name of heaven," continued he, throwing him a pistole, "tell me what you have seen, and I will pledge you the word of a gentleman that not one of your words shall escape from my heart."

The old man read so much truth and so much grief in the

face of the young man, that he made him a sign to listen, and repeated in a low voice:

"It was scarcely nine o'clock when I heard a noise in the street, and was wondering what it could be, when on coming to my door, I found that somebody was endeavoring to open it. As I am very poor, and am not afraid of being robbed, I went and opened the gate and saw three men at a few paces from it. In the shade was a carriage with two horses, and a man held three saddle horses. These horses evidently belonged to the three men, who were dressed as cavaliers.

"'Ah! my worthy gentlemen,' cried I, 'what do you want?'

"'Have you a ladder?' said the one who appeared to be the leader of the party.

"'Yes, monsieur, the one with which I gather my fruit.'

"'Lend it to us, and go into your house again; there is a crown for the annoyance we have caused you. Only remember this, if you speak a word of what you may see or what you may hear (for you will look and you will listen, I am quite sure, however we may threaten you), you are lost.'

"At these words he threw me a crown, which I picked up, and he took the ladder.

"After shutting the gate behind them, I pretended to return to the house, but I immediately went out at a back door, and stealing along in the shade of the hedge, I gained yonder clump of elder, from which I could hear and see everything.

"The three men brought the carriage up quietly, and took out of it a little man, stout, short, elderly, and commonly dressed in clothes of a dark color, who ascended the ladder very carefully, looked suspiciously in at the window of the pavilion, came down as quietly as he had gone up, and whispered:

"'It is she!'

"Immediately he who had spoken to me approached the door of the pavilion, opened it with a key he had in his hand, closed the door and disappeared, while at the same time the other two men ascended the ladder. The little old man remained at the coach door, the coachman took care of his horses, the lackey held the saddle horses.

"All at once great cries resounded in the pavilion, and a woman came to the window and opened it, as if to throw herself out of it; but as soon as she perceived the other two men, she fell back and they got into the chamber.

"Then I saw no more; but I heard the noise of breaking furniture. The woman screamed and cried for help. But her cries were soon stifled; two of the men appeared, bearing the woman in their arms, and carried her to the carriage, into which the little old man got after her. The leader closed the window, came out an instant after at the door, and satisfied himself that the woman was in the carriage: his two companions were already on horseback; he sprang into his saddle, the lackey took his place by the coachman, the carriage went off at a quick pace, escorted by the three horsemen, and all was over—from that moment I have neither seen nor heard anything."

D'Artagnan, entirely overcome by this terrible story, remained motionless and mute, while all the demons of anger and jealousy were howling in his heart.

"But, my good gentleman," resumed the old man, upon whom this mute despair certainly produced a greater effect than cries and tears would have done; "do not take on so, they did not kill her from you, that's a comfort."

"Do you know anything," said D'Artagnan, "of the man who led this infernal expedition?"

"I don't know him at all."

"But, as you spoke to him you must have seen him."

"Oh, it's a description of him you want?"

"Exactly so."

"A tall, dark man, with black mustaches, dark eyes, and looked like a gentleman."

"That's the man!" cried D'Artagnan, "again he, forever he! He is my demon, to all appearances. And the other?"

"Which?"

"The short one."

"Oh! he was not a gentleman, I'll answer for it; besides, he did not wear a sword, and the others treated him with no consideration."

"Some lackey," murmured D'Artagnan. "Poor girl! poor girl! what have they done with you?"

"You have promised to be secret, my good monsieur?" said the old man.

"And I repeat my promise; be satisfied, I am a gentleman. A gentleman has but his word, and I have given you mine."

With a heavy heart, D'Artagnan again bent his way toward the ferry. Sometimes he hoped it could not be Madame Bonacieux, and that he should find her the next day at the Louvre; sometimes he feared she had had an intrigue with

another, who, in a jealous fit, had surprised her and carried
her off. His mind was torn by doubt, grief, and despair.

"Oh! if I had my three friends here!" cried he, "I should
have, at least, some hopes of finding her; but who knows what
is become of them themselves?"

It was past midnight; the next thing was to find Planchet.
D'Artagnan went successively into all the cabarets in which
there was light, but could not meet with Planchet in any of
them.

At the sixth he began to reflect that the search was rather
hazardous. D'Artagnan had appointed six o'clock in the
morning with his lackey, and wherever he might be, he was
doing as he had bidden him.

Besides, it came into the young man's mind, that by
remaining in the environs of the spot on which this sad event
had passed, he should, perhaps, have some light thrown upon
the mysterious affair. At the sixth cabaret, then, as we said,
D'Artagnan stopped, asked for a bottle of wine of the best
quality, and placing himself in the darkest corner of the
room, determined thus to wait till daylight; but this time
again his hopes were disappointed, and although he listened
with all his ears, he heard nothing, amid the oaths, coarse
jokes, and abuse which passed between the laborers, servants,
and carters, who comprised the honorable society of which he
formed a part, which could put him at all upon the traces of
her who had been stolen from him. He was compelled, then,
after having swallowed the contents of his bottle, to pass the
time as well as to avoid suspicion, to fall into the easiest position in his corner, and to sleep, whether well or ill. D'Artagnan, be it remembered, was only twenty years old, and at that
age sleep has its imprescriptible rights, which it imperiously
insists upon, even in the saddest hearts.

Toward six o'clock, D'Artagnan awoke with that uncomfortable feeling which generally follows a bad night. He was
not long in making his toilette; he examined himself to see if
advantage had not been taken of his sleep, and having found
his diamond ring on his finger, his purse in his pocket, and
his pistols in his belt, he got up, paid for his wine, and went
out to try if he could have any better luck in his search after
his lackey than he had had the night before. The first thing
he perceived through the damp gray mist was honest Planchet,
who, with the two horses in hand, awaited him at the door of
a little blind cabaret, before which D'Artagnan had passed
without even suspecting its existence.

CHAPTER XXV.

PORTHOS.

INSTEAD of returning directly home, D'Artagnan alighted at the door of M. de Tréville, and ran quickly up the stairs. This time he was determined to relate all that had passed. He would doubtless give him good advice in the whole affair; and besides, as M. de Tréville saw the queen almost every day, he might be able to get from her majesty some intelligence of the poor young woman, whom they were doubtless making pay very dearly for her devotedness to her mistress.

M. de Tréville listened to the young man's account with a seriousness which proved that he saw something else in this adventure beside a love affair; and when D'Artagnan had finished:

"Hum!" said he, "all this savors of his eminence, a league off."

"But what is to be done?" said D'Artagnan.

"Nothing, absolutely nothing, at present, but quitting Paris, as I told you, as soon as possible. I will see the queen; I will relate to her the details of the disappearance of this poor woman, of which she is, no doubt, ignorant. These details will guide her on her part, and, on your return, I shall perhaps have some good news to tell you."

D'Artagnan knew that, although a Gascon, M. de Tréville was not in the habit of making promises, and that when by chance he did promise, he generally more than kept his word. He bowed to him, then, full of gratitude for the past and for the future, and the worthy captain, who, on his side, felt a lively interest in this young man, so brave and so resolute, pressed his hand kindly, while wishing him a pleasant journey.

Determined to put the advice of M. de Tréville in practice instantly, D'Artagnan directed his course toward the Rue des Fossoyeurs, in order to superintend the packing of his valise. On approaching the house, he perceived M. Bonacieux, in morning costume, standing at his door. All that the prudent Planchet had said to him the preceding evening recurred to the mind of D'Artagnan, who looked at him with more attention than he had done before. In fact, in addition to that yellow, sickly paleness which indicates the insinuation of the bile in the blood, and which might, besides, be accidental, D'Artagnan remarked something perfidiously significant in

the play of the wrinkled features of his countenance. A
rogue does not laugh in the same way that an honest man
does; a hypocrite does not shed the same sort of tears as fall
from the eyes of a man of good faith. All falsehood is a
mask, and however well-made the mask may be, with a little
attention we may always succeed in distinguishing it from the
true face.

It appeared, then, to D'Artagnan, that M. Bonacieux wore
a mask, and likewise that that mask was very disagreeeable to
look upon.

In consequence of this feeling of repugnance, he was about
to pass without speaking to him, but, as he had done the day
before, M. Bonacieux accosted him.

"Well, young man," said he, "we appear to pass rather
gay nights! Seven o'clock in the morning! Peste! you seem
to reverse ordinary customs, and come home at the hour when
other people are going out."

"No one can reproach you for anything of the kind,
Master Bonacieux," said the young man; "you are a model
for regular people. It is true that when a man possesses a
young and pretty wife, he has no need to seek hapiness elsewhere; happiness comes to meet him, does it not, Monsieur
Bonacieux?"

Bonacieux became as pale as death, and grinned a ghastly
smile.

"Ah! ah!" said Bonacieux, "you are a jocular companion! But where the devil were you gadding last night,
my young master? It does not appear to be very clean in the
crossroads."

D'Artagnan glanced down at his boots, all covered with
mud, but that same glance fell upon the shoes and stockings
of the mercer, and it might have been said they had been
dipped in the same mud-heap; both were stained with splashes
of mud of the same appearance.

Then a sudden idea crossed the mind of D'Artagnan.
That little stout man, short and elderly, that sort of lackey,
dressed in dark clothes, treated without consideration by the
men wearing swords who composed the escort, was Bonacieux
himself! The husband had presided over the carrying off of
his wife!

A terrible inclination immediately took possession of
D'Artagnan to seize the mercer by the throat and strangle
him; but as we have said, he was, occasionally, a very prudent
youth, and he restrained himself. The revolution, however,
which had appeared upon his countenance, was so visible,

that Bonacieux was terrified at it, and he endeavoured to draw back a step or two, but being before the flap of the door, which was shut, the obstacle compelled him to keep his place.

"Ah! ah! but you are joking, my worthy man!" said D'Artagnan. "It appears to me that if my boots want a sponge, your stockings and shoes stand in equal need of a brush. May you not have been philandering a little also, Master Bonacieux? Oh! the devil! that's unpardonable in a man of your age, and who, besides, has such a pretty young wife as yours is!"

"Oh lord! no," said Bonacieux; "but yesterday I went to Saint Mandé, to make some inquiries after a servant, as I cannot possibly do without one, and the roads were so bad that I brought back all this mud, which I have not yet had time to remove."

The place named by Bonacieux as that which had been the object of his journey was a fresh proof in support of the suspicions D'Artagnan had conceived. Bonacieux had named Mandé, because Mandé was in an exactly opposite direction to Saint Cloud. This probability afforded him his first consolation. If Bonacieux knew where his wife was, the mercer might, at any time, by the employment of extreme means, be forced to open his teeth and allow his secret to escape. The question, then, only was to change this probability into a certainty.

"I beg your pardon, my dear Monsieur Bonacieux, if I don't stand upon ceremony," said D'Artagnan, "but nothing makes one so thirsty as want of sleep; I am parched with thirst; allow me to take a glass of water in your apartment; you know that is never refused among neighbors."

And without waiting for the permission of his host, D'Artagnan went quickly into the house, and cast a rapid glance at the bed. The bed had not been slept in. Bonacieux had not been to bed. He had only been back an hour or two; he had accompanied his wife to the place of her confinement, or else, at least, to the first relay.

"Many thanks to you, Master Bonacieux," said D'Artagnan, emptying his glass: "that is all I wanted of you. I will now go up into my room, I will make Planchet brush my boots, and when he has done, I will, if you like, send him to you to brush your shoes."

And he left the mercer quite astonished at his singular farewell, and asking himself if he had not been a little inconsiderate.

At the top at the stairs he found Planchet in a great fright.

"Ah! monsieur!" cried Planchet, as soon as he perceived his master, "here is more trouble! I thought you would never come in!"

"What's the matter now, Planchet?"

"Oh! I give you a hundred, I give you a thousand times to guess, monsieur, the visit I have received in your absence."

"When?"

"About half an hour ago, while you were at M. de Tréville's."

"Who has been here? Come, speak."

"M. de Cavois."

"M. de Cavois?"

"In person."

"The captain of his eminence's guards?"

"Himself."

"Did he come to arrest me?"

"I have no doubt he did, monsieur, for all his carrrying manner."

"Was he so polite, then?"

"All honey, monsieur."

"Indeed!"

"He came, he said, on the part of his eminence, who wished you well, and to beg you to follow him to the Palais Cardinal."*

"What did you answer him?"

"That the thing was impossible, seeing that you were not at home, as he might perceive."

"Well, what did he say then?"

"That you must not fail to call upon him in the course of the day; and then he added, in a low voice, 'Tell your master that his eminence is very well disposed toward him, and that his fortune perhaps depends upon this interview.'"

"The snare is not very skillfully set for the cardinal," replied the young man smiling.

"Oh! yes, I saw the snare, and I answered you would be quite in despair, on your return.

"'Where is he gone to?' asked M. de Cavois.

"'To Troyes, in Champagne,' I answered.

"'And when did he set out?'

"'Yesterday evening.'"

---

*M. Dumas calls it the Palais Royal, but it was called the Palais Cardinal before Richelieu had given it to the king; indeed, I doubt whether it was built at all at the period of this story.—TRANS.

"Planchet, my friend," interrupted D'Artagnan, "you are really a jewel of a man."

"You will understand, monsieur, I thought there would be still time, if you wish, to see M. de Cavois, to contradict me by saying you were not yet gone; the falsehood would then lie at my door, and as I am not a gentleman, I may be allowed to lie."

"Be of good heart, Planchet, you shall preserve your reputation as a man of truth; in a quarter of an hour we will set off."

"That's just the advice I was going to give, monsieur: and where are we going, may I ask, without being too curious?"

"*Pardieu!* in the opposite direction to that which you said I was gone. Besides, are you not as anxious to learn news of Grimaud, Mousqueton, and Bazin, as I am to know what has become of Athos, Porthos, and Aramis?"

"Oh! yes, monsieur," said Planchet, "and I will go as soon as you please; indeed, I think provincial air will suit us much better just now than the air of Paris. So then——"

"So then, pack up our necessaries, Planchet, and let us be off. On my part, I will go out with my hands in my pockets, that nothing may be suspected. You can join me at the Hotel des Gardes. Apropos, Planchet, I think you are right with respect to our host, and that he is decidedly a frightfully low wretch."

"Ah! monsieur! you may take my word when I tell you anything. I am a physiognomist, I assure you!"

D'Artagnan went out first, as had been agreed upon; then, in order that he might have nothing to reproach himself with, he directed his steps toward the residence of his three friends: no news had been received of them; only a letter, all perfumed, and of an elegant writing in small characters, was come for Aramis. D'Artagnan took charge of it. Ten minutes afterward, Planchet joined him at the stables of the Hotel des Gardes. D'Artagnan, in order that there might be no time lost, had saddled his horse himself.

"That's well," said he to Planchet, when the latter added the portmanteau to the equipment; "now saddle the other three horses ."

"Do you think, then, monsieur, that we shall travel faster with two horses apiece?" said Planchet, with his cunning air.

"No master joker," replied D'Artagnan, "but with our four horses we may bring back our three friends, if we should have the good fortune to find them living."

"Which must be a great chance," replied Planchet, "but we must not despair of the mercy of God."

"Amen!" cried D'Artagnan, getting into his saddle.

As they went from the Hotel des Gardes, they separated, leaving the street at opposite ends, one having to quit Paris by the barrier of La Villette, and the other by the barrier Mont-Martre, with an understanding to meet again beyond St. Denis, a strategetic maneuver which, having been executed with equal punctuality, was crowned with the most fortunate results. D'Artagnan and Planchet entered Pierrefitte together.

Planchet was more courageous, it must be admitted, by day than by night. His natural prudence, however, never forsook him for a single instant; he had forgotten not one of the incidents of the first journey, and he looked upon everybody he met on the road as an enemy. It followed that his hat was forever in his hand, which procured him some severe reprimands from D'Artagnan, who feared that his excess of politeness would lead people to think he was the lackey of a man of no consequence.

Nevertheless, whether the passengers were really touched by the urbanity of Planchet, or whether this time nobody was posted on the young man's road, our two travelers arrived at Chantilly without any accident, and alighted at the hotel of the Grand Saint Martin, the same they had stopped at on their first journey.

The host, on seeing a young man followed by a lackey with two led horses, advanced respectfully to the door. Now, as they had already traveled eleven leagues, D'Artagnan thought it time to stop, whether Porthos were or were not in the hotel. And then perhaps it would not be prudent to ask at once what had become of the musketeers. It resulted from these reflections that D'Artagnan, without asking intelligence of any kind, alighted, recommended the horses to the care of his lackey, entered a small room destined to receive such as wished to be alone, and desired the host to bring him a bottle of his best wine, and as good a breakfast as possible, a desire which further corroborated the high opinion the aubergiste had formed of the traveler at first sight.

D'Artagnan was therefore served with a miraculous celerity.

The regiment of the guards was recruited among the first gentlemen of the kingdom, and D'Artagnan, followed by a lackey with four magnificent horses, could not fail to make a sensation. The host desired to wait upon him himself, which

D'Artagnan perceiving, ordered two glasses to be brought, and commenced the following conversation:

"*Ma foi!* my good host," said D'Artagnan, filling the two glasses, "I asked for a bottle of your best wine, and if you have deceived me, you will be punished by that you have sinned in, for seeing that I hate drinking by myself, you shall drink with me. Take your glass then, and let us drink. But what shall we drink to, so as to avoid wounding any susceptibility? Let us drink to the prosperity of your establishment."

"Your lordship does me much honor," said the host, "and I thank you sincerely for your kind wish."

"But don't mistake," said D'Artagnan, "there is more selfishness in my toast than perhaps you may think; for it is only in prosperous establishments that one is well received; in hotels that do not flourish, everything is in confusion, and the traveler is a victim to the embarrassments of his host: now I travel a great deal, particularly on this road, and I wish to see all aubergistes making a fortune."

"I was thinking," said the host, "that it was not the first time I had had the honor of seeing monsieur."

"Bah! I have passed, perhaps, ten times through Chantilly, and out of the ten times I have stopped three or four times at your house at least. Why, I was here only ten or twelve days ago; I was conducting some friends, three or four musketeers, one of whom, by-the-by, had a dispute with a stranger, an unknown, a man who sought a quarrel with him for I don't know what."

"Ah! exactly so," said the host; "I remember it perfectly. Is it not M. Porthos, that your lordship means?"

"Yes; that is my companion's name. Good heavens! my dear host; I hope nothing has happened to him?"

"Your honor must have observed that he could not continue his journey."

"Why, to be sure, he promised to rejoin us, and we have seen nothing of him."

"He has done us the honor to remain here."

"What! he has done you the honor to remain here?"

"Yes, monsieur, in this hotel; and we are even a little uneasy——"

"On what account?"

"Certain expenses he has been at."

"Well; but whatever expenses he may have incurred, I am sure he is in a condtion to pay them."

"Ah! monsieur, you infuse balm into my mind! We have

made considerable advances; and this morning only the surgeon declared that if M. Porthos did not pay him, he should look to me, as it was I who had sent for him."

"What, is Porthos wounded, then?"

"I cannot tell you, monsieur."

"What! you cannot tell me! surely you ought to be able to tell me better than any other person."

"Yes; but in our situation we must not say all we know; particularly when we have been warned that our ears should answer for our tongues."

"Well! can I see Porthos?"

"Certainly, monsieur. Take the stairs on your right; go up the first flight, and knock at No. 1. Only warn him that it is you."

"Warn him! why should I do that?"

"Because, monsieur, some mischief might happen to you."

"Of what kind, in the name of wonder?"

"M. Porthos may imagine you belong to the house, and in a fit of passion might run his sword through you, or blow out your brains."

"What have you done to him, then?"

"We asked him for money."

"The devil!—ah! I can understand that; it is a demand that Porthos takes very ill when he is not in funds; but I know he ought to be so at present."

"We thought so too, monsieur; as our concern is carried on very regularly, and we make our bills every week, at the end of eight days we presented our account; but it appeared we had chosen an unlucky moment, for at the first word on the subject, he sent us to all the devils; it is true he had been playing the day before."

"Playing the day before!—and with whom?"

"Lord! who can say, monsieur? With some gentleman who was traveling this way, to whom he proposed a game of lansquenet."

"That's it then! and the foolish fellow has lost all he had."

"Even to his horse, monsieur; for when the gentleman was about to set out, we perceived that his lackey was saddling M. Porthos' horse, as well as his master's. When we observed this to him, he told us to trouble ourselves with our own business, as this horse belonged to him. We also informed M. Porthos of what was going on; but he told us we were scoundrels, to doubt a gentleman's word; and that as he had said the horse was his, there could be no doubt that it was so."

"That's Porthos all over," murmured D'Artagnan.

"Then," continued the host, "I replied that from the moment we seemed not destined to come to a good understanding with respect to payment, I hoped that he would have, at least, the kindness to grant the favor of his custom to my brother host of the Aigle d'Or; but M. Porthos replied, that my hotel being the best, he should remain where he was.

"This reply was too flattering to allow me to insist on his departure. I confined myself then to begging him to give up his chamber, which is the handsomest in the hotel, and to be satisfied with a pretty little closet on the third floor. But to this M. Porthos replied, that as he every moment expected his mistress, who was one of the greatest ladies of the court, I might easily comprehend that the chamber he did me the honor to occupy in my house was itself very mean for the visit of such a personage.

"Nevertheless, while acknowledging the truth of what he said, I thought proper to insist; but without even giving himself the trouble to enter into any discussion with me, he took one of his pistols, laid it on his table, day and night, and said that at the first word that should be spoken to him about removing, either within the house or out of it, he would blow out the brains of the person who should be so imprudent as to meddle with a matter which only concerned himself. So from that time, monsieur, nobody enters his chamber but his servant."

"What! Mousqueton is here, then?"

"Oh! yes, monsieur; five days after your departure, he came back, and in a very bad condition, too; it appears that he had met with disagreeables, likewise, on his journey. Unfortunately he is more nimble than his master; so that for the sake of his master, he sets us all at defiance; and as he thinks we might refuse what he asked for, he takes all he wants without asking at all."

"Well, it's a fact," said D'Artagnan, "I always observed a great degree of intelligence and devotedness to his master in Mousqueton."

"Very possibly, monsieur: but suppose if I should happen to be brought in contact, only four times a year, with such intelligence and devotedness—why, I should be a ruined man."

"No! for Porthos will pay you."

"Hum!" said the host, in a doubting tone.

"Why, it is not to be imagined that the favorite of a great

lady will be allowed to be inconvenienced for such a paltry
sum as he owes you."

"If I durst say what I believe on that head——"

"What you believe?"

"I ought rather to say: what I know."

"What you know?"

"Ay; even what I am sure of."

"Well: tell me what this is you are so sure of?"

"I would say, that I know this great lady."

"You?"

"Yes; I."

"And how did you become acquainted with her?"

"Oh! monsieur, if I could believe I might trust in your
discretion."

"Speak: by the word of a gentleman, you shall have no
cause to repent of your confidence."

"Well, monsieur, you may conceive that uneasiness makes
us do many things."

"What have you done?"

"Oh! nothing that I had not a right to do in the character
of a creditor."

"Go on!"

"Instead of putting the letter in the post, which is never
safe, I took advantage of one of my lads being going to Paris,
and I ordered him to convey the letter to this duchess himself. This was fulfilling the intentions of M. Porthos, who
had desired us to be so careful of this letter, was it not?"

"Nearly so."

"Well, monsieur, do you know who this great lady is?"

"No; I have heard Porthos speak of her, that's all."

"Do you know who this pretended duchess is?"

"I repeat to you, I don't know her."

"Why, she is the wife of a procureur of the Châtelet, monsieur, named Madame Coquenard; who, although she is at
least fifty, still gives herself jealous airs. It struck me as very
odd, that the princess should live in the Rue aux Ours."

"But how do you know all this?"

"Because she flew into a great passion on receiving the letter, saying that M. Porthos was a fickle, inconstant man, and
that she was sure it was on account of some woman he had
received this wound."

"What, has he been wounded then?"

"Oh! good Lord! what have I said?"

"You said that Porthos was wounded."

"Yes, but he has forbidden me so strictly to say so!"

"And why so?"

"Zounds! monsieur, only because he had boasted that he would perforate the stranger with whom you left him in dispute where he pleased, whereas the stranger, on the contrary, in spite of all his rhodomontades, quickly brought him on his back. Now, as M. Porthos is a very vainglorious man, he insists that nobody shall know he has received this wound, except the duchess, whom he endeavored to interest by an account of his adventure."

"It is a wound, then, that confines him to his bed?"

"Ah! and something like a wound, too! I assure you. Your friends's soul must stick pretty tight to his body."

"Were you there, then?"

"Monsieur, I followed them from curiosity, so that I saw the combat without the combatants seeing me."

"And what took place?"

"Oh! the affair was not long, I assure you. They placed themselves in guard: the stranger made a feint and a lunge, and that so rapidly, that when M. de Porthos came to the *parade,* he had already three inches of steel in his breast. He immediately fell backward. The stranger placed the point of his sword at his throat; and M. Porthos, finding himself at the mercy of his adversary, allowed himself to be conquered. Upon which the stranger asked his name, and learning that it was Porthos, and not M. D'Artagnan, he assisted him to rise, brought him back to the hotel, mounted his horse, and disappeared."

"So it was with M. D'Artagnan this stranger meant to quarrel?"

"It appears so."

"And do you know what has become of him?"

"No; I never saw him until that moment; and have not seen him since."

"Very well! now I know all that I wish to know. Porthos' chamber is, you say, on the first story, No. 1?"

"Yes, monsieur, the handsomest in the auberge; a chamber that I could have occupied ten times over."

"Well, well, be satisfied," said D'Artagnan, laughing; "Porthos will pay you with the money of the Duchess Coquenard."

"Oh! monsieur, procureuse or duchess, if she will but draw her purse-strings, it will be all the same; but she positively answered that she was tired of the exigencies and infidelities of M. Porthos, and that she would not send him a denier."

"And did you convey this answer to your guest?"

"We took good care not to do that; he would have found out how we had delivered the letter."

"So that he is still in expectation of his money?"

"Oh! *mon Dieu!* yes, monsieur! Yesterday he wrote again, but it was his servant who this time put his letter in the post."

"Do you say the procureuse is old and ugly?"

"Fifty at least, monsieur, and not at all handsome, according to Pathaud's account."

"In that case, you may be quite at ease: she will soon be softened; besides, Porthos cannot owe you much."

"How, not much! Twenty good pistoles, already, without reckoning the doctor. Bless you, he denies himself nothing; it may easily be seen he has been accustomed to live pretty well."

"Never mind! if his mistress abandons him, he will find friends, I will answer for it. So, my dear host, be not uneasy, and continue to take all the care of him that his situation requires."

"Monsieur has promised me not to open his mouth about the procureuse, and not to say a word of the wound?"

"That's a thing agreed upon; you have my word."

"Oh! he would kill me! I am sure he would!"

"Don't be afraid: he is not so much of a devil as he appears to be."

Saying these words, D'Artagnan went upstairs, leaving his host a little better satisfied with respect to two things in which he appeared to be very much interested—his debt and his life.

At the top of the stairs, upon the most conspicuous door of the corridor, was traced in black ink a gigantic "No. 1;" D'Artagnan knocked, and upon being desired to come in, entered the chamber.

Porthos was in bed, and was playing a game at lansquenet with Mousqueton, to keep his hand in, while a spit loaded with partridges was turning before the fire, and, at each side of a large chimney-piece, over two chafing-dishes, were boiling two stewpans, from which exhaled a double odor of *gibelotte* and *matelotte,* very grateful to the olfactory nerves. In addition to this, he perceived that the top of a wardrobe and the marble of a commode were covered with empty bottles.

At the sight of his friend, Porthos, uttered a loud cry of joy; and Mousqueton, rising respectfully, yielded his place to him, and went to give an eye to the two stewpans, of which he appeared to have the particular inspection.

"Ah! *pardieu!* is that you!" said Porthos to D'Artagnan. "You are right welcome, my dear fellow! I hope you will excuse my not coming to meet you. But," added he, looking at D'Artagnan, with a certain degree of uneasiness, "you know what has happened to me?"

"Not exactly."

"Has the host told you nothing, then?"

"I asked after you, and came up as soon as I could."

Porthos seemed to breathe more freely.

"And what has happened to you, my dear Porthos?" continued D'Artagnan.

"Why, on making a thrust at my adversary, whom I had already hit three times, and with whom I meant to finish by a fourth, I put my foot on a stone, slipped, and strained my knee."

"Indeed!"

"Honor! Luckily for the rascal, for I should have left him dead on the spot, I assure you."

"And what became of him?"

"Oh! I don't know; he had enough, and set off without waiting for the rest. But you, my dear D'Artagnan, what has happened to you?"

"So that this strain of the knee," continued D'Artagnan, "my dear Porthos, keeps you here in bed?"

"*Mon Dieu!* that's all; I shall be about again in a few days."

"Why did you not have yourself conveyed to Paris? Living here must be cruelly wearisome."

"That was my intention; but, my dear friend, I have one thing to confess to you."

"What is that?"

"It is, that, as I found it cruelly wearisome, as you say, and as I had the seventy-five pistoles in my pocket which you had distributed to me, in order to amuse myself, I invited a gentleman who was traveling this way to walk up, and proposed a cast of dice with him. He accepted my challenge, and, *ma foi!* my seventy-five pistoles quickly passed from my pocket to his, without reckoning my horse, which he won into the bargain. But you, I want to know about you, D'Artagnan?"

"What can you expect, my dear Porthos; a man is not privileged in all ways," said D'Artagnan; "you know the proverb: 'Unlucky at play, lucky in love.' You are too fortunate in your love, for play not to take its revenge; what consequence can the reverses of fortune be to you?—have you not, happy rogue as you are, have you not your duchess, who cannot fail to come to your assistance?"

"Well! you see, my dear D'Artagnan, with what ill-luck I play," replied Porthos; "with the most careless air in the world I wrote to her to send me fifty louis, or so, of which I stood absolutely in need, on account of my accident."

"Well!"

"Well! she must be at her country-seat, for she has not answered me."

"Indeed!"

"No; so I yesterday addressed another letter to her, still more pressing than the first; but you are come, my dear fellow, let us speak of you. I confess I began to be very uneasy on your account."

"But your host behaves very well toward you, as it appears, friend Porthos," said D'Artagnan, directing the sick man's attention to the full stewpans and the empty bottles.

"So, so!" replied Porthos. "It is not above four days ago since the impertinent jackanapes gave me his bill, and I was forced to turn both him and his bill out of the door; so that I am here something in the fashion of a conqueror, holding my position, as it were, by conquest. So, you see, being in constant fear of being forced in that position, I am armed to the teeth."

"And yet," said D'Artagnan, laughing, "it appears to me that from time to time you must make sorties." And he again pointed to the bottles and the stewpans.

"No, not I, unfortunately!" said Porthos. "This miserable strain confines me to my bed, but Mousqueton forages, and brings in provisions. Friend Mousqueton, you see that we have a reinforcement arrived, and we must have an increase of provisions."

"Mousqueton," said D'Artagnan, "you must render me a service."

"Of what kind, monsieur?"

"You must give your recipe to Planchet; I may be besieged in my turn, and I shall not be sorry for him to be able to let me enjoy the same advantages with which you gratify your master."

"Lord, monsieur! there is nothing more easy," said Mousqueton, with a modest air. "It only requires to be sharp, that's all. I was brought up in the country, and my father, in his leisure time, was something of a poacher."

"And how did he occupy the rest of his time?"

"Monsieur, he carried on a trade, which I have always found pretty productive."

"What was that?"

"As it was a time of war between the Catholics and the Huguenots, and as he saw the Catholics exterminate the Huguenots and the Huguenots exterminate the Catholics, and all in the name of religion, he adopted a mixed belief, which permitted him to be sometimes a Catholic, sometimes a Huguenot. Now, he was accustomed to walk, with his fowling-piece on his shoulder, behind the hedges which border the roads, and when he saw a Catholic coming alone, the Protestant religion immediately prevailed in his mind. He lowered his gun in the direction of the traveler; then, when he was within ten paces of him, he commenced a conversation which almost always ended by the traveler's abandoning his purse to save his life. I must at the same time say that when he saw a Huguenot coming, he felt himself urged with such an ardent Catholic zeal that he could not understand how, a quarter of an hour before, he had been able to have any doubts upon the superiority of our holy religion. For my part, I am, monsieur, a Catholic; my father, faithful to his principles, having made my elder brother a Huguenot."

"And what was the end of this worthy man?" asked D'Artagnan.

"Oh! of the most unfortunate kind, monsieur. One day he was surprised in a hollow way between a Huguenot and a Catholic, with both of whom he had before had to do, and who both knew him again; so they united against him and hung him on a tree; then they came and boasted of their fine exploit in the cabaret of the next village, where my brother and I were drinking."

"And what did you do?" said D'Artagnan.

"We let them tell their story out," replied Mousqueton. "Then, as in leaving the cabaret they took different directions, my brother went and hid himself on the road of the Catholic, and I on that of the Huguenot. Two hours after, all was over; we had done the business of both of them, admiring the foresight of our poor father, who had taken the precaution to bring each of us up in a different religion."

"Well, I must allow, as you say, your father must have been a very intelligent fellow. And you say in his leisure moments the worthy man was a poacher?"

"Yes, monsieur, and it was he who taught me to lay a snare and ground a line. The consequence is that when I

saw our shabby host wanted to feed us upon lumps of fat
meat fit for laborers, which did not at all suit such delicate
stomachs as ours, I had recourse to a little of my old trade.
While walking near the wood of Monsieur le Prince, I laid a
few snares in the runs; and while reclining on the banks of
his highness' pieces of water, I slipped a few lines into his
fish ponds. So that now, thanks be to God! we do not want,
as monsieur can testify, for partridges, rabbits, carp, or eels—
all light, wholesome food, suitable for sick persons."

"But the wine," said D'Artagnan, "who furnishes the
wine? That, at least, must be your host?"

"That is to say, yes and no."

"How yes and no?"

"He furnishes it, it is true, but he does not know that he
has that honor."

"Explain yourself, Mousqueton, your conversation is full
of instructive things."

"This is it, monsieur. It has so chanced that I have met
with a Spaniard in my peregrinations, who had seen many
countries, and among them the New World."

"What the deuce connection can the New World have
with the bottles which are on the commode and the press?"

"Patience, monsieur, everything will come in its turn."

"You are right, Mousqueton, I leave it to you."

"This Spaniard had in his service a lackey who had accompanied him in his voyage to Mexico. This lackey was my
compatriot, and we became the more intimate from there
being many resemblances of character between us. We loved
sporting of all kinds better than anything, so that he related
to me how, in the plains of the Pampas, the natives hunt
the tiger and the wild bull with simple running nooses, which
they throw round the necks of those terrible animals. At
first I would not believe that they could attain such a degree
of skill as to throw to a distance of twenty or thirty paces
the end of a cord with such nicety; but in face of the proof
I was obliged to acknowledge the truth of the recital. My
friend placed a bottle at the distance of thirty paces, and at
each cast he caught the neck of the bottle in his running
noose. I practiced this exercise, and as nature has endowed
me with some faculties, at this day I can throw the *lasso*
with any man in the world. Well, do you understand, monsieur? Our host has a well-furnished cellar, the key of
which never leaves him; only this cellar has a loophole.
Now, through this loophole I throw my *lasso*, and as I now
know which part of the cellar the best wine is in, that's my

point for sport. Thus you see, monsieur, what the New World has to do with the bottles which are on the commode and the clothes-press. Now, will you taste our wine, and, without prejudice, say what you think of it?"

"Thank you, my friend, thank you; unfortunately I have just breakfasted."

"Well," said Porthos, "arrange your table, Mousqueton, and while we breakfast, D'Artagnan will relate to us what has happened to him during the ten days since he left us."

"Willingly," said D'Artagnan.

While Porthos and Mousqueton were breakfasting with the appetites of convalescents, and with that brotherly cordiality which unites men in misfortune, D'Artagnan related how Aramis, being wounded, was obliged to stop at Crèvecœur, how he had left Athos fighting at Amiens with four men who accused him of being a coiner, and how he, D'Artagnan, had been forced to run the Count de Wardes through the body in order to reach England.

But there the confidence of D'Artagnan stopped; he only added, that on his return from Great Britain, he had brought back four magnificent horses, one for himself, and one for each of his companions; then he informed Porthos that the one which was intended for him was already installed in the stable of the hotel.

At this moment Planchet entered, to inform his master that the horses were sufficiently refreshed, and that it would be possible to sleep at Clermont.

As D'Artagnan was tolerably reassured with regard to Porthos, and as he was anxious to obtain news of his two other friends, he held out his hand to the wounded man, and told him he was about to resume his route in order to prosecute his researches. For the rest, as he reckoned upon returning through Chantilly, if, in seven or eight days, Porthos were still at the hotel of the Grand St. Martin, he would call for him on his way.

Porthos replied that, according to all probability, his sprain would not permit him to depart yet awhile. Besides, it was necessary he should stay at Chantilly, to wait for the answer from his duchess.

D'Artagnan wished that that answer might be prompt and favorable; and after having again recommended Porthos to the care of Mousqueton, and paid his expenses at the hotel, he resumed his route with Planchet, who was already relieved of one of his led horses.

CHAPTER XXVI.

ARAMIS' THESIS.

D'ARTAGNAN had said nothing to Porthos of his wound or of his procureuse. Our Béarnais was a prudent lad, however young he might be. Consequently he had appeared to believe all that the vainglorious musketeer had told him; convinced that no friendship will hold out against a surprised secret, particularly when pride is deeply interested in that secret; besides, we feel always a sort of mental superiority over those with whose lives we are better acquainted than they are aware of. Now, in his projects of intrigue for the future, and determined as he was to make his three friends the instruments of his fortune, D'Artagnan was not sorry at getting in his grasp beforehand the invisible strings by which he reckoned upon moving them.

And yet, as he journeyed along, a profound sadness weighed upon his heart; he thought of that young and pretty Madame Bonacieux, who was to have paid him so richly for all his devotedness; but, let us hasten to say that this sadness possessed the young man less from the regret of the happiness he had missed, than from the fear he entertained that some serious misfortune had befallen the poor woman. For himself, he had no doubt she was a victim of the cardinal's vengeance, and, as was well known, the vengeance of his eminence was terrible. How he had found grace in the eyes of the minister, was what he himself was ignorant of, but, without doubt, what M. de Cavois would have revealed to him, if the captain of the guards had met with him at home.

Nothing makes time pass more quickly or more shortens a journey than a thought which absorbs in itself all the faculties of the organization of him who thinks. The external existence then resembles a sleep of which this thought is the dream. By its influence, time has no longer measure, space has no longer distance. We depart from one place and arrive at another—that is all. Of the interval passed through nothing remains in the memory but a vague mist in which a thousand confused images of trees, mountains, and landscapes are lost. It was as a prey to this hallucination that D'Artagnan traveled, at whatever pace his horse pleased, the six or eight leagues that separated Chantilly from Crèvecœur, without his being able to remember, on his arrival in the

village, any of the things he had passed or met with on the
road.

There only his memory returned to him, he shook his
head, perceived the cabaret at which he had left Aramis,
and putting his horse to a trot, he shortly pulled up at the
door.

This time it was not a host, but a hostess who received
him; D'Artagnan was a physiognomist; his eye took in at a
glance the plump, cheerful countenance of the mistress of
the place, and he at once perceived there was no occasion for
dissembling with her, or of fearing anything on the part of
one blessed with such a joyous physiognomy.

"My good dame," asked D'Artagnan, "can you tell me
what is become of one of my friends, whom we were obliged
to leave here about twelve days ago?"

"A handsome young man, three or four and twenty years
old, mild, amiable, and well made?"

"Exactly the man: wounded, moreover in the shoulder?"

"Just so. Well, monsieur, he is still here!"

"Ah! *Pardieu!* my dear dame," said D'Artagnan, springing from his horse, and throwing the bridle to Planchet,
"you restore me to life; where is this dear Aramis? let me
embrace him! I am quite anxious to see him again."

"I beg your pardon, monsieur, but I doubt whether he can
see you at this moment."

"Why so? Has he got a lady with him?"

"Jesus! what do you mean by that? Poor lad! No,
monsieur, he has not got a lady with him!"

"With whom is he, then?"

"With the curé of Montdidier and the superior of the
Jesuits of Amiens."

"Good heavens!" cried D'Artagnan, "is the poor fellow
worse, then?"

"Oh! no, monsieur, quite the contrary; but after his illness grace touched him, and he determined to enter into
orders."

"Oh! that's it!" said D'Artagnan, "I had forgotten that
he was only a musketeer for the time."

"Is monsieur still anxious to see him?"

"More so than ever."

"Well, monsieur has only to take the right-hand stair case
in the yard and knock at No. 5, on the second floor."

D'Artagnan walked quickly in the direction pointed out,
and found one of those exterior staircases that are still to be
seen in the yards of our old-fashioned auberges. But there

was no getting thus at the place of sojourn of the future abbé; the defiles of the chamber of Aramis were neither more nor less guarded than the gardens of Armida: Bazin was stationed in the corridor, and barred his passage with so much the more intrepidity, that, after many years of trial, Bazin found himself near arriving at a result of which he had ever been ambitious.

In fact, the dream of poor Bazin had always been to serve a churchman, and he waited with impatience the moment, always contemplated in the future, when Aramis would throw aside the uniform and assume the cassock. The daily renewed purpose of the young man, that the moment would not long be delayed, had alone kept him in the service of a musketeer, a service in which, he said, his soul was in constant jeopardy.

Bazin was then at the height of joy. According to all probability, this time his master would not retract. The union of physical pain with moral uneasiness had produced the effect so long desired; Aramis, suffering at once in body and mind, had at length fixed his eyes and his thoughts upon religion, and he had considered as a warning from heaven the double accident which had happened to him, that is to say, the sudden disapperance of his mistress and the wound in his shoulder.

It may be easily understood, that in the present disposition of his master, nothing could be more disagreeable to Bazin than the arrival of D'Artagnan, which might cast his master back again into that vortex of mundane affairs that had so long carried him away. He resolved then to defend the door bravely; and as, betrayed by the mistress of the auberge, he could not say that Aramis was absent, he endeavored to prove to the newcomer that it would be the height of indiscretion to disturb his master in his pious conference, which had commenced with the morning, and would not be, as Bazin said, terminated before night.

But D'Artagnan took very little heed of the eloquent discourse of Master Bazin, and as he had no desire to support a polemic discussion with his friend's valet, he simply moved him out of the way with one hand, and with the other turned the handle of the door, No. 5.

The door opened, and D'Artagnan penetrated into the chamber.

Aramis, in a black gown, his head enveloped in a sort of round, flap cap, not much unlike a calotte, was seated before an oblong table, covered with rolls of paper and enormous

volumes in folio; at his right hand was placed the superior of
the Jesuits, and on his left the *curé* of Montdidier. The
curtains were half drawn, and only admitted the mysterious
light calculated for beatific reveries. All the mundane objects that generally strike the eye on entering the room of a
young man, particularly when that young man is a musketeer, had disappeared as if by enchantment, and, for fear, no
doubt, that the sight of them might bring his master back to
ideas of this world, Bazin had laid his hands upon sword,
pistols, plumed hat, and embroideries and laces of all kinds
and sorts.

But in their stead and place, D'Artagnan thought he perceived in an obscure corner a discipline cord suspended from
a nail in the wall.

At the noise made by D'Artagnan on entering, Aramts
lifted up his head and beheld his friend. But to the great
astonishment of the young man, the sight of him did not produce much effort upon the musketeer, so completely was his
mind detached from the things of this world.

"Good-day to you, dear D'Artagnan; believe me, I am
very glad to see you."

"So am I delighted to see you," said D'Artagnan,
"although I am not yet sure that it is Aramis I am speaking
to."

"To himself, my friend, to himself; but what makes you
doubt?"

"I was afraid I had made a mistake in the chamber, and
that I had found my way into the apartment of some churchman; then another error seized me on seeing you in company
with these gentleman—I was afraid you were dangerously ill."

The two men in black, who guessed D'Artagnan's meaning, darted at him a glance which might have been thought
threatening; but D'Artagnan took no heed of it.

"I disturb you, perhaps, my dear Aramis," continued
D'Artagnan, "for by what I see, I am led to believe you are
confessing to these gentlemen."

Aramis colored imperceptibly.

"You disturb me! oh! quite the contrary, dear friend, I
swear; and as a proof of what I say, permit me to declare I
am rejoiced to see you safe and sound."

"Ah! he'll come round!" thought D'Artagnan, "that's
not bad!"

"For this gentleman, who is my friend, has just escaped
from a serious danger," continued Aramis with unction,

pointing to D'Artagnan with his hand, and addressing the
two ecclesiastics.

"Give God praise, monsieur," replied they, bowing.

"I have not failed to do so, your reverences," replied the
young man, returning their salutation.

"You arrive very apropos, D'Artagnan," said Aramis,
"and by taking part in our discussion, may assist us with
your intelligence. M. de Principal of Amiens, M. le Curé of
Montdidier, and I, are arguing upon certain theological questions, with which we have been much interested; I shall be
delighted to have your opinion."

"The opinion of the man of the sword can have very little
weight," replied D'Artagnan, who began to get uneasy at the
turn things were taking, "and you had better be satisfied,
believe me, with the knowledge of these gentlemen."

The two men in black bowed in their turn.

"On the contrary," replied Aramis, "your opinion will be
very valuable; the question is this: Monsieur le Principal
thinks that my thesis ought to be dogmatic and didactic."

"Your thesis! are you then making a thesis?"

"Without doubt," replied the Jesuit: "in the examination
which precedes ordination, a thesis is always requisite."

"Ordination!" cried D'Artagnan, who could not believe
what the hostess and Bazin had successively told him; and he
gazed, half-stupefied, upon the three persons before him.

"Now," continued Aramis, taking the same graceful position in his easy-chair that he would have assumed in a *ruelle,*
and complacently examining his hand, which was as white and
plump as that of a woman, and which he held in the air to
cause the blood to descend from it, "now, as you have heard,
D'Artagnan, M. le Principal is desirous that my thesis should
be dogmatic, while I, for my part, would rather it should be
ideal. This is the reason why M. le Principal has proposed to
me the following subject, which has not yet been treated upon,
and in which I perceive there is matter for magnificent developments: *'Utraque manus in benedicendo clericis infe-
rioribus necessaria est.'*"

D'Artagnan, whose erudition we are well acquainted with,
evinced no more interest on hearing this quotation, than he
had at that of M. de Tréville, in allusion to the presents he
fancied he had received from the Duke of Buckingham.

"Which means," resumed Aramis, that he might perfectly
understand the matter; "'The two hands are indispensable
for priests of the inferior orders, when they bestow the
benediction.'"

"An admirable subject!" cried the Jesuit.

"Admirable and dogmatic!" repeated the curate, who, about as strong as D'Artagnan with respect to Latin, carefully watched the Jesuit, in order to keep step with him, and repeated his words like an echo.

As to D'Artagnan, he remained perfectly insensible to the enthusiasm of the two men in black.

"Yes, admirable! *prorsus admirabile!*" continued Aramis; "but which requires a profound study of both the Scriptures and the Fathers. Now, I have confessed to these learned ecclesiastics, and that in all humility, that the duties of mounting guard and the service of the king have caused me to neglect study a little. I should find myself, therefore, more at my ease, *facilius natans,* in a subject of my own choice, which would be to these hard theological questions what morals are to metaphysics in philosophy."

D'Artagnan began to be tired, and so did the *curé*.

"See what an exordium!" cried the Jesuit.

"Exordium," repeated the *cure* for the sake of saying something. *"Quemadmodum inter cœlorum immensitatem."*

Aramis cast a glance upon D'Artagnan, to see what effect all this produced, and found his friend gaping enough to split his jaws.

"Let us speak French, worthy father," said he to the Jesuit, "M. D'Artagnan will enjoy our conversation the more."

"Yes," replied D'Artagnan; "I am fatigued with riding, and all this Latin confuses me."

"Certainly," replied the Jesuit, a little thrown out, while the *cure,* greatly delighted, turned upon D'Artagnan a look full of gratitude; "well, let us see what is to be derived from this gloss.

"Moses, the servant of God—he was but a servant, please to understand! Moses blessed with the hands; he held out both his arms, while the Hebrews beat their enemies, and then he blessed them with his two hands. Besides, what does the gospel say: *'Imponite manus,'* and not *'manum:'* place the hands and not the hand."

"Place the hands," repeated the *cure,* with the proper gesture.

"St. Peter, on the contrary, of whom the popes are the successors," continued the Jesuit: *'Porrige digitos:'* present the fingers. Do you see that, now?"

"Certes," replied Aramis, in a pleased tone, "but the thing is subtle."

"The fingers!" resumed the Jesuit, "St. Peter blessed with

the fingers. The pope, therefore, blesses with the fingers. And with how many fingers does he bless? With *three* fingers, to be sure; one for the Father, one for the Son, and one for the Holy Ghost."

All crossed themselves; D'Artagnan thought it was proper to follow this example.

"The pope is the successor of St. Peter, and represents the three divine powers; the rest, *ordines inferiores,* of the ecclesiastical hierarchy, bless in the name of the holy archangels and angels. The most humble clerks, such as our deacons and sacristans, bless with *goupillons* (brushes for sprinkling holy water), which resemble an infinite number of blessing fingers. There is the subject simplified. *Argumentum omni denudatum ornamento.* I could make of that subject two volumes of the size of this—" and, in his enthusiasm, he struck a St. Chrysostom in folio, which made the table bend beneath its weight.

D'Artagnan trembled.

"Certes," said Aramis, "I do justice to the beauties of this thesis; but, at the same time, I perceive it would be overwhelming for me. I had chosen this text—tell me, dear D'Artagnan, if it is not to your taste: *'Non inutile est desiderium in oblatione:'* or, still better, 'A little regret is not unsuitable in an offering to the Lord.'"

"Stop there!" cried the Jesuit, "for that thesis touches closely upon heresy: there is a proposition almost like it in the 'Angustinus' of the heresiarch Jansenius, whose book will, sooner or later, be burnt by the hands of the hangman. Take care, my young friend, you are inclining toward false doctrines; my young friend, you will be lost!"

"You will be lost," said the *curé,* shaking his head sorrowfully.

"You approach that famous point of free will, which is a mortal rock. You face the insinuations of the Pelagians and the demi-Pelagians."

"But, my reverend—" replied Aramis, a little amazed by the shower of arguments that poured upon his head.

"How will you prove," continued the Jesuit, without allowing him to speak, "that we ought to regret the world when we offer ourselves to God? Listen to this dilemma: God is God, and the world is the devil. To regret the world is to regret the devil; that is my conclusion."

"And, that is mine, also," said the *curé.*

"But for heaven's sake—" resumed Aramis.

"Desideras diabolum, unhappy man," cried the Jesuit.

"He regrets the devil! Ah! my young friend," added the *curé*, groaning, "do not regret the devil, I implore you!"

D'Artagnan felt himself bewildered; he appeared to be in a mad-house, and that he was becoming as mad as those he saw. He was, however, forced to hold his tongue, from not comprehending half the language they employed.

"But listen to me, then," resumed Aramis, with politeness mingled with a little impatience. "I do not say I regret; no, I will never pronounce that sentence, which would not be orthodox."

The Jesuit raised his hands toward heaven, and the curate did the same.

"No, but pray grant me that it is acting with an ill grace to offer to the Lord only that with which we are perfectly disgusted? Don't you think so, D'Artagnan?"

"*Pardieu!* I think so, indeed," cried he.

The Jesuit and the *curé* quite started from their chairs.

"This is the point I start from, it is a syllogism; the world is not wanting in attractions, I quit the world, then I make a sacrifice; now, the Scripture says positively, 'Make a sacrifice unto the Lord.'"

"That is true," said his antagonists.

"And then," said Aramis, pinching his ear to make it red, as he rubbed his hands to make them white, "and then I made a certain rondeau upon it last year, which I showed to M. de Voiture, and that great man paid me a thousand handsome compliments upon it."

"A rondeau!" said the Jesuit disdainfully.

"A rondeau!" said the *curé* mechanically.

"Repeat it! repeat it!" cried D'Artagnan; "it will make a little change."

"Not so, for it is religious," replied Aramis; "it is theology in verse."

"The devil!" said D'Artagnan.

"Here it is," said Aramis, with a little look of diffidence, which, however, was not exempt from a shade of hypocrisy:

> "Vous qui pleurez un passé plein de charmes,
> Et qui trainez des jours infortunés,
> Tous vos malheurs se verront terminés.
> Quand à Dieu seul vous offrirez vos larmes.
> Vous qui pleurez!

> "You who weep for pleasures fled,
> Whilst dragging on a life of care,

All your woes will melt in air,
If at God's feet your tears you shed.
        You who weep!"

D'Artagnan and the *cure* appeared pleased. The Jesuit persisted in his opinion.

"Beware of a profane taste in your theological style. What says Augustin on this subject: *Severus sit clericorum verbo.*"

"Yes, let the sermon be clear," said the *curé.*

"Now," hastily interrupted the Jesuit, on seeing that his acolyte was going astray, "now, your thesis would please the ladies; it would have the success of one of M. Patru's pleadings."

"I hope to God it may!" cried Aramis, transported.

"There it is," cried the Jesuit; "the world still speaks within you in a loud voice, *altissimâ voce.* You follow the world, my young friend, and I tremble lest grace prove not efficacious."

"Be satisfied, my reverend father, I can depend upon myself."

"Mundane presumption!"

"I know myself, father; my resolution is irrevocable."

"Then you persist in continuing that thesis?"

"I feel myself called upon to treat that, and no other, I will see about the continuation of it, and to-morrow I hope you will be satisfied with the corrections I shall have made in consequence of your advice."

"Work slowly," said the *cure;* "we leave you in an excellent tone of mind."

"Yes, the ground is all sown," said the Jesuit, "and we have not to fear that one portion of the seed may have fallen upon stone, another upon the highway, or that the birds of heaven have eaten the rest, *aves cœli comederunt illam.*"

"Plague stifle you and your Latin!" said D'Artagnan, who began to feel all his patience exhausted.

"Farewell, my son," said the *curé,* "till to-morrow."

"Till to-morrow, my rash young friend," said the Jesuit. "You promise to become one of the lights of the church; heaven grant that this light prove not a devouring fire!"

D'Artagnan, who, for an hour past, had been gnawing his nails with impatience, was beginning to attack the flesh.

The two men in black rose, bowed to Aramis and D'Artagnan, and advanced toward the door. Bazin, who had been standing listening to all this controversy with a pious jubliation, sprang toward them, took the breviary of the *cure* and the missal of the Jesuit, and walked respectfully before them, to clear their way.

Aramis conducted them to the foot of the stairs, and then immediately came up again to D'Artagnan, whose senses were still in a state of confusion.

When left alone, the two friends at first observed an embarrassed silence; it, however, became necessary for one of them to break it the first, and as D'Artagnan appeared determined to leave that honor to his companion—

"You see," said Aramis, "that I am returned to my original ideas."

"Yes; efficacious grace has touched you, as that gentleman said just now."

"Oh, these plans of retreat have been formed for a long time; you have often heard me speak of them, have you not, my friend?"

"Yes; but I must confess that I always thought you were joking."

"With such sort of things! Oh, D'Artagnan!"

"The devil! Why, people joke with death."

"And people are wrong, D'Artagnan; for death is the door which leads to perdition or to salvation."

"Granted; but, if you please, let us not theologize, Aramis; you must have had enough for to-day; as for me, I have almost forgotten the little Latin I have ever known. Then I confess to you that I have eaten nothing since ten o'clock this morning, and I am devilish hungry."

"We will dine directly, my friend; only you must please to remember that this is Friday: now, on such a day I cannot eat meat or see it eaten. If you can be satisfied with my dinner, it consists of cooked tetragones and fruits."

"What do you mean by tetragones?" asked D'Artagnan eagerly.

"I mean spinach," replied Aramis; "but, on your account I will add some eggs, and that is a serious infraction of the rule, for eggs are meat, since they engender chickens."

"This feast is not very succulent; but never mind, I will put up with it for the sake of remaining with you."

"I am grateful to you for the sacrifice," said Aramis; "but if your body be not greatly benefited by it, your soul will, be assured."

"And so, Aramis, you are decidedly going into the church? What will our two friends say? What will M. de

Tréville say? They will treat you as a deserter, I warn you."

"I do not enter the church—I re-enter it; I deserted the church for the world, for you know that I committed violence upon myself when I became a musketeer."

"Who—I? I know nothing about it."

"You don't know how I quitted the seminary?"

"Not at all."

"This is my history, then; besides, the Scriptures say, 'Confess yourselves to one another,' and I confess to you, D'Artagnan."

"And I give you absolution beforehand; you see, I am a good sort of a man."

"Do not jest with holy things, my friend."

"Go on, then; I'll listen."

"I had been at the seminary from nine years old; in three days I should have been twenty; I was about to become an abbé, and all was told.

"One evening, I had gone, according to custom, to a house which I frequented with much pleasure; when one is young, what can be expected?—one is weak. An officer who saw me, with a jealous eye, reading the 'Lives of the Saints' to the mistress of the house, entered suddenly, and without being announced. That evening I had translated an episode of Judith, and had just communicated my verses to the lady, who made me all sorts of compliments, and leaning on my shoulder, was reading them a second time. Her *pose*, which, I must admit, was rather free, wounded this gentleman's feelings. He said nothing, but when I went out he followed, and quickly came up with me.

"'Monsieur l'Abbé,' said he, 'do you like blows with a cane?'

"'I cannot say, monsieur,' answered I; 'no one has ever dared to give me any.'

"'Well, listen to me, then, Monsieur l'Abbé: if you venture again into the house in which I have met you this evening, I will dare, myself, Monsieur l'Abbé.'

"I really think I must have been frightened; I became very pale, I felt my legs fail me, I sought for a reply, but could find none—I was silent.

"The officer waited for this reply, and, seeing it so long coming, he burst into a laugh, turned upon his heel, and re-entered the house.

"I returned to my seminary.

"I am a gentleman born—my blood is warm, as you may

have remarked, my dear D'Artagnan; the insult was terrible, and, however unknown to the rest of the world, I felt it live and fester at the bottom of my heart. I informed my superiors that I did not feel myself sufficiently prepared for ordination, and, at my request, the ceremony was postponed for a year.

"I sought out the best fencing-master in Paris; I made an agreement with him to take a lesson every day, and every day during a year I took that lesson. Then, on the anniversary of the day on which I had been insulted, I hung my cassock on a peg, assumed the costume of a cavalier, and went to a ball given by a lady friend of mine, and to which I knew my man was invited. It was Rue des Francs-Bourgeois, close to La Force.

"As I expected, my officer was there. I went up to him, as he was singing a love ditty and looking tenderly at a lady, and interrupted him exactly in the middle of the second couplet.

"'Monsieur,' said I, 'is it still unpleasant to you that I should frequent a certain house of La Rue Payenne? And would you still bestow a caning upon me if I took it into my head to disobey you?'

"The officer looked at me with astonishment, and then said:

"'What is your business with me, monsieur? I do not know you.'

"'I am,' said I, 'the little abbé, who reads the 'Lives of the Saints,' and translates Judith into verse.'

"'Ah, ah! I recollect now,' said the officer, in a jeering tone; 'well, what do you want with me?'

"'I want you to spare time to take a walk with me.'

"'To-morrow morning, if you like, and with the greatest pleasure.'

"'No, not to-morrow morning, but immediately, if you please.'

"'If you absolutely insist upon it——'

"'I do—I insist upon it.'

"'Come, then. Ladies,' said the officer, 'do not disturb yourselves; allow me time just to kill this gentleman, and I will return and finish the last couplet.'

"We went out. I took him to the Rue Payenne, to exactly the same spot where, a year before, at the very same hour, he had paid me the compliment I have related to you. It was a superb moonlight night. We immediately drew, and at the first pass I laid him stark dead."

"The devil!" cried D'Artagnan.

"Now," continued Aramis, "as the ladies did not see the
singer come back, and as he was found in the Rue Payenne,
with a great sword-wound through his body, it was supposed
that I had accommodated him thus, and the matter created
some scandal, which obliged me to renounce the cassock for a
time. Athos, whose acquaintance I made about that period,
and Porthos, who had, in addition to my lessons, taught me
some effetive tricks of fence, prevailed upon me to solicit
the uniform of a musketeer. The king entertained great regard for my father, who had fallen at the siege of Arras, and
the uniform was granted. You may understand that the
moment is arrived for me to re-enter into the bosom of the
church."

"And why to-day, rather than yesterday, or to-morrow?
What has happened to you to-day, to create all these melancholy ideas?"

"This wound, my dear D'Artagnan, has been a warning
to me from heaven."

"This wound? Bah! it is nearly healed, and I am sure
that it is not that which at the present moment gives you the
most pain."

"What do you think it is, then?" said Aramis, blushing.

"You have one in your heart, Aramis, one deeper and
more painful, a wound made by a woman."

The eye of Aramis kindled, in spite of himself.

"Ah," said he, dissembling his emotion under a feigned
carelessness, "do not talk of such things. What! I think of
such things, and suffer love pains? *Vanitas vanitatum!*
According to your idea, then, my brain is turned! And for
whom?—for some grisette, some *fille-de-chambre*, with whom
I have trifled in some garrison! Fie!"

"I crave your pardon, my dear Aramis, but I thought you
aimed higher."

"Higher? And who am I, to nourish such ambition?—a
poor musketeer, a beggar and unknown, who hates slavery,
and finds himself ill-placed in the world."

"Aramis, Aramis!" cried D'Artagnan, looking at his friend
with an air of doubt.

"Dust I am, and to dust I return. Life is full of humili-
ations and sorrows," continued he, becoming still more melancholy; "all the ties which attach him to life break in the
hand of man, particularly the golden ties. Oh, my dear
D'Artagnan," resumed Aramis, giving to his voice a slight
tone of bitterness, "trust me, conceal your wounds when you

have any; silence is the last joy of the unhappy. Beware of giving any one the clue to your griefs; the curious suck our tears as flies suck the blood of a wounded hart."

"Alas! my dear Aramis," said D'Artagnan, in his turn heaving a profound sigh, "that is my history you are relating!"

"How?"

"Yes; a woman whom I love, whom I adore, has just been torn from me by force. I do not know where she is; I have no means of ascertaining where she has been taken to. She is perhaps a prisoner; she is perhaps dead!"

"Yes, but you have at least this consolation, that you can say to yourself she has not quitted you voluntarily; that if you learn no news of her, it is because all communication with you is interdicted; while I——"

"While what?"

"Nothing," replied Aramis, "nothing."

'So you renounce the world, then, forever; that is a settled thing; a resolution decreed?"

"Forever! You are my friend to-day, to-morrow you will be no more to me than a shadow; or rather, even, you will no longer exist for me. As for the world, it is a sepulchre, and nothing else."

"The devil! All this is very sad."

"What is to be said? My vocation commands me, it carries me away." D'Artagnan smiled, but made no answer. Aramis continued.

"And yet, while I do belong to the earth, I should wish to speak of you and of our friends."

"And on my part," said D'Artagnan, "I should have wished to speak of you, but I find you so completely detached from everything! Love you cry fie upon! friends are shadows! the world is a sepulchre!"

"Alas! you will find it so yourself," said Aramis, with a sigh.

"Well, then let us say no more about it," said D'Artagnan; "and let us burn this letter, which, no doubt, announces to you some fresh infidelity of your grisette or your *fille-de-chambre.*"

"What letter?" cried Aramis eagerly.

"A letter which was sent to your abode in your absence, and which was given to me for you."

"But from whom is that letter?"

"Oh! from some heart-broken waiting-woman, some desponding grisette; from Madame de Chevreuse's *fille-de-*

chambre, perhaps, who was obliged to return to Tours with her mistress, and who, in order to appear smart and attractive, stole some perfumed paper, and sealed her letter with a duchess' coronet."

"What do you say?"

"Well! I really think I must have lost it," said the young man maliciously, while pretending to search for it. "But fortunately the world is a sepulchre; the men, and consequently the women, are but shadows, and love is a sentiment upon which you cry fie! fie!"

"D'Artagnan! D'Artagnan!" cried Aramis, "you are killing me!"

"Well! here it is at last!" said D'Artagnan, as he drew the letter from his pocket.

Aramis sprang toward him, seized the letter, read it, or rather devoured it, his countenance absolutely beaming with delight.

"This same waiting-maid seems to have an agreeable style," said the messenger carelessly.

"Thanks, D'Artagnan, thanks!" cried Aramis, almost in a state of delirium. "She was forced to return to Tours; she is not faithless; she still loves me! Dear friend, let me embrace you; happiness almost stifles me!"

And the two friends began to dance round the venerable St. Chrysostom, kicking about famously the sheets of the thesis, which had fallen on the floor.

At that moment Bazin entered with the spinach and the omelette.

"Be off, you scoundrel!" cried Aramis, throwing his *calotte* in his face; "return to whence you came; take back those horrible vegetables, and that poor kickshaw! Order a larded hare, a fat capon, a *gigot à l'ail* and four bottles of the best old Burgundy!"

Bazin, who looked at his master, without comprehending the cause of this change, in a melancholy manner, allowed the omelette to slip in to the spinach, and the spinach on to the floor.

"Now is the moment to consecrate your existence to the King of Kings," said D'Artagnan, "if you persist in offering him a civility. *Non inutile desiderium oblatione.*"

"Get to the devil with your Latin. Let us drink, my dear D'Artagnan, *morbleu!* let us drink while the wine is fresh, let us drink heartily, and while we do so tell me something about what is doing in the world yonder."

CHAPTER XXVII.

THE WIFE OF ATHOS.

"WELL, we have now to search for Athos," said D'Artagnan to the vivacious Aramis, when he had informed him of all that had passed since their departure from the capital, and a good dinner had made one of them forget his thesis and the other his fatigue.

"Do you think, then, that any harm can have happened to him?" asked Aramis. "Athos is so cool, so brave, and handles his sword so skillfully."

"There is no doubt of all that; nobody has a higher opinion of the courage and skill of Athos than I have; but I like better to hear my sword clang against lances than against staves: I fear lest Athos should have been beaten down by a mob of serving-men: those fellows strike hard, and don't leave off in a hurry. This is my reason for wishing to set out again as soon as I possibly can."

"I will try to accompany you," said Aramis, "though I scarcely feel in a condition to mount on horseback. Yesterday I undertook to employ that cord which you see hanging against the wall, but pain prevented my continuing the pious exercise."

"That's the first time I ever heard of anybody trying to cure gunshot wounds with a cat-o'-nine-tails; but you were ill, and illness renders the head weak; therefore you may be excused."

"When do you mean to set out?"

"To-morrow, at daybreak; sleep as soundly as you can to-night, and to-morrow, if you are strong enough, we will take our departure together."

"Till to-morrow, then," said Aramis; "for, iron-nerved as you are, you must stand in need of repose."

The next morning, when D'Artagnan entered Aramis' chamber, he found him standing at the window.

"What are you looking at there?" asked D'Artagnan.

"*Ma foi!* I am admiring three magnificent horses which the stable lads are leading about; it would be a pleasure worthy of a prince to travel upon such horses."

"Well, my dear Aramis, you may enjoy that pleasure, for one of those three horses is your."

"Ah! bah! which of them?"

"Which of the three you like, I have no preference."

"And the rich caparison, is that mine, too?"

"Without doubt it is."

"You are laughing, D'Artagnan."

"No; I have left off laughing now you speak French again."

"What, those rich holsters, that velvet housing, that saddle studded with silver, are they all mine?"

"Yours, and nobody else's, as the horse which is pawing the ground in eagerness is mine, and the other horse which is caracoling belongs to Athos."

"Peste! they are three superb animals!"

"I am glad they please you."

"Why, it must have been the king who made you such a present?"

"To a certainty it was not the cardinal; but don't trouble yourself about where they come from, be satisfied that one of them is your property."

"I choose that which the red-headed boy is leading."

"Have it then."

"*Vive Dieu!* That is enough to drive away all my pains; I could ride upon him with thirty balls in my body. What handsome stirrups! Hola! Bazin, come here this minute."

Bazin made his appearance at the door, dull and spiritless.

"Furbish my sword, put my hat to rights, brush my cloak, and load my pistols!" said Aramis.

"That last order is useless," interrupted D'Artagnan; "there are loaded pistols in your holsters."

Bazin sighed.

"Come, Master Bazin, make yourself easy; people gain the kingdom of heaven in all conditions of life."

"Monsieur was already such a good theologian," said Bazin, almost weeping; "he might have become a bishop, perhaps a cardinal."

"Well! but my poor Bazin, reflect a little; of what use is it to be a churchman, pray? You do not avoid going to war by that means; you see the cardinal is about to make the next campaign, helm on head and partisan in hand; and M. de Nogaret de la Valette, what do you say of him? he is a cardinal likewise; ask his lackey how often he has had to prepare lint for him."

"Alas!" sighed Bazin, "I very well know, monsieur, that everything is turned topsy-turvy in the world nowadays."

While this dialogue was going on, the two young men and the poor lackey went down into the yard.

"Hold my stirrup, Bazin," cried Aramis.

And Aramis sprang into his saddle with his usual grace and lightness; but, after a few vaults and curvets of the noble animal, his rider felt his pains come on so insupportably, that he turned pale, and became unsteady in his seat. D'Artagnan, who, forseeing such an event, had kept his eye on him, sprang toward him, caught him in his arms, and assisted him to his chamber.

"That's well, my dear Aramis, take care of yourself," said he, "I will go alone in search of Athos."

"You are a man of brass," replied Aramis.

"No: I have good luck, that is all; but how do you mean to pass your time till I come back? no more theses, no more glosses upon the fingers, or upon benedictions, hem!"

Aramis smiled: "I will make verses," said he.

"Yes, I dare say; verses perfumed with the odor of the billet from the attendant of Madame de Chevreuse. Teach Bazin prosody, that will consol him. As to the horse, ride him a little every day, till you become accustomed to him and recover your strength."

"Oh, make yourself easy on that head," replied Aramis, "you will find me ready to follow you."

They took leave of each other, and in ten minutes, after commending his friend to the cares of the hostess and Bazin, D'Artagnan was trotting along in the direct of Amiens.

How was he going to find Athos, even should he find him at all? The position in which he had left him was critical; he might, very probably, have succumbed. This idea, while darkening his brow, drew several sighs from him, and caused him to formulate to himself a few vows of vengeance. Of all his friends, Athos was the eldest, and the least resembling him in appearance, in his tastes and sympathies. And yet he entertained a marked preference for this gentleman. The noble and distinguished aid of Athos, those flashes of greatness, which from time to time broke out from the shade in which he voluntarily kept himself, that unalterable equality of temper, which made him the most pleasant companion in the world, that forced and malign gayety, that bravery which might have been termed blind if it had not been the result of the rarest coolness—such qualities attracted more than the esteem, more than the friendship of D'Artagnan, they attracted his admiration.

Indeed, when placed beside M. de Tréville, the elegant and noble courtier, Athos, in his most cheerful days, might advantageously sustain a comparison; he was but of middle height; but his person was so admirably shaped, and so well proportioned, that more than once, in his struggles with Porthos, he had overcome the giant whose physical strength was proverbial among the musketeers; his head, with piercing eyes, a straight nose, a chin cut like that of Brutus—had altogether an indefinable character of grandeur and grace; his hands, of which he took little care, were the envy of Aramis, who cultivated his with almond paste and perfumed oil; the sound of his voice was at once penetrating and melodious, and then, that which was inconceivable in Athos, who was always retiring, was that delicate knowledge of the world, and of the usages of the most brilliant society, those manners of a high family which appeared, as if unconsciously to himself, in his least actions.

If a repast were on foot, Athos presided over it better than any other, placing every guest exactly in the rank which his ancestors had earned for him, or that he had made for himself. If a question in heraldry were started, Athos knew all the noble families of the kingdom, their genealogy, their alliances, their arms, and the origin of their arms. Etiquette had no minutiæ which were unknown to him; he knew what were the rights of the great landowners; he was profoundly versed in venery and falconry, and had, one day, when conversing on this great art, astonished even Louis XIII. himself, who took a pride in being considered a past-master in it.

Like all the great nobles of that period, he rode and fenced to perfection. But still further, his education had been so little neglected, even with respect to scholastic studies, so rare at this time among gentlemen, that he smiled at the scraps of Latin which Aramis sported, and which Porthos pretended to understand; twice or thrice even, to the great astonishment of his friends, he had, when Aramis allowed some rudimental error to escape him, replaced a verb in its right tense and a noun in its case; besides all which, his probity was irreproachable, in an age in which soldiers compounded so easily with their religion and their consciences, lovers with the rigorous delicacy of our days, and the poor with God's seventh commandment. This Athos, then, was a very extraordinary man.

And yet this nature so distinguished, this creature so beautiful, this essence so fine, was seen to turn insensibly toward material life, as old men turn toward physical and moral imbecility. Athos in his hours of privation—and these hours were frequent—was extinguished as to the whole of the luminous portion of him, and his brilliant side disapeared as if in profound darkness.

Then the demi-god having vanished, he remained scarcely a man. His head hanging down—his eye dull—his speech slow and painful, Athos would look for hours together at his bottle, his glass, or at Grimaud, who accustomed to obey him by signs, read in the faint glance of his master his least desire, and satisfied it immediately. If the four friends were assembled at one of these moments, a word, thrown forth occasionally with a violent effort, was the share Athos furnished to the conversation. In exchange for his silence, Athos alone drank enough for four, and without appearing to be otherwise affected by wine, than by a more marked contraction of the brow, and by a deeper sadness.

D'Artagnan, whose inquiring disposition we are acquainted with, had not—whatever interest he had in satisfying his curiosity on this subject—been able to assign any cause for these fits, or for the periods of their recurrence. Athos never received any letters, Athos never had concerns with which all his friends were unacquainted.

It could not be said that it was wine which produced this sadness, for, in truth, he only drank to combat this sadness, which wine only, as we have said, rendered still darker. This excess of bilious humor could not be attributed to play, for, unlike Porthos, who accompanied the variations of chance with songs or oaths, Athos, when he had won, remained as impassable as when he had lost. He had been known, in the circle of the musketeers, to win in one night three thousand pistoles; lose to the gold embroidered belt of gala days; re-win all this, with the addition of a hundred louis, without his beautiful eyebrow being heightened or lowered half a line, without his hands losing their pearly hue, without his conversation, which was cheerful that evening, ceasing for a moment to be calm and agreeable.

Neither was it, as with our neighbors the English, an atmospheric influence which darkened his countenance, for the sadness generally became more intense toward the fine season of the year: June and July were the terrible months with Athos.

On account of the present he had no care, he shrugged his shoulders when people spoke of the future; his secret then was with the past, as D'Artagnan had often vaguely said.

This mysterious shade spread over his whole person, rendered still more interesting the man whose eyes or mouth had never, even in the most complete intoxication, revealed anything, however skillfully questions had been put to him.

"Well," thought D'Artagna, "poor Athos is perhaps at this moment dead, and dead by my fault, for it was I who dragged him into this affair, of which he did not know the origin, of which he will be ignorant of the result, and from which he can derive no advantage."

"Without reckoning, monsieur," added Planchet to his master's audibly expressed reflections, "that we perhaps owe our lives to him. Do you remember how he cried: 'On, D'Artagnan! on! I am taken?' And when he had discharged his two pistols, what a terrible noise he made with his sword! One might have said that twenty men, or rather twenty mad devils, were fighting."

And these words redoubled the eagerness of D'Artagnan, who excited his horse, which stood in need of no excitement, and they proceeded at a rapid pace. About eleven o'clock in the morning they perceived Amiens, and at half-past eleven they were at the door of the accursed auberge.

D'Artagnan had often meditated against the perfidious host one of those hearty vengeances which offer consolation while being hoped for. He entered the hostelry with his hat pulled over his eyes, his left hand on the pummel of the sword, and cracking his whip with his right hand.

"Do you remember me?" said he to the host, who advanced, bowing, toward him.

"I have not that honor, monseigneur," replied the latter, his eyes being dazzled by the brilliant style in which D'Artagnan traveled.

"What! do you mean to say you don't know me?"

"No, monseigneur."

"Well! two words will refresh your memory. What have you done with that gentleman against whom you had the audacity, about twelve days ago, to make an accusation of passing bad money?"

The host became as pale as death; D'Artagnan having assumed a threatening attitude, and Planchet having modeled himself upon his master.

"Ah! monseigneur! do not mention it," cried the host, in the most pitiable voice imaginable; "ah! seigneur, how dearly have I paid for that fault! Unhappy wretch as I am!"

"That gentleman, I say, what is become of him?"

"Deign to listen to me, monseigneur, and be merciful! Sit down, I beg!"

D'Artagnan, mute with anger and uneasiness, took a seat

in the threatening attitude of a judge; Planchet looking fiercely over the back of his *fauteuil*.

"Here is the history, monseigneur," resumed the trembling host, "for I now recollect you: it was you who rode off at the moment I had that unfortunate difference with the gentleman you speak of."

"Yes, it was I; so you may plainly perceive that you have no mercy to expect if you do not tell me the whole truth."

"Condescend to listen to me, and you shall know it all."

"I am listening to you."

"I had been warned by the authorities that a celebrated coiner of bad money would arrive at my auberge, with several of his companions, all disguised as guards or musketeers. I was furnished with a description of your horses, your lackeys, your countenances—nothing was omitted."

"Go on! go on!" said D'Artagnan, who quickly conceived whence such an exact description had come.

"I took then, in conformity with the orders of the authorities, who sent me a reinforcement of six men, such measures as I thought necessary to get possession of the persons of the pretended coiners."

"Again!" said D'Artagnan, whose ears were terribly wounded by the repetition of this word *coiners*.

"Pardon me, monseigneur, for saying such things, but they form my excuse. The authorities had terrified me, and you know that an aubergiste must keep on good terms with the authorities."

"But, once again, that gentleman, where is he? What is become of him? is he dead? is he living?"

"Patience, monseigneur, we are coming to it. There happened then that which you know, and of which your precipitate departure," added the host, with a *finesse* that did not escape D'Artagnan, "appeared to authorize the issue. That gentleman, your friend, defended himself desperately. His lackey, who, by an unforseen piece of ill-luck, had quarreled with the people belonging to the authorities, disguised as stable-lads——"

"Miserable scoundrel!" cried D'Artagnan, "you were all in the plot then! and I really don't know what prevents me from exterminating you all!"

"Alas! monsieur, you will soon see we were not so. Monsieur, your friend (I ask your pardon for not calling him by the honorable name which no doubt he bears, but we do not know that name), monsieur, your friend, having placed two men *hors de combat* with his pistols, retreated, fighting with his sword, with which he disabled one of my men, and stunned me with a blow of the flat side of it."

"But, you infernal villain! when will you come to the end?" cried D'Artagnan; "Athos, what is become of Athos?"

"While fighting and retreating, as I have told monseigneur, he found the door of the cellar stairs behind him, and as the door was open, he took out the key, and barricaded himself inside. As we were sure of finding him there, we left him alone."

"Yes," said D'Artagnan, "you did not particularly wish to kill him, and so were satisfied with detaining him a prisoner."

"Good God! a prisoner, monseigneur? Why, he imprisoned himself, and I will be upon my oath he did. In the first place he had made rough work of it; one man was killed on the spot, and two others were severely wounded. The dead man, and the two that were wounded, were carried off by their companions, and I have heard nothing of either the one or the other since. As for myself, as soon as I recovered my senses, I went to M. the governor, to whom I related all that had passed, and whom I asked what I should do with my prisoner. But M. the governor was all astonishment, he told me he knew nothing about the matter, that the orders I had received did not come from him, and that if I had the audacity to mention his name as being concerned in this disturbance he would have me hanged. It appears that I made a mistake, monsieur, that I had arrested the wrong person, and that he whom I ought to have arrested had escaped."

"But Athos!" cried D'Artagnan, whose impatience was increased by the state of abandonment in which the authorities left the matter; "Athos! where is he?"

"As I was anxious to repair the wrongs I had done the prisoner," resumed the aubergiste, "I took my way straight to the cellar, in order to set him at, liberty. Ah! monsieur he was no longer a man, he was a devil! To my offer of liberty, he replied that it was nothing but a snare, and that before he came out he intended to impose his own conditions. I told him, very humbly—for I could not conceal from myself the scrape I had got into by laying hands on one of his majesty's musketeers—I told him I was quite ready to submit to his conditions.

"'In the first place,' said he, 'I insist upon having my lackey placed with me, fully armed.' We hastened to obey this order; for you will please to understand, monsieur, we were disposed to do everything your friend could desire. M.

Grimaud (he told us his name, he did, although he does not talk much), M. Grimaud, then, went down to the cellar, wounded as he was; then his master, having received him, barricaded the door afresh, and ordered us to remain quietly in our own bar."

"Well where is Athos now?" cried D'Artagnan.

"In the cellar, monsieur."

"What you good-for-nothing scoundrel! What! have you kept him in the cellar all this time?"

"Merciful heaven! No, monsieur! We keep him in the cellar! You do not know what he is about in the cellar! Ah! if you could but persuade him to come out, monsieur, I should owe you the gratitude of my whole life; I should adore you as my patron saint!"

"Then he is there? I shall find him there?"

"Without doubt you will, monsieur; he persists in remaining there. We every day pass through the loophole some bread at the end of a fork, and some meat when he asks for it; but alas! it is not of bread and meat that he makes the greatest consumption. I once endeavored to go down with two of my servants, but he flew into a terrible rage. I heard the noise he made in loading his pistols, and his servant in loading his musketoon. Then, when we asked them what were their intentions, the master replied that he had forty charges to fire, and that he and his lackey would fire to the last one, before he would allow a single soul of us to set foot in the cellar. Upon this I went and complained to the governor, who replied that I only had what I deserved, and that it would teach me to insult honorable gentleman who took up their abode in my house."

"So that from that time—" replied D'Artagnan, totally unable to refrain from laughing at the pitiable face of the host.

"So that from that time, monsieur," continued the latter, "we have led the most miserable life imaginable; for you must know, monsieur, that all our provisions are in the cellar, there is our wine in bottles, and our wine in the piece; beer, oil, grocery, bacon, and large sausages; and as we are prevented from going down, we are forced to refuse food and drink to the travelers who come to the house, so that our hostelry is daily going to ruin. If your friend remains another week in my cellar I shall be a ruined man."

"And not more than justice, neither, you stupid man; could you not perceive by our appearance that we were people of quality, and not coiners—say?"

"Yes, monsieur, you are right," said the host. "But, hark! hark! there he is in a passion again!"

"Somebody has disturbed him, no doubt," said D'Artagnan.

"But he must be disturbed," cried the host; "here are two English gentlemen just arrived."

"Well?"

"Well! the English like good wine, as you may know, monsieur; these have asked for the best. My wife then requested permission of M. Athos to go into the cellar to satisfy these gentlemen; and he, as usual, has refused. Ah! good heaven! there is the Sabbath louder than ever!"

D'Artagnan, in fact, heard a great noise on the side next the cellar. He rose, and, preceded by the host, wringing his hands, and followed by Planchet with his musketoon, ready for action, he approached the scene of action.

The two gentlemen were exasperated; they had had a long ride, and were dying with hunger and thirst.

"But this is a tyranny!" cried one of them, in very good French, though with a foreign accent, "that this madman will not allow these good people access to their own wine! Nonsense! let us break open the door, and if he is too far gone in his madness, well! we will kill him."

"Softly, gentlemen!" said D'Artagnan, drawing his pistols from his belt, "there is nobody to be killed, if you please."

"Good! good!" cried Athos, from the other side of the door, "let them just come in, these devourers of little children, and we shall see."

Brave as they appeared to be, the two English gentlemen looked at each other hesitatingly; it might be said that there was in that cellar one of those hungry ogres, the gigantic heroes of popular legends, into whose cavern nobody could force their way with impunity.

There was a moment of silence; but at length the two Englishmen felt ashamed to draw back, and the more angry one descended the five or six steps which led to the cellar, and gave a kick against the door enough to split a wall.

"Planchet," said D'Artagnan, cocking his pistols, "I will take charge of the one at the top, you look to the one below. Now, gentlemen, if it's battle you want, you shall have it."

"Good God!" cried the hollow voice of Athos, "I can hear D'Artagnan, I think."

"Yes!" cried D'Artagnan, exalting his voice, in his turn, "I am here, my friend!"

"Ah! ah! then," replied Athos, "we will give it to these breakers-in of doors!"

The gentlemen had drawn their swords, but they found themselves taken between two fires; they still hesitated an instant; but, as before, pride prevailed, and a second kick split the door from bottom to top.

"Stand on one side, D'Artagnan, stand on one side," cried Athos, "I am going to fire!"

"Gentlemen!" exclaimed D'Artagnan, whom reflection never abandoned, "gentlemen, think of what you are about! Patience, Athos! You are running your heads into a very silly affair; you will be riddled. My lackey and I will have three shots at you, and you will get as many from the cellar; you will then have our swords, with which, I can assure you, my friend and I can play tolerably well. Let me conduct your business and my own. You shall soon have something to drink, I give you my word."

"If there is any left," grumbled the jeering voice of Athos. The host felt a cold sweat creep down his back.

"What! if there is any left!" murmured he.

"What, the devil! there must be plenty left," replied D'Artagnan; "be satisfied of that; these two can never have drunk all the cellar. Gentlemen, return your swords to their scabbards."

"We will, provided you replace your pistols in your belt."

"Willingly."

And D'Artagnan set the example. Then turning toward Planchet, he made him a sign to uncock his musketoon.

The Englishmen, overcome by these peaceful proceedings, sheathed their swords grumblingly. The history of Athos' imprisonment was then related to them; and as they were really gentleman, they pronounced the host in the wrong.

"Now, gentlemen," said D'Artagnan, "go up to your room again; and in ten minutes, I will answer for it, you shall have all you desire."

The Englishmen bowed, and went upstairs.

"Now I am alone, my dear Athos," said D'Artagnan, "open the door, I beg of you."

"Instantly," said Athos.

Then was heard a great noise of fagots being removed, and of the groaning of posts; these were the counterscarps and bastions of Athos, which the besieged demolished himself.

An instant after, the broken door was removed, and the pale face of Athos appeared, who with a rapid glance took a survey of the environs.

D'Artagnan threw himself on his neck and embraced him.

tenderly; he then endeavored to draw him from his moist abode, but, to his surprise, perceived that Athos staggered.

"Why, you are wounded?" said he.

"I! not at all; I am dead drunk, that's all, and never did a man set about getting so better. *Vive Dieu!* my good host! I must at least have drunk for my part a hundred and fifty bottles."

"*Misericorde!*" cried the host, "if the lackey has drunk only half as much as the master, I am a ruined man."

"Grimaud is a well-bred lackey; he would never think of faring in the same manner as his master; he only drank from the butt: hark! I don't think he put the faucet in again. Do you hear it? It is running now."

D'Artagnan burst into a loud laugh, which changed the trembling of the host into a burning fever.

In the meantime, Grimaud appeared in his turn behind his master, with his musketoon on his shoulder, and his head shaking like one of those drunken satyrs in the pictures of Rubens. He was moistened before and behind with a liquid which the host recognized as his best olive oil.

The *cortége* crossed the public room and proceeded to take possession of the best apartment in the house, which D'Artagnan occupied by authority.

In the meantime the host and his wife hurried down with lamps into the cellar, which had so long been interdicted to them, and where a frightful spectacle awaited them.

Beyond the fortifications through which Athos had made a breach in order to get out, and which were composed of fagots, planks, and empty casks, heaped up according to all the rules of the strategic art, they found, swimming in puddles of oil and wine, the bones and fragments of all the hams they had eaten; while a heap of broken bottles filled the whole left-hand corner of the cellar, and a tun, the cock of which was left running, was yielding, by this means, the last drop of its blood. "The image of devastation and death," as the ancient poet says, "reigned as over a field of battle."

Of sixty large sausages, that had been suspended from the joists, scarcely any remained.

Then the lamentations of the host and hostess pierced the vault of the cellar. D'Artagnan himself was moved by them; Athos did not even turn his head.

But to grief succeeded rage. The host armed himself with a spit, and rushed into the chamber occupied by the two friends.

"Some wine!" said Athos, on perceiving the host.

"Some wine!" cried the stupefied host, "some wine! why you have drunk more than a hundred pistoles' worth! I am a ruined man, lost, destroyed!"

"Bah!" said Athos, "why, we were always dry."

"If you had been contented with drinking, why, well and good; but you have broken all the bottles."

"You pushed me upon a heap which rolled down. That was your fault."

"All my oil is lost!"

"Oil is a sovereign balm for wounds, and my poor Grimaud here was obliged to dress those you had inflicted on him."

"All my sausages gnawed!"

"There is an enormous number of rats in that cellar."

"You shall pay me for all this," cried the exasperated host.

"You triple ass!" said Athos, rising; but he sank down again immediately; he had tried his strength to the utmost. D'Artagnan came to his relief, with his whip in his hand.

The host drew back and burst into tears.

"This will teach you," said D'Artagnan, "to treat the guests God sends you in a more courteous fashion."

"God! say the devil!"

"My dear friend," said D'Artagnan, "if you stun us in this manner, we will all four go and shut ourselves up in your cellar, and see if the mischief be as great as you say."

"Oh! gentlemen!" gentlemen!" said the host, "I have been wrong. I confess it, but, pardon to every sin! you are a gentleman and I am a poor aubergiste, you will have pity on me."

"Ah! if you speak in that way," said Athos, "you will break my heart, and the tears will flow from my eyes as the wine flowed from the casks. We are not such devils as we appear to be. Come hither, and let us talk the matter over."

The host approached with hesitation.

"Come hither, I say, and don't be afraid," continued Athos. "At the moment I was about to pay you, I had placed my purse on the table."

"Yes, monsieur."

"That purse contained sixty pistoles, where is it?"

"Deposited in the justice's office; they said it was bad money."

"Very well; get my purse back and keep the sixty pistoles."

"But monseigneur knows very well that justice never lets go that which it once lays hold of. If it were bad money, there might be some hopes; but unfortunately they are all good pieces."

"Manage the matter as well as you can, my good man; it does not concern me, the more so as I have not a livre left."

"Come," said D'Artagnan, "let us try further; Athos' horse, where is that?"

"In the stable."

"How much is it worth?"

"Fifty pistoles at most."

"It's worth eighty, take it, and there ends the matter."

"What!" cried Athos, "are you selling my horse? my Bajazet? and pray upon what shall I make my campaign? upon Grimaud?"

"I have brought you another," said D'Artagnan.

"Another?"

"And a magnificent one, too!" cried the host.

"Well, since there is another finer and younger, why, you may take the old one, and let us have some wine."

"Which?" asked the host, quite cheerful again.

"Some of that at the bottom, near the laths; there are twenty-five bottles of it left, all the rest were broken by my fall. Bring up six of them."

"Why, this man is a tun!" said the host aside; "if he only remains here a fortnight, and pays for what he drinks, my affairs will soon be right again."

"And don't forget," said D'Artagnan, "to bring up four bottles of the same sort for the two English gentlemen."

"And now," said Athos, "while they are bringing up the wine, tell me, D'Artagnan, what has become of the others, come!"

D'Artagnan related how he had found Porthos in bed with a strained knee, and Aramis at a table between two theologians. As he finished, the host entered with the wine and a ham, which, fortunately for him, had been left out of the cellar.

"That's well!" said Athos, filling his glass and that of his friend; "here's to Porthos and Aramis! but you, D'Artagnan, what is the matter with you, and what has happened to you personally? You don't look happy!"

"Alas!" said D'Artagnan, "it is because I am the most unfortunate of all!"

"You! unfortunate!" said Athos; "come! how the devil can you be unfortunate? let us see that."

"Presently!" said D'Artagnan.

"Presently! and why presently? Now, that's because you

think I am drunk, D'Artagnan. But, take this with you, my ideas are never so clear as when I have had plenty of wine. Speak, then, I am all ears."

D'Artagnan related his adventure with Madame Bonacieux. Athos listened to him with perfect immobility of countenance; and, when he had finished:

"Trifles, all that;" said Athos, "nothing but trifles!" That was Athos' expression.

"You always say trifles, my dear Athos!" said D'Artagnan, "and that comes very ill from you, who have never been in love."

The drink-deadened eye of Athos flashed, but it was only for a moment—it became dull and vacant as before.

"That's true," said he quietly, "for my part I have never loved."

"Acknowledge then, you stone-hearted man," said D'Artagnan, "that you have no right to be so hard upon us whose hearts are tender."

"Tender hearts! wounded hearts!" said Athos.

"What do you say?"

"I say that love is a lottery, in which he who wins, wins death! You are very fortunate to have lost, believe me, my dear D'Artagnan. And if I may be allowed to advise you, it will be to lose always."

"Oh! but she seemed to love me so!"

"She seemed, did she?"

"Oh! she did love me!"

"You boy! why, there lives not a man who has not believed, as you do, that his mistress loved him, and there lives not a man who has not been deceived by his mistress."

"Except you, Athos, who never had one."

"That's true," said Athos, after a moment's silence, "that's true! I never had one! I!—I!—Drink!"

"But then, philosopher as you are," said D'Artagnan, "it is your duty to instruct me, to support me; I stand in need of being taught and consoled."

"Consoled! for what?"

"For my misfortune."

"Your misfortune is laughable," said Athos, shrugging his shoulders; "I should like to know what you would say if I were to relate to you a real tale of love!"

"Which concerns you?"

"Either me or one of my friends, what matters?"

"Tell it, Athos, tell it."

"Drink! I shall tell it better if I drink."

"Drink and relate, then."

"Not a bad idea!" said Athos, emptying and filling his glass, "the two things go marvelously well together."

"I am all attention," said D'Artagnan.

Athos collected himself, and in proportion as he did so, D'Artagnan saw that he became paler; he was at that period of intoxication in which vulgar drinkers fall and sleep. He kept himself upright and dreamed, without sleeping. This somnambulism of drunkenness had something frightful in it.

"You particularly wish it?" asked he.

"I beg you will," said D'Artagnan.

"Be it done then, as you desire. One of my friends, please to observe, not myself," said Athos, interrupting himself with a melancholy smile; "one of the counts of my province, that is to say, of Berry, noble as a Dandolo or a Montmorency, at twenty-five years of age, fell in love with a girl of sixteen, beautiful as fancy can paint. Through the ingenuousness of her age beamed an ardent mind, a mind not of the woman, but of the poet; she did not please, she intoxicated; she lived in a small town with her brother, who was a curé. Both had recently come into the country; they came nobody knew whence; but when seeing her so lovely and her brother so pious, nobody thought of asking whence they came. They were said, however, to be of good extraction. My friend, who was lord of the country, might have seduced her, or he might have seized her forcibly, at his will, for he was master; who would have come to the assistance of two strangers, two unknown persons? Unfortunately, he was an honorable man, he married her. The fool! the ass! the idiot."

"How so, if he loved her?" asked D'Artagnan.

"Wait!" said Athos. "He took her to his château, and made her the first lady in the province; and, in justice, it must be allowed, she supported her rank becomingly."

"Well?" asked D'Artagnan, quite excited.

"Well, one day when she was hunting with her husband," continued Athos, in a low voice, and speaking very quickly, "she fell from her horse and fainted; the count flew to her help, and as she appeared to be oppressed by her clothes, he ripped them open with his poniard, and in so doing laid bare her shoulder: and now, guess, D'Artagnan," said Athos, with a maniacal burst of laughter, "guess what she had upon her shoulder."

"How can I tell?" said D'Artagnan.

"A *fleur-de-lis*," said Athos. "She was branded!"

And Athos emptied at a single draught the glass he held in his hand.

"Horror!" cried D'Artagnan. "What *do* you tell me?"

"Truth! my friend—the angel was a demon: the poor young girl had been a thief!"

"And what did the count do?"

"The count was of the highest noblesse; he had, on his estates the right of high and low justice; he tore the dress of the countess to pieces, he tied her hands behind her, and hanged her on a tree!"

"Heavens! Athos! a murder!" cried D'Artagnan.

"Yes, a murder—no more"—said Athos, as pale as death. "But, methinks, they let me want wine!" and he seized the last bottle that was left, by the neck, put it to his mouth, and emptied it at a single draught as he would have emptied an ordinary glass.

Then he let his head sink upon his two hands, while D'Artagnan stood up before him, terrified, stupefied.

"That has cured me of beautiful, poetical, and loving women," said Athos, after a considerable pause, raising his head, and forgetting to continue the apologue of the count— "God grant you as much! Drink!"

"Then she is dead?" stammered D'Artagnan.

"*Parbleu!*" said Athos. "But hold out your glass. Some ham, my man!" cried Athos; "we don't half drink!"

"And her brother?" added D'Artagnan timidly.

"Her brother?" replied Athos.

"Yes, the priest."

"Oh, I inquired after him for the purpose of hanging him likewise, but he was beforehand with me, he had quitted the curacy instantly."

"Was it ever known who this miserable fellow was?"

"He was doubtless the first lover, and the accomplice of the fair lady, a worthy man, who had pretended to be a curé for the purpose of getting his mistress married, and securing her a position. He has been hanged and quartered before this time, I hope."

"Good God! good God!" cried D'Artagnan, quite stunned by the relation of this horrible adventure.

"Taste some of this ham, D'Artagnan; it is exquisite," said Athos, cutting a slice, which he placed on the young man's plate. "What a pity it is there were only four like this in the cellar, I should have drunk fifty bottles more."

D'Artagnan could no longer endure this conversation,

which had terrified away his senses; he felt quite bewildered, and allowing his head to sink upon his hand, he pretended to sleep.

"These young fellows can none of them drink," said Athos, looking at him with pity, "and yet this is one of the best of them, too!"

CHAPTER XXVIII.

THE RETURN.

D'ARTAGNAN was astounded by the terrible confidence of Athos; and yet many things appeared very obscure to him in this partial revelation; in the first place, it had been made by a man quite drunk, to one who was half drunk, and yet, in spite of the uncertainty which the vapor of three or four bottles of Burgundy carried with it to the brain, D'Artagnan, when awaking on the following morning, had every word of Athos as present to his memory as if they fell from his mouth; they had been impressed upon his mind. All this doubt only gave rise to a more lively desire of arriving at a certainty, and he went into his friend's chamber with a fixed determination of renewing the conversation of the preceding evening; but he found Athos quite himself again, that is to say, the most shrewd and impenetrable of men. Besides which the musketeer, after having exchanged a hearty shake of the hand with him, broached the matter first.

"I was pretty drunk yesterday, D'Artagnan," said he, "I can tell that by my tongue, which was swollen and hot this morning, and by my pulse, which was very tremulous; I would lay a wager I uttered a thousand absurdities."

And while saying this he looked at his friend with an earnestness that embarrassed him.

"No," replied D'Artagnan, "if I recollect what you said, it was nothing out of the common way."

"Indeed! you surprise me, I thought I had related a most lamentable history to you?" And he looked at the young man as if he would read to the very depths of his heart.

"*Ma foi!*" said D'Artagnan, "it would appear that I was more drunk than you, since I remember nothing of the kind."

But this did not deceive Athos, and he resumed:

"You cannot have failed to remark, my dear friend, that every one has his particular kind of drunkenness, sad or gay;

my drunkenness is always sad, and when I am thoroughly intoxicated my mania is to relate all the dismal histories which
my foolish nurse infused into my brain.   That is my failing,
a capital failing, I admit; but, with that exception, I am a
good drinker."

Athos spoke this in so natural a manner, that D'Artagnan
was shaken in his conviction.

"Oh, it is that, then," replied the young man, anxious to
find out the truth, "it is that, then, I remember, as we remember a dream—we were speaking of hanging people."

"Ah! you see how it is," said Athos, becoming still paler,
but yet attempting to laugh, "I was sure it was so—the
hanging of people is my nightmare."

"Yes, yes," replied D'Artagnan, "I remember now; yes,
it was about—stop a minute—yes, it was about a woman."

"That's it," replied Athos, becoming almost livid, "that
is my grand history of the fair lady, and when I relate that, I
must be drunk indeed."

"Yes, that was it," said D'Artagnan, "the history of a
tall, fair lady, with blue eyes."

"Yes, who was hanged."

"By her husband, who was a nobleman of your acquaintance," continued D'Artagnan, looking intently at Athos.

"Well, you see how a man may compromise himself when
he does not know what he says," replied Athos, shrugging
his shoulders as if he thought himself an object of pity.   "I
certainly never will get drunk again D'Artagnan—it is too
bad a habit."

D'Artagnan remained silent.

Then Athos, changing the conversation all at once:

"By-the-by, I thank you for the horse you have brought
me," said he.

"Is it to your mind?" asked D'Artagnan.

"Yes; but it is not a horse for hard work."

"You are mistaken; I have ridden him nearly ten leagues
in less than an hour and a half, and he appeared no more
distressed than if he had only made the tour of the Place
Saint Sulpice."*

"Ah, ah! you begin to awaken my regret."

"Regret?"

* I endeavor to translate as faithfully as is consistent with spirit,
therefore beg the reader to hold me responsible for such wonders
as this; as a pretty good English horseman, I must confess I never
met with such a horse: all these circumstances are exaggerated—TRANS.

"Yes; I have parted with him."

"How?"

"Why, here is the simple fact: this morning I awoke at six o'clock: you were still fast asleep, and I did not know what to do with myself; I was still stupid from our yesterday's debauch. As I came into the public room, I saw one of our Englishmen bargaining with a dealer for a horse, his own having died yesterday from bleeding. I drew near, and found he was bidding a hundred pistoles for a fine chestnut nag. *'Pardieu!'* said I; 'my good gentleman, I have a horse to sell, too.'

" 'Ay, and a very fine one! I saw him yesterday—your friend's lackey was leading him.'

" 'Do you think he is worth a hundred pistoles?'

" 'Yes; will you sell him to me for that sum?'

" 'No; but I will play with you for him.'

" 'You will play with me?'

" 'Yes.'

" 'At what?'

" 'At dice.'

"No sooner said than done, and I lost the horse. Ah, ah! but please to observe I won back the caparison," cried Athos.

D'Artagnan looked much disconcerted.

"This vexes you?" said Athos.

"Well, I must confess it does," replied D'Artagnan. "That horse was to have assisted in making us known in the day of battle. It was a pledge—a remembrance. Athos, you have done very wrong."

"But, my dear friend, put yourself in my place," replied the musketeer. "I was hipped to death: and still further, upon my honor, I don't like English horses. If all the consequence is to be recognized, why the saddle will suffice for that; it is quite remarkable enough. As to the horse, we can easily find some excuse for its disappearance. What the devil! a horse is mortal; suppose mine had had the glanders, or the farcy?"

D'Artagnan could not smile.

"It vexes me greatly," continued Athos, "that you attach so much importance to these animals, for I am not yet at the end of my story."

"What else have you done?"

"After having lost my own horse, nine against ten—see how near!—I formed an idea of staking yours."

"Yes—but you stopped at the idea, I hope?"

"No; for I put it in execution that very minute."

"And the consequence?" said D'Artagnan, in great anxiety.

"I threw, and I lost."

"What, my horse?"

"Your horse; seven against eight; a point short—you know the proverb."

"Athos, you are not in your right senses—I swear you are not."

"My dear lad, it was yesterday, when I was telling you silly stories, that you ought to have told me that, and not this morning. I lost him, then, with all his appointments and furniture."

"Really, this is frightful!"

"Stop a minute; you don't know all yet. I should make an excellent gambler if I were not too hot-headed; but I became so, just as if I were drinking; well, I was hot-headed then——"

"Well, but what else could you play for—you had nothing left?"

"Oh! yes, yes, my friend; there was still that diamond left which sparkles on your finger, and which I had observed yesterday."

"This diamond;" said D'Artagnan, placing his hand eagerly on his ring.

"And as I am a connoisseur in such things, having had a few of my own once, I estimated it at a thousand pistoles."

"I hope," said D'Artagnan, half dead with fright, "you made no mention of my diamond?"

"On the contrary, my dear friend, this diamond became our only resource; with it I might regain our horses and their furniture, and, still further, money to pay our expenses on the road."

"Athos, you make me tremble!" cried D'Artagnan.

"I mentioned your diamond then to my adversary, who had likewise remarked it. What the devil! do you think you can wear a star from heaven on your finger and nobody observe it? Impossible!"

"Oh! go on, go on!" said D'Artagnan, "for upon my honor, you will kill me with your careless coolness."

"We divided, then, this diamond into ten parts, of a hundred pistoles each."

"You are laughing at me, and want to try me!" said D'Artagnan, whom anger began to take by the hair, as Minerva takes Achilles, in the "Iliad."

"No, I am not joking, *mordieu!* I should like to have seen you

in my place! I had been fifteen days without seeing a human
face, and had been left to brutalize myself with the company
of nothing but bottles."

"That was no reason for staking my diamond!" replied
D'Artagnan, closing his hand with a nervous spasm.

"But hear the end. Ten throws of a hundred pistoles
each—ten throws, without revenge; in thirteen throws I lost
all—in thirteen throws. The number thirteen was always
fatal to me; it was on the 13th of the month of July
that——"

"*Ventrebleu!*" cried D'Artagnan, rising from the table,
the history of the present day making him forget that of the
preceding one.

"Patience, patience!" said Athos; "I had a plan. The
Englishman was an original; I had seen him conversing that
morning with Grimaud, and Grimaud had told me that he
had made him proposals to enter into his service. I staked
Grimaud—the silent Grimaud—divided into ten portions."

"Well, what next?" said D'Artagnan, laughing in spite of
himself.

"Grimaud himself, understand! and with the ten parts of
Grimaud, which are not worth a ducatoon, I won back the
diamond. Tell me, now, whether you don't think persistence
is a virtue?"

"*Ma foi!* but this a droll story," cried D'Artagnan, a
little consoled, and holding his sides with laughter.

"You may easily guess, that finding the luck turned, I
again staked the diamond."

"The devil!" said D'Artagnan, becoming again angry.

"I won back your furniture, then your horse, then my
furniture, then my horse, and then I lost again. To make
short, I regained your furniture and then mine. That's where
we left off. That was a superb throw, so I left off there."

D'Artagnan breathed as if the whole hostelry had been removed from off his chest.

"Then I understand," said he timidly, "the diamond is
safe?"

"Intact, my dear friend; *plus* the furniture of your Bu-
cephalus and mine."

"But what is the use of horse-furniture without horses?"

"I have an idea concerning them."

"Athos, you keep me in a fever."

"Listen to me. You have not played for a long time,
D'Artagnan."

"Neither have I any inclination to play."

"Swear to nothing. You have not played for a long time, I said; you ought, then, to have a good hand."

"Well, what then?"

"Well! the Englishman and his companion are still here. I remarked that he regretted the horse-furniture very much. You appear to think much of your horse. In your place, now, I would stake the funiture against the horse."

"But he will not be satisfied with one equipment."

"Stake both, *pardieu!* I am not selfish, if you are."

"You would do so?" said D'Artagnan, undecided, so strongly did the confidence of Athos begin to prevail, unknown to himself.

"*Parole d'honneur,* in one single throw."

"But having lost the horses, I am particularly anxious to preserve the furniture."

"Stake your diamond, then!"

"This! No, thank you! that's quite another thing. Never! never!"

"The devil!" said Athos. "I would propose to you to stake Planchet, but as that has already been done, the Englishman would not, perhaps, be willing."

"Decidedly, my dear Athos, I should like better not to risk anything."

"That's a pity," said Athos coolly; "the Englishman is overflowing with pistoles. Good Lord! try one throw; one throw is soon thrown."

"And if I lose?"

"You will win, I tell you."

"But if I lose?"

"Well, you will surrender the furniture."

"I will try one throw," said D'Artagnan.

Athos went in search of the Englishman, whom he found in the stable, examining the furniture with a greedy eye. The opportunity was good. He proposed the conditions—the two furnitures against one horse, or a hundred pistoles, to choose. The Englishman calculated fast: the two furnitures were worth three hundred pistoles to them: he consented.

D'Artagnan threw the dice with a trembling hand, and turned up the number three; his paleness terrified Athos, who, however, contented himself with saying:

"That's a sad throw, comrade; you will have the horses fully equipped, monsieur."

The Englishman, quite triumphant, did not even give himself the trouble to shake the dice; he threw them on the table without looking at them, so sure was he of victory; D'Artagnan himself had turned on one side to conceal his ill-humor.

"There! there! there!" said Athos, with his quiet tone; "that throw of the dice is extraordinary. I have only witnessed such a one four times in my life. Two aces, gentlemen!"

The Englishman looked, and was seized with astonishment; D'Artagnan looked, and was seized with pleasure.

"Yes," continued Athos, "four times only; once at the house of M. Créquy; another time at my own house in the country, in my château at——, when I had a château; a third time at M. de Tréville's, where it surprised us all; and the fourth time at a cabaret, where it fell to my lot, and where I lost a hundred louis and a supper on it."

"Then monsieur takes his horse back again," said the Englishman.

"Certainly," said D'Artagnan.

"Then there is no revenge?"

"Our conditions said no revenge, you will please to recollect."

"That is true; the horse shall be restored to your lackey, monsieur."

"A moment!" said Athos; "with your permission, monsieur, I wish to speak a word with my friend."

"If you please."

Athos drew D'Artagnan on one side.

"Well, tempter! what more do you want with me?" said D'Artagnan; "you want me to throw again, do you not?"

"No; I would wish you to reflect a little before you decide."

"Upon what?"

"You mean to take your horse, do you not?"

"Without doubt, I do."

"You are wrong, then. I would take the hundred pistoles; you know you have staked the furniture against the horse or a hundred pistoles, at your choice."

"Yes."

"Well, then, I would take the hundred pistoles."

"And I will take the horse."

"In which, I repeat, you are wrong. What is the use of one horse, for us two? I could not get up behind: we should look like the two sons of Amyon, who have lost their brother. You cannot think of humiliating me by riding by my side, prancing along upon that magnificent charger. For my part,

I should not hesitate a moment, but take the hundred pistoles. We want money to carry us back to Paris."

"I am much attached to that horse, Athos."

"And there, again, you are wrong; a horse slips and injures a joint, a horse stumbles and breaks his knees to the bone, a horse eats out of a manger in which a glandered horse has eaten; there is a horse, or rather a hundred pistoles, lost: a master must feed his horse, while, on the contrary, the hundred pistoles feed their master."

"But how shall we get back to Paris?"

"Upon our lackeys' horses, *pardieu!* Never think of our steeds; anybody may see by our carriage that we are people of condition."

"Very pretty figures we shall cut upon ponies, while Aramis and Porthos will be caracoling upon their war steeds!"

"Aramis and Porthos!" cried Athos, and laughed more loudly than was his custom.

"What are you laughing at?" asked D'Artagnan, who did not at all comprehend the hilarity of his friend.

"Never mind—do one thing or the other," said Athos.

"Your advice then is——"

"To take the hundred pistoles, D'Artagnan; with the hundred pistoles we can live well to the end of the month: we have undergone a great deal of fatigue, remember, and a little rest will do us no harm."

"I rest! oh, no, Athos, the moment I am in Paris, I shall prosecute my researches after that unfortunate woman.

"Well, you may be assured that your horse will not be half so serviceable to you for that purpose as the good louis d'or; take the hundred pistoles, my friend, take the hundred pistoles!"

D'Artagnan only required one reason, to be satisfied. This last reason appeared convincing. Besides, he feared that by resisting longer he should appear selfish in the eyes of Athos: he acquiesced, then, and chose the hundred pistoles, which the Englishman paid down immediately.

They then determined to depart. Peace with the landlord, in addition to Athos' old horse, cost six pistoles; D'Artagnan and Athos took the nags of Planchet and Grimaud, and the two lackeys started on foot, carrying the saddles on their heads.

However ill our two friends were mounted, they soon got far in advance of their servants, and arrived at Crèvecœur. From a distance they perceived Aramis, seated in a melan-

choly manner at his window, looking out, like *Sister Anne,*
at the dust in the horizon.

"Holo! ha! Aramis! what the devil are you doing there!"
cried they.

"Ah! is that you, D'Artagnan, and you, Athos?" said the
young man. "I was reflecting upon the rapidity with which
the blessings of this world leave us, and my English horse,
which has just disappeared amid a cloud of dust, has furnished
me with a living image of the fragility of things of the
earth. Life itself may be resolved into three words: *Erat,
est, fuit.*"

"Which means——" said D'Artagnan, who began to suspect the truth.

"Which means, that I have just been duped; sixty louis for
a horse, which, by the manner in which he goes, can do at
least five leagues an hour."

D'Artagnan and Athos burst into a loud laugh.

"My dear D'Artagnan," said Aramis, "don't be too angry
with me, I beg of you, necessity has no law; besides, I am
the person punished, as that rascally horse-dealer has robbed
me of fifty pistoles at least. Ah! you fellows are good man-
agers! you ride on your lackeys' horses, and have your own
gallant steeds led along carefully by hand, at short stages."

At the same instant a market-cart, which had for some
minutes appeared upon the Amiens road, pulled up at the
auberge, and Planchet and Grimaud got out of it with the
saddles on their heads. The carter was going to Paris, and
had agreed, on condition of being prevented from feeling
thirst upon the road, to convey the lackeys and their burdens
thither.

"How is all this?" said Aramis, on seeing them arrive
—"nothing but saddles?"

"Now, do you understand?" said Athos.

"Oh, yes! all alike. I retained my furniture by instinct.
Hola! Bazin! bring my new saddle, and carry it with those
of these gentlemen."

"And what have you done with your curés?" asked D'Artagnan.

"Why, I invited them to a dinner the next day," replied
Aramis; "they have some capital wine here; please to observe
that in passing, I did my best to make them drunk; then
the curé forbade me to quit my uniform, and the Jesuit en-
treated me to get him made a musketeer."

"Without a thesis!" cried D'Artagnan, "without a thesis!
for my part, I request the thesis may be suppressed!"

"From that time," continued Aramis, "I have lived very agreeably. I have begun a poem in verse of one syllable! that is rather difficult, but the merit in all things consists in the difficulty. The matter is tasty. I will read the first canto to you; it has four hundred verses, and lasts a minute."

"*Ma foi!* my dear Aramis!" said D'Artagnan, who detested verses almost as much as he did Latin; "add to the merit of the difficulty that of the brevity, and you are sure that your poem will at least have two merits."

"Ah; but you will see," continued Aramis, "that it breathes irreproachable passion. And so, my friends, we are returning to Paris? Bravo! I am ready, we are going to rejoin that good fellow, Porthos! so much the better. You can't think how I have missed him, the great simpleton. He would not sell his horse, not for a kingdom; I think I can see him now, mounted upon his superb animal and seated in his handsome saddle, looking like the Great Mogul!"

They made a halt for an hour, to refresh their horses: Aramis discharged his bill, placed Bazin in the cart with his comrades, and they set forward to join Porthos.

They found him up, less pale than when D'Artagnan left him, and seated at a table, on which, though he was alone, was spread enough for four persons; this dinner consisted of viands nicely dressed, choice wines, and superb fruit.

"Ah! *pardieu!*" said he, rising, "you come in the nick of time; gentlemen, I was just beginning the potage, and you will dine with me."

"Oh, oh!" said D'Artagnan, "these bottles are not the fruits of Mousqueton's *lasso!* besides, here is a *fricandeau piqué,* and a *filet de bœuf!*"

"I am recruiting myself," said Porthos, "I am recruiting myself; nothing weakens a man more than these cursed strains. Did you ever suffer from a strain, Athos?"

"Never!—only I remember that in our affair of the Rue Férou, I received a sword-wound, which at the end of fifteen or eighteen days produced exactly the same effect."

"But this dinner was not intended for you alone, Porthos?" said Aramis.

"No," said Porthos. "I expected some gentlemen of the neighborhood, who have just sent me word they could not come; you will take their places, and I shall not lose by the exchange. Holo, Mousqueton! seats, and order the number of bottles to be doubled."

"Do you know what we are eating here?" said Athos, at the expiration of about ten minutes.

"*Pardieu!*" replied D'Artagnan, "for my part I am eating *veau pique aux cardons* and *à la moelle.*"

"And I some *filets d'agneau,*" said Porthos.

"And I a *blanc de volaille,*" said Aramis.

"You are all mistaken, gentlemen," answered Athos, with a serious countenance; "you are all eating horse-flesh."

"Eating what?" said D'Artagnan.

"Horse-flesh!" said Aramis, with a look of disgust.

Porthos alone made no reply.

"Yes, real horse; are we not, Porthos, eating a horse—and perhaps his saddle."

"No, no, gentlemen, I have kept the furniture," said Porthos.

"*Ma foi!*" said Aramis, "we are all bad alike; one would think we acted upon agreement."

"What could I do?" said Porthos; "this horse made my visitors ashamed of theirs, and I don't like to humble people!"

"Then your duchess is still taking the waters?" asked D'Artagnan.

"Yes, still," replied Porthos. "And the governor of the province, one of the gentlemen I expected to-day, seemed to have such a wish for him, that I gave him to him."

"Gave him?" cried D'Artagnan.

"Lord yes, gave it to him, you can't call it anything but a gift," said Porthos, "for the animal was worth at least a hundred and fifty louis, and the stingy fellow would only give me eighty!"

"Without the saddle?" said Aramis.

"Yes, without the saddle."

"You will please to observe, gentlemen," said Athos, "that Porthos has made the best bargain of any of us."

And then commenced a roar of laughter in which they all joined, to the astonishment of poor Porthos: but when he was informed of the cause of their hilarity, his laughter, according to custom, was more vociferous than anybody's.

"So, then, there is one comfort, we are all in cash," said D'Artagnan.

"Well, for my part," said Athos, "I found Aramis' Spanish wine so good that I sent on a hamper of sixty bottles of it with the lackeys: that has weakened my purse not a little."

"And I," said Aramis, "you can imagine that I had given

almost my last sou to the church of Montdidier and the
Jesuits of Amiens; that I, moreover, had formed engagements
which I ought to have kept. I have ordered masses for myself, and for you, gentlemen, which will be said, gentlemen,
and for which I have not the least doubt you will be very
much the better."

"And I," said Porthos, "do you think my strain cost me
nothing? without reckoning Mousqueton's wound, on account
of which the surgeon was obliged to come twice a day, and
who charged the double on account of Mousqueton's having
allowed himself to be wounded in a part which people generally only show to an apothecary; so I advised him to try never
to get wounded there any more."

"Ay, ay!" said Athos, exchanging a smile with D'Artagnan and Aramis; "it is very clear you acted nobly with
regard to the poor lad; that is like a good master."

"In short," said Porthos, "when all my expenses are paid,
I shall have, at most, thirty crowns left."

"And I about ten pistoles," said Aramis.

"Well, then, it appears that we are the Crœsuses of the
society. How much have you left of your hundred pistoles,
D'Artagnan?"

"Of my hundred pistoles? Why, in the first place, I gave
you fifty."

"You did?"

"*Pardieu!* yes."

"Ah! yes, so you did; I recollect now."

"Then I paid the host six."

"What an animal that host was! Why did you give him
six pistoles?"

"Why, you told me to give them to him yourself!"

"Ah! so I did; but I am too good-natured. In brief, how
much have you left?"

"Twenty-five pistoles," said D'Artagnan.

"And I," said Athos, taking some small change from his
pocket, "I——"

"You? why, nothing!"

"*Ma foi!* so little that it is not worth reckoning with the
general stock."

"Now, then, let us calculate how much we possess in all."

"Porthos?"

"Thirty crowns."

"Aramis?"

"Ten pistoles."

"And you, D'Artagnan?"

"Twenty-five."

"That makes in all?" said Athos.

"Four hundred and seventy-five livres!" said D'Artagnan, who reckoned like an Archimedes.

"Then on our arrival in Paris we shall still have four hundred, besides the furniture," said Porthos.

"But our troop horses?" said Aramis.

"Well! of the four lackeys' horses we will make two for the masters, for which we will draw lots; with the four hundred livres, we will make the half of one for one of the unmounted, and then we will give the turnings out of our pockets to D'Artagnan, who has a steady hand, and will go and play in the first *tripet* we come to. There, that's arranged."

"Let us finish the dinner, then," said Porthos; "it is getting cold."

The friends having set their minds at ease with regard to the future, did honor to the repast, the remains of which were abandoned to MM. Mousqueton, Bazin, Planchet, and Grimaud.

On arriving in Paris, D'Artagnan found a letter from M. de Tréville, which informed him that, at his request, the king had promised that he should be admitted to the company of the musketeers.

As this was the height of D'Artagnan's worldly ambition, apart, be it well understood, from his desire of finding Madame Bonacieux, he ran, full of joy, to seek his comrades, whom he had left only half an hour before, but whom he found very sad and deeply preoccupied. They were assembled in council at the residence of Athos, which always indicated an event of some seriousness. M. de Tréville had intimated to them that, it being his majesty's fixed intention to open the campaign on the 1st of May, they must immediately get ready all their appointments.

The four philosophers looked at each other in a state of bewilderment. M. de Tréville never joked in matters relating to discipline.

"And what do you reckon your appointments will cost?" said D'Artagnan.

"Oh, we can scarcely venture to say. We have made our calculations with Spartan economy, and we each require fifteen hundred livres."

"Four times fifteen make sixty—ah! six thousand livres," said Athos.

"For my part, I think," said D'Artagnan, "with a

thousand livres each—I do not speak as a Spartan, but as a
procureur——"

This word procureur roused Porthos.

'Stop!" said he, "I have an idea."

"Well, that's something; for my part, I have not the
shadow of one," said Athos coolly; "but as to D'Artagnan,
the idea of belonging to *ours*, gentlemen, has driven him out
of his senses. A thousand livres! for my part, I declare I
want two thousand."

"Four times two makes eight, then," said Aramis; "it
is eight thousand that we want to complete our appointments,
of which appointments, it is true, we have already handsome
saddles."

"Besides," said Athos, waiting till D'Artagnan, who went
to thank M. de Tréville, had shut the door, "besides, there
is that beautiful ring which beams from the finger of our
friend. What the devil! D'Artagnan is too good a comrade
to leave his brothers in embarrassment while he wears the
ransom of a king on his finger."

CHAPTER XXIX.

HUNTING FOR THE EQUIPMENTS.

THE most preoccupied of the four friends was certainly
D'Artagnan, although D'Artagnan, in his quality of guard,
would be much more easily equipped than messieurs the musketeers, who were all very high; but our Gascon cadet was,
as may have been observed, of a provident and almost
avaricious character, and with that (explain the contra-
diction if you can) so vainglorious as almost to rival Porthos.
To this preoccupation of his vanity, D'Artagnan, at this moment, joined an uneasiness much less selfish. Notwithstanding all his inquiries respecting Madame Bonacieux, he could
obtain no intelligence of her. M. de Tréville had spoken of
her to the queen; the queen was ignorant where the mercer's
young wife was, but had promised to have her sought for.
But this promise was very vague, and did not at all reassure
D'Artagnan.

Athos did not leave his chamber; he made up his mind not
to take a single step to provide for his equipment.

"We have still a fortnight before us," said he to his
friends; "well, if, at the end of a fortnight, I have found

nothing, or, rather, if nothing has come to find me, as I am too good a Catholic to kill myself with a pistol-bullet, I will seek a good cause of quarrel with four of his eminence's guards or with eight Englishmen; I will fight until one of them has killed me, which, considering the number, cannot fail to happen. It will then be said of me that I died for the king, so that I shall have performed my duty without the expense of equipment."

Porthos continued to walk about, with his hands behind him, tossing his head and repeating:

"I shall follow up my idea."

Aramis, anxious, and negligently dressed, said nothing.

It may be seen by these disastrous details that desolation reigned in the community.

The lackeys, on their parts, like the coursers of Hippolytus, shared the sadness of their masters. Mousqueton collected a store of crusts; Bazin, who had always been inclined to devotion, never quitted the churches; Planchet watched the flight of flies; and Grimaud, whom the general distress could not induce to break the silence imposed by his master, heaved sighs enough to soften stones.

The three friends—for, as we have said, Athos had sworn not to stir a foot to equip himself—the three friends went out early in the morning, and returned late at night. They wandered about the streets, looking at the pavement to see whether the passengers had not left a purse behind them. They might have been supposed to be following tracks, so attentive were they wherever they went. When they met they looked desolately at each other, as much as to say, "Have you found anything?"

However, as Porthos had first found an idea, and had thought of it earnestly afterward, he was the first to act. He was a man of execution, this worthy Porthos. D'Artagnan perceived him one day walking toward the church of St. Leu, and followed him instinctively; he entered after having twisted his mustache and elongated his royal, which always announced, on his part, the most conquering resolutions. As D'Artagnan took some precautions to conceal himself, Porthos believed he had not been seen. D'Artagnan entered behind him, Porthos went and leaned against the side of a pillar; D'Artagnan, still unperceived, supported himself against the other side of it.

There happened to be a sermon, which made the church very full. Porthos took advantage of this circumstance to ogle the women: thanks to the cares of Mousqueton, the ex-

terior was far from announcing the distress of the interior:
his hat was a little napless, his feather was a little faded, his
gold lace was a little tarnished, his laces were a trifle frayed;
but in the obscurity of the church these things were not seen
and Porthos was still the handsome Porthos.

D'Artagnan observed, on the bench nearest to the pillar
against which Porthos leaned, a sort of ripe beauty, rather
yellow and rather dry, but erect and haughty, under her
black hood. The eyes of Porthos were furtively cast upon
this lady, and then roved about at large over the nave.

On her side, the lady, who from time to time blushed,
darted with the rapidity of lightning a glance toward the inconstant Porthos, and then immediately the eyes of Porthos
were sent wandering over the church anxiously. It was
plain that this was a mode of proceeding that piqued the lady
in the black hood to the quick, for she bit her lips till they
bled, scratched the top of her nose, and could not sit still in
her seat.

Porthos, seeing this, retwisted his mustache, elongated his
royal a second time, and began to make signals to a beautiful lady who was near the choir, and who not only was a
beautiful lady, but, still further, no doubt, a great lady, for
she had behind her a negro boy, who had brought the cushion
on which she knelt, and a female servant who held the coat-
of-arms marked bag, in which was placed the book from
which she read the mass.

The lady with the black hood followed through all their
wanderings the looks of Porthos, and perceived that they
stopped upon the lady with the velvet cushion, the little
negro, and the maid-servant.

During all this time Porthos played close; it was almost
imperceptible motions of his eyes, fingers placed upon the
lips, little assassinating smiles, which really did assassinate
the disdained beauty.

Then she uttered, in form of *mea culpa,* and striking her
breast, a *hum!* so vigorous that everybody, even the lady with
the red cushion, turned round toward her. Porthos paid no
attention; nevertheless, he understood it all, but was as deaf
as the pillar he leaned against.

The lady with the red cushion produced a great effect—for
she was very handsome—upon the lady with the black hood
who saw in her a rival really to be dreaded: a great effect
upon Porthos, who thought her much more pretty than the
lady with the black hood; a great effect upon D'Artagnan,
who recognized in her the lady of Meung, of Calais, and

Dover, whom his persecutor, the man with the scar, had saluted by the name of milady.

D'Artagnan, without losing sight of the lady of the red cushion, continued to watch the proceedings of Porthos, which amused him greatly; he directly guessed that the lady of the black hood was the procureur's wife of the Rue aux Ours, which was the more probable from the church of St. Leu being contiguous to that locality.

He guessed, likewise, that Porthos was taking his revenge for the defeat of Chantilly, when the procureuse had proved so refractory with respect to her purse.

But, amid all this, D'Artagnan remarked also that not one countenance responded to the gallantries of Porthos. There was nothing but chimeras and illusions; but for real love, for true jealousy, is there any reality but illusions and chimeras?

The sermon over, the procureuse advanced toward the *benitier;* Porthos went before her, and, instead of a finger, dipped his whole hand in. The procureuse smiled, thinking that it was for her that Porthos put himself to this expense; but she was cruelly and promptly undeceived: when she was only about three steps from him, he turned his head round, fixing his eyes invariably upon the lady of the red cushion, who had risen and was approaching, followed by her black boy and fille-de-chambre.

When the lady of the red cushion came close to Porthos, Porthos drew his dripping hand from the *benitier.* The fair *devote* touched the great hand of Porthos with her delicate fingers, smiled, made the sign of the cross, and left the church.

This was too much for the procureuse; she entertained no doubt that there was an affair of gallantry between this lady and Porthos. If she had been a great lady she would have fainted; but as she was only a procureuse, she contented herself with saying to the musketeer, with concentrated fury:

"Eh, Monsieur Porthos, you don't offer *me* any holy water?"

Porthos, at the sound of that voice, started like a man awakened from a sleep of a hundred years.

"Ma—madame!" cried he; "is that you? How is your husband, our dear Monsieur Coquenard? Is he still as stingy as ever? Where can my eyes have been not to have even perceived you during the two hours the sermon has lasted?"

"I was within two paces of you, monsieur," replied the procureuse; "but you did not perceive me, because you had no eyes but for the pretty lady to whom you just now gave the holy water."

Porthos pretended to be confused.

"Ah," said he, "you have remarked."

"I must have been blind if I had not."

"Yes," said Porthos, "that is a duchess of my acquaintance, with whom I have great trouble to meet, on account of the jealousy of her husband, and who sent me word that she should come to-day, solely for the purpose of seeing me in this poor church, buried in this vile quarter."

"Monsieur Porthos," said the procureuse, "will you have the kindness to offer me your arm for five minutes? I have something to say to you."

"Certainly, madame," said Porthos, winking to himself, as a gambler does who laughs at the dupe he is about to pluck.

At that moment D'Artagnan passed in pursuit of milady; he cast a passing glance at Porthos, and beheld this triumphant look.

"Eh, eh!" said he, reasoning to himself according to the strangely easy morality of the gallant period, "there is one, at least, in the road to be equipped in time."

Porthos, yielding to the pressure of the arm of the procureuse, as a bark yields to the rudder, arrived at the Cloisters Saint Magloire, a very unfrequented passage, enclosed with a turnstile at each end. In the daytime nobody was seen there but mendicants devouring their crusts, and children playing.

"Ah, Monsieur Porthos," cried the procureuse, when she was assured that no one a stranger to the population of the locality could either see or hear her, "ah, Monsieur Porthos, you are a great conqueror, it appears!"

"Who—I, madame?" said Porthos, drawing himself up proudly; "how so?"

"Look at the proofs of it, just now, and the holy water! But that must be a princess, at least, that lady with her negro boy and her maid!"

"*Pardieu!* madame, you are deceived; she is simply a duchess."

"And that running footman who waited at the door, and that carriage with a coachman in grand livery, who sat waiting on his seat?"

Porthos had seen neither the footman nor the carriage, but, with the eye of a jealous woman, Madame Coquenard had seen everything.

Porthos regretted that he had not at once made the lady of the red cushion a princess.

"Ah, you are quite the pet of the ladies, Monsieur Porthos!" resumed the procureuse with a sigh.

"Why, you may well imagine that, with the person with which nature has endowed me, I am not in want of ladies' favors."

"Good Lord! how quickly men forget!" cried the procureuse, raising her eyes toward heaven.

"Still less quickly than the women, in my opinion," replied Porthos; "as a proof, I, madame, I may say, was your victim: when wounded, dying, I was abandoned by the surgeons; I, the offspring of a noble family, who placed reliance upon your friendship, I was near dying of my wounds at first, and of hunger afterward, in a beggarly auberge at Chantilly, without you ever deigning once to reply to the burning letters I addressed to you."

"But, Monsieur Porthos," murmured the procureuse, who began to feel that, to judge by the conduct of the great ladies of the time, she was wrong.

"I! who had sacrificed the Countess de Penaflor on your account!"

"Well, I know you did."

"The Baronee de——"

"Monsieur Porthos, do not overwhelm me quite!"

"The Countess de——"

"Monsieur Porthos be generous!"

"You are right, madame, and I will not finish."

"But it was my husband who would not hear of lending."

"Madame Coquenard," said Porthos, "remember the first letter you wrote me, and which I preserve engraven in my memory."

The procureuse uttered a groan.

"Besides," said she, "the sum you require me to borrow was rather large; you said you wanted a thousand livres!"

"Madame Coquenard, I gave you the preference. I had but to write to the Duchess de——; but I don't repeat her name, for I am incapable of compromising a woman; but this I know, that I had but to write to her, and she would have sent me fifteen hundred."

The procureuse let fall a tear.

"Monsieur Porthos," said she, "I can assure you you have severely punished me; and if in the time to come you should find yourself in a similar situation, you have but to apply to me."

"Fie, madame, fie!" said Porthos, as if disgusted; "let us not talk about money, if you please; it is humiliating."

"Then you no longer love me?" said the procureuse, slowly and sadly.

Porthos maintained a majestic silence.

"And that is the only reply you make me? Alas! I but too well understand."

"Think of the offense you have committed toward me, madame! it remains *here!*" said Porthos, placing his hand on his heart, and pressing it strongly.

"I will repair it; indeed I will, my dear Porthos."

"Besides, what did I ask of you?" resumed Porthos, with a movement of the shoulders full of *bonhommie.* "A loan, nothing more! After all, I am not an unreasonable man. I know you are not rich, Madame Coquenard, and that your husband is obliged to bleed his poor clients to squeeze a few paltry crowns from them. Oh! if you were a duchess, a marquise, or a countess, it would be quite a different thing; it would be unpardonable."

The procureuse was piqued.

"Please to know, Monsieur Porthos," said she, "that my strong box, strong box of a procureuse as it may be, is better filled than those of your ruined minxes."

"That, then, doubles the offense," said Porthos, disengaging his arm from that of the procureuse; "for if you are rich, Madame Coquenard, then there is no excuse for your refusal."

"When I said rich," replied the procureuse, who saw that she had gone too far, "you must not take the word for the letter. I am not precisely rich, I am only pretty well off."

"Hold, madame," said Porthos, "let us say no more upon the subject, I beg of you. You don't know me—all sympathy is extinct between us."

"Ungrateful man as you are!"

"Ah! I advise you to complain!" said Porthos.

"Begone, then, to your beautiful duchess, I will detain you no longer."

"And she is not to be despised, in my opinion."

"Now, Monsieur Porthos, once more, and this is the last! do you love me still?"

"Alas! madame," said Porthos, in the most melancholy tone he could assume, "when we are about to enter upon a campaign, a campaign in which my presentiments tell me I shall be killed——"

"Oh! don't talk of such things!" cried the procureuse, bursting into tears.

"Something whispers me so," continued Porthos, becoming still more and more melancholy.

"Rather say that you have a new love affair."

"No, not so; I speak frankly to you. No new object affects me; and I even feel here, at the bottom of my heart, something which speaks for you. But in a fortnight's time, as you know, or as you do not know, this fatal campaign is to open; I shall be fearfully engaged in providing for my equipment. Then I am obliged to make a journey to my family, in the lower part of Brittany, to obtain the sum necessary for my departure."

Porthos observed a last struggle between love and avarice.

"And as," continued he, "the duchess you saw at the church has estates near to those of my family, we mean to make the journey together. Journeys, you know, appear much shorter when we travel two in company."

"Have you no friends in Paris, then, Monsieur Porthos?" said the procureuse.

"I thought I had," said Porthos, resuming his melancholy air; "but I have been bitterly taught that I was mistaken."

"You have some, Monsieur Porthos, you have some!" cried the procureuse, in a transport that surprised even herself; "come to our house to-morrow. You are the son of my aunt, consequently my cousin; you come from Noyon, in Picardy; you have several lawsuits and no procureur. Can you recollect all that?"

"Perfectly, madame."

"Come at dinner time."

"Very well."

"And be upon your guard before my husband, who is rather shrewd, notwithstanding his seventy-six years."

"Seventy-six years! Peste! that's a fine age!" replied Porthos.

"A great age, you mean, Monsieur Porthos. Yes, the poor man may be expected to leave me a widow, every hour," continued she, throwing a significant glance at Porthos. "Fortunately, by our marriage contract, the survivor takes everything."

"Everything?"

"Yes, all"

"You are a woman of precaution, I see, my dear Madame Coquenard," said Porthos, squeezing the hand of the procureuse tenderly.

"We are, then, reconciled, dear Monsieur Porthos?" said she, simpering.

"For life," said Porthos, in the same manner.

"Till we meet again, then, dear traitor!"

"Till we meet again, my forgetful charmer!"

"To-morrow, my angel!"

"To-morrow, flame of my life!"

CHAPTER XXX.

D'ARTAGNAN AND THE ENGLISHMAN.

D'ARTAGNAN followed milady, without being perceived by her; he saw her get into her carriage, and heard her order the coachman to drive to St. Germain.

It was useless to endeavor to keep pace on foot with a carriage drawn by two powerful horses: D'Artagnan returned then to the Rue Férou.

In the Rue de Seine he met with Planchet, who had stopped before the house of a pastry cook, and was contemplating with ecstasy a cake of the most appetizing appearance.

He ordered him to go and saddle two horses in M. de Tréville's stables, one for himself, D'Artagnan, and one for Planchet. M. de Tréville, on all common occasions, had allowed him the liberty to do so.

Planchet proceeded toward the Rue du Colombier, and D'Artagnan toward the Rue Férou. Athos was at home, emptying in solitary sadness one of his bottles of the famous Spanish wine he had brought back with him from his journey into Picardy. He made a sign for Grimaud to bring a glass for D'Artagnan, and Grimaud obeyed, still as silently as usual.

D'Artagnan related to Athos all that had passed at the church between Porthos and the procureuse, and how their comrade was probably by that time in a fair way to be equipped.

"As for me," replied Athos, to this recital, "I am quite at my ease; it will not be women that will defray the expense of my equipment."

"The more to blame you; handsome, well-bred, noble as you are, my dear Athos, neither princesses nor queens would be secure!"

"How young this D'Artagnan is!" said Athos, shrugging his shoulders, and making a sign to Grimaud to bring another bottle.

At that moment Planchet put his head modestly in at the half-open door, and told his master that the horses were ready.

"What horses?" cried Athos.

"Two horses that M. de Tréville lends me when I please, and with which I am now going to take a ride to St. Germain."

"Well, and what are you going to do at St. Germain?"

Then D'Artagnan described the meeting which, on his side, he had had at the church, and how he had found that lady who, with the seigneur in the black cloak, and with the scar near his temple, filled his mind constantly.

"That is to say, you are in love with this lady as you were with Madame Bonacieux," said Athos, shrugging his shoulders contemptuously, as if he pitied human weakness.

"I? not at all!" said D'Artagnan, "I am only curious to unravel the mystery to which she is attached. I do not know why, but I have a strong feeling that this woman, perfectly unknown to me as she is, and unknown to her as I am, has an influence over my life."

"Well, perhaps you are right," said Athos; "I do not know a woman that is worth the trouble of being sought for when she is once lost. Madame Bonacieux is lost, so much the worse for her."

"No, Athos, no, you are mistaken," said D'Artagnan; "I love my poor Constance more than ever, and if I knew the place in which she is, were it at the end of the world, I would go and free her from the hands of her enemies; but I cannot find out where she is; all my researches have proved in vain. What is to be said? I must divert my attention by something!"

"Amuse yourself, then, with milady, my dear D'Artagnan; I wish you may with all my heart, if that will amuse you."

"Hear me, Athos," said D'Artagnan, "instead of shutting yourself up here as if you were under arrest, get on horseback, and come and take a ride with me to St. Germain."

"My dear fellow," said Athos, "I ride horses when I have any; when I have none, I walk on foot."

"Well, on my part," said D'Artagnan, smiling at the misanthropy of Athos, which from any other person would certainly have offended him, "for my part, I ride what I can get; I am not so proud as you, Athos. So, *au revoir*, my proud, melancholy friend."

"*Au revoir,*" said the musketeer, making a sign to Grimaud to uncork the bottle he had just brought.

D'Artagnan and Planchet got into the saddle, and took the road to St. Germain.

As he rode along, that which Athos had said respecting Madame Bonacieux, recurred to the mind of the young man. Although D'Artagnan was not of a very sentimental character, the mercer's pretty wife had made a real impression upon his heart. As he said, he was ready to go to the end of the world to seek her: but the world being round, it has many ends, so that he did not know which way to turn; in the meantime, he was going to try to find out who milady was. Milady had spoken to the man in the black cloak, therefore she knew him. Now, in the opinion of D'Artagnan, it was certainly the man in the black cloak who had carried off Madame Bonacieux the second time, as he had carried her off the first. D'Artagnan then only half lied, which is lying but little, when he said that by going in search of milady, he at the same time went in search of Constance.

Thinking of all this, and from time to time giving a touch of the spur to his horse, D'Artagnan completed his short journey, and arrived at St. Germain. He had just passed by the pavilion in which ten years later Louis XIV. was to be born. He rode up a very quiet street, looking to the right and the left to see if he could catch any vestige of his beautiful Englishwoman, when from the terrace in front of a pretty house, which, according to the fashion of the time, had no window toward the street, he saw a face peep out with which he thought he was acquainted. This person walked along the terrace, which was ornamented with flowers. Planchet made out who it was first.

"Eh! monsieur!" said he, addressing D'Artagnan, "don't you remember that face which is gaping about yonder?"

"No," said D,Artagnan, "and yet I am certain it is not the first time I have seen it."

"*Parbleu!* I believe it is not," said Planchet; "why, it is poor Lubin, the lackey of the Count de Wardes—he whom you so well accommodated a month ago, at Calais, on the road to the governor's country-house."

"So it is!" said D'Artagnan; "I know him now. Do you think he would recollect you?"

"*Ma foi!* monsieur, he was in such trouble, that I don't think he can have retained a very clear recollection of me."

"Well, go and get into conversation with him, and make out, if you can, whether his master is dead or not."

Planchet dismounted, and went straight up to Lubin, who

did not at all remember him, and the two lackeys began to chat with the best understanding possible; while D'Artagnan turned the two horses into a lane, and went round the house, coming back to watch the conference from behind a hedge of nut-trees.

At the end of an instant's observation he heard the noise of a carriage, and speedily saw that of milady stop opposite to him. He could not be mistaken—milady was in it. D'Artagnan stooped down upon the neck of his horse, in order that he might see without being seen.

Milady put her charming fair head out of the window, and gave her orders to her female attendant.

The latter, a pretty girl of about twenty years of age, active and lively, the true soubrette of a great lady, jumped from the step—upon which, according to the custom of the time, she was seated—and took her way toward the terrace upon which D'Artagnan had perceived Lubin.

D'Artagnan followed the soubrette with his eyes, and saw her go toward the terrace. But it happened that some one in the house called Lubin, so that Planchet remained alone, looking in all directions for his master.

The femme de chambre approached Planchet, whom she took for Lubin, and holding out a little billet to him—

"For your master," said she.

"For my master?" replied Planchet, in astonishment.

"Yes—and of consequence—take it quickly."

Thereupon she ran toward the carriage, which had turned round toward the way it came, jumped upon the step and the carriage drove off.

Planchet turned the billet on all sides; then accustomed to passive obedience, he jumped down from the terrace, ran toward the lane, and at the end of twenty paces met D'Artagnan, who, having seen all, was coming to him.

"For you, monsieur," said Planchet, presenting the billet to the young man.

"For me!" said D'Artagnan, "are you sure of that?"

"*Pardieu!* monsieur, I can't be more sure. The soubrette said '*For your master;*' I have no other master but you; so—a pretty little lass, *ma foi!* is that soubrette!"

D'Artagnan opened the letter, and read these words:

"A person who takes more interest in you than she is willing to confess, wishes to know on what day it will suit you to walk in the forest? To-morrow, at the Hotel du Champ du Drap d'Or, a lackey in black and red will wait for your reply"

"Oh! oh!" said D'Artagnan, "this is rather warm; it appears that milady and I are anxious about the health of the same person. Well, Planchet, how is the good M. de Wardes! he is not dead, then?"

"Oh, no, monsieur, he is as well as a man can be with four sword-wounds in his body; for you, without question, inflicted four upon the dear gentleman, and he is still very weak, having lost almost all his blood. As I said, monsieur, Lubin did not know me, and told me our adventure from one end to the other."

"Well done, Planchet! you are the king of lackeys. Now jump up on your horse, and let us overtake the carriage."

They soon effected this. At the end of five minutes they perceived the carriage drawn up by the roadside: a cavalier, richly dressed, was close to the coach door.

The conversation between milady and the cavalier was so animated that D'Artagnan stopped on the other side of the carriage without any one but the pretty soubrette being aware of his presence.

The conversation took place in English—a language which D'Artagnan could not understand; but by the accent the young man plainly saw that the beautiful Englishwoman was in a great rage: she terminated it by an action which left no doubt as to the nature of this conversation—this was a blow with her fan, applied with such force that the little feminine weapon flew into a thousand pieces.

The cavalier broke into a loud laugh, which appeared to exasperate milady still more.

D'Artagnan thought this was the moment to interfere; he approached the other door, and taking off his hat respectfully—

"Madame," said he, "will you permit me to offer you my services? It appears to me that this cavalier has made you very angry. Speak one word, madame, and I take upon myself to punish him for the want of courtesy."

At the first word, milady turned round, looking at the young man with astonishment; and when he had finished:

"Monsieur," said she, in very good French, "I should with great confidence place myself under your protection, if the person with whom I quarrel were not my brother."

"Ah! excuse me, then," said D'Artagnan, "you must be aware that I was ignorant of that, madame!"

"What is that stupid fellow troubling himself about?" cried the cavalier, whom milady had designated as her brother, stooping down to the height of the coach window—"why does not he go about his own business?"

"Stupid fellow yourself!" said D'Artagnan, stooping in his turn on the neck of his horse, and answering on his side though the carriage window. "I do not go on, because it pleases me to stop here."

The cavalier addressed some words in English to his sister.

"I speak to you in French," said D'Artagnan; "be kind enough, then, to reply to me in the same language. You are madame's brother, I learn—be it so; but, fortunately, you are not mine."

It might be thought that milady, timid as women are in general, would have interposed in this commencement of mutual provocations, in order to prevent the quarrel from going too far; but, on the contrary, she threw herself back in her carriage, and called out coolly to the coachman, "Go on—home!"

The pretty soubrette cast an anxious glance at D'Artagnan, whose good looks seemed to have made an impression upon her.

The carriage went on, and left the two men in face of each other; no material obstacle separated them.

The cavalier made a movement as if to follow the carriage; but D'Artagnan, whose anger, already excited, was much increased by recognizing in him the Englishman of Amiens, who had won his horse and was very near winning his diamond of Athos, caught at his bridle and stopped him.

"Well, monsieur!" said he; "you appear to be more stupid than I am, for you forget there is a little quarrel to arrange between us two."

"Ah! ah!" said the Englishman; "is it you, my master? It seems you must always be playing some game or other."

"Yes; and that reminds me that I have a revenge to take. We will see, my dear monsieur, if you can handle a sword as skillfully as you can a dice-box."

"You see plainly that I have no sword," said the Englishman. "Do you wish to play the braggart with an unarmed man?"

"I hope you have a sword at home; but, at all events, I have two, and, if you like, I will throw with you for one of them."

"Quite unnecessary," said the Englishman; "I am well furnished with such sorts of playthings."

"Very well! my worthy gentleman," replied D'Artagnan; "pick out the longest, and come and show it to me this evening."

"Where?"

"Behind the Luxembourg; that's a charming spot for such amusements as the one I propose to you."

"That will do; I will be there."

"Your hour?"

"Six o'clock."

"Apropos, you have probably one or two friends?"

"Humph! I have three who would be honored by joining in the sport with me."

"Three! that's fortunate! That falls out oddly! Three is just my number!"

"Now then, who are you?" asked the Englishman.

"I am M. d'Artagnan, a Gascon gentleman, serving in the guards, in the company of M. Dessessarts. And you?"

"I am the Lord de Winter, Baron of Scheffield."

"Well, then, I am your servant, Monsieur le Baron," said D'Artagnan, "though you have names rather difficult to recollect."

And touching his horse with the spur, he cantered back to Paris.

As he was accustomed to do in all cases of any consequence, D'Artagnan went straight to the residence of Athos.

He found Athos reclining upon a large sofa, where he was waiting, as he said, for his equipment to come and find him.

He related to Athos all that had passed, except the letter to M. de Wardes.

Athos was delighted to find he was going to fight an Englishman. We are aware that that was his dream.

They immediately sent their lackeys for Porthos and Aramis, and, on their arrival, made them acquainted with the affair in hand.

Porthos drew his sword from the scabbard, and made passes at the wall, springing back from time to time, and making contortions like a dancer.

Aramis, who was constantly at work at his poem, shut himself up in Athos' closet, and begged not to be disturbed before the moment of drawing swords.

Athos by signs desired Grimaud to bring another bottle of wine.

And D'Artagnan employed himself in arranging a little plan, of which we shall hereafter see the execution, and which promised him some agreeable adventure, as might be seen by the smiles which from time to time passed over his countenance, the thoughtfulness of which they enlivened.

CHAPTER XXXI.

ENGLISH AND FRENCH.

THE hour being come, they, with their four lackeys, repaired to a spot behind the Luxembourg given up to the feeding of goats. Athos threw a piece of money to the goat-keeper to remove his flock to a distance. The lackeys were charged to act as sentinels.

A silent party soon drew near to the same enclosure, penetrated into it, and joined the musketeers: then, according to the English custom, the presentations took place.

The Englishmen were all men of rank; consequently, the extraordinary names of their adversaries were, for them, not only a matter of surprise, but of uneasiness.

"But, after all this," said Lord de Winter, when the three friends had been named, "we do not know who you are; as gentlemen, we cannot fight with such; why, they are nothing but shepherd's names."

"Therefore your lordship may suppose they are only assumed names," said Athos.

"Which only gives us a greater desire to know the real ones," replied milord.

"You gambled very willingly with us without knowing our names," said Athos, "as is plain by your having won our horses."

"That is true, but we then only risked our pistoles; this time we risk our blood: we play with anybody, but we only fight with our equals."

"And that is but just," said Athos, and he took aside that one of the four Englishmen with whom he was to fight, and communicated his name in a low voice.

Porthos and Aramis did the same.

"Does that satisfy you?" said Athos to his adversary; "do you think me sufficiently noble to do me the honor of crossing swords with me?"

"Yes, monsieur," said the Englishman, bowing.

"Well! now shall I tell you another thing?" said Athos coolly.

"What is that?" replied the Englishman.

"Why, that is, that you would have acted much more wisely if you had not required me to make myself known."

"Why so?"

"Because I am believed to be dead, and have reason for

wishing nobody should know I am living, so that I shall be obliged to kill you to prevent my secret getting wind."

The Englishman looked at Athos, believing that he was joking, but Athos was not joking the least in the world.

"Gentlemen," said Athos, addressing at the same time his companions and their adversaries, "are we ready?"

"Yes!" answered the Englishmen and the Frenchmen, as with one voice.

"Guard, then!" cried Athos.

And immediately eight swords glittered in the rays of the setting sun, and the combat began with an animosity very natural to men who had been twice enemies.

Athos fenced with as much calmness and method as if he had been practicing in a school.

Porthos, corrected, no doubt, of his too great confidence by his adventure of Chantilly, played with *finesse* and prudence.

Aramis, who had the third canto of his poem to finish made all the dispatch of a man very much pressed for time.

Athos, the first, killed his adversary: he hit him but once, but, as he had foretold, that hit was a mortal one—the sword passed through his heart.

Porthos, the second, stretched his upon the grass, with a wound through his thigh; and as the Englishman, without making any further resistance, then surrendered his sword, Porthos took him up in his arms and carried him to his carriage.

Aramis pushed his so vigorously that after going back many paces, he finished by fairly taking to his heels, and disappeared amid the hooting of the lackeys.

As to D'Artagnan, he fought purely and simply on the defensive; and when he saw his adversary pretty well fatigued, with a vigorous side-thrust he twisted the sword from his grasp, and sent it glittering into the air. The baron finding himself disarmed, gave two or three paces back, but in this movement, his foot slipped and he fell.

D'Artagnan was over him at a bound, and pointing his sword to his throat:

"I could kill you, milord," said he to the Englishman; "you are completely at my mercy, but I spare your life for the sake of your sister."

D'Artagnan was at the height of joy; he had realized the plan which he had fancied, the development of which had produced the smiles upon his face we mentioned.

The Englishman, delighted at having to do with a gentleman of such a kind disposition, pressed D'Artagnan in his arms and paid a thousand compliments to the three musketeers, and as Porthos' adversary was already installed in the carriage, and as Aramis' had run away, they had nothing to think about but the defunct.

As Porthos and Aramis were undressing him in the hope of finding his wound not mortal, a large purse dropped from his clothes. D'Artagnan picked it up and held it out to Lord de Winter.

"What the devil would you have me to do with that?" said the Englishman.

"You can restore it to his family," said D'Artagnan.

"His family will care vastly about such a trifle as that! his family will inherit fifteen thousand louis a year from him: keep the purse for your lackeys.

D'Artagnan put the purse into his pocket.

"And now, my young friend, if you will permit me, I hope to give you that name," said Lord de Winter, "on this very evening, if agreeable to you, I will present you to my sister, Lady Clarik; for I am desirous that she should take you into her good graces; and as she is not in bad odor at court, she may perhaps, on some future day, speak a word that will not prove useless to you.

D'Artagnan blushed with pleasure, and bowed a sign of assent.

At this time Athos came up to D'Artagnan:

"What do you mean to do with that purse?" whispered he.

"Why, I meant to pass it over to you, my dear Athos."

"Me? why to me?"

"The devil! why you killed him, didn't you? They are the *spolia opima*."

"I, the heir of an enemy!" said Athos, "for whom then do you take me?"

"It is the custom in war," said D'Artagnan, "why should it not be the custom in a duel?"

"Even on the field of battle, I have never done that."

Porthos shrugged his shoulders; Aramis by a movement of his lips applauded the opinion of Athos.

"Then, said D'Artagnan, "let us give the money to the lackeys, as Lord de Winter desired us to do."

"Yes," said Athos, "let us give the money to the lackeys, but not to our lackeys, to the lackeys of the Englishmen."

Athos took the purse, and threw it into the hand of the coachman.

"For you and your comrades," said he.

This greatness of spirit in a man who was quite destitute,
struck even Porthos, and this trait of French generosity repeated by Lord de Winter and his friend, was highly applauded
by every one, except MM. Grimaud, Bazin, Mousqueton, and
Planchet.

Lord de Winter, on quitting D'Artagnan, gave him his
sister's address; she lived, No. 6, Place Royale, then the
fashionable quarter, and undertook to call and take him with
him in order to introduce him. D'Artagnan appointed eight
o'clock at Athos' residence.

This introduction to Lady Clarik occupied the head of our
Gascon greatly. He remembered in what a strange manner
this woman had hitherto been mixed up in his destiny. According to his conviction, she was some creature of the
cardinal's, and yet he felt himself invincibly drawn toward
her by one of those sentiments for which we cannot account.
His only fear was that milady would recognize in him the
man of Meung and of Dover. Then she knew that he was
one of the friends of M. de Tréville, and, consequently, that
he belonged body and soul to the king, which would make him
lose a part of his advantage, since when known to milady as
he knew her, he played only an equal game with her. As
to the commencement of an intrigue between her and M. de
Wardes, our presumptuous hero gave but little heed to that
although the marquis was young, handsome, rich, and high in
'he cardinal's favor. It is not for nothing we are but twenty
years old, particularly if we were born at Tarbes.

D'Artagnan began by making his most splendid toilette;
then returned to Athos', and, according to custom, related
everything to him. Athos listened attentively to his projects;
then, shook his head, and recommended prudence to him with
a shade of bitterness.

"What!" said he, "you have just lost one woman, who,
you say, was good, charming, perfect, and here you are, running headlong after another!"

D'Artagnan felt the truth of this reproach.

"I loved Madame Bonacieux with my heart, while I only
love milady with my head," said he; "by getting introduced
to her, my principal object is to ascertain what part she plays
at court."

"The part she plays at court, *pardieu!* it is not difficult to
divine that after all you have told me. She is some emissary
of the cardinal's; a woman who will draw you into a snare,
in which you will leave your head."

"The devil! my dear Athos, you view things on the dark side, methinks."

"D'Artagnan, I mistrust women: can it be otherwise! I bought my experience dearly—particularly fair women. Milady is fair, you say?"

"She has the most beautiful light hair imaginable!"

"Ah! my poor D'Artagnan!" said Athos.

"Well, but listen to me: I want to be enlightened on a subject: then, when I shall have learned what I desire to know, I will withdraw."

"Be enlightened!" said Athos phlegmatically.

Lord de Winter arrived at the appointed time, but Athos, being warned of his coming, went into the other chamber. He found D'Artagnan alone then, and as it was nearly eight o'clock, he took the young man with him.

An elegant carriage waited below, and as it was drawn by two excellent horses, they were soon at the Place Royale.

Milady Clarik received D'Artagnan ceremoniously. Her hotel was remarkably sumptuous; and, while the most part of the English had quitted, or were about to quit France, on account of the war, milady had just been laying out much money upon her residence; which proved that the general measure which drove the English from France did not affect her.

"You see," said Lord de Winter, presenting D'Artagnan to his sister, "a young gentleman who has held my life in his hands, and who has not abused his advantage, although we had been twice enemies, although it was I who insulted him, and although I am an Englishman. Thank him then, madame, if you have any affection for me."

Milady frowned slightly, a scarcely visible cloud passed over her brow, and so peculiar a smile appeared upon her lips that the young man who saw and observed this triple shade almost shuddered at it.

The brother did not perceive this; he had turned round to play with milady's favorite monkey, which had pulled him by the doublet.

"You are welcome, monsieur," said milady, in a voice whose singular sweetness contrasted with the symptoms of ill-humor which D'Artagnan had just remarked—"you have to-day acquired eternal rights to my gratitude."

The Englishman then turned round, and described the combat without omitting a single detail. Milady listened with the greatest attention, and yet it was easily to be perceived, whatever effort she made to conceal her impressions, that this recital was not agreeable to her. The blood rose to her head, and her little foot worked with impatience beneath her robe.

Lord de Winter perceived nothing of this. When he had finished, he went to a table upon which was a salver with Spanish wine and glasses. He filled two, and by a sign, invited D'Artagnan to drink.

D'Artagnan knew it was considered disobliging by an Englishman to refuse to pledge him; therefore, drew near to the table, and took the second glass. He did not, however, lose sight of milady, and in a mirror perceived the change that took place in her face. Now that she believed herself to be no longer observed, a sentiment which resembled ferocity animated her countenance. She bit her handkerchief with all her might.

That pretty little soubrette that D'Artagnan had already observed, then came in; she spoke some words to Lord de Winter in English; and he immediately requested D'Artagnan's permission to retire, excusing himself on account of the urgency of the business that called him away, and charging his sister to obtain his pardon.

D'Artagnan exchanged a shake of the hand with Lord de Winter, and then returned to milady. Her countenance, with surprising mobility, had recovered its gracious expression, but some little red spots upon her hankerchief indicated that she had bitten her lips till the blood came. Those lips were magnificent! they might be said to be of coral.

The conversation took a cheerful turn. Milady appeared to be entirely recovered. She told D'Artagnan that Lord de Winter was her brother-in-law, and not her brother; she had married a younger brother of the family, who had left her a widow with one child. This child was the only heir to Lord de Winter, if Lord de Winter did not marry. All this showed D'Artagnan that there was a veil which enveloped something, but he could not yet see under this veil.

In addition to this, after half an hour's conversation, D'Artagnan was convinced that milady was his compatriot; she spoke French with an elegance and a purity that left no doubt on that head.

D'Artagnan was profuse in gallant speeches and protestations of devotedness. To all the simple things which escaped our Gascon, milady replied with a smile of kindness. The hour for retiring arrived. D'Artagnan took leave of milady, and left the salon the happiest of men.

Upon the stairs he met the pretty soubrette, who brushed gently against him as she passed, and then, blushing to the eyes, asked his pardon for having touched him, in a voice so sweet that the pardon was granted instantly.

D'Artagnan came again on the morrow, and was still better received than on the day before. Lord de Winter was not at home, and it was milady who this time did all the honors of the evening. She appeared to take a great interest in him, asked him whence he came, who were his friends, and whether he had not at some time thought of attaching himself to M. le Cardinal.

D'Artagnan who, as we have said, was exceedingly prudent for a young man of twenty, then remembered his suspicions regarding milady; he launched into an eulogy of his eminence, and said that he should not have failed to enter into the guards of the cardinal instead of the king's guards, if he had happened to know M. de Cavois instead of M. de Tréville.

Milady changed the conversation without any appearance of affectation, and asked D'Artagnan in the most careless manner possible, if he had never been in England.

D'Artagnan replied that he had been sent thither by M. de Tréville, to treat for a number of horses, and that he had brought back four as specimens.

Milady, in the course of her conversation, twice or thrice bit her lips; she had to deal with a Gascon who played close.

At the same hour as the preceding evening D'Artagnan retired. In the corridor he again met the pretty Kitty; that was the name of the soubrette. She looked at him with an expression of kindness which it was impossible to mistake. But D'Artagnan was so preoccupied by the mistress that he remarked nothing but her.

D'Artagnan came again on the morrow and the day after that, and each day milady gave him a more gracious welcome.

Every evening, either in the antechamber, the corridor, or on the stairs, he met the pretty soubrette. But, as we have said, D'Artagnan paid no attention to this.

CHAPTER XXXII.

A PROCUREUR'S DINNER.

HOWEVER brilliant had been the part played by Porthos in the duel, it had not made him forget the dinner of his procureuse.

On the morrow he received the last polishing brush from

the hands of Mousqueton, and took his way toward the Rue aux Ours, with the step of a man who was doubly in favor with fortune.

His heart beat, but not like D'Artagnan's, with a young and impatient love. No, a more material interest stirred his blood: he was about at last to pass that mysterious threshold, to climb those unknown stairs by which, one by one, the old crowns of Master Coquenard had ascended. He was about to see, in reality, a certain coffer, of which he had twenty times beheld the image in his dreams; a coffer, long and deep, locked, bolted, fixed in the wall; a coffer of which he had so often heard speak, and which the hands, a little wrinkled, it is true, but still not without elegance, of the procureuse were about to open to his admiring looks.

And then he, a wanderer on the earth, a man without fortune, a man without family, a soldier accustomed to auberges, cabarets, taverns, and parades, a lover of wine forced to depend upon chance treats—he was about to partake of family meals, to enjoy the pleasures of a comfortable establishment, and to give himself up to those little attentions, which the harder one is the more they please, as the old soldiers say.

To come in quality of a cousin, and seat himself every day at a good table, to smooth the yellow, wrinkled brow of the old procureur, to pluck the clerks a little by teaching them *bassette, passe-dix,* and *lansquenet,* in their utmost *finesse,* and by winning of them, by way of fee for the lesson he would give them in an hour, their savings of a month—all this was enormously delightful in prospect of Porthos.

The musketeer could not forget the evil reports which then prevailed, and which indeed have survived them, of the procureurs of the period: meanness, stinginess, fasts; but as, after all, excepting some few acts of economy, which Porthos had always found very unseasonable, the procureuse had been tolerably liberal—that is, be it understood, for a procureuse—he hoped to see a household of a highly comfortable kind.

And yet, at the very door, the musketeer began to entertain some doubts; the approach was not such as to prepossess people; an ill-smelling, dark passage, a staircase half lighted by bars through which stole a glimmer from a neighboring yard; on the first floor a low door studded with enormous nails, like the principal gate of the Grand Châtelet.

Porthos knocked with his finger; a tall, pale clerk, with a face shaded by a forest of unclipped hair, opened the door, and bowed with the air of a man forced to respect in another lofty stature, which indicated strength, military dress, which indicated rank, and a ruddy countenance, which indicated being accustomed to good living.

Another shorter clerk behind the first, another taller clerk behind the second, another stripling of twelve years old behind the third—in all, three clerks and a half, which, for the time, argued a very extensive clientage.

Although the musketeer was not expected before one o'clock, the procureuse had been upon the watch ever since twelve, reckoning that the heart, or perhaps the stomach of her lover, would bring him before his time.

Madame Coquenard therefore entered the office from the house at the same moment that her guest entered from the stairs, and the appearance of the worthy lady relieved him from an awkward embarrassment. The clerks surveyed him with great curiosity, and he, not knowing well what to say to this ascending and descending scale, remained mute.

"It is my cousin!" cried the procureuse; "come in! come in! my dear Monsieur Porthos."

The name of Porthos produced its effect upon the clerks, who began to laugh; but Porthos turned sharply round, and every countenance quickly recovered its gravity.

They arrived in the closet of the procureur, after having passed through the antechamber in which the clerks were, and the office in which they ought to have been; this last apartment was a sort of dark room, covered with waste paper. On leaving the office, the kitchen was on the right, and they entered the principal room, or, as we should now say, drawing-room.

All these chambers, which communicated with each other, did not inspire Porthos with the most favorable ideas. Words might be heard at a distance through all these open doors; and then, while passing, he had cast a rapid, investigating glance into the kitchen, and he was obliged to confess to himself, to the shame of the procureuse, and his own regret, that he did not see that fire, that bustle, which, while a good repast is about to be produced, prevails generally in that sanctuary of good living.

The procureur had without doubt been warned of his visit, as he expressed no surprise at the sight of Porthos, who advanced toward him with a sufficiently familiar air, and saluted him courteously.

"We are cousins, it appears, Monsieur Porthos?" said the procureur, rising, by supporting his weight upon the arms of his cane-chair

The old man, enveloped in a large black doublet, in which the whole of his slender body was concealed, was brisk and dry; his little gray eyes shone like carbuncles, and appeared, with his grinning mouth, to be the only part of his face in which life survived. Unfortunately, the legs began to refuse their service to this bony machine; during the last five or six months that this weakness had been felt, the worthy procureur had nearly become the slave of his wife.

The cousin was received with resignation, that was all. Master Coquenard firm upon his legs, would have declined all relationship with M. Porthos.

"Yes, monsieur, we are cousins," said Porthos, without being disconcerted, as he had never reckoned upon being received enthusiastically by the husband.

"By the female side, I believe?" said the procureur maliciously.

Porthos did not feel the ridicule of this, and took it for a piece of simplicity at which he laughed in his large mustache. Madame Coquenard, who knew that a simple procureur was a very rare variety in the species, smiled a little, and colored a great deal.

Master Coquenard had, from the arrival of Porthos, frequently cast his eyes with great uneasiness upon a large chest placed in front of his oak desk. Porthos comprehended that this chest, although it did not correspond in shape with that which he had seen in his dreams, must be the blessed coffer, and he congratulated himself that the reality was several feet higher than the dream.

Monsieur Coquenard did not carry his genealogical investigations any further; but, withdrawing his anxious look from the chest, and fixing it upon Porthos, he contented himself with saying: "Monsieur, our cousin, will do us the favor of dining with us once before his departure for the campaign, will he not, Madame Coquenard?"

This time, Porthos received the blow right in his stomach, and felt it. It appeared, likewise, that Madame Coquenard was no less affected by it on her part, for she added:

"My cousin will not return if he finds that we do not treat him kindly; but, otherwise, he has so little time to pass in Paris, and consequently to spare to us, that we must entreat him to give us every instant he can call his own previously to his departure."

"Oh my legs! my poor legs! where are you?" murmured Coquenard, and he endeavored to smile.

This succor, which Porthos received at the moment in

which he was attacked in his gastronomic hopes, inspired much gratitude in the musketeer for the procureuse.

The hour of dinner soon arrived. They passed into the eating-room, a large dark apartment situated opposite to the kitchen.

The clerks who, as it appeared, had smelled unusual perfumes in the house, were of military punctuality, and stood with their stools in their hands, quite ready to sit down. Their jaws moved preliminarily with fearful threatenings.

"Indeed!" thought Porthos, casting a glance at the three hungry clerks, for the lad was not, as might be expected, admitted to the honors of the master's table; "indeed! in my cousin's place, I would not keep such gluttonous-looking fellows as these! Why, they have the appearance of shipwrecked sailors who have had nothing to eat for six weeks."

Monsieur Coquenard entered, pushed along upon his chiar with castors by Madame Coquenard, whom Porthos assisted in rolling her husband up to the table.

He had scarcely entered when he began to agitate his nose and his jaws after the example of his clerks.

"Oh, oh!" said he; "here is a potage which is rather inviting!"

"What the devil can they smell so extraordinary in this potage?" said Porthos, at the sight of a pale *bouillon*, abundant, but perfectly free from meat, and upon the surface of which a few crusts swam about, as wide apart as the islands of an archipelago.

Madame Coquenard smiled, and upon a sign from her every one eagerly took his seat.

Master Coquenard was served first, then Porthos; afterward Madame Coquenard filled her own plate, and distributed the crusts without *bouillon* to the impatient clerks. At this moment the door of the dining-room opened of itself with a creak, and Porthos perceived the little clerk, who, not being allowed to take part in the feast, ate his dry bread in the passage, by which he gave it the double relish of the odor which came from the dining-room and the kitchen.

After the potage the maid brought in a boiled fowl, a piece of magnificance which caused the eyes of the usual guests to dilate in a manner that threatened injury to them.

"One may see that you love your family, Madame Coquenard," said the procureur, with a smile that was almost tragic: "you are certainly treating your cousin very handsomely!"

The poor fowl was thin, and covered with one of those thick bristly skins through which the teeth cannot penetrate with all their efforts. The fowl must have been sought for a long time on the perch, to which it had retired to die of old age.

"The devil!" thought Porthos, "this is poor work! I respect old age; but I don't think much of it boiled or roasted."

And he looked round to see if anybody partook of his opinion; but, on the contrary, he saw nothing but eager eyes which were devouring, in anticipation, that sublime fowl which was the object of his contempt.

Madame Coquenard drew the dish toward her, skillfully detached the two great black feet, which she placed upon her husband's plate; cut off the neck, which, with the head, she put on one side for herself; raised the wing for Porthos, and then returned to the servant who had brought it in, the animal, otherwise intact, and which had disappeared before the musketeer had had time to examine the variations which disappointment produces upon faces, according to the characters and temperaments of those who experience it.

In the place of the fowl, a dish of haricot beans made its appearance; an enormous dish, in which some bones of mutton, which, at first sight, might have been supposed to have some meat on them, pretended to show themselves.

But the clerks were not the dupes of this deceit, and their lugubrious looks settled down into resigned countenances.

Madame Coquenard distributed this dish to the young men with the moderation of a good housewife.

The time for taking wine was come. Master Coquenard poured, from a very small stone bottle, the third of a glass to each of the young men, served himself in about the same proportion, and passed the bottle to Porthos and Madame Coquenard.

The young men filled up their third of a glass with water; then, when they had drunk half the glass, they filled it up again, and continued to do so; which brought them, by the end of the repast, to the swallowing of a drink which, from the color of the ruby, had passed to that of a pale topaz.

Porthos ate his wing of the fowl very timidly, and shuddered when he left the knee of the procureuse under the table, as it came in search of his. He also drank half a glass of this sparingly served wine, and found it to be nothing but that horrible Montreuil, the terror of all practiced palates.

Master Coquenard saw him swallowing this wine undiluted, and sighed deeply.

"Will you eat any of these beans, Cousin Porthos?" said Madame Coquenard, in that tone which says, "Take my advice, don't touch them."

"Devil take me if I taste one of them!" murmured Porthos; and then aloud:

"Thank you, my dear cousin, I have no more appetite."

A general silence prevailed. Porthos was quite at a loss. The procureur repeated several times:

"Ah! Madame Coquenard! accept my compliments; your dinner has been a real feast. Lord! how I have eaten!"

Master Coquenard had eaten his potage, the black feet of the fowl, and the only mutton bone on which there was the least appearance of meat.

Porthos fancied they were mystifying him, and began to curl his mustache and knit his eyebrow; but the knee of Madame Coquenard came, and greatly advised him to be patient.

This silence and this interruption in serving, which were unintelligible to Porthos, had, on the contrary, a terrible meaning for the clerks; upon a look from the procureur, accompanied by a smile from Madame Coquenard, they arose slowly from table, folded their napkins more slowly still, bowed, and retired.

"Go, young men; go and promote digestion by working," said the procureur gravely.

The clerks being gone, Madame Coquenard rose and took from a buffet a piece of cheese, some preserved quinces, and a cake which she had herself made of almonds and honey.

Master Coquenard knitted his eyebrows because there were too many good things; Porthos bit his lips because there was not enough for a man's dinner. He looked to see if the dish of beans were gone; the dish of beans had disappeared.

"A positive feast!" cried Master Coquenard, turning about in his chair; "a real feast, *epulæ epulorum;* Lucullus dines with Lucullus."

Porthos looked at the bottle, which was near him, and hoped that with wine, bread and cheese, he might make a dinner, but wine was wanting, the bottle was empty; Monsieur and Madame Coquenard did not seem to observe it.

"This is very fine!" thought Porthos to himself, "I am prettily caught!"

He passed his tongue over a spoonful of preserves, and stuck his teeth into the sticky pastry of Madame Coquenard.

"Now," said he, "the sacrifice is consummated! Ah! if I
had not the hopes of having a peep with Madame Coquenard
into her husband's chest!"

Master Coquenard, after the luxuries of such a repast,
which he called an excess, felt the want of a siesta. Porthos
began to hope that the thing would take place at the present
sitting, and in that same locality; but the procureur
would listen to nothing; he would be taken to his chamber,
and was not satisfied till he was close to his chest, upon the
edge of which, for still greater precaution, he placed his feet.

The procureuse took Porthos into an adjoining chamber,
and they began to lay the basis of reconciliation.

"You can come and dine three times a week," said Madame
Coquenard.

"Thanks, madame!" said Porthos, "but I don't like to
abuse your kindness; besides, I must think of this equipment."

"That's true," said the procureuse, groaning—"that unfortunate equipment!"

"Alas! yes," said Porthos, "it is so."

"But of what, then, does the equipment of your corps
consist, Monsieur Porthos?"

"Oh! of many things," said Porthos, "the musketeers are,
as you know, picked soldiers, and they require many things
that are useless to the guards or the Swiss."

"But yet, detail them to me."

"Why, they may amount to—— said Porthos, who preferred discussing the total to taking them one by one.

The procureuse waited tremblingly.

"To how much?" said she, "I hope it does not exceed——"
She stopped, speech failed her.

"Oh! no," said Porthos, "it does not exceed two thousand
five hundred livres; I even think that, with economy, I could
manage it with two thousand livres."

"Good God!" cried she, "two thousand livres! why that is a
fortune!"

Porthos made a most significant grimace; Madame Coquenard understood it.

"I only wish to know the details," said she, "because having
many relations in business, I was almost sure of obtaining things at a hundred per cent. less than you could get
them yourself."

"Ah! ah!" said Porthos, "if that is what you meant to
say?"

"Yes, my dear Monsieur Porthos; thus, for instance, don't
you, in the first place want a horse!"

"Yes, a horse."

"Well, then! I can just suit you."

"Ah!" said Porthos, brightening, "that's well as regards my horse, then; but I must have the horse appointments complete, which are composed of objects that a musketeer alone can purchase, and which will not amount, besides, to more than three hundred livres."

"Three hundred livres; then put down three hundred livres," said the procureuse, with a sigh.

Porthos smiled; it may be remembered that he had the saddle which came from Buckingham; the three hundred livres then he reckoned upon putting snugly into his pocket.

"Then," continued he, "there is a horse for my lackey and my valise; as to my arms it is useless to trouble you about them, I have them."

"A horse for your lackey?" resumed the procureuse, hesitatingly; "but that is doing things in a very noble style, my friend."

"Well, madame!" said Porthos haughtily; "do you take me for a beggar?"

"No, no; I only thought that a pretty mule made sometimes as good an appearance as a horse, an it seemed to me that by getting a pretty mule for Mousqueton——"

"Well, agreed for a pretty mule," said Porthos; "you are right, I have seen very great Spanish nobles, whose whole suite were mounted on mules. But then you understand, Madame Coquenard, a mule with feathers and bells."

"Be satisfied," said the procureuse.

"Then there remains the valise."

"Oh! don't let that disturb you," cried Madame Coquenard "my husband has five or six valises, you shall choose the best; there is one in particular, which he prefers himself wherever he travels, large enough to hold all the world."

"Your valise is then empty?" asked Porthos, with simplicity.

"Certainly it is empty," replied the procureuse, really simply, on her part.

"Ah! but the valise I want," cried Porthos, "is a well-filled one, my dear."

Madame uttered fresh sighs. Molière had not written his scene in L'Avare then. Madame Coquenard has then the *pas* of Harpagan.

In short, the rest of the equipment was successively debated in the same manner; and the result of the sitting was, that Madame Coquenard should give eight hundred livres in money, and should furnish the horse and the mule, which should have the honor to carry Porthos and Mousqueton to glory.

These conditions being agreed to, Porthos took leave of Madame Coquenard. The latter wished to detain him by darting certain tender glances; but Porthos urged the commands of duty, and the procureuse was obliged to give place to the king.

The musketeer returned home as hungry as a hunter.

CHAPTER XXXIII.

SOUBRETTE AND MISTRESS.

IN the meantime, in spite of the cries of his conscience and the wise counsels of Athos, D'Artagnan became hourly more in love with milady; thus he never failed to pay his diurnal court to her, and the self-satified Gascon was convinced that sooner or later, she could not fail to respond to him.

One day when he arrived, with his head in the air, and as light at heart as a man who is in expectation of a shower of gold, he found the soubrette under the gateway of the hotel; but this time the pretty Kitty was not contented with touching him as he passed; she took him gently by the hand.

"Good!" though D'Artagnan, "she is charged with some message for me from her mistress; she is about to appoint some meeting which she had not courage to speak of." And he looked down at the pretty girl with the most triumphant air imaginable.

"I wish to say three words to you, Monsieur le Chevalier," stammered the soubrette.

"Speak, my dear, speak," said D'Artagnan; "I am all attention."

"Here? That's impossible; that which I have to say is too long, and still more, too secret."

"Well, what is to be done?"

"If Monsieur le Chevalier would follow me?" said Kitty timidly.

"Where you please, my pretty little dear."

"Come, then."

And Kitty, who had not let go the hand of D'Artagnan, led him up a little dark, winding staircase, and after ascending about fifteen steps, opened a door.

"Come in here, Monsieur le Chevalier," said she; "here we shall be alone, and can talk safely."

"And whose chamber is this, my pretty-faced friend?"

"It is mine, Monsieur le Chevalier; it communicates with my mistress' by that door. But you need not fear; she will not hear what we say; she never goes to bed before midnight."

D'Artagnan cast a glance around him. The little apartment was charming for its taste and neatness; but, in spite of himself, his eyes were directed to that door which Kitty said led to milady's chamber.

Kitty guessed what was passing in the mind of the young man, and heaved a deep sigh.

"You love my mistress, then, very dearly, Monsieur le Chevalier?" said she.

"Oh, more than I can say, Kitty! I am mad for her!"

Kitty breathed a second sigh.

"Alas! monsieur," said she, "that is a great pity!"

"What the devil do you see so pitable in it?" said D'Artagnan.

"Because, monsieur," replied Kitty, "my mistress does not love you at all."

"Hein!" said D'Artagnan, "can she have charged her to tell me so?"

"Oh, no, monsieur; out of the regard I have for you, I have taken upon myself to tell you so."

"I am much obliged, my dear Kitty, but for the intention only; for the information, you must agree, is not likely to be very pleasant."

"That is to say, you don't believe what I have told you, is it not?"

"We have always some difficulty in believing such things, my pretty dear, were it only from self-love."

"Then you don't believe me?"

"Why, I confess that, unless you give me some proof of what you advance——"

"What do you think of this?"

And Kitty drew a little note from her bosom.

"For me?" said D'Artagnan, seizing the letter.

"No; for another."

"For another?"

"Yes."

"His name! his name!" cried D'Artagnan.

"Read the address."

"Monsieur le Comte de Wardes."

The remembrance of the scene at St. Germain presented

itself to the mind of the presumptuous Gascon; as quick as
thought he tore open the letter, in spite of the cry which
Kitty uttered on seeing what he was going to do, or, rather,
what he was doing.

"Oh, good Lord! Monsieur le Chevalier," said she, "what
are you doing?"

"Who—I?" said D'Artagnan; "nothing;" and he read:

"You have not answered my first note; are you indisposed,
or have you forgot the glances you favored me with at the
ball of Madame de Guise? You have an opportunity now,
count; do not allow it to escape."

D'Artagnan became very pale: he was wounded in his self-
love; he thought that it was in his love.

"Poor, dear Monsieur D'Artagnan!" said Kitty, in a voice
full of compassion, and pressing the young man's hand again.

"You pity me, my kind little creature?" said D'Artagnan.

"That I do, and with all my heart; for I know what it is
to be in love."

"You know what it is to be in love?" said D'Artagnan,
looking at her for the first time with much attention.

"Alas! yes."

"Well, then, instead of pitying me, you would do much
better to assist me in revenging myself of your mistress."

"And what sort of revenge would you take?"

"I would triumph over her, and supplant my rival."

"I will never help you in that, Monsieur le Chevalier," said
Kitty warmly.

"Why not?"

"For two reasons."

"What are they?"

"The first is, that my mistress will never love you."

"How do you know that?"

"You have offended her to the very heart."

"I? in what can have offended her? I, who, ever since I
have known her, have lived at her feet like a slave! Speak,
I beg of you!"

"I will never confess that but to the man—who should read
to the bottom of my soul!"

D'Artagnan looked at Kitty for the second time. The young
girl was of a freshness and beauty which many duchesses
would have purchased with their coronets.

"Kitty," said he, "I will read to the bottom of your soul
whenever you like; don't let that disturb you;" and he gave
her a kiss, at which the poor girl became as red as a cherry.

"Oh, no," said Kitty, "it is not me you love—it is my mistress you love; you told me so only just now."

"And does that hinder you from telling me the second reason?"

"The second reason, Monsieur le Chevalier," replied Kitty, emboldened by the kiss in the first place, and still further by the expression of the eyes of the young man, "is—that in love, every one for herself!"

Then only D'Artagnan remembered the languishing glances of Kitty, her constantly meeting him in the antechamber, the corridor, or on the stairs, those touches of the hand every time she did meet him, and her deep sighs; but, absorbed by his desire to please the great lady, he had disdained the soubrette: he whose game is the eagle, takes no heed of the sparrow.

But this time our Gascon saw at a glance all the advantage that might be derived from the love which Kitty had just confessed so innocently—or so boldly: the interception of letters addressed to the Count de Wardes, intelligences on the spot, entrance at all hours into Kitty's chamber, which was contiguous to her mistress'. The perfidious deceiver was, as may plainly be perceived, already sacrificing in idea the poor girl to obtain milady, whether she would or not.

"Well," said he to the young girl, "are you willing, my dear Kitty, that I should give you a proof of that love of which you doubt?"

"What love?" asked the girl.

"Of that which I am ready to feel for you."

"And what is that proof?"

"Are you willing that I should this evening pass with you the time I generally spend with your mistress?"

"Oh, yes!" said Kitty, clapping her hands, "very willing."

"Well, then, come here, my dear," said D'Artagnan, establishing himself in a *fauteuil*, "come, and let me tell you that you are the prettiest soubrette I ever saw!"

And he did tell her so much, and so well, that the poor girl, who asked nothing better than to believe him, did believe him. Nevertheless, to D'Artagnan's great astonishment the pretty Kitty defended herself with resolution.

In such conversation time passes very rapidly. Twelve o'clock struck, and almost at the same time the bell was rung in milady's chamber.

"Good God!" cried Kitty, "there is my mistress calling me! Go, go directly!"

D'Artagnan rose, took his hat as if it had been his intention to obey; then, opening quickly the door of a large closet, instead of that of the staircase, he plunged into the midst of robes and lady's dressing-gowns.

"What are you doing?" cried Kitty.

D'Artagnan, who had secured the key, shut himself up in the closet without any reply.

"Well," cried milady, in a sharp voice, "are you asleep, that you don't answer when I ring?"

And D'Artagnan heard the door of communication opened violently.

Here am I, milady! here am I!" cried Kitty, springing forward to meet her mistress.

Both went into the bedroom, and, as the door of communication remained open, D'Artagnan could hear milady for some time scolding her maid. She was at length, however, appeased, and the conversation turned upon him while Kitty was assisting her mistress to undress.

"Well," said milady, "I have not seen our Gascon this evening."

"What, milady! has he not come?" said Kitty. "Can he be inconstant before being happy?"

"Oh, no; he must have been prevented by M. de Tréville or M. Dessessarts. I understand my game, Kitty; I have him safe!"

"What will you do with him, madame?"

"What will I do with him? Oh, Kitty, there is something between that man and me that he is quite ignorant of; he was very near making me lose my credit with his eminence. Oh, I will be revenged for that!"

"I thought madame loved him?"

"I love him? I detest him! A simple fool, who held the life of Lord de Winter in his hands and did not kill him, by which I missed three hundred thousand livres a year!"

"That's true," said Kitty; "your son was the only heir of his uncle, and until his coming of age you would have had the enjoyment of his fortune."

D'Artagnan shuddered to his very marrow at hearing this apparently sweet creature reproach him with that sharp voice, which she took such pains to conceal in conversation, for not having killed a man whom he had seen load her with kindness.

"For all this," continued milady, "I should long ago have revenged myself on him, if, and I don't know why, the cardinal had not requested me to conciliate him."

"Oh, yes; but madame has not favored the little woman he was so fond of?"

"What! the mercer's wife of the Rue des Fossoyeurs? Has he not already forgotten she ever existed? Fine vengeance that, *ma foi!*"

A cold sweat broke from D'Artagnan brow. Why, this woman was a monster! He resumed his listening, but unfortunately the toilet was ended.

"That will do," said milady; "go into your own room, and to-morrow endeavor again to obtain me an answer to the letter I gave you."

"For M. de Wardes?" said Kitty.

"To be sure; for M. de Wardes."

"Now, there is one," said Kitty, "who appears to me to be quite a different sort of man to that poor M. d'Artagnan."

"Go to bed, mademoiselle," said milady; "I don't like comments."

D'Artagnan heard the door close, then the noise of two bolts by which milady fastened herself in; on her side, but as softly as possible, Kitty turned the key of the lock, and then D'Artagnan opened the closet-door.

"Oh, good Lord!" said Kitty, in a low voice, "what is the matter with you? How pale you are!"

"The abominable creature!" murmured D'Artagnan.

"Silence, silence! begone!" said Kitty; "there is nothing but a wainscot between my chamber and milady's; every word that is uttered in one can be heard in the other."

"That's exactly the reason I won't go," said D'Artagnan.

"What!" said Kitty, blushing.

"Or, at least, I will go—later;" and he put his arm round her waist. D'Artagnan's love for Kitty was little more than an idea of vengeance upon milady. With a little more heart, he might have been contented with this new conquest; but the principal features of his character were ambition and pride It must, however, be confessed, in his justification, that the first use he made of the influence he had obtained over Kitty was, to endeavor to find out what had become of Madame Bonacieux; but the poor girl swore upon the crucifix to D'Artagnan, that she was entirely ignorant on that head, her mistress never admitting her into half her secrets, only she believed she was able to say she was not dead.

As to the cause which was near making milady lose the confidence of the cardinal, Kitty knew nothing about it; but this time D'Artagnan was better informed than she was: as he had seen milady on board a vessel at the moment he was leaving England, he suspected that it was, almost without a doubt, on account of the diamond studs.

But what was clearest in all this was, that the true hatred, the profound hatred, the inveterate hatred of milady, was increased by his not having killed her brother-in-law.

D'Artagnan came the next day to milady's, and finding her in a very ill-humor, had no doubt that it was having no answer from M. de Wardes that provoked her thus. Kitty came in, but milady was very cross with her. The poor girl ventured a glance at D'Artagnan, which said "See how I suffer on your account!"

Toward the end of the evening, however, the beautiful lioness became milder, she smilingly listened to the soft speeches of D'Artagnan, and even gave him her hand to kiss.

D'Artagnan, at parting, scarcely knew what to think; but as he was a youth not easily imposed upon, while continuing to pay his court to milady, he determined to carry out the little plan he had framed in his mind.

He found Kitty at the gate, and, as on the preceding evening, went up to her chamber. Kitty had been accused of negligence, and consequently severely scolded. Milady could not at all comprehend the silence of the Count de Wardes, and she ordered Kitty to come at nine o'clock in the morning to take a third letter.

D'Artagnan made Kitty promise to bring him that letter on the following morning; the poor girl promised all her lover desired; she was mad.

Things passed as they had done the night before: D'Artagnan concealed himself in his closet, milady called, undressed, sent away Kitty, and shut the door. As before. likewise, D'Artagnan returned home at five o'clock in the morning.

At eleven o'clock Kitty came to him: she held in her hand a fresh billet from milady. This time the poor girl did not even hesitate at giving up the note to D'Artagnan! she belonged, body and soul, to her handsome soldier.

D'Artagnan opened the letter, and read as follows:

"This is the third time I have written to you, to tell you that I love you. Beware that I do not write to you a fourth time, to tell you that I detest you.

"If you repent of the manner in which you have acted toward me, the young girl who brings you this will tell you how a man of spirit may obtain his pardon."

D'Artagnan colored and grew pale several times while reading this billet.

"Oh! you love her still," said Kitty, who had not taken her eyes off the young man's countenance for an instant.

"No, Kitty, you are mistaken: I do not love her; but I will revenge myself for her contempt of me."

"Oh! yes, I know what sort of vengeance! you told me that!"

"Of what consequence can it be to you. Kitty; you know it is you alone I love."

"How can I be sure of that?"

"By the scorn I will throw upon her."

D'Artagnan took a pen and wrote:

"MADAME—Until the present moment, I could not believe that it was to me your two first letters were addressed, so unworthy did I feel myself of such an honor; besides, I was so seriously indisposed, that I could not, in any case, have replied to them.

"But now I am forced to believe in the excess of your kindness, since not only your letter, but your servant, assures me that I have the good fortune to be beloved by you.

"She has no occasion to teach me the way in which a man of spirit may obtain his pardon; I will come and ask mine at eleven o'clock this evening.

"To delay it a single day would be, in my eyes, now, to commit a fresh offense—He whom you have rendered the happiest of men,

"COMTE DE WARDES."

This note was in the first place a forgery; it was likewise an indelicacy; it was even, according to our present manners, something like an infamous action; but at that period, people were not so scrupulous. Besides, D'Artagnan, from her own admission, knew milady to be treacherous in matters of more importance, and could entertain no respect for her. And yet, notwithstanding this want of respect, he felt an uncontrollable passion for this woman boiling in his veins. Passion drunk with contempt; but passion or thirst, as the reader pleases.

D'Artagnan's plan was very simple; by Kitty's chamber he gained that of his mistress; he would take advantage of the first moment of surprise, shame and terror; he might fail, but something must be left to chance. In eight days the campaign was to open, and he would be compelled to leave Paris: D'Artagnan had no time for a prolonged love siege.

"There," said the young man, handing Kitty the letter, sealed and addressed, "give that to milady; it is the Count de Wardes' reply."

Poor Kitty became as pale as death; she suspected what the letter contained.

"Listen, my dear girl," said D'Artagnan, "you cannot but perceive that all this must end, some way or other; milady may discover that you gave the first billet to my lackey instead of to De Wardes'; that it is I who have opened the others which ought to have been opened by him; milady will then turn you out of doors, and you know she is not the woman to let her vengeance stop there."

"Alas!" said Kitty, "for whom have I exposed myself to all that?"

"For me, I well know, my sweet girl," said D'Artagnan. "But I am grateful."

"But what does this note contain?"

"Milady will tell you."

"Ah! you do not love me," cried Kitty, "and I am very wretched!"

In spite of the caresses with which D'Artagnan endeavored to console her, Kitty wept for some time before she could be persuaded to give her mistress the note; but she yielded at last.

CHAPTER XXXIV.

IN WHICH THE EQUIPMENT OF ARAMIS AND PORTHOS IS TREATED OF.

SINCE the four friends had been in search of their equipments, there had been no fixed meeting. They dined without each other, wherever they might happen to be, or rather, where they could find a dinner. Duty, likewise, on its part, took up a considerable portion of the precious time which was gliding away so rapidly. Only they had agreed to meet once a week, about one o'clock, at the residence of Athos, seeing that he, in agreement with the vow he had formed, did not pass over the threshold of his door.

This was the same day as that on which Kitty went to D'Artagnan.

Soon as Kitty left him, D'Artagnan directed his steps toward the Rue Férou.

He found Athos and Aramis philosophizing. Aramis had some slight inclination to resume the cassock. Athos, according to his system, neither encouraged nor dissuaded him. Athos was an advocate that every one should be left to his own free will. He never gave advice but when it was asked; and even then he required to be asked twice.

People in general, he said, only asked advice not to follow it or if they did follow it, it was for the sake of having some one to blame for having given it.

Porthos arrived a minute after D'Artagnan, and the four friends were all assembled.

The four countenances expressed four different feelings: that of Porthos, tranquillity; that of D'Artagnan, hope; that of Aramis, uneasiness; that of Athos, carelessness.

At the end of a moment's conversation, in which Porthos hinted that a lady of elevated rank had condescended to relieve him from his embarrassment, Mousqueton entered. He came to request his master to come home instantly; his presence was very urgent.

"Is it my equipment?"

"Yes, and no," replied Mousqueton.

"Well, but can't you speak?"

"Come home, monsieur!"

Porthos rose, saluted his friends, and followed Mousqueton. An instant after, Bazin made his appearance at the door.

"What do you want with me, my friend?" said Aramis, with that mildness of language which was observable in him every time that his ideas were directed toward the church.

"A man wishes to see monsieur at home," replied Bazin.

"A man! what man?"

"A mendicant."

"Give him alms, Bazin, and bid him pray for a poor sinner."

"But this mendicant insists upon speaking to you, and pretends that you will be very glad to see him."

"Has he sent no particular message for me?"

"Yes, if M. Aramis hesitates to come," he said, "tell him I am from Tours."

"From Tours!" cried Aramis, "a thousand pardons, gentlemen, but no doubt this man brings me the news I expected."

And rising, he went off at a quick pace.

There then only remained Athos and D'Artagnan.

"I believe these fellows have managed their business. What do you think, D'Artagnan?" said Athos.

"I know that Porthos was in a fair way," replied D'Artagnan; "and as to Aramis, to tell you the truth, I have never been uneasy on his account; but you, my dear Athos, you, who so generously distributed the Englishman's pistoles, which were your legitimate property, what do you mean to do?"

"I am satisfied with having killed that man, my good lad, seeing that it is blessed bread to kill an Englishman; but if I had pocketed his pistoles, they would have weighed me down like a remorse."

"Athos! Athos! you have truly inconceivable ideas!"

"Well, leave that! What do you think of M. de Tréville's telling me, when he did me the honor to call upon me yesterday, that you associated with the suspected English, whom the cardinal protects?"

"That is to say, I visit an Englishwoman; the one I named to you."

"Oh! ay! the fair woman, on whose account I gave you advice, which, naturally, you took care not to adopt."

"I gave you my reasons."

"Yes; you look to the connection for your equipment, I think you said."

"Not at all! I have acquired a certain knowledge that that woman was concerned in the carrying off of Madame Bonacieux."

"Yes, I understand now; to find one woman you make love to another; it is the longest road, but certainly the most amusing."

D'Artagnan was on the point of telling Athos all; but one consideration restrained him. Athos was a gentleman, and was punctilious in all that concerned honor, and there were in all the plans which our lover had devised with regard to milady, he was sure, certain things that would not obtain his approbation: he was therefore silent, and as Athos was the least curious of any man on earth, D'Artagnan's confidence stopped there.

We will therefore leave the two friends, who had nothing important to communicate to each other, to follow Aramis.

Upon being informed that the person who wanted to speak to him came from Tours, we have seen with what rapidity the young man followed, or rather went before Bazin; he ran without stopping from the Rue Férou to Rue de Vaugirard.

On entering, he found a man of short stature and intelligent eyes, but covered with rags.

"Did you ask for me?" said the musketeer.

"I wish to speak with Monsieur Aramis: is that your name, monsieur?"

"Yes: you have brought me something?"

"Yes, if you can show me a certain embroidered handkerchief?"

"Here it is," said Aramis, taking a small key from his

breast, and opening a little ebony box inlaid with mother-of-pearl; "here it is, look!"

"That is right," replied the mendicant; "dismiss your lackey."

In fact, Bazin, curious to know what the mendicant could want with his master, kept pace with him as well as he could, and arrived almost at the same time he did; but this quickness was not of much use to him; at the hint from the mendicant, his master made him a sign to retire, and he was obliged to obey.

Bazin being gone, the mendicant cast a rapid glance around him, in order to be sure that nobody could either see or hear him, and opening his ragged vest, badly held together by a leather strap, he began to unsew the upper part of his doublet, from which he drew a letter.

Aramis uttered a cry of joy at the sight of the seal, kissed the superscription with an almost religious respect, and opened the epistle, which contained what follows:

"MY FRIEND: It is the will of fate that we should be still for some time separated; but the delightful days of youth are not lost beyond return. Perform your duty in camp; I will do mine elsewhere. Accept that which the bearer brings you: make the campaign like a handsome true gentleman and think of me, who tenderly kiss your dear black eyes!

"Adieu! or rather, *au revoir!*"

The mendicant continued to unsew his garments; and drew from amid his rags a hundred and fifty Spanish double pistoles, which he laid down on the table; then he opened the door, bowed, and went out before the young man, stupefied by his letter, had ventured to address a word to him.

Aramis then re-perused the letter, and perceived there was a postscript.

"P. S. You may behave politely to the bearer, who is a count and a grandee of Spain."

"Golden dreams!" cried Aramis. "Oh, beautiful life! yes, we are young, yes, we shall yet have happy days! Oh! my love, my blood, my life! all, all, all, all are thine, my adored mistress!"

And he kissed the letter with passion, without even vouchsafing a look at the gold which sparkled on the table.

Bazin scratched at the door, and as Aramis had no longer any reason to exclude him, he bade him come in.

Bazin was stupefied at the sight of the gold, and forgot that he came to announce D'Artagnan, who, curious to know who the mendicant could be, came to Aramis' residence on leaving that of Athos.

Now, as D'Artagnan used no ceremony with Aramis, seeing that Bazin forgot to announce him, he announced himself.

"The devil! my dear Aramis," said D'Artagnan, "if these are the prunes that are sent to you from Tours, I beg you will make my compliments to the gardener who gathers them."

"You are mistaken, friend D'Artagnan," said Aramis, always on his guard, "this is from my bookseller, who has just sent me the price of that poem in one-syllable verse which I began yonder."

"Ah! indeed," said D'Artagnan; "well, your bookseller is very generous, that's all I can say."

"How, monsieur?" cried Bazin, "a poem sell so dear as that! it is incredible! You can write as much as you like, you may become equal to M. Voiture and M. Benserade. I like that. A poet is as good as an abbé. Ah, Monsieur Aramis! become a poet, I beg of you."

"Bazin, my friend," said Aramis, "I believe you are interfering with my conversation."

Bazin perceived he was wrong; he bowed and went out.

"Ah!" said D'Artagnan with a smile, "you sell your productions at their weight in gold; you are very fortunate, my friend, but take care, or else you will lose that letter which is peeping out from your doublet, and which comes, no doubt from your bookseller likewise."

Aramis blushed to the eyes, crammed in the letter, and rebuttoned his doublet.

"My dear D'Artagnan," said he, "if you please, we will join our friends; as I am rich, we will to-day begin to dine together again, expecting that you will be rich in your turn."

"*Ma foi!*" said D'Artagnan, with great pleasure. "It is long since we have had a good dinner together; and I, for my part, have a somewhat hazardous expedition for this evening, and shall not be sorry, I confess, to fortify myself with a few glasses of good old Burgundy."

"Agreed, as to the old Burgundy; I have no objection to that," said Aramis, from whom the letter and the gold had removed, as by magic, his ideas of retreat.

And having put two or three double pistoles into his pocket to answer the calls of the moment, he placed the others in the ebony box, inlaid with mother-of-pearl, in which was the famous handkerchief, which served him as a talisman.

The two friends repaired to Athos' dwelling; and he, faithful to his vow of not going out, took upon him to order dinner to be brought to them; as he was perfectly acquainted with the details of gastronomy, D'Artagnan and Aramis made no difficulty in abandoning this important care to him.

They went to find Porthos, and at the corner of the Rue Bac met Mousqueton, who, with a most pitiable air, was driving before him a mule and a horse.

D'Artagnan uttered a cry of surprise, which was not quite free from joy.

"There's my yellow horse, Aramis," cried he; "look at that horse!"

"Oh, the frightful brute!" said Aramis.

"Well," replied D'Artagnan, "upon that very horse I came to Paris."

"What, does monsieur know this horse?" said Mousqueton.

"It is of a singular color," said Aramis; "I never saw one with such a hide in my life."

"I can well believe you did not," replied D'Artagnan, "and that was how I got three crowns for him; it must have been for his hide, for, *certes,* the carcass is not worth eighteen livres. But how did this horse come into your hands, Mousqueton?"

"Pray," said the lackey, "say nothing about it, monsieur; it is a frightful trick played us by the husband of our duchess!"

"How has it come about, Mousqueton?"

"Why, we are looked upon with a rather favorable eye, by a lady of quality, the Duchess of ——; but, your pardon; my master has commanded me to be discreet; she had forced us to accept, as a little keepsake, a magnificent Spanish genet and an Andalusian mule, which were beautiful to look upon; the husband heard of the affair; on their way he seized the two magnificent beasts which were being sent to us, and substituted these horrible animals in their places."

"Which you are taking back to him, I suppose?" said D'Artagnan.

"Exactly so, monsieur!" replied Mousqueton; "you may well believe that we will not accept such steeds as these in exchange for those which had been promised to us."

"No, *pardieu!* though I should like to have seen Porthos upon my yellow horse; that would give me an idea of how I looked on my arrival in Paris. But don't let us hinder you, Mousqueton; go, and perform your master's orders. Is he at home?"

"Yes, monsieur," said Mousqueton, "but in a very ill humor. Go on!" and he continued his way toward the Quai des Grands Augustins, while the two friends went to ring at the bell of the unfortunate Porthos. He, having seen them crossing the yard, took care not to answer; and they rang in vain.

In the meanwhile Mousqueton continued on his way, and crossing the Pont Neuf, still driving the two sorry animals before him, he reached the Rue aux Ours. When arrived there, he fastened, according to the orders of his master, both the horse and mule to the knocker of the procureur's door; then, without taking any heed of their future fate, he returned to Porthos, and told him that his commission was completed.

In a short time the two unfortunate beasts, who had not eaten anything since the morning, made such a noise with the knocker, that the procureur ordered his boy-clerk to go and inquire in the neighborhood to whom this horse and mule belonged.

Madame Coquenard recognized her present, and could not at first comprehend this restitution; but the visit of Porthos soon enlightened her. The anger which fired the eyes of the musketeer, in spite of his efforts to suppress it, terrified his sensitive lover. In fact, Mousqueton had not concealed from his master that he had met D'Artagnan and Aramis, and that D'Artagnan, in the yellow horse, had recognized the Béarnais pony upon which he had come to Paris, and which he had sold for three crowns.

Porthos went away after having appointed a meeting with the procureuse in the cloisters of St. Magloire. The procureur, seeing he was going, invited him to dinner; an invitation which the musketeer refused with an air of majesty.

Madame Coquenard repaired trembling to the cloisters of St. Magloire, for she guessed the reproaches that awaited her there; but she was fascinated by the lofty airs of Porthos.

All that which a man, wounded in his self love, could let fall in the shape of imprecations and reproaches upon the head of a woman, Porthos let fall upon the bowed head of his procureuse.

"Alas!" said she, "I did all for the best. One of our clients is a horsedealer; he owes money to the office, and was backward in his pay. I took the mule and the horse for what he owed us; he assured me that they were two noble steeds."

"Well, madame," said Porthos, "if he owed you more than five crowns, your horsedealer is a thief."

"There is no harm in endeavoring to buy things cheap, Monsieur Porthos," said the procureuse, seeking to excuse herself.

"No, madame, but they who so earnestly try to buy things cheap, ought to permit others to seek more generous friends." And Porthos, turning on his heels, made a step to retire.

"Monsieur Porthos! Monsieur Porthos!" cried the procureuse, "I have been wrong, I confess it, I ought not to have driven a bargain when the matter was to equip a cavalier like you."

Porthos, without reply, retreated a second step.

The procureuse fancied she saw him in a brilliant cloud, all surrounded by duchesses and marquises, who cast bags of money at his feet.

"Stop! in the name of heaven! Monsieur Porthos," cried she; "stop, and let us talk."

"Talking with you brings me misfortune," said Porthos.

"But, tell me, what do you ask?"

. "Nothing, for that amounts to the same thing as if I asked you for something."

The procureuse hung herself upon the arm of Porthos, and, in the violence of her grief, she cried out:

"Monsieur Porthos, I am ignorant of all such matters. How should I know what a horse is? How should I know what horse-furniture is?"

"You should have left it to me, then, madame, who do know what they are: but you would be parsimonious, and consequently, lend at usury."

"I have done wrong, Monsieur Porthos, but I will repair that wrong, upon my word of honor I will."

"And how will you do that?" asked the musketeer.

"Listen to me. This evening M. Coquenard is going to the house of M. Le Duc de Chaulness, who has sent for him. It is upon a consultation, which will last three hours at least; come, we shall be alone, and can make up our accounts."

"Ah! now that is speaking to the purpose, my dear!"

"You pardon me, then?"

"We shall see," said Porthos majestically.

And they separated, both saying: "Till this evening."

"The devil!" thought Porthos, as he walked away. "It appears I am getting nearer to Monsieur Coquenard's strong box at last."

CHAPTER XXXV.

A GASCON A MATCH FOR CUPID.

On the morning following the evening so fondly anticipated by both Porthos and D'Artagnan, Athos sat chewing
the cud of recollections, in which the bitter somewhat predominated over the sweet, when his meditations were pleasingly interrupted by the appearance of D'Artagnan. We say
pleasingly, for two reasons: first, that Athos took particular
pleasure in the society of the frank, shrewd Gascon; and sec-
ondly, that though the circumstances of his early life had
cast a tinge of melancholy over his tone of mind, and altered
his habits of existence, there was still a spirit of comparative
youth and natural buoyancy of temperament, which made him
hail, as a relief, the society of a man he esteemed so greatly
as he did D'Artagnan.

As to the Gascon, he was in exuberant spirits, but spirits
which, to the cool, observant eye of Athos, seemed rather
feverish than natural; his eye sparkled, his tongue was volu-
ble, his laugh was loud, but there was occasionally a nervous
twitching of the muscles of the mouth, and, altogether, an
uneasiness which denoted that his spirits resembled rather
the excitement produced by opium or wine, than the overflowing cheerfulness of youth and peace of mind.

"This seems to have been an auspicious night with you,
D'Artagnan," said Athos. "Did you visit your fascinating
Englishwoman?"

"Oh, yes," replied D'Artagnan, rubbing his hands, "and my
revenge is complete."

"Ah?" said Athos gravely. "Beware! revenge is an awkward passion to indulge in; they who employ it find it a
double-edged weapon, which, in the recoil, frequently wounds
the hand that wields it."

"*Mordieux!* I must confess that I am not quite at ease.
Milady has a deal more of a Circe than a Venus in her, however beautiful I think her. Her very love and its expression
have something mysterious in them."

"Well, we know she was a spy of the cardinal's," said
Athos. "The cardinal does not usually employ lovable people; few of us would like to take either Le Père Joseph or
his *âme damnée*, Rochefort, to our bosoms as confidential
friends; and a woman must be still more to be dreaded. With
men, we can be on our guard; against women, never."

"Peste!" said D'Artagnan; "that is it. I almost trembled while I loved. She has the strangest expression in her eyes I ever met with. Though merely gray eyes, their brilliancy is astonishing; but that brilliancy is more of the nature of the flash of a meteor, than of the moon-like luster we love in women's eyes. But I will tell you all, and then you may judge for yourself." And with his usual readiness and fluency the Gascon related to his attentive friend the adventures of the evening.

In the first place he recapitulated all that our readers know concerning the lady's warm letters to De Wardes, and D'Artagnan's forged reply.

At this period Athos' brow became clouded. In general, the eye of Athos seemed to turn toward D'Artagnan as the weary look of the town drudge seeks a break between the line of houses where he can catch a glimpse of green fields and golden sunshine; but now, it was serious to sternness.

"My dear friend, this is not like you. You are, naturally, no assassin; though anxious to win the fight, you would never forget that honor should be dearer to a combatant than victory. But look at the consequence of this victory; for the sake of a momentary gratification, you secure yourself an enemy, and no mean one, depend upon it."

"Oh," said D'Artagnan, "I have felt all that—but—but, Athos, you know what it is to be under the influence of a beautiful, artful woman."

The brow of Athos again darkened.

"But proceed," added he, gravely.

"Well, at my usual time, about nine o'clock, I presented myself, and was almost flattered into hope by my reception. I had never seen her look handsomer; her spirits were good, her laugh was cheerful, and there was none of that constrained, affected air of politeness of which I had before seen so much. But then the devil of jealously did not fail to whisper to me that all this arose from the anticipation of gratified love, and was not in any way due to me or my presence. But passion is a bad reasoner; and I said to myself, 'Well, she may love De Wardes, but if she will take all this pains to make herself agreeable to me, I must go for something, and she may not take the deception very ill.' Besides, he was hard to be courted; I was a willing slave."

"There, your usually acute philosophy was at fault, D'Artagnan. As a soldier, you ought to know there is more honor from a contested victory, than from a too easy surrender. But go on."

"Well, I perceived my billet had done its work. Kitty was ordered to bring in sherbet. Her mistress' good-humor extended even to her; she spoke more kindly to her than usual, but I could see poor Kitty was insensible to it all—her heart seemed full of the idea of my purposed revenge. As I witnessed the play of natural feeling in the countenance of one of these women, and beheld the artful blandishments of that of the other, I was not only tempted to think that fortune had made a mistake in their relative positions, but even felt my heart waver, and turn, instinctively, from art to nature. But I was committed, and had no means of honorable retreat before victory.

"At ten o'clock milady began to be uneasy. I could plainly see what was the matter. She arose, walked about, sat down again, her eyes seeming constantly to reproach the sluggish progress of the pendulum. At length, as the time drew near, there was no mistaking her; her looks said, distinctly as words, You have been very agreeable, but it is quite time you were gone. I arose, took my hat, bowed upon her hand, even ventured to kiss it, all which she not only allowed, but I was astonished to find her beautiful fingers return the respectful pressure of mine. And yet, though the fascination still continued, I was not for a moment deceived; there was no partiality for me, not even coquetry in it.

"'She must love him devilishly,' thought I, as I descended the stairs.

"But my poor little Kitty could not find it in her heart to come down to meet me; I was obliged to grope my way up the back staircase alone.

"On reaching the soubrette's little apartment, I found her seated with her head leaning on her hands, weeping bitterly. She did not notice my entrance, but when I went, in a kindly manner, to take her hand, she broke into an agony of sobbing. I soon found, from her reproaches, that milady, in the delirium of her joy, had revealed to her the contents of the supposed De Wardes' billet, and, as a reward for the manner in which she had performed her commission, had given her a purse of money.

"Kitty, on regaining her chamber, had thrown this purse contemptuously into a corner, where it lay, disgorging three or four pieces of gold upon the carpet.

"My heart smote me more than I like to own, but my plan lay too much at my heart; the only honest thing I could do toward Kitty was to give her clearly to understand that I

could not draw back, that I must go on; only adding, as a
sedative, that I was now actuated solely by revenge.

"From some little remains of modesty, milady had ordered
all the lights to be extinguished, even in her own chamber,
and M. de Wardes was to depart before day, in darkness.

"I had not been many minutes with Kitty before we heard
milady enter her own chamber, and I quickly ensconced myself
in my closet; indeed, Kitty had scarcely pushed me in, when
her mistress' little bell rang. Kitty replied to the summons,
taking care to shut the door after her; but the wainscot was
so thin I could hear almost all both the women said.

"Milady appeared intoxicated with joy. She made Kitty
repeat the minutest details of her pretended interview with
De Wardes; to which poor Kitty returned but broken answers, and I really expected, from her tone, she would begin
to cry. And yet, so selfish is happiness, milady was too much
engrossed by her own joy to mark the distress of her poor
attendant.

"A few minutes before the appointed hour, milady had all
the lights put out in her chamber, and dismissed Kitty to
hers, with an injunction to introduce the count the moment
he arrived.

"You may suppose I did not keep Kitty waiting long.

"Seeing through a chink of my hiding-place that all was
darkness, I was at the door of milady's chamber before Kitty
had closed it.

"'What is that noise? said milady.

"'It is I, De Wardes,' replied I, in a suppressed voice.

"'Well, why does he not come in?'" said milady.

"Shaking off poor Kitty, with as much kindness as I could,
I made my way into milady's chamber. And here, dear Athos,
I must confess that I scarcely knew which predominated, love
or jealousy. I had no idea what a man's feelings would be
when he has passionate protestations of love poured into his
ears, and knows that they are addressed to a rival. Oh, what
a keen, remorseless tooth has jealousy! Her love for De
Wardes seems boundless."

"Call it not love, D'Artagnan," said Athos, "it is a dese-
cration of the word; such natures as hers may be susceptible
of coarse passion, but know nothing of love."

"Well, call it what you will, she is intensely in earnest, as
you may judge. At parting, she forced this ring upon my
finger, with a request that I would return her a token of re-
sponding affection to-day; and people don't give such jewels
as this away lightly. My heart smote me, and I wished to

refuse it. She, however, would not hear of that, but replied, 'No, no; keep that ring for my sake; you will render me likewise a greater service than you are aware of by doing so,' and her voice was agitated as she spoke. What the latter part of her speech meant, I don't know; but she is full of mysteries. I remember the ring; it is, as you see, a magnificent sapphire, surrounded by brilliants. At that moment I felt ready to reveal everything, but, very strangely, she added: "'Poor dear angel! whom the monster of a Gascon was so near killing.'

"Comfortable, this! to know I was the monster.

"'Do you suffer much from your wounds?' continued she.

"'Yes, a great deal,' said I, scarcely knowing what to answer.

"'Be satisfied,' murmured she; 'I will avenge you, and cruelly.'

"'Peste!' thought I to myself; 'the time for confidence has not yet come. At our parting, which was a passionate one, another interview was agreed upon for next week."

"Your milady is doubtless an infamous creature. But since you mentioned it, my attention has been engrossed by your ring," said Athos.

"I saw you were looking at it; it is handsome, is it not?" said D'Artagnan.

"Yes," said Athos, "magnificent. It reminds me of a family jewel; I did not think two sapphires of such a fine water existed. And she gave you that ring, do you say."

"Yes, my beautiful Englishwoman, or rather Frenchwoman, for I am sure she was born in France, took it from her own finger and forced it onto mine."

"Let me look at it," said Athos; and, as he took it and examined it, he became very pale. He tried it on his little finger, which it fitted as if made for it.

A shade of anger and vengeance passed across his usually calm brow.

"It is impossible it can be she," said he. "How could this ring come into the possession of Lady Clarik? And yet it is difficult to suppose such a resemblance should exist between two jewels."

"Do you know this ring?" said D'Artagnan.

"I thought I did," replied Athos; "but, no doubt, was mistaken."

And he returned D'Artagnan the ring, without, however, ceasing to look at it.

"Pray," said Athos, after a minute, "either take off that

ring, or turn the collet inside; it recalls such recollections that I cannot keep my head cool enough to converse with you. But stop, let me look at that ring again; the one I mentioned to you had one of its faces scratched."

D'Artagnan took off the ring, giving it again to Athos.

Athos started. "Look?" said he, "is it not strange?" and he pointed out to D'Artagnan the scratch he had remembered.

"But from whom did this ring come to you, Athos?"

"From my mother, who inherited it from her mother."

"And you—sold it?" asked D'Artagnan, hesitatingly.

"No," replied Athos, with a singular smile; "I gave it away in a love affair, as it has been given to you."

D'Artagnan became pensive in his turn. He took back the ring, but put it into his pocket, and not on his finger.

"D'Artagnan," said Athos, taking his hand, "you know I love you; if I had a son, I could not love him better. Take my advice, renounce this woman."

"You are right," said D'Artagnan. "I have done with her; she terrifies me."

"Shall you have the courage?" said Athos.

"I shall," replied D'Artagnan; "and instantly."

"In truth, my young friend, you will act rightly, and God grant that this woman, who has scarcely entered into your life, may not leave a terrible trace in it!"

And Athos bowed to D'Artagnan, like a man who wishes to be left alone with his thoughts.

On reaching home, D'Artagnan found Kitty waiting for him. She was sent by her mistress to the false De Wardes. Her mistress was mad with love; she wished to know when her lover would meet her again. And poor Kitty, pale and trembling, awaited D'Artagnan's reply. The counsels of his friend, joined to the cries of his own heart, made him determine, now his pride was saved and his vengeance satisfied, not to see milady again. As a reply, he wrote the following letter:

"Do not depend upon me, madame, for the next meeting; since my convalscence I have so many affairs of this kind on my hands, that I am forced to regulate them a little. When your turn comes, I shall have the honor to inform you of it. I kiss your hands.   DE WARDES."

Not a word about the ring. Was the Gascon determined to keep it as a weapon against milady; or else, let us be frank, did he not reserve the jewel as a last resource for the equipment? We should be wrong to judge of the actions of one period from the point of view of another. That which would now be considered as disgraceful to a gentleman, was at that time quite a simple and natural affair, and the cadets of the best families were frequently kept by their mistresses. D'Artagnan gave the open letter to Kitty, who at first was unable to comprehend it, but who became almost wild with joy on reading it a second time. She could scarcely believe in her happiness; and whatever might be, considering the violent character of milady, the danger which the poor girl incurred in giving this billet to her mistress, she ran back to the Place Royale as fast as her legs could carry her.

Milady opened the letter with eagerness: but at the first words she read she became livid; she crushed the paper in her hand, and turning with flashing eyes upon Kitty:

"What is this letter?" cried she.

"The answer to madame's," replied Kitty, all in a tremble.

"Impossible!" cried milady; "it is impossible a gentleman could have written such a letter to a woman." Then all at once, starting:

"My God!" cried she, "can he have—" and she stopped. She ground her teeth; she was of the color of ashes. She endeavored to go toward the window for air, but she could only stretch forth her arms, her legs failed her, and she sank into a *fauteuil*. Kitty, fearing she was going to faint, hastened toward her, and was beginning to open her dress; but milady started up, pushing her away.

"What do you want with me?" said she; "and why do you place your hand on me?"

"I thought you were going to faint, milady," answered the terrified girl.

"I faint! I! I! do you take me for a weak, silly woman, then? When I am insulted I do not faint, I avenge myself!"

And she made a sign for Kitty to leave the room.

CHAPTER XXXVI.

DREAM OF VENGEANCE.

THAT evening milady gave orders that when M. D'Artagnan came as usual, he should be immediately admitted. But he did not come.

The next day Kitty went to see the young man again, and

related to him all that had passed on the preceding evening: D'Artagnan smiled; this jealous anger of milady was his revenge.

That evening milady was still more impatient than on the preceding one; she renewed the order relative to the Gascon; but, as before, she expected him in vain.

The next morning, when Kitty presented herself at D'Artagnan's residence, she was no longer joyous and alert, as she had been on the two preceding days, but on the contrary, as sad as possible.

D'Artagnan asked the poor girl what was the matter with her, but she, as her only reply, drew a letter from her pocket and gave it to him.

This letter was in milady's handwriting, only this time it was addressed to M. D'Artagnan, and not to M. de Wardes. He opened it, and read as follows:

"DEAR MONSIEUR D'ARTAGNAN : It is wrong thus to neglect your friends, particularly at the moment you are about to leave them for so long a time. My brother-in-law and myself expected you yesterday and the day before, but in vain. Will it be the same this evening?

"Your very grateful
"LADY CLARIK."

"That's all very simple," said D'Artagnan; "I expected this letter. My credit rises by the fall of that of the Count de Wardes."

"And will you go?" asked Kitty.

"Listen to me, my dear girl," said the Gascon, who sought for an excuse in his own eyes for breaking the promise he had made Athos; "you must understand it would be impolitic not to accept such a positive invitation. Milady, at not seeing me come again, would not be able to understand what could cause the interruption of my visits, and might suspect something: who could say how far the vengeance of such a woman would go?"

"Oh dear! oh dear!" said Kitty, "you know how to represent things in such a way that you are always in the right. You are going now to pay your court to her again, and if, this time, you succeed in pleasing her in your own name and with your own face, it will be much worse than before."

Instinct caused poor Kitty to guess a part of what was going to happen.

D'Artagnan reassured her as well as he could, and promised to remain insensible to the seductions of milady.

He desired Kitty to tell her mistress that he could not be more grateful for her kindnesses than he was, and that he would be obedient to her orders: but he did not dare to write, for fear of not being able, to such experienced eyes as those of milady, to disguise his writing sufficiently.

As nine o'clock struck, D'Artagnan was at the Place Royale. It was evident that the servants who waited in the antechamber were warned, for as soon as D'Artagnan appeared, before even he had asked if milady were invisible, one of them ran to announce him.

"Show him in," said milady, in a quick tone, but so piercing that D'Artagnan heard her in the antechamber.

He was introduced.

"I am at home to nobody," said milady; "observe, to nobody." The servant went out.

D'Artagnan cast an inquiring glance at milady. She was pale, and her eyes looked red, either from tears or want of sleep. The number of lights had been intentionally diminished, but the young woman could not conceal the traces of the fever which had devoured her during the last two days.

D'Artagnan approached her with his usual gallantry. She then made an extraordinary effort to receive him, but never did a more distressed countenance give the lie to a more amiable smile.

To the questions which D'Artagnan put concerning her health:

"Ill!" replied she, "very ill!"

"Then," replied he, "my visit is ill-timed; you, no doubt, stand in need of repose, and I will not intrude longer."

"No, no," said milady: "on the contrary. Stay, Monsieur d'Artagnan, your agreeable company will divert me."

"Oh! oh!" thought D'Artagnan. "She has never been so kind before. I must be on my guard."

Milady assumed the most agreeable air possible, and conversed with more than her usual brilliancy. At the same time the fever, which for an instant abandoned her, returned to give luster to her eyes, color to her cheeks, and vermilion to her lips. D'Artagnan was again in the presence of the Circe who had before surrounded him with her enchantments. His love, which he believed to be extinct, but which was only asleep, awoke again in his heart. Milady smiled, and D'Artagnan felt that he could damn himself for that smile. There was a moment at which he felt something like remorse.

By degrees, milady became more communicative She asked D'Artagnan if he had a mistress.

"Alas!" said D'Artagnan, with the most sentimental air he could assume, "can you be cruel enough to put such a question to me; to me, who, from the moment I saw you, have only breathed and sighed by you and for you!"

Milady smiled with a strange smile.

"Then you do love me?" said she.

"Have I any need to tell you so? can you have failed to perceive it?"

"Perhaps I have; but you know, the more hearts are worth the capture, the more difficult they are to be won."

"Oh! difficulties do not affright me," said D'Artagnan. "I shrink before nothing but impossibilities."

"Nothing is impossible," replied milady, "to true love."

"Nothing, madame?"

"Nothing," replied milady.

"The devil!" thought D'Artagnan. "The note is changed. Can she be going to fall in love with me, by chance, this fair inconstant, and be disposed to give me myself another sapphire like that which she gave me for De Wardes."

D'Artagnan drew his seat nearer to milady's.

"Well, now, let us see what you would do to prove this love of which you speak."

"All that could be required of me. Order—I am ready."

"For everything?"

"For everything," cried D'Artagnan, who knew beforehand that he had not much to risk in engaging himself thus.

"Well, now let us talk a little seriously," said milady, in her turn drawing her *fauteuil* nearer to D'Artagnan's chair.

"I am all attention, madame," said he.

Milady remained thoughtful and undecided for a moment; then, as if appearing to have formed a resolution:

"I have an enemy," said she.

"You, madame!" said D'Artagnan, effecting surprise; "is that possible? My God! good and beautiful as you are!"

"A mortal enemy."

"Indeed!"

"An enemy, who has insulted me so cruelly, that between him and me it is war to the death. May I reckon on you as an auxiliary?"

D'Artagnan at once perceived what the vindictive creature was coming to.

"You may, madame," said he, with emphasis. "My arm and my life are yours, as my love is."

"Then," said milady, "since you are as generous as you are loving—" She stopped.

"Well?" demanded D'Artagnan.

"Well," replied milady, after a moment of silence, "from the present time cease to talk of impossibilities."

"Do not overwhelm me with happiness!" cried D'Artagnan, throwing himself on his knees, and covering with kisses the hands she did not attempt to withdraw.

"Avenge me of that infamous De Wardes," said milady to herself, "and I shall soon know how to get rid of you, double fool, living sword-blade!"

"Fall voluntarily into my arms," said D'Artagnan, likewise to himself, "after having abused me with such effrontery, hypocritical, dangerous woman, and afterward I will laugh at you with him whom you wish me to kill."

D'Artagnan lifted up his head.

"I am ready," said he.

"You have understood me, then, dear Monsieur d'Artagnan," said milady.

"I could understand one of your looks."

"Then you would employ on my account your arm, which has already acquired so much renown?"

"Instantly!"

"But on my part," said milady, "how should I repay such a service? I know what lovers are; they are men who do nothing for nothing."

"You know the only reply that I desire," said D'Artagnan, "the only one worthy of you and of me!"

And he drew nearer to her.

She did not retreat.

"Interested man!" cried she, smiling.

"Ah!" cried D'Artagnan, really carried away by the passion this woman had the power to kindle in him. "Ah! that is because my happiness appears so impossible to me: and I have such fear that it should fly away from me like a dream, that I pant to make a reality of it."

"Well! merit this pretended happiness, then!"

"I am at your orders," said D'Artagnan.

"Quite certain?" said milady, with a last doubt.

"Only name to me the base man that has brought tears into your beautiful eyes!"

"Who told you that I had been weeping?" said she.

"It appeared to me——"

"Such women as I am don't weep," said milady.

"So much the better! Come, tell me what his name is?"

"Remember that his name is all my secret."

"Yet I must know his name."

"Yes, you must; see what confidence I have in you!"

"You overwhelm me with joy. What is his name?"

"You know him."

"Indeed?"

"Yes."

"It is surely not one of my friends?" replied D'Artagnan, affecting hesitation, in order to make her believe him ignorant.

"If it were one of your friends, you would hesitate then?" cried milady; and a threatening glance darted from her eyes.

"Not if it were my own brother!" cried D'Artagnan, as if carried away by his enthusiasm.

Our Gascon advanced this without risk, for he knew all that was meant.

"I love your devotedness," said milady.

"Alas! do you love nothing else in me?" asked D'Artagnan.

"I love you also, you!" said she, taking his hand.

And the warm pressure made D'Artagnan tremble; as if by the touch, that fever which consumed milady was communicated to him.

"You love me! you!" cried he. "Oh! if that were so, I should lose my reason!"

And he folded her in his arms. She made no efforts to remove her lips from his kisses, only she did not respond to them.

Her lips were cold; it appeared to D'Artagnan that he had embraced a statue.

He was not the less intoxicated with joy, electrified by love; he almost believed in the tenderness of milady; he almost believed in the crime of De Wardes. If De Wardes had at that moment been under his hand, he would have killed him.

Milady seized the desired moment.

"His name is—" said she, in her turn.

"De Wardes; I know it," cried D'Artagnan.

"And how do you know it?" asked milady, seizing both his hands, and endeavoring to read with her eyes to the bottom of his heart.

D'Artagnan felt he had allowed himself to be carried away, and that he had committed an error.

"Tell me! tell me! tell me, I say," repeated milady, "how do you know it?"

"How do I know it?" said D'Artagnan.

"Yes."

"I know it, because, yesterday, M. de Wardes, in a salon where I was, showed a ring which he said he had of you."

"Miserable scoundrel!" cried milady.

The epithet, as may be easily understood, resounded to the very bottom of the heart of D'Artagnan.

"Well?" continued she.

"Well, I will avenge you of this 'miserable scoundrel,'" replied D'Artagnan, giving himself the airs of Don Japhet of Armenia.

"Thanks! my brave friend!" cried milady; "and when shall I be avenged?"

"To-morrow—immediately—when you please!"

Milady was about to cry out, "immediately;" but she reflected that such precipitation would not be very gracious toward D'Artagnan.

Besides, she had a thousand precautions to take, a thousand counsels to give to her defender, in order that he might avoid explanations with the count before witnesses. All this was answered by an expression of D'Artagnan's.

"To-morrow," said he, "you will be avenged, or I shall be dead!"

"No!" said she, "you will avenge me; but you will not be dead. He is a contemptible fellow."

"Toward women he may be, but not toward men. I know something of him."

"But it seems you had not much to complain of your fortune in your contest with him?"

"Fortune is a courtesan; though favorable yesterday, she may turn her back to-morrow."

"Which means that you now hesitate?"

"No, I do not hesitate; God forbid! But would it be just to allow me to go to a possible death, without having given me at least something more than hope?"

Milady answered by a glance which said, "Is that all, speak then?" And then accompanying the glance with explanatory words:

"That is but too just," said she tenderly.

"Oh! you are an angel!" exclaimed the young man.

"Then all is agreed?" said she.

"Except that which I ask of you, dear love!"

"But when I tell you that you may rely on my tenderness?"

"I cannot wait till to-morrow."

"Silence! I hear my brother: it will be useless for him to find you here."

She rang the bell, and Kitty appeared.

"Go out this way," said she, opening a small private door, "and come back at eleven o'clock; we will then terminate this conversation; Kitty will conduct you to my chamber."

The poor girl was near fainting at hearing these words.

"Well! mademoiselle! what are you thinking about, standing there like a statue? Do as I bid you; show the chevalier the way; and this evening, at eleven o'clock—you have heard what I said."

"It appears that these appointments are all made for eleven o'clock," thought D'Artagnan: "that's a settled custom."

Milady held out her hand to him, which he kissed tenderly.

"But," said he, as he retired as quickly as possible from the reproaches of Kitty, "but I must not play the fool—this is certainly a very bad woman, I must be upon my guard."

CHAPTER XXXVII.

MILADY'S SECRET.

D'ARTAGNAN left the hotel instead of going up at once to Kitty's chamber, as she endeavored to persuade him to do, and that for two reasons: the first, because by this means he should escape reproaches, recriminations, and prayers; the second, because he was not sorry to have an opportunity of examining his own thoughts, and endeavoring, if possible, to fathom those of this woman.

What was the most clear in the matter was that D'Artagnan loved milady like a madman, and that she did not love him at all. In an instant D'Artagnan perceived that the best way in which he could act would be to go home and write milady a long letter, in which he would confess to her that he and De Wardes were, up to the present moment, the same, and that consequently he could not undertake, without committing suicide, to kill the Count de Wardes. But he also was spurred on by a ferocious desire of vengeance; he wished to subdue this woman in his own name; and as this vengeance appeared to him to have a certain sweetness in it, he could not make up his mind to renounce it.

He walked six or seven times round the Place Royale, turning, at every ten steps to look at the light in milady's apartment, which was to be seen through the blinds; it was evident that this time the young woman was not in such haste to retire to her apartment as she had been the first.

At length the light disappeared.

With this light was extinguished the last irresolution in the heart of D'Artagnan: he recalled to his mind the details

of the first night, and, with a beating heart and a brain on
fire, he re-entered the hotel and flew toward Kitty's chamber.

The poor girl pale as death, and trembling in all her limbs,
wished to delay her lover; but milady, with her ear on the
watch, had heard the noise D'Artagnan had made, and, opening the door:

"Come in," said she.

All this was of such incredible immodesty, of such monstrous effrontery, that D'Artagnan could scarcely believe what
he saw or what he heard. He imagined himself to be drawn
into one of those fantastic intrigues which we meet with in
our dreams.

He, however, darted not the less quickly toward milady, yielding to that magnetic attraction which the loadstone exercises
over iron.

As the door closed after them, Kitty rushed toward it.
Jealousy, fury, offended pride, all the passions in short, that
dispute the heart of an outraged woman in love, urged her to
make a revelation; but she reflected that she would be totally
lost if she confessed having assisted in such a machination,
and, above all, that D'Artagnan would also be lost to her forever. This last thought of love counseled her to make this
last sacrifice.

D'Artagnan, on his part, had gained the summit of all his
wishes: it was no longer a rival that was beloved, it was he
himself that was apparently beloved. A secret voice whispered to him, at the bottom of his heart, that he was but an
instrument of vengeance, that he was only caressed till he
had given death; but pride, but self-love, but madness silenced
this voice, and stifled its murmurs. And then our Gascon,
with that large quantity of conceit which we know he possessed, compared himself with De Wardes, and asked himself
why, after all, he should not be beloved for himself?

He was absorbed entirely by the sensations of the moment.
Milady was no longer, for him, that woman of fatal intentions
who had for a moment terrified him; she was an ardent, passionate mistress, returning his love in full measure.

But milady, who had not the same motives for forgetfulness that D'Artagnan had, was the first to return to reality,
and asked the young man if the means which were on the
morrow to bring on the rencounter between him and De
Wardes were already arranged in his mind.

But D'Artagnan, whose ideas had taken quite another course,
forgot himself like a fool, and answered gallantly, that that
was not the time to think about duels and sword-thrusts.

This coldness for the only interests that occupied her mind terrified milady, whose questions became more pressing.

Then D'Artagnan, who had never seriously thought of this impossible duel, endeavored to turn the conversation, but he could not succeed. Milady kept him within the limits she had traced beforehand with her irresistible spirit and her iron will.

D'Artagnan fancied himself very cunning when advising milady to renounce, by pardoning De Wardes, the furious projects she had formed.

But at the first word she started and exclaimed in a sharp, bantering tone, which sounded strangely:

"Are you afraid, dear D'Artagnan?"

"You cannot think me so, dear love!" replied D'Artagnan, "but now, suppose this poor Count de Wardes should be less guilty than you imagine him to be?"

"At all events," said milady seriously, "he has deceived me, and, from the moment he deceived me, he merited death."

"He shall die, then, since you condemn him!" said D'Artagnan, in so firm a tone that it appeared to milady the expression of a devotedness superior to every trial.

This reassured her.

When the faint light of dawn peeped through the blinds, milady warned D'Artagnan that it was time to depart, not forgetting to remind him of his promise to avenge her on the Count de Wardes.

"I am quite ready," said D'Artagnan; "but, in the first place, I should like to be certain of one thing."

"And what is that?" asked milady.

"That is, whether you really love me?"

"You have little reason to ask such a question, I think."

"Well, perhaps you do, and I am yours, body and soul!"

"Thanks, my brave lover; but as you are satisfied of my love, you must, in your turn satisfy me of yours. Is not that just?"

"Certainly; but if you love me as much as you say," replied D'Artagnan, "do you not entertain a little fear on my account?"

"What have I to fear?"

"Why, that I may be dangerously wounded—killed even."

"Impossible!" cried milady; "you are such a valiant man, and such an expert swordsman."

"You would not, then, prefer a means," resumed D'Artagnan, "which would equally avenge you, while rendering the combat useless?"

Milady looked at her lover in silence; the pale light of the first rays of day gave to her clear eyes a strangely frightful expression.

"Really," said she, "I believe you now begin to hesitate."

"No, I do not hesitate; but I really pity this poor Count de Wardes, since you have ceased to love him. I think that a man must be so severely punished by the loss of your love that he stands in need of no other chastisement."

"Who told you that I have loved him?" asked milady sharply.

"At least, I am now at liberty to believe, without too much fatuity, that you love another," said the young man, in a caressing tone, "and I repeat, that I am really interested for the count."

"You are?" asked milady.

"Yes, I."

"And on what account?"

"Because I alone know——"

"What?"

"That he is far from being, or rather having been, so guilty toward you, as he appears to be."

"Indeed!" said milady, in an anxious tone; "explain yourself, for I really cannot tell what you mean."

And she looked at D'Artagnan.

"Yes; I am a man of honor," said D'Artagnan, determined to come to an end, "and since your love is mine, and I am satisfied I possess it——for I do possess it, do I not?"

"Entirely; go on."

"Well, I feel as if transformed—a confession weighs on my mind."

"A confession!"

"If I had the least doubt of your love I would not make it; but you love me, do you not?"

"Without doubt I do."

"Then if, through excess of love, I have rendered myself culpable toward you, you will pardon me?"

"Perhaps."

D'Artagnan assumed his most winning smile, but it had no effect; he had alarmed milady, and she involuntarily turned from him.

"This confession," said she, growing paler and paler, "what is this confession!"

"You gave De Wardes a meeting on Thursday last, in this very room, did you not?"

"Who—I? No, certainly not!" said milady, in a tone of voice so firm, and with a countenance so unchanged, that if

D'Artagnan had not been in such perfect possession of the fact, he would have doubted.

"Do not say that which is not true, my angel," said D'Artagnan, smiling; "that would be useless."

"What do you mean? Speak! you terrify me to death."

"Be satisfied; you are not guilty toward me—I have already pardoned you."

"What next? what next?"

"De Wardes cannot boast of anything."

"How is that? You told me yourself that that ring——"

"That ring I have! The Count de Wardes of last Thursday and the D'Artagnan of to-day are the same person!"

The imprudent young man expected a surprise mixed with shame—a slight storm, which would resolve itself into tears; but he was strangely deceived, and his error was not of long duration.

Pale and trembling, milady repulsed D'Artagnan's attempted embrace by a violent blow on the chest, as she sprang from him.

It was then broad daylight.

In his eagerness to detain her, D'Artagnan had grasped her dress; but the frail cambric could not stand against two such strong wills—it was torn from her fair round shoulders, and, to his horror and astonishment, D'Artagnan recognized upon one of them, indelibly branded, the mark which is impressed by the ignominious hand of the executioner.

"Great God!" cried D'Artagnan, loosing his hold, and remaining mute, motionless, and frozen.

But milady felt herself denounced by his terror even. He had doubtless seen all. The young man now knew her secret, her terrible secret—the secret she concealed even from her maid with such care, the secret of which all the world, excepting he, was ignorant.

She turned upon him, no longer like a furious woman, but like a wounded panther.

"Ah, wretch!" cried she, "thou hast basely betrayed me! and still more, thou hast my secret! Thou shalt die!"

And she flew to a little inlaid casket which stood upon the toilet, opened it with a feverish and trembling hand, drew from it a small poniard with a golden haft and a sharp thin blade, and then threw herself with a bound upon D'Artagnan.

Although the young man was, as we know, brave, he was terrified at that wild countenance, those terribly dilated pupils, those pale cheeks, and those bleeding lips. He drew back to the other side of the room as he would have done from a serpent which was crawling toward him, and his sword coming in contact with his nervous hand, he drew it, almost unconsciously, from the scabbard.

But, without taking any heed of the sword, milady endeavored to get near enough to him to stab him, and did not stop till she felt the sharp point at her throat.

She then endeavored to seize the sword with her hands; but D'Artagnan kept it free from her grasp, and continued to present the point, sometimes at her eyes, sometimes at her breast, while he aimed at making his retreat by the door which led to Kitty's apartment.

Milady during this time continued to strike at him with her dagger with horrible fury, screaming in a superhuman manner.

As all this, however, bore some resemblance to a duel, D'Artagnan soon began to recover himself.

"Very well, pretty lady, very well," said he; "but, *pardieu!* if you don't calm yourself, I will mark you with a second *fleur-de-lis* upon one of those pretty cheeks!"

"Scoundrel! infamous scoundrel!" howled milady.

But D'Artagnan, still keeping on the defensive, drew near to Kitty's door. At the noise they made, she in overturning the furniture in her efforts to get at him, he in screening himself behind the furniture to keep out of her reach, Kitty, in great alarm, opened the door. D'Artagnan, who had constantly maneuvered to gain this point, was not at more than three paces from it. With one spring he flew from the chamber of milady into that of the maid, and, quick as lightning, he slammed-to the door, and placed all his weight against it, while Kitty bolted it.

Then milady attempted to tear down the door-case, with a strength apparently above that of a woman; but finding she could not accomplish this, she, in her fury, stabbed at the door with her poniard, the point of which repeatedly glittered through the wood. Every blow was accompanied with terrible imprecations.

"Quick, Kitty, quick!" said D'Artagnan, in a low voice, as soon as the bolts were fast, "let me get out of the hotel; for if we leave her time to turn round, she will have me killed by the servants!"

"But you can't go out so," said Kitty; "you have hardly any clothes on."

"That's true," said D'Artagnan, then first thinking of the costume he appeared in—"that's true; but dress me as well as you are able, only make haste; think, my dear girl, it's life and death!"

Kitty was but too well aware of that. In a moment she muffled him up in a large flowered robe, a capacious hood, and a cloak; she gave him some slippers, in which he placed his naked feet, and then conducted him down the stairs. It was time: milady had already rung her bell, and roused the whole hotel; the porter was drawing the cord at the moment milady cried from her window:

"Don't open the gate! don't open the gate!"

The young man sprang out while she was still threatening him with an impotent gesture. At the moment she lost sight of him, milady sank back fainting into her chamber.

CHAPTER XXXVIII.

HOW, WITHOUT INCOMMODING HIMSELF, ATHOS FOUND HIS EQUIPMENT.

D'ARTAGNAN was so completely bewildered that, without taking any heed of what would become of Kitty, he ran at full speed across half Paris, and did not stop till he came to Athos' door. The confusion of his mind, the terror which spurred him on, the cries of some of the patrol who started in pursuit of him, and the shouting of the people, who, notwithstanding the early hour, were going to their work, only made him precipitate his course.

He crossed the court, ran up the two flights to Athos' apartments, and knocked at the door enough to break it down.

Grimaud came, rubbing his half-open eyes to answer this noisy summons, and D'Artagnan sprang with such violence into the room as nearly to overturn the astonished lackey.

In spite of his habitual mutism, the poor lad this time found his speech.

"Holloa, there!" cried he; "what do you want, you strumpet? What's your business here, you hussey?"

D'Artagnan threw off his hood, and disengaged his hands from the folds of the cloak; and, at the sight of the mustaches and the naked sword, the poor devil perceived he had to deal with a man. He then concluded it must be an assassin.

"Help! murder! help!" cried he.

"Hold your tongue, you stupid fellow!" said the young man; "I am D'Artagnan—don't you know me? Where is your master?"

"You, Monsieur d'Artagnan!" cried Grimaud, "impossible!"

"Grimaud," said Athos, coming out of his apartment in a *robe de chambre,* "Grimaud, I thought I heard you permitting yourself to speak?"

"Ah, monsieur, but——"

"Silence!"

Grimaud contented himself with pointing D'Artagnan out to his master with his finger.

Athos recognized his comrade, and, phlegmatic as he was, he burst into a laugh that was quite excused by the masquerade before his eyes; petticoats falling over his shoes, sleeves tucked up, and mustaches stiff with agitation.

"Don't laugh, my friend!" cried D'Artagnan; "for heaven's sake, don't laugh, for, upon my soul, it's no laughing matter!"

And he pronounced these words with such a solemn air and with such a real appearance of terror, that Athos eagerly seized his hand, crying:

"Are you wounded, my friend? How pale you are!"

"No, but I have just met with a terrible adventure! Are you alone, Athos?"

"*Parbleu!* who do you expect to find with me at this hour?"

"Well, well!" and D'Artagnan rushed into Athos' chamber.

"Come, speak!" said the latter, closing the door and bolting it, that they might not be disturbed. "Is the king dead? Have you killed the cardinal? Why, you are quite beside yourself! Come, come, tell me; I am dying with curiosity and uneasiness!"

"Athos," said D'Artagnan, getting rid of his female garments, and appearing in his shirt, "prepare yourself to hear an incredible, an unheard-of history."

"Well, but put on that *robe de chambre* first," said the musketeer to his friend.

D'Artagnan got into the robe as quickly as he could, taking one sleeve for the other, so greatly was he still agitated.

"Well?" said Athos.

"Well," replied D'Artagnan, inclining his mouth to Athos' ear, and lowering his voice, "milady is marked with a *fleur-de-lis* upon her shoulder!"

"Ah!" cried the musketeer, as if he had received a ball in his heart.

"Are you sure," said D'Artagnan, "are you *sure* that the *other* is dead?"

"The other?" said Athos, in so inward a voice that D'Artagnan scarcely heard him.

"Yes; she of whom you told me one day at Amiens."

Athos uttered a groan, and let his head sink into his hands.

"This one is a woman of from twenty-six to twenty-eight years of age."

"Fair," said Athos, "is she not?"

"Very."

"Blue and clear eyes, of a strange brilliancy, with black eyelids and eyebrows?"

"Yes."

"Tall, well-made? She has lost a tooth, next to the eye-tooth on the left?"

"Yes."

"The *fleur-de-lis* is small, red in color, and looks as if endeavors had been made to efface it with paste of some kind?"

"Yes."

"But you say she is an Englishwoman?"

"She is called milady, but, notwithstanding that, she may be a Frenchwoman. Lord de Winter is only her brother-in-law."

"I will see her, D'Artagnan!"

"Beware, Athos, beware; you endeavored to kill her; she is a woman to return you the like, and not to fail, I promise you."

"She will not dare to say anything; that would be to denounce herself."

"She is capable of anything or everything. Did you ever see her furious?"

"No," said Athos.

"A tigress! a panther! Ah! my dear Athos, I am greatly afraid I have drawn a terrible vengeance on both of us!"

D'Artagnan then related all: the mad passion of milady and her menaces of death to him.

"You are right, and upon my soul, I would give my life for a hair," said Athos. "Fortunately, the day after to-morrow we leave Paris. We are going, according to all probability, to La Rochelle, and once gone——"

"She will follow you to the end of the world, Athos, if she recognizes you; let her then exhaust her vengeance on me alone!"

"My dear friend! of what consequence is it if she kills me?" said Athos, "do you, perchance, think I set any great store by life?"

"There is something horribly mysterious under all this,

Athos; this woman is one of the cardinal's spies, I am sure of that."

"In that case take care of yourself. If the cardinal does not hold you in high admiration for the affair of London, he entertains a great hatred for you; but as, considering everything, he cannot accuse you openly, and as hatred must be satisfied, particularly when it's a cardinal's hatred, take care of yourself! If you go out, do not go out alone; when you eat, use every precaution; mistrust, in short, everything, even your own shadow."

"Fortunately," said D'Artagnan, "all this will be only necessary till after to-morrow evening, for when once with the army, we shall have, I hope, only men to dread."

"In the meantime," said Athos, "I renounce my plan of seclusion, and wherever you go, I will go with you: you must return to the Rue de Fossoyeurs; I will accompany you."

"Yes, but however near it may be, I cannot go thither in this guise."

"That's true," said Athos, and he rang the bell.

Grimaud entered.

Athos made him a sign to go to D'Artagnan's residence, and bring back some clothes. Grimaud replied, by another sign, that he understood perfectly, and set off.

"All this will not advance your equipment," said Athos, "for, if I am not mistaken, you have left the best of your apparel at milady's, and she will certainly not have the politeness to return it to you. Fortunately you have the sapphire."

"The sapphire is yours, my dear Athos! Did you not tell me it was a family jewel?"

"Yes, my father gave two thousand crowns for it, as he once told me; it formed part of the nuptial present he made my mother; and it is magnificent. My mother gave it to me, and I, fool as I was, instead of keeping the ring as a holy relic, gave it to this wretched woman."

"Then, my friend, take back this ring, to which, it is plain, you attach much value."

"I take back the ring, after it has passed through the hands of that infamous creatue! never! that ring is defiled, D'Artagnan."

"Sell it, then."

"Sell a diamond which was the gift of my mother! I must confess I should consider that as a profanation."

"Pledge it, then; you can borrow at least a thousand crowns on it. With that sum you can extricate yourself from your present difficulties; and when you are full of

money again, you can redeem it, and take it back cleansed
from its ancient stains, as it will have passed through the
hands of usurers."

Athos smiled.

"You are a capital companion, D'Artagnan," said he;
"your never-failing cheerfulness raises poor souls in affliction.
Agreed, let us pledge the ring, but upon one condition."

"What is that?"

"That there shall be five hundred crowns for you, and five
hundred crowns for me."

"Don't think of such a thing, Athos; I don't want the
half of such a sum. I who am still only in the guards. What
do I want? A horse for Planchet, that's all, and by selling my
saddles, I shall get it. Besides, you forget that I have a ring
likewise."

"To which you attach more value than I do to mine; at
least, I have thought it seemed so."

"Yes, for in any extreme circumstance it might extricate us
from some great embarrassment, or even a great danger; it is
not only a valuable diamond, it is an enchanted talisman."

"I don't at all understand you, but I believe all you say to
be true. Let us return to my ring, or rather to yours; you
shall take half the sum that will be advanced upon it, or I
will throw it into the Seine; and I doubt, as was the case
with Polycrates, whether any fish will be sufficiently complai-
sant to bring it back to us."

"Well, I will take it, then," said D'Artagnan.

At this moment Grimaud returned, accompanied by Planchet; the latter, anxious about his master, and curious to
know what had happened to him, took advantage of the opportunity, and brought his clothes himself.

D'Artagnan dressed himself, and Athos did the same.
When about to go out, the latter made Grimaud the sign of
a person taking an aim, and the lackey immediately took
down his musketoon, and got ready to follow his master.

They arrived without accident at the Rue des Fossoyeurs.
Bonacieux was standing at the door; he cast one of his ill-
meaning, bantering looks at D'Artagnan as he passed him:

"Make haste, my dear lodger," said he; "there is a very
pretty girl waiting for you upstairs; and, you know, women
don't like to be made to wait."

"That's Kitty!" said D'Artagnan to himself, and darted
into the passage.

In fact, upon the landing leading to the chamber, and

crouching against the door, he found the poor girl, all in a tremble. As soon as she perceived him:

"You promised to protect me; you promised to save me from her anger," said she; "remember, it was you who ruined me!"

"Yes, yes, to be sure, Kitty," said D'Artagnan; "be at ease, my girl. But what happened after my departure?"

"How can I tell!" said Kitty. "The lackeys were brought by the cries she made—she was mad with passion; there exist no imprecations she did not utter against you. Then I thought she would remember it was through my chamber you had gone into hers, and that then she would suppose I was your accomplice; so I took what little money I had and the best of my things, and I got away as fast as I could."

"Poor dear girl! But what can I do with you? I am going away the day after to-morrow."

"Do what you please, Monsieur le Chevalier; help me out of Paris; help me out of France!"

"I cannot take you, however, to the siege of La Rochelle," said D'Artagnan.

"No; but you can place me in one of the provinces, with some lady of your acquaintance; in your own country, for instance."

"My dear little love! in my country the ladies do without chambermaids. But, stop; I can manage your business for you. Planchet, go and find M. Aramis; request him to come here directly. We have something very important to say to him."

"I understand," said Athos; "but why not Porthos? I should have thought that his duchess——"

"Oh! Porthos' duchess is dressed by her husband's clerks," said D'Artagnan, laughing. "Besides, Kitty would not like to live in the Rue aux Ours."

"I do not care where I live," said Kitty, "provided I am well concealed, and she does not know where I am."

"And now, Kitty, when we are about to separate, and you are no longer jealous of me——"

"Monsieur le Chevalier, far off or near, be where I may, I shall always love you."

"Where the devil will constancy take up its abode next?" said Athos to himself.

"And I also," said D'Artagnan; "I also shall always love you; be sure of that. But now, answer me; I attach great importance to the question I am about to put to you. Did you never hear talk of a young woman who was carried off one night?"

"There now! Oh! Monsieur de Chevalier, do you love that woman still?"

"No, no, it is one of my friends who loves her—M. Athos, this gentleman here."

"I?" cried Athos, with an accent like that of a man who perceives he was about to tread upon an adder.

"You, to be sure!" said D'Artagnan, pressing Athos' hand. "You know the interest we both take in this poor little Madame Bonacieux. Besides, Kitty will tell nothing; will you Kitty? You understand, my dear girl," continued D'Artagnan, "she is the wife of that frightful baboon you saw at the door as you came in."

"Oh Mon Dieu! you remind me of my fright; if he should have known me again!"

"What! know you again! Did you ever see that man before?"

"He came twice to milady's."

"That's it. And what time?"

"Why, about fifteen or eighteen days ago."

"Exactly so."

"And yesterday evening he came again."

"Yesterday evening?"

"Yes, just before you came."

"My dear Athos, we are enveloped in a network of spies! do you believe he knew you again, Kitty?"

"I pulled down my hood as soon as I saw him, but perhaps it was too late."

"Go down, Athos, he mistrusts you less than me, and see if he be still at his door."

Athos went down and returned immediately.

"He is gone," said he, "and the house door is shut."

"He is gone to make his report, and to say that the pigeons are at this moment all in the dovecote."

"Well, then, let us all fly away," said Athos, "and leave nobody here but Planchet, to bring us news."

"A minute. But Aramis, whom we have sent for!"

"That's true," said Athos, "we must wait for Aramis."

At that moment Aramis arrived.

The matter was all explained to him, and the friends gave him to understand that among all his high connections he must find a place for Kitty.

Aramis reflected for a minute, and then said, coloring: "Will it be really rendering you a service, D'Artagnan?"

"I shall be grateful to you all my life."

"Very well; Madame de Bois-Tracy asked me, for one of her friends who resides in the provinces, I believe, for a trustworthy *femme de chambre;* and if you can, my dear D'Artagnan, answer for mademoiselle——"

"Oh! monsieur, be assured that I shall be entirely devoted to the person who will give me the means of quitting Paris."

"Then," said Aramis, "this falls out very well."

He placed himself at the table, and wrote a little note which he sealed with a ring, and gave the billet to Kitty.

"And now, my dear girl," said D'Artagnan, "you know that it is not good for any of us to be here. Therefore let us separate. We shall meet again in better days, depend upon it."

"Dicers' oaths!" said Athos, while D'Artagnan went to conduct Kitty downstairs.

An instant afterward the three young men separated, agreeing to meet again at four o'clock at Athos' residence, and leaving Planchet to guard the house.

Aramis returned home, and Athos and D'Artagnan went about pledging the sapphire.

As the Gascon had foreseen, they found no difficulty in obtaining three hundred pistoles upon the ring. Still further, the Jew told them that if they would sell it to him, as it would make a magnificent pendant for earrings, he would give five hundred pistoles for it.

Athos and D'Artagnan, with the activity of two soldiers, and the knowledge of two connoisseurs, hardly required three hours to purchase the entire equipment of the musketeer. Besides, Athos was very easy, and a noble to his fingers' ends. Whenever a thing suited him, he directly paid the price asked for it, without thinking to ask for any abatement. D'Artagnan would have remonstrated at this, but Athos put his hand upon his shoulder, with a smile, and D'Artagnan understood that it was all very well for such a little Gascon gentleman as himself to drive a bargain, but not for a man who had the bearing of a prince. The musketeer met with a superb Andalusian horse, black as jet, nostrils of fire, legs clean and elegant, rising six.. He examined him, and found him sound and without blemish, he was asked a thousand livres for him.

He might, perhaps, have been bought for less; but while D'Artagnan was discussing the price with the dealer, Athos was counting the money down on the table.

Grimaud had a stout, short Picard cob, which cost three hundred livres.

But when the saddle and arms for Grimaud were purchased, Athos had not a sou left of his hundred and fifty pistoles. D'Artagnan offered his friend a part of his share, which he should return when convenient.

But Athos only replied to this proposal by shrugging his shoulders.

"How much did the Jew say he would give for the sapphire, if he purchased it?" said Athos.

"Five hundred pistoles."

"That is to say, two hundred more! a hundred pistoles for you, and a hundred pistoles for me. Well, now, that would be a real fortune to us, my friend; let us go back to the Jew's again."

"What! will you——"

"This ring would certainly only recall very bitter remembrances; then we shall never be masters of three hundred pistoles to redeem it; so that we really should lose two hundred pistoles by the bargain. Go and tell him the ring is his, D'Artagnan, and bring back the two hundred pistoles with you."

"Reflect, Athos!"

"Ready money is dear for the time that passes, and we must learn how to make sacrifices. Go, D'Artagnan, go; Grimaud will accompany you with his musketoon."

Half an hour afterward, D'Artagnan returned with the two thousand livres, and without having met with any accident.

It was thus Athos found at home resources which he did not expect.

CHAPTER XXXIX.

A VISION.

At four o'clock the four friends were all assembled at Athos' apartments. Their anxiety about their equipments had all disappeared, and each countenance only preserved the expression of its own secret inquietudes; for behind all present happiness is concealed a fear for the future.

Suddenly Planchet entered, bringing two letters for D'Artagnan.

The one was a little billet, genteelly folded, with a pretty seal in green wax, on which was impressed a dove bearing a green branch.

The other was a large square epistle, resplendent with the terrible arms of his eminence the cardinal duke.

At the sight of the little letter the heart of D'Artagnan bounded, for he believed he had seen that writing before: and although he had seen that writing but once, the memory of it remained at the bottom of his heart.

He therefore seized the little letter, and opened it eagerly.

"Be," said the letter, "on Thursday next, at seven o'clock in the evening, on the road to Chaillot, and look carefully into the carriages that pass; but if you have any consideration for your own life or that of those who love you, do not speak a single word, do not make a movement which may lead any one to believe you have recognized her, who exposes herself to everything for the sake of seeing you but for an instant."

No signature.

"That's a snare," said Athos; "don't go, D'Artagnan."

"And yet," replied D'Artagnan, "I think I recognize the writing."

"That may be forged," said Athos; "between six and seven o'clock the road to Chaillot is quite deserted; you might as well go and ride in the forest of Bondy."

"But suppose we all go," said D'Artagnan; "what the devil! they won't devour us all four; four lackeys, horses, arms, and all!"

"And, besides, it will be a good opportunity for displaying our new equipments," said Porthos.

"But if it is a woman that writes," said Aramis, "and that woman desires not to be seen, remember, you compromise her, D'Artagnan; which is not behaving like a gentleman."

"We will remain in the background; and he will advance alone."

"Yes, but a pistol-shot is easily fired from a carriage, however fast it may be going."

"Bah!" said D'Artagnan, "they will miss me; if they fire, we will ride after the carriage, and exterminate those who may be in it. They must be enemies."

"He is right," said Porthos; "battle: besides, it will be a good opportunity to try our new arms."

"Let us enjoy that pleasure," said Aramis, in his mild and careless manner.

"As you please," said Athos.

"Gentlemen," said D'Artagnan, "it is half-past four, and we have scarcely time to be on the road of Chaillot by six."

"Besides, if we go out late, nobody will see us," said Porthos, "and that will be a pity. Let us get ready, gentlemen."

"But this second letter," said Athos, "you forget that; it appears to me, however, that the seal denotes that it deserves to be opened; for my part, I declare, D'Artagnan, I think it of much more consequence than the little piece of waste paper you have so cunningly slipped into your bosom."

D'Artagnan blushed.

"Well," said he, "let us see, gentlemen, what are his eminence's commands," and D'Artagnan unsealed the letter, and read:

"M. D'Artagnan, of the King's Guards, company Dessessarts, is expected at the Palais-Cardinal, this evening at eight o'clock.

"La Houndeniere, Captain of the Guards."

"The devil!" said Athos; "here's a rendezvous much more serious than the other."

"I will go to the second, after attending the first," said D'Artagnan, "one is for seven o'clock, and the other for eight: there will be time for both."

"Hum! Now, I would not go at all," said Aramis; "a gallant knight cannot decline an appointment made by a lady; but a prudent gentleman may excuse himself from not waiting on his eminence, particularly when he has reason to believe he is not invited for courteous purposes."

"I am of Aramis' opinion," said Porthos.

"Gentlemen," replied D'Artagnan, "I have already received by M. de Cavois a similar invitation from his eminence; I neglected it, and on the morrow a serious misfortune happened to me! Constance disappeared. Whatever may ensue, I will go."

"If you are determined," said Athos, "do so."

"Yes, but the Bastille?" said Aramis.

"Bah! you will get me out, if they put me there," said D'Artagnan.

"To be sure we will," replied Aramis and Porthos, with admirable promptness and decision, as if that were the simplest thing in the world—"to be sure we will get you out, if there; but in the meantime, as we are to set off the day after to-morrow, you would do much better not to risk this Bastille."

"Let us do better than that," said Athos, "do not let us leave him during the whole evening; let each of us wait at a gate of the palace with a musketeer behind him; if we see any carriage with closed windows, and of at all suspicious appearance, come out, let us fall upon it; it is a long time since we have had a skirmish with the guards of Monsieur le Cardinal; M. de Tréville must think us dead."

"To a certainty, Athos," said Aramis, "you were meant to be a general; what do you think of the plan, gentlemen?"

"Admirable!" replied the young men in chorus.

"Well!" said Porthos, "I will run to the hotel, and engage our comrades to hold themselves in readiness by eight o'clock, the rendezvous, the Place du Palais-Cardinal; in the meantime, you see that the lackeys saddle the horses."

"I have no horse," said D'Artagnan, but that is of no consequence, I can take one of M. de Tréville's."

"That is not worth while," said Aramis, "you can have one of mine."

"One of yours! how many have you, then?" asked D'Artagnan.

"Three," replied Aramis smiling.

"Certes," cried Athos, "you are the best mounted poet of France or Navarre."

"Well, but Aramis, you don't want three horses? I cannot comprehend what induced you to buy three!"

"Therefore I only purchased two," said Aramis.

"The third then fell from the clouds, I suppose?"

"No, the third was brought to me this very morning by a groom out of livery, who would not tell me in whose service he was, and who said he had received orders from his master."

"Or his mistress," interrupted D'Artagnan.

"That makes no difference," said Aramis, coloring; "and who affirmed, as I said, that he had received orders from his mistress to place the horse in my stable, without informing me whence it came."

"It is only to poets that such things happen," said Athos gravely.

"Well, in that case, we can manage famously," said D'Artagnan; "which of the two horses will you ride; that which you bought, or the one that was given to you?"

"That which was given to me, without doubt—you cannot for a moment imagine, D'Artagnan, that I should commit such an offense toward——"

"The unknown giver," interrupted D'Artagnan.

"Or the mysterious benefactress," said Athos.

"The one you bought will then become useless to you?"

"Nearly so."

"And you selected it yourself?"

"With the greatest care; the safety of the horseman, you

know, depends almost always upon the goodness of his horse."

"Well, let me have it at the price it cost you?"

"I was going to make you the offer, my dear D'Artagnan, giving you all the time necessary for repaying me such a trifle."

"How much did it cost you?"

"Eight hundred livres."

"Here are forty double pistoles, my dear friend," said D'Artagnan, taking the sum from his pocket; "I know that this is the coin in which you were paid for your poems."

"You are full of money, then?" said Aramis.

"Money! rolling in it, my dear fellow!"

And D'Artagnan chinked the remainder of his pistoles in his pocket.

"Send your saddle, then, to the hotel of the musketeers, and your horse can be brought back with ours."

"Very well; but it is already five o'clock, so make haste."

A quarter of an hour afterward, Porthos appeared at the end of the Rue Férou, mounted upon a very handsome genet; Mousqueton followed him upon an Auvergne horse, small, but very good-looking: Porthos was resplendent with joy and pride.

At the same time, Aramis made his appearance at the other end of the street, upon a superb English charger; Bazin followed him upon a roan, leading a splendid, vigorous Mecklenburg horse; this last was D'Artagnan's.

The two musketeers met at the gate; Athos and D'Artagnan watched their approach from the window.

"The devil," cried Aramis, "you have a magnificent horse there, Porthos."

"Yes," replied Porthos, "it is the one that ought to have been sent to me at first; a bad joke of the husband's substituted the other; but the good man has been punished since, and I have obtained full satisfaction."

Grimaud then led up his master's horse; D'Artagnan and Athos came down, got into their saddles, and all four set forward: Athos upon a horse he owed to a woman, Aramis on a horse he owed to his mistress, Porthos on a horse he owed to the procureuse, and D'Artagnan on a horse he owed to his good fortune, the best mistress possible.

The lackeys followed.

As Porthos had foreseen, the cavalcade produced a good effect; and if Madame Coquenard had met Porthos, and seen what a superb appearance he made upon his handsome Spanish genet, she would not have regretted the bleeding she had inflicted upon the strong box of her husband.

Near the Louvre the four friends met with M. de Tréville, who was returning from St. Germain; he stopped them to offer his compliments upon their appointments, which in an instant drew round them a hundred gapers.

D'Artagnan took advantage of the circumstance to speak to M. de Tréville of the letter with the great red seal, and the cardinal's arms; we beg it to be understood that he did not breathe a word concerning the other.

M. de Tréville approved of the resolution he had adopted, and assured him that if on the morrow he did not appear, he himself would undertake to find him, let him be where he might.

At this moment the clock of La Samaritaine struck six: the four friends pleaded an engagement, and took leave of M. de Tréville.

A short gallop brought them to the road of Chaillot; the day began to decline, carriages were passing and repassing; D'Artagnan, keeping at some distance from his friends, darted a scrutinizing glance into every carriage that appeared, but saw no face with which he was acquainted.

At length, after waiting a quarter of an hour, and just as twilight was beginning to thicken, a carriage appeared, coming at a quick pace on the road of Sèvres; a presentiment instantly told D'Artagnan that this carriage contained the person who had appointed the rendezvous; the young man was himself astonished to find his heart beat so violently. Almost instantly a female head was put out at the window, with two fingers placed upon her mouth, either to enjoy silence or to send him a kiss; D'Artagnan uttered a slight cry of joy; this woman, or rather this apparition, for the carriage passed with the rapidity of a vision, was Madame Bonacieux.

By an involuntary movement, and in spite of the injunction given, D'Artagnan put his horse into a gallop, and in a few strides overtook the carriage; but the window was close shut, the vision had disappeared.

D'Artagnan then remembered the injunction: "If you value your own life, or that of those who love you, remain motionless, and as if you had seen nothing."

He stopped, therefore, trembling, not for himself, but for the poor woman who had evidently exposed herself to great danger by appointing this rendezvous.

The carriage pursued its way, still going at a great pace, till it dashed into Paris, and disappeared.

D'Artagnan remained fixed to the spot, astonished, and not knowing what to think. If it were Madame Bonacieux and if she was returning to Paris, why this fugitive interview, why this simple exchange of a glance, why this last kiss? If, on the other side, it were not she, which was still quite possible, for the little light that remained rendered a mistake easy; if it were not she, might it not be the commencement of some machination against him with the bait of this woman, for whom his love was known?

His three companions joined him. All had plainly seen a woman's head appear out at the window, but none of them, except Athos, knew Madame Bonacieux. The opinion of Athos was that it was Madame Bonacieux; but less preoccupied by that pretty face than D'Artagnan, he had fancied he saw a second head, a man's head, in the carriage.

"If that be the case," said D'Artagnan, "they are doubtless transporting her from one prison to another. But what can they intend to do with the poor creature, and how shall I ever meet her again?"

"My friend," said Athos gravely, "remember that it is the dead alone with whom we are not likely to meet again on this earth. You know something of that, as well as I do, I think. Now, if your mistress is not dead, if it is she we have just seen, you will meet with her again some day or other. And perhaps, my God!" added he, with that misanthropic tone which was peculiar to him, "perhaps sooner than you wish."

Half-past seven had struck, the carriage was twenty minutes behind the time appointed. D'Artagnan's friends reminded him that he had a visit to pay, but at the same time calling it to his observation that there was still time to retract.

But D'Artagnan was at the same time impetuous and curious. He had made up his mind that he would go to the Palais-Cardinal, and that he would learn what his eminence had to say to him: nothing could turn him from his purpose.

They reached the Rue St. Honoré, and in the Place du Palais-Cardinal they found the twelve convoked musketeers, walking about in expectation of their comrades. There only they made them acquainted with the matter in question.

D'Artagnan was well known in the honorable corps of the king's musketeers, in which it had been stated that he was, one day, to take his place: he was considered, beforehand, as their comrade. It resulted from these antecedents that every one entered heartily into the purpose for which they met; besides, it would not be unlikely that they should have an opportunity of playing either the cardinal or his people an ill turn, and for such expeditions these worthy gentlemen were always ready.

Athos divided them into three groups, assumed the command of one, gave the second to Aramis, and the third to Porthos, and then each group went and took a position for watching, near an entrance.

D'Artagnan, on his part, entered boldly at the front gate.

Although he felt himself ably supported, the young man was not without a little uneasiness as he ascended the great staircase, step by step. His conduct toward milady bore a strong resemblance to treachery, and he was very suspicious of the political relations which existed between that woman and the cardinal; still further, De Wardes, whom he had treated so ill, was one of the creatures of his eminence, and D'Artagnan knew, that while his eminence was terrible to his enemies, he was strongly attached to his friends.

"If De Wardes has related all our affair to the cardinal, which is not to be doubted, and if he has recognized me, which is probable, I may consider myself almost as a condemned man," said D'Artagnan, shaking his head. "But why has he waited till now? Humph! that's all plain enough: milady has laid her complaint against me with that hypocritical grief which renders her so interesting, and this last offense has made the cup overflow."

"Fortunately," added he, "my good friends are down yonder, and they will not allow me to be carried away easily. Nevertheless, M. de Tréville's company of musketeers alone cannot maintain a war against the cardinal, who disposes of the forces of all France, and before whom the queen is without power and the king without will. D'Artagnan, my friend, you are brave, you are prudent, you have excellent qualities, but the women will ruin you!"

He came to this melancholy conclusion as he entered the antechamber. He placed his letter in the hands of the usher on duty, who led him into the waiting-room, and passed on into the interior of the palace.

In this waiting-room were five or six of the cardinal's guards, who recognized D'Artagnan, and knowing that it was he who had wounded Jussac, they looked upon him with a smile of singular meaning.

This smile appeared to D'Artagnan to be of bad augury, only, as our Gascon was not easily intimidated, or rather, thanks to a great pride natural to the men of his country, he did not allow himself easily to see that which was passing in his mind, when that which was passing at all resembled fear, he placed himself haughtily in front of messieurs the guards, and waited with his hand on his hip, in an attitude by no means deficient in majesty.

The usher returned and made a sign to D'Artagnan to follow him. It appeared to the young man that that guards, on seeing him depart, whispered among themselves.

He followed a corridor, crossed a grand salon, entered a library, and found himself in the presence of a man seated at a desk and writing.

The usher introduced him and retired without speaking a word. D'Artagnan remained standing and examined this man.

D'Artagnan at first believed that he had to do with some judge examining his papers, but he perceived that the man of the desk wrote or rather corrected lines of unequal length, scanning the words on his fingers; he saw then that he was in face of a poet. At the end of an instant the poet closed his manuscript, upon the cover of which was written, *Mirame, a tragedy in five acts,* and raised his head.

D'Artagnan recognized the cardinal.

CHAPTER XL.

A TERRIBLE VISION.

THE cardinal leaned his elbow on his manuscript, his cheek upon his hand, and looked intently at the young man for a moment. No one had a more searching eye than the Cardinal de Richelieu, and D'Artagnan felt this glance penetrate his veins like a fever.

He, however, kept a good countenance, holding his hat in his hand, and awaiting the good pleasure of his eminence, without too much assurance, but without too much humility.

"Monsieur," said the cardinal, "are you a D'Artagnan from Béarn?"

"Yes, monseigneur," replied the young man.

"There are several branches of the D'Artagnans at Tarbes, and in its environs," said the cardinal; "to which do you belong?"

"I am the son of him who served in the religious wars under the great King Henry, the father of his gracious majesty."

"That is well. It is you who set out, seven or eight months

ago, from your country to try your fortune in the capital?"

"Yes, monseigneur."

"You came through Meung, where something befell you, I don't very well know what, but still something."

"Monseigneur," said D'Artagnan, "this was what happened to me——"

"Of no consequence, of no consequence!" resumed the cardinal with a smile, which indicated that he knew the story as well as he who wished to relate it; "you were recommended to M. de Tréville, were you not?"

"Yes, monseigneur, but in that unfortunate affair of Meung——"

"The letter was lost," replied his eminence; "yes, I know that; but M. de Tréville is a skillful physiognomist, who knows men at first sight; and he placed you in the company of his brother-in-law, M. Dessessarts, leaving you to hope that one day or other you should enter the musketeers."

"Monseigneur is quite correctly informed," said D'Artagnan.

"Since that time many things have happened to you: you were walking one day behind the Chartreux, when it would have been better for you if you had been elsewhere; then you took with your friends a journey to the waters of Forges; they stopped on the road, but you continued yours. That is all very simple, you had business in England."

"Monseigneur," said D'Artagnan, quite confused, "I went——"

"Hunting at Windsor, or elsewhere: that concerns nobody. I am acquainted with the circumstances, because it is my postion to know everything. On your return, you were received by an august personage, and I perceive with pleasure that you preserve the souvenir she gave you."

D'Artagnan placed his hand upon the queen's diamond, which he wore, and quickly turned the collet inward; but it was too late.

"The day after that, you received a visit from Cavois," resumed the cardinal: "he went to desire you to come to the palace; you did not return that visit, and you were wrong."

"Monseigneur, I feared I had incurred the anger of your eminence."

"How could that be, monsieur? Could you incur my anger by having followed the orders of your superiors with more intelligence and courage than another would have done? It is the people who do not obey that I punish, and not those who, like you, obey but too well. As a proof, remember the date of the day on which I caused you to be informed that I desired you to come to me, and seek in your memory for what happened to you that very night."

That was the very evening on which the carrying off of Madame Bonacieux took place; D'Artagnan trembled; and he likewise recollected that half an hour before the poor woman had passed close to him, without doubt, carried away by the same power that had caused her disappearance.

"In short," continued the cardinal, "as I have heard nothing of you for some time past, I wished to know what you were doing; besides, you owe me some thanks; you must yourself have remarked how much you have been considered in all the circumstances."

D'Artagnan bowed with respect.

"That," continued the cardinal, "arose not only from a feeling of natural equity, but likewise from a plan I have marked out with respect to you."

D'Artagnan became more and more astonished.

"I wished to explain this plan to you on the day you received my first invitation; but you did not come. Fortunately nothing is lost by this delay, and you are now about to hear it. Sit down, there, before me, M. d'Artagnan; you are quite gentleman enough not to listen standing."

And the cardinal pointed with his finger to a chair for the young man, who was so astonished at what was passing, that he awaited a second sign from his interlocutor before he obeyed.

"You are brave, Monsieur d'Artagnan," continued his eminence; "you are prudent, which is still better. I like men of head and heart. Don't be afraid," said he smiling, "by men of heart, I mean men of courage; but young as you are, and scarcely entering into the world, you have powerful enemies; if you do not take great heed, they will destroy you!"

"Alas! monseigneur!" replied the young man, "very easily, no doubt; for they are strong and well supported: while I am alone!"

"Yes, that's very true; but alone as you are, you have already done much, and will still do more, I don't doubt. And yet you have need, I believe, to be guarded in the adventurous career you have undertaken; for, if I mistake not, you came to Paris with the ambitious idea of making your fortune."

"I am at the age of extravagant hopes, monseigneur," said D'Artagnan.

"There are no extravagant hopes but for fools, monsieur, and you are a man of understanding. Now, what would you say to an ensigncy in my guards, and a company after the campaign?"

"Ah! monseigneur!"

"You accept it, do you not?"

"Monseigneur," replied D'Artagnan, with an embarrassed air.

"What! do you decline it?" cried the cardinal, with astonishment.

"I am in his majesty's guards, monseigneur, and I have no reason to be dissatisfied."

"But it appears to me that my guards are also his majesty's guards, and whoever serves in a French corps serves the king."

"Monseigneur, your eminence has ill understood my words."

"You want a pretext, do you not? I comprehend. Well, you have this excuse. Advancement, the opening campaign, the opportunity which I offer you, so much for the world; as regards yourself, safe protection; for it is fit you should know, Monsieur d'Artagnan, that I have received heavy and serious complaints against you; you do not consecrate your days and nights to the king's service alone."

D'Artagnan colored.

"In fact," said the cardinal, placing his hand upon a bundle of papers, "I have here a whole pile which concerns you. I know you to be a man of resolution, and your services, well directed, instead of leading you to ill, might be very advantageous to you. Come, reflect, and decide."

"Your goodness confounds me, monseigneur," replied D'Artagnan, "and I am conscious of a greatness of soul in your eminence that makes me mean as an earth-worm; but since monseigneur permits me to speak freely——"

D'Artagnan paused.

"Yes—speak."

"Then, I will presume to say, that all my friends are in the king's musketeers and guards, and, by an inconceivable fatality, all my enemies are in the service of your eminence; I should, therefore, be ill received here and ill regarded there, if I accepted that which monseigneur offers me."

"Do you happen to entertain the proud idea that I have not yet made you an offer equal to your merit?" asked the cardinal, with a smile of disdain.

"Monseigneur, your eminence is a hundred times too kind on my account, and, on the contrary, I think I have not proved myself worthy of your goodness. The siege of La Rochelle is about to be resumed, monseigneur; I shall serve under the eye of your eminence, and if I have the good fortune to conduct myself at that siege in such a manner as to attract your attention—then I shall a least leave behind me some brilliant action to justify the protection with which you honor me. Everything is best in its time, monseigneur; hereafter, perhaps, I shall have the right of giving myself: at present, I shall appear to sell myself."

"That is to say, you refuse to serve me, monsieur," said the cardinal, with a tone of vexation through which, however, might be seen a sort of esteem; "remain free, then, and preserve your hatreds and your sympathies."

"Monseigneur——"

"Well! well!" said the cardinal, "I don't wish you any ill; but you must be aware that it is quite trouble enough to defend and reward our friends; we owe nothing to our enemies; and let me give you a piece of advice: take good care of yourself, Monsieur d'Artagnan, for, from the moment I withdraw my hand from you, I would not give you an abode for your life."

"I will try to do so, monseigneur," replied the Gascon, with a noble confidence.

"Remember at a later period, and at a certain moment, if any mischance should happen to you," said Richelieu, with earnestness, "that it was I who came to seek you, and that I did all in my power to prevent this misfortune befalling you."

"I shall entertain, whatever may happen," said D'Artagnan, placing his hand upon his breast and bowing, "an eternal gratitude toward your eminence for that which you now do for me."

"Well, let it be then, as you have said, Monsieur d'Artagnan; we shall see each other again after the campaign; I will have my eye upon you, for I shall be there," replied the cardinal, pointing with his finger to a magnificent suit of armor he was to wear, "and on our return, well—we will settle our account!"

"Ah! monseigneur!" cried D'Artagnan, "spare me the weight of your anger; remain neuter, monseigneur, if you find that I act as a gentleman ought to act."

"Young man," said Richelieu, "if I am able to say to you again once more what I have said to you to-day, I promise you to do so."

This last expression of Richelieu's conveyed a terrible doubt; it alarmed D'Artagnan more than a menace would have done, for it was a warning. The cardinal, then, was seeking to preserve him from some misfortune which threatened him. He opened his mouth to reply, but, with a haughty gesture, the cardinal dismissed him.

D'Artagnan went out, but at the door his heart almost failed him, and he felt inclined to return. But the noble and severe countenance of Athos crossed his mind: if he made the compact with the cardinal which he required, Athos would no more give him his hand, Athos would renounce him.

It was this fear that restrained him, so powerful is the influence of a truly great character on all that surrounds it.

D'Artagnan descended by the staircase at which he had entered, and found Athos and the four musketeers waiting his appearance, and beginning to grow uneasy. With a word D'Artagnan reassured them, and Planchet ran to inform the other post that it was useless to keep guard longer, as his master had come out safe from the Palais-Cardinal.

When they reached Athos' residence, Aramis and Porthos inquired eagerly the cause of this strange interview; but D'Artagnan confined himself to telling them that M. de Richelieu had sent for him to propose to him to enter into his guards with the rank of ensign, and that he had refused.

"And you were quite right," cried Aramis and Porthos, with one voice.

Athos fell into a profound reverie and answered nothing. But when they were alone:

"You have done that which you ought to have done, D'Artagnan," said Athos—"but yet, perhaps, you have done wrong."

D'Artagnan sighed deeply, for this voice responded to a secret voice of his soul, which told him that great misfortunes awaited him.

The whole of the next day was spent in preparations for departure; D'Artagnan went to take leave of M. de Tréville. At that time it was believed that the separation of the musketeers and the guards would be but momentary, the king holding his parliament that very day, and proposing to set out the day after. M. de Tréville contented himself with asking D'Artagnan if he could do anything for him, but D'Artagnan answered that he was supplied with all he wanted.

That night assembled all the comrades of the guards of M. Dessessarts and the company of the musketeers of M. de Tréville, who had been accustomed to associate together. They were parting to meet again when it should please God, and if it should please God. The night, then, was a somewhat riotous one, as may be imagined; in such cases extreme preoccupation being only to be combated by extreme carelessness.

At the first sound of the morning trumpet the friends separated, the musketeers hastening to the hotel of M. de Tréville, the guards to that of M. Dessessarts. Each of the captains then led his company to the Louvre, where the king passed them in review.

The king was dull, and appeared ill, which took off a little from his usual lofty carriage. In fact, the evening before, a fever had seized him in the midst of the parliament, while he was holding his bed of justice. He had, not the less, decided upon setting out that same evening, and, in spite of the remonstrances that had been offered to him, he persisted in having the review, hoping, by setting it at defiance, to conquer the disease which began to lay hold of him.

The review over, the guards set forward alone on their march, the musketeers waiting for the king, which allowed Porthos time to go and take a turn, in his supurb equipment, in the Rue-aux Ours.

The procureuse saw him pass in his new uniform and upon his fine horse. She loved Porthos too dearly to allow him to part thus: she made him a sign to dismount and come to her. Porthos was magnificent, his spurs jingled, his cuirass glittered, his sword knocked proudly against his ample limbs. This time the clerks evinced no inclination to laugh, such a real ear-clipper did Porthos appear.

The musketeer was introduced to M. Coquenard, whose little gray eyes sparkled with anger at seeing his cousin all blazing new. Nevertheless, one thing afforded him inward consolation; it was expected by everybody that the campaign would a severe one: he whispered a hope to himself that this beloved relation might be killed in the course of it.

Porthos paid his compliments to M. Coquenard, and bade him farewell; Monsieur Coquenard wished him all sorts of prosperities. As to Madame Coquenard, she could not restrain her tears, but no evil impressions were taken from her grief, as she was known to be very much attached to her relations, about whom she was constantly having serious disputes with her husband.

But the real adieux were made in Madame Coquenard's chamber; they were heartrending!

As long as the procureuse could follow him with her eyes, she waved her handkerchief to him, leaning so far out of the window as to lead people to believe she was about to precipitate herself after her musketeer. Porthos received all these attentions like a man accustomed to such demonstrations; only, on turning the corner of the street, he lifted his hat gracefully, and waved it to her as a sign of adieu.

On his part, Aramis wrote a long letter. To whom? Nobody knew. Kitty, who was to set out that evening for Tours, was waiting in the next chamber.

Athos sipped the last bottle of his Spanish wine.

In the meantime, D'Artagnan was defiling with his company. On arriving at the Faubourg St. Antoine, he turned round to look gayly at the Bastille; but as it was the Bastille alone he looked at, he did not observe milady, who, mounted upon a light chestnut horse, pointed him out with her finger to two ill-looking men who came close up to the ranks to take notice of him. To a look of interrogation which they made, milady replied by a sign that that was the person. Then, certain that there could be no mistake in the execution of her orders, she turned her horse and disappeared.

The two men followed the company, and at leaving the Faubourg, St. Antoine, mounted two horses properly equipped, which a servant out of livery was holding in expectation of their coming.

CHAPTER XLI.

THE SIEGE OF LA ROCHELLE.

THE siege of La Rochelle was one of the great political events of the reign of Louis XIII., and one of the great military enterprises of the cardinal. It is then interesting, and even necessary, that we should say a few words about it, particularly as many details of this siege are connected in too important a manner with the history we have undertaken to relate, to allow us to pass it over in silence.

The political views of the cardinal, when he undertook this siege, were considerable. Let us expose them first, and then pass on to the private ones, which, perhaps, had not less influence upon his eminence than the former.

Of the important cities given up by Henry IV. to the Huguenots as places of safety, there only remained La Rochelle. It became necessary, therefore, to destroy this last bulwark of Calvinism, a dangerous leaven, with which the ferments of civil revolt and foreign war were constantly mingling.

Spaniards, English and Italian malcontents, adventurers of all nations, and soldiers of fortune of every or of no sect, flocked at the first summons to the standards of the Protestants, and organized themselves like a vast association, whose branches diverged at leisure over all parts of Europe.

La Rochelle, which had derived a new importance from the
ruin of the other Calvinist cities, was then the focus of dis-
sentious and ambitious views. Moreover, its port was the last
port in the kingdom of France open to the English, and by
closing it against England, our eternal enemy, the cardinal
completed the work of Joan of Arc and the Duke of Guise.

Thus Bassompierre, who was at once a Protestant and a
Catholic—a Protestant by conviction and a Catholic as com-
mander of the order of the Holy Ghost; Bassompierre, who
was a German by birth, and a Frenchman at heart; in short,
Bassompierre, who had a distinguished command at the siege
of La Rochelle, said, on charging at the head of several other
Protestant nobles like himself:

"You will see, gentlemen, that we shall be fools enough to
take La Rochelle."

And Bassompierre was right: the cannonade of the Isle of
Ré presaged to him the dragonades of the Cévennes; the
taking of La Rochelle was the preface to the revocation of
the Edict of Nantes.

But, we have hinted, that by the side of these views of the
leveling and simplifying minister, and which belong to history, the chronicler is forced to recognize the little aims of
the lover and the jealous rival.

Richelieu, as every one knows, had been in love with the
queen: was this love a simple political affair, or was it naturally one of those profound passions which Anne of Austria
inspired in those who approached her? That we are not able
to say; but, at all events, we have seen, by the anterior developments of this history, that Buckingham had had the
advantage over him, and in two or three circumstances, particularly that of the diamond studs, had, thanks to the
devotedness of the three musketeers, and the courage and
conduct of D'Artagnan, cruelly mystified him.

It was, then, Richelieu's object, not only to get rid of an
enemy of France, but to avenge himself on a rival; but this
vengeance ought to be great and striking, and worthy in
every way of a man who held in his hand, as his weapon for
combat, the forces of a whole kingdom.

Richelieu knew that while combating England he was combating Buckingham—that when triumphing over England,
he triumphed over Buckingham; in short, that in humiliating
England in the eyes of Europe, he humiliated Buckingham
in the eyes of the queen.

On his side, Buckingham, while pretending to maintain
the honor of England, was moved by interests exactly similar

to those of the cardinal. Buckingham, also, was pursuing a private vengeance. Buckingham could not, under any pretense, be admitted into France as an ambassador: he wished to enter it as a conqueror.

It resulted from this, that the veritable stake of this game, which two of the most powerful kingdoms played for the good pleasure of two men in love, was simply—a kind look from Anne of Austria.

The first advantage had been gained by Buckingham. Arriving unexpectedly in sight of the Isle of Ré, with ninety vessels, and nearly twenty thousand men, he had surprised the Count de Toirac, who commanded for the king in the Isle; he had, after a sanguinary conflict, effected his landing.

Allow us to observe, in passing, that in this fight perished the Baron de Chantal; that the Baron de Chantal left a little orphan girl of eighteen months old, and that this little girl was afterward Madame de Sévigné.

The Count de Toirac entered into the citadel St. Martin with his garrison, and threw a hundred men into a little fort, called the fort of La Prée.

This event had hastened the resolutions of the cardinal; and till the king and he could take the command of the siege of La Rochelle, which was determined on, he had sent monsieur to direct the first operations, and had ordered all the troops he could dispose of to march toward the theater of war. It was of this detachment, sent as vanguard, that our friend D'Artagnan formed a part.

The king, as we have said, was to follow as soon as his bed of justice had been held; but on rising from his bed of justice on the 28th of June, he felt himself attacked by fever. He was, notwithstanding, anxious to set out; but his illness becoming more serious, he was forced to stop at Villeroi.

Now, whenever the king stopped, the musketeers stopped. It resulted that D'Artagnan, who was as yet purely and simply in the guards, found himself, for the time at least, separated from his good friends, Athos, Aramis, and Porthos. This separation, which was no more than an unpleasant circumstance, would have certainly become a cause of serious uneasiness, if he had been able to guess by what unknown dangers he was surrounded.

He, however, arrived without accident in the camp established before La Rochelle, on the 10th of the month of September of the year 1627.

Everything was in the same state; the Duke of Buckingham and his English, masters of the Isle of Ré, continued to

besiege, but without success, the citadel of St. Martin and
the fort of La Prée; and hostilities with La Rochelle had
commenced, two or three days before, about a fort which the
Duke d'Angoulême had caused to be constructed near the
city.

The guards, under the command of M. Dessessarts, took
up their quarters at the Minimes; but, as we know, D'Artagnan,
preoccupied by the ambition of passing into the musketeers,
had formed but few friendships among his comrades,
and he felt himself isolated, and given up to his own
reflections.

His reflections were not very cheerful. From the time of
his arrival in Paris, he had been mixed up with public affairs;
but his own private affairs had not made any great progress,
as regarded either love or fortune. As to love, the only
woman he could have loved was Madame Bonacieux; and
Madame Bonacieux had disappeared, without his being able
to discover what had become of her. With respect to fortune,
he had made himself—he, humble as he was—an enemy of
the cardinal, that is to say, of a man before whom trembled
the greatest men of the kingdom, beginning with the king.

That man had the power to crush him, and yet he had not
done it. For a mind so perspicuous as that of D'Artagnan,
this indulgence was a light by which he caught a glimpse of
a better future.

And then he had made himself another enemy; not so
much to be feared, he thought, but, nevertheless, he instinctively
felt not to be despised; the enemy was milady.

In exchange for all this, he had acquired the protection
and good-will of the queen; but the favor of the queen was,
at the present time, an additional cause of persecution; and
her protection, it was pretty well known, protected the objects
of it very badly—as instanced in Chalais and Madame Bonacieux.

What he had clearly gained in all this was the diamond,
worth five or six thousand livres, which he wore on his finger;
and even this diamond, supposing that D'Artagnan, in his
projects of ambition, wished to keep it, to make it some day
a pledge for the gratitude of the queen, had not, in the meanwhile,
since he could not part with it, more value than the
stones he trod under his feet.

We say than the stones he trod under his feet, for D'Artagnan
made these reflections while walking solitarily along a
pretty little road which led from the camp to the village of
Angoutin. Now, these reflections had led him further than

he intended, and the day was beginning to decline, when, by the last ray of the setting sun, he thought he saw the barrel of a musket glitter from behind a hedge.

D'Artagnan had a quick eye, and a prompt understanding. He naturally supposed that that musket had not come there of itself, and that he who bore it had not concealed himself behind a hedge with any friendly intentions. He determined, therefore, to direct his course as clear from it as he could, when, on the opposite side of the road, from behind a rock, he perceived the extremity of another musket-barrel.

This was evidently an ambuscade.

The young man cast a glance at the first musket, and saw, with a certain degree of inquietude, that it was leveled in his direction; but as soon as he perceived that the orifice of the barrel was motionless, he threw himself upon the ground: at the same instant the gun was fired, and he heard the whistling of a ball pass over his head.

No time was to be lost. D'Artagnan sprang up with a bound, and at the same instant the ball from the other musket tore up the stones on the very place of the road where he had thrown himself with his face to the ground.

D'Artagnan was not one of those uselessly brave men who seek a ridiculous death, in order that it may be said of them that they did not give way a single step; besides, courage was out of the question here, D'Artagnan had fallen into a premeditated ambuscade.

"If there should be a third shot," said he, "I am a lost man."

He immediately, therefore, took to his heels, and ran toward the camp, with the swiftness of the young men of his country, so renowned for their agility; but whatever might be his speed, the first that fired, having had time to reload, fired a second shot, and this time so well aimed, that it struck his hat, and carried it ten paces from him.

As he, however, had no other hat, he picked up this as he ran, and arrived at his quarters, very pale and quite out of breath. He sat down without saying a word to anybody, and began to reflect.

This event might have three causes:

The first and the most natural was, that it might be an ambuscade of the Rochellais who might not have been sorry to kill one of his majesty's guards; in the first place, because it would be an enemy the less, and that this enemy might have a well-furnished purse in his pocket.

D'Artagnan took his hat, examined the hole made by the

ball, and shook his head. The ball was not a musket-ball—
it was an arquebus-ball. The justness of the aim had first
given him the idea that a particular kind of weapon had been
employed. This could not then, be a military ambuscade, as
the ball was not of the regular caliber.

This might be a kind remembrance of Monsieur le Cardinal.
It may be observed that at the very moment when, thanks to
the ray of the sun, he perceived the gun-barrel, he was thinking with astonishment on the forbearance of his eminence
with respect to him.

But D'Artagnan again shook his head. For people toward
whom he had but to put forth his hand, his eminence had
rarely recourse to such means.

It might be a vengeance of milady's—that was the most
probable!

He endeavored in vain to remember the faces or dress of
the assassins; he had escaped so rapidly, that he had not had
leisure to remark anything.

"Ah! my poor friends!" murmured D'Artagnan; "where
are you? How sadly I want you!"

D'Artagnan passed a very restless night. Three or four
times he started up, imagining that a man was approaching
his bed for the purpose of poniarding him. Nevertheless,
day dawned without darkness having brought any accident.

But D'Artagnan justly suspected that that which was
deferred was not lost.

D'Artagnan remained all day in his quarters, assigning as
a reason to himself that the weather was bad.

At nine o'clock next morning, the drums beat to arms.
The Duke of Orleans visited the posts. The guards were
under arms, and D'Artagnan took his place in the midst of
his comrades.

Monsieur passed along the front of the line; then all the
superior officers approached him to pay their compliments,
M. Dessessarts, captain of the guards, as well as the others.

At the expiration of a minute or two, it appeared to D'Artagnan that M. Dessessarts made him a sign to come to him;
he waited for a fresh gesture on the part of his superior, for
fear he might be mistaken; but this gesture being repeated,
he left the ranks, and advanced to receive his orders.

"Monsieur is about to ask for some men of good courage
for a dangerous mission, but which will do honor to those
who shall accomplish it, and I made you a sign in order that
you might hold yourself in readiness."

"Thanks! captain!" replied D'Artagnan, who wished for

nothing better than an opportunity for distinguishing himself under the eye of the lieutenant-general.

In fact, the Rochellais had made a sortie during the night, and had retaken a bastion of which the royal army had gained possession two days before; the matter was to ascertain, by reconnoitering, how the enemy guarded this bastion.

At the end of a few minutes, monsieur raised his voice, and said:

"I want, for this mission, three or four volunteers, led by a man who can be depended upon."

"As to the man to be depended upon, I have him under my hand, monseigneur," said M. Dessessarts, pointing to D'Artagnan; "and as to the four or five volunteers, monseigneur has but to make his intentions known, and the men will not be wanting."

"Four men of good will who will risk being killed with me!" said D'Artagnan, raising his sword.

Two of his comrades of the guards immediately sprang forward, and two other soldiers having joined them, the number was deemed sufficient; D'Artagnan declined all others, being unwilling to injure the chance of honor of those who came forward first.

It was not known whether, after the taking of the bastion, the Rochellais had evacuated it or left a garrison in it; the object then was to examine the place near enough to ascertain the thing.

D'Artagnan set out with his four companions, and followed the trench: the two guards marched abreast with him, and the two soldiers followed behind.

They arrived thus, screened by the lining of the trench, till they came within a hundred paces of the bastion! There, on turning round, D'Artagnan perceived that the two soldiers had disappeared.

He thought that, beginning to be afraid, they had stayed behind.

At the turning of the counterscarp they found themselves within about sixty paces of the bastion. The saw no one, and the bastion seemed abandoned.

The three composing our forlorn hope were deliberating whether they should proceed any further, when all at once a circle of smoke enveloped the giant of stone, and a dozen balls came whistling round D'Artagnan and his companions.

They knew all they wished to know; the bastion was guarded. A longer stay in this dangerous spot would have been useless imprudence: D'Artagnan and his two companions turned their backs, and commenced a retreat which looked very much like a flight.

On arriving at the angle of the trench which was to serve them as a rampart, one of the guards fell; a ball passed through his breast. The other, who was safe and sound, continued his way toward the camp.

D'Artagnan was not willing to abandon his companion thus, and stooped down to raise him and assist him in regaining the lines; but at this moment two shots were fired; one ball hit the head of the already wounded guard, and the other was flattened against a rock, after having passed within two inches of D'Artagnan.

The young man turned quickly round, for this attack could not come from the bastion, which was masked by the angle of the trench; the idea of the two soldiers who had abandoned him occurred to his mind, and with them that of the assassins of two evenings before; he resolved then, this time, to know what he had to trust to, and fell upon the body of his comrade as if he had been dead.

He quickly saw two heads appear above an abandoned work, within thirty paces of him; they were the heads of the two soldiers. D'Artagnan had not been deceived, these two men had only followed him for the purpose of assassinating him, hoping that the young man's death would be placed to the account of the enemy.

Only, as he might be wounded and might denounce their crime, they came up to him with the purpose of making sure of him; fortunately, deceived by D'Artagnan's trick, they neglected to reload their guns.

When they were within ten paces of him, D'Artagnan, who, in falling had taken care not to leave hold of his sword, sprang up close to them.

The assassins comprehended that if they fled toward the camp without having killed their man, they would be accused by him; therefore, their first idea was to pass over to the enemy. One of them took his gun by the barrel, and used it as he would a club; he aimed a terrible blow at D'Artagnan, who avoided it by springing on one side; but by this movement he left a passage free to the bandit, who darted off toward the bastion. As tho the Rochellais who guarded the bastion were ignorant of the intentions of the man they saw coming toward them, they fired upon him, and he fell, struck by a ball, which broke his shoulder.

In the meantime, D'Artagnan had thrown himself upon the other soldier, attacking him with his sword; the conflict was not long; the wretch had nothing to defend himself with but his discharged arquebus; the sword of the guard slipped down the barrel of the now useless weapon, and passed through the thigh of the assassin, who fell.

D'Artagnan immediately placed the point of his sword at his throat.

"Oh, do not kill me!" cried the bandit. "Pardon, pardon! my officer! and I will tell you all."

"Is your secret of enough importance for me to spare your life for it?" asked the young man, withholding his arm.

"Yes! if you think existence worth anything to a man of twenty as you are, and who may hope for everything, being handsome and brave, as you are."

"Wretch!" cried D'Artagnan, "speak, and speak quickly! who employed you to assassinate me?"

"A woman whom I don't know; but who is called milady."

"But if you don't know this woman, how do you know her name?"

"My comrade knows her, and called her so; it was with him she agreed, and not with me; he even has in his pocket a letter from that person, who attaches great importance to you, as I have heard him say."

"But how did you become concerned in this villainous affair?"

"He proposed to me to undertake it with him, and I agreed."

"And how much did she give you for this fine enterprise?"

"A hundred louis."

"Well, come!" said the young man, laughing, "she thinks I am worth something! A hundred louis! Well, that was a temptation for two miserable creatures like you; so I understand you accepted it, and I grant you my pardon; but upon one condition!"

"What is that?" said the soldier, uneasy at perceiving that all was not over.

"That you will go and fetch me the letter your comrade has in his pocket."

"Why," cried the bandit, "that is only another way of killing me, how can I go and fetch that letter under the fire of the bastion?"

"You must, however, make up your mind to go and fetch it, or you shall die by my hand."

"Pardon! Monsieur, have pity on me! In the name of that young lady you love, and whom you perhaps think is dead, but is not!" cried the bandit, throwing himself upon his knees, and leaning upon his hand, for he began to lose his strength with his blood.

"And how do you know there is a young woman that I love, or that I thought that woman dead?" asked D'Artagnan.

"By that letter which my comrade had in his pocket."

"You see, then," said D'Artagnan, "that I must have that letter; so no more delay, no more hesitation; or else, whatever may be my repugnance to soiling my sword a second time with the blood of a wretch like you, I swear by the word of a gentleman——"

And at these words D'Artagnan made so menacing a gesture that the wounded man sprang up.

"Stop, stop!" cried he, regaining strength from terror, "I will go—I will go!"

D'Artagnan took the soldier's arquebus, made him go on before him, and urged him toward his companion by pricking him behind with his sword.

It was a frightful thing to see this unfortunate being, leaving a long track of blood upon the ground he passed over, pale with approaching death, endeavoring to drag himself along without being seen, to the body of his accomplice, which lay at twenty paces from him.

Terror was so strongly painted on his face, covered with a cold sweat, that D'Artagnan took pity on him, and casting upon him a look of contempt:

"Stop!" said he, "I will show you the difference between a man of true courage and such a base creature as you; stay where you are, I will go myself."

And, with a light step, an eye on the watch, observing the movements of the enemy, and taking advantage of the accidents of the ground, D'Artagnan succeeded in reaching the second soldier.

There were two means of gaining his object; to search him on the spot, or to carry him away, making a buckler of his body, and searching him in the trench.

D'Artagnan preferred the second means, and lifted the assassin on to his shoulders at the moment the enemy fired.

A slight shock, the dull noise of three balls which penetrated the flesh, a last cry, a convulsion of agony, proved to D'Artagnan that he who had endeavored to assassinate him had saved his life.

D'Artagnan regained the trench, and threw the body down by the wounded man, who was as pale as death.

The search was instantly commenced; a leather pocketbook, a purse, in which was evidently a part of the sum which the bandit had received, with a dice-box and dice, formed the heritage of the dead man.

He threw the purse to the wounded man, and eagerly opened the pocket-book.

Among some unimportant papers he found the following letter.

"Since you have lost sight of that woman, and she is now in safety in the convent, at which you should never have allowed her to arrive, try, at least, not to miss the man; if you do, you know that my hand reaches far, and that you shall repay me very dearly the hundred louis you have had of me."

No signature. Nevertheless it was plain the letter came from milady. He consequently kept it as a piece of evidence, and, being in safety behind the angle of the trench, he began to interrogate the wounded man. He confessed that he had undertaken, with his comrade, the same that was killed, to carry off a young woman, who was to leave Paris by the barrier of La Villette; but having stopped to drink at a cabaret, they had missed the carriage by ten minutes.

"But what were you to have done with that woman?" asked D'Artagnan, with great agitation.

"We were to have conveyed her to an hotel in the Place Royale," said the wounded man.

"Yes! yes!" murmured D'Artagnan; "that's the place; milady's own residence!"

The young man tremblingly felt what a terrible thirst of vengeance urged this woman on to destroy him, as well as all who loved him, and how well she must be acquainted with the affairs of the court, since she had discovered everything. There could be no doubt she owed this information to the cardinal.

But amid all this he perceived, with a feeling of real joy, that the queen must have discovered the prison in which poor Madame Bonacieux expiated her devotedness, and that she had freed her from that prison. And the letter he had received from the young woman, with her passing along the road of Chaillot like an apparition, were now explained.

From that time, also, as Athos had predicted, it became possible to find Madame Bonacieux, and a convent was not impregnable.

This idea completely restored clemency to his heart. He

turned toward the wounded man, who had watched with intense anxiety all the various expressions of his countenance, and holding out his arm to him:

"Come," said he, "I will not abandon you thus. Lean upon me, and let us return to the camp."

"Yes," said the man, who could scarcely believe in such magnanimity, "but is not that to have me hanged?"

"You have my word," said he; "for the second time I give you your life."

The wounded man sank upon his knees, to again kiss the feet of his preserver; but D'Artagnan, who had no longer a motive for staying so near the enemy, cut short the evidences of his gratitude.

The guard who had returned at the first discharge had announced the death of his four companions. They were therefore much astonished and delighted in the regiment, when they saw the young man come back safe and sound.

D'Artagnan explained the sword-wound of his companion by a sortie which he improvised. He described the death of the other soldier, and the perils they had encountered. This recital was for him the occasion of a veritable triumph. The whole army talked of this expedition for a day, and monsieur paid him his compliments upon it. Besides this, as every great action bears its own recompense with it, the great action of D'Artagnan had for result the restoration of the tranquillity he had lost. In fact, D'Artagnan believed that he might indulge in a little tranquillity, as of his two enemies, one was killed, and the other devoted to his interests.

This tranquillity proved one thing, which was, that D'Artagnan was not yet perfectly acquainted with milady

CHAPTER XLII.

THE ANJOU WINE.

AFTER the most disheartening news of the king's health, a report of his convalescence began to prevail in the army; and as he was very anxious to be in person at the siege, it was said that as soon as he could mount on horseback he would set forward.

In the meantime, monsieur, who knew that, from one day to the other, he might expect to be removed from his command by the Duke d'Angoulême, Bassompierre, or Schomberg, who were all eager for his post, did but little, lost his days in wavering, and did not dare to attempt any great enterprise to drive the English from the Isle of Ré, where they still besieged the citadel St. Martin and the fort of La Prée, while, on their side, the French were besieging La Rochelle.

D'Artagnan, as we have said, had become more tranquil, as always happens after a past danger, particularly when that danger seems to have vanished; he only felt one uneasiness, and that was at not hearing from his three friends.

But one morning at the commencement of the month of November, everything was explained to him by this letter, dated from Villeroi:

"MONSIEUR D'ARTAGNAN: MM. Athos, Porthos, and Aramis, after having had an entertainment at my house, and enjoyed themselves very much, created such a disturbance, that the provost of the castle, a very rigid man, has ordered them to be confined for some days; but I accomplish the order they have given me, by forwarding to you a dozen bottles of my Anjou wine, with which they are much pleased: they are desirous that you should drink to their health in their favorite wine. I have done accordingly, and am, monsieur, with great respect,

"Your very humble and obedient servant,

"GODEAU,

"Messman of the Musketeers."

"That's all well!" cried D'Artagnan, "they think of me in their pleasures, as I thought of them in my troubles. Well, I will certainly drink to their health with all my heart, but I will not drink alone."

And D'Artagnan went among the guards, with whom he had formed greater intimacy than with the others, to invite them to enjoy with him this present of delicious Anjou wine which had been sent him from Villeroi.

One of the two guards was engaged that evening, and another the next: so that the meeting was fixed for the day after that.

D'Artagnan, on his return, sent the twelve bottles of wine to the *buvette* of the guards, with strict orders that great care should be taken of it; and then, on the day appointed, as the dinner was fixed for twelve o'clock, D'Artagnan sent Planchet, at nine in the morning, to assist in preparing everything for the entertainment.

Planchet, very proud of being raised to the dignity of *maître d'hôtel*, thought he would get all ready like an intel-

ligent man, and with this view called in the assistance of the
lackey of one of his master's guests, named Fourreau, and
the false soldier who had endeavored to kill D'Artagnan and
who, belonging to no corps, had entered into the service of
D'Artagnan, or rather of Planchet, since D'Artagnan had
saved his life.

The hour of the banquet being come, the two guests arrived, took their places, and the dishes were arranged upon
the table. Planchet waited, towel on arm; Fourreau un-
corked the bottles, and Brisemont, which was the name of
the convalescent, poured the wine, which was a little shaken
by its journey, carefully into glass decanters. Of this wine,
the first bottle being a little thick at the bottom, Brisemont
poured the lees into a glass, and D'Artagnan desired him to
drink it, for the poor devil had not half recovered his strength.

The guests, after having eaten the soup, were about to lift
the first glass of wine to their lips, when all at once the cannon sounded from Fort Louis and Fort Neuf; the guards,
imagining this to be caused by some unexpected attack, either
of the besieged or the English, sprang to their swords; D'Artagnan, not less forward than they, did so likewise, and all
ran out, in order to repair to their posts.

But scarcely were they out of the *buvette,* than they were
made aware of the cause of this noise: cries of "Vive le Roi!
Vive Monsieur le Cardinal!" resounded on every side, and the
drums were beaten in all directions.

In short, the king, impatient as we have said he was, had
come by forced marches, and had arrived at that moment
with all his household and a reinforcement of ten thousand
troops: his musketeers preceded and followed him. D'Artagnan, placed in line with his company, saluted with an
expressive gesture his three friends, whose eyes soon discovered him, and M. de Tréville, who recognized him at once.

The ceremony of the arrival over, the four friends were
soon together.

"Pardieu!" cried D'Artagnan, "you could not have arrived
in better time; the dinner cannot have had time to get cold!
can it, gentlemen?" added the young man turning to the
two guards, whom he introduced to his friends.

"Ah! ah!" said Porthos, "it appears we are feasting, then!"
"I hope," said Aramis, "there are no women of your party."
"Is there any drinkable wine in your tavern?" asked Athos.
"Well, *pardieu!* there is your own, my dear friend," re-
plied D'Artagnan.
"Our wine!" said Athos, astonished.

"Yes, that you sent me."

"We send you wine?"

"Yes; nonsense, you know what I mean; the wine from the hills of Anjou."

"Yes, I know what wine you mean."

"The wine you prefer."

"Doubtless, when I can get neither champagne nor chambertin."

"Well! in the absence of champagne and chambertin, you must content yourselves with that."

"And so, connoisseurs in wine as we are, we have sent you some Anjou wine, eh! have we?" said Porthos.

"Not exactly, it is the wine that was sent me on your account."

"On our account?" said the three musketeers.

"Did you send this wine, Aramis?" said Athos.

"No; and you, Porthos?"

"No; and you, Athos?"

"Well, but if it was not you, it was your messman," said D'Artagnan.

"Our messman!"

"Yes, your messman, Godeau, the messman of the musketeers."

"*Ma foi!* never mind where it comes from," said Porthos, "let us taste it, and if it is good, let us drink it."

"No," said Athos, "don't let us drink wine which comes from an unknown source."

"You are right, Athos," said D'Artagnan. "Did none of you order Godeau to send me some wine?"

"No! and yet you say he has sent you some as from us?"

"Here is his letter," said D'Artagnan, and he presented the note to his comrade.

"That is not his writing!" said Athos, "I know it; before we left Villeroi, I settled the accounts of the regiment."

"It is a false letter altogether," said Porthos, "we have not been confined."

"D'Artagnan," said Aramis, in a reproachful tone, "how could you believe that we had made a disturbance?"

D'Artagnan grew pale, and a convulsive trembling shook all his limbs.

"Thou alarmest me!" said Athos, who never used *thee* and *thou* but upon very particular occasions, "what has happened?"

"Hasten! hasten! my friend!" cried D'Artagnan, "a horrible suspicion crosses my mind! can this be another vengeance on the part of that woman?"

It was now Athos' turn to become pale.

D'Artagnan rushed toward the *buvette,* the three musketeers and the two guards following him.

The first object that met the eyes of D'Artagnan, on entering the *buvette,* was Brisemont, stretched upon the ground and rolling in horrible convulsions.

Planchet and Fourreau, as pale as death, were endeavoring to render him assistance; but it was plain that all assistance was useless: all the features of the dying man were distorted with agony.

"Ah!" cried he, on perceiving D'Artagnan, "ah! this is frightful! you pretend to pardon me, and you poison me!"

"I!" cried D'Artagnan, "I, wretched man! what can you mean by that?"

"I say that it was you who gave me the wine, I say that it was you who desired me to drink it, I say you wished to avenge yourself on me, and I say that it is horrible!"

"Do not think so, Brisemont," said D'Artagnan; "do not think so; I swear to you, I protest——"

"Oh! but God is above! God will punish you! My God! grant that he may one day suffer what I suffer!"

"Upon the Gospel," said D'Artagnan, throwing himself down by the dying man, "I swear to you that the wine was poisoned and that I was going to drink of it as you did."

"I do not believe you," cried the soldier, and he expired amid horrible tortures.

"Frightful! frightful!" murmured Athos, while Porthos broke the bottles and Aramis gave orders, a little too late, that a confessor should be sent for.

"Oh! my friends," said D'Artagnan, "you come once more to save my life, not only mine, but that of these gentlemen. Gentlemen," continued he, addressing the guards, "I request you will be silent with regard to this adventure; great personages may have had a hand in what you have seen, and, if talked about, the evil would only recoil upon us."

"Ah! monsieur!" stammered Planchet, more dead than alive, "ah! monsieur! what an escape I have had!"

"How, sirrah! you were going to drink my wine, were you!"

"To the health of the king, monsieur; I was going to drink a small glass of it, if Fourreau had not told me I was called."

"Alas!" said Fourreau, whose teeth chattered with terror, "I wanted to get him out of the way that I might drink by myself!"

"Gentlemen," said D'Artagnan, addressing the guards,

"you may easily comprehend that such a feast can but be very dull, after what has taken place; so accept my excuses, and put off the party till another day, I beg of you."

The two guards courteously accepted D'Artagnan's excuses, and perceiving that the four friends desired to be alone, retired.

When the young guardsman and the three musketeers were without witnesses, they looked at each other with an air which plainly expressed that every one of them perceived the seriousness of their situation.

"In the first place," said Athos, "let us leave this chamber; the dead are not agreeable company, particularly when they have died a violent death."

"Planchet," said D'Artagnan, "I commit the body of this poor devil to your care. Let him be interred in holy ground. He committed a crime, it is true; but he repented of it."

And the four friends quitted the room, leaving Planchet and Fourreau the charge of paying the mortuary honors to Brisemont.

The host gave them another chamber, and served them with fresh eggs and some water, which Athos went himself to draw at the fountain. In a few words, Porthos and Aramis were informed of past events.

"Well!" said D'Artagnan to Athos, "you see, my dear friend, that this is war to the death!"

Athos shook his head.

"Yes, yes," replied he, "I perceive that plainly; but do you really believe it is she?"

"I am sure of it."

"Nevertheless, I confess I still doubt."

"But the *fleur-de-lis* on her shoulder?"

"She is some Englishwoman who has committed a crime in France, and has been branded in consequence."

"Athos, she is your wife, I tell you," repeated D'Artagnan; "only reflect how much your description agrees with mine."

"Yes, but I should think the other must be dead, I hanged her so effectually."

It was D'Artagnan who now shook his head in his turn.

"But, in either case, what is to be done?" said the young man.

"It is impossible to remain thus, with a sword hanging eternally over one's head," said Athos; "we must emancipate ourselves from this position."

"Well, but how?"

"Listen; you must try to have an interview with her, and

enter into an explanation with her; say to her: 'Peace or war, my word of honor of a gentleman never to say anything of you, never to do anything against you—on your side, a solemn oath to remain neuter with respect to me if not, I will apply to the chancellor, I will apply to the king, I will apply to the hangman, I will move the courts against you, I will denounce you as branded, I will bring you to trial, and if you are acquitted—well—by the honor of a gentleman I will kill you, at the corner of some wall, as I would a mad dog.'"

"I like the means well enough," said D'Artagnan, "but where and how to meet with her?"

"Time, dear friend, time brings round opportunity, opportunity is the martingal of man: the more we have ventured, the more we gain when we know how to wait."

"Yes, but to wait surrounded by assassins and poisoners."

"Bah!" said Athos, "God has preserved us hitherto, God will preserve us still."

"Yes, we; we, besides, are men; and everything considered, it is our lot to risk our lives; but she," added he in an undertone.

"What she?" asked Athos.

"Constance?"

"Madame Bonacieux! ah! that's true," said Athos, "my poor friend, I had forgotten you were in love."

"Well, but," said Aramis, "have you not learned by the letter you found on the assassin, that she is in a convent? She may be very comfortable in a convent; and as soon as the siege of Rochelle is terminated, I promise you, on my part——"

"Good!" cried Athos, "good! yes, Aramis, we all know that your views have a religious tendency."

"I am only a musketeer for the time," said Aramis humbly.

"Ay, it is some time since he heard from his mistress," said Athos, in a low voice; "but take no notice, we know all about that."

"Well!" said Porthos, "it appears to me that the means are very simple."

"What are they?" said D'Artagnan.

"Don't you say she is in a convent?" replied Porthos.

"Yes."

"Well, as soon as the siege is over, we'll carry her off from that convent."

"But we must first learn what convent she is in."

"That's true," said Porthos.

"But, I think I have it," said Athos. "Don't you say, D'Artagnan, that it is the queen who has made choice of the convent for her?"

"I believe so, at least."

"In that case, Porthos will assist us."

"How, I pray you?"

"Why, by your marquise, your duchess, your princess; she must have a long arm."

"Hush!" said Porthos, placing a finger on his lips, "I believe her to be a cardinalist; she must know nothing of the matter."

"Then," said Aramis, "I take upon myself to obtain intelligence of her."

"You, Aramis!" cried the three friends, "how?"

"By the queen's almoner, with whom I am very intimately acquainted," said Aramis, coloring

And upon this assurance, the four friends, who had finished their modest repast, separated, with the promise of meeting again that evening; D'Artagnan returned to the Minimes, and the three musketeers repaired to the king's quarters, where they had to prepare their lodging.

CHAPTER XLIII.

THE AUBERGE OF THE COLUMBIER ROUGE.

In the meanwhile, the king, although scarcely arrived, who was in such haste to face the enemy, and who, with more reason than the cardinal, showed his hatred for Buckingham, commanded every disposition to be made to drive the English from the Isle of Ré, and afterward to press the siege of La Rochelle; but, notwithstanding his earnest wish, he was delayed by the dissensions which broke out between MM. Bassompierre and Schomberg against the Duke d'Angoulême.

MM. Bassompierre and Schomberg were marshals of France, and claimed their right of commanding the army under the orders of the king; but the cardinal, who feared that Bassompierre, a Huguenot at heart, might press the English and Rochellais, his brothers in religion, but feebly, supported the Duke d'Angoulême, whom the king, at his instigation, had named lieutenant-general. The result was, that, to avoid seeing MM. Bassompierre and Schomberg desert the army, a separate command was forced to be given to each: Bassom-

pierre took up his quarters to the north of the city between
La Leu and Dompierre; the Duke d'Angoulême to the east,
from Dompierre to Perigny; and M. de Schomberg to the
south, from Perigny to Angoutin.

The quarters of monsieur were at Dompierre. The quarters of the king were sometimes at Etre, sometimes at La
Jairie. The cardinal's quarters were upon the downs, at the
bridge of La Pierre, in a simple house without any entrench-
ment.

So that monsieur watched Bassompierre; the king, the
Duke d'Angoulême; and the cardinal, M. de Schomberg.

As soon as this organization was established, they set about
driving the English from the Isle.

The conjuncture was favorable; the English, who required,
above everything, good living, in order to be good soldiers,
only eating salt meat and bad biscuit, had many sick in their
camp; still further, the sea, very bad at this period of the
year on all the coasts of the ocean, destroyed every day some
little vessel or other, and the shore, from the point of L'Arguillon to the trenches, was at every tide literally covered
with the wrecks of pinnaces, roberges and feluccas; it resulted
that even if the king's troops remained quietly in their camp,
it was evident that some day or other, Buckingham, who only
continued in the isle from obstinacy, would be obliged to raise
the siege.

But as M. de Toirac gave information that everything was
preparing in the enemy's camp for a fresh assault, the king
judged that it would be best to put an end to the affair, and
gave the neccessary orders for a decisive action.

It not being our intention to make a journal of the siege,
but, on the contrary only to describe such of the events of it
as are connected with the history we are relating, we will
content ourselves with saying in two words that the expedition succeeded, to the great astonishment of the king, and the
great glory of Monsieur le Cardinal. The English, repulsed
foot by foot, beaten in all the rencounters, and defeated in
the passage of L'Ile de Loix, were obliged to re-embark, leaving on the field of battle two thousand men, among whom
were five colonels, three lieutenant-colonels, two hundred and
fifty captains, and twenty gentlemen of rank, four pieces of
cannon, and sixty colors, which were taken to Paris by Claude
de St. Simon, and suspended with great pomp in the vaults
of Nôtre Dame.

Te Deums were sung in the camp, and afterward throughout France.

The cardinal was left master of carrying on the siege without having, at least at the present, anything to fear on the part of the English.

But, as we have just said, this repose was but for the moment.

An envoy of the Duke of Buckingham, named Montague, was taken, and proof was obtained of a league between the empire, Spain, England, and Lorraine.

This league was directed against France.

Still further, in Buckingham's quarters, which he had been forced to abandon more precipitately than he expected, papers were found which confirmed this league, and which, as the cardinal asserts in his memoirs, strongly compromised Madame de Chevreuse, and consequently the queen.

It was upon the cardinal that all the responsibility fell, for there is no being a despotic minister without responsibility; all, therefore, of the vast resources of his genius were at work night and day, and engaged in listening to the least report that was to be heard in any of the great kingdoms of Europe.

The cardinal was acquainted with the activity, and, more particularly, with the hatred, of Buckingham; if the league which threatened France triumphed, all his influence would be lost; Spanish policy and Austrian policy would have their representatives in the cabinet of the Louvre, where they had as yet but partisans; and he, Richelieu, the French minister, the national minister, would be ruined. The king, who, while obeying him like a child, hated him as a child hates his master, would abandon him to the personal vengeance of monsieur and the queen; he would then be lost, and France, perhaps, with him. All this must be guarded against.

Thus, couriers, becoming every instant more numerous, succeeded each other, day and night, in the little house of the bridge of La Pierre, in which the cardinal had established his residence.

These were monks who wore the frock with such an ill grace, that it was easy to perceive they belonged to the church militant; women, a little inconvenienced by their costume of pages, and whose large trousers could not entirely conceal their rounded forms: and peasants with blackened hands and fine limbs, savoring of the man of quality a league off.

In addition to these there were less agreeable visits, for two or three times reports were spread that the cardinal had nearly been assassinated.

It is true that the enemies of the cardinal said that it was he himself who set these bungling assassins to work, in order to have, if wanted, the right of using reprisals—but we must not believe everything ministers say, nor everything their enemies say.

But these attempts did not prevent the cardinal, to whom his most inveterate detractors have never denied personal bravery, from making nocturnal excursions, sometimes to communicate to the Duke d'Angoulême some important orders; sometimes to go and confer with the king; and sometimes to have an interview with a messenger whom he did not wish to see at home.

On their part, the musketeers, who had not much to do with the siege, were not under very strict orders, and led a joyous life. This was the more easy for our three companions in particular, as being friends of M. de Tréville's they obtained from him permission to be absent after the closing of the camp.

Now, one evening, when D'Artagnan, who was in the trenches, was not able to accompany them, Athos, Porthos, and Aramis, mounted upon their battle-steeds, enveloped in their war cloaks, with their hands upon their pistol-butts, were returning from a *buvette* which Athos had discovered two days before upon the route to La Jairie, called the Colombier Rouge, following the road which led to the camp, and quite upon their guard, as we have stated, for fear of an ambuscade, when at about a quarter of a league from the village of Boinar, they fancied they heard the sound of horses approaching them. They immediately all three halted, closed in, and waited, occupying the middle of the road. At the end of an instant, and as the moon broke from behind a cloud, they saw, at a turning of the road, two horsemen who, on perceiving them, stopped in their turn, appearing to deliberate whether they should continue their route or go back. The hesitation created some suspicion in the three friends, and Athos, advancing a few paces in front of the others, cried in a firm voice.

"Who goes there?"

"Who goes there, yourselves?" replied one of the horsemen.

"That is not an answer," replied Athos. "Who goes there? Answer, or else we charge."

"Beware of what you are about, gentlemen!" said a clear voice, which appeared accustomed to command.

"It is some superior officer, making his night-rounds," said Athos, "what do you mean to do, gentlemen?"

"Who are you?" said the same voice in the same commanding tone; "answer in your turn, or you may repent of your disobedience."

"King's musketeers," said Athos, still more convinced that he who interrogated them had the right to do so.

"Of what company?"

"Company of Tréville."

"Advance, and render me an account of what you are doing here at this time of night."

The three companions advanced rather humbly, for all were now convinced that they had to do with some one more powerful than themselves, leaving Athos the post of speaker.

"Your pardon, *mon officer!*" said Athos; "but we were ignorant of whom we were speaking to, and you may see that we were keeping good guard."

"Your name?" said the officer, a part of whose face was covered by his cloak.

"But yourself, monsieur," said Athos, who began to be annoyed by this inquisition, "give me, I beg you, the proof that you have the right to question me."

"Your name?" repeated the cavalier a second time, letting his cloak fall, and leaving his face uncovered.

"Monsieur le Cardinal!" cried the stupefied musketeers.

"Your name?" cried the cardinal for the third time.

"Athos!" said the musketeer.

The cardinal made a sign to his attendant, who drew near to him:

"These three musketeers shall follow us," said he in an under voice, "I am not willing it should be known I have left the camp; and by following us we shall be certain they will tell nobody."

"We are gentlemen, monseigneur," said Athos, "require our parole, and give yourself no uneasiness. Thank God! we can keep a secret."

"You have a quick ear, Monsieur Athos," said the cardinal; "but now listen to this; it is not from mistrust that I request you to follow me, but for my security; your companions are, no doubt MM. Porthos and Aramis."

"Yes, your eminence," said Athos, while the two musketeers who had remained behind, advanced, hat in hand.

"I know you, gentlemen," said the cardinal, "I know you; I know you are not quite my friends, and I am sorry you are not so; but I know you are brave and loyal gentlemen, and that confidence may be placed in you. Monsieur Athos, do me, then, the honor to accompany me, you and your **two** friends, and then I shall have on escort to excite envy in his majesty, if we should meet him."

The three musketeers bowed to the necks of their horses.

"Well, upon my honor," said Athos, "your eminence is right in taking us with you; we have seen several ill-looking faces on the road, and we have even had a quarrel at the Colombier Rouge with four of those faces."

"A quarrel, and what for, gentlemen?" said the cardinal; "you know I don't like quarrels."

"And that is the reason why I have the honor to inform your eminence of what has happened; for you might learn it from others, and upon a false account, believe us to be in fault."

"What have been the results of your quarrel?" said the cardinal, knitting his brow.

"My friend Aramis, here, has received a slight sword-wound in the arm, but not enough to prevent him, as your eminence may see, from mounting to the assault to-morrow, if your eminence orders an escalade."

"But you are not the men to allow sword-wounds to be inflicted upon you thus," said the cardinal; "come, be frank, gentlemen, you have given a good account of some persons; confess, you know I have the right of giving absolution."

"Who? I! monseigneur?" said Athos. "I did not even draw my sword, but I took him who offended me round the body, and threw him out of the window; it appears that in falling," continued Athos, with some hesitation, "he broke his thigh."

"Ah! Ah!" said the cardinal; "and you, Monsieur Porthos?"

"I, monseigneur, knowing that duelling is prohibited, I seized a bench, and gave one of these brigands such a blow, that I believe his shoulder is broken."

"Very well!" said the cardinal; "and you, Monsieur Aramis?"

"For my part, monseigneur, being of a very mild disposition, and being likewise, of which monsiegneur, perhaps, is not aware, about to enter into orders, I endeavored to appease my comrades, when one of these wretches gave me a wound with a sword, treacherously, across my left arm; then I admit my patience failed me; I drew my sword in my turn, and as he came back to the charge, I fancied I felt that in throwing himself upon me, he let it pass through his body: I only know, for a certainty, that he fell, and that he appeared to be borne away with his two companions."

"The devil, gentlemen!" said the cardinal, "three men placed *hors de combat* in a cabaret squabble! you don't do your work by halves; and pray what was this quarrel about?"

"These fellows were drunk," said Athos, "and knowing there was a lady who had arrived at the cabaret this evening, they wanted to force her door."

"Force her door!" said the cardinal, "and for what purpose?"

"To do her violence, without doubt," said Athos; "I have had the honor of informing your eminence that these men were drunk."

"And was this lady young and handsome?" asked the cardinal, with a certain degree of anxiety.

"We did not see her, monseigneur," said Athos.

"You did not see her! ah! very well," replied the cardinal quickly; "you acted quite rightly in defending the honor of a woman; and as I am going to the Colombier Rouge myself, I shall know whether you have told me the truth or not."

"Monseigneur," said Athos haughtily, "we are gentlemen, and to save our heads we would not be guilty of a falsehood."

"Therefore, I do not doubt what you say, Monsieur Athos, I do not doubt it for a single instant; but," added he, to change the conversation, "was this lady alone?"

"The lady had a cavalier shut up with her," said Athos, "but as notwithstanding the noise, this cavalier did not show himself, it is to be presumed that he is a coward."

"Judge not rashly, says the Gospel," replied the cardinal. Athos bowed.

"And now, gentlemen, that's all very well," continued the cardinal. "I know what I wish to know; follow me."

The three musketeers passed behind his eminence, who again enveloped his face in his cloak, and put his horse in motion, keeping at from eight to ten paces in advance of his companions.

They soon arrived at the silent, solitary auberge; no doubt the host knew what illustrious visitor he expected, and had consequently sent intruders out of the way.

At ten paces from the door the cardinal made a sign to his attendant and the three musketeers to halt; a saddled horse was fastened to the window-shutter, the cardinal knocked three times, and in peculiar manner.

A man, enveloped in a cloak, came out immediately, and exchanged some rapid words with the cardinal; after which he mounted his horse, and set off in the direction of Surgères, which was likewise that of Paris.

"Advance, gentlemen," said the cardinal.

"You have told me the truth, gentlemen," said he, addressing the musketeers, "and it will not be my fault if our rencounter of this evening be not advantageous to you: in the meantime, follow me."

The cardinal alighted, the three musketeers did so likewise; the cardinal threw the bridle of his horse to his attendant, the three musketeers fastened their horses to the shutter.

The host stood at the door; for him, the cardinal was only an officer coming to visit a lady.

"Have you any chamber on the ground flood where these gentlemen can wait, near a good fire?" said the cardinal.

The host opened the door of a large room, in which an old bad stove had just been replaced by a large and excellent chimney.

"I have this, monsieur," said he.

"That will do," replied the cardinal; "come in, gentlemen, and be kind enough to wait for me; I shall not be more than half an hour."

And while the three musketeers entered the ground-floor room, the cardinal, without asking further information, ascended the staircase like a man who has no need of having his road pointed out to him.

CHAPTER XLIV.

THE UTILITY OF STOVE-PIPES.

It was evident that without suspecting it, and actuated solely by their chivalric and adventurous character, our three friends had just rendered a service to some one the cardinal honored with his particular protection.

Now, who could that some one be? That was the question the three musketeers put to each other; then, seeing that none of the replies could throw any light on the subject, Porthos called the host, and asked for dice.

Porthos and Aramis placed themselves at the table and began to play. Athos walked about, in a contemplative mood.

While thinking and walking, Athos passed and repassed before the pipe of the stove, broken in half, the other extremity of which passed into the upper chamber; and every time he passed, he heard a murmur of words, which at length fixed his attention. Athos went close to it, and distinguished some words that appeared to merit so great an interest that he

made a sign to his friends to be silent, remaining himself bent
with his ear directed to the opening of the lower orifice.

"Listen, milady," said the cardinal, "the affair is important; sit down, and let us talk it over."

"Milady!" murmured Athos.

"I am listening to your eminence with the greatest attention," replied a female voice that made the musketeer start.

"A small vessel with an English crew, whose captain is mine,
awaits you at the mouth of the Charente, at Fort de la Pointe;
he will set sail to-morrow morning."

"I must go thither to-night, then?"

"Instantly! that is to say, when you have received my instructions. Two men, whom you will find at the door, on
going out, will serve you as escort; you will allow me to leave
first, and, half an hour after, you can go away in your turn."

"Yes, monseigneur. Now let us return to the mission with
which you wish to charge me, and as I desire to continue to
merit the confidence of your eminence, deign to expose it to
me in clear and precise terms, so that I may not commit any
error."

There was an instant of profound silence between the two
interlocutors; it was evident the cardinal was weighing beforehand the terms in which he was about to speak, and that
milady was collecting all her faculties to comprehend the things
he was about to say, and to engrave them in her memory
when they should be spoken.

Athos took advantage of this moment to tell his two companions to fasten the door on the inside, and to make them a
sign to come and listen with him.

The two musketeers, who loved their ease, brought a chair
for each of themselves and one for Athos. All three then sat
down with their heads together, and their ears on the watch.

"You will go to London," continued the cardinal; "when
arrived in London you will seek Buckingham."

"I must beg your eminence to observe," said milady, "that
since the affair of the diamond studs, about which the duke
always suspected me, his grace has been very mistrustful of
me."

"Well, this time," said the cardinal, "it is not the question
to steal his confidence, but to present yourself frankly and
loyally as a negotiator."

"Frankly and loyally," repeated milady, with an unspeakable expression of duplicity.

"Yes, frankly and loyally," replied the cardinal, in the same
tone; "all this negotiation must be carried on openly."

"I will follow your eminence's instruction to the letter; I only wait your giving them."

"You will go to Buckingham on my part, and you will tell him I am acquainted will all the preparations he has made, but that they give me no uneasiness, since, at the first step he takes, I will ruin the queen."

"Will he believe that your eminence is in a position to accomplish the threat you make him?"

"Yes, for I have the proofs."

"I must be able to present these proofs to his appreciation."

"Without doubt; and you will tell him I will publish the account of Bois-Robert and of the Marquis de Beautru, upon the interview which the duke had at the residence of Madame la Connétable with the queen, on the evening Madame la Connétable gave a masked *fête;* you will tell him, in order that he may not doubt of anything, that he came there in the costume of the Great Mogul, which the Chevalier de Guise was to have worn, and that he purchased this exchange for the sum of three thousand pistoles."

"Very well, monseigneur."

"All the details of his coming into and going out of the palace on the night when he introduced himself in the character of an Italian fortune-teller, you will tell him in order that he may not doubt the correctness of my information: that he had under his cloak a large white robe, sown over with black tears, death's heads, and crossbones; for in case of a surprise, he was to pass for the Phantom of the White Lady, who, as all the world knows, appears at the Louvre every time any great event is about to be accomplished."

"Is that all, monseigneur?"

"Tell him also that I am acquainted with all the details of the adventure at Amiens, that I will have a little romance made of it, wittily turned, with a plan of the garden, and portraits of the principal actors in that nocturnal romance."

"I will tell him that."

"Tell him, further, Montague is in my power, that Montague is in the Bastille; no letters were found upon him, it is true, but that nature may make him say much of what he knows, and even—what he does not know."

"Exactly."

"Then add, that his grace has, in his precipitation to quit the Isle of Ré, forgotten and left behind him in his lodging a certain letter from Madame de Chevreuse, which singularly compromises the queen, inasmuch as it proves not only that her majesty can love the enemies of France, but that she can conspire with the enemies of France. You recollect perfectly all I have told you, do you not?"

"Your eminence will judge: the ball of Madame la Conné-table; the night at the Louvre; the evening at Amiens; the arrest of Montague; the letter of Madame de Chevreuse."

"That's it," said the cardinal—"that's it; you have an ex-cellent memory, milady."

"But," resumed the lady, to whom the cardinal had ad-dressed this flattering compliment, "if, in spite of all these reasons, the duke does not give way, and continues to menace France?"

"The duke is in love to madness, or rather to folly," re-plied Richelieu, with great bitterness; "like the ancient pal-adins, he has only undertaken this war to obtain a look from his lady-love. If he becomes certain that this war will cost the honor, and perhaps the liberty of the lady of his thoughts, as he says, I will answer for it he will look at it twice."

"And yet," said milady, with a persistance that proved she wished to see clearly to the end of the mission with which she was about to be charged, "and yet, if he persists?"

"If he persists?" said the cardinal; "that is not probable."

"It is possible," said milady.

"If he. persists—" His eminence made a pause, and re-sumed: "If he persists—well, then I shall hope for one of those events which change the destinies of states."

"If your eminence would quote to me some one of these events in history," said milady, "perhaps I should partake of your confidence in the future."

"Well, here, then, for example," said Richelieu. "When in 1610, for a cause almost similar to that which moves the duke, the King Henry IV., of glorious memory, was about, at the same time, to invade Flanders and Italy to attack Austria on both sides—well, did there not happen an event which saved Austria? Why should not the King of France have the same chance as the emperor?"

"Your eminence means, I presume, the knife-stab of the Rue de la Féronnerie?"

"Exactly so," said the cardinal.

"Does not your eminence fear that the punishment inflicted upon Ravaillac may deter any one who might entertain the idea of imitating him?"

"There will be, in all times and in all countries, particu-larly if religious divisions exist in those countries, fanatics who ask nothing better than to become martyrs. Ay, and ob-serve, it just recurs to me that the Puritans are furious against

Buckingham, and their preachers designate him as the Anti-Christ."

"Well?" said milady.

"Well," continued the cardinal, in an indifferent tone, "the only thing to be sought for, at this moment, is some woman, handsome, young and clever, who has cause of quarrel with the duke. The duke has had many affairs of gallantry, and if he has succeeded in many amours by his promises of eternal constancy, he must likewise have sown the seeds of many hatreds by his eternal infidelities."

"No doubt," said milady coolly, "such a woman may be found."

"Well, such a woman, who would place the knife of Jacques Clement, or of Ravaillac, in the hands of a fanatic, would save France."

"Yes, but she would be the accomplice of an assassination."

"Were the accomplices of Ravaillac, or of Jacques Clement, ever known?"

"No, for perhaps they were too high for any one to dare to look for them where they were; the Palais de Justice would not be burned down for everybody, monseigneur."

"You think, then, that the fire at the Palais de Justice was not caused by chance?" asked Richelieu, in the tone with which he would have put a question of no importance.

"I, monseigneur?" replied milady; "I think nothing—I quote a fact, that is all; only I say that if I were named Mademoiselle de Montpensier, or the Queen Mary de Medici, I should take less precautions than I take, being simply called Lady Clarik."

"That is but just," said Richelieu; "what do you require, then?"

"I require an order which would ratify beforehand all that I should think proper to do for the greatest good of France."

"But, in the first place, this woman I have described must be found, who is desirous of avenging herself upon the duke."

"She is found," said milady.

"Then the miserable fanatic must be found who will serve as an instrument of God's justice."

"He will be found."

"Well," said the cardinal, "then it will be time to claim the order which you just now required."

"Your eminence is right," replied milady; "and I have been wrong in seeing in the mission with which you honor me, anything but that which it really is—that is to say, to announce to his grace, on the part of your eminence, that you are acquainted with the different disguises by the means of which he succeeded in approaching the queen during the *fete* given by Madame la Connétable; that you have proofs of the interview granted at the Louvre by the queen to a certain Italian astrologer, who was no other than the Duke of Buckingham; that you have ordered a little romance of a satirical nature to be written upon the adventures of Amiens, with a plan of the gardens in which those adventures took place, and portraits of the actors who figured in them; that Montague is in the Bastille, and that the torture may make him say things he remembers, and even things he has forgotten; that you possess a certain letter from Madame de Chevreuse, found in his grace's lodging, which singularly compromises not only her who wrote it, but her in whose name it was written. Then, if he persists, notwithstanding all this, as that is, as I have said, the limit of my mission, I shall have nothing to do but to pray God to work a miracle for the salvation of France. That is it, is it not, monseigneur, and I shall have nothing else to do?"

"That is it," replied the cardinal dryly.

"And now," said milady, without appearing to remark the change of the duke's tone toward her, "now that I have received the instructions of your eminence as concerns your enemies, monseigneur will permit me to say a few words to him of mine?"

"Have you enemies, then?" asked Richelieu.

"Yes, monseigneur, enemies against whom you owe me all your support, for I made them by serving your eminence."

"Who are they?" replied the duke.

"In the first place, there is a little intriguing woman, named Bonacieux."

"She is in the prison of Nantes."

"That is to say, she was there," replied milady; "but the queen has obtained an order from the king, by means of which she has been conveyed to a convent."

"To a convent?" said the duke.

"Yes, to a convent."

"And what convent?"

"I don't know: the secret has been well kept."

"But I will know!"

"And your eminence will tell me in what convent that woman is?"

"I see nothing inconvenient in that," said the cardinal.

"Well, now I have an enemy much more to be dreaded by me than this little Madame Bonacieux."

"Who is that?"

"Her lover."

"What is his name?"

"Oh, your eminence knows him well," cried milady, carried away by her anger. "He is the evil genius of both of us: it is he who, in a rencounter with your eminence's guards, decided the victory in favor of the king's musketeers; it is he who gave three desperate wounds to De Wardes, your emissary, and who caused the affair of the diamond studs to fail; it is he who, knowing it was I who had Madame Bonacieux carried off, has sworn my death."

"Ah, ah!" said the cardinal. "I know whom you mean."

"I mean that wretch D'Artagnan."

"He is a bold fellow," said the cardinal.

"And it is because he is a bold fellow that he is the more to be feared."

"I must have," said the duke, "a proof of his connection with Buckingham."

"A proof!" cried milady; "I will find you ten."

"Well, then, it becomes the simplest thing in the world; get me that proof, and I will send him to the Bastille."

"So far good, monseigneur; but afterward?"

"When once in the Bastille there is no afterward!" said the cardinal, in a low voice. "Ah, *pardieu!*" continued he, "if it were as easy for me to get rid of my enemy as it is easy to get rid of yours, and if it were against such people you required impunity!"

"Monseigneur," replied milady, "a fair exchange—existence for existence, man for man; give me one, I will give you the other."

"I don't know what you mean, nor do I even desire to know what you mean," replied the cardinal; "but I wish to please you, and see nothing inconvenient in giving you what you ask for with respect to so mean a creature; the more so as you tell me this paltry D'Artagnan is a libertine, a duelist, and a traitor."

"An infamous scoundrel, monseigneur, an infamous scoundrel!"

"Give me paper, a pen, and some ink, then," said the cardinal.

"Here they are, monseigneur."

There was a moment of silence, which proved that the cardinal was employed in seeking the terms in which he should write the note, or else in writing it. Athos, who had not lost a word of the conversation, took his two companions by the hand, and led them to the other end of the room.

"Well," said Porthos, "what do you want, and why do you not let us listen to the end of the conversation?"

"Hush!" said Athos, speaking in a low voice; " we have heard all it was necessary we should hear; besides, I don't prevent you from listening, but I must be gone."

"You must be gone!" said Porthos; "and if the cardinal asks for you, what answer can we make?"

"You will not wait till he asks; you will speak first, and tell him that I am gone on the lookout, because certain expressions of our host's have given me reason to think the road is not safe; I will say two words about it to the cardinal's attendant likewise; the rest concerns myself, don't be uneasy about that."

"Be prudent, Athos," said Aramis.

"Be easy on that head," replied Athos, "you know I am cool enough."

Porthos and Aramis resumed their places by the stove-pipe.

As to Athos, he went out without any mystery, took his horse, which was tied with those of his friends to the fastenings of the shutters, in four words convinced the attendant of the necessity of a vanguard for their return, carefully examined the priming of his pistols, drew his sword, and took, like a forlorn hope, the road to the camp.

CHAPTER XLV.

A CONJUGAL SCENE.

As Athos had foreseen, it was not long before the cardinal came down; he opened the door of the room in which the musketeers were, and found Porthos playing an earnest game at dice with Aramis. He cast a rapid glance round the room, and perceived that one of his men was missing.

"What is become of M. Athos?" asked he.

"Monseigneur," replied Porthos, "he is gone as a scout, upon some words of our host, which made him believe the road was not safe."

"And how have you amused yourself, M. Porthos?"

"I have won five pistoles of Aramis, monseigneur."

"Well, now will you return with me?"

"We are at your eminence's orders."

"To horse, then, gentlemen; for it is getting late."

The attendant was at the door, holding the cardinal's horse

by the bridle. At a short distance, a group of two men and three horses appeared in the shade; these were the two men who were to conduct milady to the fort of La Pointe, and superintend her embarkation.

The attendant confirmed to the cardinal what the two musketeers had already said with respect to Athos. The cardinal made an approving gesture, and retook his route with the same precautions he had used in coming.

Let us leave him to follow the road to the camp protected by his attendant and the two musketeers, and return to Athos.

For some distance he maintained the pace at which he started, but when out of sight, he turned his horse to the right, made a circuit, and came back within twenty paces of a high hedge, to watch the passage of the little troop; having recognized the laced hats of his companions and the golden fringe of the cardinal's cloak, he waited till the horsemen had turned the angle of the road, and having lost sight of them, he returned at a gallop to the auberge, which was opened to him without hesitation.

The host recognized him.

"My officer," said Athos, "has forgotten to give a piece of very important information to the lady, and has sent me back to repair his forgetfulness."

"Go up," said the host, "she is still in her chamber."

Athos availed himself of the permission, ascended the stairs with his lightest step, gained the landing, and through the open door perceived milady putting on her hat.

He went straight into the chamber and closed the door after him.

At the noise he made in bolting it, milady turned round.

Athos was standing before the door, enveloped in his cloak, with his hat pulled down over his eyes.

"Who are you? and what do you want?" cried she.

"Humph!" murmured Athos, "it is certainly she!"

And letting fall his cloak, and raising his hat, he advanced toward milady.

"Do you know me, madame?" said he.

Milady made one step forward, and then drew back, as if she had seen a serpent.

"So far well," said Athos, "I perceive you know me."

"The Count de la Fère!" murmured milady, becoming exceedingly pale, and drawing back till the wall prevented her going any further.

"Yes, milady," replied Athos, "the Count de la Fère in person, who comes expressly from the other world to have the

pleasure of paying you a visit. Sit down, madame, and let
us talk, as the cardinal said."

Milady, under the influence of inexpressible terror, sat down
without uttering a word.

"You certainly are a demon sent upon the earth!" said
Athos. "Your power is great, I know; but you also know
that with the help of God men have often conquered the most
terrible demons. You have once before thrown yourself in
my path! I thought I had crushed you, madame; but either
I was deceived, or hell has resuscitated you!"

Milady, at these words, which recalled frightful remembrances, hung down her head, with a suppressed groan.

"Yes, hell has resuscitated you," continued Athos, "hell has
made you rich, hell has given you another name, hell has
almost made you another countenance; but it has neither effaced
the stains from your soul nor the brand mark from your body!"

Milady arose as if moved by a powerful spring, and her
eyes flashed lightning. Athos remained sitting.

"You believed me to be dead, did you not, as I believed
you to be? and the name of Athos as well concealed the Count
de la Fère, as the name of Milady Clarik concealed Anne de
Beuil! Was it not so you were called when your honored
brother married us? Our position is truly a strange one,"
continued Athos, laughing, "we have only lived up to the
present time because we believed each other to be dead, and
because a remembrance is less oppressive than a living creature,
though a remembrance is sometimes a devouring thing!"

"But," said milady, in a hollow, faint voice, "what brings
you back to me? and what do you want with me?"

"I wish to tell you, that while remaining invisible to your
eyes, I have not lost sight of you."

"You know what I have done and been?"

"I can relate to you, day by day, your actions, from your
entrance into the service of the cardinal to this evening."

A smile of incredulity passed over the pale lips of milady.

"Listen! It was you who cut off the two diamond studs
from the shoulder of the Duke of Buckingham; it was you
who had Madame Bonacieux carried off; it was you who, in
love with De Wardes, and thinking to pass the night with
him, opened the door to M. d'Artagnan; it was you, believing that De Wardes had deceived you, wished to have him
killed by his rival; it was you who, when this rival had discovered your infamous secret, wished to have him killed in
his turn by two assassins, whom you sent in pursuit of him;
it was you who, finding the balls had missed their mark, sent

poisoned wine with a forged letter, to make your victim believe that that wine came from his friends; in short, it was
you who have but now, in this chamber, seated in this chair
I now fill, made an engagement with the Cardinal de Richelieu to cause the Duke of Buckingham to be assassinated, in
exchange for the promise he has made you to allow you to
assassinate D'Artagnan.

Milady was livid.

"You must be Satan!" cried she.

"Perhaps," said Athos; "but, at all events, listen well to
this. Assassinate the Duke of Buckingham, or cause him to
be assassinated, I care very little about that! I don't know
him: besides, he is an Englishman; but do not touch with the
tip of your finger a single hair of D'Artagnan, who is a faithful friend, whom I love and defend, or, I swear to you by
the head of my father, the crime which you shall have endeavored to commit, or shall have committed, shall be the
last."

"M. d'Artagnan has cruelly insulted me," said milady, in a
hollow tone; "M. d'Artagnan shall die!"

"Indeed! is it possible to insult you, madame?" said Athos,
laughing, "he has insulted you, and he shall die!"

"He shall die!" replied milady; "she first, he afterward."

Athos was seized with a kind a vertigo; the sight of this
creature, who had nothing of the woman about her, recalled
devouring remembrances; he thought that one day, in a less
dangerous situation than the one in which he was now placed,
he had already endeavored to sacrifice her to his honor; his
desire for blood returned, burning his brain, and pervading
his frame like a raging fever; he arose in his turn, reached
his hand to his belt, drew forth a pistol, and cocked it.

Milady, pale as a corpse, endeavored to cry out; but her
swollen tongue could utter no more than a hoarse sound, which
had nothing human in it, and seemed the rattle of a wild beast:
fixed against the dark tapestry, she appeared with her hair in
disorder, like a horrid image of terror.

Athos slowly raised his pistol, stretched out his arm, so that
the weapon, almost touched milady's forehead, and then, in
a voice the more terrible from having the supreme calmness
of a fixed resolution:

"Madame," said he, "you will this instant deliver to me the
paper the cardinal signed; or, upon my soul, I will blow your
brains out."

With another man, milady might have preserved some doubt;
but she knew Athos: nevertheless, she remained motionless.

THE THREE MUSKETEERS

"You have one second to decide," said he.

Milady saw by the contraction of his countenance that the trigger was about to be pulled; she reached her hand quickly to her bosom, drew out a paper, and held it toward Athos.

"Take it," said she, "and be accursed!"

Athos took the paper, returned the pistol to his belt, approached the lamp, to be assured that it was the paper, unfolded it, and read:

"It is by my order, and for the good of the state, that the bearer of this has done what he has done.
"December 3d, 1627.   RICHELIEU."

"And now," said Athos, resuming his cloak, and putting on his hat, "now that I have drawn your teeth, viper, bite if you can."

And he left the chamber without once looking behind him.

At the door he found the two men, and the spare horse which they held.

"Gentlemen," said he, "monseigneur's order is, you know, to conduct that woman, without losing time, to the fort of La Pointe, and never to leave her till she is on board."

As these orders agreed effectively with the order they had received, they bowed their heads in sign of assent.

With regard to Athos, he leaped lightly into the saddle, and set out at full gallop; only, instead of following the road, he took across the fields, urging his horse to the utmost, and stopping occasionally to listen.

In one of those halts, he heard the steps of several horses on the road. He had no doubt it was the cardinal and his escort. He immediately made a new point in advance, rubbed his horse down with some heath and leaves of trees, and came and placed himself across the road, at about two hundred paces from the camp.

"Who goes there?" cried he, as soon as he perceived the horseman.

"That is our brave musketeer, I think," said the cardinal.

"Yes, monseigneur," said Porthos, "it is he."

"Monsieur Athos," said Richelieu, "receive my thanks for the good guard you have kept. Gentlemen, we are arrived; take the gate on the left; the watchword is, 'Roi et Ré.'"

On saying these words, the cardinal saluted the three friends with an inclination of his head, and took the right hand, followed by his attendant; for, that night, he himself slept in the camp.

"Well!" said Porthos and Aramis, together, as soon as the cardinal was out of hearing; "well! he signed the paper she required!"

"I know he did," said Athos, "since here it is."

And the three friends did not exchange a single word till they got to their quarters, except to give the watchword to the sentinels.

They sent Mousqueton to tell Planchet that his master was requested, the instant he left the trenches, to come to the quarters of the musketeers.

Milady, as Athos had foreseen, on finding the two men that awaited her, made no difficulty in following them; she had had for an instant an inclination to be reconducted to the cardinal, and relate everything to him; but a revelation, on her part, would bring about a revelation on the part of Athos; she might say that Athos had hung her; but then Athos would tell that she was branded: she thought it was best to preserve silence, to set off discreetly, to accomplish her difficult mission with her usual skill; and then, all things being performed to the satisfaction of the cardinal, to come back and claim her vengeance.

In consequence, after having traveled all night, at seven o'clock she was at Fort Le Pointe; at eight o'clock she had embarked; and at nine the vessel, which, with letters of marque from the cardinal, was supposed to be sailing for Bayonne, raised anchor and steered its course toward England.

CHAPTER XLVI.

THE BASTION SAINT-GERVAIS.

On arriving at the lodging of his three friends, D'Artagnan found them assembled in the same chamber: Athos was meditating, Porthos was twisting his mustaches, Aramis was reading prayers in a charming little *livre d'heures,* bound in blue velvet.

"*Pardieu!*" said he, "gentlemen! I hope what you have to tell me is worth the trouble; or else, I warn you, I will not pardon you for making me come here instead of getting a little rest, after a night spent in taking and dismantling a bastion. Ah! why were you not there, gentlemen; it was warm work!"

"We were in a place where it was not very cold!" replied

Porthos, giving his mustache a twist which was peculiar to him.

"Hush !" said Athos.

"Oh ! oh !" said D'Artagnan, comprehending the slight frown of the musketeer; "it appears there is something fresh abroad."

"Aramis," said Athos, "you went to breakfast the day before yesterday, at the auberge of the Parpaillot, I beileve?"

"Yes."

"How did you fare?"

"For my part, I ate but little; the day before yesterday was a fish day, and they had nothing but meat."

"What !" said Athos, "no fish at a seaport?"

"They say," said Aramis, resuming his pious studies, "that the dyke which the cardinal is making drives them all out into the open sea."

"But that is not quite what I mean to ask you," replied Athos: "I want to know if you were left alone, and nobody interrupted you."

"Why, I think there were not many intruders; yes, Athos, I know what you mean, we shall do very comfortably at the Parpaillot."

"Let us go to the Parpaillot, then; for here the walls are like sheets of paper."

D'Artagnan, who was accustomed to his friend's manner of acting, and who perceived immediately by a word, a gesture, or a sign from him, that the circumstances were serious, took Athos' arm, and went out without saying anything; Porthos followed, chatting with Aramis.

On their way they met with Grimaud: Athos made him a sign to come with him: Grimaud, according to custom, obeyed in silence; the poor lad had nearly come to the pass of forgetting how to speak.

They arrived at the *buvette* of the Parpaillot: it was seven o'clock in the morning, and daylight began to appear: the three friends ordered breakfast, and went into a room in which, the host said, they would not be disturbed.

Unfortunately, the hour was badly chosen for a private conference; the morning drum had just been beaten; every one shook off the drowsiness of night, and, to dispel the humid morning air, came to take a drop at the *buvette:* dragoons, Swiss, guards, musketeers, light-horseman, succeeded each other with a rapidity which might answer the purpose of the host very well, but agreed badly with the views of the four friends. Thus they replied very curtly to the salutations, healths, and jokes of their companions.

"I see how it will be," said Athos; "we shall get into some

pretty quarrel or other, and we don't stand in need of one just now. D'Artagnan, tell us what sort of a night you have had, and we will describe ours afterward."

"Ah! yes," said a light-horseman, with a glass of *eau-de-vie* in his hand, which he degustated slowly; "ah! yes! I hear you gentlemen of the guards have been in the trenches to-night, and that you did not get much the best of the Rochellais."

D'Artagnan looked at Athos to know if he ought to reply to this intruder who mixed unasked in their conversation.

"Well!" said Athos, "don't you head M. de Busigny, who does you the honor to ask you a question? Relate what has passed during the night, since these gentlemen desire it."

"Have you not taken a bastion?" said a Swiss, who was drinking rum out of a beer glass.

"Yes, monsieur," said D'Artagnan, bowing, "we have had that honor: we even have, as you may have heard, introduced a barrel of powder under one of the angles, which, in blowing up, made a very pretty breach; without reckoning that, as the bastion was not of yesterday, all the rest of the building was much shaken."

"And what bastion is it?" asked a dragoon, with his saber run through a goose, which he was taking to be cooked.

"The bastion Saint-Gervais," replied D'Artagnan, "from behind which the Rochellais annoyed our workmen."

"Was the affair hot?"

"Yes, moderately so; we lost five men, and the Rochellais eight or ten."

"*Blazempleu!*" said the Swiss, who, notwithstanding the admirable collection of oaths possessed by the German language, had acquired a habit of swearing in French.

"But it is probable," said the light-horseman, "that they will send pioneers this morning to reinstate the bastion."

"Yes, that's probable," said D'Artagnan.

"Gentlemen," said Athos, "I have a wager to propose."

"Ah! ah! a wager!" cried the Swiss.

"What is it?" said the light-horseman.

"Stop a bit," said the dragoon, placing his saber like a spit upon the two large iron dogs which held the fire in the chimney—"Stop a bit, I am in it. You master host! a dripping pan immediately, that I may not lose a drop of the fat of this estimable bird."

"You are quite right," said the Swiss; "goose-grease is good with pastry."

"There!" said the dragoon. "Now for the wager. We are all attention, M. Athos."

"Ah! now for the wager!" said the light-horseman.

"Well, Monsieur de Busigny, I will bet you," said Athos, "that my three companions, MM. Porthos, Aramis, and D'Artagnan, and myself, will go and breakfast in the bastion Saint-Gervais, and we will remain there an hour, by the watch, whatever the enemy may do to dislodge us."

Porthos and Aramis looked at each other; they began to comprehend.

"Well, but," said D'Artagnan, in Athos' ear, "you are going to get us all killed without mercy."

"We are much more likely to be killed," said Athos, "if we do not go."

"*Ma foi!* gentlemen," said Porthos, turning round upon his chair, and twisting his mustache, "that's a fair bet, I hope."

"I take it," said M. de Busigny; "now let us fix the stake."

"Why, you are four, gentlemen," said Athos, "and we are four; a dinner for eight—will that do?"

"Capitally," replied M. de Busigny.

"Perfectly well," said the dragoon.

"That's just the thing," said the Swiss. The fourth auditor, who, during all this conversation had played a mute part, made a sign of the head to show that he acquiesced in the proposition.

"The breakfast for these gentlemen is ready," said the host.

"Well, bring it in," said Athos.

The host obeyed. Athos called Grimaud, pointed to a large basket which lay in a corner, and made a sign to him to wrap the viands up in the napkins.

Grimaud perceived that it was to be a breakfast on the grass, took the basket, packed up the viands, added the bottles, and then took the basket on his arm.

"But where are you going to eat my breakfast?" said the host.

"Of what consequence is that to you, if you are paid for it?" said Athos, and he threw two pistoles majestically on to the table.

"Shall I give you the change, *mon officer?*" said the host.

"No, only add two bottles of champagne, and the difference will be for the napkins."

The host had not quite so good a bargain as he at first hoped for, but he made amends by slipping in two bottles of Anjou wine instead of two bottles of champagne.

"Monsieur de Busigny," said Athos, "will you be so kind as to set your watch with mine, or permit me to regulate mine by yours?"

"Which you please, monsieur!" said the light-horseman, drawing from his fob a very handsome watch, surrounded with diamonds; "half-past seven," said he.

"Thirty-five minutes after seven," said Athos, "by which you perceive I am five minutes faster than you."

And bowing to all the astonished persons present, the young men took the road to the bastion St. Gervais, followed by Grimaud, who carried the basket, ignorant of where he was going, but, in the passive obedience which Athos had taught him, not even thinking of asking.

As long as they were within the camp, the four friends did not exchange one word; besides, they were followed by the curious, who hearing of the wager, were anxious to know how they would come out of it. But when once they had passed the line of circumvallation, and found themselves in the open plain, D'Artagnan, who was completely ignorant of what was going forward, thought it was time to demand an explanation.

"And now, my dear Athos," said he, "do me the kindness to tell me where we are going?"

"Why, you see plainly enough we are going to the bastion."

"But what are we going to do there?"

"Why, you know, equally well, we are going to breakfast there."

"But why did we not breakfast at the Parpaillot?"

"Because we have some very important matters to communicate to each other, and it was impossible to talk five minutes in that auberge without being annoyed by all those importunate fellows, who keep coming in, saluting you, and addressing you; yonder," said Athos, pointing to the bastion, "they will, at least, not come and disturb us."

"It appears to me," said D'Artagnan, with that prudence which allied itself in him so naturally with excessive bravery, "it appears that we could have found some retired place on the downs or the seashore."

"Where we should have been seen all four conferring together, so that at the end of a quarter of an hour the cardinal would have been informed by his spies that we were holding a council."

"Yes," said Aramis, "Athos is right: *Animadvertuntur in desertis.*"

"A desert would not have been amiss," said Porthos, "but the matter was where to find it."

"There is no desert where a bird cannot pass over one's head, where a fish cannot leap out of the water, where a rabbit cannot come out of its burrow, and I believe that bird, fish, and rabbit would be all spies of the cardinal. Better, then, follow up our enterprise, from which, besides, we cannot retreat without shame; we have made a wager, which could not be forseen, and of which I defy any one to guess the true cause; we are going, in order to win it, to remain an hour in the bastion. We either shall be or shall not be attacked. If we are not, we shall have all the time to talk, and nobody will hear us, for, I will answer for it the walls of the bastion have no ears; if we are attacked, we will talk of our affairs just the same, and while defending ourselves, we shall cover ourselves with glory. You see that everything is to our advantage."

"Yes," said D'Artagnan, "but I think there is very little doubt that one of us will catch a ball."

"Well!" replied Athos, "I am sure you ought to know that the balls most to be dreaded are not from open enemies."

"But, for such an expedition, we surely ought to have brought our muskets."

"You are stupid, friend Porthos, why should we load ourselves with a useless burden?"

"For my part, I don't think a good musket, twelve cartridges, and a powder flask very useless things, in face of an enemy."

"Well," replied Athos, "have you not heard what D'Artagnan said?"

"What did he say to the purpose?"

"D'Artagnan said that in the attack of last night, eight or ten Frenchmen were killed, and as many Rochellais."

"What then?"

"The bodies were not plundered, were they? it appears the conquerors had something else to do."

"Well?"

"Well! we shall find their muskets, their cartridges, and their flasks, and instead of four musketoons and twelve balls, we shall have fifteen guns and a hundred charges to fire."

"Oh! Athos!" said Aramis, "truly, thou art a great man." Porthos bowed, in a sign of agreement. D'Artagnan alone did not appear to be quite satisfied.

Grimaud, no doubt, shared the misgivings of the young man, for, seeing that they continued to advance toward the bastion, a circumstance which he had not at first suspected, he pulled his master by the skirt of his coat.

"Where are we going?" asked he, by a gesture.

Athos pointed to the bastion.

"But," said the still silent Grimaud, in the usual dialect current between him and his master, "we shall leave our skins behind us."

Athos raised his eyes, and pointed with his finger toward heaven.

Grimaud put his basket on the ground, and sat down with a shake of the head.

Athos took a pistol from his belt, looked to see if it was properly primed, cocked it, and placed the muzzle close to Grimaud's ear.

Grimaud was on his legs again, as if by magic. Athos then made him a sign to take up his basket, and to walk on first. Grimaud obeyed. All that Grimaud gained by this pantomime of a minute, was to pass from the rear-guard to the vanguard.

When arrived at the bastion, the four friends turned round.

More than three hundred soldiers of all kinds were assembled at the gate of the camp; and in a separate group might be distinguished M. de Busigny, the dragoon, the Swiss, and the fourth wagerer.

Athos took off his hat, placed it on the end of his sword, and waved it in the air.

All the spectators returned him his salute, accompanying this politeness with a loud hurrah! which was audible at the bastion.

After which they all four disappeared in the bastion, Grimaud having preceded them.

CHAPTER XLVII.

THE COUNCIL OF THE MUSKETEERS.

As Athos had forseen, the bastion was only occupied by a dozen of dead bodies, French and Rochellais.

"Gentlemen," said Athos, who had assumed the command of the expedition, "while Grimaud is laying out the breakfast, let us begin by collecting the guns and cartridges together; we can talk while performing that necessary task. These gentlemen," added he, pointing to the bodies, "cannot hear us."

"But we could throw them into the ditch," said Porthos,

"after having assured ourselves they have nothing in their pockets."

"Yes," said Athos, "that's Grimaud's business."

"Well, then," cried D'Artagnan, "pray, let Grimaud search them, and throw them over the walls at once."

"I desire he will do no such things," said Athos, "they may be useful to us."

"These bodies useful to us? Why, Athos, you are mad!" said Porthos.

"Judge not rashly, say the Gospel and the cardinal," replied Athos; "how many guns, gentlemen?"

"Twelve," replied Aramis.

"How many cartridges?"

"A hundred."

"That's quite as many as we shall want: let us load the guns."

The four musketeers went to work, and as they were loading the last musket, Grimaud announced that the breakfast was ready.

Athos replied, still by gestures, that that was well, and indicated to Grimaud, by pointing to a kind of pepper-castor, that he was to stand as sentinel. Only, to alleviate the tediousness of the duty, Athos allowed him to take a loaf, two cutlets, and a bottle of wine.

"And now, to table," said Athos.

The four friends sat down upon the ground, with their legs crossed, like Turks or tailors.

"And now," said D'Artagnan, "as there is no longer a fear of being overheard, I hope you are going to let me into this momentous secret."

"I hope, at the same time, to procure you amusement and glory, gentlemen," said Athos. "I have induced you to take a very pleasant walk; here is a delicious breakfast, and five hundred persons yonder, as you may see through the loopholes, taking us for heroes or madmen, two classes of imbeciles sufficiently resembling each other."

"But the secret! the secret!" said D'Artagnan.

"The secret is," said Athos, "that I saw milady last night."

D'Artagnan was lifting a glass to his lips, but at the name of milady his hand shook so that he was obliged to put the glass on the ground again, for fear of spilling the contents.

"You say your wi——"

"Hush!" interrupted Athos, "you forget, D'Artagnan, you forget that these gentlemen are not so initiated as you are in my family affairs. I have seen milady."

"Where?" demanded D'Artagnan.

"Within two leagues of this place, at the auberge of the Colombier Rouge."

"In that case I am a lost man," said D'Artagnan.

"Not quite so yet," replied Athos; "for by this time she must have left the shores of France."

D'Artagnan breathed again.

"But, after all," asked Porthos, "who is milady?"

"A very charming woman!" said Athos, sipping a glass of sparkling wine. "A scoundrel of a host!" cried he, "he has given us Anjou wine instead of champagne, and fancies we know no better! Yes," continued he, "a very charming woman, who entertained kind views toward our friend D'Artagnan, who, on his part, has given her some offense for which she endeavored to revenge herself, a month ago, by having him killed by two musket shots; a week ago, by trying to poison him; and yesterday, by demanding his head of the cardinal."

"What! by demanding my head of the cardinal?" cried D'Artagnan, pale with terror.

"Yes, that is as true as the Gospel," said Porthos; "I heard her with my own ears."

"So did I," said Aramis.

"Then," said D'Artagnan, letting his arm fall, as if overcome by discouragement, "it is useless to struggle any longer; I may as well blow my brains out, and put an end to the matter at once."

"That's the last folly to be committed," said Athos, "seeing that that is the only one for which there is no remedy."

"But I can never escape," said D'Artagnan, "with such enemies. First, there is my unknown man of Meung; then De Wardes, to whom I have given three wounds; next milady, whose secret I have discovered; and, last and worst, the cardinal, whose vengeance I have balked."

"Well," said Athos, "that only makes four; and we are four—one for one."

"*Pardieu!* if we may believe the signs Grimaud is making, we are about to have to do with a very different number of folks."

"What's the matter, Grimaud?" said Athos. "Considering the seriousness of the circumstance, I permit you to speak, my friend; but be laconic, I beg. What do you see?"

"A troop."

"Of how many persons?"

"Twenty men."

"What sort of men?"

"Sixteen pioneers, four soldiers."

"How far distant?"

"Five hundred paces."

"Good! We have just time to finish this fowl, and to drink one glass of wine to your health, D'Artagnan!"

"To your health," repeated Porthos and Aramis.

"Well, then, to my health! although I am very much afraid that your good wishes will not be of great service to me."

"Bah!" said Athos, "God is great, as the followers of Mahomet say; and the future is in His hands."

Then, swallowing the contents of his glass, which he put down close to him, Athos arose carelessly, took the musket next to him, and drew near to one of the loopholes.

Porthos, Aramis, and D'Artagnan followed his example. As to Grimaud, he received orders to place himself behind the four friends, in order to reload their weapons.

At the expiration of a minute the troop appeared; they advanced along a sort of narrow channel of the trench, which kept up a means of communication between the bastion and the city.

"*Pardieu!*" said Athos, "it was hardly worth while to disturb ourselves for twenty fellows, armed with pickaxes, mattocks and shovels! Grimaud had only need have made them a sign to go away, and I am convinced they would have left us alone."

"I doubt that," replied D'Artagnan; "for they are advancing very resolutely. Besides, in addition to the pioneers, there are four soldiers and a brigadier armed with muskets."

"That's because they don't see us," said Athos.

"*Ma foi?*" said Aramis, "I must confess I feel a great repugnance to fire on these poor devils of bourgeois."

"He is a bad priest," said Porthos, "who feels pity for heretics!"

"In truth," said Athos, "Aramis is right—I will warn them."

"What the devil are you going about?" cried D'Artagnan, "you will be shot!"

But Athos took no heed of his advice; and, mounting on the breach, with his musket in one hand, and his hat in the other:

"Gentlemen," said he, addressing the soldiers and the pioneers, who, astonished at his appearance, stopped at fifty paces from the bastion, and bowing courteously to them; "gentlemen, a few friends and myself are about to breakfast in this bastion. Now, you know nothing is more disagreeable than being disturbed when one is at breakfast. We request you, then, if you really have business here, to wait till we have finished our repast, or to come again a short time hence; unless, which would be far better, you form the salutary resolution to quit the side of the rebels, and come and drink with us to the health of the king of France."

"Take care, Athos!" cried D'Artagnan; "don't you see they are preparing to fire?"

"Yes, yes," said Athos; "but they are only bourgeois— very bad marksmen, and who will be sure not to hit me."

In fact, at the same instant, four shots were fired, and the balls were flattened against the wall round Athos, but not one hit him.

Four shots replied to them, almost instantaneously, but much better aimed than those of the aggressors; three soldiers fell dead, and one of the pioneers was wounded.

"Grimaud," said Athos, still on the breach, "another musket!"

Grimaud immediately obeyed. On their part, the three friends had reloaded their arms; another discharge followed the second; the brigadier and two pioneers fell dead; the rest of the troop took to flight.

"Now gentlemen, a sortie!" cried Athos.

And the four friends rushed out of the fort, gained the field of battle, picked up the four soldiers' muskets and the half-pike of the brigadier; and, convinced that the fugitives would not stop till they got to the city, turned again toward the bastion, bearing with them the trophies of their victory.

"Reload the muskets, Grimaud," said Athos, "and we, gentlemen, will go on with our breakfast, and resume our conversation. Where were we?"

"You were saying," said D'Artagnan, "that after having demanded my head of the cardinal, milady, had left the shores of France. Where is she going to?" added he, considerably interested in the itinerary milady followed.

"She is going into England," said Athos.

"With what view?"

"With the view of assassinating, or causing to be assassinated, the Duke of Buckingham."

D'Artagnan uttered an exclamation of surprise and astonishment.

"But this is infamous!" cried he.

"As to that," said Athos, "I beg you to believe that I care very little about it. Now you have done, Grimaud, take our

brigadier's half-pike, tie a napkin to it, and plant it at the
top of our bastion, that these rebels of Rochellais may see
that they have to deal with brave and loyal soldiers of the
king."

Grimaud obeyed without replying.   An instant afterward,
the white flag was floating over the heads of the four friends:
a thunder of applause saluted its appearance: half the camp
was at the barrier.

"But why do you care so little whether Buckingham be
killed or not? The duke is our friend."

"The duke is an Englishman, the duke is fighting against
us; let her do what she likes with the duke; I care no more
about him than an empty bottle."

And Athos threw fifteen paces from him an empty bottle,
from which he had poured the last drop into his glass.

"Ay, but stop a minute, I will not give up Buckingham
thus," said D'Artagnan, "he gave us some very fine horses."

"And, moreover, very handsome saddles," said Porthos,
who at the moment wore the lace of his on his cloak.

"Besides," said Aramis. "God desires the conversion, and
not the death of a sinner."

"*Amen!*" said Athos, "and we will return to that subject
presently, if such be your pleasure: but that which, for the
moment, engaged my attention most earnestly, and I am sure
you will understand me, D'Artagnan, was the getting from
this woman a kind of signed carte-blanche, which she had
extorted from the cardinal, and by means of which she could
with impunity get rid of you and perhaps of us."

"But this creature must be a demon!" said Porthos, holding
out his plate to Aramis, who was cutting up a fowl.

"And this carte-blanche," said D'Artagnan, "this carte-
blanche, does it remain in her hands?"

"No, it passed into mine; I will not say without trouble,
for if I did I should tell a lie."

"My dear Athos, I shall give over counting the number of
times I am indebted to you for my life."

"Then it was to go to her you left us?" said Aramis.

"Exactly so."

"And you have that letter of the cardinal's?"

"Here it is," said Athos.

And he took the invaluable paper from the pocket of his
uniform.

D'Artagnan unfolded it with a hand, the trembling of
which he did not even attempt to conceal, and read:

"It is by my order and for the good of the state, that the bearer of the present has done what he has done.

"December 5, 1627.   RICHELIEU."

"In fact," said Aramis, "it is an absolution in all its forms."

"That paper must be torn to pieces," said D'Artagnan, who fancied he read in it his sentence of death.

"On the contrary," said Athos, "it must be preserved carefully; I would not give this paper for as many gold pieces as would cover it."

"And what is she going to do now?" asked the young man.

"Why," replied Athos, carelessly, "she is probably going to write to the cardinal that a damned musketeer, named Athos, has taken her *protection* from her by force; she will advise him, in the same letter, to get rid of his two friends, Aramis and Porthos, at the time he disposes of them. The cardinal will remember that these are the same men that have so often crossed his path; and then, some fine morning, he will arrest D'Artagnan, and for fear he should feel lonely, he will send us to keep him company in the Bastile."

"It appears to me you are making but very dull jokes, friend Athos," said Porthos.

"I am not joking."

"Do you know," said Porthos, "that to twist that damned milady's neck would be a less sin than to twist those of these poor devils of Huguenots, who have committed no other crimes than singing the Psalms in French that we sing in Latin?"

"What says the abbé?" asked Athos quietly.

"I say I am entirely of Porthos' opinion," replied Aramis.

"And I am sure I am so too," said D'Artagnan.

"Fortunately, she is a good way off," said Porthos, "for I confess she would make me very uncomfortable if she were here."

"She makes me uncomfortable in England as well as in France," said Athos.

"She makes me uncomfortable wherever she is," said D'Artagnan.

"But, when you had her in your power, why did you not drown her, or strangle her, or hang her?" said Porthos, "it is only the dead that don't come back again."

"You think so, do you, Porthos?" replied the musketeer, with a sad smile, which d'Artagnan alone understood.

"I have an idea," said D'Artagnan.

"What is it?" said the musketeers.

"To arms!" cried Grimaud.

The young men sprang up, and seized their muskets.

This time a small troop advanced, consisting of from twenty to five-and-twenty men; but they were no longer pioneers, they were soldiers of the garrison.

"Shall we return to the camp?" said Porthos. "I don't think the sides are equal."

"Impossible, for three reasons," replied Athos; "the first is, we have not finished breakfast; the second, we have still some very important things to talk about; and the third, it yet wants ten minutes before the hour will be elapsed."

"Well, then," said Aramis, "we must form a plan of battle."

"That's very simple," replied Athos, "as soon as the enemy are within musket-shot we must fire upon them; if they continue to advance, we must fire again, we fire as long as we have loaded guns; if such as then remain of the troop persist in coming to the assault, we will allow the besiegers to go into the ditch, and then we will push down upon their heads that strip of wall which seems only to keep its perpendicular by a miracle."

"Bravo!" cried Porthos; "decidedly, Athos, you were born to be a general, and the cardinal, who fancies himself a great captain, is nothing to you."

"Gentlemen," said Athos, "no divided attention, I beg; let each one pick out his man."

"I cover mine," said D'Artagnan.

"And I mine," said Porthos.

"And I *idem*," said Aramis.

"Fire! then," said Athos.

The four muskets made one report, but four men fell.

The drum immediately beat, and the little troop advanced in charging step.

Then the shots were repeated, without regularity, but always aimed with the same correctness. Nevertheless, as if they had been aware of the numerical weakness of the friends, the Rochellais continued to advance in quick time.

Upon every three shots at least two men fell; but the march of those left untouched was not slackened.

When arrived at the foot of the bastion, there was still more than a dozen of the enemy; a last discharge welcomed them, but did not stop them; they jumped into the ditch, and prepared to scale the breach.

"Now, my friends" said Athos, "finish that at a blow! to the wall! to the wall!"

And the four friends, seconded by Grimaud, pushed with

the barrels of their muskets an enormous sheet of the wall, which bent over as if acted upon by the wind, and, becoming detached from its base, fell with a horrible crash into the ditch. Then a fearful cry was heard, a cloud of dust mounted toward heaven, and all was over!

"Can we have destroyed them all, from the first to the last?" said Athos.

"*Ma foi!* it appears so," said D'Artagnan.

"No," cried Porthos; "there go three or four limping away."

In fact, three or four of these unfortunate men, covered with dirt and blood, were flying along the hollow way, and at length regained the city; these were all that were left of the little troop.

Athos looked at his watch.

"Gentlemen," said he, "we have been here an hour, and our wager is won; besides, we will be fair players; besides, D'Artagnan has not told us his idea yet."

And the musketeer, with his usual coolness, went and reseated himself before the remains of the breakfast.

"My idea?" said D'Artagnan.

"Yes; you said you had an idea," said Athos.

"Oh! I remember now," said D'Artagnan. "Well, I will go into England for a second time; I will go and find M. Buckingham."

"You shall not do that, D'Artagnan," said Athos coolly.

"And why not? Have I not been there once?"

"Yes; but at that period we were not at war; at that period M. de Buckingham was an ally, and not an enemy. What you now contemplate doing would amount to treason."

D'Artagnan perceived the force of this reasoning, and was silent.

"But," said Porthos, "I think I have an idea, in my turn."

"Silence for M. Porthos' idea!" said Aramis.

"I will ask leave of absence of M. de Tréville, on some pretext or other, which you must find out, as I am not very clever at pretexts. Milady does not know me; I will get access to her without her suspecting me, and when I catch my beauty alone, I will strangle her."

"Well," replied Athos, "I am not far from approving the idea of M. Porthos."

"For shame! for shame!" said Aramis—"kill a woman? No, listen to me; I have the best idea."

"Let us see your idea, Aramis," said Athos, who entertained much deference for the young musketeer.

"We must acquaint the queen."

"Ah, *ma foi!* yes!" said Porthos and D'Artagnan at the same time; "we are coming nearer to it now."

"Acquaint the queen!" said Athos; "and how will you do that? Have we any relations with the court? Could we send any one to Paris without its being known in the camp? From hence to Paris it is a hundred and forty leagues; before our letter was at Angers we should be in a dungeon."

"As to remitting a letter with safety to her majesty," said Aramis coloring, "I will take that upon myself. I know a clever person at Tours——"

Aramis stopped on seeing Athos smile.

"Well, do you not adopt this means, Athos?" said D'Artagnan.

"I do not reject it altogether," said Athos; "but I wish to remind Aramis that he cannot quit the camp, and that nobody but one of ourselves is safe; that two hours after the messenger has set out all the capuchins, all the alguazils, all the black caps of the cardinal, will know your letter by heart, and you and your clever person will be arrested."

"Without reckoning that the queen would save M. de Buckingham, but would take no heed of us."

"Gentlemen," said D'Artagnan, "what Porthos says is full of sense."

"Ah, ah! but what's going on in the city yonder?" said Athos.

"They are beating the *générale.*"

The four friends listened, and all plainly heard the sound of the drum.

"You will see they are going to send a whole regiment against us," said Athos.

"You don't think of holding out against a whole regiment, do you?" said Porthos.

"Why not?" said the musketeer. "I feel myself quite in a humor for it; and I could hold out before a whole army if we had had the precaution to bring a dozen more bottles of wine."

"Upon my word, the drums draws near," said D'Artagnan.

"Let it come," said Athos. "It is a quarter of an hour's journey from hence to the city, consequently a quarter of an hour's journey from the city hither; that is more than time enough for us to advise a plan. If we go from this place, we shall never find another so suitable. Ah! stop! I have it, gentlemen—the right idea has just occurred to me."

"Tell us what it is, then."

"Allow me to give Grimaud some indispensable orders."
Athos made a sign for his lackey to draw near.

"Grimaud," said Athos, pointing to the bodies which lay
under the wall of the bastion, "take those gentlemen, set
them up against the wall, put their hats upon their heads,
and their guns in their hands."

"Oh, the great man!" cried D'Artagnan; "I comprehend
now."

"You comprehend?" said Porthos.

"And do you comprehend, Grimaud?" said Aramis.

Grimaud made a sign in the affirmative.

"That's all that's necessary," said Athos; "now for my
idea."

"I should like, however, to comprehend," said Porthos.

"Not at all necessary."

"Athos' idea! Athos' idea!" cried Aramis and D'Artagnan
at the same time.

"This milady—this woman—this creature—this demon, has
a brother-in-law, as I think you have told me, D'Artagnan?"

"Yes, I know him very well; and I also believe that he has
not a very warm affection for his sister-in-law."

"There is no harm in that; if he detested her, it would be
all the better," replied Athos.

"In that case we are as well off as we wish."

"And yet," said Porthos, "I should like to comprehend
what Grimaud is about."

"Silence, Porthos!" said Aramis.

"What is her brother's name?"

"Lord de Winter."

"Where is he now?"

"He returned to London at the first rumor of the war."

"Well, that's just the man we want," said Athos; "it is
him we must warn. We will have him informed that his
sister-in-law is on the point of having some one assassinated,
and we beg of him not to lose sight of her. There is in
London, I hope, some establishment like that of the Made-
lonnettes, or of the Filles Repenties. He must place his
sister in one of these, and we shall be in peace."

"Yes," said D'Artagnan, "until she gets out again."

"Ah, *ma foi!*" said Athos, "you require too much, D'Artagnan, I have given you all I had, and I beg leave to tell
you that that is the bottom of my sack."

"But I think it would be still better," said Aramis, "to
inform the queen and M. de Winter at the same time."

"Yes; but who is to carry the letter to Tours, and who to London?"

"I answer for Bazin," said Aramis.

"And I for Planchet," said D'Artagnan.

"Ay," said Porthos, "if we cannot leave the camp, our lackeys may."

"To be sure they may, and this very day, we will write the letters," said Aramis; "give them money, and set them forward."

"We will give them money?" replied Athos. "Have you any money, then?"

The four friends looked at each other, and a cloud came over the brows which but lately had been so cheerful.

"Quick! quick!" cried D'Artagnan, "I see black points and red points moving yonder. What! did you talk of a regiment, Athos? It is an army!"

"*Ma foi!* yes," said Athos, "there they are. Think of the sneaks coming without beat of drum or sound of trumpet. Ah, ah! have you finished Grimaud?"

Grimaud made a sign in the affirmative and pointed to a dozen bodies which he had set up in the most picturesque attitudes; some supported arms, others seems to be taking aim, and the remainder appeared merely to be sword in hand.

"Bravo!" said Athos; "that does honor to your imagination."

"Ay, I dare say it's all very well," said Porthos, "but I should like to comprehend."

"Let us decamp first, and you can comprehend afterward."

"Stop one minute, gentlemen; give Grimaud time to collect the breakfast things."

"Ah, ah!" said Aramis, "the black points and the red points are visibly enlarging; I am of D'Artagnan's opinion— we have no time to lose to regain our camp."

"*Ma foi!*" said Athos, "I have nothing more to say against a retreat; we betted upon one hour, and we have stayed an hour and a half. Nothing can be said; let us be off, gentlemen, let us be off!"

Grimaud went on before with the basket; the four friends followed, at about ten paces behind him.

"What the devil shall we do now, gentlemen?" cried Athos.

"Have you forgotten anything?" said Aramis.

"The white flag, *morbleu!* we must not leave a flag in the hands of the enemy, even if that flag be but a napkin."

And Athos ran back to the bastion, mounted the platform

and bore off the flag; but as the Rochellais were arrived within
musket range, they opened a terrible fire upon this man, who
appeared to expose himself for pleasure's sake.

But Athos might be said to bear a charmed life; the balls
passed and whistled all round him; not one hit him.

Athos waved his flag, turning his back to the city guards,
and saluting those of the camp. On both sides loud cries
arose—on the one side cries of anger, on the other cries of
enthusiasm.

A second discharge followed the first, and three balls, by passing through it, made the napkin really a flag. Cries were heard
from the camp, "Come down! come down!"

Athos came down; his friends, who anxiously awaited him,
saw him return with joy.

"Come along, Athos, come along!" cried D'Artagnan; "now
we have found everything except money, it would be stupid
to be killed."

But Athos continued to march majestically, whatever obser-
vations his companions made; and they, finding their ob-
servations useless, regulated their pace by his.

Grimaud and his basket were far in advance, out of the
reach of the balls.

At the end of an instant, a furious firing was heard.

"What's that?" asked Porthos, "what are they firing at
now? I hear no balls, and I see nobody!"

"They are firing upon Grimaud's dead company," replied
Athos.

"But the dead cannot return their fire."

"Certainly not; they will then fancy it is an ambuscade, they
will deliberate, and by the time they have found out the joke
we shall be out of the reach of their balls. That renders it
useless to get a pleurisy by too much haste."

"Oh, I comprehend now," said the astonished Porthos.

"That's lucky," said Athos, shrugging his shoulders.

On their part, the French, on seeing the four friends return in common marching step, uttered cries of enthusiasm.

At length a fresh discharge was heard, and this time the
balls came rattling among the stones around the friends, and
whistling sharply in their ears. The Rochellais had at last
taken possession of the bastion.

"These Rochellais are bungling fellows," said Athos; "how
many have we killed of them—a dozen?"

"Or fifteen."

"How many did we crush under the wall?"

"Eight or ten."

"And in exchange for all that not even a scratch! Ah! but what is the matter with your hand, D'Artagnan? It bleeds, seemingly."

"Oh, it's nothing," said D'Artagnan.

"A spent ball?"

"Not even that."

"What is it, then?"

We have said that Athos loved D'Artagnan like a child, and this somber and inflexible character felt the anxiety of a parent for the young man.

"Only grazed a little," replied D'Artagnan; "my fingers were caught between two stones, that of the wall and that of my ring, and the skin was broken."

"That comes of wearing diamonds, my master," said Athos disdainfully.

"Ah, to be sure," cried Porthos, "there is a diamond; why the devil then, do we plague ourselves about money, when there is a diamond?"

"Stop a bit!" said Aramis.

"Well thought of, Porthos; this time you have an idea."

"Certainly I have," said Porthos, drawing himself up at Athos' compliment; "as there is a diamond, let us sell it."

"But," said D'Artagnan, "it is the queen's diamond."

"The stronger reason why it should be sold," replied Athos; "the queen saving M. de Buckingham, her lover, nothing more just; the queen saving us, her friends, nothing more moral; let us sell the diamond. What says Monsieur l'Abbé? I don't ask Porthos; his opinion has been given."

"Why, I think," said Aramis, coloring as usual, that this ring not coming from a mistress, and, consequently, not being a love token, D'Artagnan may sell it."

"My dear Aramis, you speak like theology personified. Your opinion, then, is——"

"That the diamond may be sold."

"Well, then," said D'Artagnan gayly, "let us sell the diamond, and say no more about it."

The fusillade continued; but the friends were out of reach, and the Rochellais only fired for the discharge of their consciences.

"*Ma foi!* is was time that idea came into Porthos' head—here we are at the camp! therefore, gentlemen, not a word more of this affair. We are observed—they are coming to meet us; we shall be borne in in triumph."

In fact, as we have said, the whole camp was in motion. More than two thousand persons had assisted, as at a spectacle, at this fortunate but wild undertaking of the four friends, an undertaking of which they were far from suspecting the real motive. Nothing was heard but cries of *"Vivent les mousquetaires! vivent les gardes!"* M. de Busigny was the first to come and shake Athos by the hand, and acknowledge that the wager was lost. The dragoon and the Swiss followed him, and all their comrades followed the dragoon and the Swiss. There was nothing but felicitations, pressures of the hand, and embraces; there was no end to the inextinguishable laughter at the Rochellais. The tumult at length became so great that the cardinal fancied there must be some riot, and sent La Houdinière, his captain of the guards, to inquire what was going on.

The affair was described to the messenger with all the effervescence of enthusiasm.

"Well?" asked the cardinal, on seeing La Houdinière return.

"Well, monseigneur," replied the latter, "three musketeers and a guard laid a wager with M. de Busigny, that they would go and breakfast in the Bastion St. Gervais, and while breakfasting, they held it for two hours against the enemy, and have killed I don't know how many Rochellais."

"Did you inquire the names of those three musketeers?"

"Yes, monseigneur."

"What are their names?"

"MM. Athos, Porthos, and Aramis."

"Still my three brave fellows!" murmured the cardinal. "And the guard?"

"M. D'Artagnan."

"Still my young scapegrace. Positively, these four men must be mine."

That same evening, the cardinal spoke to M. de Tréville of the exploit of the morning, which was the talk of the whole camp. M. de Tréville, who had received the account of the adventure from the mouths of the heroes of it, related it in all its details to His Eminence, not forgetting the episode of the napkin.

"That's well! Monsieur de Tréville," said the cardinal: pray let that napkin be sent to me. I will have three *fleur-de-lis* embroidered on it in gold, and will give it to your company as a standard."

"Monseigneur," said M. de Tréville, "that will hardly be doing justice to the guards; M. D'Artagnan is not mine; he serves under M. Dessessarts."

"Well, then, take him," said the cardinal; "when four men

are so much attached to each other, it is only fair that they should serve in the same company."

That same evening M. de Tréville announced this good news to the three musketeers and D'Artagnan, inviting all four to breakfast with him next morning.

D'Artagnan was beside himself with joy. We know that the dream of his life had been to become a musketeer. The three friends were likewise greatly delighted.

"*Ma foi!*" said D'Artagnan to Athos, "that was a triumphant idea of yours! As you said, we have acquired glory, and were enabled to carry on a conversation of the greatest importance."

"Which we can resume now without anybody suspecting us, for, with the help of God, we shall henceforth pass for cardinalists."

That evening D'Artagnan went to present his compliments to M. Dessessarts, and inform him of his promotion.

M. Dessessarts, who esteemed D'Artagnan, made him offers of service, as this change would bring on expenses for equipment.

D'Artagnan respectfully declined, but thinking the opportunity a good one, he begged him to have the diamond he put into his hand valued, as he wished to turn it into money.

The next day, by two o'clock, M. Dessessarts' valet came to D'Artagnan's lodging and gave him a bag containing seven thousand livres.

This was the price of the queen's diamond.

CHAPTER XLVIII.

A FAMILY AFFAIR.

ATHOS had discovered the word: *family affair*. A family affair was not subject to the investigation of the cardinal; a family affair concerned nobody; people might employ themselves in a family before all the world.

Thus Athos had discovered the word: family affair.

Aramis had discovered the idea: the lackeys.

Porthos had discovered the means: the diamond.

D'Artagnan alone had discovered nothing; he, ordinarily the most inventive of the four; but it must be also said that the name alone of milady paralyzed him.

Ah! yes, but we were mistaken; he had discovered a pur-
chaser for his diamond.

The breakfast at M. de Tréville's was as gay and cheerful
as possible. D'Artagnan already wore his uniform; for being
nearly of the same size of Aramis, and Aramis being so liberally paid by the bookseller who purchased his poem, as to
allow him to have bought double of everything, he yielded
his friend a complete equipment.

D'Artagnan would have been at the height of his wishes
if he had not constantly seen milady, like a dark cloud, hovering in the horizon.

After breakfast, it was agreed that they should meet again
in the evening at Athos' lodgings, and would there terminate
the affair.

D'Artagnan passed the day in exhibiting his musketeer's
uniform in every street of the camp.

In the evening, at the appointed hour, the four friends met;
there only remained three things to be decided upon.

What they should write to milady's brother.

What they should write to the clever person at Tours.

And which should be the lackeys to carry the letters.

Every one offered his own: Athos talked of the discretion
of Grimaud, who never spoke a word but when his master
unlocked his mouth. Porthos boasted of the strength of
Mousqueton, who was big enough to thrash four men of
ordinary size. Aramis, confiding in the address of Bazin,
made a pompous eulogium upon his candidate; and D'Artagnan had entire faith in the bravery of Planchet, and reminded
them of the manner in which he had conducted himself in
the ticklish affair of Boulogne.

These four virtues disputed the prize for a length of time,
and gave birth to magnificent speeches, which we do not
repeat here, for fear they should de deemed too long.

"Unfortunately," said Athos, "he whom we send must possess
in himself alone the four qualities united."

"But where is such a lackey to be found?"

"Not to be found!" cried Athos; "I know that; take
Grimaud then."

"Take Mousqueton!"

"Take Bazin!"

"Take Planchet; Planchet is brave and shrewd; they are
two qualities out of the four."

"Gentlemen," said Aramis, "the principal question is not
to know which of our four lackeys is the most discreet, the

strongest, the cleverest, or the most brave; the matter is to know which loves money the best."

"What Aramis says is very sensible," replied Athos; "we must speculate upon the faults of people, and not upon their virtues. Monsieur l'Abbé, you are a great moralist!"

"Doubtless," said Aramis; "for we not only require to be well served, in order to succeed, but, moreover, not to fail; for, in case of failure, heads are in question, not for our lackeys——"

"Speak lower, Aramis," said Athos.

"That's correct; not for the lackeys," resumed Aramis, "but for the masters! Are our lackeys sufficiently devoted to us to risk their lives for us? No."

"*Ma foi!*" said D'Artagnan, "I would almost answer for Planchet."

"Well, my dear friend, add to his natural devotedness a good sum of money, and then, instead of answering for him once, answer for him twice."

"Why, good God! you will be deceived just the same," said Athos, who was an optimist when things were concerned, and a pessimist when men were in question. "They will promise everything for the sake of the money, and on the road fear will prevent them from acting. Once taken, they will be pressed; when pressed, they will confess everything What the devil, we are not children! To go to England" (Athos lowered his voice), "all France—covered with the spies and creatures of the cardinal—must be crossed; a pass for embarkation must be obtained; and the party must be acquainted with English, to inquire the way to London. Really, I think the thing is very difficult!"

"Not at all," cried D'Artagnan, who was anxious the matter should be accomplished; "on the contrary, I think it is very easy. It should be, no doubt. *Parbleu!* if we write to Lord de Winter about affairs of vast importance, of the horrors of the cardinal——"

"Speak lower!" said Athos.

"Of the intrigues and secrets of state," continued D'Artagnan, complying with the recommendation; "there can be no doubt we shall be all broken on the wheel; but, for God's sake, do not forget, as you yourself said, Athos, that we only write to him concerning a family affair; that we only write to him to entreat that as soon as milady arrives in London, he will put it out of her power to injure us. I will write to him then nearly in these terms."

"Let us see," said Athos, assuming a critical look.

"Monsieur, and dear friend——"

"Ah! yes! 'dear friend' to an Englishman," interrupted Athos; "capitally commenced! Bravo, D'Artagnan! Only with that word you would be quartered, instead of being broken on the wheel."

"Well! perhaps. I will say, then, monsieur, quite short."

"You may even say, milord," replied Athos, who stickled for propriety.

"Milord, do you remember the little goat pasture of the Luxembourg?"

"Good, the Luxembourg! It might be believed to be an allusion to the queen-mother! That's ingenious," said Athos.

"Well, then! we will put simply, 'Milord, do you remember a certain little inclosure where your life was spared?' "

"My dear D'Artagnan, you will never make anything but a very bad secretary. 'Where your life was spared!' For shame! that's unworthy. A man of spirit is not to be reminded of such services. A benefit reproached is an offense committed.

"The devil," said D'Artagnan, "you are insupportable! If the letter must be written under your censure, I renounce the task."

"And you will do right. Handle the musket and the sword, my dear fellow; you will come off splendidly at those two exercises; but pass the pen over to M. l'Abbé, that's his province."

"Ay, ay," said Porthos, "pass the pen over to Aramis, who writes theses in Latin."

"Well so be it," said D'Artagnan, "draw up this note for us, Aramis; but, by our holy father the pope! be concise, for I shall prune you in my turn, I warn you."

"I ask no better," said Aramis, with that ingenuous air of confidence which every poet has in himself; "but let me be properly acquainted with the subject; I have heard, by this means and that, that this sister-in-law was a vile woman; I have obtained a proof of it by listening to her conversation with the cardinal."

"Lower! *sacre bleu!*" said Athos.

"But," continued Aramis, "the details escape me."

"And me also," said Porthos.

D'Artagnan and Athos looked at each other for some time in silence. At length, Athos, after apparently serious reflection, and becoming more pale than usual, made a sign of assent to D'Artagnan, who by it understood he was at liberty to speak.

"Well, this is what you have to say," said D'Artagnan; " 'Milord, your sister-in-law is an infamous woman, who has wished to have you killed, that she might inherit your wealth. But she could not marry your brother, being already married in France, and having been—' " D'Artagnan stopped, as if seeking for the word, and looking at Athos.

"Repudiated by her husband."

"Because she had been branded," continued D'Artagnan.

"Bah!" cried Porthos, "impossible! What do you say, she wanted to have her brother-in-law killed?"

"Yes."

"And she was previously married?" asked Aramis.

"Yes."

"And her husband found out that she had a *fleur-de-lis* on her shoulder?" cried Porthos.

"Yes."

These three yeses had been pronounced by Athos, each with a deeper intonation.

"And who has seen this *fleur-de-lis?*" said Aramis.

"D'Artagnan and I, or rather, to observe the chronological order, I and D'Artagnan," replied Athos.

"And does the husband of this frightful creature still live?" said Aramis.

"He still lives."

"Are you quite sure of it?"

"I am he."

There was a moment of cold silence, during which every one was affected, according to his nature.

"This time," said Athos, first breaking the silence, "D'Artagnan has given us an excellent programme, and the letter must be written at once."

"The devil! you are right, Athos," said Aramis, "and it is rather a difficult matter. M. the Chancellor himself would be puzzled how to write such a letter, and yet M. the Chancellor draws up a *procès-verbal* very agreeably. Never mind! be silent, I will try."

Aramis accordingly took the pen, reflected for a few moments, wrote eight or ten lines, in a charming, little, female hand, and then, with a voice soft and slow, as if each word had been scrupulously weighed, he read the following:

"MILORD: The person who writes these few lines had the honor of crossing swords with you in the little enclosure of the Rue d'Enfer. As you have several times since declared yourself the friend of that person, he thinks it his duty to respond to that friendship by sending you important advice.

Twice you have nearly been the victim of a near relation whom you believe to be your heir, because you are ignorant that before she contracted a marriage in England, she was already married in France. But the third time, which is this, you may succumb. Your relation left La Rochelle for England during the night. Watch her arrival, for she has great and terrible projects. If you require to know positively what she is capable of, read her past history upon her left shoulder."

"Well, now that will do wonderfully well," said Athos; "really, my dear Aramis, you have the pen of a secretary of state. Lord de Winter will now be upon his guard, if the letter should reach him; and even if it should fall into the hands of the cardinal, we shall not be compromised. But as the lackey who goes may make us believe he has been to London and may stop at Châtelherault, let us give him only half the sum promised him with the letter, with an agreement that he shall have the other half in exchange for the reply. Have you the diamond?" continued Athos.

"I have what is still better: I have the value of it," said D'Artagnan, throwing the bag upon the table. At the sound of the gold, Aramis raised his eyes, and Porthos started; as to Athos, he remained impassible.

"How much is there in that little bag?"

"Seven thousand livres, in louis of twelve francs."

"Seven thousand livres!" cried Porthos; "that poor little diamond was worth seven thousand livres?"

"It appears so," said Athos, "since here they are; I don't suppose that our friend D'Artagnan has added any of his own to the amount."

"But, gentlemen, in all this," said D'Artagnan, "we do not think of the queen. Let us take some heed of the welfare of her dear Buckingham. That is the least we owe her."

"That's true," said Athos, "but that falls to Aramis."

"Well," replied the latter, blushing, "what must I say?"

"Oh! that's simple enough," replied Athos; "write a second letter for that clever personage that lives at Tours."

Aramis resumed his pen, reflected a little, and wrote the following lines, which he immediately submitted to the approbation of his friends:

"My dear cousin."

"Ah! ah!" said Athos, "this clever person is your relation then?"

"Cousin-german."

"Go on, to your cousin, then!"

Aramis continued:

"My Dear Cousin: His Eminence the cardinal, whom God preserve for the happiness of France and the confusion of the enemies of the kingdom, is on the point of putting an end to the heretic rebellion of La Rochelle; it is probable that the succor of the English fleet will never even arrive in sight of the place; I will even venture to say that I am certain M. de Buckingham will be prevented from setting out by some great event. His Eminence is the most illustrious politician of times past, of times present, and probably of times to come. He would extinguish the sun, if the sun incommoded him. Give these happy tidings to your sister, my dear cousin. I have dreamed that that cursed Englishman was dead. I cannot recollect whether it was by steel or by poison; only of this I am sure, I have dreamed he was dead, and you know my dreams never deceive me. Be assured, then, of seeing me soon return."

"Capital," cried Athos; "you are the king of poets, my dear Aramis; you speak like the Apocalypse, and you are as true as the Gospel. There is nothing now to do but to put the address to this letter."

"That's soon done," said Aramis.

He folded the letter fancifully, and took up his pen and wrote:

"To Mademoiselle Michon, seamstress, Tours."

The three friends looked at each other and laughed; they were caught.

"Now," said Aramis, "you will please to understand, gentlemen, that Bazin alone can carry this letter to Tours; my cousin knows nobody but Bazin, and places confidence in nobody but him; any other person would fail. Besides, Bazin is ambitious and learned; Bazin has read history, gentlemen, he knows that Sixtus Quintus bêcame pope after having kept pigs; well! as he means to enter the church at the same time as myself, he does not despair of becoming pope in his turn, or at least a cardinal; you can understand that a man who has such views, will never allow himself to be taken, or if taken, will undergo martyrdom rather than speak."

"Very well," said D'Artagnan, "I consent to Bazin, with all my heart, but grant me Planchet; milady had him one day turned out of doors, with sundry blows of a good stick, to accelerate his motions; now Planchet has an excellent memory, and I will be bound that sooner than relinquish any possible means of vengeance, he will allow himself to be beaten to death. If your affairs of Tours are your affairs, Aramis, those of London are mine. I request, then, that Planchet may be chosen, more particularly as he has already been to London with me, and knows how to speak very correctly: *London, sir, if you please, and my master, Lord D'Artagnan.* With that, you may be satisfied, he can make his way, both going and returning."

"In that case," said Athos, "Planchet must receive seven hundred livres for going, and seven hundred livres for coming back; and Bazin, three hundred livres for going, and three hundred livres for returning; that will reduce the sum to five thousand livres; we will each take a thousand livres to be employed as seems good to each, and we will leave a fund of a thousand livres, under the guardianship of Monsieur l'Abbé here, for extraordinary occasions or common wants. Will that do?"

"My dear Athos," said Aramis, "you speak like Nestor, who was, as every one knows, the wisest among the Greeks."

"Well, then," said Athos, "it is agreed; Planchet and Bazin shall go; everything considered, I am not sorry to retain Grimaud; he is accustomed to my ways, and I am particular; yesterday's affair must have shaken him a little, his voyage would overset him quite."

Planchet was sent for, and instructions were given him; the matter had been named to him by D'Artagnan, who had, in the first place, pointed out the money to him, then the glory, and then the danger.

"I will carry the letter in the lining of my coat," said Planchet; "and if I am taken I will swallow it."

"Well, but then you will not be able to fulfill your commission," said D'Artagnan.

"You will give me a copy of it this evening, which I shall know by heart before the morning."

D'Artagnan looked at his friends, as if to say, "Well, what did I promise you?"

"Now," continued he, addressing Planchet, "you have eight days to get an interview with Lord de Winter, you have eight days to return in, in all sixteen days; if, on the sixteenth day after your departure, at eight o'clock in the evening, you are not here, no money, even if it be but five minutes past eight——"

"Then, monsieur," said Planchet, "you must buy me a watch."

"Take this," said Athos, with his usual careless generosity, giving him his own, "and be a good lad. Remember, if you talk, if you babble, if you get drunk, you risk your master's head, who has so much confidence in your fidelity, and who answers for you. But remember, also, that if, by your fault, any evil happens to M. D'Artagnan, I will find you, wherever you may be, and that for the purpose of ripping up your belly."

"Oh, monsieur!" said Planchet, humiliated by the suspicion, and, moreover, terrified at the calm air of the musketeer.

"And I," said Porthos, rolling his large eyes, "remember, I will skin you alive."

"Ah! monsieur!"

"And I," said Aramis, with his soft, melodious voice, "remember that I will roast you at a slow fire like a savage."

"Ah! monsieur!"

And Planchet began to weep; we will not venture to say whether it was from terror, created by the threats, or from tenderness, at seeing four friends so closely united.

D'Artagnan took his hand.

"See, Planchet," said he, "these gentlemen only say this out of affection for me; at bottom, they all respect you."

"Ah, monsieur," said Planchet; "I will succeed, or I will consent to be cut in quarters; and if they do cut me in quarters, be assured that not a morsel of me will speak."

It was determined that Planchet should set out the next day, at eight o'clock in the morning, in order, as he had said, that he might, during the night, learn the letter by heart. He gained just twelve hours by this engagement; he was to be back on the sixteenth day, by eight o'clock in the evening.

In the morning, as he was mounting on horseback, D'Artagnan, who felt at the bottom of his heart a partiality for the duke, took Planchet aside.

"Listen," said he to him; "when you have given the letter to Lord de Winter, and he has read it, you will further say to him, 'Watch over His Grace Lord Buckingham, for they wish to assassinate him.' But this, Planchet, is so serious and important, that I have not informed my friends that I would intrust this secret to you; and, for a captain's commission, I would not write it."

"Be satisfied, monsieur," said Planchet, "you shall see whether confidence can be placed in me or not."

And, mounted on an excellent horse, which he was to leave at the end of twenty leagues, to take the post, Planchet set off at a gallop, his spirits a little depressed by the triple promise made him by the musketeers; but otherwise as light-hearted as possible.

Bazin set out the next day for Tours, and was allowed eight days to perform his commission in.

The four friends, during the period of these two absences, had, as may well be supposed, the eye on the watch, the nose to the wind, and the ear on the listen. Their days were passed in endeavoring to catch all that was said, in observing the proceedings of the cardinal, and in looking out for all the couriers that arrived. More than once an involuntary trembling seized them when called upon for any unexpected service. They had, besides, to look constantly to their own proper safety; milady was a phantom which, when it had once appeared to people, did not allow them to sleep very quietly.

On the morning of the eighth day, Bazin, fresh as ever, and smiling according to custom, entered the cabaret of Parpaillot as the four friends were sitting down to breakfast, saying, as had been agreed upon:

"Monsieur Aramis, here is the answer from your cousin."

The four friends exchanged a joyful glance, half of the work was done; it is true, however, that it was the shortest and the most easy part.

Aramis, blushing in spite of himself, took the letter, which was in a large, coarse hand, and not particular for its orthography.

"Good God!" cried he, laughing, "I quite despair of my poor Michon; she will never write like M. de Voiture."

"What do you mean by poor Michon?" said the Swiss, who was chatting with the four friends when the letter arrived.

"Oh, *pardieu!* less than nothing," said Aramis: "a little charming seamstress, whom I love dearly, and from whose hand I requested a few lines as a sort of keepsake."

"The devil!" said the Swiss, "if the lady is as great as her writing is large, you are a lucky fellow, comrade!"

Aramis read the letter, and passed it to Athos.

"See what she writes to me, Athos," said he.

Athos cast a glance over the epistle, and to disperse all the suspicions that might have been created, read aloud:

"My Cousin: My sister and I are skillful in interpreting dreams, and even entertain great fear of them; but of yours it may be said, I hope, every dream is an illusion. Adieu! Take care of yourself; and act so that we may, from time to time, hear you spoken of.   Aglae Michon."

"And what dream does she mean?" asked the dragoon, who had approached during the reading.

"Yes; what's the dream?" said the Swiss.

"Well, *pardieu!*" said Aramis, "it was only this—I had a dream, and I related it to her."

"Yes, yes," said the Swiss; "it's simple enough to relate a dream when you have one; but I never dream."

"You are very fortunate," said Athos, rising; "I wish I could say as much!"

"Never!" replied the Swiss, enchanted that a man like Athos could envy him anything. "Never! never!"

D'Artagnan, seeing Athos rise, did so likewise, took his arm, and went out.

Porthos and Aramis remained behind to encounter the quolibets of the dragoon and the Swiss.

As to Bazin, he went and laid down on a truss of straw; and as he had more imagination than the Swiss, he dreamed that Aramis, having become pope, adorned his head with a cardinal's hat.

But, as we have said, Bazin had not, by his fortunate return, removed more than a part of the uneasiness which weighed upon the four friends. The days of expectation are long, and D'Artagnan, in particular, would have wagered that the days were forty-hour hours long. He forgot the necessary slowness of the navigation, he exaggerated to himself the power of milady. He gave to this woman, who appeared to him equal to a demon, auxiliaries as supernatural as herself; at the least noise, he imagined that he was about to be arrested, and that Planchet was being brought back to be confronted with himself and his friends. Still further; his confidences in the worthy Picard, at one time so great, diminished day by day. This anxiety became so great that it even extended to Aramis and Porthos. Athos alone remained impassible, as if no danger hovered over him, and as if he respired his usual atmosphere.

On the sixteenth day, in particular, these signs were so visible in D'Artagnan and his two friends, that they could not remain quiet in one place, and they wandered about, like ghosts, on the road by which Planchet was expected.

"Really," said Athos, "you are not men, but children, to let a woman terrify you so. And what does it amount to, after all? To be imprisoned. Well, but we should be taken out of prison; Madame Bonacieux got out. To be decapitated? Why, every day in the trenches, we go cheerfully to expose ourselves to worse than that, for a bullet may break a

leg, and I am convinced a surgeon would give us more pain
in cutting off a thigh than an executioner would in cutting
off a head. Wait quietly, then; in two hours, in four, in six
hours at least, Planchet will be here; he promised to be here,
and I have very great faith in Planchet's promises. I think
him a very good lad."

"But if he does not come?" said D'Artagnan.

"Well, if he does not come, it will be because he has been
delayed, that's all. He may have fallen from his horse, he
may have slipped down on the deck, he may have traveled so
fast against the wind as to have produced a violent cold. ·Eh!
gentlemen, let us reckon upon accidents. Life is a chaplet of
little miseries, which the philosopher unstrings with a smile.
Be philosophers, as I am, gentlemen; sit down to the table,
and let us drink; nothing makes the future look so bright as
surveying it through a glass of chambertin."

"That's all very well," replied D'Artagnan, "but I am tired
of fearing, when I open a fresh bottle, that the wine may
come from her ladyship's cellar."

"You are very diffident," said Athos; "such a beautiful
woman!"

"A woman of mark!" said Porthos, with his loud laugh.

Athos started, passed his hand over his brow to remove the
drops of perspiration that burst forth, and rose in his turn
with a nervous movement he could not express.

The day, however, passed away, and the evening came on
slowly, but it did come; the *buvettes* were filled with drinkers.
Athos, who had pocketed his share of the diamond, seldom
quitted the Parpaillot. He had found in M. de Busigny,
who, by the by, had given them a magnificent dinner, a
partner worthy of his company. They were playing together,
as usual, when seven o'clock struck; the patrols were heard
passing to double the posts; at half-past seven the retreat was
sounded.

"We are lost," said D'Artagnan in Athos' ear.

"You mean to say we have lost," said Athos quietly, drawing four pistoles from his pocket, and throwing them on the
table. "Come, gentlemen," said he, "they are beating the
tattoo—to bed, to bed!"

And Athos went out of the Parpaillot, followed by D'Artagnan. Aramis came behind, giving his arm to Porthos.
Aramis mumbled verses to himself, and Porthos, from time
to time, pulled a hair or two from his mustache, in sign of
despair.

But, all at once, a shadow appeared in the darkness, the

outline of which was familiar to D'Artagnan, and a well-known voice said:

"Monsieur, I have brought your cloak; it is chilly this evening."

"Planchet!" cried D'Artagnan, beside himself with joy.

"Planchet!" repeated Aramis and Porthos.

"Well, yes, Planchet, to be sure," said Athos, "what is there so astonishing in that? He promised to be back by eight o'clock, and eight is just now striking. Bravo! Planchet, you are a lad of your word, and if ever you leave your master, I will promise you a place in my service."

"Oh! no, never," said Planchet, "I will never leave M. D'Artagnan."

At the same time D'Artagnan felt that Planchet had slipped a note into his hand.

D'Artagnan felt a strong inclination to embrace Planchet as he had embraced him on his departure; but he feared lest this mark of affection bestowed upon his lackey in the open street might appear extraordinary to passengers, and he restrained himself.

"I have a note," said he to Athos and his friends.

"That's well," said Athos, "let us go home and read it."

The note burned in the hand of D'Artagnan; he wished to increase their speed; but Athos took his arm and passed it under his own, and the young man was forced to regulate his pace by that of his friend.

At length they reached the tent, lit a lamp, and while Planchet stood at the entrance, that the four friends might not be surprised, D'Artagnan, with a trembling hand, broke the seal and opened the so anxiously expected letter.

It contained half a line in a hand perfectly British, and of a conciseness as perfectly Spartan.

"*Thank you, be easy.*"

"Which means what?"

"Thank you, be easy," said D'Artagnan.

Athos took the letter from the hands of D'Artagnan, drew near to the lamp, set fire to it, and did not leave hold of it till it was reduced to ashes.

Then, calling Planchet:

"Now, my lad," said he, "you may claim your seven hundred livres, but you did not run much risk with such a note as that."

"I am not to blame for having tried every means to compress it," said Planchet.

"Well!" cried D'Artagnan, "tell us all about it."

"Lord, monsieur, that's a long job!"

"You are right, Planchet," said Athos; "besides, the tattoo has been sounded, and we should be observed if we kept a light burning longer than the others."

"So be it," said D'Artagnan. "Go to bed, Planchet, and sleep soundly."

"*Ma foi*, monsieur! that will be the first time I have done so these sixteen days!"

"Or I either!" said D'Artagnan.

"Or I either!" said Porthos.

"Or I either!" said Aramis.

"Well! if I must tell you the truth—or I either!" said Athos.

CHAPTER XLIX.

FATALITY.

IN the meantime, milady, drunk with passion, roaring on the deck like a lioness that has been embarked, had been tempted to throw herself into the sea that she might regain the coast, for she could not get rid of the idea that she had been insulted by D'Artagnan, and threatened by Athos, and had left France without being revenged of both. This idea soon became so insupportable to her, that at the risk of whatever terrible consequences might result to herself from it, she implored the captain to put her on shore; but the captain, eager to escape from his false position, placed between French and English cruisers, like that bat between the mice and the birds, was in great haste to gain the coast of England, and positively refused to obey what he took for a woman's caprice, promising his passenger, who had been particularly recommended to him by the cardinal, to land her, if the sea and the French permitted him, at one of the ports of Brittany, either at Lorient or Brest; but the wind was contrary, the sea bad, they laveered, and kept off shore. Nine days after leaving the Charente, pale with fatigue and vexation, milady saw only the blue coasts of Finisterre appear.

She calculated that to cross this corner of France and return to the cardinal, it would take her at least three days; and another day for landing, and it would make four; add these to the nine others, that would be thirteen days lost— thirteen days—during which so many important events might pass in London. She reflected, likewise, that the cardinal would be furious at her return, and, consequently, would be more disposed to listen to the complaints made against her than to the accusations she brought against others.

She allowed the vessel to pass Lorient and Brest without repeating her request to the captain, who, on his part, took care not to remind her of it. Milady, therefore, continued her voyage, and on the very day that Planchet embarked at Portsmouth for France, the messenger of His Eminence entered the port in triumph.

All the city was agitated by an extraordinary movement— four large vessels, recently built, had just been launched. Standing on the jetty, his clothes richly laced with gold, glittering, as was customary with him, with diamonds and precious stones, his hat ornamented with a white feather which drooped upon his shoulder, Buckingham was seen surrounded by a staff almost as brilliant as himself.

It was one of those rare and beautiful days in which England remembers that there is a sun. The star of day, pale, but nevertheless still splendid, was declining toward the horizon, empurpling at once the heavens and the sea with bands of fire, and casting upon the towers and the old houses of the city a last ray of gold, which made the windows sparkle like the reflection of a conflagration. Milady, on respiring that sea breeze, so much more lovely and balsamic as the land is approached, while contemplating all the power of those preparations she was commissioned to destroy, all the power of that army which she was to combat alone—she, a woman— with a few bags of gold, compared herself mentally to Judith, the terrible Jewess, when she penetrated into the camp of the Assyrians, and beheld the enormous mass of chariots, horses, men and arms, which a gesture of her hand was to dissipate like a cloud of smoke.

They entered the road, but as they drew near, in order to cast anchor, a little cutter, formidably armed, approached the merchant vessel, in appearance a coast-guard, and dropping its boat into the sea, the latter directed its course to the ladder. This boat contained an officer, a mate, and eight rowers —the officer alone got on board, where he was received with all the deference inspired by the uniform.

The officer conversed a few instants with the captain, gave him several papers, of which he was the bearer, to read, and, upon the order of the merchant-captain, the whole crew of the vessel, both passengers and sailors, were called upon deck.

When this species of summons was made, the officer inquired aloud the point of the brig's departure, of its route, of its landings, and to all these questions the captain replied without difficulty and without hesitation. Then the officer began to pass in review all the persons, one after the other, and stopping when he came to milady, surveyed her very closely, but without addressing a single word to her.

He then went up to the captain, again said a few words to him; and, as if from that moment the vessel was under his command, he ordered a maneuver which the crew executed immediately. Then the vessel resumed its course, still escorted by the little cutter, which sailed side by side with it, menacing it with the mouths of its six cannon; the boat followed in the wake of the ship, a speck near the enormous mass.

During the examination of milady by the officer, as may well be imagined, milady, on her part, was not less scrutinizing in her glances. But, however great was the power of this woman, with eyes of flame, in reading the hearts of those whose secrets she wished to divine, she met this time with a countenance of such impassibility, that no discovery followed her investigation. The officer who had stopped before her, and studied her with so much care, might have been about twenty-five or twenty-six years of age; he was of pale complexion, with clear blue eyes, rather deeply set; his mouth, fine and well cut, remained motionless in its correct lines; his chin, strongly marked, denoted that strength of will which, in the ordinary Britannic type, denotes mostly nothing but obstinacy; a brow a little receding, as is proper for poets, enthusiasts, and soldiers, was scarcely shaded by short thin hair, which, like the beard which covered the lower part of his face, was of a beautiful, deep chestnut color.

When they entered the port, it was already night. The fog increased the darkness, and formed round the stern lights and the lanterns of the jetty a circle like that which surrounds the moon when the weather threatens to become rainy. The air they breathed was heavy, humid, and cold.

Milady, that woman so courageous and firm, shivered in spite of herself.

The officer desired to have milady's packages pointed out to him, and ordered them to be placed in the boat: when this operation was completed, he invited her to descend by offering her his hand.

Milady looked at this man, and hesitated.

"Who are you, sir," asked she, "who have the kindness to occupy yourself so particularly on my account?"

"You may perceive, madame, by my uniform, that I am an officer in the English navy," replied the young man.

"But is it the custom for the officers in the English navy to place themselves at the service of their female compatriots, when they land in a port of Great Britain, and carry their gallantry so far as to conduct them ashore?"

"Yes, milady, it is the custom, not from gallantry but prudence, that in time of war, foreigners are conducted to particular hotels, in order that they may remain under the *surveillance* of the government, until perfect information be obtained relative to them."

These words were pronounced with the most exact politeness, and the most perfect calmness. Nevertheless, they had not the power of convincing milady.

"But I am not a foreigner, sir," said she, with an accent as pure as ever was heard between Portsmouth and Manchester; "my name is Lady Clarik, and this measure——"

"This measure is general, madame; and you will endeavor in vain to evade it."

"I will follow you, then, sir."

And accepting the hand of the officer, she commenced the descent of the ladder, at the foot of which the boat waited. The officer followed her. A large cloak was spread at the stern; the officer requested her to sit down upon this cloak, and placed himself beside her.

"Row on!" said he, to the sailors.

The eight oars fell at once into the sea, making but one single sound, giving one single stroke, and the boat seemed to fly over the surface of the waters.

At the expiration of five minutes they gained the land.

The officer sprang out of the boat, and offered his hand to milady. A carriage was in waiting.

"Is this carriage for us?" asked milady.

"Yes, madame," replied the officer.

"The hotel, then, is at some distance?"

"At the other end of the town."

"Very well," said milady; and she got resolutely into the carriage. The officer saw that the baggage was fastened carefully behind the carriage; and this operation being performed, he took his place beside milady, and shut the door.

Immediately, without any order being given, or his place of destination indicated, the coachman set off at a rapid pace, and plunged into the streets of the town.

So strange a reception naturally gave milady ample matter for reflection; so, seeing that the young officer did not seem

at all disposed for conversation, she reclined in her corner of the
carriage; and, one after the other, passed in review all
the suppositions which presented themselves to her mind.

At the end of a quarter of an hour, however, surprised at
the length of the journey, she leaned forward toward the
window to see whither she was being conducted.   Houses were
no longer to be seen; trees appeared in the darkness like great
black phantoms running after one another.

Milady shuddered with apprehension.

"But we are no longer in the town, sir," said she.

The young officer preserved profound silence.

"I beg you to understand, sir, I will go no further, unless
you tell me whither you are taking me."

This threat obtained no reply.

"Oh; but this is outrageous!" cried milady.   "Help! help!
help!"

No voice replied to hers; the carriage continued to roll on
with rapidity; the officer appeared a statue.

Milady looked at the officer with one of those terrible expressions peculiar to her countenance, and which so rarely
failed of their effect; anger made her eyes flash in the
darkness.

The young man remained impassible.

Milady endeavored to open the door, in order to throw herself out.

"Take care, madame," said the young man coldly, "you
will kill yourself if you attempt to jump out."

Milady reseated herself, foaming with rage; the officer
leaned forward, looked at her in his turn, and appeared surprised to see that face, but just before so beautiful, distorted
with passion and become almost hideous.   The artful creature
at once comprehended that she was injuring herself by allowing him thus to read her soul; she collected her features, and
in a complaining voice said:

"In the name of heaven, sir! tell me if it is to you, if it is
to your government, if it is to an enemy I am to attribute
the violence that is done me?"

"No violence will be offered to you, madame, and what
happens to you is the result of a very simple measure which
we are obliged to adopt with all who land in England."

"Then you don't know me, sir?"

"It is the first time I have had the honor of seeing you."

"And, upon your honor, you have no cause of hatred against
me?"

"None, I swear to you."

There was so much serenity, coolness, mildness even, in the voice of the young man, that milady felt reassured.

At length, after a journey of near an hour, the carriage stopped before an iron gate, which enclosed an avenue leading to a château, severe in form, massive and isolated. Then, as the wheels rolled over a fine gravel, milady could hear a vast roaring; which she at once recognized as the noise of the sea, dashing against some steep coast.

The carriage passed under two arched gateways, and at length stopped in a large, dark, square court; almost immediately, the door of the carriage was opened, the young man sprang lightly out and presented his hand to milady, who leaned upon it, and in her turn alighted with tolerable calmness.

"Still, then, I am a prisoner," said milady, looking around her, and bringing back her eyes with a most gracious smile to the young officer; "but I feel assured it will not be for long," added she; "my own conscience and your politeness, sir, are the guarantees of that."

However flattering this compliment was, the officer made no reply; but drawing from his belt a little silver whistle, such as boatswains use in ships of war, he whistled three times, with three different modulations: immediately several men appeared, who unharnessed the smoking horses, and put the carriage into a coach-house.

The officer then, with the same calm politeness, invited the lady to enter the house. She, with a still smiling countenance, took his arm, and passed with him under a low arched door, which, by a vaulted passage, lighted only at the farther end, led to a stone staircase, turning round an angle of stone: they then came to a massive door, which, after the introduction of a key into the lock, by the young officer, turned heavily upon its hinges, and disclosed the chamber destined for milady.

With a single glance the prisoner took in the apartment in its minutest details. It was a chamber whose furniture was at once proper for a prisoner or a free man; and yet, bars at the windows and outside bolts at the door decided the question in favor of the prison.

In an instant all the strength of mind of this creature, though drawn from the most vigorous sources, abandoned her; she sank into a large chair, with her arms crossed, her head hanging down, and expecting every instant to see a judge enter to interrogate her.

But no one entered except two marines, who brought in

her trunks and packages, deposited them in a corner of the room, and retired without speaking.

The officer presided over all these details with the same calmness milady had observed in him, never pronouncing a word, and making himself obeyed by a gesture of his hand or a sound of his whistle.

It might have been said that between this man and his inferiors spoken language did not exist, or had become useless.

At length milady could hold out no longer; she broke the silence:

"In the name of heaven, sir!" cried she, "what does all this that is passing mean? Put an end to my doubts; I have courage enough for any danger I can forsee, for every misfortune which I can comprehend. Where am I, and why am I here? if I am free, why these bars and these doors? If I am a prisoner, what crime have I committed?"

"You are here in the apartment destined for you, madame. I received orders to go and take charge of you at sea, and to conduct you to this château; this order I believe I have accomplished, with all the exactness of a soldier, but also with the courtesy of a gentleman. There terminates, at least to the present moment, the duty I had to fulfill toward you, the rest concerns another person."

"And who is that other person?" asked milady warmly; "can you not tell me his name?"

At the moment a great jingling of spurs was heard upon the stairs; some voices passed, and faded away, and the sound of one footstep approached the door.

"That person is here, madam," said the officer, leaving the entrance open, and drawing himself up in an attitude of respect.

At the same time the door opened; a man appeared in the opening. He was without a hat, wore a sword, and carried a handkerchief in his hand.

Milady thought she recognized this shadow in the shade; she supported herself with one hand upon the arm of the chair, and advanced her head as if to meet a certainty.

The stranger advanced slowly, and as he advanced, after entering into the circle of light projected by the lamp, milady involuntarily drew back.

Then, when she had no longer any doubt:

"What! my brother," cried she, in a state of stupor, "is it you?"

"Yes, fair lady!" replied Lord de Winter, making a bow, half courteous, half ironical: "it is I, myself."

"But this Château, then?"

"Is mine."

"This chamber?"

"Is yours."

"I am your prisoner, then?"

"Nearly so."

"But this is a frightful abuse of power!"

"No high-sounding words! let us sit down and chat qui-etly, as brother and sister ought to do."

Then, turning toward the door, and seeing that the young officer was waiting for his last orders:

"That is all quite well," said he, "I thank you; now leave us alone, Master Felton."

CHAPTER L.

CHAT BETWEEN BROTHER AND SISTER.

DURING the time that Lord de Winter took to shut the door, close a shutter, and draw a chair near his sister-in-law's *fauteuil,* milady, anxiously thoughtful, plunged her glance into the depths of possibility, and discovered all the plan, of which she could not even get a glance as long as she was igno-rant into whose hands she had fallen. She knew her brother to be a worthy gentleman, a bold hunter, and intrepid player, enterprising with women, but by no means remarkable for his skill in the business of intrigues. How had he discovered her arrival? caused her to be seized? Why did he detain her?

Athos had dropped some words which proved that the con-versation she had had with the cardinal had fallen into strange ears; but she could not suppose that he had dug a counter mine so promptly and so boldly. She rather feared that her preceding operations in England might have been discovered. Buckingham might have guessed that it was she who had cut off the two studs, and avenged himself for that little treachery; but Buckingham was incapable of going to any excess against a woman, particularly if that woman was supposed to have acted from a feeling of jealousy.

This supposition appeared to her the most reasonable; it seemed that they wanted to revenge the past, and not to go to meet the future. At all events, she congratulated herself upon having fallen into the hands of her brother-in-law, with

whom she reckoned she could deal very easily, rather than
into the hands of a direct and intelligent enemy.

"Yes, let us chat, brother," said she, with a kind of cheerfulness, decided as she was to draw from the conversation, in
spite of all the dissimulation Lord de Winter could bring to
it, the information of which she stood in need to regulate her
future conduct.

"You were, then, determined to come to England again,"
said Lord de Winter, "in spite of the resolutions you so often
manifested in Paris never to set your foot more on British
ground?"

Milady replied to this question by another question.

"Before everything," said she, "how happen you to have
watched me so closely, as to be beforehand aware, not only of
my arrival, but still more, of the day, the hour, and the port,
at which I should arrive?"

Lord de Winter adopted the same tactics as milady, thinking that as his sister-in-law employed them they must be the
best.

"But tell me, my dear sister," replied he, "what are you
come to do in England?"

"Come for! why to see you," replied milady, without
knowing how much she aggravated, by this reply, the suspicions which D'Artagnan's letter had given birth to in the
mind of her brother-in-law, and only desiring to gain the
good will of her auditor by a falsehood.

"Humph! to see me?" said De Winter, as if doubtingly.

"To be sure, to see you. What is there astonishing in
that?"

"And you had no other object in coming to England but
to see me?"

"No."

"So it was for my sake alone you have taken the trouble to
cross the channel?"

"For your sake only."

"The deuce! what tenderness, my sister!"

"Why, am I not your nearest relation?" demanded milady,
with a tone of the most touching ingenuousness.

"And my only heir, are you not?" said Lord de Winter in
his turn, fixing his eyes on those of milady.

Whatever command she had over herself, milady could not
help starting, and as, in pronouncing the last words, Lord de
Winter placed his hand upon the arm of his sister, this start
did not escape him.

In fact, the blow was direct and severe. The first idea

that occurred to milady's mind was that she had been betrayed
by Kitty, and that she had described to the baron the interested aversion of which she had imprudently allowed some
marks to escape her before her servant; she also recollected
the furious and imprudent attack she had made upon D'Artagnan when he spared the life of her brother.

"I do not comprehend, my lord," said she, to gain time
and make her adversary speak out. "What do you mean to
say? Is there any secret meaning concealed beneath your
words?"

"Oh! good lord! no," said Lord de Winter, with an apparent *bonhomie,* "you wish to see me, and you come to England.
I learn this desire, or rather I suspect that you feel it, and,
in order to spare you all the annoyances of a nocturnal arrival
in a port, and all the fatigues of landing, I send one of my
officers to meet you, I place a carriage at his orders, and he
brings you hither to this castle, of which I am governor,
whither I come every day, and where, in order to satisfy our
mutual desire of seeing each other, I have prepared you a
chamber. What is there more astonishing in all that I have
said to you, than in that which you have told me?"

"No, all that I think astonishing is that you should be
aware of my coming."

"And yet that is the most simple thing in the world, my
dear sister: have you not observed that the captain of your
little vessel, on entering the road, sent forward, to obtain
permission to enter the port, a little boat bearing his log-book
and the register of his crew? I am commandant of the port;
they brought me that book. I recognized your name in it.
My heart told me what your mouth has just confirmed, that
is to say, with what views you have exposed yourself to the
dangers of so perilous a sea, or at least, so troublesome at this
moment, and I sent my cutter to meet you. You know the
rest."

Milady comprehended that Lord de Winter lied, and was
only the more alarmed.

"Brother," continued she, "was not that Milord Buckingham whom I saw on the jetty, this evening, as we entered
the port?"

"Himself. Ah! I can understand how the sight of him
struck you," replied Lord de Winter: "you came from a
country where he must be very much talked of, and I know
that his armaments against France greatly engaged the attention of your friend the cardinal."

"My friend the cardinal!" cried milady, seeing that, upon

this point as upon the other, Lord de Winter seemed perfectly well informed.

"Is he not your friend?" replied the baron negligently; "ah! I crave your pardon, I thought he was; but we will return to my lord duke presently, let us not depart from the sentimental turn our conversation had taken: you came, you say, to see me?"

"Yes."

"Well! I reply to you that you shall be attended to to the height of your wishes, and that we shall see each other every day."

"Am I then to remain here eternally?" demanded milady with terror.

"Do you find yourself ill-lodged, sister? Ask for anything you want, and I will hasten to have you furnished with it."

"But I have neither my women, nor my servants."

"You shall have all that, madame. Tell me on what footing your household was established by your first husband, and, although I am only your brother-in-law, I will arrange it upon a similar one."

"My first husband!" cried milady, looking at Lord de Winter, with eyes almost starting from their sockets.

"Yes, your French husband; I don't speak of my brother. If you have forgotten, as he is still living, I can write to him, and he will send me information on the subject."

A cold sweat burst from the brow of milady.

"You are joking!" said she in a hollow, broken voice.

"Do I look as if I were?" asked the baron, rising and going a step backward.

"Or rather you insult me," continued she, pressing with her stiffened hands the two arms of her chair, and raising herself up upon her wrists.

"I insult you!" said Lord de Winter with contempt; "in truth, madam, do you think that can be possible?"

"In truth, sir," said milady, "you must be either drunk or mad: leave the room, sir, and send me a woman."

"Women are very indiscreet, sister! cannot I serve you as a waiting maid? by that means, all our secrets would be kept in the family."

"Insolent wretch!" cried milady, and, as if acted upon by a spring, she rushed toward the baron, who awaited her attack with his arms crossed, but one hand upon the hilt of his sword.

"Come! come!" said he, "I know you are accustomed to

assassinate people, but I shall defend myself, I give you notice, even against you."

"No doubt you would!" said she; "you have all the appearance of being coward enough to lift your hand against a woman."

"Perhaps I have, and I have an excuse, for mine would not be the first man's hand that has been placed upon you, I imagine."

And the baron pointed with a slow accusing gesture to the left shoulder of milady, which he almost touched with his finger.

Milady uttered a deep inward shriek, and retreated to a corner of the room, like a panther which draws back to take its spring.

"Oh! groan and shriek as much as you please," cried Lord de Winter, "but don't try to bite, for I warn you the thing would be to your prejudice; there are here no procureurs who regulate successions beforehand; there is no knight-errant to come and seek a quarrel with me, on account of the fair lady I detain a prisoner; but I have judges quite ready, who will quickly dispose of a woman so shameless, as, although already married, to come and steal, a bigamist, into the bed of my brother, and these judges, I warn you, will soon pass you over to a hangman that will make both your shoulders alike."

The eyes of milady darted such flashes, that although he was a man, and armed, before an unarmed woman, he felt the chill of fear glide through his whole frame; he, however, not the less continued, but with increasing warmth:

"Yes, I can very well understand that after having inherited the fortune of my brother, it would be very agreeable to you to be my heir likewise; but know, beforehand, if you kill me, or cause me to be killed, my precautions are taken: not a penny of what I posses will pass into your hands. Were you not already rich enough, you who possess nearly a million? and could you not stop your fatal career, if you did not do evil for the supreme delight of doing it? Oh! be assured, if the memory of my brother were not sacred to me, you should rot in a state dungeon, or satisfy the curiosity of sailors at Tyburn: I will be silent, but you must endure your captivity quietly: in fifteen or twenty days I shall set out for La Rochelle, with the army; but before my departure, a vessel which I will see sail, will take you hence and convey you to our colonies of the south; and be assured that you shall be accompanied by one who will blow your brains out at the first attempt you may make to return to England or to the continent."

Milady listened with an attention that dilated her inflamed eyes.

"Yes, at present," continued Lord de Winter, "you will remain in this castle: the walls of it are thick, the doors strong, and the bars solid; besides which your window opens immediately over the sea: the men of my crew, who are devoted to me for life and death, mount guard around this apartment, and watch all the passages that lead to the castle-yard; and even if you gained the yard, there would still be three iron gates for you to pass through. The word given is positive; a step, a gesture, a word, on your part, denoting an effort to escape, and you are to be fired upon; if they kill you, English justice will be under an obligation to me for having saved it trouble. Ah! I see your features are resuming their calmness, your countenance is recovering its assurance: fifteen days, twenty days, say you, bah! I have an inventive mind, before that is expired some idea will occur to me; I have an infernal spirit, I shall meet with a victim. Before fifteen days are gone by, you say to yourself, I shall be away, from here! Well try!"

Milady, finding her thoughts betrayed, dug her nails into her flesh to subdue every emotion that might give to her physiognomy any expression beyond that of pain.

Lord de Winter continued:

"The officer who commands here in my absence you have already seen, and therefore know him; he knows how, as you must have observed, to obey an order, for you did not, I am sure, come from Portsmouth hither without endeavoring to make him speak. What did you say to him? Could a statue of marble have been more impassable and more mute? You have already tried the power of your seductions upon many men, and, unfortunately, you have always succeeded; but I give you leave to try them upon this one: *pardieu!* if you succeed with him, I pronounce you the demon himself."

He went toward the door and opened it hastily.

"Call Master Felton," said he. "Wait a minute longer, and I will introduce him to you."

There followed between these two personages a strange silence, during which the sound of a slow and regular step was heard approaching; shortly a human form appeared in the shade of the corridor, and the young lieutenant, with whom we are already acquainted, stopped at the door, to receive the orders of the baron.

"Come in, my dear John," said Lord de Winter, "come in, and shut the door."

The young officer entered.

"Now," said the baron, "look at this woman: she is young, she is beautiful, she possesses all earthly seductions. Well, she is a monster, who, at twenty-five years of age, has been guilty of as many crimes as you could read of in a year in the archives of our tribunals: her voice prejudices her hearers in her favor, her beauty serves as a bait to her victims, her body even pays what she promises—I must do her that justice: she will endeavor to seduce you, perhaps she will endeavor to kill you. I have extricated you from misery, Felton, I have caused you to be named lieutenant, I once saved your life, you know on what occasion; I am for you not only a protector, but a friend; not only a benefactor, but a father; this woman is come back again into England for the purpose of conspiring against my life; I hold this serpent in my power; well! I call upon you, and say to you: Friend Felton, John, my child, guard me, and more particularly guard yourself against this woman: swear by your hopes of salvation to keep her safely for the chastisement she has merited. John Felton, I trust in thy word! John Felton, I put faith in thy loyalty!"

"My lord," said the young officer, summoning to his mild countenance all the hatred he could find in his heart; "my lord, I swear all shall be done as you desire."

Milady received this look like a resigned victim: it was impossible to imagine a more submissive or a more mild expression than that which prevailed on her beautiful countenance. Lord de Winter himself could scarcely recognize the tigress who, a minute before, appeared preparing for fight.

"She is not to leave this chamber, understand, John; she is not to correspond with any one, she is to speak to no one but you—if you will do her the honor to address a word to her."

"That is quite sufficient, my lord! I have sworn."

"And now madame, try to make your peace with God, for you are adjudged by men!"

Milady let her head sink, as if crushed by this sentence. Lord de Winter went out, making a sign to Felton, who followed him, shutting the door after him.

One instant after, the heavy step of a marine was heard in the corridor; his axe in his girdle and his musket on his shoulder, he commenced his watch.

Milady remained for some minutes in the same position,

for she thought they might perhaps be examining her through the keyhole; she then slowly raised her head, which had resumed its formidable expression of menace and defiance, ran to the door to listen, looked out of her window, and, returning to bury herself again in her large *fauteuil*—

She reflected.

CHAPTER LI.

OFFICER.

IN the meanwhile, the cardinal looked anxiously for news from England; but no news arrived but such as were annoying and threatening.

Although La Rochelle was invested, however certain success might appear, thanks to the precautions taken, and above all to the dyke, which prevented the entrance of any vessel into the besieged city, the blockade might last for a long time yet; which was a great affront to the king's arms, and a great inconvenience to the cardinal, who had no longer, it is true, to embroil Louis XIII. with Anne of Austria, for that affair was done, but he had to accomodate matters between M. de Bassompierre and the Duke d'Angoulême.

As to monsieur, who had begun the siege, he left to the cardinal the task of finishing it.

The city, notwithstanding the incredible perseverance of its mayor, had attempted a sort of mutiny to surrender; the mayor had hung the mutineers. This execution quieted the ill-disposed, who resolved to allow themselves to die of hunger, this death always appearing to them more slow and less sure than strangulation.

On their side, from time to time, the besiegers took the messengers which the Rochellais sent to Buckingham, or the spies which Buckingham sent to the Rochellais. In one case or the other, the trial was soon over. M. le Cardinal pronounced the single word—hanged! The king was invited to come and see the hanging. The king came languidly, placing himself in a good situation to see all the details: this amused him sometimes a little, and made him endure the siege with patience; but it did not prevent his getting very tired, or from talking at every moment of returning to Paris; so that if the messengers and the spies had failed, his eminence, notwithstanding all his imagination, would have found himself very much embarrassed.

Nevertheless, time passed on, and the Rochellais did not surrender; the last spy that was taken was the bearer of a letter. This letter told Buckingham that the city was at an extremity; but instead of adding, "If your succor does not arrive within fifteen days, we will surrender," it added, quite simply, "If your succor does not arrive within fifteen days, we shall be all dead with hunger when it does arrive."

The Rochellais, then, had no hope but in Buckingham—Buckingham was their Messiah. It was evident that if they one day learned in a certain manner that they must not reckon upon Buckingham, their courage would fail with ther hope.

He looked, then, with great impatience for the news from England which would announce to him that Buckingham would not come.

The question of carrying the city by assault, though often debated in the council of the king, had been always rejected.

In the first place, La Rochelle appeared impregnable; then the cardinal, whatever he might have said, very well knew that the horror of the blood shed in this rencounter, in which Frenchmen would combat against Frenchmen, was a retrograde movement of sixty years impressed upon his policy, and the cardinal was at that period what we now call a man of progress. In fact, the sacking of La Rochelle, and the assassination of three or four thousand insurgents who would allow themselves to be killed, would resemble too closely, in 1628, the Massacre of St. Bartholomew in 1572; and then, above all this, this extreme measure, to which the king, good Catholic as he was, was not at all repugnant, always fell before this argument of the besieging generals—La Rochelle is impregnable except by famine.

The cardinal could not drive from his mind the fear he entertained of his terrible emissary, for he comprehended the strange qualities of this woman, sometimes a serpent, sometimes a lion. Had she betrayed him? Was she dead? He knew her well enough in all cases to know that, while acting for him or against him, as a friend or an enemy, she would not remain motionless without great impediments; but whence did these impediments arise? That was what he could not know.

And yet he reckoned, and with reason, on milady. He had divined in the past of this woman the terrible things which his red mantle alone could cover; and he felt that, from one cause or another, this woman was his own, as she could look to no other but himself for a support superior to the danger which threatened her.

He resolved, then, to carry on the war alone, and to look for no success foreign to himself, but as we look for a fortunate chance. He continued to press the raising of the famous dyke, which was to starve La Rochelle; in the meanwhile, he cast his eyes over that unfortunate city, which contained so much deep misery and so many heroic virtues, and recalling the saying of Louis XI., his political predecessor, as he himself was the predecessor of Robespierre, he repeated this maxim of Tristan's gossip: "Divide to reign."

Henry IV., when besieging Paris had loaves and provisions thrown over the walls; the cardinal had little notes thrown over, in which he represented to the Rochellais how unjust, selfish, and barbarous was the conduct of their leaders; these leaders had corn in abundance, and would not let them partake of it; they adopted as a maxim—for they, too, had maxims—that it was of very little consequence that women, children, and old men should die, so long as the men who were to defend the walls remained strong and healthy. Up to that time, whether from devotedness, or from want of power to react against it, this maxim, without being generally adopted, was, nevertheless, passed from theory to practice; but the notes did it injury. The notes reminded the men that the children, women, and old men whom they allowed to die, were their sons, their wives, and their fathers; and that it would be more just for every one to be reduced to the common misery, in order that one same position should give birth to unanimous resolutions.

These notes had all the effect that he who wrote them could expect, in that they induced a great number of the inhabitants to open private negotiations with the royal army.

But at the moment when the cardinal saw his means already fructify, and applauded himself for having put it in action, an inhabitant of Rochelle, who had contrived to pass the royal lines, God knows how, such was the watchfulness of Bassompierre, Schomberg, and the Duke d'Angoulême, themselves watched over by the cardinal—an inhabitant of Rochelle, we say, entered the city, coming from Portsmouth, and saying, that he had seen a magnificent fleet ready to sail within a week. Still further, Buckingham announced to the mayor, that at length the great league was about to declare itself against France, and that the kingdom would be at once invaded by the English, Imperial and Spanish armies. This letter was read publicly in all the places of the city, copies

were put up at the corners of the streets, and they even who
had begun to open negotiations interrupted them, being resolved to await the succor so pompously announced.

This unexpected circumstance brought back Richelieu's
former inquietudes, and forced him, in spite of himself, once
more to turn his eyes to the other side of the sea.

During this time, exempt from these inquietudes of its
only and true leader, the royal army led a joyous life, neither
provisions nor money being wanting in the camp; all the
corps rivaled each other in audacity and gayety. To take
spies and hang them, to make hazardous expeditions upon
the dyke or the sea, to imagine wild plans, and to execute
them coolly, such was the pastime which made the army find
these days short, which were not only so long for the Rochellais, a prey to famine and anxiety, as even for the cardinal,
who blockaded them so closely.

Sometimes when the cardinal, always on horseback, like
the lowest gendarme of the army, cast a pensive glance over
those works, so slowly keeping pace with his wishes, which
the engineers, brought from all the corners of France, were
executing under his orders, if he met a musketeer of the
company of Tréville, he drew near and looked at him in a
peculiar manner, and not recognizing in him one of our four
companions, he turned his penetrating look and profound
thoughts in another direction.

One day, on which, oppressed with a mortal weariness of
mind, without hope in the negotiations with the city, without
news from England, the cardinal went out, without any other
aim but to go out, accompanied only by Cahusac and La
Houdinière, strolling along the beach. Mingling the immensity of his dreams with the immensity of the ocean, he
arrived, his horse going at a foot's pace, on a hill, from the
top of which he perceived, behind a hedge, reclining on the
sand, and catching in its passage one of those rays of the sun
so rare at this period of the year, seven men surrounded by
empty bottles. Four of these men were our musketeers, preparing to listen to a letter one of them had just received.
This letter was so important that it made them abandon
their cards and their dice on the drum-head.

The other three were occupied in opening an enormous
flagon of Collicure wine; these were the lackeys of these
gentlemen.

The cardinal was, as we have said, in very low spirits, and
nothing, when he was in that state of mind, increased his
depression so much as gayety in others. Besides, he had

another strange fancy, which was always to believe that the causes of his sadness created the gayety of others. Making a sign to La Houdinière and Cahusac to stop, he alighted from his horse, and went toward these suspected merry companions, hoping, by means of the sand which deadened the sound of his steps, and of the hedge which concealed his approach, to catch some words of this conversation which appeared so interesting; at ten paces from the hedge he recognized the talkative Gascon, and as he had already perceived that these men were musketeers, he did not doubt that the three others were those called the inseparables, that is to say, Athos, Porthos, and Aramis.

It may be supposed that his desire to hear the conversation was augmented by this discovery; his eyes took a strange expression, and with the step of a tiger-cat, he advanced toward the hedge; but he had not been able to catch more than a few vague syllables without any positive sense, when a sonorous and short cry made him start, and attracted the attention of the musketeers.

"Officer!" cried Grimaud.

"You are speaking, you scoundrel!" said Athos, rising upon his elbow, and fascinating Grimaud with his angry look.

Grimaud therefore added nothing to his speech, but contented himself with pointing his index finger in the direction of the hedge, denouncing by his gesture the cardinal and his escort.

With a single bound the musketeers were on their feet, and saluted with respect.

The cardinal seemed furious.

"It appears that messieurs the musketeers keep guard," said he. "Are the English expected by land, or do the musketeers consider themselves superior officers?"

"Monseigneur," replied Athos, for, amid the general fright he alone had preserved the noble calmness and coolness that never forsook him—"monseigneur, the musketeers, when they are not on duty, or when their duty is over, drink and play at dice, and they are certainly superior officers for their lackeys."

"Lackeys!" grumbled the cardinal; "lackeys, who have the word given to warn their masters when any one passes, are not lackeys, they are sentinels."

"Your eminence may perceive that, if we had not taken this precaution, we should have been exposed to allowing you to pass without presenting you our respects, or offering you our thanks, for the favor you have done us in uniting us.

D'Artagnan," continued Athos, "you, who but lately were so anxious for such an opportunity for expressing your thanks to monseigneur, here it is, avail yourself of it."

These words were pronounced with that imperturbable phlegm which distinguished Athos in the hour of danger, and with that excessive politeness which made of him, at certain moments, a king more majestic than kings by birth.

D'Artagnan came forward and stammered out a few words of gratitude, which soon expired under the gloomy looks of the cardinal.

"It does not signify, gentlemen," continued the cardinal, without appearing to be in the least diverted from his first intention by the incident which Athos had started—"it does not signify, gentlemen; I do not like simple soldiers, because they have the advantage of serving in a privileged corps, thus to play the great lords; discipline is the same for them as for everybody else."

Athos allowed the cardinal to finish his sentence completely, and, bowing in sign of assent, he resumed in his turn:

"Discipline, monseigneur, has, I hope, in no way been forgotten by us. We are not on duty, and we believed that not being on duty we were at liberty to dispose of our time as we pleased. If we are so fortunate as to have some particular duty to perform for your eminence, we are ready to obey you. Your eminence may perceive," continued Athos, knitting his brow, for this sort of investigation began to annoy him, "that we have not come out without our arms."

And he showed the cardinal, with his finger, the four muskets, piled near the drum upon which were the cards and dice.

"Your eminence may believe," added D'Artagnan, "that we would have come to meet you, if we could have supposed it was monseigneur coming toward us with so few attendants."

The cardinal bit his mustache, and even his lips a little.

"Do you know what you look like, all together, as you are, armed, and guarded by your lackeys?" said the cardinal: "you look like four conspirators."

"Oh! so far, monseigneur, that's true," said Athos; "we do conspire, as your eminence might have seen the other day, only we conspire against the Rochellais."

"Ay! ay! *messieurs les politiques!*" replied the cardinal, knitting his brow in his turn, "the secret of many unknown things might perhaps be found in your brains, if we could read in them, as you were reading that letter which you concealed as soon as you saw me coming."

The color mounted to the face of Athos, and he made a step toward his eminence.

"We might be led to think that you really suspected us, monseigneur, and that we were undergoing a real interrogatory; if it be so, we trust your eminence will deign to explain yourself, and we should then at least be acquainted with our real position."

"And if it were an interrogatory," replied the cardinal, "others besides you have undergone such, Monsieur Athos and have replied to them."

"Thus, I have told your eminence that you had but to question us, and we are ready to reply."

"What was that letter you were about to read, Monsieur Aramis, and which you so promptly concealed?"

"A woman's letter, monseigneur."

"Ah! yes, I understand, we must be discreet with this sort of letter; but nevertheless, we may show them to a confessor, and, you know, I have taken orders."

"Monseigneur," said Athos, with a calmness the more terrible, from his risking his head when he made this reply, "the letter is a woman's letter, but it is neither signed Marion de Lorme, nor Madame d'Arguillon."

The cardinal became as pale as death; a fiery gleam darted from his eyes; he turned round as if to give an order to Cahusac and Houdinière. Athos saw the movement; he made a step toward the muskets, upon which the other three friends had fixed their eyes as men ill-disposed to allow themselves to be taken. The cardinal's party consisted of only three; the musketeers, lackeys included, numbered seven; he judged that the match would be so much the less equal, if Athos and his companions were really plotting; and by one of those rapid turns which he always had at command, all his anger faded away into a smile.

"Well! well!" said he, "you are brave young men, proud in daylight, faithful in darkness; we can find no fault with you for watching over yourselves, when you watch so carefully over others. Gentlemen, I have not forgotten the night in which you served me as an escort to the Colombier Rouge: if there were any danger to be apprehended on the road I am going, I would request you to accompany me; but as there is none, remain where you are, finish your bottles, your game, and your letter. Adieu, gentlemen!"

And remounting his horse, which Cahusac led to him, he saluted them with his hand, and rode away.

The four young men, standing and motionless, followed

him with their eyes, without speaking a single word, until he had disappeared.

Then they looked at each other.

The countenances of all gave evidence of terror; for, notwithstanding the friendly adieu of his eminence, they plainly perceived that the cardinal went away with rage in his heart.

Athos alone smiled with a self-possessed, disdainful smile.

When the cardinal was out of hearing and sight:

"That Grimaud kept bad watch!" cried Porthos, who had a great inclination to vent his ill-humor on somebody.

Grimaud was about to reply to excuse himself. Athos lifted his finger, and Grimaud was silent.

"Would you have given up the letter, Aramis?" said D'Artagnan.

"I!" said Aramis, in his most flute-like tone; "I had made up my mind; if he had insisted upon the letter being given up to him, I would have presented the letter to him with one hand, and with the other I would have run my sword through his body."

"I expected as much," said Athos; "and that was why I threw myself between you and him. In good truth, this man is very much to blame to talk in this manner to other men; one would say he had never had to do with any but women and children."

"My dear Athos, I admire your behavior very much, but nevertheless, we were in the wrong, after all."

"How, in the wrong!" said Athos. "Whose, then, is the air we breathe? Whose is the ocean upon which we look? Whose is the sand upon which we were reclining? Whose is that letter of your mistress? Do these belong to the cardinal? Upon my honor, this man fancies the world belongs to him; there you stood, stammering, stupefied, annihilated! one might have supposed that the Bastille appeared before you, and that the gigantic Medusa had converted you into stone. Is being in love conspiring? You are in love with a woman whom the cardinal has caused to be shut up, and you wish to get her out of the hands of his eminence; that's a match you are playing with the cardinal: this letter is your game, why should you expose your game to your adversary? That is never done. Let him find it out if he can! We can find out his!"

"Well, that's all very sensible, Athos," said D'Artagnan.

"In that case, let there be no more question of what's past, and let Aramis resume the letter from his cousin, where the cardinal interrupted him."

Aramis drew the letter from h ispocket, the three friends surrounded him, and the three lackeys grouped themselves again near the wine-jar.

"You had only read a line or two," said D'Artagnan; "begin the letter again, then."

"Willingly," said Aramis.

"MY DEAR COUSIN : I think I shall make up my mind to set out for Stenay, where my sister has placed our little servant in the convent of the Carmelites; this poor child is quite resigned, as she knows she cannot live elsewhere without the salvation of her soul being in danger. Nevertheless, if the affairs of your family are arranged, as we hope they will be, I believe she will run the risk of being damned, and will return to those she regrets, particularly as she knows they are always thinking of her. In the meanwhile, she is not very wretched; what she most desires is a letter from her intended. I know that such sort of provisions pass with difficulty through convent gratings; but after all, as I have given you proofs, my dear cousin, I am not unskilled in such affairs, and I will take charge of the commission. My sister thanks you for your good and eternal remembrance. She has experienced much inquietude; but she is now at length a little reassured, having sent her secretary yonder, in order that nothing may happen unexpectedly.

"Adieu, my dear cousin; let us hear from you as often as you can, that is to say, as often as you can with safety. I embrace you. MARY MICHON."

"Oh! what do I not owe you, Aramis?" said D'Artagnan. "Dear Constance! I have at length, then, intelligence of you; she lives, she is in safety in a convent, she is at Stenay! Where is Stenay, Athos?"

"Why, a few leagues from the frontiers of Alsace, in Lorraine; the siege once over, we shall be able to make a tour in that direction."

"And that will not be long, it is to be hoped," said Porthos; "for they have this morning hung a spy who confessed that the Rochellais had come to the leather of their shoes. Supposing, that after having eaten the leather they eat the soles, I cannot see anything else they have left, unless they eat one another."

"Poor fools!" said Athos, emptying a glass of excellent Bordeaux wine, which, without having, at that period, the reputation it now enjoys, merited it no less: "poor fools! as if the Catholic religion was not the most advantageous and the most agreeable of all religions! It's all one," resumed he, after having smacked his tongue against his palate, "they are brave fellows! But what the devil are you about, Aramis?" continued Athos; "why, you are squeezing that letter into your pocket!"

"Yes," said D'Artagnan, "Athos is right, it must be burned; and yet if we burn it, who knows whether Monsieur le Cardinal has not a secret to interrogate ashes?"

"He must have one," said Athos.

"What will you do with the letter, then?" asked Porthos.

"Come here, Grimaud," said Athos. "As a punishment for having spoken without permission, my friend, you will please to eat this piece of paper; then to recompense you for the service you will have rendered us, you shall afterward drink this glass of wine; here is the letter, first, eat heartily." Grimaud smiled; and with his eyes fixed upon the glass which Athos held in his hand, he ground the paper well between his teeth, and then swallowed it.

"Bravo! Master Grimaud!" said Athos, "and now take this; that's well! we dispense with your saying thank you."

Grimaud silently swallowed the glass of Bordeaux wine; but his eyes raised toward heaven spoke, during the whole time this delicious occupation lasted, a language which, for being mute, was not the less expressive.

"And now," said Athos, "unless Monsieur le Cardinal should form the ingenious idea of ripping up Grimaud, I think we may be pretty much at our ease respecting the letter."

In the meantime his eminence continued his melancholy ride, murmuring between his mustaches:

"These four men must positively be mine."

CHAPTER LII.

THE FIRST DAY OF CAPTIVITY.

LET us return to milady, whom a glance thrown upon the coast of France has made us lose sight of for an instant.

We shall find her still in the despairing attitude in which we left her, plunged in an abyss of dismal reflection, a dark hell, at the gate of which she has almost left hope behind; for, for the first time she doubts, for the first time she fears.

On two occasions her fortune has failed her, on two occasions she has found herself discovered and betrayed; and on these two occasions, it was before the fatal genius, sent doubtlessly by heaven to combat her, that she has succumbed: D'Artagnan has conquered her; her, that invincible power of evil.

He has deceived her in her love, humbled her in her pride, thwarted her in her ambition, and now he ruins her fortune, deprives her of liberty, and even threatens her life. Still more, he has lifted the corner of her mask, that ægis with which she covered herself, and which rendered her so strong.

D'Artagnan has turned aside from Buckingham, whom she hates as she hates all she has loved, the tempest with which Richelieu threatened him in the person of the queen. D'Artagnan had passed himself upon her as De Wardes, for whom she had conceived one of those tigress-like fancies common to women of her character. D'Artagnan knows that terrible secret which she has sworn no one shall know without dying. In short, at the moment in which she has just obtained from Richelieu a *carte blanche* by the means of which she is about to take vengeance on her enemy, this precious paper is torn from her hands, and it is D'Artagnan who holds her prisoner, and is about to send her to some filthy Botany Bay, some infamous Tyburn of the Indian Ocean.

All this she owes to D'Artagnan, without doubt; from whom can come so many disgraces heaped upon her head, if not from him? He alone could have transmitted to Lord de Winter all these frightful secrets, which he has discovered one after another, by a train of fatalities. He knows her brother-in-law, he must have written to him.

What hatred she distils! There, motionless, with her burning, fixed glances in her desert apartment, how well the outbursts of passion, which at times escape from the depths of her chest with her respiration, accompany the sound of the surf which rises, growls, roars, and breaks itself, like an eternal and powerless despair, against the rocks upon which is built this dark and lofty castle! How many magnificent projects of vengeance she conceives by the light of the flashes which her tempestuous passion casts over her mind, against Madame Bonacieux, against Buckingham, but, above all, against D'Artagnan—projects lost in the distance of the future!

Yes, but in order to avenge herself she must be free; and to be free a prisoner has to pierce a wall, detach bars, cut through a floor—all undertakings which a patient and strong

man may accomplish, but before which the feverish irrita-
tions of a woman must give way. Besides, to do all this, time
is necessary—months, years—and she has ten or twelve days,
as Lord de Winter, her fraternal and terrible gaoler, told her.

And yet, if she were a man, she would attempt all this,
and, perhaps, might succeed; why, then, did heaven make
the mistake of placing that manlike soul in that frail and
delicate body?"

The first moments of her captivity were terrible; a few convulsions of rage which she could not suppress paid her debt
of feminine weakness to nature. But by degrees she overcame
the outbursts of her mad passion; the nervous tremblings
which agitated her frame disappeared, and she remained
folded within herself, like a fatigued serpent reposing.

"Why, I must have been mad to allow myself to be carried
away so," says she, plunging into the glass, which reflects
back to her eyes the burning glance by which she appears to
interrogate herself. "No violence; violence is the proof of
weakness. In the first place, I have never succeeded by that
means; perhaps if I employed my strength against women, I
should have a chance to find them weaker than myself, and
consequently to conquer them. But it is with men that my
struggle is, and I am but a woman for them. Let us struggle
like a woman, then; my strength is in my weakness."

Then, as if to render an account to herself of the changes
she could impose upon her countenance, so mobile and so expressive, she made it take all expressions, from that of passionate anger, which convulsed her features, to that of the
most sweet, most affectionate, and most seducing smile.
Then her hair assumed successively under her skillful hands,
all the undulations she thought might assist the charms of
her face. At length she murmured, satisfied with herself:

"Come, nothing is lost. I am still beautiful."

It was then nearly eight o'clock in the evening. Milady
perceived a bed; she calculated that the repose of a few hours
would not only refresh her head and her ideas, but still
further, her complexion. A better idea, however, came into
her mind before going to bed. She had heard something
said about supper. She had already been an hour in this
apartment; they could not be long before they brought her
her repast. The prisoner was determined not to lose any
time; she resolved to make that very evening some attempts
to ascertain the nature of the ground she had to work upon, by
studying the characters of the people to whose guardianship
she was committed.

A light appeared under the door; this light announced the reappearance of her goalers. Milady, who had arisen, threw herself quickly into the *fauteuil*, her head thrown back, her beautiful hair unbound and disheveled, her bosom half bare beneath her crumpled laces, one hand on her heart and the other hanging down.

The bolts were drawn, the door groaned upon its hinges, steps sounded in the chamber and drew near.

"Place that table there," said a voice, which the prisoner recognized as the voice of Felton.

The order was obeyed.

"You will bring lights, and relieve the sentinel," continued Felton.

And this double order which the young man gave to the same individuals, proved to milady that her servants were the same men as her guards—that is to say, soldiers.

Felton's orders were, for the rest, executed with a silent rapidity that gave a good idea of the state in which he kept up discipline.

At length Felton, who had not looked at milady, turned toward her.

"Ah! ah!" said he, "she is asleep, that's well; when she wakes she can sup." And he made some steps toward the door.

"But, my lieutenant!" said a soldier, a little less stoical than his officer, and who had approached milady, "this woman is not asleep."

"What! not asleep!" said Felton, "what is she doing then?"

"She has fainted away; her face is very pale, and I have listened in vain; I can't hear her breathe."

"You are right," said Felton, after having looked at milady from the spot on which he stood, without moving a step toward her: "Go and tell Lord de Winter that his prisoner has fainted. The case not having been foreseen, I don't know what to do."

The soldier went out to obey the orders of his officer; Felton sat down upon the *fauteuil* which was by chance near the door, and waited without speaking a word, without making a gesture. Milady possessed that great art, so much studied by women, of looking through her long eyelashes without appearing to open the lids; she perceived Felton, who sat with his back toward her. She continued to look at him during nearly ten minutes, and in these ten minutes the impassable guardian never turned round once.

She then thought that Lord de Winter would come, and by

his presence give fresh strength to her gaoler: her first trial
was lost; she acted like a woman who reckons upon her
resources; she consequently raised her head, opened her eyes
and sighed deeply.

At this sigh Felton turned round.

"Ah! you have awakened again, madame," he said; "then
I have nothing more to do here. If you want anything you
can ring."

"Oh! my God! my God! how I have suffered," said milady,
in that harmonious voice, which like that of the ancient en-
chantresses, charmed all those they wished to destroy.

And she assumed, upon sitting up in the *fauteuil,* a still
more graceful and voluptuous position than that she had exhibited when reclining.

Felton rose.

"You will be served thus, madame, three times a day,"
said he; "in the morning at nine o'clock, in the day at one
o'clock, and in the evening at eight. If that does not suit
you, you can point out what other hours you prefer, and in
this respect your wishes will be complied with."

"But am I to remain always alone in this vast and dismal
chamber?" asked milady.

"A woman of the neighborhood has been sent for, who
will be to-morrow at the castle, and will return as often as
you desire her presence."

"I thank you, sir," replied the prisoner humbly.

Felton made a slight bow, and directed his steps toward
the door. At the moment he was about to go out, Lord de
Winter appeared in the corridor, followed by the soldier who
had been sent to inform him of the fainting of milady. He
held a phial of salts in his hand.

"Well, what's going on here," said he in a jeering voice,
on seeing the prisoner sitting up, and Felton about to go out.
"is this dead woman come to life again already? *Pardieu,*
Felton, my lad, did you not perceive that you were taken for
a novice, and that the first act was being performed of a comedy of which we shall doubtless have the pleasure of following out all the developments?"

"I imagined that might be the case, my lord," said Felton;
"but as the prisoner is a woman, after all, I wished to pay
her the attention that every man of gentle birth owes to a
woman, if not on her account, at least on my own."

Milady shuddered through her whole system. These words
of Felton's passed like ice through her veins.

"So," replied De Winter, laughing, "that beautiful hair

so skillfully disheveled, that white skin and that languishing look, have not yet seduced you, you heart of stone?"

"No, my lord," replied the impassable young man; "your lordship may be assured that it requires more than the tricks and coquetry of a woman to corrupt me."

"In that case, my brave lieutenant, let us leave milady to find out something else, and go to supper; but remember she has a fruitful imagination, and the second act of the comedy will not be long after the first."

And at these words Lord de Winter passed his arm through that of Felton, and led him out, laughing.

"Oh! I will be a match for you!" murmured milady between her teeth; "be assured of that, you poor should-be monk, you poor converted soldier, who have cut your uniform out of a monk's frock!"

"Apropos," resumed De Winter, stopping at the door, "you must not, milady, let this check take away your appetite. Taste that fowl and those fish; 'pon honor, they are not poisoned. I agree very well with my cook, and he is not to be my heir; I have full and perfect confidence in him. Do as I do. Adieu! dear sister! till your next fainting fit!"

This was all that milady could endure: her hands became clenched, she ground her teeth inwardly, her eyes followed the motion of the door as it closed behind Lord de Winter and Felton, and the moment she was alone a fresh fit of despair seized her; she cast her eyes upon the table, saw the glittering of a knife, rushed toward it and clutched it; but her disappointment was cruel; the blade was blunt, and of flexible silver.

A burst of laughter resounded from the other side of the ill-closed door, and the door was reopened.

"Ha! ha! ha!" cried Lord de Winter; "ha! ha! ~! don't you see, my brave Felton, don't you see what I to.. you? That knife was for you, my lad; she would have killed you. Observe, this is one of her peculiarities, to get rid thus, after one fashion or another, of all the people who inconvenience her. If I had listened to you, the knife would have been pointed and of steel. Then it would have been all over with Felton; she would have cut your throat, and, after that, the throat of everybody else. Look at her, John, see how well she knows how to handle a knife."

In fact, milady still held the harmless weapon in her clenched hand, but these last words, this supreme insult, relaxed her hands, her strength, and even her will. The knife fell to the ground.

"You were right, my lord," said Felton, with a tone of profound disgust, which sounded to the very bottom of the heart of milady; "you were right, my lord; I was in the wrong."

And both left the room afresh.

But this time milady lent a more attentive ear than the first, and she heard their steps die away in the distance of the corridor.

"I am lost," murmured she; "I am lost! I am in the power of men upon whom I can have no more influence than upon statues of bronze or granite; they know me by heart, and are cuirassed against all my weapons. It is, however, impossible that this should end as they have decreed!"

In fact, as the last reflection, this instinctive return to hope, indicated sentiments of weakness or fear did not dwell long in her ardent spirit. Milady sat down to table, ate of several dishes, drank a little Spanish wine, and felt all her resolution return.

Before she went to bed she had commented upon, analyzed, turned on all sides, examined on all points, the words, the gestures, the signs, and even the silence of her interlocutors, and from this profound, skillful, and anxious study, it resulted that Felton was, everything considered, the more vulnerable of her two persecutors.

One expression, above all, recurred to the mind of the prisoner:

"If I had listened to you," Lord de Winter had said to Felton.

Felton, then, had spoken in her favor, since Lord de Winter had not been willing to listen to Felton.

"Weak or strong," repeated milady, "that man has a spark of pity in his soul; of that spark I will make a flame that will devour him.

As to the other, he knows me, he fears me, and knows what he has to expect of me, if ever I escape from his hands; it is useless then to attempt anything with him.

"But, Felton, that's another thing; he is a young, ingenuous, pure man, who seems virtuous; him there are means of destroying."

And milady went to bed and fell asleep, with a smile upon her lips. Any one who had seen her sleeping, might have said she was a young girl dreaming of the crown of flowers she was to wear on her brow at the next *fête*.

CHAPTER LIII.

THE SECOND DAY OF CAPTIVITY.

MILADY dreamed that she at length had D'Artagnan in her power, that she was present at his execution, and it was the sight of his odious blood, flowing beneath the axe of the executioner, which spread that charming smile upon her lips. She slept as a prisoner sleeps who is rocked by his first hope.

In the morning, when they entered her chamber, she was still in bed. Felton remained in the corridor; he brought with him the woman of whom he had spoken the evening before, and who had just arrived; this woman entered, and approaching milady's bed, offered her services.

Milady was habitually pale; her complexion might therefore deceive a person who saw her for the first time.

"I am in a fever," said she; "I have not slept a single instant during all this long night—I am in frightful pain: are you likely to be more humane to me than others were to me yesterday? All I ask is, permission to remain in bed."

"Would you like to have a physician sent for?" said the woman.

Felton listened to this dialogue without speaking a word.

Milady reflected that the more people she had around her, the more she should have to work upon, and the more strict would be the watch Lord de Winter kept over her; besides, the physician might declare the malady was feigned, and milady, after having lost the first trick of the game, was not willing to lose the second.

"Go and fetch a physician!" said she; "what could be the good of that? These gentlemen declared yesterday that my illness was a comedy; it would be just the same to-day, no doubt; for, since yesterday evening they have had plenty of time to send for a doctor."

"Then," said Felton, who became impatient, "say yourself, madame, what treatment you wish to be pursued."

"Eh! how can I tell? My God! I know that I am in pain, that's all: give me anything you ilke, it is of very little consequence to me."

"Go and fetch Lord de Winter," said Felton, tired of these eternal complaints.

"Oh! no, no!" cried milady; "no, sir, do not call him, I conjure you. I am well, I want nothing; do not call him."

She gave so much vehemence, such prevailing eloquence to this exclamation, that Felton, in spite of himself, advanced some steps into the room.

"He is come!" thought milady.

"If you *really* are in pain," said Felton, "a physician shall be sent for; and if you deceive us, well! why it will be the worse for you, but at least we shall not have to reproach ourselves with anything."

Milady made no reply, but turning her beautiful head round upon her pillow, she burst into tears, and uttered heart-breaking sobs.

Felton surveyed her for an instant with his usual impassability; then, seeing that the crisis threatened to be prolonged, he went out; the woman followed him, and Lord de Winter did not appear.

"I fancy I begin to see my way," murmured milady, with a savage joy, burying herself under the clothes to conceal from anybody who might be watching her this burst of inward satisfaction.

Two hours passed away.

"Now it is time that the malady should be over," said she; "let me rise, and obtain some success this very day; I have but ten days, and this evening two of them will be gone."

In the morning, when the woman and Felton came, they had brought her breakfast; now she thought they could not be long before they came to clear the table, and that Felton would then come back.

Milady was not deceived: Felton reappeared, and without observing whether she had or had not touched her repast, he made a sign that the table should be carried out of the room, it being brought in ready covered.

Felton remained behind: he held a book in his hand.

Milady, reclining in a *fauteuil*, near the chimney, beautiful, pale, and resigned, looked like a holy virgin awaiting martyrdom.

Felton approached her, and said:

"Lord de Winter, who is a Catholic, as well as yourself, madame, thinking that the privation of the rites and ceremonies of your church might be painful to you, has consented that you should read every day the ordinary of *your mass*, and here is a book which contains the ritual of it."

At the manner in which Felton laid the book upon the little table near which my lady was sitting, at the tone in which he pronounced the two words, *your mass*, at the dis-

dainf·l smile which he accompanied them, milady raised
her head, and looked more attentively at the officer.

Then, by that plain arrangement of the hair, by that costume of extreme simplicity, by the brow polished like marble,
but as hard and impenetrable as it, she recognized one of
those dark Puritans she had so often met with, as well at the
court of King James as that of the king of France, where, in
spite of the remembrance of the Saint Bartholomew, they
sometimes came to seek refuge.

She then had one of those sudden inspirations which people
of genius alone have in great crises, in supreme moments
which are to decide their fortunes or their lives.

Those two words, *your mass,* and a simple glance cast upon
Felton, revealed to her all the importance of the reply she
was about to make.

But, with that rapidity of intelligence which was peculiar
to her, this reply, ready arranged, presented itself to her lips:

"I!" said she, with an accent of disdain in unison with
that which she had remarked in the voice of the young officer,
"I, sir; *my mass!* Lord de Winter, the corrupted Catholic,
knows very well that I am not of his religion, and this is a
snare he wishes to lay for me!"

"And of what religion are you, then, madame?" asked
Felton, with an astonishment which, in spite of the empire
he held over himself, he could not entirely conceal.

"I will tell it," cried milady, with a feigned exultation,
"on the day when I shall have suffered sufficiently for my
faith."

The look of Felton revealed to milady the full extent of the
space she had opened for herself by this single word.

The young officer, however, remained mute and motionless:
his look alone had spoken.

"I am in the hands of mine enemies," continued she, with
that tone of enthusiasm which she knew was familiar to the
Puritans: "well, let my God save me, or let me perish for
my God! That is the reply I beg you to make to Lord de
Winter. And as to this book," added she, pointing to the
ritual with her finger, but without touching it, as if she must
be contaminated by the touch, "you may carry it back and
make use of it yourself; for, doubtless, you are doubly the
accomplice of Lord de Winter; the accomplice in his persecutions, the accomplice in his heresies."

Felton made no reply, took the book with the same appearance of repugnance which he had before manifested, and retired pensively.

Lord de Winter came toward five o'clock in the evening; milady had had time, during the whole day, to trace her plan of conduct. She received him like a woman who had already recovered all her advantages.

"It appears," said the baron, seating himself in the *fauteuil* opposite to that occupied by milady, and stretching out his legs carelessly upon the hearth, "it appears we have made a little apostasy!"

"What do you mean, sir?"

"I mean to say that, since we last met, you have changed your religion; you have not, by chance, married a Protestant for a third husband, have you?"

"Explain yourself, my lord," replied the prisoner, with majesty; "for, though I hear your words, I declare I do not understand them."

"Then it is, that you have no religion at all; I like that best," replied Lord de Winter, laughing.

"It is certain that that is the most accordant with your own principles," replied milady coldly.

"Well, I confess it is all perfectly the same to me."

"Oh! you need not avow this religious indifference, my lord, your debaucheries and crimes would gain credit for it."

"What! you talk of debaucheries, Madame Messalina! Lady Macbeth! Either I misunderstand you, or *pardieu!* you are pretty impudent!"

"You only speak thus because you know you are listened to, sir," coldly replied milady; "and you wish to interest your gaolers and your hangmen against me."

"My gaolers! and my hangmen! Heyday, madame! you are getting quite into a poetical tone, and the comedy of yesterday is turning this evening to a tragedy. As to the rest, in eight days you will be where you ought to be, and my task will be completed."

"Infamous task! impious task!" cried milady, with the exultation of a victim provoking the judge.

"*Parole d'honneur!*" said De Winter, rising, "I think the hussey is going mad! Come, come, calm yourself, Madame Puritan, or I'll remove you to a dungeon. *Pardieu!* it's my Spanish wine that has got into your head, is it not? But, never mind, that sort of intoxication is not dangerous, and will have no consequences."

And Lord de Winter retired swearing, which at that period was a very cavalier-like habit.

Felton was, in fact, behind the door, and had not lost one word of this scene.

Milady had guessed as much.

"Yes, go! go!" said she to her brother; "the consequences are drawing near, on the contrary; but you, weak fool! will not see them until it will be too late to shun them."

Silence was re-established—two hours passed away; milady's supper was brought in, and she was found deeply engaged in saying her prayers aloud; prayers which she had learned of an old servant of her second husband, a most austere Puritan. She appeared to be in ecstasy, and did not pay the least attention to what was going on around her. Felton made a sign that she should not be disturbed; and when all was arranged, he went out quietly with the soldiers.

Milady knew she might be watched, so she continued her prayers to the end; and it appeared to her that the soldier who was on duty at her door did not march with the same step, and seemed to listen.

For the moment she required no more; she arose, placed herself at table, ate but little, and drank only water.

An hour after, her table was cleared; but milady remarked that this time Felton did not accompany the soldiers.

He feared, then, to see her too often.

She turned toward the wall to smile; for there was in this smile such an expression of triumph that this single smile would have betrayed her.

She allowed, therefore, half an hour to pass away; and as at that moment all was silence in the old castle, as nothing was heard but the eternal murmur of the waves—that immense respiration of the ocean—with her pure, harmonious, and powerful voice, she began the first couplet of the psalm then in greater favor with the Puritans:

"Thou leavest thy servants, Lord!
    To see if they be strong,
But soon thou dost afford
    Thy hand to conduct them along."

These verses were not excellent—very far from it, even; but, as it is well known, the Puritans did not pique themselves upon their poetry.

While singing, milady listened. The soldier on guard at her door stopped, as if he had been changed into stone. Milady was then able to judge of the effect she had produced.

Then she continued her singing with inexpressible fervor and feeling; it appeared to her that the sounds spread to a distance beneath the vaulted roofs, and carried with them a magic charm to soften the hearts of her gaolers. It, how-

ever, likewise appeared that the soldier on duty—a zealous
Catholic, no doubt, shook off the charm, for through the
door—

"Hold your tongue, madame!" said he; "your song is as
dismal as a *De profundis;* and if, besides the pleasure of
being in garrison here, we must hear such things as these, no
mortal can hold out."

"Silence!" then said another stern voice, which milady
recognized as that of Felton; "what business is it of yours,
you stupid fellow! Did anybody order you to prevent that
woman from singing? No; you were told to guard her—to
fire at her if she attempted to fly. Keep her there; if she
flies, kill her; but don't exceed your orders."

An expression of unspeakable joy lightened the countenance
of milady, but this expression was fleeting as the reflection of
lightning, and, without appearing to have heard the dialogue,
of which she had not lost a word, she began again, giving to
her voice all the charm, all the power, all the seduction, the
demon had bestowed upon it:

> "For all my tears and all my cares,
>   My exile and my chains,
> I have my youth, I have my prayers,
>   And God who counts my pains."

Her voice, of immense power and of sublime expression,
gave to the rude, unpolished poetry of these psalms a magic
and an effect which the most exalted Puritans rarely found
in the songs of their brethren, and which they were forced
to ornament with all the resources of their imagination.
Felton believed he heard the singing of the angel who consoled the three Hebrews in the furnace.

Milady continued:

> "But the day of our liberation
>   Will come, just and powerful Sire!
> And if it cheat our expectation,
>   To death and martyrdom we can still aspire."

This verse, into which the terrible enchantress threw her
whole soul, completed the trouble which had seized the heart
of the young officer; he opened the door quickly, and milady
saw him appear, pale as usual, but with his eyes inflamed and
almost wild.

"Why do you sing thus, and with such a voice?" said he.

"I crave your pardon, sir," said my lady, with mildness;

"I forgot that my songs are out of place in this mansion. I have, perhaps, offended you in your religious opinions; but it was without wishing to do so, I assure you. Pardon me, then, a fault which is perhaps great, but which certainly was involuntary."

Milady was so beautiful at this moment—the religious ecstasy in which she appeared to be plunged gave such an expression to her countenance, that Felton was so dazzled that he fancied he beheld the angel whom he had just before only heard.

"Yes, yes," said he, "you disturb—you agitate the people who inhabit the castle."

And the poor, senseless young man was not aware of the incoherence of his words, while milady was reading, with her lynx's eyes, the very depths of his heart.

"I will be silent then," said milady, casting down her eyes, with all the sweetness she could give to her voice, with all the resignation she could impress upon her manner.

"No, no, madame," said Felton; "only do not sing so loud, particularly at night."

And at these words Felton, feeling that he could not long maintain his severity toward his prisoner, rushed out of the room.

"You have done right, lieutenant," said the soldier "such songs disturb the mind; and yet we become accustomed to them—her voice is so beautiful!"

CHAPTER LIV.

THE THIRD DAY OF CAPTIVITY.

FELTON had fallen, but there was still another step to be taken—he must be retained, or, rather, he must be left quite alone; and milady but obscurely perceived the means which could lead to this result.

Still more must be done: he must be made to speak, in order that he might be spoken to; for milady very well knew that her greatest seduction was in her voice, which so skillfully ran over the whole gamut of tones, from human speech to celestial language.

And yet, in spite of all this seduction, milady might fail; for Felton was forewarned, and that against the least chance. From that moment she watched all his actions, all his words,

to the simplest glance of his eyes, to his gestures, even to a
respiration that could be interpreted as a sigh; in short, she
studied everything, as a skillful comedian does, to whom a
new part has been assigned in a line he has not been accustomed to.

With Lord de Winter her plan of conduct was more easy;
she had laid that down the preceding evening. To remain
silent and dignified in his presence; from time to time to
irritate him by an affected disdain, by a contemptuous word;
to provoke him to threats and violence, which would produce
a contrast with her own resignation—such was her plan.
Felton would see all; perhaps he would say nothing, but he
would see.

In the morning, Felton came as usual; but milady allowed
him to preside over all the preparations for the breakfast
without addressing a word to him. At the moment he was
about to retire, she was cheered with a ray of hope, for she
thought he was about to speak; but his lips moved without
any sound passing from his mouth, and, making a powerful
effort over himself, he sent back to his heart the words that
were about to escape from his lips, and went out.

Toward midday, Lord de Winter came to her apartment.

It was a tolerably fine winter's day, and a ray of that pale
English sun, which lightens but does not warm, passed through
the bars of her prison.

Milady was looking out at the winodw, and pretended not
to hear the door as it opened.

"Ah, ah!" said Lord de Winter, "after having played
comedy, after having played tragedy, we are now playing
melancholy, eh?"

The prisoner made no reply.

"Yes, yes," continued Lord de Winter, "I understand—
you would like very well to be at liberty on that beach! you
would like very well to be in a good ship, dancing upon the
waves of that emerald-green sea; you would like very well,
either on land or on the ocean, to lay for me one of those
nice little ambuscades you are so skillful in planning. Patience, patience! in four days time the shore will be beneath
your foot, the sea will be open to you—more open than will,
perhaps, be agreeable to you; for in four days England will
be relieved of your presence."

Milady joined her hands, and raising her fine eyes toward
heaven—

"Lord, lord!" said she, with an angelic meekness of gesture
and tone, "pardon this man, as I myself pardon him!"

"Yes, pray, accursed woman!" cried the baron; "your prayer is so much the more generous from your being, I swear to you, in the power of a man who will never pardon you!" And he left the room.

At the moment he went out, a piercing glance darted through the opening of the nearly closed door, and she perceived Felton, who drew quickly on one side to prevent being seen by her.

Then she threw herself upon her knees, and began to pray. "My God, my God!" said she, "you know in what holy cause I suffer; give me, then, the strength to support my sufferings."

The door opened gently; the beautiful supplicant pretended not to hear the noise, and, in a voice broken by tears, she continued:

"God of vengeance! God of goodness! will you allow the frightful projects of this man to be accomplished?"

Then only she feigned to hear the sound of Felton's steps, and rising quick as thought, she blushed, as if ashamed of being surprised on her knees.

"I do not like to disturb those who pray, madame," said Felton seriously; "do not disturb yourself on my account, I beseech you."

"How do you know I was praying, sir?" said milady, in a voice interrupted by sobs. "You were deceived, sir; I was not praying."

"Do you think, then, madame," replied Felton, in the same serious voice, but with a more mild tone, "do you think I assume the right of preventing a creature from prostrating herself before her Creator? God forbid! God forbid! Besides, repentence becomes the guilty; whatever crimes they may have committed, for me the guilty are sacred at the feet of God!"

"Guilty! I?" said milady, with a smile which might have disarmed the angel of the last judgment. "Guilty! oh, my God, thou knowest whether I am guilty! Say I am condemned, sir, if you please; but you know that God, who loves martyrs, sometimes permits the innocent to be condemned."

"Were you condemned, were you innocent, were you a martyr," replied Felton, "the greater would be the necessity for prayer; and I myself will aid you with my prayers."

"Oh, you are a just man!" cried milady, throwing herself on her knees at his feet; "I can hold out no longer, for I fear I shall be wandering in strength in the moment at which

I shall be forced to undergo the struggle, and confess my
faith. Listen, then, to the supplication of a despairing woman.
You are abused, sir, but that is not the question; I only ask
you one favor, and if you grant it me, I will bless you in this
world and in the next."

"Speak to the master, madame," said Felton; "happily, I
am neither charged with the power of pardoning nor punish-
ing; it is upon one higher placed than I am that God has laid
this responsibility."

"To you—no, to you alone! Listen to me, rather than
contribute to my destruction, rather than contribute to my
ignominy."

"If you have merited this shame, madame, if you have
incurred this ignominy, you must submit to it as an offering
to God."

"What do you say? Oh, you do not understand me!
When I speak of ignominy, you think I speak of some punishment or other, of imprisonment or death! Would to heaven
it were no more! Of what consequence to me is imprisonment or death?"

"It is I who no longer understand you, madame," said
Felton.

"Or rather, who pretend not to understand me, sir!"
replied the prisoner, with a smile of doubt.

"No, madame, upon the honor of a soldier, upon the faith
of a Christian."

"What! you are ignorant of Lord de Winter's designs
upon me?"

"I am unacquainted with them."

"Impossible; you are his confidant!"

"I never lie, madame."

"Oh, he conceals them too little for you not to divine
them."

"I seek to divine nothing, madame; I wait till I am confided in, and, apart from that which Lord de Winter has said
to me before you, he has confided nothing to me."

"Why, then," cried milady, with an incredible tone of
truthfulness, "why, then, you are not his accomplice—you do
not know that he destines me to a disgrace which all the pun-
ishments of the world cannot equal in horror?"

"You are deceived, madame," said Felton, blushing;
"Lord de Winter is not capable of such a crime."

"Good!" said milady to herself; "without knowing what
it is, he calls it a crime!"

Then aloud:

"The friend of the infamous is capable of everything."

"Whom do you call the infamous?" asked Felton.

"Are there, then, in England two men to whom such an epithet can be applied?"

"You mean George Villiers?" said Felton, whose looks became agitated.

"Whom Pagans and infidel Gentiles call Duke of Buckingham," replied milady; "I could not have thought that there was an Englishman in all England who would have required so long an explanation to make him understand of whom I was speaking."

"The hand of the Lord is stretched over him," said Felton, "he will not escape the chastisement he deserves."

Felton did but express, with regard to the duke, the feeling of execration which all the English had vowed to him whom the Catholics themselves called the extortioner, the pillager, the *débauché;* and whom the Puritans styled simply Satan.

"Oh! my God! my God!" cried milady; "when I supplicate you to pour upon this man the chastisement which is his due, you know that it is not my own vengeance I pursue, but the deliverance of a whole nation that I implore!"

"Do you know him, then?" asked Felton.

"At length he interrogates me!" said milady to herself, at the height of joy at having obtained so quickly such a result. "Oh! know him! yes! to my misfortune, to my eternal misfortune!" and milady wrung her hands, as if arrived at the very paroxysm of grief.

Felton no doubt felt within himself that his strength was abandoning him, and he made several steps toward the door: but the prisoner, whose eye was never off him, sprang in pursuit of him, and stopped him.

"Sir," cried she, "be kind, be clement, listen to my prayer; that knife, which the fatal prudence of the baron deprived me of, because he knows the use I would make of it; oh! hear me to the end! that knife, give it to me for a minute only, for mercy's, for pity's sake! I will embrace your knees! you shall shut the door that you may be certain I contemplate no injury to you! my God! to you! the only just, good, and compassionate being I have met with!—to you! my saviour, perhaps! one minute, that knife, one minute, a single minute, and I will restore it to you through the grating of the door; only one minute, Master Felton, and you will have saved my honor!"

"To kill yourself!" cried Felton, with terror, forgetting to withdraw his hands from the hands of the prisoner; "to kill yourself?"

"I have told, sir," murmured milady, lowering her voice, and allowing herself to sink overpowered to the ground, "I have told my secret! He knows all! My God, I am lost!"

Felton remained standing, motionless and undecided.

"He still doubts," thought milady, "I have not been earnest enough."

Some one was heard in the corridor, milady recognized the step of Lord de Winter.

Felton recognized it also, and made a step toward the door.

Milady sprang toward him.

"Oh! not a word," said she in a concentrated voice, "not a word of all that I have said to you to this man, or I am lost, and it would be you—you——"

Then as the steps drew near she became silent, for fear of being heard, applying, with a gesture of infinite terror, her beautiful hand to Felton's mouth.

Felton gently pushed milady from him, and she sank into a chair.

Lord de Winter passed before the door without stopping, and the sound of his footsteps soon died away in the distance.

Felton, as pale as death, remained some instants with his ear turned and listening; then, when the sound was quite extinct, he breathed like a man awaking from a dream, and rushed out of the apartment.

"Ah!" said milady, listening in her turn to the noise of Felton's steps, which faded away in a direction opposite to those of Lord de Winter; "ah! at length thou art mine!"

Then her brow darkened.

"If he tells the baron," said she, "I am lost, for the baron, who knows very well that I shall not kill myself, will place me before him, with a knife in my hand, and he will discover that all this despair is but played."

She went, and placed herself before the glass, and looked at herself attentively; never had she appeared more beautiful.

"Yes! yes!" said she smiling, "but he won't tell him!"

In the evening Lord de Winter accompanied the supper.

"Sir," said milady, "is your presence an indispensable accessory of my captivity? could you not spare me the increase of tortures which your visits inflict upon me?"

"How! my dear sister!" said Lord de Winter, "did not you sentimentally inform me, with that pretty mouth of yours, so cruel to me to-day, that you came to England solely for the pleasure of seeing me at your ease, an enjoyment of which you told me you so sensibly felt the privation, that you had risked everything for it—bad seas, tempests, and captivity? Well! here I am, be satisfied: besides, this time, my visit has a motive."

Milady trembled—she thought Felton had told all; perhaps, never in her life had this woman, who had experienced so many opposite and powerful emotions, felt her heart beat so violently.

She was seated; Lord de Winter took a chair, drew it toward her, and sat down close beside her; then taking a paper out of his pocket, he unfolded it slowly.

"Here," said he, "I want to show you the kind of passport which I have drawn up, and which will serve you henceforward as a numero of order in the life I consent to leave you."

Then turning his eyes from milady to the paper, he read:

"'Order to conduct to——;' the name is blank," interrupted Lord de Winter; "if you have any preferene you can point it out to me; and if it be not within a thousand leagues of London, attention will be paid to your wishes. I will begin again, then: 'Order to conduct to——, the person named Charlotte Backson, branded by the justice of the kingdom of France, but liberated after chastisement; she is to dwell in this place, without ever going more than three leagues from it. In case of any attempt to escape, the penalty of death is to be applied. She will receive five shillings per day, for lodging and food.'"

"That order does not concern me," replied milady coldly, "since it bears another name than mine."

"A name!—have you a name, then?"

"I bear that of your brother."

"Ay, but you are mistaken; my brother is only your second husband, and your first is still living. Tell me his name, and I will put it in the place of the name of Charlotte Backson. No?—you will not?—you are silent? Well! then you must be registered as Charlotte Backson."

Milady remained silent; only this time it was no longer from affectation, but from terror: she believed the order to be about to be executed; she thought that Lord de Winter had hastened her departure; she thought she was condemned to set off that very evening. Everything, in her mind, was lost for an instant, when all at once she perceived that no signature was attached to the order. The joy she felt at this discovery was so great she could not conceal it.

"Yes, yes," said Lord de Winter, who perceived what was passing in her mind; "yes, you look for the signature, and you say to yourself, 'All is not lost, for that order is not signed; it is only shown to me to me to terrify me; that's all.' You are mistaken; to-morrow this order will be sent to the Duke of Buckingham; after to-morrow, it will return signed by his hand and marked with his seal; and four-and-twenty hours afterward, I will answer for its being carried into execution. Adieu, madame; that is all I had to say to you."

"And I reply to you, sir, that this abuse of power, this exile under a false name, is infamous!"

"Would you like better to be hung in your true name, milady? You know that the English laws are inexorable on the abuse of marriage! speak freely: although my name, or rather that of my brother, would be mixed up with the affair, I will risk the scandal of a public trial, to make myself certain of getting rid of you."

Milady made no reply, but became as pale as a corpse.

"Oh! I see you prefer peregrination. That's well, milady; and there is an old proverb that says: 'Traveling forms youth.' *Ma foi!* you are not wrong after all; and life is sweet. That's the reason why I take such care you shall not deprive me of mine. There only remains, then, the question of the five shillings to be settled; you think me rather parsimonious—don't you? That's because I don't care to leave you the means of corrupting your jailers. Besides you will always have your charms left to seduce them with. Employ them, if your check with regard to Felton has not disgusted you with attempts of that kind."

"Felton has not told him," said milady to herself; "nothing is lost, then."

"And now, madame, till I see you again. To-morrow I will come and announce to you the departure of my messenger."

Lord de Winter rose, saluted her ironically, and left the room.

Milady breathed again; she had still four days before her; four days would quite suffice to complete the seduction of Felton.

A terrible idea, however, rushed into her mind; she thought that Lord de Winter would, perhaps, send Felton himself to get the order signed by the Duke of Buckingham; in that case, Felton would escape her; for, in order to secure success, the magic of a continuous seduction was necessary. Never-

theless, as we have said, one circumstance reassured her—
Felton had not spoken.

As she would not appear to be agitated by the threats of
Lord de Winter, she placed herself at table and ate.

There, as she had done the evening before, she fell on her
knees and repeated her prayers aloud. As on the evening
before, the soldier stopped his march to listen to her.

Soon after, she heard lighter steps than those of the sentinel, which came from the bottom of the corridor, and stopped
before her door.

"That is he," said she.

And she began the same religious chant which had so strongly
excited Felton the evening before.

But, although her voice, sweet, full, and sonorous, vibrated
as harmoniously and as affectingly as ever, the door remained
shut. It appeared, however, to milady, that in one of the
furtive glances she darted, from time to time, at the grating
of the door, she thought she saw the ardent eyes of the young
man through the narrow opening. But whether this was a
reality or not, he had, this time, sufficient self-command not
to enter.

Only, a few instants after she had finished her religious
song, milady thought she heard a profound sigh; then the
same steps she had heard approach, departed slowly, as if
with regret.

CHAPTER LV.

THE FOURTH DAY OF CAPTIVITY.

THE next day, when Felton entered milady's apartments,
he found her standing, mounted upon a chair, holding in her
hands a cord made by means of torn cambric handkerchiefs,
twisted into a kind of rope one with another, and tied at the
ends; at the noise Felton made in entering, milady leaped
lightly to the ground, and endeavored to conceal behind her
the improvised cord she held in her hand.

The young man was still more pale than usual, and his eyes,
reddened by want of sleep, denoted that he had passed a'
feverish night.

Nevertheless, his brow was armed with a sternness more
severe than ever.

He advanced slowly toward milady, who had sat down, and

taking an end of the murderous rope, which by mistake or else by design, she allowed to appear.

"What is this, madame?" he asked coldly.

"That? Nothing," said milady, smiling with that painful expression which she knew so well how to give to her smile; "*ennui* is the mortal enemy of prisoners; I was *ennuyée*, and I amused myself with twisting that rope."

Felton turned his eyes toward the part of the wall of the apartment before which he had found milady standing in the chair in which she was now seated, and over her head he perceived a gilt-headed screw, fixed in the wall for the purpose of hanging up clothes or arms.

He started, and the prisoner saw that start; for, though her eyes were cast down, nothing escaped her.

"What were you doing, standing in that chair?" asked he.

"Of what consequence can that be to you?" replied milady.

"But," replied Felton, "I wish to know."

"Do not question me," said the prisoner, "you know that we true Christians are forbidden to speak falsely."

"Well, then," said Felton, "I will tell you what you were doing, or rather what you were going to do; you were going to complete the fatal work you cherish in your mind; remember, madame, if our God forbids us to speak falsely, he much more severely forbids us to commit suicide."

"When God sees one of his creatures persecuted unjustly, placed between suicide and dishonor, believe me, sir," replied milady in a tone of deep conviction, "God pardons suicide: for then suicide becomes martyrdom."

"You say either too much or too little; speak, madame, in the name of heaven, explain yourself."

"That I may relate my misfortunes to you, for you to treat them as fables; that I may tell you my projects, for you to go and denounce them to my persecutor: no, sir; besides, of what importance is the life or death of a condemned wretch to you? You are only responsible for my body, are you? and provided you produce a carcass that may be recognized as mine, they will require no more of you; nay, perhaps even, you will have a double reward."

"I, madame I!" cried Felton; "to suppose that I should ever accept the price of your life! Oh! you cannot think what you say!"

"Let me act as I please, Felton, let me act as I please," said milady, becoming excited; "every soldier must be ambitious, must he not? You are now a lieutenant—you will follow me to the grave with the rank of captain."

"What have I then done to you," said Felton, much agitated, "that you should load me with such a responsibility before God and before men? In a few days you will be away from this place; your life, madame, will then no longer be under my care, and," added he with a sigh, "then you can do what you will with it."

"So," cried milady, as if she could not resist giving utterance to a holy indignation, "you, a pious man, you who are called a just man, you ask but one thing—and that is that you may not be inculpated, annoyed, by my death!"

"It is my duty to watch over your life, madame, and I will watch over it."

"But do you understand the mission you are fulfilling. A sufficiently cruel one if I am guilty, but what name can you give it, what name will the Lord give it, if I am innocent?"

"I am a soldier, madame, and perform the orders I have received."

"Do you believe, then, that at the last day of judgment God will separate blind executioners from iniquitous judges! You are not willing that I should kill my body, and you make yourself the agent of him who would kill my soul!"

"But I repeat it again to you," replied Felton in great emotion; "no danger threatens you; I will answer for Lord de Winter as for myself."

"Senseless man!" cried milady, "poor senseless man! who dares to answer for another man, when the wisest, when those most after God's own heart, hesitate to answer for themselves; and who ranges himself on the side of the strongest and the most fortunate, to crush the weakest and the most unfortunate."

"Impossible, madame, impossible," murmured Felton, who felt to the bottom of his heart the justness of this argument: "a prisoner, you shall not recover your liberty by my means; living, you shall not lose your life by my means!"

"Yes," cried milady, "but I shall lose that which is much dearer to me than life, I shall lose my honor, Felton; and it is you, you whom I make responsible, before God and before men, for my shame and my infamy."

This time Felton, impassable as he was, or appeared to be, could not resist the secret influence which had already taken possession of him; to see this woman, so beautiful, fair as the brightest vision, to see her by turns overcome with grief and threatening to resist at once the ascendency of grief and beauty, it was too much for a visionary, it was too much for a brain weakened by the ardent dreams of an ecstatic faith, it was too much for a heart corroded by the love of heaven that burns, by the hatred of men that devours.

Milady saw the trouble, she felt by intuition the flame of the opposing passions which burned with the blood in the veins of the young fanatic; and, like a skillful general, who, seeing the enemy ready to surrender, marches toward him with a cry of victory, she rose, beautiful as an antique priestess, inspired like a Christian virgin, her arms extended, her throat uncovered, her hair disheveled, holding with one hand her robe modestly drawn over her breast, her look illumined by that fire which had already created such disorder in the veins of the young Puritan, she stepped toward him, crying out with a vehement air, and in her melodious voice, to which, on this occasion, she communicated a terrible energy:

"Let his victim to Baal be sent,
To the lions the martyr be thrown.
Thy God shall teach thee to repent!
From the abyss he'll give ear to my moan."

Felton stood before this strange apparition, like one petrified.

"Who art thou? who art thou?" cried he, clasping his hands; "art thou a messenger from God, art thou a minister from hell, art thou an angel or a demon, callest thou thyself Eloa or Astarte?"

"Do you not know me, Felton? I am neither an angel nor a demon, I am a daughter of earth, I am a sister of thy faith, that is all."

"Yes! yes!" said Felton, "I doubted, but now I believe!"

"You believe, and still you are an accomplice of that child of Belial, who is called Lord de Winter! You believe, and yet you leave me in the hands of my enemies, of the enemy of England, of the enemy of God! You believe, and yet you deliver me up to him who fills and defiles the world with his heresies and debaucheries, to that infamous Sardanapalus, whom the blind call the Duke of Buckingham, and whom true believers name Antichrist!"

"I deliver you up to Buckingham! I! what mean you by that?"

"They have eyes," cried milady, "and they will not see; they have ears, and they will not hear."

"Yes! yes!" said Felton, passing his hands over his brow,

covered with sweat, as if to remove his last doubt; "yes, I recognize the voice which speaks to me in my dreams; yes, I recognize the features of the angel that appears to me every night, crying to my soul, which cannot sleep: 'Strike, save England, save thyself, for thou wilt die without having disarmed God!' Speak! speak!" cried Felton, "I can understand you now."

A flash of terrible joy, but rapid as thought, gleamed from the eyes of milady.

However fugitive this homicide flash, Felton saw it, and started as if its light had revealed the abysses of this woman's heart. He recalled, all at once, the warnings of Lord de Winter, the seductions of milady, her first attempts after her arrival; he drew back a step, and hung down his head, without, however, ceasing to look at her: as if, fascinated by this strange creature, he could not remove his eyes from her eyes.

Milady was not a woman to misunderstand the meaning of this hesitation. Under her apparent emotions, her icy coolness never abandoned her. Before Felton replied, and before she should be forced to resume this conversation, so difficult to be sustained in the same exalted tone, she let her hands fall, and as if the weakness of the woman overpowered the enthusiasm of the inspired fanatic—

"But no," said she, "it is not for me to be the Judith to deliver Bethulia from this Holofernes. The sword of the eternal is too heavy for my arm. Allow me then to avoid dishonor by death, let me take refuge in martyrdom. I do not ask you for liberty, as a guilty one would, nor for vengeance, as a pagan would. Let me die, that is all I supplicate you, I implore you on my knees; let me die, and my last sigh shall be a blessing for my saviour."

At hearing that voice, so sweet and suppliant, at viewing that look, so timid and downcast, Felton reproached himself. By degrees the enchantress had clothed herself with that magic adornment which she assumed and threw aside at will, that is to say, beauty, meekness, and tears, and above all, the irresistible attraction of mystical voluptuousness, the most devouring of all voluptuousness.

"Alas!" said Felton, "I can do but one thing, which is, to pity you, if you prove to me you are a victim! Lord de Winter alleges cruel accusations against you. You are a Christian, you are my sister in religion; I feel myself drawn toward you, I, who have never loved any one but my benefactor, I, who have met with nothing but traitors and impious men. But you, madame, so beautiful in reality, you, so pure in appearance, must have committed great iniquities for Lord de Winter to pursue you thus."

"They have eyes," repeated milady, with an accent of indescribable grief, "and they will not see; they have ears, and they will not hear."

"But," cried the young officer, "speak! speak, then!"

"Confide my shame to you," cried milady, with the blush of modesty upon her countenance, "for often the crime of one becomes the shame of another; confide my shame to you, a man, and I a woman! Oh!" continued she, placing her hand modestly over her beautiful eyes, "never! never! I could not!"

"But to me, to a brother?" said Felton.

Milady looked at him for some time with an expression which the young man took for doubt, but which, however, was nothing but observation, or rather the will to fascinate.

Felton, in his turn a suppliant, clasped his hands.

"Well then," said milady, "I confide in my brother, I will dare to——"

At this moment the steps of Lord de Winter were heard; but this time the terrible brother-in-law of milady did not content himself, as on the preceding day, with passing before the door and going away again; he stopped, exchanged two words with the sentinel, then the door opened, and he appeared.

During these two words, Felton drew back suddenly, and when Lord de Winter entered, he was at several paces from the prisoner.

The baron entered slowly, carrying a scrutinizing glance from milady to the young officer.

"You have been a long time here, John," said he; "has this woman been relating her crimes to you? In that case I can comprehend the length of the conversation."

Felton started, and milady felt she was lost if she did not come to the assistance of the disconcerted Puritan.

"Ah! you fear your prisoner should escape," said she; "well! ask your worthy gaoler what favor I was but this instant soliciting of him."

"You were soliciting a favor?" said the baron suspiciously.

"Yes, my lord," replied the young man, in some confusion.

"And what favor, pray?" asked Lord de Winter.

"A knife, which she would return to me through the grating of the door, a minute after she had received it," replied Felton.

"There is some one then concealed here, whose throat this amiable lady is desirous of cutting," said De Winter in an ironical, contemptuous tone.

"There is myself," replied milady.

"I have given you the choice between America and Tyburn," replied Lord de Winter; "choose Tyburn, milady; believe me, the cord is more certain than the knife."

Felton grew pale, and made a step forward, remembering that at the moment he entered milady had a rope in her hand.

"You are right," said she, "I have often thought of it;" then she added, in a low voice, "and I will think of it again."

Felton felt a shudder run to the marrow of his bones; probably Lord de Winter perceived this emotion.

"Mistrust yourself, John," said he; "I have placed reliance upon you, my friend; beware; I have warned you. But be of good courage, my lad, in three days we shall be delivered from this creature, and where I shall send her to, she can hurt nobody."

"You hear him!" cried milady with vehemence, so that the baron might believe she was addressing heaven, and that Felton might understand she was addressing him.

Felton hung down his head and appeared buried in thought.

The baron took the young officer by the arm, turning his head over his shoulder, so as not to lose sight of milady till he was gone out.

"Alas!" said the prisoner, when the door was shut, "I am not so far advanced as I expected, I fear. De Winter has changed his usual stupidity into a prudence hitherto foreign to him—it is the desire of vengeance, and new desires form a man! As to Felton, he hesitates. Ah! he is not a man like that cursed D'Artagnan. A Puritan only adores virgins, and he adores them by clasping his hands. A musketeer loves women, and he loves them by clasping his arms round them."

Milady waited then with much impatience, for she feared the day would pass away without her seeing Felton again. But, in an hour after the scene we have just related, she heard some one speaking in a low voice at the door; soon after the door opened, and she perceived Felton.

The young man advanced into the room with a quick step, leaving the door open behind him, and making a sign to milady to be silent; his face was much agitated.

"What do you want with me?" said she.

"Listen," replied Felton in a low voice; "I have just sent

away the sentinel, that I might remain here, without its being known I was come here, that I might speak to you without having that I say to you overhead by others. The baron has just related a frightful history to me."

Milady assumed her smile of a resigned victim, and shook her head.

"Either you are a demon," continued Felton, "or the baron, my benefactor, my father, is a monster. I have known you four days, I have loved him four years; I therefore may hesitate between you; but be not alarmed at what I say, I want to be convinced. To-night, after twelve, I will come and see and listen to you, and you will convince me."

"No, Felton, no, my brother, the sacrifice is too great, and I feel what it must cost you. No, I am lost, do not be lost with me. My death will be much more eloquent than my life, and the silence of the corpse will convince you much better than the words of the prisoner."

"Be silent, madame," cried Felton, "and do not speak to me thus: I came to entreat you to promise me upon your honor, to swear to me by what you hold most sacred, that you will make no attempt upon your life."

"I will not promise," said milady, "for no one has more respect for a promise or an oath than I have, and if I make a promise I must keep it."

"Well," said Felton, "only promise till after you have seen me again. If, when you have seen me again, you still persist—well! then you shall be free, and I myself will give you the weapon you desire."

"Well!" said milady, "for your sake I will wait."

"Swear it."

"I swear I will, by our God. Are you satisfied?"

"I am," said Felton; "till night, then."

And he darted out of the room, shut the door, and waited in the corridor, the soldier's half-pike in his hand, and as if he had mounted guard in his place.

When the soldier returned, Felton gave him back his weapon.

Then, through the grating to which she had drawn near, milady saw the young man cross himself with a delirious fervor, and depart in an apparent transport of joy.

As for her, she returned to her place with a smile of savage contempt upon her lips, and repeated, blaspheming, that terrible name of God, by which she had just sworn without ever having learned to know Him.

"My God!" said she, "what a senseless fanatic! my God, it is I, I, and he who will help me to avenge myself."

CHAPTER LVI.

THE FIFTH DAY OF CAPTIVITY.

MILADY had however achieved a half-triumph, and the success obtained doubled her strength.

It was not a difficult thing to conquer, as she had hitherto done, men prompt to allow themselves to be seduced, and whom the gallant education of a court led quickly into her snares; milady was handsome enough not to find much resistance on the part of the flesh, and she was sufficiently skillful to prevail over all the obstacles of the mind.

But this time she had to contend with a wild nature, concentrated and insensible by the power of austerity; religion and its observances had made Felton a man inaccessible to ordinary seductions. There fermented in that heated brain plans so vast, projects so tumultuous, that there remained no room for any capricious or material love, that sentiment which is fed by leisure and grows with corruption. Milady had then made a breach, with her false virtue, in the opinion of a man horribly prejudiced against her, and by her beauty in the heart of a man hitherto chaste and pure. In short, she had acquired a knowledge of her means, till this instance unknown to herself, by this experiment, made upon the most rebellious subject that nature and religion could submit to her study.

Many a time, nevertheless, during the evening, she despaired of fate and of herself: she did not invoke God, we very well know, but she had faith in the genius of evil, that immense sovereignty which reigns in all the details of human life, and by which, as in the Arabian fable, a single pomegranate seed is sufficient to reconstruct a ruined world.

Milady, being well prepared for the reception of Felton, was able to erect her batteries for the next day. She knew she had only two days left; that when once the order was signed by Buckingham—and Buckingham would sign it the more readily from its bearing a false name, and that he could not, therefore, recognize the woman in question—once this order signed, we say, the baron would make her embark immediately, and she knew very well that women condemned to transportation employ arms much less powerful in their seductions than the pretendedly virtuous woman whose beauty is enlightened by the sun of the world, which style of beauty the voice of fashion lauds, and whom a halo of aristocracy

gilds with its enchanting splendors. To be a woman condemned to a painful and disgraceful punishment is no im-
pediment to beauty, but it is an obstacle to the regaining of
power. Like all persons of real genius, milady was acquainted with what suited her nature and her means. Poverty
was destruction to her—degradation took away two-thirds of
her greatness. Milady was only a queen among queens. The
pleasure of satisfied pride was necessary for her domination.
To command inferior beings was rather a humiliation than a
pleasure for her.

She should certainly return from her exile—she did not
doubt that a single instant; but how long might this exile
last? For an active, ambitious nature, like that of milady,
days not spent in mounting are inauspicious days! what word,
then, can be found to describe those in which they descend?
To lose a year, two years, three years, is to talk of an eter-
nity; to return after the death or disgrace of the cardinal,
perhaps; to return when D'Artagnan and his friends, happy
and triumphant, should have received from the queen the
reward they had well acquired by the services they had rendered her—there were devouring ideas that a woman like
milady could not endure. For the rest, the storm which raged
within her doubled her strength, and she would have burst
the walls of her prison if her body had been able to take for
a single instant the proportions of her mind.

Then that which spurred her on additionally in the midst
of all this was the remembrance of the cardinal. What must
the mistrustful, restless, suspicious cardinal think of her
silence; the cardinal, not merely her only support, her only
prop, her only protector in the present, but still further,
the principal instrument of her future fortune and vengeance? She knew him—she knew that at her return it would
be in vain to tell him of her imprisonment, in vain to enlarge
upon the sufferings she had undergone—the cardinal would
reply, with the sarcastic calmness of the skeptic, strong at
once by power and genius, "You should not have allowed
yourself to be taken."

Then milady collected all her energies, murmuring in the
depths of her soul the name of Felton, the only beam of
light that penetrated to her in the hell into which she was
fallen; and, like a serpent which folds and unfolds its rings
to ascertain its strength, she enveloped Felton beforehand in
the thousand meshes of her inventive imagination.

Time, however, passed away; the hours, one after another,
seemed to awaken the clock as they passed, and every blow of

the brass hammer resounded upon the heart of the prisoner. At nine o'clock de Winter made his customary visit, examined the window and the bars, sounded the floor and the walls, looked to the chimney and the doors, without, during this long and minute examination, he or milady pronouncing a single word.

Doubtless both of them understood that the situation had become too serious to lose time in useless words and aimless passion.

"Well," said the baron, on leaving her, "you will not escape this night!"

At ten o'clock, Felton came and placed the sentinel; milady recognized his step. She was as well acquainted with it now as a mistress is with that of the lover of her heart, and yet milady at the same time detested and despised this weak fanatic.

That was not the appointed hour—Felton would not come in. Two hours after, as the clock struck twelve, the sentinel was relieved.

This time it was the hour, and from this moment milady waited with impatience.

The new sentinel commenced his walk in the corridor.

At the expiration of ten minutes Felton came.

Milady was all attention.

"Listen," said the young man to the sentinel; "on no pretense leave the door, for you know that last night my lord punished a soldier for having quitted his post for an instant, although I, during his absence, watched in his place."

"Yes, I know he did," said the soldier.

"I recommend you, therefore, to keep the strictest watch For my part, I am going to pay a second visit to this woman who, I fear, entertains sinister intentions upon her own life, and I have received orders to watch her."

"Good!" murmured milady; "the austere Puritan has learned to lie!"

As to the soldier, he only smiled.

"Zounds! lieutenant," said he, "you are not very unlucky in being charged with such commissions, particularly if my lord has authorized you to look in her bed!"

Felton blushed; under any other circumstances he would have reprimanded the soldier for indulging in such a joke, but his conscience murmured too highly to allow his mouth to dare to speak.

"If I call, come in," said he; "if any one comes, call me."

"I will, lieutenant," said the soldier.

Felton entered milady's apartment. Milady arose.

"You are come, then!" said she.

"I promised you I would come," said Felton, "and I am come."

"You promised me other things besides."

"What? my God!" said the young man, who, in spite of his self-command, felt his knees tremble, and the sweat start from his brow.

"You promised to bring a knife, and to leave it with me after our conversation."

"Say no more of that, madame," said Felton; "there is no situation, however terrible it may be, which can authorize one of God's creatures to inflict death upon itself. I have reflected, and I cannot, must not be capable of such a sin."

dered her—there were devouring ideas that a woman like in her *fauteuil*, with a smile of disdain; "and I also have reflected!"

"Upon what? To what purpose?"

"That I can have nothing to say to a man who does not keep his word."

"Oh! my God!" murmured Felton.

"You may retire," said milady; "I shall not speak."

"Here is the knife!" said Felton, drawing from his pocket the weapon which, according to his promise, he had brought, but which he hesitated to give to the prisoner.

"Let me see it," said milady.

"For what purpose?"

"Upon my honor I will instantly return it to you; you shall place it on that table, and you remain between it and me."

Felton held the weapon to milady, who examined the temper of it attentively, and who tried to point on the tip of her finger.

"Well," said she, returning the knife to the young offcer, "this is fine and good steel; you are a faithful friend, Felton."

Felton took back the weapon, and laid it upon the table, as had been agreed.

Milady followed him with eyes, unable to refrain from a gesture of satisfaction.

"Now," said she, "listen to me."

The recommendation was useless: the young officer stood upright before her, awaiting her words, as if to devour them.

"Felton," said milady, with a solemnity full of melancholy, "if your sister, the daughter of your father, said to you:

" 'Still young, unfortunately handsome, I was dragged into a snare, I resisted; ambushes and violences were multiplied around me, I resisted; the religion I serve, the God I adore, were blasphemed because I called upon that religion and that God, I resisted; then outrages were heaped upon me, and as my soul was not subdued, it was determined to defile my body forever. In short——' "

Milady stopped, and a bitter smile passed over her lips.

"In short," said Felton, "in short, what did they do?"

"At length, one evening, my enemy resolved to paralyze the resistance he could not conquer; one evening he mixed a powerful narcotic with my water. Scarcely had I finished my repast, when I felt myself sink by degrees into a strange torpor. Although I was without suspicion, a vague fear seized me, and I endeavored to struggle against sleep. I arose; I endeavored to run to the window, and call for help, but my limbs refused their office. It appeared as if the ceiling sank upon my head, and crushed me with its weight! I stretched out my arms, I endeavored to speak; I could only utter inarticulate sounds, and irresistable faintness came over me; I supported myself by a *fauteuil,* feeling that I was about to fall, but this support was soon useless, for my weak arms. I fell upon one knee, then upon both. I tried to pray, but my tongue was frozen; God, doubtless, neither heard nor saw me, and I sank down upon the floor, a prey to a sleep which resembled death.

"Of all that passed in that sleep, or the time which glided away while it lasted, I have no remembrance; the only thing I recollect is, that I awoke in bed, in a round chamber, the furniture of which was sumptuous, and into which light only penetrated by an opening in the ceiling. No door gave entrance to the room: it might be called a magnificent prison.

"It was a long time before I was able to make out what place I was in, or to take account of the details I describe; my mind appeared to strive in vain to shake off the heavy darkness of the sleep from which I could not rouse myself. I had vague perceptions of a space traveled over, of the rolling of a carriage, of a horrible dream, in which my strength had become exhausted; but all this was so dark and so indistinct in my mind, that these events seemed to belong to another life than mine, and yet mixed with mine by a fantastic duality.

"At times, the state into which I was fallen appeared so strange that I thought I was dreaming. I arose tremblingly, my clothes were near me on a chair; I neither remembered having undressed myself, nor going to bed. Then by degrees the reality broke upon me, full of modest terrors: I was no longer in the house I had dwelt in. As well as I could judge by the light of the sun, the day was already two-thirds gone. It was the evening before that I had fallen asleep; my sleep then must have lasted twenty-four hours! What had taken place during this long sleep?

"I dressed myself as quickly as possible; my slow and stiff motions all attested that the effects of the narcotic were not all yet dissipated. The chamber was evidently furnished for the reception of a woman; and the most finished coquette could not have formed a wish which, an casting her eyes round the apartment, she would not have found accomplished.

"Certainly, I was not the first captive that had been shut up in this splendid prison; but you may easily comprehend, Felton, that the more superb the prison the greater was my terror.

"Yes, it was a prison, for I endeavored in vain to get out of it. I sounded all the walls in the hopes of discovering a door, but everywhere the walls returned a full and flat sound.

"I made the tour of the room at least twenty times, in search of an outlet of some kind; there was none—I sank exhausted with fatigue and terror into a *fauteuil*.

"In the meantime, night came on rapidly, and with night my terrors increased: I did not know whether I had better remain where I was seated; it appeared that I was surrounded with unknown dangers, into which I was about to fall at every instant. Although I had eaten nothing since the evening before, my fears prevented my feeling hunger.

"No noise from without, by which I could measure the time, reached me; I only supposed it must be seven or eight o'clock in the evening, for we were in the month of October, and it was quite dark.

"All at once, the noise of a door turning on its hinges made me start; a globe of fire appeared above the glazed opening of the ceiling, casting a strong light into my chamber, and I perceived with terror that a man was standing within a few paces of me.

"A table, with two covers, bearing a supper ready prepared, stood, as if by magic, in the middle of the apartment.

"That man was he who had pursued me during a whole year, who had vowed my dishonor, and who, by the first words that issued from his mouth, gave me to understand he had accomplished it the preceding night."

"Infamous villain!" murmured Felton.

"Oh, yes, infamous vallain!" cried milady, seeing the interest which the young officer, whose soul seemed to hang on her lips, took in this strange recital.

"Oh, yes, the infamous villain! he believed that, by having triumphed over me in my sleep, all was completed; he came, hoping that I should accept my shame, as my shame was consummated; he came to offer his fortune in exchange for my love.

"All that the heart of a woman could contain of haughty contempt and disdainful words I poured out upon this man. Doubtless he was accustomed to such reproaches, for he listened to me calm and smiling, with his arms crossed over his breast; then, when he thought I had said all, he advanced toward me; I sprang toward the table, I seized a knife, I placed it to my breast.

"'Make one step more,' said I, 'and, in addition to my dishonor, you shall have my death to reproach yourself with!'

"There was no doubt, in my look, my voice, my whole person, that truth of gesture, of *pose* and action which carries conviction to the most perverse minds, for he stopped.

"'Your death!' said he; 'or, no, you are too charming a mistress to allow me to consent to lose you thus, after what has happened. Adieu, my charmer; I will wait to pay you my next visit till you are in a better humor.'

"At these words he blew a whistle: the globe of fire which lighted the room reascended and disappeared; I found myself again in complete darkness. The same noise of the door opening and shutting was repeated the instant afterward, the flaming globe descended afresh, and I was completely alone.

"This moment was frightful; if I had had any doubts of my misfortune, these doubts had vanished in an overwhelming reality: I was in the power of a man whom I not only detested, but despised; of a man capable of anything, and who had already given me a fatal proof of what he was able to do."

"But who, then, was this man?" asked Felton.

"I passed the night in a chair, starting at the least noise; for toward midnight the lamp went out, and I again was in darkness. But the night passed away, without any fresh attempt on the part of my persecutor; day came—the table had disappeared, only I had still the knife in my hand.

"This knife was my only hope.

"I was worn out with fatigue; want of sleep inflamed my eyes; I had not ventured to sleep a single instant. The light of day reassured me; I went and threw myself on the bed, without parting with the liberator knife, which I concealed under my pillow.

"When I awoke, a fresh table was served.

"This time, in spite of my terrors, in spite of my agony, I began to feel a devouring hunger—it was forty-eight hours since I had taken any nourishments; I ate some bread and some fruit; then remembering the narcotic mixed with the water I had drunk, I would not touch that which was placed on the table, but filled my glass at a marble fountain fixed in the wall, over my toilet.

"And yet, notwithstanding these precautions, I remained for some time in a terrible agitation of mind. But my fears were ill-founded; I passed the day without experiencing anything of the kind I dreaded.

"I took the precaution to half empty the carafe, in order that my suspicion might not be noticed.

"The evening came on, and with it darkness; but, however profound was this darkness, my eyes began to be accustomed to it; I saw the table sink through the floor; a quarter of an hour after it reappeared, bearing my supper; and in an instant, thanks to the lamp, my chamber was once more lighted.

"I was determined to eat only such objects as could not possibly have anything soporific introduced into them: two eggs and some fruit composed my repast, then I drew another glass of water from my protecting fountain, and drank it.

"After swallowing a mouthful or two, it appeared to me not to have the same taste that it had in the morning: a suspicion instantly seized me—I stopped, but I had already drunk half a glassful of it.

"I threw the rest away with horror and waited, with the dew of fear upon my brow.

"There was no doubt that some invisible witness had seen me draw the water from that fountain, and had taken advantage of my confidence in it, the better to assure my ruin, so cruelly resolved upon, so cruelly pursued.

"Half an hour had not passed when the same symptoms began to appear; only, as I had only drunk half a glass of the water, I contended longer, and, instead of falling entirely asleep, I sank into a state of drowsiness, which left me a perception of what was passing around me, while depriving me of the strength either to defend myself or to fly.

"I dragged myself toward the bed, to seek the only defense I had left—my perserver knife—but I could not reach the bolster; I sank on my knees, my hands clasped round one of the bedposts; then I felt that I was lost."

Felton became frightfully pale, and a convulsive tremor crept through his whole body.

"And what was most terrible," continued milady, her voice altered, as if she still experienced the same agony as at that awful minute, "was that at this time I retained a consciousness of the danger that threatened me; was that my soul, if I may say so, waked in my sleeping body; was that I saw, was that I heard. It is true that all was like a dream, but it was not the less frightful.

"I saw the lamp ascend, and leave me in darkness; then I heard the so well-known creaking of the door, although I had heard that door open but twice.

"I felt instinctively that some one approached me: it is said that the doomed wretch in the deserts of America thus feels the approach of the serpent.

"I endeavored to make an effort, I attempted to cry out; by an incredible effort of will I even raised myself up, but only to sink down again immediately, and to fall into the arms of my persecutor."

"Tell me who this man was!" cried the young officer.

Milady saw at a single glance all the painful feelings she inspired in Felton, by dwelling on every detail of her recital; but she would not spare him a single pang. The more profoundly she wounded his heart, the more certainly he would avenge her. She continued, then, as if she had not heard his exclamation, or as if she thought the moment was not yet come to reply to it.

"Only this time it was no longer an inert body, without feeling, that the villain had to deal with; I have told you that, without being able to regain the complete exercise of my faculties, I retained the sense of my danger. I struggled, than, with all my strength, and doubtless opposed, weak as I was, a long resistance, for I heard him cry out:

"'These miserable Puritans! I knew very well that they tired out their executioners, but I did not think they had been so strong against their lovers!'

"Alas! this desperate resistance could not last long; I felt my strength fail, and this time it was not my sleep that enabled the villain to prevail, but my swooning."

Felton listened without uttering any word or sound but a kind of inward expression of agony; the sweat streamed down his marble brow, and his hand, under his coat, tore his breast in nervous excitement.

"My first impulse, on coming to myself, was to feel under my pillow for the knife I had not been able to reach; if it had not been useful for defense, it might at least serve in expiation.

"But on taking this knife, Felton, a terrible idea occurred to me. I have sworn to tell you all, and I will tell you all; I have promised you the truth—I will tell it, were it to destroy me."

"The idea came into your mind to avenge yourself on this man, did it not?" cried Felton.

"Yes," said milady. "The idea was not that of a Christian, I knew; but, without doubt, that eternal enemy of our souls, that lion roaring constantly around us, breathed it into my mind. In short, what shall I say to you, Felton?" continued milady, in the tone of a woman accusing herself of a crime. "This idea occurred to me, and did not leave me; it is of this homicidal thought that I now bear the punishment."

"Continue! continue!" said Felton; "I am eager to see you attain your vengeance!"

"Oh, I resolved that it should take place as soon as possible; I had no doubt he would return the following night. During the day I had nothing to fear.

"When the hour of breakfast came, therefore, I did not hesitate to eat and drink. I determined to make believe to sup, but to take nothing; I was forced, then, by the nourishment of the morning, to combat the fast of the evening.

"Only I concealed a glass of water, which formed part of my breakfast, thirst having been the chief of my sufferings when I had remained forty-eight hours without eating or drinking.

"The day passed away, without having any other influence on me than to strengthen the resolution I had formed; only I took care that my face should not betray the thoughts of my heart, for I had no doubt I was watched; several times, even, I felt a smile upon my lips. Felton, I dare not tell you at what idea I smiled; you would hold me in horror——"

"Go on! go on!" said Felton; "you see plainly that I listen, and that I am anxious to know the end."

"Evening came, the ordinary events were accomplished: during the darkness, as before, my table was covered, then the lamp was lighted, and I sat down to table; I only ate some fruit; I pretended to pour out water from the carafe, but I only drank that which I had saved in my glass; the substitution was made so carefully that my spies, if I had any, could have no suspicion of it.

"After supper, I exhibited the same marks of languor as on the preceding evenings; but this time, as if I yielded to fatigue, or as if I had become familiarized with danger, I dragged myself towards my bed, let my robe fall, and got in.

"I found my knife where I had placed it, under my pillow, and, while feigning to sleep, my hand grasped the handle of it convulsively.

"Two hours passed away without anything fresh occurring this time. Oh, my God! who could have said so the evening before! I began to fear that he would not come!

"At length I saw the lamp rise softly, and disappear in the depths of the ceiling; my chamber was filled with darkness and obscurity, but I made a strong effort to penetrate this darkness and obscurity.

"Nearly ten minutes passed; I heard no other noise but the beating of my own heart.

"I implored heaven that he might come.

"At length I heard the well-known noise of the door which opened and shut; I heard, notwithstanding the thickness of the carpet, a step which made the floor creak; I saw, notwithstanding the darkness, a shadow which approached my bed."

"Make haste make haste!" said Felton; "do you not see that every one of your words burns me like molten lead."

"Then," continued milady, "then I collected all my strength, I recalled to my mind that the moment of vengeance, or, rather, of justice, had struck. I looked upon myself as another Judith: I gathered myself up, my knife in my hand, and when I saw him near me, stretching out his arms to find his victim, then, with the last cry of agony and despair, I struck him in the middle of his breast.

"The miserable villain! he had foreseen all! his breast was covered with a coat of mail: the knife was bent against it.

"'Ah! ah!' cried he, seizing my arm, and wrestling from me the weapon that had so ill-seconded my design, 'you want to take my life, do you, my pretty Puritan! but that's more than dislike, that's ingratitude! Come, come, calm yourself, my sweet girl! I thought you were become kinder. I am not one of these tyrants who detain women by force. You don't love me; with my usual fatuity, I doubted of it; now I am convinced. To-morrow you shall be free.'

"I had but one wish, and that was that he should kill me.

" 'Beware!' said I, 'for my liberty is your dishonor.'

" 'Explain yourself, my pretty Sibyl.'

" 'Yes; for no sooner shall I have left this place, than I will tell everything; I will proclaim the violence you have used toward me; I will describe my captivity. I will denounce this palace of infamy. You are placed on high, my lord. but tremble! Above you there is the king; above the king there is God!'

"However perfect master he was over himself my persecutor allowed a movement of anger to escape him. I could not see the expression of his countenance, but I felt the arm upon which my hand was placed tremble.

" 'Then you shall not leave this place,' said he.

" 'So be it,' cried I, 'then the place of my punishment will be that of my tomb. So be it, I will die here, and you will see if a phantom that accuses is not more terrible than a living being that threatens.'

" 'You shall have no weapon left in your power.'

" 'There is a weapon which despair has placed within the reach of every creature that has the courage to make use of it. I will allow myself to die with hunger.'

" 'Come, come,' said the wretch, 'is not peace much better than such a war as that? I will restore you to liberty this moment; I will proclaim you a piece of immaculate virtue; I will name you the Lucretia of England.'

" 'And I will say that you are the Sextus; I will denounce you before men as I have denounced you before God; and if it be necessary that, like Lucretia, I should sign my accusation with my blood, I will sign it.'

" 'Ah!' said my enemy, in a jeering tone, 'that's quite another thing. *Ma foi!* everything considered, you are very well off here, you shall want for nothing, and if you choose to die of hunger—why, that will be your own fault.'

"At these words he retired; I heard the door open and shut, and I remained overwhelmed, still less, I confess it, by my grief than by the shame of not having avenged myself.

"He kept his word. All the day, all the next night passed away, without my seeing him again. But I also kept my word with him, and I neither ate nor drank; I was, as I had told him, resolved to die of hunger.

"I passed the day and the night in prayer, for I hoped that God would pardon me my suicide.

"The second night the door opened; I was lying on the floor, for my strength began to abandon me.

"At the noise I raised myself up on one hand.

" 'Well!' said a voice which vibrated in too terrible a manner in my ear not to be recognized; 'well! are we softened a little, will we not pay for our liberty with a single promise of silence? Come, I am a good sort of a prince,' added he, 'and although I am not very partial to Puritans, I do them justice, as well as to female Puritans, when they are pretty. Come, take a little oath for me on the cross, I won't ask anything more of you.'

" 'Upon the cross,' cried I, rising up, for at that abhorred voice I had recovered all my strength; 'upon the cross! I swear that no promise, no menace, no force, no torture shall close my mouth; upon the cross! I swear to denounce you everywhere as a murderer, as a despoiler of honor, as a base coward; upon the cross! I swear, if I ever leave this place, to call down vengeance upon you from the whole human race.'

" 'Beware!' said the voice, in a threatening accent that I had never yet heard, 'I have an extraordinary means, which I will not employ, but in the last extremity, to close your mouth, or at least to prevent any one from believing a word you may utter.'

"I mustered all my strength to reply to him with a burst of laughter.

"He saw that, from that time, it was an exterminal war, a war to the death between us.

" 'Listen,' said he, 'I give you the rest of the night and the day of to-morrow; reflect, promise to be silent, and riches, consideration, even honor shall surround you; threaten to speak, and I will condemn you to infamy.'

" 'You,' cried I, 'you!'

" 'To interminable, ineffaceable infamy!'

" 'You,' repeated I. Oh! I declare to you, Felton, I thought him mad!

" 'Yes, I,' replied he.

" 'Oh! leave me,' said I, 'begone, if you do not desire to see me dash my head against that wall before your eyes!'

" 'Very well! it is you own doing; till to-morrow evening, then!'

" 'Till to-morrow evening, then,' replied I, allowing myself to fall, and biting the carpet with rage.

Felton leaned for support upon a piece of furniture, and milady saw, with the joy of a demon, that his strength would fail him, perhaps before the end of her recital.

CHAPTER LVII.

MEANS FOR CLASSICAL TRAGEDY.

AFTER a moment of silence employed by milady in observing the young man who listened to her, milady continued her recital.

"It was nearly three days since I had eaten or drunk anything, I suffered frightful torments; at times there passed before me clouds which pressed my brow, which veiled my eyes; this was delirium.

"When the evening came, I was so weak that at every time that I fainted I thanked God, for I thought I was about to die.

"In the midst of one of these faintings, I heard the door open; terror recalled me to myself.

"He entered the apartment, followed by a man in a mask; he was masked likewise; but I knew his step, I knew his voice, I knew him by that imposing carriage that hell has bestowed upon his person for the curse of humanity.

"'Well!' said he to me, 'have you made your mind up to take the oath I have requested of you?'

"'You have said it, Puritans have but one word; mine you have heard, and that is to pursue you on earth to the tribunal of men, in heaven to the tribunal of God.'

"'You persist, then?'

"'I swear it before the God who hears me; I will take the whole world as a witness of your crime, and that until I have found an avenger.'

"'You are a prostitute,' said he in a voice of thunder, 'and you shall undergo the punishment of prostitutes! Disgraced in the eyes of the world you shall invoke, try to prove to that world that you are neither guilty nor mad!'

"Then, addressing the man who accompanied him:

"'Executioner,' said he, 'do your duty.'"

"Oh! his name, his name!" cried Felton, "tell it me!"

"Then, in spite of my cries, in spite of my resistance, for I began to comprehend that there was a question of something worse than death, the executioner seized me, threw me on the floor, fastened me with his bonds, and suffocated by sobs, almost without sense, invoking God, who did not listen to me, I uttered all at once a frightful cry of pain and shame; a burning fire, a red-hot iron, the iron of the executioner, was imprinted on my shoulder."

Felton uttered a groan.

"Here," said milady, rising with the majesty of a queen—"here, Felton, behold the new martyrdom invented for a pure young girl, the victim of the brutality of a villain. Learn to know the heart of men, and henceforth make yourself less easily the instrument of their unjust vengeances."

Milady, with a rapid gesture, opened her robe, tore the cambric that covered her bosom, and red with feigned anger and simulated shame, showed the young man the ineffaceable impression which dishonored that beautiful shoulder.

"But," cried Felton, "that is a fleur-de-lis which I see there."

"And therein consisted the infamy." replied milady. "The brand of England!—it would be necessary to prove what tribunal had imposed it on me, and I could have made a public appeal to all the tribunals of the kingdom; but the brand of France!—oh! by it, by it I was really branded indeed!"

This was too much for Felton.

Pale, motionless, overwhelmed by this frightful revelation, dazzled by the superhuman beauty of this woman, who unveiled herself before him with an immodesty which appeared to him sublime, he ended by falling on his knees before her, as the early Christmas did before those pure and holy martyrs whom the persecution of the emperors gave up in the circus to the sanguinary lubricity of the populace. The brand disappeared, the beauty alone remained.

"Pardon! pardon!" cried Felton, "oh! pardon!"

Milady read in his eyes, love! love!

"Pardon for what?" asked she.

"Pardon me for having joined with your persecutors."

Milady held out her hand to him.

"So beautiful! so young!" cried Felton, covering that hand with his kisses.

Milady let one of those looks fall upon him which make a slave of a king.

Felton was a Puritan; he abandoned the hand of this woman to kiss her feet.

He no longer loved her, he adored her.

When this crisis was past, when milady appeared to have resumed her self-possession, which she had never lost; when Felton had seen her cover again with the veil of chastity those treasures of love which were only concealed from him to make him desire them the more ardently—

"Ah! now," said he, "I have only one thing to ask of

you, that is, the name of your true executioner, for, for me there is but one; the other was an instrument, that was all."

"What, brother!" cried milady, "must I name him again, have you not divined who he is?"

"What!" cried Felton, "he!—again he!—always he! What! —the truly guilty?"

"The truly guilty," said milady, "is the ravager of England, the persecutor of true believers, the base ravisher of the honor of so many women, he who, to satisfy a caprice of his corrupt heart, is about to make England shed so much blood, who protects the Protestants to-day and will betray them to-morrow——"

"Buckingham! it is, then, Buckingham!" cried Felton, in a high state of exasperation.

Milady concealed her face in her hands, as if she could not endure the shame which this name recalled to her.

"Buckingham, the executioner of this angelic creature!" cried Felton. "And thou hast not hurled thy thunder at him, my God! and thou hast left him noble, honored, powerful, for the ruin of us all!"

"God abandons him who abandons himself," cried milady.

"But he will draw down upon his head the punishment reserved for the damned!" said Felton, with increasing warmth: "he wills that human vengeance should precede heavenly justice."

"Men fear him and spare him."

"I!" said Felton, "I do not fear him, nor I will I spare him!"

The soul of milady was as if bathed in an infernal joy.

"But how can Lord de Winter, my protector, my father," asked Felton, "possibly be mixed up with all this?"

"Listen, Felton," resumed milady, "for by the side of base and contemptible men there are often found great and generous natures. I had an affianced husband, a man whom I loved, and who loved me; a heart like yours, Felton, a man like you. I went to him and told him all; he knew me, that man did, and did not doubt an instant. He was a nobleman, a man equal to Buckingham, in every respect. He said nothing, he only girded on his sword, enveloped himself in his cloak, and went straight to Buckingham Palace."

"Yes, yes," said Felton; "I understand how he would act: but with such men it is not the sword, it is the poniard that should be employed."

"Buckingham had left England the day before, sent am.

bassador to Spain, to demand the hand of the Infanta for King
Charles I., who was then only Prince of Wales. My affianced
husband returned.

" 'Hear me,' said he; 'this man is gone, and for the moment has, consequently, escaped my vengeance; but let us be
united, as we were to have been, and then leave it to Lord de
Winter to maintain his own honor and that of his wife.' "

"Lord de Winter!" cried Felton.

"Yes," said milady, "Lord de Winter; and now you can
understand it all, can you not? Buckingham remained
nearly a year absent. A week before his return Lord de
Winter died, leaving me his sole heir. Whence came the
blow? God who knows all, knows without doubt; but as for
me, I accuse nobody."

"Oh! what an abyss! what an abyss!" cried Felton.

"Lord de Winter died without revealing anything to his
brother. The terrible secret was to be concealed till it burst
like a clap of thunder, over the head of the guilty. Your
protector had seen with pain this marriage of his elder brother
with a portionless girl. I was sensible that I could look for no
support from a man disappointed in his hopes of an inheritance. I went to France, with a determination to remain there
for the rest of my life. But all my fortune is in England.
Communication being closed by the war, I was in want of
everything. I was then obliged to come back again. Six
days ago I landed at Portmouth."

"Well?" said Felton.

"Well. Buckingham heard by some means, no doubt, of
my return. He spoke of me to Lord de Winter, already
prejudiced against me; and told him that his sister-in-law
was a prostitute, a branded woman. The noble and pure
voice of my husband was no longer there to defend me.
Lord de Winter believed all that was told him, with so much
the more facility from its being his interest to believe it. He
caused me to be arrested, had me conducted hither, and
placed me under your guard. You know the rest. The day
after to-morrow he banishes me, he transports me; the day
after to-morrow he exiles me among the infamous. Oh! the
scheme is well laid! the plot is clever! my honor will not survive it! You see, then, Felton, I can do nothing but die!
Felton, give me that knife."

And, at these words, as if all her strength was exhausted,
milady sank weak and languishing into the arms of the young
officer, who, intoxicated with love, anger, and hitherto unknown sensations of delight, received her with transport,

pressed her against his heart, all trembling at the breath from that charming mouth, bewildered by the contact with that beautiful bosom.

"No, no," said he, "no, you shall live honored and pure, you shall live to triumph over your enemies."

Milady put him from her slowly with her hand, while drawing him nearer with her look; but Felton, in his turn, embraced her more closely, imploring her like a divinity.

"Oh, death! death!" said she, lowering her voice and her eyelids; "oh, death rather than shame! Felton, my brother, my friend, I conjure you!"

"No," cried Felton, "no; you shall live, and you shall be avenged."

"Felton, I bring misfortune to all who surround me! Felton, abandon me! Felton, let me die!"

"Well, then, we live and die together!" cried he, gluing his lips to those of the prisoner.

Several strokes resounded on the door; this time milady really pushed him away from her.

"Hark!" said she; "we have been overheard; some one is coming! all is over! we are lost!"

"No," said Felton; "it is only the sentinel warning me that they are about to change guard."

"Then run to the door and open it yourself."

Felton obeyed, this woman was now his whole thought, his whole soul.

He found a sergeant commanding a watch patrol.

"Well! what is the matter!" asked the young lieutenant.

"You told me to open the door if I heard anyone cry out!" said the soldier; "but you forgot to leave me the key. I heard you cry out, without understanding what you said. I tried to open the door, but it was locked inside; then I called the sergeant."

"And here I am," said the sergeant.

Felton, quite bewildered, almost mad, stood speechless.

Milady plainly perceived that it was now her turn to come forward: she ran to the table, and seizing the knife which Felton had laid down:

"And by what right will you prevent me from dying?" said she.

"Great God!" exclaimed Felton, on seeing the knife glitter in her hand.

At that moment a burst of ironical laughter resounded through the corridor. The baron, attracted by the noise, in his *robe-de-chambre*, his sword under his arm, stood in the doorway.

"Ah! ah!" said he; "here we are, arrived at the last act of the tragedy. You see, Felton, the drama has gone through all the phases I named; but be at ease, no blood will flow."

Milady perceived that all was lost unless she gave Felton an immediate and terrible proof of her courage.

"You are mistaken, my lord, blood will flow; and may that blood fall back on those who cause it to flow!"

Felton uttered a cry, and rushed toward her; he was too late milady had stabbed herself.

But the knife had fortunately, we ought to say skillfully, come in contact with the steel busk, which at that period, like a cuirass, defended the chests of the women; it had glided down it, tearing the robe, and had penetrated slantingly between the flesh and the ribs.

Milady's robe was not the less stained with blood in a second. Felton snatched away the knife.

"See, my lord," said he, in a deep, gloomy tone, "here is a woman who was under my guard, and who has killed herself!"

"Be at ease, Felton," said Lord de Winter, "she is not dead; demons do not die so easily. Be at ease, and go and wait for me in my chamber."

"But, my lord——"

"Go, sir, I command you."

At this injunction from his superior, Felton obeyed; but, in going out, he put the knife into his bosom.

As to Lord de Winter, he contented himself with calling the woman who waited on milady, and when she was come, he recommended the prisoner, who was still fainting, to her care, and left her alone with her.

But as, all things considered, notwithstanding his suspicions, the wound might be serious, he immediately sent off a man and horse to fetch a doctor.

CHAPTER LVIII.

ESCAPE.

As Lord de Winter had thought, milady's wound was not dangerous. So soon as she was left alone with the woman whom the baron had summoned to her assistance, she opened her eyes.

It was, however, necessary to affect weakness and pain; not a very difficult task for so finished an actress as milady. Thus the poor woman was completely the dupe of the prisoner, whom, notwithstanding her entreaties to the contrary, she persisted in watching during the remainder of the night.

But the presence of this woman did not prevent milady from thinking.

There was no longer a doubt that Felton was convinced: Felton was hers. If an angel appeared to that young man as an accuser of milady, he would take him, in the disposition of mind he was then in, for a messenger from the demon.

Milady smiled at this thought, for Felton was from that time her only hope—her only means of safety.

But Lord de Winter might have suspected him—Felton himself might now be watched!

Toward four o'clock in the morning the doctor arrived; but since the time my lady had stabbed herself, however short, the wound had closed. The doctor could, therefore, measure neither the direction nor the depth of it; he only satisfied himself that, by milady's pulse, the case was not serious.

In the morning, milady, under the pretense of not having slept well in the night, and wanting rest, sent away the woman who attended her.

She had one hope; which was, that Felton would appear at the breakfast hour; but Felton did not come.

Were her fears realized? Was Felton, suspected by the baron, about to fail her at the decisive moment? She had only one day left. Lord de Winter had announced her embarkation for the 23d, and it was now the morning of the 22d.

Nevertheless she still waited patiently till the hour for dinner.

Although she had eaten nothing in the morning, the dinner was brought in at its usual time; milady then perceived with terror that the uniform of the soldiers that guarded her was changed.

Then she ventured to ask what had become of Felton.

She was told that he had left the castle an hour before, on horseback. She inquired if the baron was still at the castle. The soldier replied that he was, and that he had given orders to be informed if the prisoner wished to speak to him.

Milady replied that she was too weak at present, and that her only desire was to be left alone.

The soldier went out, leaving the dinner-table covered.

Felton was sent away; the marines were removed; Felton was, then, mistrusted!

This was the last blow to the prisoner.

Left alone, she got up. The bed in which she had remained from prudence, and that she might be believed to be seriously wounded, burned her like a bed of fire. She cast a glance at the door: the baron had had a plank nailed over the grating; he no doubt feared that, by this opening, she might still, by some diabolical means succeed in corrupting her guards.

Milady smiled with joy. She was free now to give way to her transports without being observed. She traversed the chamber with the fury of mad woman, or of a tigress shut up in an iron cage. Certes, if the knife had been left to her power, she would now have thought, not of killing herself, but of killing the baron.

At six o'clock, Lord de Winter came in: he was armed at all points. This man, in whom milady, till that time, had only seen a sufficiently simple gentleman, had become an admirable gaoler: he appeared to foresee everything, to divine everything, to prevent everything.

A single look at milady informed him of all that was passing in her mind.

"Ay!" said he, "I see; but you shall not kill me to-day; you have no longer a weapon; and besides, I am on my guard. You began to pervert my poor Felton; he was yielding to your infernal influence; but I will save him—he will never see you again—all is over. Get your clothes together, to-morrow you shall go. I had fixed the embarkation for the 24th; but I have reflected that the more promptly the affair takes place, the more certain it will be. To-morrow, by twelve o'clock, I shall have the order for your exile, signed—'Buckingham.' If you speak a single word to any one before being on shipboard, my sergeant will blow your brains out; he has orders to do so; if, when on board, you speak a single word to any one before the captain permits you, the captain will have you thrown into the sea—that is agreed upon.

"*Au revoir*, then—that is all I have to say to-day. To-morrow I will see you again, to take my leave of you." And at these words the baron went out. Milady had listened to all this menacing tirade with a smile of disdain on her lips, but rage in her heart.

The supper was served; milady felt that she stood in need of all her strength; she did not know what might take place during this night, which approached so menacingly; for large masses of cloud rolled over the face of the heavens, and distant lightning announced a storm.

The storm came on about ten o'clock: milady felt a consolation in seeing nature partake of the disorder of her heart; the thunder growled in the air like the passion and anger in her thoughts: it appeared to her that the blast as it swept along disheveled her brow, as it bowed the branches of the trees and bore away their leaves; she howled as the hurricane howled, and her voice was lost in the great voice of nature, who also seemed to groan with despair.

All at once she heard a tap at her window, and by the help of a flash of lightning she saw the face of a man appear behind the bars.

She ran to the window and opened it.

"Felton!" cried she—"I am saved!"

"Yes!" said Felton; "but be silent! be silent! I must have time to file through these bars. Only take care that I am not seen through the grating of the door."

"Oh! it is a proof that the Lord is on our side, Felton," replied milady; "they have closed up the grating with a board."

"That is well, God has made them senseless!" said Felton.

"But what must I do?" asked milady.

"Nothing! nothing! only shut the window. Go to bed, or at least lie down in your clothes; as soon as I have done I will knock on one of the panes of glass. But are you strong enough to follow me?"

"Oh, yes!"

"Your wound?"

"Gives me pain, but will not prevent my walking."

"Be ready, then, at the first signal."

Milady shut the window, extinguished the lamp, and went, as Felton had desired her, to lie down on the bed. Amid the moaning of the storm she heard the grinding of the file upon the bars, and by the light of every flash she perceived the shadow of Felton through the window.

She passed an hour apparently, unable to breathe, panting, with a cold sweat upon her brow, and her heart oppressed by frightful agony at every movement she heard in the corridor.

There are hours which last a year.

At the expiration of an hour, Felton tapped again.

Milady sprang out of bed and opened the window. Tw

bars removed formed an opening large enough for a man to pass through.

"Are you ready?" asked Felton.

"Yes. Must I take anything with me?"

"Money, if you have any."

"Yes, fortunately, they have left me all I had."

"So much the better, for I have expended all mine in hiring a vessel."

"Here!" said milady, placing a bag full of loius in Felton's hands.

Felton took the bag and threw it to the foot of the wall.

"Now," said he, "will you come?"

"I am ready."

Milady mounted upon a chair, and passed the upper part of her person through the window; she saw the young officer suspended over the abyss by a ladder of ropes. For the first time an emotion of terror reminded her that she was a woman. The dark space frightened her.

"I expected this," said Felton.

"Oh! it's nothing! it's nothing!" said milady; "I will descend with my eyes shut."

"Have you confidence in me?" said Felton.

"How can you ask me such a question?"

"Put your two hands together. Cross them—that's right."

Felton tied her two wrists together with a handkerchief, and then over the handkerchief with a cord.

"What are you doing?" asked milady with surprise.

"Pass your arms around my neck, and fear nothing."

"But I shall make you lose your balance, and we shall both be dashed to pieces."

"Don't be afraid; I am a sailor."

Not a second was to be lost; milady passed her arms round Felton's neck, and let herself slip out of the window. Felton began to descend the ladder slowly, step by step; notwithstanding the weight of their bodies, the blast of the hurricane made them wave in the air.

All at once Felton stopped.

"What is the matter?" asked milady.

"Silence," said Felton, "I hear footsteps."

"We are discovered!"

There was a silence of several seconds.

"No," said Felton, "it is nothing."

"But what noise was that then?"

"That of the patrol going their round."

"Where is their round?"

"Just under us."

"They will discover us!"

"No; if it does not lighten, they will not."

"But they will run against the ladder."

"Fortunately it is too short by six feet."

"Here they are! my God!"

"Silence!"

Both remained suspended, motionless and breathless, within twenty paces of the ground, while the patrol passed beneath them, laughing and talking.

This was a terrible moment for the fugitives.

The patrol passed: the noise of their retreating footsteps and the murmur of their voices soon died away.

"Now," said Felton, "we are safe."

Milady breathed a deep sigh and fainted.

Felton continued to descend. When arrived at the bottom of the ladder, and he found no more support for his feet, he clung with his hands; at length, arrived at the last step, he hung by his hands and touched the ground. He stooped down, picked up the bag of money, and carried it in his teeth. Then he took milady in his arms and set off briskly in the direction opposite to that which the patrol had taken. He soon left the path of the rounds, descended across the rocks, and when arrived on the edge of the sea, whistled.

A similar signal replied to him, and five minutes after a boat appeared, rowed by four men.

The boat approached as near as it could to the shore, but there was not depth of water enough for it to touch; and Felton walked into the sea up to his middle, being unwilling to trust his precious burden to anybody.

Fortunately the storm began to die away, but still the sea was disturbed; the little boat bounded over the waves like a nutshell.

"To the sloop," said Felton, "and row quickly."

The four men bent to their oars, but the sea was too rough to let them take much hold of it.

They, however, left the castle behind: that was the principal thing. The night was extremely dark, it was almost impossible to distinguish the shore from the boat, it was therefore less likely to distinguish the boat from the shore.

A black point floated on the sea—that was the sloop.

While the boat was advancing with all the speed its four rowers could give it, Felton united the cord, and then the handkerchief which bound milady's hands together. When

her hands were loosed, he took some sea-water and sprinkled
it over her face.

Milady breathed a sigh and opened her eyes.

"Where am I?" said she.

"Saved," replied the young officer.

"Oh! saved! saved!" cried she. "Yes, there are the
heavens, here is the sea! the air I breathe is the air of liberty!
Ah! thanks, Felton, thanks!"

The young man pressed her to his heart.

"But what is the matter with my hands?" asked milady,
"it seems as if my wrists had been crushed in a vice?"

Milady held out her arms, and her wrists appeared bruised.

"Alas!" said Felton, looking at those beautiful hands and
shaking his head sorrowfully.

"Oh! it's of no consequence; it's nothing!" cried milady.
"I remember now."

Milady looked around her as if in search of something.

"Is it there," said Felton, touching the bag of money with
his foot.

They drew near to the sloop. A sailor on watch hailed the
boat, the boat replied:

"What vessel is that?" asked milady.

"The one I have hired for you."

"Where is it to take me to?"

"Where you please, after you have put me on shore at
Portsmouth."

"What are you going to do at Portsmouth?" asked milady.

"To accomplish the orders of Lord de Winter," said Felton,
with a gloomy smile.

"What orders?" said milady.

"Do you not understand?" asked Felton.

"No; explain yourself, I beg."

"As he mistrusted me, he determined to guard you himself, and sent me in his place to get Buckingham to sign the
order for your transportation."

"But if he mistrusted you, how could he confide such an
order to you?"

"How could I be supposed to know what I was the
bearer of?"

"That's true! And you are going to Portsomuth?"

"I have no time to lose: to-morrow is the 23d and Buckingham sets sail to-morrow with his fleet."

"He sets sail to-morrow! Where for?"

"For La Rochelle."

"He must not sail!" cried milady, forgetting her usual presence of mind.

"Be satisfied," relied Felton; "he will not sail."

Milady started with joy; she could read to the depths of the heart of this young man; the death of Buckingham was there written at full length.

"Felton," cried she, "you are as great as Judas Maccabeus! If you die, I will die with you; that is all I am able to say to you."

"Silence!" cried Felton; "we are arrived."

They were, in fact, close to the sloop.

Felton ascended first, and gave his hand to milady, while the sailors supported her, for the sea was still much agitated.

An instant after they were on the deck.

"Captain," said Felton, "this is the person of whom I spoke to you, and whom you must convey safe and sound to France."

"For a thousand pistoles," said the captain.

"I have paid you five hundred of them."

"That's correct," said the captain.

"And here are the other five hundred," replied milady, placing her hand upon the bag of gold.

"No," said the captain, "I make but one bargain; and I have agreed with this young man that the other five hundred shall not be due to me till we arrive at Boulogne."

"And shall we arrive there?"

"Safe and sound," said the captain, "as true as my name's Jack Butler."

"Well!" said milady, "if you keep your word, instead of five hundred, I will give you a thousand pistoles."

"Hurrah! for you, then, my pretty lady," cried the captain; "and may God often send me such passengers as your ladyship."

"In the meanwhile," said Felton, "convey me to the little bay of——you know it was agreed you should put in there."

The captain replied by ordering the necessary maneuvers, and toward seven o'clock in the morning the little vessel cast anchor in the bay that had been named.

During this passage Felton related everything to milady; how, instead of going to London, he had hired the little vessel; how he had returned; how he had scaled the wall by fastening cramps in the interstices of the stones as he ascended to give him foothold; and how, when he had reached the bars, he fastened his ladder: milady knew the rest.

On her side, milady was going to endeavor to encourage Felton in his project; but at the first words that issued from her mouth, she plainly saw that the young fanatic stood more in need of being moderated than urged on.

It was agreed that milady should wait for Felton till ten o'clock; if he did not return by ten o'clock, she was to sail without him.

In that case, and supposing he was at liberty, he was to rejoin her in France, at the convent of the Carmelites, at Béthune.

CHAPTER LIX.

WHAT TOOK PLACE AT PORTSMOUTH ON AUGUST 23D, 1628.

FELTON took leave of milady as a brother about to go for a mere walk takes leave of his sister, kissing her hand.

His whole person appeared in its ordinary state of calmness; only an unusual fire beamed from his eyes, like the effects of a fever; his brow was more pale than it generally was; his teeth were clenched, and his speech had a short dry accent, which indicated that something dark was at work within him.

As long as he remained in the boat which conveyed him to land, he kept his face toward milady, who, standing on the deck, followed him with her eyes. Both felt relieved from the fear of pursuit, nobody ever came into milady's apartment before nine o'clock; and it would require three hours to go from the castle to London.

Felton jumped on shore, climbed the little ascent which led to the top of the beach, saluted milady a last time, and took his course toward the city.

At the end of a hundred paces, the ground began to decline again, and he could, on turning round, only see the mast of the sloop.

He immediately ran in the direction of Portsmouth, which he saw at nearly half a league before him, standing out in the haze of the morning, with its houses and towers.

Beyond Portsmouth, the sea was covered with vessels, whose masts, like a forest of poplars, bent with each breath of the wind.

Felton, in his rapid walk, repassed in his mind all which

two years of meditation and a long residence among partisans furnished of accusations, true or false, against the favorite of James I. and Charles I.

When he compared the public crimes of this minister, startling crimes, European crimes, if so we may say, with the private and unknown crimes with which milady had charged him, Felton found that the more culpable of the two men which formed the character of Buckingham was the one of whom the public knew not the life. This was because his love, so strange, so new, and so ardent, made him view the infamous and imaginary accusations of Lady de Winter as we view, through a magnifying glass, as frightful monsters atoms in reality imperceptible by the side of an ant.

The rapidity of his walk heated his blood still more; the idea that he left behind him, exposed to a frightful vengeance, the woman he loved, or rather that he adored as a saint, the emotion he had experienced, present fatigue, all together exalted his mind above human feeling.

He entered Portsmouth about eight o'clock in the morning; the whole population was on foot; drums were beating in the streets and the port; the troops about to be embarked were marching toward the sea.

Felton arrived at the palace of the admiralty, covered with dust, and streaming with perspiration. His countenance usually so pale, was purple with heat and passion. The sentinel wanted to repulse him, but Felton called to the officer of the post, and drawing from his pocket the letter of which he was the bearer—

"A pressing message from the Lord de Winter," said he.

At the name of Lord de Winter, who was known to be one of his grace's most intimate friends, the officer of the post gave orders for Felton to be allowed to pass, who, besides wore the uniform of a naval officer.

Felton darted into the palace.

At the moment he entered the vestibule, another man was entering likewise, covered with dust, and out of breath, leaving at the gate a post-horse, which, as soon as he had alighted from it, sank down exhausted.

Felton and he addressed Patrick, the duke's confidential *valet-de-chambre,* at the same moment. Felton named Lord de Winter, the unknown would not name anybody, and asserted that it was to the duke alone he should make himself known. Each was anxious to gain admission before the other.

Patrick, who knew Lord de Winter was in affairs of duty

and in relations of friendship with the duke, gave the preference to him who came in his name. The other was forced to wait, and it was easily to be seen how he cursed the delay.

The *valet-de-chambre* led Felton through a large hall, in which waited the deputies from La Rochelle, headed by the Prince of Soubise, and introduced him into a closet, where Buckingham, just out of the bath, was finishing his toilet, on which, as at all times, he bestowed extraordinary attention.

"Lieutenant Felton, on the part of the Lord de Winter," said Patrick.

"From Lord de Winter!" repeated Buckingham; "let him come in."

Felton entered. At that moment Buckingham was throwing upon a couch a rich *robe-de-chambre* worked with gold, to put on a blue velvet doublet embroidered with pearls.

"Why did not the baron come himself?" demanded Buckingham; "I expected him this morning."

"He desired me to tell your grace," replied Felton, "that he very much regretted not having that honor, but that he was prevented by the guard he is obliged to keep at the castle."

"Yes, I know," said Buckingham; "he has a prisoner."

"It is of that prisoner I wish to speak of your grace," replied Felton.

"Well, then, speak!"

"That which I have to say of her can only be heard by yourself, my lord!"

"Leave us, Patrick," said Buckingham, "but remain within sound of the bell. I will call you presently."

Patrick went out.

"We are alone, sir," said Buckingham; "speak!"

"My lord," said Felton, "the Baron de Winter wrote to you the other day to request you to sign an order of embarkation relative to a young woman named Charlotte Backson."

"Yes, sir, and I answered him, that if he would bring or send me that order, I would sign it."

"Here it is, my lord."

"Give it to me," said the duke.

And, taking it from Felton, he cast a rapid glance over the paper, and perceiving that it was the one that had been mentioned to him, he placed it on the table, took a pen, and prepared to sign it.

"I ask your pardon, my lord," said Felton, stopping the duke; "but does your grace know that the name of Charlotte Backson is not the true name of this young woman?"

"Yes, sir, I do know it," replied the duke, dipping the pen in the ink.

"Then your grace knows her real name?" asked Felton in a sharp tone.

"Yes, I know that too;" and the duke put the pen to the paper. Felton grew pale.

"And, knowing that real name, my lord," replied Felton, "will you sign it all the same?"

"Doubtless, I will," said Buckingham, "and rather twice than once."

"I cannot believe," continued Felton, in a voice that became more sharp and rough, "that your grace knows that it is to Lady de Winter this relates."

"I do know it, perfectly well, although I must confess I am astonished that you know it."

"And will your grace sign that order without remorse?" Buckingham looked at the young man with much *hauteur*.

"Do you know, sir, that you are asking me very strange questions, and that it is very silly, on my part, to answer them?"

"Reply to them, my lord," said Felton; "the circumstances are more serious than perhaps you imagine."

Buckingham reflected that the young man, coming from Lord de Winter, perhaps spoke in his name, and softened his manner a little.

"Doubtless without any remorse," said he, "the baron knows, as well as myself, that Lady de Winter is a very guilty woman, and it is treating her very favorably to remit her punishment to transportation."

The duke put his pen to the paper again.

"You will not sign that order, my lord!" said Felton, making a step toward the duke.

"I will not sign this order!" said Buckingham, "and why not?"

"Because you will consult your own consience, and you will do justice to my lady."

"I should do justice to my lady by sending her to Tyburn," said the duke; "my lady is an infamous woman."

"My lord, Lady de Winter is an angel; you know that she is, and I demand her liberty of you."

"Why, the man must be mad to talk to me in this manner!" said Buckingham.

"My lord, excuse me! I speak as I am able; I restrain myself all I can. But, my lord, think of what you are about to do, and beware of going too far!"

"What do you say? God pardon me!" cried Buckingham. "I really think the man threatens me!"

"No, my lord, I still pray, and I say to you: one drop of water suffices to make the full vase overflow, one slight fault may draw down punishment upon the head spared amidst many crimes."

"Master Felton," said Buckingham, "you will please to withdraw, and place yourself under arrest immediately."

"You shall hear me to the end, my lord. You have seduced this young girl, you have outraged, defiled her; repair your crimes toward her, let her go free, and I will require nothing else of you."

"You will require!" said Buckingham, looking at Felton with astonishment, and dwelling upon each syllable of the words as he pronounced them.

"My lord," continued Felton, becoming more excited as he spoke—"my lord, beware! all England is tired of your iniquities; my lord, you have abused the royal power, which you have almost usurped; my lord, you are held in horror by God and men; God will punish you hereafter, but I will punish you here."

"Well! this is too much!" cried Buckingham, making a step toward the door.

Felton barred his passage.

"I ask it humbly of you, my lord," said he; "sign the order for the liberation of Lady de Winter; reflect, she is a woman you have dishonored."

"Withdraw, sir," said Buckingham, "or I will call my attendant, and have you placed in irons."

"You shall not call," said Felton, throwing himself between the duke and the bell placed upon a *gueridon* incrusted with silver; "beware, my lord, you are in the hands of God!"

"In the hands of the devil, you mean!" cried Buckingham, raising his voice so as to attract the notice of his people without absolutely calling.

"Sign, my lord, sign the liberation of Lady de Winter," said Felton, holding a paper to the duke.

"What, by force! you are joking! hilloa! Patrick!"

"Sign, my lord!"

"Never."

"Never?"

"Who waits there?" cried the duke aloud, and at the same time sprang toward his sword.

But Felton did not give him time to draw it; he held the knife with which milady had stabbed herself, open in his bosom; at one bound he was upon the duke.

At that moment Patrick entered the room, crying:

"A letter from France, my lord."

"From France!" cried Buckingham, forgetting everything on thinking from whom that letter came.

Felton took advantage of this moment, and plunged the knife into his side up to the handle.

"Ah, traitor!" cried Buckingham, "thou hast killed me!"

"Murder!" screamed Patrick.

Felton cast his eyes round for means of escape, and seeing the door free, he rushed into the next chamber, in which, as we said, the deputies from La Rochelle were waiting, crossed it as quickly as possible, and precipitated himself toward the staircase; but upon the first step he met Lord de Winter, who, seeing him pale, confused, livid, and stained with blood both upon his hands and face, seized him, crying:

"I knew it! I guessed it! but too late by a minute, unfortunate, unfortunate that I am!"

Felton made no resistance; Lord de Winter placed him in the hands of the guards, who led him, while awaiting fresh orders, to a little terrace looking out upon the sea: and then the baron hastened to the duke.

At the cry uttered by the duke and the scream of Patrick, the man whom Felton had met in the antechamber, rushed into the closet.

He found the duke reclining upon a sofa, with his hand pressed upon the wound.

"Laporte," said the duke in a faint voice, "Laporte, do you come from her?"

"Yes, monsieur," replied the faithful cloak-bearer of Anne of Austria, "but too late perhaps."

"Silence! Laporte, you may be overheard: Patrick, let no one enter: oh! I cannot tell what she says to me! my God! I am dying."

And the duke fainted.

In the meanwhile, Lord de Winter, the deputies, the leaders of the expedition, the officers of Buckingham's household, had all made their way into the chamber; cries of despair resounded on all sides. The news, which filled the palace with tears and groans soon became known, and was spread throughout the city.

The report of a cannon announced that something new and unexpected had taken place.

Lord de Winter tore his hair in agony.

"Too late by a minute!" cried he, "too late by a minute! oh! my God! my God! what a misfortune!"

He had been informed at seven o'clock in the morning that a ladder of ropes was floating from one of the windows of the castle; he had hastened to milady's chamber, found it empty, the window open, and the bars filed, had remembered the verbal caution D'Artagnan had transmitted to him by his messenger, had trembled for the duke, and running to the stable, without taking time to have a horse saddled, had jumped upon the first he came to, had galloped off at full speed, had alighted in the courtyard, had ascended the stairs precipitately, and on the top step, as we have said, had met Felton.

The duke, however, was not dead; he recovered a little, opened his eyes, and hope revived in all hearts.

"Gentlemen," said he, "leave me alone with Patrick and Laporte. Ah! is that you, De Winter! you sent me a strange madman this morning; see what a state he was placed me in!"

"Oh, my lord!" cried the baron, "I shall never console myself for it."

"And you would be quite wrong, my dear De Winter," said Buckingham, holding out his hand to him. "I do not know the man who deserves being regretted during the whole life of another man—but leave us, I pray you."

The baron went out sobbing with grief.

There only remained in the closet of the wounded duke, Laporte and Patrick. A doctor was being sought for, but none was yet found.

"You will live, milord, you will live!" repeated the faithful servant of Anne of Austria, on his knees before the duke's sofa.

"What has she written to me?" said Buckingham feebly, streaming with blood, and suppressing his agony to speak of her he loved; "what has she written to me? Read me her letter."

"Oh! milord!" said Laporte.

"Obey, Laporte; do you not see I have no time to lose?"

Laporte broke the seal, and placed the paper before the eyes of the duke; but Buckingham in vain endeavored to make out the writing.

"Read!" said he, "read! I cannot see, read then! for soon,

perhaps, I shall not hear, and I shall die without knowing what she has written to me."

Laporte made no more difficulty, and read:

"MILORD: By that which, since I have known you, I have suffered by you and for you, I conjure you, if you have any care for my repose, to interrupt those great armaments which you are preparing against France, to put an end to a war, of which it is publicly said religion is the ostensible cause, and of which, it is generally whispered, your love for me is the concealed and real cause. This war may not only bring great catastrophes upon England and France, but misfortunes upon you, milord, for which I should never console myself.

"Be careful of your life, which is menaced, and which will be dear to me from the moment I am not obliged to see an enemy in you.   Your affectionate,
                                        "ANNE."

Buckingham collected all his remaining strength to listen to the reading of the letter; then, when it was ended, as if he had met with a bitter disappointment.

"Have you nothing else to say to me yourself, Laporte?" asked he.

"Yes, milord! the queen charged me to tell you to be very careful, for she has been informed that your assassination would be attempted."

"And is that all? is that all?" replied Buckingham impatiently.

"She likewise charged me to tell you that she still loved you."

"Ah!" said Buckingham, "God be praised! my death, then, will not be to her as the death of a stranger."

Laporte burst into tears.

"Patrick," said the duke, "bring me the casket in which the diamond studs were kept."

Patrick brought the object desired, which Laporte recognized as having belonged to the queen.

"Now the *sachet* of white satin, upon which her cipher is embroidered in pearls."

Patrick again obeyed.

"Here, Laporte," said Buckingham, "these are the only remembrances I ever received from her, this silver casket and these letters. You will restore them to her majesty: and as

a last memorial"—(he looked round for some valuable object)
—"you will add——"

He still sought; but his eyes, darkened by death, met with
nothing but the knife which had fallen from the hand of
Felton, still smoking with the blood spread over its blade.

"And you will add to them this knife," said the duke,
pressing the hand of Laporte. He had just strength enough
to place the *sachet* at the bottom of the silver casket, and to
let the knife fall into it, making a sign to Laporte that he
was no longer able to speak; and then, in a last convulsion,
with which he had not the power to contend, he slipped off
the sofa on the floor.

Patrick uttered a loud cry.

Buckingham endeavored to smile a last time; but death
arrested his wish, which remained engraven on his brow like
a last kiss of love.

At this moment the duke's surgeon arrived, quite terrified;
he was already on board the admiral's ship, from which he
had been obliged to be fetched.

He approached the duke, took his hand, held it for an
instant in his own, and letting it fall—

"All is useless," said he, "he is dead."

"Dead! dead!" screamed Patrick.

At this cry all the crowd came again into the apartment,
and throughout the palace and town there was nothing but
consternation and tumult.

As soon as Lord de Winter saw Buckingham was dead, he
ran to Felton, whom the soldiers still guarded on the terrace
of the palace.

"Miserable wretch!" said he, to the young man, who since
the death of Buckingham had regained that coolness and self-
possesion which never after abandoned him; "miserable
wretch! what hast thou done?"

"I have avenged myself!" said he.

"Avenged yourself!" said the baron; "rather say that you
have served as an instrument to that accursed woman; but I
swear to you, that this crime shall be her last crime."

"I don't know what you mean," replied Felton, quietly;
"and I am ignorant of whom you are speaking, my lord: I
killed the Duke of Buckingham because he twice refused you
yourself to appoint me captain; I have punished him for his
injustice, that is all."

De Winter, quite stupefied, looked on while the soldiers
bound Felton, and could not tell what to think of such
insensibility.

One thing alone, however, threw a shade over the pallid brow of Felton. At every noise he heard, the simple Puritan fancied he recognized the step and voice of milady coming to throw herself into his arms, to accuse herself, and meet death with him.

All at once he started—his eyes became fixed upon a point of the sea, which the terrace upon which he was overlooked; with the eagle glance of a sailor, he had recognized there, where another would have only seen a gull hovering over the waves, the sail of the sloop, which was directed toward the coast of France.

He grew deadly pale, placed his hand upon his heart, which was breaking, and at once perceived all the treachery.

"One last favor, my lord!" said he, to the baron.

"What is that?" replied his lordship.

"What o'clock is it?"

The baron drew out his watch.

"It wants ten minutes to nine."

Milady had advanced her departure by an hour and a half; as soon as she heard the cannon which announced the fatal event, she had ordered the anchor to be weighed.

The vessel was making way under a blue sky at a great distance from the coast.

"God has so willed it!" said he, with the resignation of a fanatic; but without, however, being able to take his eyes from that ship, on board of which he doubtless fancied he could distinguish the white phantom of her to whom he had sacrificed his life.

De Winter followed his look, observed his feelings, and guessed all.

"Be punished *alone*, in the first place, miserable man!" said Lord de Winter to Felton, who was being dragged away with his eyes turned toward the sea, "but I swear to you, by the memory of my brother whom I loved so much, that your accomplice is not saved."

Felton hung down his head without pronouncing a syllable

As to Lord de Winter he descended the stairs rapidly, and went straight to the port.

CHAPTER LX.

IN FRANCE.

THE first fear of the King of England, Charles I., on learning the death of the duke, was that such terrible news might discourage the Rochellais; he endeavored, says Richeleiu in his memories, to conceal it from them as long as possible, closing all the ports of his kingdom, and carefully keeping watch that no vessel should go out until the army which Buckingham was getting together had set sail, taking upon himself, in default of Buckingham, to superintend its departure.

He carried the strictness of this order so far as to detain in England the ambassadors of Denmark, who had taken leave, and the ordinary ambassador of Holland, who was to take back to the port of Flushing the Indian merchantmen of which Charles I. had made restitution to the United Provinces.

But as he did not think of giving this order till five hours after the event, that is to say, till two o'clock in the afternoon, two vessels had already left the port: the one bearing, as we know, milady, who already anticipating the event, was further confirmed in that belief by seeing the black flag flying at the mast head of the admiral's ship.

As to the second vessel, we will tell hereafter whom it carried, and how it set sail.

During all this time, nothing fresh occurred in the camp at La Rochelle; only the king, who grew weary everywhere, but perhaps a little more so in the camp than in any other place, resolved to go incognito and spend the festival of St. Louis at St. Germain's, and asked the cardinal to order him an escort of twenty musketeers only. The cardinal who sometimes became weary of the king, granted this leave of absence with great pleasure to his royal lieutenant, who promised to return about the 15th of September.

M. de Tréville, upon being informed by his eminence, made up his portmanteau, and as, without knowing the cause, he knew the great desire and even imperative want that his friends had to return to Paris, he fixed upon them, of course, to form part of the escort.

The four young men heard the news a quarter of an hour after M. de Tréville, for they were the first to whom he communicated it. It was then that D'Artagnan appreciated the favor the cardinal had conferred upon him by making him at last pass into the musketeers, for without that circumstance he would have been forced to remain in the camp, while his companions left it.

It must be admitted that this impatience to return toward Paris had for cause the danger which Madame Bonacieux would run of meeting at the convent of Béthune with milady, her mortal enemy. Aramis, therefore had written immediately to Marie Michon, the seamstress at Tours, who had such fine acquaintances, to obtain from the queen authority for Madame Bonacieux to leave the convent, and to retire either into Lorraine or Belgium. They had not long to wait for an answer; a week after, Aramis received the following letter:

"MY DEAR COUSIN: With this you will receive the order from my sister to withdraw our little servant from the convent of Béthune, the air of which you think does not agree with her. My sister sends you this order with great pleasure, for she is very partial to the little girl, and to whom she intends to be more serviceable hereafter.

"I salute you,
"MARIE MICHON."

In this letter was inclosed an order conceived in these terms:

"The superior of the convent of Béthune will place in the hands of the person who shall present this note to her, the novice who entered the convent upon my recommendation, and under my patronage.   ANNE.
"At the Louvre, August 10, 1628."

It may be easily imagined how the relationship between Aramis and a seamstress who called the queen her sister amused the young men; but Aramis, after having blushed up to the eyes at the gross jokes of Porthos, begged his friends not to revert to the subject again, declaring that if another single word were said to him about it, he would never again implore his cousin to interfere in such affairs.

There was no further question, therefore, of Marie Michon among the four musketeers, who, besides, had what they wanted: that was, the order to withdraw Madame Bonacieux from the convent of the Carmelites of Béthune. It was true that this order would not be of great use to them while they were in camp at La Rochelle, that is to say, at the other end of France; therefore, D'Artagnan was going to ask leave of absence of M. de Tréville, confiding to him candidly the importance of his departure, when the news was transmitted to him, as well as to his three friends, that the king was about to set out for Paris with an escort of twenty musketeers and that they formed part of the escort.

Their joy was great. The lackeys were sent on before

with the baggage, and they set out on the morning of the 16th.

The cardinal accompanied his majesty from Surgères to Mauzé, and there the king and his minister took leave of each other with great demonstrations of friendship.

The king, however, who sought amusement, while traveling as fast as possible, for he was anxious to be in Paris by the 23d, stopped from time to time to fly the pie, a pastime for which the taste had been formerly communicated to him by De Luynes, and for which he had always preserved a great predilection. Out of the twenty musketeers, sixteen, when the thing happened, rejoiced greatly at this relaxation, but the other four cursed it heartily. D'Artagnan in particular had a perpetual buzzing in his ears, which Porthos explained thus:

"A very great lady told me that that means somebody is talking of you somewhere."

At length the escort passed through Paris on the 23d, in the night; the king thanked M. de Tréville, and permitted him to distribute leaves of absence for four days, upon condition that the favored parties should not appear in any public place, under penalty of the Bastille.

The four first leaves granted, as may be imagined, were to our four friends. Still further, Athos obtained of M. de Tréville six days instead of four, and introduced into these six days two more nights, for they set out on the 24th, at five o'clock in the evening, and, as a further kindness, M. de Tréville post-dated the leave to the twenty-fifth in the morning.

"Good Lord!" said D'Artagnan, who, as we have often said, never doubted of anything—"it appears to me that we are making a great trouble of a very simple thing: in two days, and by knocking up two or three horses (which I care little about, as I have plenty of money), I am at Béthune, I present my letter from the queen to the superior, and I bring back the dear treasure I go to seek, not into Lorraine, not into Belgium, but to Paris; where she will be much better concealed, particularly while the cardinal is at La Rochelle. Well, once returned from the campaign, half by the protection of her cousin, half in favor of what we have personally done for her, we shall obtain from the queen what we desire. Remain, then, where you are, and do not exhaust yourselves with useless fatigue: myself and Planchet, that is all that such a simple expedition as this requires."

To this Athos replied quietly:

"We, also, have money left; for I have not yet drunk all my share of the diamond, and Porthos and Aramis have not eaten theirs. We are, therefore, in a condition to knock up four horses as well as one. But consider, D'Artagnan," added he, in a tone so solemn that it made the young man shudder, "consider that Béthune is a city at which the cardinal has appointed to meet a woman, who, wherever she goes, brings misery with her. If you had only to deal with four men, D'Artagnan, I would allow you to go alone; you have to do with that woman—we will go, and I hope to God that, with our four lackeys, we may be in sufficient number."

"You terrify me, Athos!" cried D'Artagnan; "my God! what do you fear?"

"Everything!" replied Athos.

D'Artagnan examined the countenances of his companions, which, like that of Athos, wore an impression of deep anxiety, and they continued their route as fast as their horses could carry them, but without adding another word.

On the evening of the 25th, as they were entering Arras, and as D'Artagnan was dismounting at the auberge of the Herse d'Or to drink a glass of wine, a horseman came out of the posting-yard, where he had just had a relay, starting off at a gallop, and with a fresh horse, and taking the road to Paris. At the moment he was passing through the gateway into the street, the wind blew open the cloak in which he was enveloped, although it was the month of August, and lifted his hat, which the traveler seized with his hand at the moment it had left his head, and pulled it down eagerly over his eyes.

D'Artagnan, who had his eyes fixed upon this man, became very pale, and let his glass fall.

"What is the matter, monsieur?" said Planchet. "Oh, come, gentlemen, gentlemen! my master is ill!"

The three friends hastened toward D'Artagnan, but, instead of finding him ill, met him running toward his horse. They stopped him at the door.

"Where the devil are you going to now, in this fashion?" cried Athos.

"It is he!" cried D'Artagnan, pale with passion, and with the sweat on his brow, "it is he! let me overtake him!"

"He! but what he?" asked Athos.

"He—that man!"

"What man?"

"That cursed man, my evil genius, whom I have always met with when threatened by some misfortune—he who accompanied the horrible woman when I met her for the first time—he whom I was seeking when I offended our Athos— he whom I saw on the very morning Madame Bonacieux was carried off! I have seen him! that is he! I recognized him when his cloak blew open!"

"The devil!" said Athos, musingly.

"To horse, gentlemen! to horse! let us pursue him; we shall overtake him!"

"My dear friend," said Aramis, "remember that it is in an opposite direction to that in which we are going, that he has a fresh horse, and ours are fatigued, so that we shall disable our own horses without a chance of overtaking him. Let the man go, D'Artagnan; let us save the woman."

"Monsieur, monsieur!" cried the stableman, running out and looking after the unknown—"monsieur, here is a paper which dropped out of your hat! monsieur!"

"Friend," said D'Artagnan, "a half-pistole for that paper!"

"Ma foi! monsieur, with great pleasure! here it is!"

The stableman, delighted with the good day's work he had done, went into the yard again; D'Artagnan unfolded the paper.

"Well?" eagerly demanded all his three friends.

"Nothing but one word!" said D'Artagnan.

"Yes," said Aramis, "but that one word is the name of some town or village."

"*Armentières!*" read Porthos; "Armentières—I don't know such a place."

"And that name of a town or village is written in her hand!" cried Athos.

"Come on, then! come on, then!" said D'Artagnan; "let us keep that paper carefully—perhaps I have not thrown away my half-pistole. To horse, my friends, to horse!"

And the four friends galloped off on the road to Béthune.

CHAPTER LXI.

THE CONVENT OF THE CARMELITES AT BÉTHUNE.

GREAT criminals bear about them a kind of predestination which makes them surmount all obstacles, which makes them escape all dangers, till the moment which a wearied Providence has marked as the rock of their impious fortunes.

It was thus with milady. She passed through the cruisers of both nations, and arrived at Boulogne without accident.

When landing at Portsmouth, milady was an English-woman, whom the persecutions of the French drove from La Rochelle; when landing at Boulogne, after a two days' passage, she passed for a Frenchwoman, whom the English persecuted at Portsmouth, out of their hatred for France.

Milady had, likewise, her best of passports—her beauty, her noble appearance, and the liberality with which she distributed her pistoles. Freed from the usual formalities by the affable smile and gallant manners of an old governor of port, who kissed her hand, she only remained long enough at Boulogne to put into the post a letter, conceived in the following terms:

"To his Eminence Monseigneur the Cardinal de Richelieu, in his camp before Rochelle.

"Monseigneur, let your eminence be reassured; his grace the Duke of Buckingham *will not set out* for France.

"Boulogne, evening of the 25th. MILADY DE . . . .

"P.S.—According to the desire of your eminence, I am going to the convent of the Carmelites of Béthune, where I will await your orders."

Accordingly, that same evening, milady commenced her journey; night overtook her; she stopped, and slept at an auberge; at five o'clock the next morning she again proceeded, and in three hours after entered Béthune.

She inquired for the convent of the Carmelities, and went to it immediately.

The superior came out to her; milady showed her the cardinal's order; the abbess assigned her a chamber, and had breakfast served.

All the past was effaced from the eyes of this woman, and her looks, fixed on the future, beheld nothing but the high fortunes reserved for her by the cardinal, whom she had so successfully served, without his name being in any way mixed up with the sanguinary affair. The ever-new passions which consumed her gave to her life the appearance of those clouds which float in the heavens, reflecting sometimes azure, sometimes fire, sometimes the opaque blackness of the tempest, and which leave no traces upon the earth behind them but devastation and death.

After breakfast the abbess came to pay her a visit. There is very little amusement in the cloister, and the good superior was eager to make acquaintance with her new pensioner. Milady wished to please the abbess. Now this was a very easy matter for a woman so really superior as she was, she endeavored to be agreeable, and she was charming, winning the good superior by her varied conversation and by the graces spread over her whole person.

The abbess, who was the daughter of a noble house, took particular delight in histories of the court, which so seldom travel to the extremities of the kingdom, and which, above all, have so much difficulty in penetrating the walls of convents, at whose gates the noise of the world appears to die away.

Milady, on the contrary, was quite conversant in all aristocratic intrigues, amid which she had constantly lived for five or six years; she made it her business, then, to amuse the good abbess with the mundane practices of the court of France, mixed with the extravagant devotions of the king: she made for her the scandalous chronicle of the lords and ladies of the court, whom the abbess knew perfectly by name, touched lightly on the amours of the queen and the Duke of Buckingham, talking a great deal to induce her auditor to talk a little.

But the abbess contented herself with listening and smiling, without replying a word. Milady, however, saw that this style of conversation amused her very much, and continued; only she now turned to chat in the direction of the cardinal.

But she was greatly embarrassed—she did not know whether the abbess was a royalist or a cardinalist; she therefore confined herself to a prudent middle course. But the abbess, on her part, maintained a reserve still more prudent, contenting herself with making a profound inclination of the head every time that the fair traveler pronounced the name of his eminence.

Milady began to conceive she should soon grow weary of a convent life; she resolved then, to risk something, in order that she might know how to act afterward. Desirous of seeing how far the discretion of the good abbess would go, she began to tell a story, obscure at first, but very circumstantial afterward, of the cardinal, relating the amours of the minister with Madame d'Aiguillon, Marion de Lorme, and several other women of gallantry.

The abbess listened more attentively, grew animated by degrees, and smiled.

"Good!" thought milady; "she takes a pleasure in my

conversation. If she is a cardinalist, she has no fanaticism in her partiality."

She then went on to describe the persecutions exercised by the cardinal upon his enemies. The abbess only crossed herself, without approving or disapproving.

This confirmed milady in her opinion that the abbess was rather a royalist than a cardinalist; milady, therefore, continued, heightening her narrations more and more.

"I am very little acquainted with all these matters," said the abbess at length; "but however distant from the court we may be, however remote from the interests of the world we may be placed, we have very sad examples of what you have related; and one of our pensioners has suffered much from the vengeance and persecutions of Monsieur le Cardinal."

"One of your pensioners!" said milady; "oh, my God! poor woman, I pity her, then."

"And you have reason to do so, for she is much to be pitied: imprisonment, menaces, ill treatment, she has suffered everything. But after all," resumed the abbess, "Monsieur le Cardinal has, perhaps, plausible motives for acting thus; and though she has the look of an angel, we must not always judge people by appearances."

"Good!" said milady to herself; "who knows! I am about perhaps, to discover something here; I am in the vein."

And she tried to give her countenance an appearance of perfect candor.

"Alas!" said milady, "I know it is so. It is said that we must not trust to the physiognomy; but in what, then, shall we place confidence, if not in the most beautiful work of the Lord? As for me, I shall be deceived all my life, perhaps, but I shall always have faith in a person whose countenance inspires me with sympathy."

"You would, then, be tempted to believe," said the abbess, "that this young person was innocent?"

"M. le Cardinal does not always pursue crimes," said she; "there are certain virtues that he pursues more severely than certain offences."

"Permit me, madame, to express my surprise," said the abbess.

"Upon what occasion?" said milady, with the utmost ingenuousness.

"Upon the language you hold."

"What do you find so astonishing in that language?" said milady, smiling.

"You are the friend of the cardinal, for he sends you hither, and yet——"

"And yet I speak ill of him," replied milady, finishing the thought of the superior.

"At least, you don't speak well of him."

"That is because I am not his friend," said she, sighing, "but his victim!"

"Well, but this letter by which he recommends you to me?"

"Is an order for me to confine myself to a sort of prison, from which he will release me by one of his satellites."

"But why have you not fled?"

"Whither should I go? Do you believe there is a spot on the earth which the cardinal cannot reach, if he takes the trouble to stretch forth his hand? If I were a man, certainly that would be possible, but what can a woman do? This young pensioner of yours, has she endeavored to fly?"

"No, that is true; but she—that is another thing, for I believe she is detained in France by some love affair."

"Ah," said milady, with a sigh, "if she is in love, she is not altogether wretched."

"Then," said the abbess, looking at her with increasing interest, "I behold another poor persecuted woman?"

"Alas! yes," said milàdy.

The abbess looked at her for an instant with uneasiness, as if a fresh thought had arisen in her mind.

"You are not an enemy of our holy faith?" said she, hesitatingly.

"Who—I?" cried milady—"I a Protestant! Oh, no! I attest the God who hears us, that, on the contrary, I am a fervent Catholic!"

"Then, madame," said the abbess, smiling, "be reassured; the house in which you are shall not be a very hard prison, and we will do all in our power to make you in love with your captivity. You will find here, moreover, the young woman of whom I spoke, who is persecuted, no doubt, in consequence of some court intrigue. She is amiable and well-behaved."

"What is her name?"

"She was sent to me by some one of high rank, under the name of Kitty. I have not endeavored to discover her other name."

"Kitty!" cried milady; "what! are you sure?"

"That she is called so? Yes, madame. Do you know her?"

Milady smiled to herself at the idea which had occurred to her, that this might be her old waiting-maid. There was connected with the remembrance of this girl a remembrance of anger; and a desire of vengeance disordered the features of milady, but which, however, immediately recovered the calm and benevolent expression which this woman of a hundred faces had for a moment allowed them to lose.

"And when can I see this young lady, for whom I already feel so great a sympathy?" asked milady.

"Why, this evening," said the abbess; "to-day even. But you have been traveling these four days, as you told me: this morning you rose at five o'clock; you must stand in need of repose. Go to bed and sleep, at dinner-time we will call you."

Although milady would very willingly have gone without sleep, sustained as she was by all the excitements that a fresh adventure awakened in her heart, ever thirsting for intrigues, she nevertheless accepted the offer of the superior: during the last fifteen days she had experienced so many and such various emotions, that if her frame of iron was still capable of supporting fatigue, her mind required repose.

She therefore took leave of the abbess, and went to bed, softly rocked by the ideas of vengeance which the name of Kitty had naturally brought back to her thoughts. She remembered that almost unlimited promise which the cardinal had given her if she succeeded in her enterprise. She had succeeded, D'Artagnan was then in her power!

One thing alone frightened her; that was, the remembrance of her husband, the Count de la Fère, whom she had thought dead, or at least expatriated, and whom she found again in Athos, the best friend of D'Artagnan.

But also, if he was the friend of D'Artagnan, he must have lent him his assistance in all the proceedings by the means of which the queen had defeated the projects of his eminence; if he was the friend of D'Artagnan, he was the enemy of the cardinal; and she, doubtless, should succeed in enveloping him in the folds of the vengeance by which she hoped to destroy the young musketeer.

All these hopes were so many sweet thoughts for milady; so, rocked by them, she soon fell asleep.

She was awakened by a soft voice, which sounded at the foot of her bed. She opened her eyes, and saw the abbess, accompanied by a young woman, with light hair and a delicate complexion, who fixed upon her a look full of benevolent curiosity.

The face of the young woman was entirely unknown to her; each examined the other with great attention, while exchanging the customary compliments; both were very handsome, but of quite different styles of beauty. Milady, however, smiled on observing that she excelled the young woman by far in her high air and aristocratic bearing. It is true that the habit of a novice, which the young woman wore, was not very advantageous in a contest of this kind.

The abbess introduced them to each other; then, when this formality was gone through, as her duties called her to the church, she left the two young women alone.

The novice, seeing milady remained in bed, was about to follow the example of the superior; but milady stopped her.

"How, madame," said she, "I have scarcely seen you, and you already wish to deprive me of your company, upon which I had reckoned a little, I must confess, during the time I have to pass here?"

"No, madame," replied the novice, "only I thought I had chosen my time ill; you were asleep—you are fatigued."

"Well," said milady, "what can people who are asleep wish for? a happy awakening. This awakening you have given me; allow me then to enjoy it at my ease;" and taking her hand, she drew her toward the chair by the bedside.

The novice sat down.

"How unfortunate I am!" said she; "I have been here six months, without the shadow of an amusement, you arrive, and your presence was likely to afford me delightful company, and I expect, according to all probability, from one moment to another, to leave the convent."

"Are you then going soon?" asked milady.

"At least I hope so," said the novice, with an expression of joy which she made no effort to disguise.

"I think I learned you had suffered persecutions from the cardinal," continued milady "that would have been another motive for sympathy between us."

"What I have heard then from our good mother is true; you have likewise been a victim of that wicked priest?"

"Hush!" said milady; "let us not, even here, speak thus of him; almost all my misfortunates arise from my having said nearly what you have said, before a woman whom I thought my friend, and who betrayed me. Are you also the victim of a treachery?"

"No," said the novice, "but of my devotedness; of a devotedness to a woman I loved, for whom I would have laid down my life, for whom I would still do so."

"And who has abandoned you, is that it?"

"I have been sufficiently unjust to believe so; but during the last two or three days I have obtained proof to the contrary, for which I thank God! for it would have cost me very dear to think that she had forgotten me. But you, madame, you appear to be free: and if you were inclined to fly, it only rests with yourself to do so."

"Whither would you have me go, without friends, without money, in a part of France with which I am unacquainted, and where I have never been before?"

"Oh!" cried the novice, "as to friends you would have them wherever you went, you appear so good and are so beautiful!"

"That does not prevent," replied milady, softening her smile as to give it an angelic expression, "my being alone or being persecuted."

"Hear me," said the novice; "we must trust in heaven; there always comes a moment when the good you have done pleads your cause before God; and, see, perhaps, it is a happiness for you, humble and powerless as I am, that you have met with me: for, if I leave this place; well! I have powerful friends, who, after having exerted themselves on my account, may also exert themselves for you."

"Oh! when I said I was alone," said milady, hoping to make the novice speak by speaking of herself, "it is not for want of some highly-placed friends; but these friends themselves tremble before the cardinal: the queen herself does not dare to oppose the terrible minister: I have proof that her majesty, notwithstanding her excellent heart, has more than once been obliged to abandon persons who had served her, to the anger of his eminence."

"Trust me, madame, the queen may appear to have abandoned those persons; but we must not put faith in appearances: the more they are persecuted, the more she thinks of them; and often, when they the least expect it, they receive proofs of a kind remembrance."

"Alas!" said milady, "I believe so; the queen is so good!"

"Oh! you know her, then! that lovely and noble queen, by your speaking of her thus!" cried the novice, warmly.

"That is to say," replied milady, driven into her intrenchments, "that I have not the honor of knowing her personally; but I know a great number of her most intimate friends; I am acquainted with M. de Putange; I met M. Dujart in England: I know M. de Tréville."

"M. de Tréville!" exclaimed the novice, "do you know M. de Tréville?"

"Yes, perfectly well, intimately even."

"What, the captain of the king's musketeers?"

"Yes, the captain of the king's musketeers."

"Oh! why then, only see!" cried the novice, "we shall soon be well acquainted, almost friends; if you know M. de Tréville, you must have visited him?"

"Often!" said milady, who having entered this track, and perceiving that falsehood succeeded, was determined to carry it on.

"If you have visited him, you must have met some of his musketeers?"

"All such as he is in the habit of receiving!" replied milady, for whom this conversation began to have a real interest.

"Name a few of those you know, and you will find they are my friends."

"Well!" said milady, a little embarrassed, "I know M. de Sauvigny, M. de Courtviron, M. de Ferrusac."

The novice let her speak, but observing she stopped—

"Don't you know," said she, "a gentlemen of the name of Athos?"

Milady became as pale as the sheets in which she was reclining, and mistress as she was of herself, could not help uttering a cry, seizing the hand of the novice, and devouring her with her looks.

"What is the matter? Good God!" asked the poor woman; "have I said anything that has hurt your feelings?"

"No, no; but the name struck me; because I also have known that gentleman, and it appeared strange to me to meet with a person who appears to know him well."

"Oh, yes, well! very well! not only him, but some of his friends: MM. Porthos and Aramis."

"Indeed! you know them, likewise! I know them," cried milady, who began to feel a chill penetrate to her heart.

"Well! if you know them, you know that they are good and worthy gentlemen; why do you not apply to them, if you stand in need of support?"

"That is to say," stammered milady, "I am not really very intimate with any of them; I know them from having heard one of their friends, a Monsieur d'Artagnan, say a great deal about them."

"You know M. d'Artagnan!" cried the novice, in her turn seizing the hands of milady, and fixing her eyes upon her.

Then, remarking the strange expression of milady's countenance:

"Pardon me, madame," said she, "you know him, by what title?"

"Why," replied milady, considerably embarrassed, "why by the title of friend."

"You are deceiving me, madame," said the novice; "you have been his mistress!"

"It is you who have been his mistress, madame," cried milady, in her turn.

"I!" said the novice.

"Yes, you; I know you now: you are Madame Bonacieux." The young woman drew back in surprise and terror.

"Oh, do not deny it! answer!" continued milady.

"Well yes, madame," said the novice; "are we rivals?"

The countenance of milady was illuminated by so savage a joy, that under any other circumstance Madame Bonacieux would have fled away in terror; but she was absorbed by her jealousy.

"Speak, madame!" resumed Madame Bonacieux, with an energy of which she might not have been thought to be capable, "have you been, or are you his mistress?"

"Oh, no!" cried milady, with a tone that admitted no doubt of her truth; "never! never!"

"I believe you," said Madame Bonacieux; "but why, then, did you cry out so?"

"Do you not understand?" said milady, who had already overcome her agitation, and recovered all her presence of mind.

"How can I understand? I know nothing."

"Can you not understand that M. d'Artagnan, being my friend, might take me into his confidence?"

"Indeed!"

"Do you not perceive that I know all? Your being carried off from the little house at St. Germain, his despair, that of his friends, and their useless inquiries up to this moment! How could I help being astonished, when, without having the least expectation of such a thing, I meet you face to face; you, of whom we have so often spoken together, you, whom he loves with all his soul; you, whom he had taught me to love before I had seen you! Ah! dear Constance, I have found you then, I see you at last!"

And milady stretched out her arms to Madame Bonacieux, who, convinced by what she had just said, saw nothing in this woman, whom an instant before she had believed to be her rival, but a sincere and devoted friend.

"Oh! pardon me! pardon me!" cried she, sinking upon the shoulders of milady; "pardon me! I love him so dearly!"

These two women held each other for an instant in a close embrace. Certes, if milady's strength had been equal to her hatred, Madame Bonacieux would have never escaped alive from that embrace.

But not being able to stifle her, she smiled upon her.

"Oh! dear, pretty, good little creature!" said milady, "how delighted I am to have found you! Let me look at you!" And, while saying these words, she absolutely devoured her with her eyes. "Oh! yes, it is you indeed! From what he has told me, I know you now; I recognize you perfectly."

The poor young woman could not possibly suspect what was passing of frightful cruelty behind the rampart of that pure brow, behind those brilliant eyes, in which she read nothing but interest and compassion.

"Then you know what I have suffered," said Madame Bonacieux, "since he has told you what he has suffered: but to suffer for him is happiness."

Milady replied mechanically, "Yes, that is happiness."

She was thinking of something else.

"And then," continued Madame Bonacieux, "my punishment is drawing to a close: to-morrow, this evening perhaps, I shall see him again; and then the past will no longer exist."

"This evening?" asked milady, roused from her reverie by these words; "what do you mean? Do you expect any news from him?"

"I expect him himself."

"Him himself! D'Artagnan here!"

"Yes, him himself!"

"But that's impossible! He is at the siege of La Rochelle, with the cardinal; he will not return before the taking of the city."

"Ah! you fancy so; but is there anything impossible for my D'Artagnan, the noble and loyal gentleman?"

"Oh, I cannot believe you!"

"Well, read, then!" said the unhappy young woman, in the excess of her pride and joy, presenting a letter to milady.

"Humph! the writing of Madame de Chevreuse!" said milady to herself. "Ah! I always thought there was some intelligence carried on on that side." And she greedily read the following few lines:

"My Dear Child: Hold yourself in readiness. *Our friend* will see you soon, and he will only see you to release you from that imprisonment in which your safety required you should be concealed. Prepare, then, for your departure, and never despair of us.

"Our charming Gascon has just proved himself as brave and faithful as ever. Tell him that certain parties are grateful to him for the warning he has given."

"Yes, yes," said milady, "the letter is precise. Do you know what that warning was?"

"No; I only suspect he was warned the queen against some fresh machinations of the cardinal."

"Yes, that's it, no doubt!" said milady, returning the letter to Madame Bonacieux, and allowing her head to sink in a pensive manner upon her bosom.

At that moment the galloping of a horse was heard.

"Oh!" cried Madame Bonacieux, darting to the window, "can it be he?"

Milady remained still in bed, petrified by surprise; so many unexpected things happened to her all at once, that for the first time she was at a loss.

"Ho! ho!" murmured she; "can it be he?" And she remained in bed with her eyes fixed.

"Alas! no," said Madame Bonacieux: "it is a man I don't know; and yet he seems to be coming here. Yes, he has checked his horse—he stops at the gate—he rings."

Milady sprang out of bed.

"Are you sure it is not he?" said she.

"Oh! yes—very sure!"

"Perhaps you did not see him plainly?"

"Oh! if I were to see the plume of his hat, the end of his cloak, I should know him!"

Milady continued to dress herself.

"Never mind! The man is coming here, do you say?"

"Yes, he is come in."

"He must come either to you or to me."

"Good God! how agitated you seem!"

"Yes, I admit I am so. I have not your confidence; I am in dread of the cardinal."

"Hush!" said Madame Bonacieux; "somebody is coming."

In fact, the door opened, and the superior entered.

"Do you come from Boulogne?" demanded she of milady.

"Yes, I do," replied she, endeavoring to recover her self-possession; "Who wants me?"

"A man who will not tell his name, but who comes from the cardinal."

"And who wishes to speak with me?" asked milady.

"Who wishes to speak to a lady recently come from Boulogne."

"Then let him come in, if you please."

"Good God! good God!" cried Madame Bonacieux; "can it be any bad news?"

"I am afraid so."

"I will leave you with this stranger, but as soon as he is gone, if you will permit me, I will return."

"Certainly! I beg you will." The superior and Madame Bonacieux retired. Milady was left alone, with her eyes fixed upon the floor. An instant after, the jingling of spurs was heard upon the stairs, steps drew near, the door opened, and a man appeared.

Milady uttered a cry of joy: this man was the Count de Rochefort, the *âme damnée* of the cardinal.

CHAPTER LXII.

TWO VARITIES OF DEMONS.

"AH!" cried milady and Rochefort together, "is that you?"

"Yes it is."

"And you come?"—asked milady.

"From La Rochelle—and you?"

"From England."

"Buckingham?"

"Dead or desperately wounded, as I left without being able to obtain anything of him. A fanatic has just assassinated him."

"Ah!" said Rochefort, with a smile "this is a fortunate chance—one that will delight his eminence! Have you informed him of it?"

"I wrote to him from Boulogne. But what brings you here?"

"His eminence was uneasy, and sent me to inquire after you."

"I only arrived yesterday."

"And what have you been doing since yesterday?"

"I have not lost my time."

"Oh! I have no fear of that."

"Do you know whom I have found here?"

"No."

"Guess."

"How can I?"

"That young woman whom the queen took out of prison."

"The mistress of that fellow D'Artagnan?"

"Yes, Madame Bonacieux, with whose retreat the cardinal was unacquainted."

"Upon my word!" said De Rochefort, "here is a chance that may be paired with the other! Truly, Monsieur le Cardinal is a privileged man!"

"Imagine my astonishment," continued milady, "when I found myself face to face with this•woman."

"Does she know you?"

"No."

"Then she looks upon you as a stranger?"

Milady smiled.

"I am her best friend."

"Upon my honor, it is only you, my fair countess, that can perform such miracles!"

"And it is well I can, chevalier," said milady; "for do you know what is going on here?"

"No."

"She is about to be taken away to-morrow, or the day after, with an order from the queen."

"Indeed! And who is going to do that?"

"D'Artagnan and his friends."

"They certainly will go so far we shall be obliged to put them into the Bastille at last."

"Why is it not done already?"

"Why, because M. le Cardinal has a weakness with respect to these men which I cannot at all account for."

"Indeed!"

"Yes."

"Well then! tell him this, Rochefort: tell him that our conversation at the auberge of the Colombier Rouge was overheard by these four men; tell him that, after his departure, one of them came up to me, and took from me, by violence, the safe-conduct which he had given me; tell him they warned Lord de Winter of my passage to England; that this time they had nearly made me fail in my mission, as they did in the affair of the studs; tell him that, among these four men, two only are to be feared—D'Artagnan and Athos: tell him that the third, Aramis, is the lover of Madame de Chevreuse; he may be left alone, we know his secret, and it may be useful; as to the fourth, Porthos, he is a fool, a simpleton, a blustering booby, not worth troubling himself about."

"But these four men must be now at the siege of La Rochelle?"

"I thought so too, but a letter which Madame Bonacieux had received from Madame la Connétable, and which she has had the imprudence to show me, leads me to believe that these four men, on the contrary, are on the road hither to take her away."

"The devil! what's to be done?"

"What did the cardinal say with respect to me?"

"I was to take your despatches, written or verbal, to return post; and when he shall know what you have done, he will think of what you have to do."

"I must then remain here?"

"Here, or in the environs."

"You cannot take me with you?"

"No; the order is imperative: near the camp, you might be recognized; and your presence, you must be aware, would compromise the cardinal."

"Then I must wait here or in this neighborhood?"

"Only tell me, beforehand, where you will wait for commands from the cardinal: let me know always where to find you."

"But, observe, it is probable I may not be able to remain here."

"Why not?"

"You forgot that my enemies may arrive at any minute."

"That's true; but then, is this little woman to escape his eminence?"

"Bah!" said milady, with a smile that only belonged to herself, "did not I tell you I was her best friend?"

"Ah that's true, likewise; I may then tell the cardinal, with respect to this little woman——"

"That he may be at ease."

"Is that all?"

"He will know what that means."

"He will guess, at least. Now, then, what had I better do?"

"Set off back again directly; it appears to me that the news you bear is worth the trouble of a little diligence."

"My chaise broke down coming into Lilliers."

"I am glad of that."

"Why, glad of that?"

"Yes, I am; I want your chaise."

"And how shall I travel, then——"

"On horseback."

"You talk very much at your ease; a hundred and eighty leagues?"

"What's that?"

"Well, that may be done; and then?"

"Then? why, in passing through Lilliers you will send me your chaise, with an order to your servant to place himself at my disposal."

"Well."

"You have, no doubt, about you some order from the cardinal?"

"I have my *full power.*"

"Show it to the abbess, and tell her that some one will come and fetch me, either to-day or to-morrow, and that I am to follow the person who presents himself in your name."

"Very well."

"Don't forget to treat me harshly, in speaking of me to the abbess."

"To what purpose?"

"I am a victim of the cardinal. I must inspire confidence in that poor little Madame Bonacieux."

"That's true. Now, will you make me a report of all that has happened?"

"Why, I have related the events to you, you have a good memory, repeat what I have told you; a paper may be lost."

"You are right; only let me know where to find you, that I may not lose my time in hunting for you about the neighborhood."

"That's correct; wait a minute."

"Do you want a map?"

"Oh! I know this country well."

"You? when were you here before?"

"I was brought up here."

"Indeed!"

"It is worth something, you see, to have been brought up somewhere."

"You will wait for me, then?"

"Let me reflect a little: ay, that will do, at Armentières.'

"Where is that Armentières?"

"A little town upon the Lys; I only shall have to cross the river, and I shall be in a foreign country."

"Just so! but it is understood you will only cross the river in case of danger."

"Certainly not."

"And in that case, how shall I know where you are?"

"You do not want your lackey?"

"No."

"Is he to be depended on?"

"Perfectly."

"Give him to me, then; nobody knows him; I will leave him at the place I may quit, and he will conduct you to me."

"And you say you will wait for me at Armentières?"

"At Armentières."

"Write that name on a piece of paper, lest I should forget it; there is no fear of compromising yourself in that; a name of a town, is it not?"

"Eh! who knows? never mind," said milady, writing the name upon half a sheet of paper; "I will commit myself."

"That will do," said Rochefort, taking the paper from milady, folding it, and placing it in the lining of his hat; "besides, to make sure, I will do as children do, for fear of losing the paper, repeat the name as I go along. Now, is that all?"

"I believe so."

"Let us see; Buckingham dead, or grievously wounded; your conversation with the cardinal overheard by the four musketeers; De Winter warned of your arrival at Portsmouth; D'Artagnan and Athos to the Bastille; Aramis the lover of Madame de Chevreuse; Porthos a fool; Madame Bonacieux found again; to send you the chaise as soon as possible; to place my lackey at your disposal; to make you out to be a victim of the cardinal, in order that the abbess may entertain no suspicion; Armentières, on the banks of the Lys. Is that all correct?"

"In good truth, my dear chevalier, you are a miracle of memory. Apropos, add one thing——"

"What is that?"

"I saw some very pretty woods which come close to the convent garden; say that I may be permitted to walk in those woods; who knows? perhaps I shall stand in need of a back door to go out at."

"You think of everything."

"And you forget one thing."

"What's that?"

"To ask me if I want any money."

"That's true, how much do you want?"

"All you have in gold."

"I have five hundred pistoles, or thereabouts."

"I have as much; with a thousand pistoles we may face everything. Empty your pockets."

"There it is, then."

"That's well! when do you start?"

"In an hour—time to eat a morsel, during which I shall send some one to look for a post-horse."

"All well! Adieu, chevalier!"

"Adieu, countess!"

"Commend me to the cardinal!"

"Commend me to Satan!"

Milady and Rochefort exchanged a smile and separated.

An hour afterward, Rochefort set out at his horse's best speed; five hours after that he passed through Arras.

Our readers already know that he was recognized by D'Artagnan, and how that recognition, by inspiring fear in the four musketeers, had given fresh activity to their journey.

CHAPTER LXIII.

THE DROP OF WATER.

Rochefort had scarcely departed, when Madame Bonacienx re-entered. She found milady with a smiling countenance.

"Well," said the young woman, "what you dreaded has happened; this evening, or to-morrow, the cardinal will send some one to take you away!"

"Who told you that, my dear?" said milady.

"I heard it from the mouth of the messenger himself."

"Come and sit down close to me," said milady; "and let me be assured no one can hear us."

"Why do you take all these precautions?"

"You shall know."

Milady arose, went to the door, opened it, looked in the corridor, and then returned and seated herself close to Madame Bonacieux.

"Then," said she, "he has well played his part."

"Who has?"

"He who just now presented himself to the abbess as a messenger from the cardinal."

"It was, then, a part he was playing?"

"Yes, my dear."

"That man, then, was not——"

"That man," said milady, lowering her voice, "is my brother!"

"Your brother!" said Madame Bonacieux.

"Mind, no one must know this secret, my dear, but yourself. If you reveal it to any one whatever, I shall be lost, and perhaps you likewise!"

"Oh! good God!"

"Listen to me; this is what has happened. My brother, who was coming to my assistance, to take me away, by force, if it were necessary, met with the emissary of the cardinal, who was coming in search of me. He followed him. When arrived at a solitary and retired part of the road, he drew his sword and required the messenger to deliver up to him the papers of which he was the bearer; the messenger resisted; my brother killed him."

"Oh!" said Madame Bonacieux, with a shudder.

"Remember, that was the only means. Then my brother determined to substitute cunning for force. He took the papers, and presented himself here as the emissary of the cardinal, and in an hour or two a carriage will come to take me away by the orders of his eminence."

"I understand: your brother sends this carriage."

"Exactly so; but that is not all. That letter you have received, and which you believe to be from Madame de Chevreuse——"

"Well?"

"It is a forgery."

"How can that be?"

"Yes, a forgery; it is a snare to prevent your making any resistance when the persons come to fetch you."

"But it is D'Artagnan that will come!"

"Do not deceive yourself. D'Artagnan and his friends are detained at the siege of La Rochelle."

"How do you know that?"

"My brother met some emissaries of the cardinal in the uniform of musketeers. You would have been summoned to the gate, you would have thought you went to meet friends, you would have been carried off, and conducted back again to Paris."

"Oh! good God! My senses fail me amid such a chaos of iniquities. I feel, if this continues," said Madame Bonacieux, raising her hands to her forehead, "I shall go mad!"

"Stop——"

"What?"

"I hear a horse's steps, it is my brother setting off again. I should like to offer him a last salute. Come?"

Milady opened the window, and made a sign to Madame Bonacieux to join her. The young woman complied.

Rochefort passed at a gallop.

"Adieu, brother!" cried milady.

The chevalier raised his head, saw the two young women, and without stopping waved his hand in a friendly way to milady.

"Dear, good George!" said she, closing the window with an expression of countenance full of affection and melancholy.

And she resumed her seat, as if plunged in reflections entirely personal.

"Dear lady," said Madame Bonacieux, "pardon me for interrupting you; but what do you advise me to do? Good heaven! You have more experience than I have. Speak; I will listen to your advice with the greatest gratitude."

"In the first place," said milady, "it is possible that I may be deceived, and D'Artagnan and his friends may really come to your assistance."

"Oh! that would be too much!" cried Madame Bonacieux; "so much happiness is not destined for me!"

"Then you perceive it would be only a question of time, a sort of race, which should arrive first. If your friends are the more speedy, you will be saved; if the satellites of the cardinal are so, you will be lost!"

"Oh! yes, yes! lost beyond redemption! What am I to do? what am I to do?"

"There would be a very simple means, very natural——"

"What? Speak!"

"To wait, concealed in the neighborhood, until you have satisfied yourself who the men were who came to ask for you."

"But where can I wait?"

"Oh! there is no difficulty in that; I shall stop and conceal myself at a few leagues from hence, until my brother can rejoin me. Well! I can take you with me; we can conceal ourselves, and wait together."

"But I shall not be allowed to go; I am almost a prisoner here."

"As I am supposed to go in consequence of an order from the cardinal, no one will believe you are anxious to follow me."

"Well?"

"Well! the carriage is at the door, you bid me adieu, you get upon the step to embrace me a last time; my brother's servant, who comes to fetch me, is told how to proceed; he makes a sign to the postillion, and we set off at a gallop."

"But D'Artagnan! D'Artagnan! if he should come."

"Well! shall we not know it?"

"How?"

"Nothing more easy. We will send my brother's servant back to Béthune, and, as I told you we can trust in him, he shall assume a disguise, and place himself in front of the convent. If the emissaries of the cardinal arrive, he will take no notice; if they are M. d'Artagnan and his friends, he will bring them to us."

"He knows them, then?"

"Doubtless he does. Has he not seen M. d'Artagnan at my house?"

"Oh! yes, yes, you are right; in this way all may go well—all may be for the best; but do not go far from this place."

"Seven or eight leagues at most; we will keep on the frontiers, for instance; and at the first alarm we can leave France."

"And what can we do there?"

"Wait."

"But if they come?"

"My brother's carriage will be here first."

"If I should happen to be at any distance from you when the carriage comes for you; at dinner or supper, for instance?"

"Do one thing."

"What is that?"

"Tell your good superior, that in order that we may be as much together as possible, you beg her to allow you to take your meals with me."

"Will she permit it?"

"What inconvenience can it be to her?"

"Oh, delightful! in this way we shall not be separated for an instant."

"Well! go down to her then to make your request. I feel my head a little confused; I will take a turn in the garden."

"Do; and where shall I find you?"

"Here, within an hour."

"Here, in an hour; oh! you are so kind! and I am so grateful!"

"How can I avoid interesting myself for one who is so beautiful, and so amiable? Besides, are you not the beloved of one of my best friends?"

"Dear D'Artagnan, oh! how he will thank you!"

"I hope so. Now then, all is agreed; let us go down."

"You are going into the garden?"

"Yes."

"Go along this corridor, down a little staircase and you are in it."

"That will do—thank you!"

And the two women parted, exchanging affectionate smiles

Milady had told the truth—her head was confused; for her ill-arranged plans clashed against each other like a chaos. She required to be alone in order to bring her thoughts a little in order. She saw vaguely into futurity; but she stood in need of a little silence and quiet to give all her ideas, at present in confusion, a distinct form and a regular plan.

What was most pressing was, to get Madame Bonacieux away, and convey her to a place of safety, and there, matters so falling out, make her a hostage. Milady began to have doubts of the issue of this terrible duel, in which her enemies showed as much perserverance as she did inveterate animosity.

Besides, she felt as we feel when a storm is coming on— that this issue was near, and could not fail to be terrible.

The principal thing for her then was, as we have said, to keep Madame Bonacieux in her power. Madame Bonacieux was the very life of D'Artagnan; more than his life, was the life of the woman he loved; this was, in case of ill fortune, a means of treating and obtaining good conditions.

Now, this point was settled: Madame Bonacieux, without any suspicion, accompanied her and, once concealed with her at Armentières, it would be easy to make her believe that D'Artagnan was not come to Béthune. In a fortnight, at most, Rochefort would be back again; during that fortnight, besides, she should have time to think how she could best be revenged upon the four friends. She entertained no fear of being dull, thank God! for she should enjoy the sweetest pastime events could offer to a woman of her character—the perfecting of a cruel vengeance.

While revolving all this in her mind, she cast her eyes around her, and arranged the topography of the garden in her head. Milady was like a good general, who contemplates at the same time victory and defeat, and who is quite prepared, according to the chances of the battle, to march forward, or to beat a retreat.

At the end of an hour, she heard a soft voice calling her; it was Madame Bonacieux's. The good abbess had naturally consented to her request; and as a commencement, they were to sup together.

On reaching the courtyard, they heard the noise of a carriage, which stopped at the gate.

Milday listened.

"Do you hear anything?" said she.

"Yes, the rolling of a carriage."

"It is the one my brother sends for us."

"Oh! my God!"

"Come; come! courage!"

The bell of the convent gate was rung—milady was not mistaken.

"Go up to your chamber," said she to Madame Bonacieux; "you have perhaps some jewels you would like to take with you."

"I have his letters," said she.

"Well! go and fetch them, and come to my apartment; we will snatch some supper; we shall perhaps travel part of the night and must keep our streugth up."

"Great God!" said Madame Bonacieux, placing her hand upon her bosom: "my heart beats so I cannot walk."

"Courage, my dear, courage! remember that in a quarter of an hour you will be safe; and think that what you are about to do is for his sake."

"Yes, yes, everything for his sake. You have restored my courage by a single word; go up, I will be with you directly."

Milady ran up to her apartment quickly; she there found Rochefort's lackey and gave him his instructions.

He was to wait at the gate; if, by chance, the musketeers should appear, the carriage was to set off as fast as possible pass round the convent, and go and wait for milady at a little village which was situated at the other side of the wood. In this case milady was to cross the garden and gain the village on foot. We have already said milady was perfectly acquainted with this part of France.

If the musketeers did not appear, things were to go on as had been agreed; Madame Bonacieux was to get into the carriage as if to bid her adieu, and she was to take away Madame Bonacieux.

Madame Bonacieux came in; and, to remove all suspicion, if she had any, milady repeated to the lackey, before her, the latter part of her instructions.

Milady made some questions about the carriage; it was a chaise with three horses, driven by a postilion; Rochefort's lackey preceded it, as a courier.

Milady was wrong in fearing that Madame Bonacieux would have any suspicions; the poor young woman was too pure to suppose that any female could be guilty of such perfidy; besides, the name of the Countess de Winter, which she had heard the abbess pronounce, was perfectly unknown to her, and she was even ignorant that a woman had had so great and so fatal a share in the misfortune of her life.

"You see," said she, when the lackey was gone out, "everything is ready. The abbess suspects nothing, and believes that

I am fetched by the orders of the cardinal. The man is gone to give his last orders; take a mouthful to eat, drink half a glass of wine, and let us be gone."

"Yes," said Madame Bonacieux mechanically; "let us be gone."

Milady made her a sign to sit down before her, poured out a small glass of Spanish wine for her, and helped her to the wing of a chicken.

"See!" said she, "if everything is not propitious; here is night coming on; by daybreak we shall have gained our retreat, and nobody can have any suspicion where we are. Come, courage—take something."

Madame Bonacieux ate a few mouthfuls mechanically, and just touched the glass with her lips.

"Come! come!" said milady, lifting hers to her mouth, "do as I do."

But, at the moment the glass touched her lips, her hand remained suspended; she heard something on the road which sounded like the rattling of a distant gallop, and which drew nearer; and, almost at the same time, she heard the neighing of horses.

This noise acted upon her joy like the storm which awakens the sleeper in the midst of a happy dream; she grew pale, and ran to the window, while Madame Bonacieux, rising all in a tremble, supported herself upon her chair to avoid falling.

Nothing was yet to be seen, only they heard the galloping draw nearer.

"Oh! my God!" said Madame Bonacieux, "what is that noise?"

"That of either our friends or our enemies," said milady, with her terrible coolness; "stay where you are, I will tell you."

Madame Bonacieux remained standing, mute, motionless, and pale as a statue.

The noise became stronger, the horses could not be more than a hundred paces distant; if they were not yet to be seen, it was because the road made an elbow. The noise became so distinct that the horses might be counted by the sound of their hoofs.

Milady looked as if her eyes would start; it was just light enough to allow her to see those who were coming.

All at once, at the turning of the road, she saw the glitter of laced hats and the waving of feathers; she counted two, then five, then eight horsemen; one of them preceded the rest by double the length of his horse

Milady uttered a stifled groan. In the first horseman she recognized D'Artagnan.

"Oh! heavens! oh! heavens!" cried Madame Bonacieux, "what is it? what is it?"

"What is the uniform of the cardinal's guards, not an instant to be lost. Let us fly, let us fly!"

"Oh! yes! let us fly!" repeated Madame Bonacieux, but without being able to make a step, fixed to the spot she stood on by terror.

They heard the horsemen pass under the windows.

"Come, then! why, come then!" cried milady, endeavoring to drag her along by the arm. "Thanks to the garden, we yet can fly; I have the key; but make haste! in five minutes it will be too late!"

Madame Bonacieux endeavored to walk, made two steps, and sank upon her knees.

Milady endeavored to raise and carry her, but could not succeed.

At this moment they heard the rolling of the carriage, which at the approach of the musketeers, set off at a gallop. Then three or four shots were fired.

"For the last time, will you come?" cried milady.

"Oh heavens! oh heavens you see my strength fails me, you see plainly I cannot walk: fly alone!"

"Fly alone! and leave you here! no, no, never!" cried milady.

All at once she remained still, a livid flash darted from her eyes; she ran to the table, poured into Madame Bonacieux's glass the contents of a ring, which she opened with singular quickness.

It was a grain of a reddish color, which melted immediately. Then, taking the glass with a firm hand:

"Drink, said she, "this wine will give you strength, drink!"

And she put the glass to the lips of the young woman, who drank mechanically.

"This is not the way that I wished to avenge myself," said milady, replacing the glass upon the table with an infernal smile, "but, *ma foi!* we do what we can!" And she rushed out of the room. Madame Bonacieux saw her go without being able to follow her; she was like those people who dream they are pursued, and who in vain endeavor to walk.

A few moments passed, a great noise was heard at the gate; every instant Madame Bonacieux expected to see milady; but she did not return.

Several times, with terror, no doubt, the cold sweat burst from her burning brow.

At length she heard the grating of the hinges of the opening gates, the noise of boots spurs resounded on the stairs; there was a great murmur of voices, which continued to draw near, and among which it appeared to her she heard her own name pronounced.

All at once she uttered a loud cry of joy, and darted toward the door, she had recognized the voice of D'Artagnan.

"D'Artagnan! D'Artagnan!" cried she, "is it you? This way! this way!"

"Constance! Constance!" replied the young man, "where are you? where are you?"

At the same moment, the door of the cell yielded to a shock, rather than was opened; several men rushed into the chamber; Madame Bonacieux had sunk into a *fauteuil*, without the power of moving.

D'Artagnan threw a yet smoking pistol from his hand, and fell on his knees before his mistress; Athos replaced his in his belt; Porthos and Aramis, who held their drawn swords in their hands, returned them to their scabbards.

"Oh! D'Artagnan! my beloved D'Artagnan! thou art come, then, at last, thou hast not deceived me! it is indeed thee!"

"Yes, yes, dear Constance! united at last!"

"Oh! it was in vain *she* told me you would not come. I hoped silently; I was not willing to fly; oh! how rightly I have done! how happy I am!"

At this word *she,* Athos, who had seated himself quietly, started up.

"*She!* what she?" asked D'Artagnan.

"Why, my companions; she who, from friendship for me, wished to take me from my persecutors, she who, mistaking you for the cardinal's guards, has just fled away."

"Your companion!" cried D'Artagnan, becoming more pale than the white veil of his mistress, "of what companion are you speaking, dear Constance?"

"Of her whose carriage was at the gate, of a woman who calls herself your friend, of a woman to whom you have told everything."

"But her name, her name!" cried D'Artagnan; "my God! can you not remember her name?"

"Yes, it was pronounced before me once; stop—but—it is very strange—oh! my God! my head swims—I cannot see!"

"Help! help! my friends! her hands are icy cold," cried

D'Artagnan, "she will faint! great God, she is losing her senses!"

While Porthos was calling for help with all the power of his strong voice, Aramis ran to the table to get a glass of water; but he stopped at seeing the horrible alteration that had taken place in the countenance of Athos, who, standing before the table, his hair rising from his head, his eyes fixed in stupor, was looking at one of the glasses and appeared a prey to the most horrible doubt.

"Oh!" said Athos, "oh! no, it is impossible! God would not permit such a crime!"

"Water! water!" cried D'Artagnan, "water!"

"Oh! poor woman! poor woman!" murmured Athos, in a broken voice.

Madame Bonacieux opened her eyes under the kisses of D'Artagnan.

"She revives!" cried the young man. "Oh! my God! my God! I thank thee!"

"Madame!" said Athos, "madame, in the name of heaven, whose empty glass is this?"

"Mine, monsieur," said the young woman in a dying voice.

"But who poured out the wine for you that was in this glass?"

"*She.*"

"But who was *she?*"

"Oh! I remember," said Madame Bonacieux, "*the Countess de Winter.*"

The four friends uttered one and the same cry, but that of Athos dominated over all the rest.

At that moment the countenance of Madame Bonacieux became livid, a fearful agony pervaded her frame, and she sank panting into the arms of Porthos and Aramis.

D'Artagnan seized the hands of Athos with an anguish difficult to be described.

"What! what! do you believe?" His voice was stifled by sobs.

"I believe everything," said Athos, biting his lips till the blood sprang, to avoid sighing.

"D'Artagnan! D'Artagnan! where art thou? Do not quit me, thou seest that I am dying!" cried Madame Bonacieux.

D'Artagnan let fall the hands of Athos which he still held clasped in both his own, and hastened to her.

Her beautiful face was distorted with agony, her glassy eyes were fixed, a convulsive shuddering shook her whole body, the sweat flowed from her brow.

"In the name of heaven, run, call; Aramis! Porthos! call for help!"

"Useless!" said Athos, "useless! for the poison which *she* pours out there is no counter-poison!"

"Yes! yes! help! help!" murmured Madame Bonacieux, "help!"

Then, collecting all her strength, she took the head of the young man between her hands, looked at him for an instant as if her whole soul passed in that look, and, with a sobbing cry, pressed her lips to his.

"Constance! Constance!" cried D'Artagnan wildly.

A sigh escaped from the mouth of Madame Bonacieux, and dwelt for an instant on the lips of D'Artagnan—that sigh was the soul so chaste and so loving reascending to heaven.

D'Artagnan held nothing but a corpse pressed in his arms.

The young man uttered a cry and fell by the side of his mistress as pale and as senseless as she was.

Porthos wept, Aramis pointed toward heaven, Athos made the sign of the cross.

At that moment a man appeared in the doorway almost as pale as those in the chamber, looked round him and saw Madame Bonacieux dead, and D'Artagnan fainting.

He appeared just at that moment of stupor which follows great catastrophes.

"I was not deceived," said he; "here is M. d'Artagnan, and you are his friends, Messieurs Athos, Porthos, and Aramis."

The persons whose names were thus pronounced looked at the stranger with astonishment, all three thought they knew him.

"Gentlemen," resumed the newcomer, "you are, as I am, in search of a woman, who," added he, with a terrible smile, "must have passed this way, for I see a corpse!"

The three friends remained mute, for although the voice as well as the countenance reminded them of some one they had seen, they could not remember under what circumstances.

"Gentlemen," continued the stranger, "since you do not recognize a man who probably owes his life to you twice, I must name myself; I am the Lord de Winter, brother-in-law of that woman."

The three friends uttered a cry of surprise.

Athos rose, and offering him his hand:

"You are welcome, milord," said he, "you are one of us."

"I set out five hours after her from Portsmouth," said Lord de Winter. "I arrived three hours after her at Boulogne, I missed her by twenty minutes at St. Omer; at last at Lilliers I lost all trace of her. I was going about at hazard, inquiring of everybody, when I saw you gallop past; I recognized M. d'Artagnan. I called to you, but you did not answer me; I wished to follow you, but my horse was too much fatigued to permit me to overtake you. And yet, it appears that in spite of all your diligence you have arrived too late."

"You see!" said Athos, pointing to Madame Bonacieux dead, and to D'Artagnan, whom Porthos and Aramis were endeavoring to recall to life.

"Are they then both dead?" asked Lord de Winter sternly.

"No," replied Athos, "fortunately M. d'Artagnan has only fainted."

"Ah! I am glad to hear that!" said Lord de Winter.

At that moment D'Artagnan opened his eyes.

He tore himself from the arms of Porthos and Aramis, and threw himself like a madman on the corpse of his mistress.

Athos rose, walked toward his friend with a slow and solemn step, embraced him tenderly, and as he burst into violent sobs, he said to him, with his noble and persuasive voice:

"Friend, be a man! women weep for the dead, men avenge them!"

"Oh, yes!" cried D'Artagnan, "yes! if it be to avenge her, I am ready to follow you."

Athos took advantage of this moment of strength which the hope of vengeance restored to his unfortunate friend, to make a sign to Porthos and Aramis to go and fetch the superior.

They met her in the corridor, in great trouble and agitation at such strange events; she called for some of the nuns, who against all rules, found themselves in the presence of five men.

"Madame," said Athos, passing his arm under that of D'Artagnan, "we abandon to your pious care the body of that unfortunate woman. She was an angel on earth before being an angel in heaven. Treat her as one of your sisters. We will return some day to pray over her grave!"

D'Artagnan concealed his face in the bosom of Athos, and sobbed aloud.

"Weep!" said Athos, "weep! thou poor heart, full of love, youth, and life! Alas! would that I were able to weep as thou dost!"

And he drew away his friend, affectionate as a father, consoling as a priest, great as a man who has suffered much.

All five, followed by their lackeys, leading their horses, took their way to the town of Béthune, whose faubourg they perceived, and stopped before the first auberge they came to.

"But," said D'Artagnan, "shall we not pursue that woman?"

"Presently," said Athos; "I have measures to take."

"She will escape us," replied the young man; "she will escape us; and it will be your fault, Athos."

"I will be accountable for her," said Athos.

D'Artagnan had so much confidence in the word of his friend, that he hung down his head, and entered the auberge, without making a reply.

Porthos and Aramis looked at each other without comprehending whence Athos derived this assurance.

Lord de Winter believed he spoke in this manner to soothe the grief of D'Artagnan.

"Now, gentlemen," said Athos, when he had ascertained there were five chambers disengaged in the hotel, "let every one retire to his own apartment; D'Artagnan requires to be alone, to weep and to sleep. I take charge of everything, be all of you at ease."

"It appears, however," said Lord de Winter, "that if there be any measure to be taken against the countess, it particularly concerns me: she is my sister-in-law."

"And I," said Athos—*"she is my wife!"*

D'Artagnan smiled, for he was satisfied Athos was sure of his vengeance, when he revealed such a secret as that; Porthos and Aramis looked at each other, and changed color. Lord de Winter thought Athos was mad.

"Now, all retire to your chambers," said Athos, "and leave me to act. You must perceive that in my quality of a husband this concerns me in particular. Only, D'Artagnan, if you have not lost it, give me the piece of paper which fell from that man's hat, upon which is written the name of the village of——"

"Ah!" said D'Artagnan, "I comprehend now; that name written in her hand."

"You see, then," said Athos, "there is a God in heaven, still!"

CHAPTER LXIV.

THE MAN WITH THE RED CLOAK.

THE despair of Athos had given place to a concentrated grief, which only rendered more lucid the brilliant mental faculties of that extraordinary man.

Possessed by one single thought, that of the promise he had made, and of the responsibility he had taken upon himself, he retired the last to his chamber, begged the host to procure him a map of the province, bent over it, examined every line traced upon it, perceived that there were four different roads from Béthune to Armentières, and called all the four valets.

Planchet, Grimaud, Bazin, and Mousqueton presented themselves, and received clear, positive, and serious orders from Athos.

They were to set out for Armentières the next morning at daybreak, and to go to Armentières—each by a different route. Planchet, the most intelligent of the four, was to follow that by which the carriage had gone, upon which the four friends had fired, and which was accompanied, as may be remembered, by Rochefort's servant.

Athos set the lackeys to work first, because, since these men had been in the service of himself and his friends, he had discovered in each of them different and essential qualities.

Then, lackeys who ask questions inspire less mistrust than masters; and meet with more sympathies among those they address.

Besides, milady knew the masters, and did not know the lackeys; while, on the contrary, the lackeys knew milady perfectly well.

All four were to meet the next day, at eleven o'clock; if they had discovered milady's retreat, three were to remain on guard, the fourth was to return to Béthune, to inform Athos, and serve as a guide to the four friends.

These dispositions arranged, the lackeys retired.

Athos then arose from his chair, girded on his sword, enveloped himself in his cloak, and left the hotel; it was nearly ten o'clock. At ten o'clock in the evening, it is well known, the streets in provincial towns are very little frequented; Athos, nevertheless, was visibly anxious to find some one of whom he could ask a question. At length he met a belated passenger, went up to him, and spoke a few words to him;

the man he addressed drew back with terror, and only answered the musketeer by an indication. Athos offered them a half a pistole to accompany him, but the man refused.

Athos then plunged into the street the man had pointed to with his finger; but arriving at four crossroads, he stopped again, visibly embarrassed. Nevertheless, as the crossroads offered him a better chance than any other place of meeting somebody, he stood still. In a few minutes a night-watch passed. Athos repeated to him the same question he had asked the first person he had met; the night-watch evinced the same terror, refused, in his turn, to accompany Athos, and only pointed with his hand to the road he was to take.

Athos walked in the direction indicated, and reached the faubourg, situated at the extremity of the city, opposite to that by which he and his friends had entered it. There he again appeared uneasy and embarrassed, and stopped for the third time.

Fortunately a mendicant passed, who, coming up to Athos to ask charity, Athos offered him half a-crown to accompany him where he was going. The mendicant hesitated at first, but at the sight of the piece of silver which shone in the darkness, he consented, and walked on before Athos.

When arrived at the angle of a street, he pointed to a small house, isolated, solitary, and dismal. Athos went toward the house, while the mendicant, who had received his reward, hobbled off as fast as his legs could carry him.

Athos went round the house before he could distinguish the door, amid the red color in which it was painted; no light appeared through the chinks of the shutters, no noise gave reason to believe that it was inhabited—it was dark and silent as the tomb.

Three times Athos knocked without receiving any answer. At the third knock, however, steps was heard inside; the door at length was opened, and a man of high stature, pale complexion, and black hair and beard, appeared.

Athos and he exchanged some words in a low voice, then the tall man made a sign to the musketeer that he might come in. Athos immediately took advantage of the permission, and the door was closed after them.

The man whom Athos had come so far to seek, and whom he had found with so much trouble, introduced him into his laboratory, were he was engaged in fastening together with iron wire the dry bones of a skeleton. All the frame was adjusted, except the head, which lay upon the table.

All the rest of the furniture indicated that the inhabitant

of this house was engaged in the study of the natural sciences; there were large bottles filled with serpents, ticketed according to their species; dried lizards shone like emeralds set in great squares of black wood; and bunches of wild odoriferous herbs, doubtless possessed of virtues unknown to common men, were fastened to the ceiling and hung down in the corners of the apartment.

But there was no family, no servant; the tall man inhabited this house alone.

Athos cast a cold and indifferent glance upon the objects we have described, and, at the invitation of him he came to seek, he sat down near him.

Then he explained to him the cause of his visit, and the service he required of him; but scarcely had he expressed his request, than the unknown, who remained standing before the musketeer, drew back with signs of terror, and refused. Then Athos took from his pocket a small paper, upon which were written two lines, accompanied by a signature and a seal, and presented them to him who had given too prematurely these signs of repugnance. The tall man had scarcely read these lines, seen the signature, and recognized the seal, when he bowed to denote that he had no longer any objection to make, and that he was ready to obey.

Athos required no more; he arose, bowed, went out, returned by the same way he came, re-entered the hotel, and went to his apartment.

At daybreak D'Artagnan came to him, and asked him "What was to be done?"

"Wait!" replied Athos.

Some minutes after, the superior of the convent sent to inform the musketeers that the burial would take place at midday. As to the poisoner, they had heard no tidings of her whatever; only she must have made her escape through the garden, upon the sand of which her footsteps could be traced and the door of which had been found shut; the key had disappeared.

At the hour appointed, Lord de Winter and the four friends repaired to the convent: the bells tolled, the chapel was open, but the grating of the choir was closed. In the middle of the choir the body of the victim, clothed in her novitiate dress, was exposed. On each side of the choir, and behind the gratings opening upon the convent, was assembled the whole community of the Carmelites, who listened to the divine service, and mingled their chants with the chants of the priests, without seeing the profane, or being seen by them.

At the door of the chapel D'Artagnan felt his courage fail again, and returned to look for Athos, but Athos had disappeared.

Faithful to his mission of vengeance, Athos had requested to be conducted to the garden; and there upon the sand, following the light steps of this woman, who had left a bloody track wherever she had gone, he advanced toward the gate which led into the wood, and, causing it to be opened, he went out into the forest.

Then all his suspicions were confirmed—the road by which the carriage had disappeared went round the forest. Athos followed the road for some time with his eyes fixed upon the ground; slight stains of blood, which came from the wound inflicted upon the man who accompanied the carriage as a courier, or from one of the horses, were to be seen on the road. At the end of about three-quarters of a league, within fifty paces of Festubert, a larger bloodstain appeared; the ground was trampled by horses. Between the forest and this accursed spot, a little behind the trampled ground, was the same track of small feet as in the garden; the carriage, then, had stopped here. At this spot milady had come out of the wood, and got into the carriage.

Satisfied with this discovery, which confirmed all his suspicions, Athos returned to the hotel, and found Planchet impatiently waiting for him.

Everything was as Athos had foreseen.

Planchet had followed the road; like Athos, he had discovered the stains of blood; like Athos, he had remarked the spot where the horses had stopped; but he had gone further than Athos, so that at the village of Festubert, while drinking at an auberge, he had learned, without asking a quesion, that the evening before, at about half-past eight, a wounded man, who accompanied a lady traveling in a post-chaise, had been obliged to stop, being unable to go any further. The wound was attributed to thieves who had stopped the chaise in the wood. The man remained in the village; the lady had had a relay of horses, and continued her journey.

Planchet went in search of the postilion who had driven her, and found him. He had taken the lady as far as Fromelles, and from Fromelles she had set out for Armentières. Planchet took the crossroad, and by seven o'clock in the morning he was at Armentières.

There was but one hotel, that of the post. Planchet went and presented himself as a lackey out of place, who was in search of a situation. He had not chatted ten minutes with

the people of the auberge before he learned that a lady had
come here about eleven o'clock the night before, alone; had
engaged a chamber, had sent for the master of the hotel, and
told him that she was desirous to remain for some time in
that neighborhood.

Planchet did not want to know any more. He hastened
to the rendezvous, found the lackeys at their posts, placed
them as sentinels at all the issues of the hotel, and came to
find Athos, who had just received his information when his
friends returned.

All their countenance were melancholy and anxious, even
the mild countenance of Aramis.

"What is to be done?" said D'Artagnan.

"Wait," replied Athos.

Every one went to his own apartment.

At eight o'clock in the evening Athos ordered the horses
to be saddled, and had Lord de Winter and his friends informed that they must prepare for the expedition.

In an instant all five were ready. Every one examined his
arms, and put them in order. Athos came down the last,
and found D'Artagnan already mounted, and growing impatient.

"Patience!" cried Athos; "one of our party is still
wanting."

The four horseman looked round them with astonishment,
for they sought uselessly in their minds who this other person
they wanted could be.

At this moment Planchet brought out Athos' horse; the
musketeer leaped lightly into the saddle.

"Wait for me," cried he; "I will soon be back;" and set
off at a gallop.

In a quarter of an hour he returned, accompanied by a tall
man, masked, and enveloped in a large red cloak.

Lord de Winter and the three musketeers looked at each
other inquiringly. None of them could give the others any
information, for all were ignorant who this man could be;
nevertheless, they felt convinced that this ought to be so, as
it was done by Athos.

At nine o'clock, guided by Planchet, the little cavalcade
set out, taking the route the carriage had taken.

It was a melancholy sight, that of these six men, traveling
in silence, each plunged in his own thoughts, sad as despair,
dark as punishment.

CHAPTER LXV.

TRIAL.

It was a stormy and dark night; vast clouds covered the heavens, concealing the stars; the moon would not rise much before midnight.

Occasionally, by the light of a flash of lightning, which gleamed along the horizon, the road appeared before them, white and solitary; the flash extinct, all remained in darkness.

At every instant Athos was forced to restrain D'Artagnan, constantly in advance of the little troop, and to beg him to keep his rank, which, at the end of a minute, he again departed from. He had but one thought, which was to go forward, and he went.

They passed in silence through the little village of Festubert, where the wounded servant was, and then skirted the wood of Richebourg; when arrived at Herlier, Planchet, who led the column, turned to the left.

Several times Lord de Winter, Porthos, or Aramis, endeavored to enter into conversation with the man in the red cloak; but to every interrogation put to him he bowed, without making any reply. The travelers then comprehended that there must be some reason why the unknown preserved such a silence, and said no more to him.

The storm came on, the flashes succeeded each other more rapidly, the thunder began to growl, and the wind, the precursor of a hurricane, whistled in the plumes and the hair of the horsemen.

The cavalcade trotted on more sharply.

A little before they came to Fromilles the storm burst in all its fury upon them; they unfolded their cloaks. They had still three leagues to travel, and they performed it amid torrents of rain.

D'Artagnan took off his hat, and could not be persuaded to make use of his cloak: he found ease in feeling the water trickle over his burning brow, and down his feverish body.

At the moment the little troop had passed Goskal, and were approaching the port, a man, sheltered beneath a tree, left the trunk of it, with which he had been confounded in the darkness, and advanced into the middle of the road, with his finger on his lips.

Athos recognized Grimaud.

"What's the matter?" cried Athos; "has she left Armentières?"

Grimaud made a sign in the affirmative. D'Artagnan ground his teeth.

"Silence, D'Artagnan!" said Athos. "I have charged myself with this affair; it is for me, then, to interrogate Grimaud."

"Where is she?" asked Athos.

Grimaud stretched out his hands in the direction of the Lys.

"Far from here?" asked Athos.

Grimaud showed his master his forefinger bent.

"Alone?" asked Athos.

Grimaud made a sign that she was.

"Gentlemen," said Athos, "she is alone, within half a league of us, in the direction of the river."

"That's well," said D'Artagnan; "lead us on, Grimaud."

Grimaud took his course across the country, and acted as a guide to the cavalcade.

At the end of about five hundred paces they came to a rivulet, which they forded.

By the aid of the lightning they could perceive the village of Enguinghem.

"Is she there?" asked D'Artagnan of Athos.

Grimaud shook his head negatively.

"Silence, then!" cried Athos.

And the troop continued their route.

Another flash enlightened all around them; Grimaud extended his arm, and by the blue splendor of the serpent of fire they distinguished a little isolated house, on the banks of the river, within a hundred paces of a ferry.

A light was seen at one window.

"This is the place," said Athos.

At this moment a man, who had been crouching in a ditch, jumped up and came toward them. It was Mousqueton; he pointed with his finger to the window with the light in it.

"She is there," said he.

"And Bazin?" asked Athos.

"While I kept my eye on the window, he guarded the door."

"All is well!" said Athos; "you are good and faithful servants."

Athos sprang from his horse, gave the bridle to Grimaud, and advanced toward the window, after having made a sign to the rest of the troop to go toward the door.

The little house was surrounded by a low quickset hedge of two or three feet high; Athos sprang over the hedge, and went up to the window, which was without shutters, but had the half-curtain drawn closely.

He got upon the skirting-stone to enable him to look over the curtain.

By the light of a lamp he saw a woman enveloped in a mantle of a dark color, seated upon a joint-stool near the dying embers of a fire; her elbows were placed upon a mean table, and she leaned her head upon her two hands, which were white as ivory.

He could not distinguish her countenance, but a sinister smile passed over the lips of Athos; he could not be deceived —it was the woman he sought.

At this moment one of the horses neighed; milady raised her head, saw the pale face of Athos close to the window, and screamed with terror.

Athos, perceiving that she knew him, pushed the window with his knee and hand; it yielded—the frame and glass were broken to shivers.

And Athos, like the specter of vengeance, sprang into the room.

Milady rushed to the door and opened it; but, still more pale and menacing than Athos, D'Artagnan stood on the sill of it.

Milady drew back, uttering a cry; D'Artagnan, believing she might have means of flight, and fearing she should escape, drew a pistol from his belt; but Athos raised his hand.

"Put back that weapon, D'Artagnan," said he; "this woman must be judged, not assassinated. Wait but a little, my friend, and you shall be satisfied. Come in, gentlemen."

D'Artagnan obeyed, for Athos had the solemn voice and the powerul gesture of a judge sent by the Lord himself. Behind D'Artagnan entered Porthos, Aramis, Lord de Winter, and the man in the red cloak.

The four lackeys guarded the door and the window.

Milady had sunk into a chair, with her hands extended, as if to conjure away this terrible apparition. On perceiving her brother-in-law, an agonized cry of surprise and fright burst from her lips.

"What do you want?" screamed milady.

"We want," said Athos, "Charlotte Backson, who first was called Countess de la Fère, and afterward Lady de Winter, Baroness de Scheffield."

"That is I! that is I!" murmured milady, in extreme terror; "what do you want with me?"

"We want to judge you according to your crime," said

Athos; "you shall be free to defend yourself; justify yourself
if you can. Monsieur D'Artagnan, it is for you to accuse
her first."

D'Artagnan advanced.

"Before God and before men," said he, "I accuse this
woman of having poisoned Constance Bonacieux, who died
yesterday evening."

He turned toward Porthos and Aramis.

"We bear witness to this," said the two musketeers, with
one voice.

D'Artagnan continued:

"Before God and before men, I accuse this woman of having attempted to poison me, in wine which she sent me from
Villeroi, with a forged letter, as if that wine came from my
friends. God preserved me, but a man named Brisemont
died in my place."

"We bear witness to this," said Porthos and Aramis, in the
same manner as before.

"Before God and before men, I accuse this women of having urged me to murder the Baron de Wardes; and of having
employed assassins to shoot me; from whom I was again preserved by God's providence; but, as none can bear witness to
these facts, I attest them myself—I have done," and M:
d'Artagnan passed to the other side of the room, to Porthos
and Aramis.

"It is your turn, milord," said Athos.

The baron came forward.

"Before God and before men," said he, "I accuse this
woman of having been the means of the assassination of the
Duke of Buckingham."

"The Duke of Buckingham assassinated!" cried all present, with one voice.

"Yes," said the baron—"assassinated. Upon receiving the
warring letter you wrote to me, I caused this woman to be
arrested, and gave her in charge to a loyal servant; she corrupted this man, she placed the poniard in his hand, she
made him kill the duke; and at this moment, perhaps, the
assassin is paying with his head for the crime of this fury!"

A shudder crept through the frames of the judges at the
revelation of such unheard-of crimes.

"That is not all," resumed Lord de Winter; "my brother,
who made you his heir, died in three hours, of a strange disorder, which left livid traces behind it all over the body.
Sister, how did your husband die?"

"Horror! horror!" cried Porthos and Aramis.

"Assassin of Buckingham, assassin of Felton, assassin of my brother, I demand justice upon you, and I swear that if it be not granted to me, I will execute it myself."

And Lord de Winter ranged himself by the side of D'Artagnan, leaving the place free for another accuser.

Milady let her head sink between her two hands, and endeavored to recall her ideas, which whirled about in a mortal vertigo.

"It is my turn," said Athos, himself trembling as the lion trembles at the sight of the serpent; "it is my turn. I married that woman when she was a young girl; I married her in opposition to the wishes of all my family; I gave her my wealth, I gave her my name; and one day I discovered that this woman was branded; this woman was marked with a fleur-de-lis on her left shoulder."

"Oh!" said milady, "I defy you to find any tribunal which pronounced such an infamous sentence against me. I defy you to find him who executed it."

"Silence!" cried a hollow voice. "It is for me to reply to that!" And the man in the red cloak came foward in his turn.

"What man is that? what man is that?" cried milady, suffocated by terror, her hair unknotting, and rising over her livid countenance as if alive.

All eyes were turned toward this man; for to all except Athos he was unknown.

And even Athos looked at him with as much stupefaction as the rest, for he could not conceive how he could in any way be mixed up with the horrible drama which was then being unfolded.

After having approached milady with a slow and solemn step, so that the table alone separated them, the unknown took off his mask.

Milady for some time examined with increasing terror that pale face, enframed in its black hair, beard and whiskers, the only expression of which was icy impassability—all at once:

"Oh! no, no!" cried she, rising and retreating to the very wall; "no, no! it is an infernal apparition! It cannot be he! Help, help!" screamed she, turning toward the wall, as if she would tear an opening with her hands.

"Who are you, then?" cried all the witnesses of this scene.

"Ask that woman," said the man in the red cloak; "for you may plainly see she knows me!"

"The executioner of Lille! the executioner of Lille!" cried

milady, a prey to wild terror, and clinging with her hands to
the wall to avoid falling.

Every one drew back, and the man in the red cloak remained
standing alone in the middle of the room.

"Oh! pardon! pardon!" cried the miserable woman, falling
on her knees.

The unknown waited for silence, and then—

"I told you so; I was sure she would know me," resumed
he. "Yes, I am the executioner of Lille, and this is my
history."

All eyes were fixed upon this man, whose words were listened to with anxious attention.

"That woman was formerly a young maiden as beautiful as
she is now. She was a nun in the convent of the Benedictines
of Templemar. A young priest, of a simple and trustful
heart, performed the duties of the, church of that convent.
She undertook his seduction, and succeeded: she would have
seduced a saint.

"Their vows were sacred and irrevocable. Their connectioı.
could not last long without ruining both. She prevailed upon
him to leave the country; but to leave the country, to fly together, to reach another part of France, where they might live
at ease; because unknown, money was necessary; neither of
them had any. The priest stole the sacred vases, and sold
them; but as they were preparing to escape together, they
were both arrested.

"Within a week she seduced the son of the jailer, and got
away. The young priest was condemned to ten years imprisonment, and to be branded. I was executioner of the city of Lille,
as this woman has said, and the guilty man, gentlemen, was my
brother!

"I then swore that this woman who had ruined him, who was
more than his accomplice, since she had induced him to commit
the crime, should at least share his punishment. I suspected
where she was concealed. I followed her, I caught her, I
bound her, and I impressed the same disgraceful mark upon
her that I had branded upon my poor brother.

"The day after I returned to Lille, my brother, in his turn,
succeeded in making his escape; I was accused of complicity,
and was condemned to remain in his place till he should be
again a prisoner. My poor brother was ignorant of this sentence; he rejoined this woman; they fled together into Berry,
and there he obtained a little curacy. This woman passed for
his sister.

"The lord of the estate upon which the church of the curacy

was situated saw this pretended sister, and became enamored of her; so much so, that he offered to marry her. Then she left him she had ruined, for him she was destined to ruin, and became the Countess de la Fère——"

All eyes were turned toward Athos, whose real name that was, and who made a sign with his head that all was true that the executioner had said.

"Then," resumed he, "mad, desperate, determined to get rid of an existence from which she had taken away everything, both honor and happiness, my poor brother returned to Lille, and learning the sentence which had condemned me in his place, surrendered himself, and hung himself that same night, from the iron bar of the loophole of his prison.

"To render justice to them who had condemned me, they kept their word. As soon as the identity of my brother was proved, I was set at liberty.

"That is the crime of which I accuse her; that is the cause of her being branded."

"Monsieur D'Artagnan," said Athos, "what is the penalty you demand against this woman?"

"The punishment of death," replied D'Artagnan.

"Milord de Winter," continued Athos, "what is the penalty you demand against this woman?"

"The punishment of death," replied Lord de Winter.

"Messieurs Porthos and Aramis," again said Athos, "you who are her judges, what is the sentence you pronounce upon this woman?"

"The punishment of death," replied the musketeers, in a stern, hollow voice.

Milady uttered a frightful shriek, and dragged herself along several paces toward her judges upon her knees.

Athos stretched out his hand toward her.

"Charlotte Backson, Countess de la Fère, Milady de Winter," said he, "your crimes have wearied men on earth and God in heaven. If you know any prayer, say it; for you are condemned, and you shall die."

At these words, which left no hope, milady raised herself up to her full height, and endeavored to speak, but her strength failed her; she felt that a powerful and implacable hand seized her by the hair, and dragged her away as irrevocably as fatality drags man: she did not, therefore, even attempt to make the least resistance, and went out of the cottage.

Lord de Winter, D'Artagnan, Athos, Porthos, and Aramis, went out close behind her and the executioner. The lackeys followed their masters, and the chamber was left solitary, with

its broken window, its open door, and its smoky lamp burning
dimly on the table.

CHAPTER LXVI.

EXECUTION.

It was near midnight; the moon, lessened by its decline
and reddened by the last traces of the storm, arose behind
the little town of Armentières, which showed against its pale
light the dark outline of its houses, and the outline of its
high belfry. In front of them the Lys rolled its waters like
a river of melted lead; while on the other side was a black
mass of trees, cutting a stormy sky, invaded by large coppery
clouds, which created a sort of twilight amid the night. On
the left was an old abandoned mill, with its motionless wings
from the ruins of which an owl threw out its shrill, period-
ical, and monotonous cry. On the right and on the left of the
road, which the dismal *cortège* pursued, appeared a few low,
stunted trees, which looked like deformed dwarfs crouching
down to watch men traveling at this sinister hour.

From time to time a broad sheet of lightning opened the
horizon in its whole width, darted like a serpent over the black
mass of trees, and, like a terrible scimitar, divided the heavens
and the waters into two parts. Not a breath of wind now
disturbed the heavy atmosphere. A deathlike silence oppressed
all nature, the soil was humid and glittering with the rain which
had recently fallen, and the refreshed herbs threw forth their
perfume with additional energy.

Two of the lackeys now led, or rather dragged, along milady by her arms; the executioner walked behind them, and
Lord de Winter, D'Artagnan, Porthos, and Aramis walked
behind the executioner. Planchet and Bazin came last.

The two lackeys led milady to the banks of the river. Her
mouth was mute; but her eyes spoke with their inexpressible
eloquence, supplicating by turns each of those she looked at.

Being a few paces in advance, she whispered to the lackeys:
"A thousand pistoles to each of you, if you will assist my
escape; but if you deliver me up to your masters, I have, near
at hand, avengers who will make you pay for my death very
dearly."

Grimaud hesitated; Mousqueton trembled in all his mem-
bers.

Athos, who heard milady's voice, came sharply up; Lord de Winter did the same.

"Change these lackeys," said he, "she has spoken to them, they are no longer safe."

Planchet and Bazin were called forward, and took the places of Grimaud and Mousqueton.

When they arrived on the banks of the river, the executioner approached milady, and bound her hands and feet.

Then she broke silence to cry out:

"You are base cowards, miserable assassins, ten men combined to murder one woman; beware! if I am not saved I shall be avenged."

"You are not a woman," said Athos, coldly and sternly, "you do not belong to the human species: you are a demon escaped from hell, to which place we are going to send you back again."

"Ah! you virtuous men!" said milady, "but please to remember that he who shall touch a hair of my head is himself an assassin."

"The executioner can kill, madam, without being on that account an assassin," said the man in the red cloak, striking upon his immense sword; "this is the last judge; that is all: *Nachrichter*, as our neighbors, the Germans, say."

And as he bound her while saying these words, milady uttered two or three wild cries, which produced a strange and melancholy effect in flying away into the night, and losing themselves in the depths of the woods.

"If I am guilty, if I have committed the crimes you accuse me of," shrieked milady, "take me before a tribunal; you are not judges; you cannot condemn me!"

"Why, I did offer you Tyburn," said Lord de Winter, "why did you not accept it?"

"Because I am not willing to die!" cried milady, struggling, "because I am too young to die!"

"The woman you poisoned at Béthune was still younger than you, madame, and yet she is dead," said D'Artagnan.

"I will enter a cloister, I will become a nun," said milady.

"You were in a cloister," said the executioner, "and you left it to destroy my brother."

Milady uttered a cry of terror, and sank upon her knees.

The executioner took her up in his arms, and was carrying her toward the boat.

"Oh! my God!" cried she, "my God! are you going to drown me?"

These cries had something so heartrending in them, that M.

d'Artagnan, who had been at first the most eager in pursuit of milady, sank down on the stump of a tree, and leaned down his head, covering his ears with the palms of his hands; and yet, notwithstanding, he could not help hearing her cry and threaten.

D'Artagnan was the youngest of all these men; his heart failed him.

"Oh! I cannot behold this frightful spectacle!" said he; "I cannot consent that this woman should die thus!"

Milady heard these few words, and caught at a shadow of hope.

"D'Artagnan! D'Artagnan!" cried she, "remember that I loved you!"

The young man rose, and made a step toward her.

But Athos rose, likewise, drew his sword, and placed himself between them.

"One step further, M. d'Artagnan," said he, "and, dearly as I love you, we cross swords."

M. d'Artagnan sank on his knees and prayed.

"Come!" continued Athos, "executioner, do your duty."

"Willingly, monseigneur," said the executioner; "for, as I am a good Catholic, I firmly belive I am acting justly in performing my functions on this woman."

"That's well."

Athos made a step toward milady.

"I pardon you," said he, "the ill you have done me; I pardon you for my blasted future, my lost honor, my defiled love, and my salvation forever compromised by the despair into which you have cast me. Die in peace!"

Lord de Winter advanced in his turn.

"I pardon you," said he, "the poisoning of my brother, the assassination of his grace the Duke of Buckingham; I pardon you the death of poor Felton, I pardon you the attempts upon my own person. Die in peace."

"And I," said M. d'Artagnan. "Pardon me, madame, for having by a trick, unworthy of a gentleman, provoked your anger; and I, in exchange, pardon you for the murder of my poor love, and your cruel vengeance against me. I pardon you, and I weep for you. Die in peace."

"I am lost!" murmured milady, in English; "I must die!"

Then she rose up herself, and cast around her one of those piercing looks which seemed to dart from an eye of flame.

She saw nothing.

She listened, and she heard nothing.

"Where am I to die?" said she.

"On the other bank," replied the executioner.

Then he placed her in the boat, and as he was going to set foot in it himself, Athos handed him a purse of gold.

"Here," said he, "is the pay for the execution, that it may be plain we act as judges."

"That is correct," said the executioner; "and now, in her turn, let this woman see that I am not fulfilling my trade, but my duty."

And he threw the money into the river.

The boat moved off toward the left-hand shore of the Lys, bearing the guilty woman and the executioner; all the others remained on the right-hand bank, where they fell on their knees.

The boat glided along the ferry-rope under the shadow of a pale cloud which hung over the water at the moment.

The troop of friends saw it gain the opposite bank; the persons cut the red-tinted horizon with a black shade.

Milady, during her passage, had contrived to untie the cord which fastened her feet; on coming near to the bank, she jumped lightly on shore and took to flight.

But the soil was moist: on gaining the top of the bank, she slipped and fell upon her knees.

She was struck, no doubt, with a superstitious idea: she conceived that heaven denied its succor, and she remained in the attitude she had fallen in, with her head drooping and her hands clasped.

Then they saw from the other bank the executioner raise both his arms slowly, a moonbeam fell upon the blade of the large sword, the two arms fell with a sudden force: they heard the hissing of the scimitar and the cry of the victim, then a truncated mass sank beneath the blow.

The executioner then took off his red cloak, spread it upon the ground, laid the body in it, threw in the head, tied all up with the four corners, lifted it on to his back, and got into the boat again.

When he arrived in the middle of the stream, he stopped the boat, and suspending his burden over the water:

"Let the justice of God be done!" cried he with a loud voice.

And he let the body drop into the depths of the water, which closed over it.

Within three days the four musketeers were in Paris; they had not exceeded their leave of absence, and that same evening went to pay their customary visit to M. de Tréville.

"Well gentlemen," said the brave captain, "I hope you have enjoyed your excursion."

"Prodigiously!" replied Athos, for himself and his companions.

CHAPTER LXVII.

CONCLUSION.

On the sixth of the following month, the king, in compliance with the promise he had made the cardinal to return to La Rochelle, left his capital still in amazement at the news which began to spread of Buckingham's assassination.

Although warned that the man she had loved so much was in great danger, the queen, when his death was announced to her, would not believe the fact, and even imprudently exclaimed:

"It is false: he has just written to me!"

But the next day she was obliged to receive this fatal intelligence as truth; Laporte, detained in England, as every one else had been, by the orders of Charles I., arrived, and was the bearer of the duke's last dying present to the queen.

The joy of the king was great, he did not even give himself the trouble to dissemble it, and displayed it with affectation before the queen. Louis XIII., like all weak minds, was miserably wanting in generosity.

But the king soon again became dull and indisposed; his brow was not one of those that are clear for long together; he felt that by returning to his camp, he was about to resume his state of slavery; nevertheless, he did return.

The cardinal was for him the fascinating serpent, and he was the bird which flies from branch to branch, without being able to escape.

The return to La Rochelle, therefore, was profoundly dull. Our four friends, in particular, astonished their comrades; they traveled together, side by side, with spiritless eyes and heads depressed. Athos alone, from time to time, raised his expansive brow; a flash kindled in his eyes, and a bitter smile passed over his lips; then, like his comrades, he sank again into his reveries.

As soon as the escort arrived in any city, when they had conducted the king to his quarters, the four friends either retired to their own, or to some secluded cabaret, where they neither drank nor played; they only conversed in a low voice, looking around attentively that no one overheared them.

One day, when the king had halted to fly the pie, and the four friends, according to their custom, instead of following the sport, had stopped at a cabaret on the highroad, a man, coming from La Rochelle on horseback, pulled up at the door to drink a glass of wine, and darted a searching glance into the chamber in which the four musketeers were sitting.

"Hilloa! Monsieur d'Artagnan!" said he, "is not that you I see yonder?"

D'Artagnan raised his head and uttered a cry of joy. It was the man he called his phantom, it was his unknown of Meung, of the Rue des Fossoyeurs, and of Arras.

D'Artagnan drew his sword, and sprang toward the door.

But this time, instead of avoiding him, the unknown jumped from his horse, and advanced to meet D'Artagnan.

"Ah! monsieur!" said the young man, "I have met with you, then, at last! this time, I will answer for it, you shall not escape me!"

"Neither is it my intention, monsieur, for this time I was seeking you; in the name of the king, I arrest you."

"How! what do you say?" cried D'Artagnan.

"I say that you must surrender your sword to me, monsieur, and that without resistance; the safety of your head depends upon your compliance."

"Who are you, then?" demanded D'Artagnan, lowering the point of his sword, but without yet surrendering it.

"I am the Chevalier de Rochefort," answered the other, "the equerry of Monsieur the Cardinal de Richelieu, and I have orders to conduct you to his eminence."

"We are returning to his eminence, Monsieur de Chevalier," said Athos, advancing; "and you will please to accept the word of M. d'Artagnan, that he will go straight to La Rochelle."

"I must place him in the hands of guards who will take him to the camp."

"We will be his guards, monsieur, upon our words, as gentlemen; but, upon our words as gentlemen, likewise," added Athos, knitting his brow, "M. d'Artagnan shall not leave us."

The Chevalier de Rochefort cast a glance backward, and saw that Porthos and Aramis had placed themselves between him and the gate; he therefore was convinced that he was completely at the mercy of these four men.

"Gentlemen," said he, "if M. d'Artagnan will surrender his sword to me, and join his word to yours, I will be satisfied with your promise to convey M. d'Artagnan to the quarters of Monseigneur the Cardinal."

"You have my word, monsieur, and here is my sword."

"This suits me better," said Rochefort, "as I wish to continue my journey."

"If it is for the purpose of rejoining milady," said Athos coolly, "it is useless; you will not find her."

"What is become of her then?" asked Rochefort eagerly.

"Come back with us to the camp and you shall know."

Rochefort remained for a moment undecided, then, as they were only a day's journey from Surgères, to which place the cardinal was to come to meet the king, he resolved to follow Athos' advice and go with them. Besides, this return presented him the advantage of watching over his prisoner.

They resumed their route.

On the morrow, at three o'clock in the afternoon, they arrived at Surgères. The cardinal there awaited Louis XIII. The minister and the king exchanged numerous caresses, felicitating each other upon the fortunate chance which had freed France from the inveterate enemy who set on all Europe against her. After which, the cardinal, who had been informed that D'Artagnan was arrested, and who was anxious to see him, took leave of the king, inviting him to come the next day to view the labors of the dyke, which were completed.

On returning in the evening to his quarters at the bridge of La Pierre, the cardinal found D'Artagnan, without his sword, and the three musketeers armed, standing before the door of the house.

This time, as he was well attended, he looked at them sternly, and made a sign with his eye and hand for D'Artagnan to follow him.

D'Artagnan obeyed.

"We shall wait for you, D'Artagnan," said Athos, loud enough for the cardinal to hear him.

His eminence bent his brow, stopped for an instant, and then kept on his way, without uttering a single word.

D'Artagnan entered after the cardinal, and behind D'Artagnan the door was guarded.

His eminence went to the chamber which served him as a closet, and made a sign to Rochefort to bring in the young musketeer.

Rochefort obeyed and retired.

D'Artagnan remained alone in front of the cardinal; this was his second interview with Richelieu, and he afterward confessed that he felt well assured it would be his last.

Richelieu remained standing, leaning against the mantelpiece; a table was between him and D'Artagnan.

"Monsieur," said the cardinal, "you have been arrested by my orders."

"So I have been informed, monseigneur."

"Do you know why?"

"No, monseigneur, for the only thing for which I could be arrested is still unknown to your eminence."

Richelieu looked steadfastly at the young man.

"Indeed!" said he, "what does that mean?"

"If monseigneur will have the goodness to tell me, in the first place, what crimes are imputed to me, I will then tell your eminence what I have really done."

"Crimes are imputed to you that have brought down much more lofty heads than yours, monsieur," said the cardinal.

"What are they, monseigneur?" said D'Artagnan, with a calmness that astonished the cardinal himself.

"You are charged with having corresponded with the enemies of the kingdom; you are charged with having surprised state secrets; you are charged with having endeavored to thwart the plans of your general."

"And who charges me with this, monseigneur?" said D'Artagnan, who had no doubt the accusation came from milady—"a woman branded by the justice of the country—a woman who has espoused one man in France and another in England—a woman who poisoned her second husband, and who attempted both to poison and assassinate me!"

"What is all this, monsieur?" cried the cardinal, astonished; "and what woman are you speaking of thus?"

"Of Milady de Winter," replied D'Artagnan—"yes, of Milady de Winter, of whose crimes your eminence is doubtless ignorant, because you have honored her with your confidence."

"Monsieur," said the cardinal, "if Milady de Winter has committed the crimes you lay to her charge, she shall be punished."

"She is punished, monseigneur."

"And who has punished her?"

"We have."

"Is she in prison?"

"She is dead."

"Dead!" repeated the cardinal, who could not believe what he heard; "dead! Did you say she was dead?"

"Three times she attempted to kill me, and I pardoned her; but she murdered the woman I loved. Then my friends and I took her, tried her, and condemned her."

D'Artagnan then related the poisoning of Madame Bonacieux in the convent of the Carmelites of Béthune, the trial in the solitary house, and the execution on the banks of the Lys.

A shudder crept through the body of the cardinal, who, it may be observed, was not easily made to shudder.

But all at once, as if undergoing the influence of a secret thought, the countenance of the cardinal, till that moment gloomy, cleared up by degrees, and recovered perfect serenity.

"So," said the cardinal, in a tone that contrasted strongly with the severity of his words, "you have constituted yourselves judges, without remembering that they who punish without license to punish, are assassins?"

"Monseigneur, I swear to you that I never for an instant had the intention of defending my head against you; I willingly will submit to any punishment your eminence may please to inflict upon me; I do not hold life dear enough to be afraid of death."

"Yes, I know you are a man of a stout heart, monsieur," said the cardinal, in an almost kind tone; "I can therefore tell you beforehand you shall be tried, and even condemned."

"Another might reply that he had his pardon in his pocket. I will content myself with saying, Issue your orders, monseigneur; I am ready."

"Your pardon?" said Richelieu, surprised.

"Yes, monseigneur," said D'Artagnan.

"And signed by whom—by the king?"

And the cardinal pronounced these words with a singular expression of contempt.

"No; by your eminence."

"By me? You must be mad, monsieur!"

"Monseigneur will doubtless recognize his own writing."

And D'Artagnan presented to the cardinal the precious piece of paper which Athos had forced from milady, and which he had given to D'Artagnan, to serve him as a safeguard.

His eminence took the paper, and read in a slow voice, dwelling upon every syllable:

"It is by my orders that the bearer of this paper has done what he has just done.

"At the camp of Rochelle, this fifth of August, 1628.

"RICHELIEU."

The cardinal, after having read these two line, sank into a profound reverie; but he did not return the paper to D'Artagnan.

"He is meditating what sort of punishment he shall put me to death by," said D'Artagnan to himself. "Let him; *ma foi!* he shall see how a gentleman can die!"

The young musketeer was then in an excellent disposition to suffer heroically.

Richelieu still continued thinking, twisting and untwisting the paper in his hands.

At length he raised his head, fixed his eagle look upon that loyal, open, and intelligent countenance, read upon that face, furrowed with tears, all the sufferings he had endured in the course of the last month, and reflected for the third or fourth time how much that youth of twenty-one years of age had before him, and what resources his activity, his courage, and his shrewd understanding might offer to a good master.

In another respect the crimes, the strength of mind, and the infernal genius of milady had more than once terrified him; he felt something like a secret joy at having got rid of this dangerous accomplice.

He slowly tore the paper which D'Artagnan had generously placed in his hand.

"I am lost!" said D'Artagnan to himself.

And he bowed profoundly before the cardinal, like a man who says, "Lord, thy will be done!"

The cardinal went up to the table, and, without sitting down, wrote a few lines upon a parchment of which two-thirds were already filled up, and affixed his seal to it.

"That is my condemnation," thought D'Artagnan; "he will spare me the *ennui* of the Bastille, or the tediousness of a trial. That's very kind of him."

"Here, monsieur," said the cardinal to the young man, "I have taken from you one signed blank to give you another. The name is wanting in this commission; you can write it yourself."

D'Artagnan took the paper hesitatingly, and cast his eyes over it; it was a lieutenant's commission in the musketeers.

D'Artagnan fell at the feet of the cardinal.

"Monseigneur," said he, "my life is yours—henceforward dispose of it. But this favor which you bestow upon me I do not merit; I have three friends who are more meritorious and more worthy——"

"You are a brave youth, D'Artagnan," interrupted the cardinal, tapping him familiarly on the shoulder, charmed at having subdued this rebellious nature. "Do with this commission what you will; only remember that, though the name be a blank, it was to you that I gave it."

"I shall never forget it," replied D'Artagnan; "your eminnence may be certain of that."

The cardinal turned round, and said in a loud voice:

"Rochefort!"

The chevalier, who no doubt was near the door, entered immediately.

"Rochefort," said the cardinal, "you see M. d'Artagnan— I receive him among the number of my friends; embrace, then, and be prudent, if you have any wish to preserve your heads."

Rochefort and D'Artagnan saluted coolly; but the cardinal was there observing them with his vigilant eye.

They left the chamber at the same time.

"We shall meet again, shall we not, monsieur?"

"When you please," said D'Artagnan.

"An opportunity will offer itself," replied Rochefort.

"What's that?" said the cardinal, opening the door.

The two men smiled at each other, shook hands, and bowed to his eminence.

"We were beginning to grow impatient," said Athos.

"Well, here I am, my friends," replied D'Artagnan, "not only free, but in favor."

"Tell us all about it."

"This evening."

Accordingly, that same evening D'Artagnan repaired to the quarters of Athos, whom he found in a fair way of emptying a bottle of Spanish wine, an occupation which he religiously went through every night.

He related all that had taken place between the cardinal and himself, and, drawing the commission from his pocket.

"Here, my dear Athos," said he, this belongs to you naturally."

Athos smiled with one of his sweet and expressive smiles.

"My friend," said he, "for Athos this is too much; for the Count de la Fère it is too little; keep the commission—it is yours; alas! you have purchased it dearly enough."

D'Artagnan left Athos' chamber, and went to that of Porthos.

He found him clothed in a magnificent dress covered with splendid embroidery, admiring himself before a glass.

"Ah, ah! is that you, friend D'Artagnan?" exclaimed he; "how do you think these garments fit me, eh?"

"Wonderfully well," said D'Artagnan; "but I am come to offer you a dress which will become you still better."

"What's that?" asked Porthos.

"That's a lieutenant of musketeers."

D'Artagnan related to Porthos the substance of his interview with the cardinal, and, taking the commission from his pocket:

"Here, my friend," said he, "write your name upon it, and become my officer."

Porthos cast his eyes over the commission, and returned it to D'Artagnan, to the great astonishment of the young man.

"Yes," said he, "yes, that would flatter me very much, but I should not have time enough to enjoy the distinction. During our expedition to Béthune the husband of my duchess died, so that, my dear friend, the coffer of the defunct holding out its arms to me, I shall marry the widow; look here, I at this moment was trying on the wedding suit. No, keep the lieutenancy, my dear fellow, keep it."

And he returned the commission to D'Artagnan.

The young man then entered the apartment of Aramis.

He found him kneeling before a *prie-Dieu*, with his head leaning upon an open book of prayer.

He described to him his interview with the cardinal, and, for the third time drawing the commission from his pocket:

"You, our friend, our intelligence, our invisible protector," said he, "accept this commission; you have merited it more than any of us by your wisdom and your counsels, always followed by such happy results."

"Alas! my dear friend," said Aramis, "our late adventures have disgusted me with life and with the sword; this time my determination is irrevocably taken: after the siege I shall enter the house of the Lazarists. Keep the commission, D'Artagnan—the profession of arms suits you; you will be a brave and adventurous captain."

D'Artagnan, his eye moist with gratitude, though beaming with joy, went back to Athos, whom he found still at table, contemplating the charms of his last glass of Malaga by the light of his lamp.

"Well," said he, "and they likewise have refused me!"

"That, my dear friend, is because nobody is more worthy than yourself."

And he took a pen, wrote the name of D'Artagnan on the commission, and returned it to him.

"I shall then no longer have friends," said the young man, "alas! nothing but bitter recollections."

And he let his head sink upon his hands, while two large tears rolled down his cheeks.

"You are young," replied Athos, "and your bitter recollections have time to be changed into sweet remembrances."

EPILOGUE.

LA ROCHELLE, deprived of the assistance of the English fleet, and of the reinforcements promised by Buckingham, surrendered after a siege of a year. On the 28th of October, 1628, the capitulation was signed.

The king made his entrance into Paris on the 23d of December of the same year. He was received in triumph, as if he came from conquering an enemy, and not Frenchmen. He entered by the Fauborg St. Jacques under the verdant triumphal arches.

D'Artagnan took possession of his rank. Porthos left the service, and in the course of the following year married Madame Coquenard; the so much coveted coffer contained 800, 000 livres.

Mousqueton had a magnificent livery and enjoyed the satisfaction he had been ambitious of all his life—that of standing behind a gilded carriage.

Aramis after a journey into Lorraine disappeared all at once, and ceased to write to his friends; they learned at a later period, by Madame de Chevreuse, who told it to two or three of her intimates, that he had taken the habit in a convent of Nancy. Bazin became a lay brother.

Athos remained a musketeer under the command of D'Artagnan till the year 1631, at which period, after a journey which he made to Couraine, he also quitted the service under the pretext of having inherited a small property in Rousillon.

Grimaud followed Athos.

D'Artagnan fought three times with Rochefort, and wounded him at each encounter.

"I shall most likely kill you at the fourth," said he to him, holding out his hand to assist him to rise.

"We had much better leave off as we are, both for you and for me," answered the wounded man. *Corbleu!* I am much more your friend than you think; for, from our very first encounter, I could, by saying a word to the cardinal, have had your throat cut!"

They this time embraced heartily, and without retaining any malice.

Planchet obtained from Rochefort the rank of sergeant in the guards.

M. Bonacieux lived on very quietly, perfectly ignorant what had become of his wife, and caring very little about the

matter. One day he had the imprudence to intrude himself
upon the memory of the cardinal; the cardinal had him informed that he would provide for him, so that he should
never want for anything in the future. In fact, M. Bonacieux
having left his house at seven o'clock in the evening to go to
the Louvre, never appeared again in the Rue des Fossoyeurs;
the opinion of those who seemed t be the best informed was
that he was fed and lodged in some royal castle, at the expense
of his generous eminence.

THE END.

NOTE.—For the information of the reader, Dumas' Historical
Romances should be read in their chronological order, as follows: 1st.
The Three Musketeers. 2d. Twenty Years After. 3d. The Vicomte
de Bragelonne. 4th. Ten Years Later. 5th. Louise de la Vallière.
6th. The Man in the Iron Mask.